ORDINARY MONSTERS

ORDINARY MONSTERS

J. M. MIRO

FLATIRON
BOOKS
NEW YORK

ORDINARY MONSTERS. Copyright © 2022 by Ides of March Creative Inc. All rights reserved. Printed in the United States of America. For information, address Flatiron Books, 120 Broadway, New York, NY 10271.

www.flatironbooks.com

Designed by Donna Sinisgalli Noetzel

Library of Congress Cataloging-in-Publication Data

Names: Miro, J. M., author.
Title: Ordinary monsters / J.M. Miro.
Description: First edition. | New York : Flatiron Books, 2022. |
    Series: The talents trilogy ; book 1
Identifiers: LCCN 2021055568 | ISBN 9781250833662 (hardcover) |
    ISBN 9781250862181 (international, sold outside the U.S., subject to
    rights availability) | ISBN 9781250833747 (ebook)
Subjects: LCGFT: Fantasy fiction. | Novels.
Classification: LCC PS3613.I764 O73 2022 | DDC 813/.6—
    dc23/eng/20220114
LC record available at https://lccn.loc.gov/2021055568

Our books may be purchased in bulk for promotional, educational, or business use. Please contact your local bookseller or the Macmillan Corporate and Premium Sales Department at 1-800-221-7945, extension 5442, or by email at MacmillanSpecialMarkets@macmillan.com.

First U.S. Edition: 2022
First International Edition: 2022

10 9 8 7 6 5 4 3 2 1

For Dave Balchin

And when men could no longer sustain them,
the giants turned against them
and devoured mankind.

—THE BOOK OF ENOCH

The THING
on the
COBBLESTONE STAIR

·

1874

LOST CHILDREN

The first time Eliza Grey laid eyes on the baby was at dusk in a slow-moving boxcar on a rain-swept stretch of the line three miles west of Bury St Edmunds, in Suffolk, England. She was sixteen years old, unlettered, unworldly, with eyes dark as the rain, hungry because she had not eaten since the night before last, coatless and hatless because she had fled in the dark without thinking where she could run to or what she might do next. Her throat still bore the marks of her employer's thumbs, her ribs the bruises from his boots. In her belly grew his baby, though she did not know it yet. She had left him for dead in his nightshirt with a hairpin standing out of his eye.

She'd been running ever since. When she came stumbling out of the trees and glimpsed across the darkening field the freight train's approach she didn't think she could make it. But then somehow she was clambering the fence, somehow she was wading through the watery field, the freezing rain cutting sidelong into her, and then the greasy mud of the embankment was heavy and smearing her skirts as she fell, and slid back, and frantically clawed her way forward again.

That was when she heard the dogs. She saw the riders appear out of the trees, figures of darkness, one after another after another, single file behind the fence line, the black dogs loose and barking and hurtling out ahead. She saw the men kick their horses into a gallop, and when she grabbed the handle of the boxcar and with the last of her strength swung herself up, and in, she heard the report of a rifle, and something sparked stinging past her face, and she turned and saw the rider with the top hat, the dead man's terrifying father. He was standing in his stirrups and lifting the rifle again to take aim and she rolled desperately in the straw away from the door and lay panting in the gloom as the train gathered speed.

She must have slept. When she came to, her hair lay plastered along her neck, the floor of the boxcar rattled and thrumped under her, rain was blowing in through the open siding. She could just make out the walls of lashed crates, stamped with Greene King labels, and a wooden pallet overturned in the straw.

There was something else, some kind of light left burning just out of sight, faint, the stark blue of sheet lightning, but when she crawled over she saw it was not a light at all. It was a baby, a little baby boy, glowing in the straw.

All her life she would remember that moment. How the baby's face flickered, a translucent blue, as if a lantern burned in its skin. The map of veins in its cheeks and arms and throat.

She crawled closer.

Next to the baby lay its black-haired mother, dead.

What governs a life, if not chance?

Eliza watched the glow in the little creature's skin slowly seep away, vanish. In that moment what she had been and what she would become stretched out before her and behind her in a single long continuous line. She crouched on her hands and knees in the straw, swaying with the boxcar, feeling her heart slow, and she might almost have thought she had dreamed it, that blue shining, might almost have thought the afterglow in her eyelids was just tiredness and fear and the ache of a fugitive life opening out in front of her. Almost.

"Oh, what are you, little one?" she murmured. "Where did you come from?"

She was herself not special, not clever. She was small like a bird, with a narrow pinched face and too-big eyes and hair as brown and coarse as dry grass. She knew she didn't matter, had been told it since she was a little girl. If her soul belonged to Jesus in the next world, in this one her flesh belonged to any who would feed it, clothe it, shelter it. That was just the world as it was. But as the cold rain clattered and rushed past the open railway siding, and she held the baby close, exhaustion opening in front of her like a door into the dark, she was surprised by what she felt, how sudden it was, how uncomplicated and fierce. It felt like anger and was defiant like anger, but it was not anger. She had never in her life held anything so helpless and so unready for the world. She started to cry. She was crying for the baby and crying for herself and for what she could not undo, and after a time, when she was all cried out, she just held the baby and stared out at the rain.

Eliza Mackenzie Grey. That was her name, she whispered to the baby, over and over, as if it were a secret. She did not add: *Mackenzie because of my father, a good man taken by the Lord too soon.* She did not say: *Grey because of who my mama married after, a man big as my da, handsome like the devil with a fiddle, who talked sweet in a way Mama thought she liked but who wasn't the same as his words.* That man's charm had faded into drink only weeks after the wedding night until bottles rolled underfoot in their miserable tenement up north in Leicester and he'd taken to handling Eliza roughly in the mornings in a way she, still just a girl, did not understand, and which hurt her and made her feel ashamed. When she was sold out as a domestic at the age of thirteen, it was her mother who did the selling, her mother who sent her to the agency, dry-eyed, white-lipped like death, anything to get her away from that man.

And now this other man—her employer, scion of a sugar family, with his fine waistcoats and his pocket watches and his manicured whiskers, who had called her to his study and asked her name, though she had worked at the house two years already by then, and who knocked softly at her room two nights ago holding a candle in its dish, closing the door behind him before she could get out of bed, before she could even ask what was the matter—now he lay dead, miles away, on the floor of her room in a mess of black blood.

Dead by her own hand.

In the east the sky began to pale. When the baby started to cry from hunger, Eliza took out the only food she had, a crust of bread in a handkerchief, and she chewed a tiny piece to mush and then passed it to the baby. It sucked at it hungrily, eyes wide and watching hers the while. Its skin was so pale, she could see the blue veins underneath. Then she crawled over and took from the dead mother's petticoat a small bundle of pound notes and a little purse of coins and laboriously she unsleeved and rolled the mother from her outerwear. A leather cord lay at her throat, with two heavy black keys on it. Those Eliza did not bother with. The mauve skirts were long and she had to fold up the waist for the fit and she mumbled a prayer for the dead when she was done. The dead woman was soft, full-figured, everything Eliza was not, with thick black hair, but there were scars over her breasts and ribs, grooved and bubbled, not like burns and not like a pox, more like the flesh had melted and frozen like that, and Eliza didn't like to imagine what had caused them.

The new clothes were softer than her own had been, finer. In the early light, when the freight engine slowed at the little crossings, she jumped off with the baby in her arms and walked back up the tracks to the first platform she came to. That was a village called Marlowe, and because it was as good a name as any, she named the baby Marlowe too, and in the only lodging house next to the old roadhouse she paid for a room, and lay herself down in the clean sheets without even taking off her boots, the baby a warm softness on her chest, and together they slept and slept.

In the morning she bought a third-class ticket to Cambridge, and from there she and the baby continued south, into King's Cross, into the smoke of darkest London.

The money she had stolen did not last. In Rotherhithe she gave out a story that her young husband had perished in a carting accident and that she was seeking employment. On Church Street she found work and lodging in a waterman's pub alongside its owner and his wife, and was happy for a time. She did not mind the hard work, the scrubbing of the floors, the stacking of jars, the weighing and sifting of flour and sugar from the barrels. She even found she had a good head for sums. And on Sundays she would take the baby all the way across Bermondsey to Battersea Park, to the long grass there, the Thames just visible through the haze, and together they would splash barefoot in the puddles and throw rocks at the geese while the wandering poor flickered like candlelight on the paths. She was almost showing by then and worried all the time, for she knew she was pregnant with her old employer's child, but then one morning, crouched over the chamber pot, a fierce cramping took hold in her and something red and slick came out and, however much it hurt her, that was the end of that.

Then one murky night in June a woman stopped her in the street. The reek of the Thames was thick in the air. Eliza was working as a washergirl in Wapping by then, making barely enough to eat, she and the baby sleeping under a viaduct. Her shawl was ragged, her thin-boned hands blotched and red with sores. The woman who stopped her was huge, almost a giantess, with the shoulders of a wrestler and thick silver hair worn in a braid down her back and eyes as small and black as the polished buttons on a good pair of boots. Her name, she said, was Brynt. She spoke with a broad, flat American accent. She said she knew she was a sight but Eliza and the baby should not be alarmed for who among them did not have some difference, hidden though it might be, and was that not the wonder of God's hand in the world? She had worked sideshows for years, she knew the effect she could have on a person, but she followed the good Reverend Walker now at the Turk's Head Theatre and forgive her for being forward but had Eliza yet been saved?

And when Eliza did not reply, only stared up unspeaking, that huge woman, Brynt, folded back the cowl to see the baby's face, and Eliza felt a sudden dread, as if Marlowe might not be himself, might not be quite right, and she pulled him away. But it was just the baby, smiling sleepily up. That was when Eliza spied the tattoos covering the big woman's hands, vanishing up into her sleeves, like a sailor just in from the East Indies. Creatures entwined, monstrous faces. There was ink on the woman's throat too, as if her whole body might be colored.

"Don't be afraid," said Brynt.

But Eliza was not frightened; she just had not seen the like before.

Brynt led her through the fog down an alley and across a dripping court to a ramshackle theater leaning out over the muddy river. Inside, all was smoky, dim. The room was scarcely bigger than a railway carriage. She saw the good Reverend Walker in shirtsleeves and waistcoat stalking the little stage, candlelight playing on his face, as he called to a crowd of sailors and streetwalkers about the apocalypse to come, and when the preaching was done he began to peddle his elixirs and unguents and ointments. Later Eliza and the baby were taken to where he sat behind a curtain, toweling his forehead and throat, a thin man, in truth little bigger than a boy. His hair was gray, his eyes were ancient and afire. His soft fingers trembled as he unscrewed the lid of his laudanum.

"There's but the one Book of Christ," he said softly. He raised a bleary bloodshot stare. "But there's as many kinds of Christian as there is folk who did ever walk this earth."

He made a fist and then he opened his fingers wide.

"The many out of the one," he whispered.

"The many out of the one," Brynt repeated, like a prayer. "These two got nowhere to stay, Reverend."

The reverend grunted, his eyes glazing over. It was as if he were alone, as if he had forgotten Eliza entirely. His lips were moving silently.

Brynt steered her away by the elbow. "He's just tired now, is all," she said. "But he likes you, honey. You and the baby both. You want someplace to sleep?"

They stayed. At first just for the night, and then through the day, and then until the next week. She liked the way Brynt was with the baby, and it was only Brynt and the reverend after all, Brynt handling the labor, the reverend mixing his elixirs in the creaking old theater, *arguing with God through a closed door*, as Brynt would say. Eliza had thought Brynt and the reverend lovers but soon she understood the reverend had no interest in women and when she saw this she felt at once a great relief. She handled the washing and the hauling and even some of the cooking, though Brynt made a face each night at the smell of the pot, and Eliza also swept out the hall and helped trim the stage candles and rebuilt the benches daily out of boards and bricks.

It was in October when two figures pushed their way into the theater, sweeping the rain from their chesterfields. The taller of the two ran a hand down his dripping beard, his eyes hidden under the brim of his hat. But she knew him all the same. It was the man who had hunted her with dogs, back in Suffolk. Her dead employer's father.

She shrank at the curtain, willing herself to disappear. But she could not take her eyes from him, though she had imagined this moment, dreamed it so many times, woken in a sweat night after night. She watched, unable to move, as he walked the perimeter of the crowd, studying the faces, and it was like she was just waiting for him to find her. But he did not look her way. He met his companion again at the back of the theater and unbuttoned his chesterfield and withdrew a gold pocket watch on a chain as if he might be late for some appointment and then the two of them pushed their way back out into the murk of Wapping and Eliza, untouched, breathed again.

"Who were they, child?" Brynt asked later, in her low rumbling voice, the lamplight playing across her tattooed knuckles. "What did they do to you?"

But she could not say, could not tell her it was *she* who had done to *them*, could only clutch the baby close and shiver. She knew it was no coincidence, knew in that moment that he hunted her still, would hunt her for always. And all the good feeling she had felt, here, with the reverend and with Brynt, was gone. She could not stay, not with them. It would not be right.

But she didn't leave, not at once. And then one gray morning, carrying the washing pail across Runyan's Court, she was met by Brynt, who took from her big skirts a folded paper and handed it across. There was a drunk sleeping in the muck. Washing strung up on a line. Eliza opened the paper and saw her own likeness staring out.

It had come from an advertisement in a broadsheet. Notice of reward, for the apprehension of a murderess.

Eliza, who could not read, said only, "Is it me name on it?"

"Oh, honey," said Brynt softly.

And Eliza told her then, told her everything, right there in that gloomy court. It came out halting at first and then in a terrible rush and she found as she spoke that it was a relief, she had not realized how hard it had been, keeping it secret. She told of the man in his nightshirt, the candle fire in his eyes, the hunger there, and the way it hurt and kept on hurting until he was finished, and how his hands had smelled of lotion and she had fumbled in pain for her dresser and felt . . . *something*, a sharpness under her fingers, and hit him with it, and only saw what she had done after she had pushed him off her. She told about the boxcar too and the lantern that was not a lantern and how the baby had looked at her that first night, and she even told about taking the banknotes from the dead mother, and the fine clothes off her stiffening body. And when she was done, she watched Brynt blow out her cheeks and sit heavily on an overturned pail with her big knees high and her belly rolling forward and her eyes crushed shut.

"Brynt?" she said, all at once afraid. "Is it a very large reward, what they's offering?"

At that Brynt lifted her tattooed hands and stared from one to the other as if to descry some riddle there. "I could see it in you," she said quietly, "the very first day I saw you there, on the street. I could see there was a something."

"Is it a very large reward, Brynt?" she said again.

Brynt nodded.

"What do you aim to do? Will you tell the reverend?"

Brynt looked up. She shook her huge head slowly. "This world's a big place, honey. There are some who think you run far enough, you can outrun anything. Even your mistakes."

"Is—is that what you think?"

"Aw, I been running eighteen years now. You can't outrun your own self."

Eliza wiped at her eyes, ran the back of her wrist over her nose. "I didn't mean to do it," she whispered.

Brynt nodded at the paper in Eliza's hand. She started to go, and then she stopped.

"Sometimes the bastards just plain deserve it," she said fiercely.

Meanwhile Marlowe, black-haired, coltish, grew. His skin stayed eerily white, a stark unhealthy pallor, as if he'd never known sunlight. Yet he grew into a sweet toddler, with a smile that could open a purse and eyes as blue as a Suffolk sky. But there was something else in him sometimes, a temper, and as he got older Eliza would sometimes see him screw his face up into a fury and stamp his foot when he did not get his way, and she'd wonder what sort of a devil was in him. At such times he'd scream and holler and grab whatever was nearest, a fig of coal, an inkwell, anything, and smash it to pieces. Brynt tried to tell her that this was the normal way of a child, that two-year-olds all went through it, there was nothing the matter with him, but Eliza was not so sure.

For there was that one night in St Georges Street, when he wanted something—what was it, a stick of licorice in a shop-front window?—and Eliza, tired maybe, or just distracted, had told him no, firmly, and dragged him by the hand away through the crowds. There was a wide cobblestone stair leading down to Bolt Alley and she dragged him to it. "I want it! I want it!" he was crying. He'd scowled at her with such darkness and poison then. And she'd felt a heat bloom in her palm and fingers where she gripped his, and she'd stopped in the middle of the cobbled stair in the faint yellow of a gas lamp above, and seen that same blue shine coming out of him, and a most excruciating pain came over her hand. Marlowe was glaring at her in anger, fuming, watching her face twist in agony. And she'd screamed and pushed him away, and there in the shadows was a figure in a cloak, at the bottom of the cobblestone stair, and it turned and stared up at them, as still and unmoving as a pillar of darkness, but it had no face, only smoke, and she'd shuddered to see it—

But then Marlowe's anger was gone, the blue shine was gone. He was peering up at her where he had fallen in the muck, peering up in confusion, and fear contorted his little pale face, and he started to cry. She cradled her hand against her chest and wrapped it in her shawl and drew the child close with her good arm, crooning softly, feeling both ashamed and afraid, and she looked around but the thing on the stairs below was gone.

Then Marlowe was six and they had lost the theater in Wapping to the rents and were all living in a miserable room off Flower and Dean Street, in Spitalfields, but it seemed to her that maybe Brynt had been wrong, maybe it was possible to outrun your mistakes after all. It had been two years since the advertisements in the broadsheets had stopped appearing. From Spitalfields Eliza trudged all the way down to the Thames to mudlark in the thick deep gluey muck of the river at low tide, Brynt being too heavy to manage it, Marlowe still far too young. But he would run alongside the coal wagons in the foggy streets, picking up the little rocks of coal from the cobblestones, sliding under the legs of the horses and dodging the ironshod wheels, while Brynt stood behind the bollards watching him with worried eyes. Eliza liked very little about Spitalfields, it was dark and vicious, but she did like the way Marlowe survived it, the toughness in him, the way he learned watchfulness, his large eyes dark with knowing. And sometimes at night he still climbed onto the bug-riddled mattress beside her and she listened to his heart beating very fast and it was like it had been before, when he was a baby, uncomplicated and sweet and good.

But not always. In the spring of that year she had come upon him crouched in a trash-strewn alley off Thrawl Street, holding his left wrist in his right hand, and that shine started out from his hands and his throat and his face, just as had happened all those years ago. The glow was blue and bleeding through the fog. When he took his hand away, his skin for just a moment was bubbling and oozing. Then it smoothed itself back to normal. Eliza cried out, despite herself, she couldn't help it, and Marlowe turned guiltily and pulled his sleeve down and like that the shine was gone.

"Mama . . . ?" he said.

They were alone in that alley but she could hear the silk wagons creaking not ten paces from them in the fog-thick street beyond and the roar and shouting of men at their selling carts.

"Oh my heart," she murmured. She kneeled beside him, uncertain what more to say. She did not think he would remember that day when he'd burned her hand. Whether he knew what he did or not, she could not be sure, but she knew it was not a good thing in this world to be different. She tried to explain this to him. She said every person has two destinies granted them by God and that it is a person's task in this life to choose the one or the other. She looked into his little face and saw his cheeks white in the cold and his black hair long over his ears and she felt an overwhelming sadness.

"You always have a choice, Marlowe," she said. "Do you understand me?"

He nodded. But she did not think he understood at all.

When he spoke, his voice was little more than a whisper. "Is it bad, Mama?" he asked.

"Oh, honey. No."

He thought for a moment. "Because it's from God?"

She chewed her lip. Nodded.

"Mama?"

"Yes?"

"What if I don't want to be different?"

She told him he must never be afraid of who he was but that he must hide it, this blue shining, whatever it was. *Even from the reverend? Yes. Even from Brynt? Even from Brynt.* She said its purpose would make itself known to him in time but until such day there were those who would put it to their own ends. And many others who would fear it.

That was the year the reverend started coughing up blood. A leech in Whitechapel said a dryer clime might aid him but Brynt just ducked her head, storming out into the fog. The reverend had come out of the American deserts as a boy, she explained later, angrily, and all he wanted now was to go back to the deserts to die. As they drifted slowly through the gaslit nights, his face looked grayer, his eyes more and more yellow, until he stopped even the pretense of mixing his elixirs and just sold straight whiskey, telling any who would listen that it had been blessed by a holy man in the Black Hills of Agrapur, though Eliza did not think his customers cared, and even this lie he told wearily, unconvincingly, like a man who no longer believed in his truth or their truth or any truth at all.

The reverend collapsed in the rain one night, while weaving sickly on a crate, hollering to the passersby on Wentworth Road for the salvation of their souls, and Brynt carried him in her arms back to the rookery. The rain came in through the roof in several places and the wallpaper was long since peeled away and mold grew in a fur around the window. It was in that room on the seventh day of his raving that Eliza and Marlowe heard a soft knock at their door and she rose and opened it, thinking it might be Brynt, and she saw instead a strange man standing there.

A corona of gray light from the landing beyond haloed his beard and the edges of his hat so that his eyes were lost to shadow when he spoke.

"Miss Eliza Grey," he said.

It was not an unkind voice, almost gentle, the sort of voice she imagined might come from a grandfather in a children's story.

"Yes," she said slowly.

"Is it Brynt back?" Marlowe called. "Mama? Is it Brynt?"

The man took off his hat then and turned his face sideways to see past her and all at once she caught sight of his face, the long red scar over one eye, the meanness in it. He was wearing a white flower in his lapel. She started to shut the door but he put out a big hand, almost without effort, and let himself inside, and then he shut the door at his back.

"We haven't yet been acquainted, Miss Grey," he said. "I do believe that will be rectified in time. Who is this, then?"

He was looking at Marlowe where he stood in the middle of the room holding a little brown stuffed bear close to his chest. That bear was missing one eye and the stuffing was coming out of one leg, but it was the boy's only treasure. He was staring up at the stranger with a blank expression on his pallid face. It was not fear, not yet. But she saw that he sensed something was wrong.

"It's all right, sweet," she said. "You go on back to the reverend. It's only a gentleman what wants some business with me."

"A gentleman," the man murmured, as if amused by it. "Who might you be, son?"

"Marlowe," said the boy sturdily.

"And how old are you, Marlowe?"

"Six."

"And who is that on the mattress back there?" he said, waving his hat at the reverend where he lay, sweating and delirious, face turned to the wall.

"Reverend Walker," said Marlowe. "But he's sick."

"Go on," said Eliza quickly, her heart in her throat. "Go on sit with the reverend. Go."

"Are you a policeman?" said Marlowe.

"*Marlowe*," she said.

"Why, yes I am, son." The man turned his hat in his fingers, studying the boy, and then he met Eliza's gaze. His eyes were hard and small and very dark. "Where's the woman?" he said.

"What woman?"

He raised his hand above his head, to Brynt's height. "The American. The wrestler."

"If you wish to speak with her—"

"I don't," he said. There was a crooked chair at the wall and he set his hat down and caught his reflection in the clouded window and paused and ran a hand over his mustache. Then he looked around with a measured eye. He was dressed in a green checkered suit, and his fingers were stained with ink, like a bank clerk's. The white flower, Eliza saw now, was wilted.

"What is it you want, then?" she said, trying to keep the fear from her voice.

He smiled at that. He folded his jacket back and she saw the revolver at his hip. "Miss Grey, there is a gentleman of some doubtful provenance, residing at present in Blackwell Court, who's been asking all across Spitalfields about you. He says you are the recipient of an inheritance, and he wishes to locate you."

"Me?"

His eyes glittered. "You."

"It can't be. I got no kin anywhere."

"Of course you don't. You are Eliza Mackenzie Grey, formerly of Bury St Edmunds, under notice as a fugitive from the law for the killing of a man—your employer—are you not?"

Eliza felt her cheeks color.

"There's a considerable reward out. No mention of a child, though."
He looked at Marlowe with an unreadable expression. "I don't much
imagine the gentleman will want him too. I can find a suitable position
for him somewhere. Apprentice work. Keep him away from the work-
houses. It would be a sight better than here, with your dying reverend
and his crazy American."

"Brynt isn't crazy," said Marlowe from the corner.

"Sweet," said Eliza desperately, "you go on over to Cowett's and ask
for Brynt, all right? Tell her the reverend wants her." She went toward
the door to usher him out when she heard a hollow click, and froze.

"Step away from the door now, that's a girl."

The man had leveled his revolver in the faint gray light leaking in
through the window. He put back on his hat.

"You don't much resemble a killer," he said. "I'll grant you that."

He had taken out a slender pair of nickel-plated wrist irons with
his free hand from the pocket of his waistcoat, and in a moment he
was alongside her, grabbing her roughly by the arm, fastening the irons
at her right wrist and reaching for her left. She tried to resist.

"Don't—" she tried to say.

Marlowe, across the room, got to his feet. "Mama?" he said. "Mama!"

The man was pushing Eliza toward the door, ignoring her boy,
when Marlowe came at him. He looked so small. She watched almost
in slow motion as he reached up and grabbed the man's wrist with
both his little hands, as if to hold him back. The man turned, and for
what seemed a long moment to Eliza, though it could not have been
more than seconds, he stared down at the boy in amazement and then
in wonder and then something in his face twisted into a kind of horror.
Marlowe was shining. The man dropped the revolver and opened his
mouth to scream but he did not scream.

Eliza in the struggle had fallen back against the wall. Marlowe's face was turned from her so she could not see him, but she could see the man's arm where the boy held it, could see how it had begun to bubble and then to soften like hot wax. His neck twisted, his legs gave out, and then somehow he was pouring down around himself, gelid, heavy, thick like molasses, his green suit bulging in weird places, and within moments what had been a powerful man in his prime was reduced to a lumpen twist of flesh, his face a rictus of agony, his eyes wide and staring from the melt that had been his head.

In the stillness, Marlowe let go of the wrist. The blue shine faded. The man's arm stood rigid out from the frozen mess of flesh.

"Mama?" said Marlowe. He looked over at her, and he started to cry.

The shabby room was very cold, very damp. She went to him and held him as best she could with the wrist irons still locked, feeling how he shook, and she was shaking also. He buried his face in her shoulder, and no part of her had felt before what was in her just then—not the horror, not the pity, not the love.

But she was not afraid, not of her little boy.

She found the keys to the irons in the man's waistcoat pocket. She rolled Marlowe in their good blanket and lit the last of the coal in the scuttle and rocked him to sleep at the reverend's bedside, the ruined body of the bounty hunter on the floor beneath the window. The boy slept easily, exhausted. Brynt was still away, working, maybe, until morning. When Marlowe was asleep Eliza rolled the misshapen body into their other blanket and stuffed the revolver in too and then dragged him with difficulty to the door and down the creaking stairs, his heels thumping at each step, thumping even as she struggled over the stoop into the black of the alley behind.

The men would not stop coming for her, whoever they were. In

Wapping, in Spitalfields, wherever. They would wear different faces and be of any age and carry any kind of firearm but the money offered would always be what it was and too much for a person to deny.

Eliza did not go back inside. She thought of Marlowe whom she loved and she knew with a sudden clarity that he would be safer by far with Brynt. Brynt, who knew the ways of the world, who was not wanted by bounty hunters, who had talked of returning to America one day. It seemed now like a kind of dream. In Blackwell Court two streets over there waited a man with a pint in his fist and a weapon in his pocket and he would be awake even at this hour. She drew her filthy shawl closer around herself. She gripped her elbows in her crossed hands. She walked down the dripping cobblestones through the fog and then into the street. Her heart was breaking but she did not let herself slow or turn or look back at the cracked window of their rented room for fear of what she would see, the small figure silhouetted there, wrapped in a blanket, his pale hand pressed to the glass.

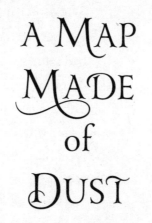

A Map Made of Dust

1882

2

LITTLE FIRES

It felt like little fires in his flesh. That is what he tried to explain to them. That it *hurt*.

His name was Charlie Ovid and he was maybe sixteen years old by the judge's reckoning and despite a lifetime of whippings and beatings and brutality there was not a scar anywhere on his body. At six feet he was as tall as he would ever be but still lean through the chest like a boy. His arms were wiry with muscle. He did not himself know why his body fixed itself the way it did but he did not think it had anything to do with Jesus, and he knew enough to know it was better kept to himself. His mama was black and his daddy was white in a world that looked at him a monster.

He could tell neither his age nor the month of his birth but he was smarter than they thought and he could even read some and write out his own name in careful letters if they gave him the time to do it. He was born in London, England, but his father had dreams of California, of a better world for them all. Maybe he'd even have found it, had he lived long enough to get there. But he'd died in their wagon train in Texas, south of the Indian Territory, leaving Charlie and his mother stranded, with only enough coin to get them back east again past Louisiana. After that they were just two more drifting black folk in a country full of them and when his mother took sick and died five years later, she left him nothing but her wedding ring. That ring was silver with a crest of crossed hammers in front of a fiery sun, and Charlie, not even ten years old, would hold it and turn it in his fingers in the lantern light, remembering the smell of her, wondering at his father who had given it to her in love, trying to imagine who he had been. Charlie still had that ring, hidden on his person. No one was taking that from him.

His mother had known what he could do, the healing. She'd loved him anyway. But he'd tried his best to keep it a secret from everyone else, and that—as much as the healing—had kept him alive. He had survived the river work south of Natchez, Mississippi, and the dark shanties that had sprung up nearer River Forks Road in that same town but here, standing manacled in the darkness of an old warehouse shift room, he was not sure he would survive this. Everything he'd ever known or lost or suffered in his brief life had taught him the same solitary truth: everyone leaves you, eventually. In this world, you only got yourself.

He wore neither shoes nor coat and his homespun shirt was stiff with his own blood and his trousers were ragged. He was being kept in the warehouse and not in the jail on account of the fear the sheriff's wife had of him. He was pretty sure that was it. For two weeks now he'd been kept manacled at the ankles and his wrists cuffed in front. The deputy marshal would come some days with other white men holding clubs and chains and they would set the lantern down on the floor and in the crazy shadows beat him for the sport of it and then watch laughing in amazement as the wounds closed over. But even as he healed, the blood was real, the pain he felt was real. The terror as he lay crying in the darkness was real.

Later he could do little but lurch, clanking from wall to wall in the near dark, feeling the little fires where his wounds had been, the tears and snot drying on his face, careful not to knock over the bucket of his own night soil. His wrists were so narrow the irons had kept sliding off until the sheriff brought in a set made special by the blacksmith, and those ones fit. The only furniture in the room was a bench suspended from the wall on rusting chains and he would lie out on it when he thought it must be night and try sometimes to sleep.

He was lying on it that day when he heard voices in the street outside. It was not mealtime, he knew that much. Mealtime came but twice a day and it was the deputy marshal who brought it over on a tray covered in cheesecloth straight from the sheriff's kitchen up the street and the deputy marshal would sometimes make a point of spitting in it before setting it down. Charlie hated him, hated and feared him, the casual cruelty in him and the way he called Charlie mongrel and his coarse laugh. But most of all it was the look in the man's eye that frightened Charlie, the look that said he, Charlie, was just an animal, that he was not even a person at all.

From outside there came the banging of tumblers in the big warehouse door and then the slow heavy tread of boots approaching. Charlie got to his feet, cringing, afraid.

He had killed a man. A white man. That is what they told him. It was that Mr. Jessup who stalked the wharf of the riverboat shipping lines going south to New Orleans and north to St. Louis with a whip singing in his fist, just like it was still 1860, just like no war had ever happened and nothing had been abolished and freedom wasn't yet the lie it would be proven to be. The man he killed deserved it, he was sure of that, he felt no remorse. But the thing of it was, he did not remember the killing. He knew it had happened because at the hearing everybody had said he had done it, even old Benji, with his sad eyes and trembling hands. *In broad daylight, yessir. On the lumber platforms, yessir.* Charlie was being whipped for some transgression or other and it went on so long he could feel the slashes beginning to close over and when Mr. Jessup saw it too and swore and started calling down the devil on him Charlie turned in fear, turned too quickly, it must have been, and he knocked into Mr. Jessup and the man had fallen onto the pier and struck his head funny and that was that. But when they tried to shoot him for it Charlie just started breathing again almost at once and the bullets oozed back out of his flesh in front of the executioner's very eyes. And when they tied him to a post a second time and took their aim they still could not kill him and they did not now know what to do with him.

Now the footsteps had stopped and Charlie heard the scrape and jangle of the keys on their ring and then the heavy door with its iron locks shook. The sound of a club striking the metal clashed and echoed.

"On your feet!" the deputy marshal shouted. "You got visitors, boy. Straighten up."

Charlie flinched and moved to the rear wall so that the cold bricks were against his back. He held his hands in front of his face, shaking. No one came to visit him, ever.

He took a deep frightened breath.

The door swung open.

Alice Quicke, tired, sore-knuckled, world-weary, was standing in the white sunlight outside the ruined warehouse in Natchez, glaring up the steep street as her partner, Coulton, ambled toward her. Four nights earlier, in a wharf-side eatery in New Orleans, she had found it necessary to acquaint a man's nose with the brass railing of the bar, and only Coulton's revolver and a hasty exit had prevented real bloodshed. Sometimes men made themselves at home in women's clothing in a way she had less and less patience for as she got older. She was over thirty now and she'd never been married and never wanted to be. She'd lived by violence and her own wits since she was a girl and that seemed good enough to her. She preferred trousers to bustles and corsets, and wore over her wide shoulders a long oilskin coat, cut for a night watchman, with the sleeves folded back off her wrists. It'd been black once, faded now almost to gray in places, with tarnished silver buttons. Her yellow hair was greasy and tangled, cut to a manageable length by her own hand. She was almost pretty, maybe, with a heart-shaped face and fine features, but her eyes were hard, and her nose had been broken years ago and badly set, and she did not smile enough for the attentions of men to linger. That was fine by her. She was a female detective and it was hard enough to get taken seriously without having her goddamn hand kissed at every turn.

Coulton, up the street, was in no hurry. She watched him drift casually under the leafy green poplars, fanning his bowler hat as he went, one thumb hooked in his waistcoat. All around her lay the shabby riverside stillness of a city still pretty in all its architecture, all of it built on the backs of slaves, pretty like a poisonous flower. Coulton was coming from the sheriff's house, from the little brick jail beside it.

She was beginning to hate this job.

She had located her first orphan, a girl named Mary, in a rooming house in Sheffield, England, last March. The second one went missing before they even got to Cape Town, South Africa. Alice found his grave newly dug, red gravel, no grass, a little wooden marker. Dead of a fever, the burial paid for by a Ladies' Aid society. Coulton told her about others who'd come from Oxford, Belfast, Whitechapel itself. In June she and Coulton had sailed for Baltimore and collected a girl from a workhouse there and later sailed south for New Orleans and booked passage on a riverboat steamer upriver and now they were here, in Mississippi, looking for one Charles Ovid, whoever that was.

She didn't know more than that because she'd been given nothing but the kid's name and the address of the Natchez city courthouse. That was how it worked. She didn't ask questions, she just got on with it. Sometimes she was only given a street, or a neighborhood, or the city itself. It didn't matter. She always found them.

Coulton was wearing a yellow-checkered suit despite the heat and his whiskers stood out in a frazzle at his jaw. He was as good as bald but he combed what hair he had left across his scalp and was always reaching up, smoothing it into place. He was maybe the most reliable man she'd ever known, stout and polite like a good Englishman, straight out of the middle classes. But Alice had also seen him move with a fury through a smoky pub in Deptford leaving bodies in his wake and she knew not to underestimate him.

"He's not here," Coulton said now, coming up. "They're holding him in a warehouse." He waved his bowler slowly by its brim, mopped his face with a handkerchief. "Sheriff's wife didn't want his like in with the others, it seems."

"Because he's black?"

"Not that. I expect they have plenty of his kind in the jug."

She waited.

"I'll have to sit down with the local judge, hear what he has to say," he went on. "The sheriff's arranged it for later this evening. Legally speaking, the lad ain't property, but I get the impression he's the next best thing to it. Near as I can figure, depot sort of owns him."

"What'd he do?"

"Killed a white man."

Alice looked up.

"Aye. Some sort of accident at the dockyards where he was working. A confrontation with an overseer and the man fell off the platform and hit his head. Dead, just like that. No great loss to the world maybe. Sheriff doesn't believe it was done on *purpose*, but he also says it doesn't matter to him, what happened happened, you can't have it happening again. Now here's the thing. Lad's already been tried and found guilty. His sentence was carried out."

"Carried out—?"

Coulton opened his hands wide. "They shot him. Six days ago. It didn't take."

"What do you mean, it didn't take?"

Coulton peered calmly back at the jail, his eyes shadowed. "Well, lad's still breathing. I reckon that's their meaning. Sheriff's wife says the lad can't be hurt."

"I bet he'd say different."

"Aye."

"And that's why he's locked up in a warehouse. Because they don't want the good folk getting all worked up."

"Miss Quicke, they don't want the good folk even to *know*. Far as the town of Natchez is concerned, Charles Ovid was shot dead in the jail six days ago. The lad's already buried."

Can't be hurt. Alice blew out her cheeks. She loathed the small-minded superstitions of little towns, had done so all her life. She knew these people wanted a reason, any reason, to hit and keep on hitting a black kid who'd killed a white man. Bullshit about it not leaving a mark was as good as any.

"So what're they going to do now?" she said. "I mean, if we didn't show up offering to take him off their hands, what would they do with him?"

"I reckon they'd go ahead and bury him."

She paused. "But if they can't kill him—"

Coulton held her eye.

And then she understood. They would bury him *alive*. She let her gaze drift off over his shoulder. "This fucking place," she said.

"Aye." Coulton squinted out at whatever it was she was watching, saw nothing, looked up at the cloudless sky.

There were two men approaching now from up the street, silhouetted and rippling in the heat. They came on foot without horses, both wearing suits, the taller man cradling a rifle crosswise in front of him. The sheriff and his deputy, she supposed. "What would you like to do to them?" she said softly.

Coulton put his bowler back on, turned. "The very same as you, Miss Quicke," he said. "But our employers would not approve. Justice is just a bucket with a hole in the bottom, as my father used to say. You ready?"

Alice rubbed her knuckles.

She'd worked with Frank Coulton for thirteen months and had come nearly to trust him, as much as she trusted anyone at least. He'd found her through an advertisement she had posted in the *Times*. He'd climbed the water-buckled stairs of her tenement in Deptford, clutching the clipping in the pocket of his chesterfield, his breath standing out like smoke in the cold. He wished to inquire, he'd explained in a quiet voice, after her credentials. A yellow fog rolled past in the dripping alley outside. He'd heard things, he went on, had heard she'd been trained by the Pinkertons in Chicago, that she'd beaten a man unconscious with her bare fists on the East India Docks. Was there any truth to such reports?

Truth, she'd thought in disgust. What did the word even mean?

Truth: she'd survived as a pickpocket on the streets of Chicago from the age of fourteen. Truth: she had a mother incarcerated in an asylum for the criminally deranged whom she had not seen in nearly twenty years, and no other family in all the world. She was eighteen when she picked the wrong pocket and the hand that seized her wrist turned out to belong to Allan Pinkerton, private detective, railroad man, intelligence agent for the Union cause, but instead of turning her in he took a shine to her and invited her to his offices, and to her own surprise she went. He trained her in the art of undercover operatives. She did that for eight years and you could ask any of two dozen bastards sitting in jail somewhere if she was good at it and they would spit and wipe their mouths and concede it by the hate in their eyes. But when Pinkerton's sons rose to power she was let go, all because she was a *woman*, and therefore *delicate*, and therefore not *right* for *detective work*. She put her fist through the wall of William Pinkerton's office when he fired her.

"Your fucking *wall* is delicate," she said to him.

But after that she could only get work at racetracks up and down the Eastern Seaboard and when that too dried up she bought a ticket on a liner bound for London, England, because where else and why not. There she discovered a city so dark with vice and cutthroats and foggy gaslit alleys that even a female detective from Chicago with hair the yellow of murky sulfur and fists like mallets could find plenty of doing needing to be done.

The sheriff and his deputy came down the hot street, nodding politely as they neared. The deputy was whistling, badly and off-key.

"Mr. Coulton," said the sheriff. "We could've walked down together. And you must be Mrs.—"

"*Miss* Quicke," said Coulton, introducing her. "Don't let her fine looks deceive you, gentlemen. I bring her for my protection."

The sheriff seemed to find this amusing. The deputy was cradling his rifle, studying Alice like a strange creature washed up out of the river, but there was no contempt in it, no hostility. He saw her watching and smiled shyly.

"We don't get many visitors from overseas no more," said the sheriff. "Not since the war. Was a time we saw all sorts of folk, Frenchmen,

Spaniards. Even a Russian countess lived here for a time, ain't that right, Alwyn? She had different customs, too."

The deputy, Alwyn, blushed. "My daddy always said so," he said. "But that was before my recollection. I ain't married neither, miss."

Alice bit back her retort. "Where's the boy?" she said instead.

"Ah, yes. You're here for Charlie Ovid." The sheriff's face darkened with regret. "Come on, then." He stopped a moment and adjusted his hat and frowned. "Now, I don't know I should be doing this. But seeing as how you come all this way, and you'll be talking to Judge Diamond later, I don't know that it's a problem neither. But I don't want you talking about what you see. It's kindly a sore point around here, this boy. He's the damnedest thing."

"An abomination is what he is," muttered the deputy. "Like one of them things in the Bible."

"What things?" said Alice.

He blushed again. "Satan's minions. Them monsters he made."

She stopped and faced him and stared up the length of him. "That's not in the Bible," she said. "You mean Leviathan and Behemoth?"

"They's the ones."

"Those are God's monsters. God made them."

The deputy looked unsure. "Aw, I don't think—"

"You should."

The sheriff was unlocking the heavy warehouse door, lock by lock. "England, you said," he murmured. "That's a distance and a half to come for a little old black boy."

"Aye," said Coulton at the sheriff's elbow, offering nothing more.

The sheriff paused at the last lock, glanced back. "You know, there ain't any way the judge is going to let this boy go," he said pleasantly. "Not with you or with anybody."

"I hope you're mistaken," said Coulton.

"I don't say it to be personal, now." The sheriff offered a smile. "I always did want to see England someday. The missus, she says, 'Maybe it's time you hung up your spurs, Bill, and we took ourselves a voyage.' Her parents come over from Cornwall once upon a time, you see. Now, I don't know if I'm just too old to go wandering about the world like a tinker. But it seems a distance and a half, you ask me."

The warehouse was dark and smelled faintly of sour cotton and rust. The air was stifling, thick. Just inside the door on nails in the wall hung two old lanterns and the deputy took down one and opened its glass door and lit it with a flint and then they shut the door behind them. The light swung loosely in the man's fist. Alice sighted the outlines of great machinery in the gloom, hooks and chains hanging in long loops from the rafters. The sheriff led them across the warehouse floor to a grimy corridor, its walls punctured with holes as if from bullets, daylight streaming through. There were the outlines of doors along the opposite wall and at the end a single thick iron door with several locks and here the sheriff paused.

The deputy set down the lantern, swung the butt of his rifle against the door. "On your feet!" he shouted through. "You got visitors, boy. Straighten up."

He turned shyly to Alice. "I don't know that he's all there, miss. Don't be alarmed by him none. He's a bit like an animal."

Alice said nothing.

The door swung open. Inside all was darkness. A terrible stench wafted out, a stink of unwashed flesh and filth and feces.

"Good God," muttered Coulton. "This is he?"

The sheriff held a handkerchief to his mouth and nodded gravely.

The deputy held the lantern out before him, entering cautiously. Alice could make out the figure of the boy now, hunched against the far wall. He was tall and skinny. She could see the glint of light on the manacles at his wrists, the chain at his ankles. As she slipped inside she caught sight of his ragged trousers, his shirt crusted brown with dried blood, the terror in his eyes. But his face was smooth, fine-boned, unbruised and unswollen, his eyelashes long and dark. She'd been expecting a terrible damage; it was strange. His small ears stuck out from his head like little handles. He raised his hands in front of him, as if to ward off a blow, as if the light pained him. The chains rustled softly as he breathed.

"I never saw nothing like him in all my life," said the deputy, almost with admiration. He was talking to Alice. "Wouldn't none of us believe it if we hadn't seen it with our own eyes. All that blood's his own, but you won't find a mark on him. You take a club to him, he just gets back up. You take a knife to him, he just heals right in front of you. I swear, it's almost enough to make a man believe in the devil."

"Yes it is," muttered Alice, glaring at the deputy in the bad light.

"Go on, Alwyn," said the sheriff. "Show them."

The boy cowered.

"By God, Mr. Coulton—!" Alice said, too loudly.

Coulton held out a hand to stop the deputy. "That won't be necessary, Alwyn," he said, in his calm way. "We believe you. It's the reason we're here."

He reached into his pocket and withdrew the letter with their instructions, written from their employer in London. He unfolded the papers, held them to the light. Alice could see the Cairndale crest, stamped prominently upon the envelope. The wax seal like a thumbprint of blood.

Charles Ovid was staring at the envelope too, Alice saw. He had gone very still, watchful like a cat, his eyes shining in the darkness.

The shift room was long but narrow. Alice stepped forward, feeling a great disgust rising in her at the thought of these two men, of this poor boy. Whatever Coulton was saying, she knew that injuries didn't just heal over on their own. Hell, some of them never healed. She knew a little about that, too.

She pulled off her gloves. Her knuckles were red and bruised. She was looking at the boy's manacles. "You can start by taking these off," she called over her shoulder. She looked back. "Alwyn, is it?"

No one moved. The sheriff glanced at Coulton.

"It's all right, sir," said Coulton, sliding the letter back into his waistcoat pocket. "I assure you. It's just for the examination."

The deputy moved to the far end and kneeled and unlocked the ankle irons and then stood and removed the wristlets. He stepped back, his hands full of the loops of chain.

Alice walked over and stood in front of Ovid and reached out and took his hands in her own. They were soft, unhurt. She was surprised that there were no calluses. In the gloom, he was trembling.

"Is that better?" she murmured, looking up at him.

Ovid said nothing.

"Miss," called the sheriff sharply. "It won't do for a lady like yourself to be touching his kind. Not here, not in Natchez. Step back, please."

Alice ignored him. She tilted the boy Ovid's chin in the light until she caught his eye. Despite everything he had suffered, despite his trembling and the way he cowered, his eyes when he looked at her were cool, intelligent, unfrightened. He had the fierce stillness of a kid who'd had only himself to rely on. The others maybe didn't see this. But she did.

"Miss—" called the sheriff.

"Charles Ovid," she whispered. She could not keep the outrage from her voice. "Charlie, is it? My name is Alice. This is Mr. Coulton. The people we work for sent us here to help you, to take you away from all this. So that no one will hurt you like this again."

She felt rather than heard the sheriff approach. He slipped his big hand under her arm, not roughly, and pulled her out of the boy's reach.

"You'll take that up with the judge," he said. "But until then, we'll keep things right and proper here."

But Alice was watching Charlie Ovid.

If he understood her, he gave no sign; he just flinched as the sheriff emerged, and lowered his eyes, and went on trembling in the lantern light.

Later that evening, Alice and Coulton sat in the judge's chambers, in the fine stone courthouse off the treed square. She wore a long blue dress and a corset threaded tightly at her ribs and she fidgeted and struggled for breath, hating it, hating her soft hair just washed and ringed into curls, hating the rouge on her lips. The low sun was coming in through the windows, getting tangled in the curtains. The judge walked around the room, turning on the gas sconces one by one, and then he came back to his desk and sat down. He had walked over from his dinner and was still in his shirtsleeves. He looked at Alice, looked at Coulton.

"Fine evening," he said, smoothing his long mustache.

The desk was of walnut and absolutely empty and it gleamed in the red glow of the setting sun. He was a heavy man, with a soft juddering neck, and when he set his big hands down in front of him Alice marveled at their alabaster whiteness.

"I don't know what the sheriff has told you, Your Honor," Coulton began politely. "We're representatives of the Cairndale Institute, in Edinburgh. We're here for the Ovid boy."

He withdrew the documents and letters of testimony from the satchel beside his chair, and handed them across. The judge studied them, one by one.

"It's some sort of a clinic, now, is that it?"

"Yes, sir."

The judge nodded. "Bill says you want to take that boy back with you. Is that it?"

"Yes, sir."

"What I don't understand," he said, "is how on God's green earth your institute ever heard tell of this boy. You must have left Edinburgh, what, four weeks ago? Six? He hadn't killed a soul yet. I can't kindly imagine there's a register on earth that has account of him even existing. That boy isn't even a ghost, Mr. Coulton."

Coulton nodded. "That's so, Your Honor."

"Well?"

Coulton glanced at Alice, glanced away. "Cairndale makes it a point to research into possible cases. They can trace through paternity some of those." Coulton opened his hands wide. "I don't pretend to understand their methods, sir. I do know the institute has been looking for Charles Ovid's family for some years, ever since an uncle of his came to their attention."

The judge tapped two fingers on the papers, turned his face to the window. "You know we killed that boy twice already," he murmured. "I do believe Bill's frightened of him."

"Three times," said Alice.

Coulton folded one leg over the other, smoothed out his trousers. He turned his hat in his hands. "It's a medical condition, Your Honor. Nothing more. You're an educated man, sir, if I may say so. You know how easily folk can be frightened by what they don't understand."

The judge inclined his head. "Not just folk. That boy frightens me too." The light was going and now the shadows from the gaslights picked up his craggy face, the tired lines at his eyes. "And how do I square this with the problem of justice? Charles Ovid killed a man."

"Yes, sir, he did."

"A *white* man," interjected Alice. "Isn't that the real issue?"

"A white man, yes, ma'am. Now, I knew Hank Jessup some. He wasn't a gentleman maybe, but he was honest and upright. Saw him in church every Sunday. And I have a town full of outraged citizens writing me angry letters about the direction this county is going in. Half of them are in the mood for a good old-fashioned lynching."

"And the other half—?" Alice muttered acidly.

"Charlie Ovid was executed last week, in private," said Coulton, cutting her short. "No one knows differently."

"That ain't exactly true. There's Bill and Alwyn, for starters. Little Jimmy Mac was in the jail that night. And there's the wives, Bill's and Alwyn's wives. I'd bet a blind man a dollar they know."

"Don't forget the men your deputy was letting in all week, to beat on the boy," Alice added bitterly.

The judge paused. He looked at her.

"Your Honor," Coulton said quickly. "If you'll permit me. Who's going to believe there's a black kid who can't be hurt chained up in the Natchez jail? It sounds like something out of the Bible. It sounds like a blooming miracle. It's just not possible, never mind what your deputies' wives say at their teas. Folk will gossip, it's what they do. But if you speak out, and tell everyone the boy has been executed, who'll question that?"

"That would be a lie," said the judge.

"Would it?" Coulton grunted, smoothing out his trouser leg. "The only problem you have is a walking corpse you just can't seem to dispose of. That boy died. He stopped breathing. It doesn't matter that he came back to life. The sentence was carried out, justice was served. I don't pretend it isn't a strange affair. But in the matter of justice, I don't see any problem. I know other folk might disagree, seeing him walking around still. But it just might be that we're a kind of answer. The clinic we represent is in Scotland, and I can assure you, if you release him to us, this boy will never be returning to Natchez, Mississippi. His condition is still not well understood. But what has been observed is that, ultimately, it proves fatal. The boy has only a few years left to live."

"A few years."

"Yes, sir."

"Then why wouldn't I just commute the boy's sentence to ten years' hard labor?"

"Wouldn't that seem a light punishment, to your constituents?"

Alice watched the judge absorb it all. All her life she'd known men like this man, men who knew what they knew with such satisfied certainty, who would rather look at a pretty thing and be admired by it than hear it speak, and it occurred to her, briefly, that perhaps that is what she should do, admire him, make pleasing sounds, coo and blink her eyes. But she would not do that.

The judge in the gloom was studying them over his steepled fingers. Then he sighed and turned and looked out the window. "My missus makes an apple pie like you never tasted in your life," he said. "It's won blue ribbons at the Confederate Daughters Picnic three years in a row. And right now there's a piece of it sitting cold on a plate in my kitchen. I'm sorry you came all this way, I am."

Coulton cleared his throat, stood. Alice stood too, the dress sweeping her ankles. Coulton was turning his hat in his fingers. "Would you take the night to think it over, sir? We could come back in the morning—"

"Mr. Coulton. I agreed to meet with you out of politeness, that's all."

"Your Honor—"

The judge held up a hand.

"Only way your boy's leaving that cell," he said quietly, "is in a pine-wood box. And I don't care if he's still moving inside it or not."

"Son of a bitch," hissed Alice, as they descended the courthouse steps. She was pulling at her corset, reaching under her skirts in a most unladylike fashion to unhook a stay or two and in that way catch her breath. It was already dark, the day's heat baking back up out of the streets, the cicadas loud in the warm night. "I put on a dress for that?"

"Aye, and look at you. Let's hope we don't run into that deputy, Alwyn. His tongue'd just about touch his toes, seeing you all dolled up."

She bit back her retort. She was still too angry to be distracted. "Is what you said in there true? That poor boy only has a few years to live?"

Coulton sighed. "Charlie Ovid will outlast us all," he said.

"They're all so goddamn certain the kid is like Jesus. It just makes it worse for him. Why are they all so goddamn certain he can't get hurt?"

"Oh, he can get hurt. He just heals, is all."

There was something in the way Coulton said this that gave her pause. "You believe it?"

He shrugged. "I didn't see a mark on him. Did you?"

"Maybe if you'd lifted up his shirt. Or maybe his legs were all a mess. How close did you look?"

He sighed. "Close enough to know the world isn't the way I want it to be," he said softly. "Listen. I need you to get yourself changed, then send your trunks down to the jetty. Settle our bill. I'll meet you at the hotel in an hour. I think we're done with the good town of Natchez."

Alice stopped. She stood in the grass of the empty square under a statue of some fallen Confederate general and after a moment Coulton stopped too, and turned, and came walking slowly back.

"I'm not leaving without that kid," she said.

A carriage passed in the street, its lanterns swaying. When it was gone, Coulton stepped closer.

"Nor am I," he said fiercely.

It was nine o'clock when they left the hotel lobby and walked along the boardwalk of Silver Street to the river and then along the back alleys to the old warehouse. It loomed up dark and rusting in the southern moonlight. They stood a long time in the shadows and then crossed the road without speaking, Coulton's greatcoat pocket heavy and jangling. Alice kept a wary eye out for anyone on the streets. But there was no one.

It took Coulton only a minute to kneel in front of the thick door and pick the locks. He stood and looked at Alice quietly and then pulled the door open and slipped into the darkness and Alice followed. They did not carry a light, but they walked sure-footed along the passage they had been in earlier that day, and at the boy Ovid's cell Coulton again withdrew his ring of picks and deftly twisted the locks open.

It was utterly black inside. Alice could see nothing for a long moment and she wondered what Charles Ovid could see, staring out at them, as he must be. Coulton cleared his throat and whispered, "Charlie, lad? Are you in here?" and Alice feared for a sudden long silent moment that the boy had been taken away.

But then she heard a sigh in the darkness, and the sound of chains clinking, and she saw the boy step into the faint halo of moonlight. He did not seem surprised to see them.

"Let me get these off you," muttered Coulton.

Alice was looking up at the boy carefully. Now that her eyes were adjusting to the darkness she slipped into his cell, speaking softly and slowly. "We're here for you, we're here to get you out," she said. "Will you come with us?"

But Ovid only stood looking at them in the darkness. There was something in his calm watchfulness that Alice found unnerving. "The . . . papers," he whispered. His voice was low, raspy, like it hadn't been used in a long time. "Where are they?"

Coulton blinked. "What papers? What's he mean?"

Suddenly Alice understood. "Your letter from Cairndale. You showed it to the sheriff. Where is it?"

Coulton took the envelope out of his waistcoat, unfolded the letter.

"It won't make sense to you, lad. It's just instructions, release papers, legal documents—"

But Ovid ignored the letter and took the envelope instead, and he ran his fingers lightly over the Cairndale crest: twin hammers crossed in front of a fiery sun. "What is this?" he whispered.

"Lad, we don't have time for—" Coulton began.

"It's the coat of arms for the Cairndale Institute, Charles," said Alice. "That's our employer. It's who we work for." A thought occurred to her. "Have you seen this symbol before? Do you know it, does it mean something to you?"

Ovid wet his lips. It seemed he was about to speak but then all at once he raised his face and listened in the darkness.

"He's coming," whispered the boy.

Alice froze.

And then she heard it too: the scrape of a man's boots in the warehouse, approaching. She slid noiselessly to the cell door and closed it softly and leaned up against the wall behind it. Coulton took up his position beside her. He had wrapped the chains around one fist. Now the man had started to whistle and Alice recognized the whistle: it was the deputy, Alwyn.

Coulton was patting his pockets. "Did you bring your gun?" he hissed.

But Alice had not. She'd left it behind on purpose, knowing that if it were fired, the sound would give them away, would draw too much attention. She didn't need anything but her fists, anyway.

But all at once Ovid was in front of them, a swift movement, he was fumbling in Coulton's pocket and Coulton, astonished, just let him do it, staring as the boy withdrew the sharpest of Coulton's lockpicks. He crouched on the edge of his bench and rolled up his sleeves and then he gripped the pick in his right fist like a fork and suddenly, in the darkness, without making a sound, he stabbed his left forearm, working the pick deep into the flesh, carving a ragged cut downward to his wrist.

"Jesus—!" Alice hissed.

The blood dripped blackly in the darkness and she could see the boy grimacing, his teeth clenched, the bubbles of snot as he breathed sharply through his nose. And then he dropped the pick to the floor with a clatter and dug his fingers deep into his own flesh and pulled out of the slick a thin six-inch piece of metal.

A blade.

And then, a minute later, to Alice's amazement, the cut in the boy's arm began to stitch itself together, flesh by flesh, until there was only the blood in a long smear and the mess of his shirt and the floor, slippery underfoot.

It felt like a dream. Ovid got to his feet. He said nothing. He stood trembling and fierce in front of the door with the blade gripped low in his right hand, and he waited.

Then an orange light spilled out from under the door and the heavy locks were unlocking, one by one, and the deputy was calling out in a cheerful voice, "Hiya, boy, looks like you ain't leaving us so soon after all," and then the door was swinging wide, and for a moment it blocked Alice's view so that she couldn't see Ovid, couldn't see the deputy as he shuffled in, could only see the fall of the lantern light and hear the man grunt in surprise and then there was a clatter of something falling and the lantern smashing to the floor and then darkness.

Alice was around the door at once, fists doubled, but the deputy was already dead. The blade was deep in his neck. Ovid stared down at him.

"God*damn*it," she swore. "What *was* that?"

But Coulton was unfazed. "Let me see that, son." He grabbed Ovid by the wrist and turned his arm this way and that until the boy pulled away.

The boy kneeled over the dead man and pulled the blade free from the body with a sucking noise and he wiped it on his own trousers and then he slid it inside his shirt for the keeping. "Why'd you come back for me?" he whispered. His gestures were calm but his voice sounded shaken.

Alice, still stunned, didn't know what to say. "Because it's our job," she said at last. "And because no one else was going to."

"You shouldn't have."

"Why not?"

"I wouldn't have."

"We don't have time for this," Coulton interrupted. "Riverboat leaves in fifteen minutes. We got to go."

Alice held the boy's eye for a long quiet moment. "Maybe someday you will," she said. "Maybe someday there'll be somebody to go back for."

Coulton was already taking off his greatcoat, handing across his bowler. Ovid looked ridiculous in the clothing, far too tall for it, Alice thought, but there was nothing to be done about it. Alice pulled off the deputy's boots and Ovid put them on. They needed to keep to the shadows and pray for quiet streets. Alice figured they would have maybe ten minutes at most before the deputy's absence was noticed and someone came looking. She tugged at the sleeves of the greatcoat for the boy and she buttoned it fast over his bloodied shirt and she turned up the collar and she grunted.

"All right," she said. "Let's go."

Coulton waved them forward. They hurried through the warehouse and back outside into the moonlit street, then slid along the silvering wall and down toward the river. The air felt clean, impossibly good to Alice, after the close reek of the warehouse cell. She was trying not to think of what she had just seen, of the boy and his forearm, the blade buried in it. Trying and failing.

At the river wharf Alice could see the big paddle steamer lit up over the water, the water reflecting the shine, the men quietly moving around below with the freight and the ropes. Coulton led them up a long ramp and into a little ticketing house, and there he spoke in low tones to a man behind the counter, and after a few minutes they hurried back out and up the gangway to the steamer. Ovid had his hat pulled low and his collar high and his hands thrust into the greatcoat pockets but he was still, to Alice's eye, clearly a black kid, absurd in his big empty boots and too-short clothes. But whatever arrangements Coulton had made worked; no one stopped them; and within a few minutes they were on board the paddleboat and following a porter down a corridor to their staterooms and then they heard the shouting of the workers below, and the ropes were cast off, and the paddle steamer pulled slowly, powerfully, out into the currents of the dark Mississippi.

She and Coulton ate a late dinner on the riverboat, the only two dining so.

They had left the boy Ovid in Coulton's cabin, pretending to sleep, his wrists unbound, in the belief he would not trust them if they did not trust him first. In the saloon the gaslights were turned low, the paddle whumping faintly in the darkness beyond. A black waiter leaned against the brass railing of the bar watching them in the mirror. Coulton chewed his steak in small bites, stacking his cheeks with potatoes and gravy. Alice had little appetite.

"Did you know?" she asked. "Did you know he could do that?"

Coulton held her eye. "I did not," he said softly.

She was shaking her head. "That deputy tried to explain it. He tried to tell us."

"These kids, these orphans. They're none of them normal. It doesn't make them monsters."

She thought about it. "Doesn't it though?" She looked up. "Isn't that exactly what it makes them?"

"No," he said firmly.

She sat with her hands folded in her lap and stared at her plate. It was true, there was about all of them, all of those orphans, something strange, unaccountable, not to be talked about by her or by Coulton. Wisps of rumor followed them out of their old lives.

"He could've got away at any time," she said then, in a slow voice. "He had a knife *inside* him. The whole time. Why didn't he try to run before?" She looked up. She thought of how unsurprised Coulton had been back in the cell and she felt suddenly foolish, like she'd been lied to. "What exactly *is* the Cairndale Institute, Mr. Coulton? And don't tell me these children are *afflicted*. Who is it I'm working for?"

"We're the good guys," he said quietly.

"Sure."

"We are."

"Everyone thinks they're the good guys."

But Coulton was serious. He smoothed the stray hairs over his scalp, frowning. "I told Mrs. Harrogate, before we left, that you ought to know more. She wasn't certain you were ... committed. But I reckon it's time. You just keep your questions clear in your own head, and you can ask her yourself, when you're back in London."

"She wants to meet with me?"

"Aye."

Alice was surprised; she'd met her employer only the once. But she was satisfied with that. She picked up her fork and knife. "I don't know how you stand it," she said, changing the subject. "These people. That judge. I'd have thrown him out of his own damn window."

"What good would that have done us?"

"It'd have done me good."

"I know this world some, Miss Quicke. Here courtesy is more important than truth. More important than being right."

She thought of the boy in rags, shivering in that warehouse. "Courtesy," she muttered.

"Aye." Coulton gave her a grin. "That's maybe a tricky one for you."

"I can be courteous."

"Sure."

"What? I can."

Coulton paused in his chewing. He swallowed and took a drink of wine and then he wiped at his mouth and met her eye. "I never in my entire life met a person more like a boil on a baker's bright red backside than you, Alice Quicke. And I mean that in the nicest way possible." He reached into his coat pocket and withdrew a small folded slip of paper. "Messenger lad delivered this to the hotel," he said, chewing again. "New assignment. Name's Marlowe. You're to go to the Beecher and Fox Circus in Remington, Illinois."

"Remington."

"Aye."

"My mother's asylum's in Remington. Or just outside it."

Coulton watched her. "Is it a problem?"

She hesitated, then shook her head. "It'll be fine. It's just the wrong end of the backside, is all." She paused. "Wait. *I'm* to go? You're not coming?"

"I'll be escorting the Ovid boy back to London." Coulton withdrew a new envelope from his pocket. "There's a ticket in here for a riverboat to St. Louis, sailing at first light. Don't worry, it doesn't put in at Natchez. You'll take the railway up to Remington. You'll also find some testimonials I've taken the liberty of writing out for you, documents and the like. Also the address in London where you'll find Mrs. Harrogate. Wire her directly, if anything comes up. Also some bills to cover expenses, also two second-class tickets for a steamer out of New York in eighteen days' time." He took another bite of his steak. "And an account of how this Marlowe lad was stolen by his nursemaid as a babe and ferreted out of England, and how his family has hired you to track him down, et cetera et cetera."

She glanced through the papers. "There's an identifying mark?"

"A birthmark. Aye."

"That's unusual."

He nodded.

"How much of this is true?"

"Some. Enough."

"But he's just another orphan?"

"Aye."

"As long as I don't get there and find him pulling things out of his fucking arms."

Coulton smiled.

She took another bite, chewed. "Why am I doing this one alone?"

Coulton looked at her. She was surprised by the emotion in his face. "There've been ... inquiries," he said, reluctant. "I heard about it right before we left Liverpool. A man, asking questions. About Mississippi, about US currencies. He's got an *interest*, you might say, in the children we been collecting. Certainly in the Ovid boy. I half feared we'd see him here in Natchez. I'll be watching for him on the way back."

She studied Coulton's face in the quiet. "He's a detective?"

Coulton shook his head. "Used to be associated with the institute. His name is Marber. Jacob Marber."

"Jacob ... Marber."

"Aye."

There was something in the way Coulton spoke that made her pause. She adjusted the knife and fork on her plate, thinking about it. "You knew him," she said.

"I knew *of* him. He had a . . . reputation." Coulton picked at his hands. "Jacob Marber is a dangerous man, Miss Quicke. If he's hunting Charlie Ovid, it's best the lad is taken off to London quick. You should be all right with this Marlowe boy, out in Illinois." Coulton grimaced, as if deciding whether to say more. "Marber blamed the institute for something, something that happened. I don't know what it was. Someone died, I think. It doesn't matter. We lost track of him years ago, haven't heard from him since. There are those who still think he's dead. I don't. He was too good at what he did, one of the best."

"Which was?"

Coulton met her eye. "Same as what we do. Except his methods were bloodier."

Alice thought it over. "How will I know him? If I see him?"

"You'll know him. He'll be the one what scares you."

"I don't scare."

Coulton sighed. "You do. You just don't know it yet."

Alice folded her hands in her lap, suddenly chilled. She watched their reflections in the warped glass of the riverboat window, the great wide currents of the Mississippi all around them out there in the darkness, the waiter where he stood with his wrists crossed at his back. The plush green armchairs and the dying ferns. All of it in the hazy glow of the gaslights in their sconces.

"He'll be disappointed then, your Mr. Marber," she said. "If he goes to Remington."

Coulton smiled tiredly at her toughness, and his smile faded as he pushed his plate aside and got to his feet. He wiped his greasy fingers in the napkin.

"It would be best you were far from there, if he does," he said quietly.

3

THE KID AT THE END
OF THE WORLD

It'd been thirteen months since Brynt had last had the Dream. But it was back, bad as ever, and it frightened her so much that every night now she tried not to sleep, tried to sit up until morning with a strong coffee in their dark wagon, watching Marlowe's little face breathing in the bunk, telling herself in the moonlight that nothing was the matter, nothing was wrong, they were safe.

But every night, in the end, her eyes would get heavy, her chin would nod, and the Dream would take over.

Always it started the same. She was crouched in her childhood wardrobe, trying to hide. The acrid reek of mothballs, the rustle of hanging clothes. Somehow she was little again, a girl, though she had never been little, not really. It was her uncle's rooming house in San Francisco, it was night, and when she opened the wardrobe a crack with her finger, she could see moonlight streaming in. Though she was a little girl she was also somehow herself too, old Brynt, careworn, tired, and little Marlowe was with her, crying softly with fear. Slowly she climbed out of the wardrobe, took Marlowe by the hand, slowly she held a finger to her lips for quiet.

There was something in the apartment house with them.

They made their way to the hall. Steep narrow stairs, silver light from the moon on the landing. All the doors to the rooms standing open in shadow. And Brynt and the child's slow, impossibly slow descent, step by creaking step, Brynt straining to hear with all her concentrated intensity for the sounds of that other in the house, that *thing*, wherever it might be.

And then she heard it. Footsteps overhead. A darkness emerged onto the third floor, walking slowly, flecks of shadow swarming around it. Brynt started to run, taking the stairs two at a time, dragging the boy along behind her. But now the darkness was coming, impossibly fast, it reached out a long, long arm and there were fingers, pale, and curled, and strangely elongated, and all the light seemed to be sucked up into that hand. Marlowe screamed. The shadow had no face; and where the mouth should have been, all was—

Brynt sat up. She felt the blanket tangled in her bulk, the sweat on her face cooling in the dimness. Starlight was pouring in through the high, narrow window. She brushed the hair from her face.

Marlowe.

He wasn't in his bed. She lurched down out of the bunk in a panic, the circus wagon creaking and shuddering under her weight, and thrust her way through the ragged curtain. Marlowe was eating a biscuit with butter at the narrow table, a book of engravings open in front of him. They were Doré's engravings from Dante's *Inferno*, eerie souls twisting in torment, a gift from the reverend long ago, the only book in the wagon aside from the Bible. She felt her heart in her chest slow.

"You all right, honey?" she said, in a forced voice. "What're you doing?"

"Reading."

She eased herself down beside him. "Couldn't sleep?"

"You were talking again," he said. "Was it that dream again?"

She looked at him. She nodded.

"Was I in it?"

Again she nodded.

The starlight was silver in his black hair, in the sleeves of his sleeping gown. He looked at her with dark, serious eyes. His face was so pale, he might have been one of the dead. "Did I help you this time?" he asked.

"Yes you did, honey," she lied. "You just keep on saving me."

"Good," he said sturdily, and folded himself into her arms.

She ran a hand through his hair. The last time she had suffered the Dream like this was the week the reverend had died, in that damp moldering room in Spitalfields, more than a year ago now. He had held on for two years after that dark week, when Marlowe's mother had vanished in the fog, Brynt trying to look out for the both of them all the while, the little boy and the dying man, angry at Eliza half the time, afraid for her the rest. She always kept thinking maybe Eliza would come back but she never did. The child never spoke of that night, hardly spoke of his mother at all, in fact, and then only at bedtime, when he was sleepy. Of course Brynt knew Eliza Mackenzie Grey was not his mother, not really, but the poor girl had saved the child from abandonment and cared for him no matter how hard it got and loved him as if he were her own flesh and blood. If that wasn't mothering then Brynt did not know what was.

But now the Dream was back. Brynt sat with Marlowe at the night table and felt a kind of tingling in her fingertips, almost like a foreboding, almost as if the weather were about to change, and because of this she knew something was coming, something bad, and they were not ready.

Marlowe wasn't like other children.

Brynt knew that, of course she knew that. For one thing, obviously, there was the glowing. His skin would start shining that eerie blue color and he'd get this quiet look in his eyes and there was no trick in it, none at all. Not that Mr. Beecher or Mr. Fox knew the truth of it—a performer was entitled to their own secrets, their own tricks, after all. Most likely they assumed the kid was painted in some sort of luminescent paint, iridium, maybe, like she'd seen spiritualists use on their ridiculous ectoplasm, back in drawing room seances in England. Never mind that the shining was stranger than that, more beautiful, as if it went right through a person, as if you could see through his skin to the bright veins and bones and lungs and everything.

He'd said to her once, while she was painting her own face for the night's stage, that he was afraid of what he could do. "What if I can't stop it, Brynt? What if one time I can't?"

And that was the other thing about him: the way he seemed to worry so. It wasn't like any eight-year-old she'd ever known. "Can't stop what, honey?" she'd asked.

"What happens to me. The shining. What if one night it just gets worse?"

"Then we can use you to find things in the dark."

He'd looked at her in the little mirror with such a serious look on his face.

"You just let me worry for the both of us," she'd said. "All right?"

"Mama used to say I could choose what I did. That it was up to me."

"That's right."

"But it isn't always, is it? A choice, I mean. You can't always choose."

It was like he'd been thinking about something else, something darker, more disturbing, and she'd wondered all at once if it was his mother, if it was Eliza he was thinking about.

"Sometimes we don't get to choose," she'd said gently. "That's true."

"Yeah," he'd said.

She'd looked at him then, really *looked* at him. The way he was regarding his own gray face in the mirror, biting his lip, the shock of black hair falling over his forehead. And she'd put down her paint and drawn him in close.

"Oh, honey," she'd said, like she often did, whenever she didn't know what else to say.

Now she was holding her skirts in one hand and picking her way through the morning muck and guylines, seeking Mr. Beecher's office. Marlowe half ran alongside her to keep up.

Beecher was the managing partner and paymaster. Brynt had decided in the night that she would have to talk to him anyhow, that it was time, but then in the morning, right after breakfast, a girl had knocked at their wagon with word that she and the boy were wanted at Mr. Beecher's office, *right away, if you please.* Brynt did not go in for coincidences, she believed there was a shape to the world and to its happenings, whether she could see it or not, and she'd thought of that night's dream and of the feeling that was in her still and she'd frowned and reached for her hat.

Everywhere reeked of wet horses and hay. There were trash and playbills trampled in the mud. Figures squatted on the steps of the traveling wagons, unshaven, turning coffee in tin cups. These were those whose gifts did not belong in the world. Geeks and clowns, palm readers and fire-eaters. They followed her with dark eyes. She and Marlowe had worked the sideshow stages here for six weeks now and still they were outsiders, strangers, keeping to themselves mostly, but Brynt didn't mind, preferred it in fact. She had been among such people all her life and knew they were no worse than any others, no more like her than anyone, never mind their own strangeness. People were people, and mostly that meant they took what they could, whenever they could.

She had always been different, all her life.

"You're like a left foot," her uncle used to say. That was when she was just a girl, back in San Francisco, living those days in the apartment house he superintended. Her uncle had been a pugilist, famous in some circles, winning fight after fight until one night he didn't, and then beginning the long slow slide into headaches, and fists so swollen they couldn't close right, and a slurring speech. He'd raised her to fight and by the age of ten she would already hunt the biggest boy in any street and sometimes it seemed fighting was all she'd ever known. She'd loved him though, her uncle, loved his big gentle ways, how he never made her feel anything but normal, despite her size and her great strength. It surprised her sometimes to think about her life, how much of the world she had seen, meeting the reverend in San Francisco in the year after her uncle died, going with him south to Mexico. That was where she first inked her skin. Later she and the reverend sailed for England, traveled Spain, returned to England. Now that she was back in America she understood that no place was her own.

She trudged brooding across the fairground, Marlowe leaping and skipping across the mud. A strangeness was in her heart. A hammer rang out in the cold air, twice, then twice again, like a warning. An ancient clown in shirtsleeves raised his face from a water barrel, razor open in his hand. He nodded gravely at them as they passed. Away at a fence line a woman wearing a frock coat over a pair of long underwear was hauling a pail of water. Out beyond loomed a reef of cloud dark against a darker sky.

Whatever it was Mr. Beecher wanted, she could not guess. But she was herself thinking that she and Marlowe had been working the sideshow over a month now, and that was too long by half, and it was time to be moving on.

There were three of them. They were seated around Beecher's desk in the mud-spattered tent he called his office and they all turned as one when she entered. She had to dip her head because of the low entrance and she reached out a hand and felt Marlowe take two of her fingers in his little fist. One of them was a woman, dressed in a blue velvet dress, a wide-brimmed hat placed delicately on her yellow curls so that her eyes were in shadow. Under the hem of her skirt Brynt glimpsed mud-spattered boots. As her eyes adjusted, she saw the woman's nose had been broken long ago and set crookedly and her eyes were full of flint so that Brynt understood she was neither delicate nor refined. She had an air of ferocity and suspicion that Brynt, in other circumstances, might have been drawn to.

Mr. Fox, ever the gentleman, stood politely as Brynt came in, but Beecher just leaned back in his chair, chewing at his cigar in the gloom.

"And here she is, Big Brynt herself," Beecher said insolently. "Good of you to bring the kid, sweetheart. This here is Miss Alice Quicke, a private detective from—"

"England," said the stranger, who was looking at Marlowe curiously.

"—the distant isles of fairest England. Miss Quicke was just explaining how easy it is to mistake, ah, what was it? Yes. One stolen boy for another."

"I never said stolen," she said quietly.

Brynt hesitated, peering at their faces, letting her eyes adjust. Then she turned to the third among them. "Mr. Fox, sir," she said. "What is this regarding?"

"The boy, Miss Brynt. Your Marlowe. Correct me when I say you are not his blood relative, yes?" When she said nothing, Mr. Fox cleared his throat apologetically. "Please, sit. I'm sure there is an explanation to it all. Hello, son."

Marlowe peered around, silent.

The tent was narrow, lit by an ancient lantern at the corner of the desk. It occurred to Brynt she could go, she knew this, she could just turn around and go, taking Marlowe with her, and not one of the three could stop her, she'd wager, not even the detective woman. She remembered the bad business Eliza had been mixed up in, back in England, and didn't know if there was some connection to it, but she didn't really care to find out.

But she didn't go. The lumbered boards underfoot were loose and scrawled with dried clay and they banged up under her bulk as she came forward and reversed the empty chair and hiked her skirts and sat, her massive arms folded up over the chairback.

"His real name is Stephen Halliday," said the woman, Miss Quicke. She glanced uneasily at Marlowe where he leaned into Brynt's arm and then back to Brynt. "Would it be better if he weren't here, at present? For his sake?" But when no one moved, least of all Brynt, and Marlowe just stayed quietly listening, she seemed to decide some argument inside herself and went on. "Stephen Halliday was kidnapped by his nursemaid eight years ago. That was in Norfolk, England. His family is eager to get him back. I am here on their behalf. I have papers, of course."

She took from her inner pocket a thick envelope tied with twine and gave it across. Brynt unfolded the documents and, while everyone waited, she began to read. From time to time she would grimace despite herself and look up. The envelope held various forms and files stamped and certified both in London and New York City, not all of which Brynt could understand, but most attesting to the identity and history of the missing boy. There were also testimonials and official licenses for the woman, Miss Alice Quicke, signed by one Lord Halliday, recognizing her as the lawful private investigator in the affair. Marlowe, it seemed, was heir to the vast Halliday estates in the east of England. He had been abducted when just a baby and vanished into the smoke of greater London and the family had been hunting him ever since. Identifiable by a birthmark on his back in the shape of a key.

Brynt, dizzy, felt the heat coming to her face. She knew that mark.

"I'm sorry," said Miss Quicke quietly. "The family is grateful to you, of course."

"No," said Brynt.

It was all she could think to say, and it came out quickly, despite herself, and as soon as she said it she was sorry. She saw Mr. Beecher run a finger over his mustache, look across at Mr. Fox. The cigar fumed between his teeth. She thought of the Dream and her sense that something bad was coming and she tried to locate it but she did not think it was this. Slowly she rolled up her sleeves, baring her thick tattooed forearms. What was wrong with her? It was his real family. His real mother. His *home*.

Miss Quicke watched closely, as if all this were playing out on Brynt's face before her. "I am sorry, Miss Brynt. It's a legal injunction. It's not a request."

"She'll set the law on you," said Mr. Fox. "On all of us."

"What law?" said Brynt, collecting herself. "The law in England isn't the law here."

"Knowing the boy's identity," Miss Quicke continued, "but refusing to give him over, ma'am, would make you an accessory to the abduction. And Mr. Fox and Mr. Beecher too, and their entire enterprise here. You could spend a decade in jail. Or worse."

"Dear me," murmured Beecher, enjoying himself. "Oh, oh. Or worse."

"We are prepared to compensate you, of course," Miss Quicke continued.

Brynt folded a protective hand around Marlowe's shoulders. "Compensate?"

"Financially. For loss of income."

"For loss of income?"

Mr. Fox took off his spectacles. He had the long arms and legs of a field spider, the same small furry head. "Marlowe, son. Take up your shirt and turn around."

The boy unlooped his suspenders and lifted his shirt and turned. Brynt heard Miss Quicke breathe in sharply. His torso was dazzlingly pale, like it had never known sunlight. And in the small of his back was a red birthmark in the shape of a key.

"It's him," said Mr. Beecher. He looked at Mr. Fox in amazement. "He's the Halliday boy."

Felix Fox put on his spectacles and inspected the mark and took off his spectacles. He made a sound low in his throat but did not speak.

No one said anything.

Mr. Fox rubbed at his face, looking like a man who did not want to say what he was about to say. "Brynt," he said. "There's money behind all this. Money and powerful folk convinced this is their boy. Do you imagine it will stop?" He squinted his watery eyes. "You know it yourself."

Brynt was thinking much the same thing.

Miss Quicke pulled on her gloves and then she kneeled before the boy. She did not touch him. "Your real name is Stephen, child," she said. "Stephen Halliday. You went missing when you were a baby. I was hired to find you and bring you back to your parents in England."

"They will be very glad to know you are safe, son," said Mr. Fox. "Miss Quicke is here to help you, you can trust her. It's all right. She is fine people."

All this the boy listened to in silence, watching their mouths carefully. He gave no indication of understanding except the way he reached for Brynt's hand, gripped it hard.

Miss Quicke stood. "Why doesn't he speak? Is he deaf?"

"Deaf!" Beecher grinned. "Good God! He's not that, surely?"

Mr. Fox folded his arms, eager now to be done with it all. "There's no law anywhere on earth wouldn't say the boy's better off with his kin, Brynt." He furrowed his brow. "Miss Quicke means to leave in the morning. I trust there'll be no need to take this matter further. You'll have the boy ready, Brynt."

"Ready—?" Brynt looked up, as if coming back to herself. "Ready?"

"Ah," said Beecher quickly. "But we do have certain details to discuss yet. Compensation and such. As was proposed. There is a contract, after all."

"Agreed," said Miss Quicke.

Beecher held up a long gray hand. "And the boy plays this afternoon's and night's set. He is ours until morning."

"Very well."

The boy tucked in his shirt, pulled up his suspenders. Then he stood staring at the woman detective, Miss Quicke.

"Son—?" said Mr. Fox.

Marlowe did not answer. The tent was quiet.

"Marlowe," Miss Quicke said slowly, cautiously. "I know this must be confusing. You must have questions for me."

He stared at her with great intensity, his eyes pale and blue. As if searching her face for some clue as to the nature of her truer self. She suffered his scrutiny in silence, white gloves folded chastely in front of her, as if somehow she understood that it was important not to move and not to look away. All this Brynt watched from across the tent. She saw his long dark eyelashes, the dusting of freckles across his nose, the tuft of hair that stuck out from his head, knowing each feature perfectly. He was so small for eight, she thought. Or maybe that was just what eight looked like.

At last Miss Quicke flinched, glanced uncertainly around. "What does he want?" she said.

Brynt watched her like an adder.

"Madam—" Fox began.

But before he could finish his thought the boy leaned up, as if in answer, and whispered something very soft to the woman. She glanced at Brynt, and her face was sad.

Then the woman, Miss Quicke, kneeled back down.

"Oh, sweetheart, no," she said to the boy. "No, Brynt has to stay here."

Alice Quicke walked out of Beecher's tent wanting to punch something, preferably her employer, Mrs. Harrogate, in her fat face, or Frank Coulton maybe, anything really, but hating her work regardless and what she had to do for it and who she had to do it to.

That poor kid, she thought. That poor woman, with her tattoos and her sad eyes. As she ducked under a guyline and made her way back through the mud toward the big top and the road back into Remington she understood that she'd had enough, that she was finished with all of it, the tracking down of the orphans, the lies. It wasn't only this kid, the sadness of it all. It was also that Ovid boy back in Mississippi, the one who had dug into his own arm and taken out of it a blade. And Coulton's warning about the man Jacob Marber, somewhere in the world, hunting these kids? Jesus.

No, she'd finish this last job, escort this Marlowe boy back to England. And then she'd tell Harrogate her decision: she was done.

Thing was, she'd only met the woman, Mrs. Harrogate, the one time, at the Grand Metropolitan Hotel on the Strand, back at the very beginning of it all. The hotel was dark, with glittering mirrors flaring in the electric lights, polished mahogany wainscotting, candelabra suspended in fiery wheels from the rafters, the works. Tall marble columns at the reception desk and a velvet-lined elevator cage with a kid in uniform operating the gears. Alice had followed Coulton in, up to the fourth floor, with a Colt Peacemaker in one pocket and a set of brass knuckles in the other.

He took her down a long, oppressively furnished corridor, stopping to work a key in the lock of a wide door, and then they were inside a sitting room, with half-opened doors on the far side and a small Chinese table of lacquered red wood with a teapot steaming on a silver tray, and at the far window, with her back to them, a middle-aged woman dressed in black.

"Miss Quicke," she said, turning. "I have heard such interesting things about you. Do come in. Mr. Coulton will take your coat."

"I'll keep it," said Alice. Her hand was in her pocket, on the revolver.

The woman introduced herself: Mrs. Harrogate, long-widowed, and merely one representative of the Cairndale Institute, its proxy here in London, so to speak. Alice had watched her carefully. She looked rather like a housekeeper, except for the expression in her eyes. She might have been forty, she might have been fifty. She glided forward on the carpet, her hands clasped before her, reddened as if scrubbed with lye, fingers devoid of rings or jewels. A purple birthmark covered her cheek and the bridge of her nose and one eye, making her expression difficult to read. But her lips were downturned, as if she had just tasted something sour, and there was in her dark eyes a ruthlessness. She wore no makeup, only a slender silver crucifix over her breasts.

"I am ugly," she said matter-of-factly.

Alice flushed. "No," she said.

Mrs. Harrogate gestured to a sofa, then seated herself; Alice, after a moment, sat too. The man Coulton stepped forward and poured out the tea and then dissolved back into the shadows, and as he did so Mrs. Harrogate explained what she wanted Alice to do. It was all quite straightforward, she said, if perhaps a little unusual. The Cairndale Institute was a charitable organization interested in the welfare of certain children, children who suffered from a rare disorder, who would not be able to get treatment elsewhere. Alice's job would be to help track these children down; she would be provided with names and places. Once they had been found, Mr. Coulton would then bring them back to Mrs. Harrogate, here in the City. And she would see that they were taken safely up to the institute. Alice would answer directly to Mr. Coulton; he would see that she was paid in full, as well as expenses covered, etc. Alice's contract would last through the year, to be renewed should her services still be required. It was all perfectly legal, of course, but discretion was required. Mrs. Harrogate trusted the terms would prove satisfactory.

Alice stared at the dark tea in her teacup but did not drink. She was thinking about the children.

"Ah," murmured Mrs. Harrogate. "You are wondering, what if they don't wish to come?"

Alice nodded.

"We are not in the business of kidnapping, Miss Quicke. If the children do not wish to come, then they do not come. Though I do not foresee that happening. Mr. Coulton can be most . . . persuasive."

Alice looked up. "What is that supposed to mean?"

"Well. You are here, are you not?"

Alice felt the color rise to her cheeks. "It's hardly the same."

Mrs. Harrogate smiled and sipped her tea. "The children will suffer if they do not get treatment, Miss Quicke," she said after a moment. "That fact tends to convince a person rather swiftly."

"And their parents? Do they come also?"

Mrs. Harrogate hesitated, the teacup half-lifted to her lips. "These children," she said, "are all unfortunates." She leaned forward, as if sharing a secret. "They are without parents, dear. They are quite alone in the world."

"All of them?"

"All of them." Mrs. Harrogate frowned. "It seems to be one of the conditions."

"Of your institute?"

"Of the affliction."

"It is contagious, then?"

Mrs. Harrogate smiled thinly. "It is not a plague, Miss Quicke. You will not catch it; you will not grow ill. You needn't worry about that."

Alice wasn't sure she understood. She tried to imagine going out into the world and taking children, one by one, like some kind of monster out of a fairy tale. She shook her head slowly. There was always other work. "I don't know that this is what I do," she said reluctantly.

"What? Help children?"

"Steal them."

Mrs. Harrogate smiled thinly. "Let's not be dramatic, my dear. Perhaps it would help if I told you what I know. I'm not in perfect knowledge about it. You will have heard, perhaps, of the Royal Society, yes? It was the beginning of an organized scientific approach here, in England, to the world around us. At one of its earliest meetings, a blind girl was brought before them, a girl with a most inexplicable affliction: it appeared she could see the dead. None of the scientists were deceived; such frauds had been perpetrated for centuries; but, disturbingly, none could disprove the girl's claims either. It troubled them, the anatomists most of all. The Cairndale Institute was founded some twelve months later, dedicated to phenomena that fell outside the realms of scientific investigations. In their very first month, twin sisters were brought before them from a hamlet in Wales. Both had exhibited unusual symptoms around the age of five. And there were others, other children who were similarly—how shall I say it?—*afflicted*. The institute has been working to find such children ever since, to work with them in their sickness."

"Work with them how?"

Mrs. Harrogate met her gaze. Her eyes were very dark. "Their flesh, Miss Quicke," she murmured. "It can *appear* to do strange things. Regenerate itself, transform itself."

Alice felt lost. "I don't understand."

"Nor do I. I am no expert. But I imagine, to one who has not the scientific mind, that it would appear amazing. Resembling, I don't know, a miracle."

Alice looked at the woman, suddenly wary. She was trying to gauge her meaning. "I beg your pardon?" she said softly.

"My dear?"

"Why, exactly," she asked slowly, "did you come to *me*, Mrs. Harrogate?"

"But you know why."

"There are other detectives."

"Not like you."

Alice wet her lips, beginning to understand. "And what am I, exactly?"

"A witness, of course." Mrs. Harrogate smoothed out her dress. "Come now, Miss Quicke, you do not imagine we have not done our due diligence?"

When Alice did not speak, Mrs. Harrogate reached into her handbag and withdrew a long brown envelope. She started to read from the papers in it.

"'Alice Quicke, from Chicago, Illinois,'" she read. "That is you, yes? You were raised in Adra Norn's religious community, at Bent Knee Hollow, under the care of your mother, yes?"

Alice, stunned, nodded. She had not heard that name in years.

The woman's strange face softened. "You witnessed a miracle, when you were a little girl. You saw Adra Norn walk into a fire and stand in it and then walk out of it, unburned. Oh, the story is quite famous, in certain circles. Our director, Dr. Berghast, was a correspondent of Adra Norn's. They were acquaintances for many years, in fact. It is a terrible shame what happened, what your mother did. I am so very sorry for you. And of course for your mother."

"She was crazy. Is crazy."

"Nevertheless."

Alice got to her feet. She'd heard enough. "You should be sorry for the people she burned in their beds," she said. "That's who you should reserve your pity for."

"Miss Quicke, please. Do sit down."

"I'll show myself out."

"*Sit.*"

The voice was cold, grim, deep-toned, as if it came from a much older and fiercer woman. Alice turned back in a fury but was surprised to see that Mrs. Harrogate did not appear imperious at all, just the same mild figure, the birthmark discoloring her face, her red-rubbed fingers reaching now for a second cup of tea.

"Miss Quicke," she said. "You of all people know how a life can be injured by prejudice, how swiftly fear can be aroused. These children *need* you."

Alice was still standing, her fists tight at her sides. She saw the man Coulton had unfolded his arms near the hat rack, his big hairy hands loose at his sides. Under the brim of his bowler his face was unreadable.

"And if I say no?"

But Mrs. Harrogate just smiled thinly and poured the tea.

She hadn't, of course, said no.

And now here she was, bone-tired, mud-spattered, doing the very thing she'd vowed not to do, wading among the low unfortunates of the world with her hands empty and curled at her sides, exactly like some monster in a fairy story, come to steal an eight-year-old child.

Remington lay thirty miles northeast of Bloomington, well off the trunk line, and she had got off the train in Bloomington and walked to the other end of town and purchased a ticket on the old-fashioned mail coach, leaving that night, without even first collecting her traveling cases. That had been four days ago. She'd made the journey through green fields and stands of poplar and oak in the settling twilight, watching the vast roiling storm clouds of the American Midwest mass darkly out on the horizon. It had been nearly six years since she'd left and the country had changed. She had changed.

Alice left the circus grounds, distracted. She walked down to a farrier at the edge of town and purchased an iron-shod cart and a bed of straw and the packhorse stabled out back. The packhorse was ship-ribbed and bony with sores around its mouth and one eye glassy but she did not argue the deal. Alice studied the old-fashioned leather tackle and ropes dangling from hooks above the counter and said nothing. They looked as if they had hung there since the town's founding. The farrier spat in his hand and held it out. His blond beard ragged, his palms seamed with dirt. She took it. She bought a hatchet and some blankets and a flint next door and later she stood out on the boardwalk massaging her sprained wrist, staring the length of the street to the trampled field beyond, the big top looming there, brooding. Thinking about the child. The sky overhead was white with traces of dark vapor adrift within it and when she raised her eyes she had to squint in the brightness. Later she bought from the general store a box of bread and dried jerky and a sack of wizened apples. She would take the child east, riding for Lafayette, Indiana, in the morning.

What she wasn't thinking about, what she deliberately did *not* think about, was her mother, in that asylum, not fifteen miles from where she was, her mother whom she had not seen in years, whom she had gone to visit on her last day in Illinois all those years ago, before heading east, and whom she had glimpsed walking in the grounds with a nurse, her mother gray-haired by then, stooped, her face eerily smooth and her eyes glazed and dead and her fingers fluttering in the air like little birds. Alice had stood at the end of the cloistered garden and watched her mother walk the nearby path, trailing her fingers along the stone wall in places, like a blind lady, finding her way, and Alice had not called out to her, had not gone to her, had not held her and been held.

It was still only just noon when she walked the packhorse across to the hotel. She changed out of her blue dress back into the clothes she preferred, the men's trousers and her faded greatcoat and the worn hat with the weather-bitten brim. Back in the street she climbed up onto the buckboard and settled herself with a blanket across her lap and snapped the reins and rode north out of town.

She knew the way, remembered it. The sky was still bright and as she rode it started to rain, a faint mist, but she did not slow or stop under the trees and soon the mist was gone and the world was shining. Her heart was in her throat. She wasn't afraid, exactly, but she didn't know how her mother would look when she got there, or what she'd say to her, or even if her mother would know who she was. It had been so long. God only knew what they did to the patients in those places.

When she got to the asylum she sat a long time in the old cart, the reins looped over her knuckles, her eyes scanning the dark granite facade, the windows dazzling with reflected sky. There was no sound, not even birdsong in the trees along the edge of the lawn. She didn't know what she would do, or say, wasn't even sure why she'd come. What could her mother offer her now, after all these years? What could she offer her mother?

The cart creaked and shuddered as she got down. She climbed the old steps and went in. The foyer was dim and smelled of varnish and at the big desk a nurse was seated, writing in a ledger. She raised her face as Alice came in, looking her up and down with disapproval. She was very old. Behind her desk stood the door to the wards, locked.

Alice hesitated. "I'm here to see Rachel Quicke. She's a patient. I'm her daughter."

A flicker of a frown. "Visiting day is Sunday."

"I've come a great distance," said Alice. "I've come from England. I have to be leaving again in the morning. Please."

"And you did not think to write ahead?" The nurse tapped her pencil twice, three times. She sighed. Then she reached for a big black leather-bound book behind her. "I'll need her patient identification number."

Alice shook her head. "I'm sorry, I wasn't told—"

"Of course you weren't. No one ever is. Dr. Crane doesn't believe in using their names, you see. Never mind, I will look it up. Rachel Quicke, was it?"

Alice nodded. "Yes, ma'am."

"And was she admitted recently?"

"Eighteen years ago."

The nurse glanced up. "For what reason?"

Alice paused. "Religious mania. She burned eleven people in their beds. She was trying to re-create a miracle she thought she saw."

The nurse was looking at her strangely. "Patient Seventeen," she said quietly. "You're her daughter. I didn't know she had a daughter. Did no one get in touch with you?"

"In touch—?"

The nurse closed the book softly, her eyes searching Alice's face. "Your mother was a fine lady, Miss Quicke. We all knew her. Troubled, of course. But a good person, under it all."

She didn't understand. "What're you saying?" she whispered.

The nurse stood gravely, her hands clasped in front of her. "Your mother died seven years ago. In her sleep. I'm sorry."

Seven years.

Alice said nothing. She should have felt ashamed, maybe. But there was nothing in her heart, she was empty—no sorrow, no anger, no bitterness—and this surprised her. *Maybe this is what grief is,* she thought. *Maybe this is how loss feels. Like nothing. Like wind in a hollow.*

The nurse put on a shawl and took her back outside and showed her the little graveyard on the hill and Alice walked up and stood for a time at her mother's gravestone, already weathered, still feeling nothing, wondering if she should say something, a prayer maybe, but in the end she just stared out at the sky and thought of nothing at all and then walked back to the cart and the packhorse waiting with its ears pricked, its eyes rolling nervously, and climbed back up.

When Alice got back to Remington it was night. Shadows were pooling in the street under the lights from the taverns. She could hear the circus, the thrump of drums, the faint roar of the crowds.

Upstairs in her room at the hotel she could not sleep. She folded her hands behind her head and watched the colored lanterns from the circus track across the ceiling. Thinking about Jacob Marber and what she had glimpsed in Coulton's face as he told her. Not fear exactly. Something darker and altogether more strange.

There was no sleeping after that. She dressed and sat on the edge of the bed and pulled on her boots and went out. The circus was strung with candle fire in jars of red-and-green-colored glass and there were townsmen in suits long out of fashion milling about in front of the big top and wives in hats with cloth flowers pinned into place calling their children close. A clown handed out flyers from a linen sack. Inside the big top a trombone and bass drum started up. She turned from that and in her mud-spattered coat and man's trousers drifted past and away as if in a darkness of her own making and gradually the laughter faded. At last at a stenciled tent she stopped and lifted her eyes and read the name on the sign.

She almost walked on. But whatever was in her would not leave it be. A shill selling tickets from a roll at the door studied her from his stool, hands motionless, cigarette at his lips.

Inside stood a group of men in hats and frock coats watching two girls dance. There was no music. The girls wore negligees and had black leather ribbons wound about their wrists and arms. As they danced, their hands turned in slow circles and the ribbons on their forearms moved also. It was then Alice saw they were not ribbons but snakes. The men assembled watched the snake dancers with great seriousness as if what happened there before them contained some truth about a future not yet written. When the girls were done a man with long hair braided down his back came out and bent low and attached a chain to the piercings in his nipples and with his hands on his knees lifted an anvil and duckwalked it across the stage. Then one of the snake dancers walked down among them with a wooden box of liquor bottles and glasses clinking on a cord around her neck. Under its powder her face looked haggard and used.

Just then the woman Brynt strode through the crowd. The figures parted before her, sullen, wary, and she loomed hulking over Alice and stared down at her, massive arms bare, the tattoos crawling over her skin in the firelight like strange runes.

"I want you to know," she said huskily, "he'll be ready to go in the morning. I won't keep him. It's good and right for a boy to be with his own. I'll not stand in the way of that."

There was a shine in her eyes belying her words and Alice felt a sudden sickness, seeing it, seeing her, the pain she was clearly in. Alice knew that grief.

"I'll get him there safely," she said.

Brynt grunted. And then she turned and was gone.

Later the boy, Marlowe, was brought out. He sat on a ladder-backed chair in front of the men and set his little hands on his knees like a child at his lessons. He waited. The men were quiet. The shill went along the walls, snuffing out the lanterns one by one until all the tent lay in darkness.

What a thing it was, blood and bone. The shining appeared faint at first and blue and seemed to grow out of the very air itself. Then it brightened. It was in the boy's skin. He sat utterly still, holding his left arm in his right hand, crackling with blue light while the darkness in the tent began to thrum. Alice could not look away.

The boy was not as he had been. Slowly his skin turned translucent so that she could see the inner workings of his blue lungs and his blue bones and the blue crisscrossed threads of veins all underneath his face and throat. He glared out with eyes black and hard and reflective as obsidian. She swallowed to see it, the hairs on her arms prickling. One April afternoon in Chicago when she was six she had been caught in a thunderstorm and she had felt something like it then, the electricity helixing all around her. Her mother had run out to her that day and bundled her inside with her swollen knuckles and had toweled her dry while the wood in their basement room hissed in the stove and lightning flashed in sheets over the lake. A scent of burning cedar. Rose-hip tea from Boston in chipped mugs. The oil and grease smell of her mother's skin, which Alice had not smelled in a quarter century. That. She was crying. She stood in the darkness of that tent and wiped at her eyes with the insides of her wrists. She saw in the blue glow the faces of the men gathered there were also wet with tears and she raised her eyes.

The shining boy grew brighter. And then brighter still.

4

MAN OF MANY DARKENINGS

Walter was hungry. So hungry.

Through the dark crowds and noisy carriages of Whitechapel the basket sellers walked, girls and women with long white throats, with ragged shawls like shreds of shadow. Walter lurked in the alley, watching them go. Sniffing the night air as they passed, the warm-blood smell of them. His flesh was gray and hairless, his red lips were wet. In his pockets, his fingernails were sharp as knives.

None of them knew that he watched. He liked that. But he was hunting one in particular, one among the many. A woman with burns on her body. She wasn't to know he was coming.

The crowds, shoving, shouted past. A hot-pie seller hollered his wares. Walter was trying to remember, but it hurt him to remember. There was a woman who had a weapon, or was a weapon, or something. She could hurt his dear Jacob, and it made him afraid. Walter came out at night because that is what Jacob wanted, his dear Jacob, his good Jacob. Because in the cold night fogs, reeking of sulfur, few would see him as he was.

Walter Walter Walter Walter—

But he didn't know which woman it was. The basket seller he'd followed this night had yellow hair and a gaunt face and scars all across her chest and throat like she'd rolled in fire. Was she the one who would hurt his Jacob? The crowds parted; Walter watched her weave across the street, heavy skirts trailing in the muck. The crowds closed in again. He must ask her. He must find her and make her tell him what she knew. He clambered onto a stack of crates in time to see her stagger between two lantern-lit doorways, drunk maybe, then into an alley of darkness.

—go Walter go find her make her show you what she's hiding—

Walter moistened his lips. He looked all around. Then, scuttling down, he detached himself from the shadows and slipped unnoticed through the crowds, his collar turned up, his hat pulled low.

The dark alley called to him like a song.

Walter awoke, gasping. Where was he? Last he remembered he'd been crossing the night docks in Limehouse, and before that he'd been in a drinking house near the abattoir, but he could not remember anything more. No, that wasn't true. There'd been a jetty in darkness, the slosh of the Thames, a flower seller crying in an alley. He opened a gritty eyelid: brown peeling walls, sleeping bodies in the dim corners of the room. In his fingers he was still holding a pipe, cold now, the black gum of opium long since smoked through.

Walter Wal—

He staggered to his feet, holding the wall for support. He had to get back, he had to get back to the room he rented for a ha'penny a week, under the crumbling ruins of St Anne's Court. The floor was wet. He looked down. Someone had taken his shoes.

—*ter Walter what did you bring us Walter Wal*—

The voices. Always the voices. They stopped whenever he smoked the resin but no sooner was he rising up out of its stupor, his skull throbbing, than they were back in his head, whispering, always whispering.

He couldn't tell the hour but it wasn't night anymore. Fog drifted in the lane outside. Jacob had given him a task, yes. Now he was remembering. There was a woman who could hurt him, yes. And he'd trusted Walter to find her. He stumbled in a puddle and caught himself on a bollard in the fog and then melted into the roar of Market Street. Then he was hurrying down a narrow lane between tenements and turning left and crossing a second street and ducking under the dripping awning of a tobacconist's. Down a flight of cobblestone stairs, along a steep passage. There were children huddled in doorways staring at him; there were women picking through garbage. At St Anne's Court he turned sideways and slipped past the twisted iron grille and walked gingerly over the muck, avoiding the deep puddles, the greasy sludge afloat there. There was a line of laundry strung up from a window, all of it yellowed and patched and limp in the watery fog, and under the axle of a broken cart in one corner he saw the rat man, drunk, sleeping.

Walter Walter Walter Walter Walter—

His door. It had been left open. He stumbled inside, down the three damp steps. The light from the broken window was the only light there was.

—*come to us Walter come to us bring us the keywrasse and*—

He was trying to remember. And then, there—on a shelf against the far wall—he saw them, his sweet ones, shining in the darkness. A row of three enormous glass canisters. The liquid within was a smoky green, and afloat in each like jarred fruit was the pale cranial figure of a human fetus, curled, aborted, malformed. Their eyes were open and their slow hands were pressing against the jars, they were watching him, calling to him softly.

Walter Walter what have you left in the—

That was when he turned and saw his broken cot and in the bed-clothes the yellow-haired basket seller. Her throat had been cut ear to ear, her abdomen carved open and pinned wide as if under the knife of a surgeon, as if someone had rummaged inside her, looking for something. Her eyes had been removed and laid out beside her.

—because she was hiding it she was but where is it Walter where is the hurting thing—

He closed his eyes. He opened his eyes. The light in the cellar was different. His sweet ones glowed in their glass jars, greenish and lovely. He got woozily to his feet and stood swaying over the dead girl and then he sat back down on the freezing floor and slept again and when he woke next his head was clearer and there was a visitor standing over the cot, a middle-aged woman. She was staring down at the body of the basket seller.

"It seems you've made rather a mess of things, Walter," she said matter-of-factly. "I blame myself. I ought to have come to you sooner, of course."

—she knows us Walter how does she know us—

"You know us," he said thickly. "How—?"

"Us?" She stepped into the weak gray light coming from the window, a visitor from a society and world he'd once known and knew no longer. She clutched a handbag demurely in front of her, in both her gloved fists. She wore a black collared dress, black gloves, a black hat with a blue feather, and there was a birthmark obscuring half her face. Her eyes were very dark and her voice, when she spoke, was dangerous. "We're quite alone here, Walter. I've been watching you for some time."

"Walter, Walter, little Walter," he whispered.

—*maybe she has it maybe she has the*—

"You are Walter Laster," said the woman. "Jacob Marber was your friend."

Yes, he thought, *my friend. Jacob was my friend. Is my friend. I love him.* He peered suddenly up at the woman, grateful. She had a lovely throat.

"I am Mrs. Harrogate, Walter. I am here to help you."

Yes, he thought. *Mrs. Harrogate will help us.*

But as he rose to his full height he could feel all that he was, his thoughts, his brief flicker of understanding, begin to slide back into a room in his skull, and then the door to that room was closing, and he was going away again, he was going to sleep again, and the voices were whispering, growing louder. He wanted to warn her about the voices, but he did not.

The woman walked over to his sweet ones where they turned in their jars, glowing with an otherworldly fire, and she studied them closely in the green light they cast.

—*why is she looking at us Walter what does she want Walter does she have the hurting thing*—

The hurting thing, the weapon, yes . . . She had her back to him and he shifted nearer, just an inch, just a half inch, creeping, creeping. He did not know what he was doing, oh, he was doing nothing, nothing at all, then why were his fists clenched, oh, now he could smell the lilac powder in her hair—

—*do it Walter do it now*—

"Oh, Walter," he heard the woman, Mrs. Harrogate, murmur, as if from a long way off. "I *am* disappointed. You really must try harder to control it."

—*now now now now now*—

He slid nearer. She was rummaging in her handbag. But as he

reached for her neck, her stout little figure turned fluidly in the gloom, impossibly fast, something clutched in her fist, and then a fierce pain bloomed inside his skull.

Margaret Harrogate slid the mangler's cosh back into her handbag, buttoned it fast. She had struck him so hard her wrist hurt.

Walter Laster, she thought. *Well, well.*

She knelt beside him and felt for a pulse but his wrist was cold, freezing really, cold as death, and she hesitated only a moment and then took off her hat and her gloves and laid her ear over his chest. She could not hear a heartbeat but she knew this meant nothing, less than nothing, and she carefully lifted his upper lip and saw the long yellow teeth, all the longer for the red gums that had withdrawn from them, just as she had been told would be there. His pallor was bloodless, the bluish-gray of bad milk. He was smoothly bald, his body hairless. Three red lines, like folds of skin, ringed his throat.

After that she stood, and adjusted her hat, and stepped gingerly over Walter to the dead woman on the cot. Something would need to be done about it, and like always, she supposed, it would be her having the doing of it.

She took a quick inventory of the miserable little room, the damp that was creeping up the bricks, the darkness almost like a living thing around the far wall, those strange three glowing fetuses adrift in their examination fluid. Then she got to work. There was a rag Walter had been using as a towel and she used this to scoop the dead woman's insides back into her cavity and then she stuffed the two tidy eyeballs in as well and she rolled the entire corpse in the ripped blanket and lugged it, thumping, onto the floor, the stain already leaking through. She had got none of the mess on her clothes and she stood with her hands on her hips, satisfied. Then she lifted Walter in her arms and carried him outside into the courtyard and leaned him against the wall in the mud. His frailness surprised her, how light he was, in truth little more than dust and bone. Lifting his hand was like picking up a bird's nest.

She went back down into the cellar and unbuttoned her handbag and took out the two jars of oil she'd brought and she poured them out over the bed and the wrapped body of the woman and the wood shelves. She stopped at the glass specimen jars. The fetuses floated, pale, still. She tapped a knuckle. The poor things. Teratological birth defects. There was still the pasted label on two of the jars from the Hunterian Collection at the Royal College of Surgeons. She did not know how a creature as pitiful as Walter Laster could have got inside such an institution, could have smuggled these things out. One more mystery. Well, well.

What was it that compelled her to do what she did next, a feeling, perhaps, an *intuition*, as Frank Coulton might say, something she had learned to trust in herself? She couldn't say. But she took down the third of the jars, the one with the smallest fetus, its little eyelids closed like petals, its delicate features almost human. It was heavy, far heavier than Walter, and the formaldehyde sloshed unevenly against the glass walls as she lugged it outside. Walter still lay in the mud, unmoving.

It was getting late now. Back inside, she took a long safety match from her handbag, struck it on the brick walls, dropped it into the oil-soaked bedding. The room erupted into flame. She adjusted the veil over her face, the birthmark like a purple handprint that stretched across her cheek and nose and up over one eye, which she'd lived with all her life. It wouldn't do to be stared at. Then she went calmly out, leaving the door standing open, and she scooped up Walter in one arm and draped her shawl over the jar with the other, and then, picking that up too, while the cellar whooshed and roared into flame behind her, and a drunk in the corner of the yard raised his bleary head, she made her way out through the fog to Bloom Stairs Street, there to hail a cab.

That was the thing about her job, what she did. There was a gruesomeness to it, an essential unladylike gruesomeness, which she enjoyed. Her husband, rest his soul, had seen it in her and loved her for it. Not that every day involved the burning of bodies—the kidnapping, yes, call it what it was, the *kidnapping* of opium-addled unfortunates. Homicidals. No, mostly she was a kind of manager, like in a bank, she supposed, or an insurance office, overseeing the jobs Dr. Berghast wished done in the capital and streamlining all of it for efficiency. Still, it was a life of secrecy, a life of deceit, even at its dullest. And Margaret Harrogate enjoyed it too much, was too good at it, ever to quit it.

The Cairndale Institute's building at 23 Nickel Street West, Blackfriars, was unmarked. It was an imposing five-story row house, and Margaret Harrogate was its sole occupant, drifting through the dim heavily furnished rooms, past the coal-burning fireplace, the thick warm drapes, or lurking at the street-facing bay window like an apparition. When her husband had been alive there had been maids and a cook and even a coach and horses stabled in the cavernous cobbled carriage house that made up the street-level entrance. But now it was only her, had only been her for so many years that the presence of others felt like an interruption, like a wrongness. Her days were days of institute affairs. In part that meant the filing of papers, organizing of correspondence, the occasional meeting of an institute investor. But mostly it meant that whenever Frank Coulton or his new partner, the Quicke woman, brought in an orphan, Margaret would examine the child, confirm the nature of their talent, and record her findings in one of the big institute ledgers kept in the hollow behind the coal scuttle.

Talents. That was what Dr. Berghast called them. She had seen disturbing things, biblical things: flesh, rippling like water, altering the face of a child into another's; a little boy, laying hands on a corpse and raising it, boneless, into a hulking flesh giant. Two years ago she had listened as a girl of twelve—*a bone witch*, as Dr. Berghast had described her in a letter—whistled a skeleton up out of its coffin and into a clattering dance. The stuff of nightmares. Margaret Harrogate had no such talents herself, thank the good Lord. Nor had her husband any, when he was alive. And the truth of it was, she wasn't even sure now whether she thought what the children could do was natural or unnatural, a right thing or a wrong one.

Walter Laster, though, was a wrong thing, through and through. She knew that much, could see it in his bloodless skin, hairless as a larva, and in his appetites, his fang-like teeth. He was something new; and Dr. Berghast would be intrigued.

It was her husband who'd got her involved with Cairndale, nearly thirty years ago. Or his death had done: he'd died of a fever in their second winter together. That was 1855. She had still been so young. When she'd met Henry Berghast for the first time, three weeks after the funeral, after the man had unlocked the iron gate at Nickel Street West with his own key and rang the bell with a bouquet of lilies in one hand, his hat and a leather satchel in the other, she hadn't quite known what to say. The servants were gone by then; she'd had to answer the door herself.

"My condolences, Mrs. Harrogate," he'd offered. "Your husband perhaps spoke of me?"

She looked at his handsome, powerful face, his oiled black hair, and wasn't sure that he had.

"I am the director of the Cairndale Institute; I was your husband's employer. I have something I wish to discuss, in private. Might I come in?"

"All right," she'd said, reluctant. She had led him to the sofa in the parlor and sat first, with her black gloved hands folded in her lap. She supposed he had come to evict her.

Dr. Berghast seemed ageless back then, neither young nor old, though he was already remote. There was about him a concentrated focus, almost like a perfume. His gestures were slow, deliberate. His knees and ankles clicked softly as he crossed his legs. Yet he was broad-shouldered, with a thick black beard, gray-eyed and powerful-looking. The black suit he wore was immaculate, tailored to the season's fashions, and the white rose in his lapel looked freshly cut. Margaret saw through the windows that the afternoon had turned gray and rainswept, but her visitor was not wet.

"I am exceedingly sorry for your loss," he'd begun. He'd regarded her birthmark without a trace of dismay. "Your husband didn't fear death, didn't wish it to be a cause for grieving. We spoke of it often. But what he didn't consider was how those who loved him might be expected to carry on."

"Yes," she said.

"Have you given any thought to how you will live? You are still young—"

"I am not destitute, sir. And I have a sister in Devon."

"Ah." He seemed to pause then, weighing something. He folded one elegant wrist over his knee and frowned politely. "I'd hoped you might consider another possibility. Mrs. Harrogate, we are all of us surrounded by the unseen, every day. What else is loss? What is death? Who doesn't believe in things they can't explain? God and the angels, gravity and electricity, death and the mystery of life. There are forces we understand, and forces we still do not. The Cairndale Institute cultivates and preserves one such mystery. Your husband was a great help to us in our efforts, as was his father, and his father's father before that."

She nodded mutely.

"I'm speaking of the river, the wall, the curtain, the shroud, Mrs.

Harrogate. I'm speaking of the passing from this world to the next. Death, madam. Of which we know more than we realize." He leaned in close, his voice lowering. She caught the scent of peppermint, of pipe smoke. "We need the dead more than the dead need us. But the human body is made up of nearly as much dead tissue, as living. Think of that. We carry our own deaths inside us. And who is to say, in death, that the proportions are not reversed? The chemistry of death, the physics of dying, the mathematics of the realm of the dead, these are the mysteries science hasn't yet begun to approach."

He blinked softly, liquidly. He wet his lips. He was handsome, and frightening.

"There are some few among us, Mrs. Harrogate, old now, who were gifted once, who were born with certain ineradicable . . . talents." He searched her face carefully. "The talent to manipulate dead cells, for instance. You've seen it, perhaps, in your husband's work. No? It can appear in many strange forms. It can appear to heal, or to destroy, to suspend life or to resurrect it. It's never the living tissue that is interfered with. These men and women have lived at Cairndale a long, long time. Since I was a child. Before that, even."

"Cairndale's a kind of . . . hospital?"

"A private clinic, you might call it. Most private."

Margaret Harrogate, in her widow's weeds, had stared hard at her visitor, thinking. "You are offering me his job," she said, confused. "My Mr. Harrogate's job."

"Your husband had great faith in you. It was his own wish."

Dr. Berghast got up to go. She saw the ferns arranged at the windows had not been watered, not in at least a week. From his satchel her visitor produced a thick ream of correspondence between her late husband and himself, tied with twine, and he laid it on the banquette.

"I am trusting in your discretion," he said at the hat stand. "Whatever you decide."

She read it slowly by candlelight over the following weeks. The institute, it seemed, occupied a manor house that had been built in the seventeenth century, on the edge of a loch, absorbing the property of an old monastery, all of it some distance northwest of Edinburgh. Dr. Berghast had been raised on its grounds, the son of the old director, of the same name, until he had taken on the role himself. There was much talk in her husband's letters that she didn't then understand, talk about an *orsine*, whatever that was, and the institute's guests. In time she would come to know more of such matters than she wished. But at that time, as she read, she realized only that she'd seen it once, at a distance, that first summer of her marriage, walking the length of a low crumbling wall that encircled its grounds, arm in arm with her husband. Sunlight, a sky so blue it was nearly black. That was high on a cliff of strange red clay, overlooking a dark loch, and an island beyond, the stone ribs of an ancient monastery just visible on it, and a golden-leaved tree rising up out of the ruins. There was a fine manor house on the landside shore, beyond. A stand of dwarf pines swayed darkly in the wind below. In the stone perimeter stood an archway, built maybe in the fourteenth century, green with moss, etched with strange markings, gated now with a black gate with the Cairndale crest prominent upon it, and it was there she and her young husband had stood, peering through the bars, going no further.

So it had been.

Intrigued, at a loss, she had written to Dr. Berghast that she would indeed be pleased to take on her late husband's duties. And her strange second life had begun, her life as it had been for nearly thirty years now, her life of secrets and darkness.

Her work did not often take her north, to the institute. On the rare occasions that it did, she would halt the carriage sometimes at the gate, remembering her husband, wondering at the life she might have had. The years passed; she grew old.

Then a new thing appeared, something awful. Dr. Berghast called it a drughr, a creature of shadow, neither dead nor living. She'd already heard rumors by then, of course, hints of strange goings-on at Cairndale, whispers of Dr. Berghast's *experiments*. She'd tried to stopper her ears against them. But she herself had glimpsed, on her occasional treks north, how he was changing: she knew he was afraid of *something*, something *unnatural*. And so, when he wrote to her about the drughr, warning that it was stalking the young talents, the unfound children, she too was afraid.

Which is how it all started, ten years ago: the findings. Dr. Berghast sent two men to 23 Nickel Street West to work under her instruction. They would locate the children, orphans all. Both were capable men, quiet, grim. And they would bring the orphans to her, squirming in burlap sacks if need be. Their names were Frank Coulton, whom she had met before; and Jacob Marber.

Jacob: there was a time she'd almost pitied him. Found by Dr. Berghast himself on the grim streets of Vienna, plucked out of poverty, gifted a better life. But no one had seen him in more than seven years, not since that terrible night when he'd attacked Cairndale itself. That was when it all went wrong, when he turned against the institute and slaughtered those two children on the banks of the Lye, starting in on those awful unnatural acts, what he did, what he swore he'd do, those acts from which there's no way back, not when a darkness gets into you and corrodes what you are and leaves you turned inside out, the seams showing. After that he'd vanished, stolen away off the face of the earth. Some said he'd been devoured by the drughr. But Margaret knew otherwise: she knew he'd been seduced away *by* it, had fallen under its *sway*, and that he was out there still, stalking the children, like a monster from bedtime stories.

Oh, few things frightened Margaret Harrogate. But Jacob Marber did.

All this was in Margaret Harrogate's thoughts as she wrestled Walter out of the hansom, and through the locked iron gate at 23 Nickel Street West, and up the four flights of gloomy stairs to the room she had prepared. She'd employed neither servants nor cooks since the death of her husband on account of privacy and her own solitary nature. Hard work never bothered her, even when she was a girl. But she could not abide gossip nor the superstitions of servants.

She left Walter unconscious, tied at the wrists and ankles to the strong oak posts of the undressed bed, and went back down for the glass specimen jar, and placed it, after some uncertainty, on the parlor table under the window. She took down the potted ferns, one by one, put them on the landing.

When she returned upstairs, Walter was awake, staring at her with a mix of fear and deviousness. He had somehow lost his shoes. She went to the wardrobe in the corner and took from the top shelf a pipe and a little chipped dish and a tin canister the size of an ointment jar. She unscrewed the lid and took out, with care, the small black gum of opium, and she cut off a little twist of it and smeared it in the dish. Then she untied one wrist. Walter rose up weakly onto his elbow and took the pipe without speaking, and she went out and came back with a candle and she passed the flame back and forth under the dish until the black gum began to bubble and smoke. He breathed the fumes in through the pipe, long deep drafts. Fell back in the bedsheets with a sigh.

Her usual method did not involve opium, of course. She kept a powder in small brown-paper packets in a locked drawer of her desk, a powder that encouraged the more recalcitrant of her visitors to share their truths. It got them talking. But Walter would need something stronger.

Margaret Harrogate set down the dish and blew out the candle and took the pipe from Walter's damp fingers. Then she lowered her face so that her lips were next to the shell of his ear. She knew many things already. She knew Jacob Marber had left Walter here, in the filth of London, to hunt down the keywrasse. She knew it was a weapon of such power it could destroy even what Jacob had become. She knew he feared it; and she knew he must never find it.

Slowly Walter's chin lifted. His eyelids were fluttering, translucent, as the drug took hold.

"Walter, Walter," she said softly, "go on now, tell us. Tell us about Jacob. Was he here in London with you? You must try to remember."

Walter's voice was little more than a whisper. "Jacob . . . Jacob was here. . . ."

"Yes, yes, good." She stroked his bald head gently, like a mother. "But he went away?"

"Jacob . . . he left me. . . ."

"Yes, he did, Walter," she murmured. "But where? Where is Jacob Marber now?"

5

AND BRIGHTER STILL

The stranger came down through the dust and the swale with a sinister long-legged stride and he cut up onto the road and without slowing he turned west, into town. He seemed to cast no shadow. When he passed the old Skinner place with its broken-backed barn the sun slid behind a cloud, the afternoon itself darkened. He came striding on. He wore a black coat spotted pale with road dust and a high black hat drawn low over his eyes, and a black scarf hid his face, and he seemed not to tire at all as he walked.

The blacksmith watched his approach with a feeling of foreboding and when the stranger stopped the smith straightened at his forge. His sleeves were rolled for the heat and his shirtfront was sticky at his chest. He could not explain it but he felt a deep uneasiness.

In the doorway the stranger paused, the daylight casting him into darkness.

The smith was used to travelers in distress but when his visitor didn't speak he cleared his throat and prompted, "You get into some trouble back up the road, mister? What can I help you with?"

The figure shifted, raised his eyes. He didn't lower his scarf. The smith glimpsed two burning lights, like little coals, reflecting the fires of the forge.

"I'm looking for the Beecher and Fox Circus," he whispered.

"Ah, circus folk," the smith said, swallowing. "I allowed you for a visitor in these parts. Got separated, did you? Your folk is up in Remington. Two miles west of here."

"Remington," whispered the stranger.

"You can't miss it, friend. You're not on foot, are you?"

The stranger turned his face and looked at the shod horses whickering in their stalls and then he looked back at the smith and started to remove his black gloves, finger by finger.

"No," he said softly.

Stepping soundlessly forward as he spoke, shutting the door behind him.

In the days after Marlowe's leaving, Brynt just slept, and ate, and worked. Emptily, just like there was nothing else in a life. Twice a night she'd loom in the footlights of Fox's sideshow tent, half-undressed, her silver hair braided down her back, her tattoos exposed in the candle fire, while ugly faces leered all around. Then she'd pull up the straps of her dress, stalk powerfully off the stage. A deep sadness was in her, like a drug, and it would not leave her.

The Dream, though, that had left her. It had gone away with Marlowe, in that old cart driven by the hired detective, that grim woman with the dark eyes and oilskin coat, collar rolled up against the cold, and Brynt almost missed it now, the Dream that is, never mind the man in the black cloak, his face lost to darkness, his long white fingers. Almost missed it, because it was one of those things that reminded you what you'd had, what you'd been afraid of losing all along.

The day's light was already fading. She was working in the menagerie tent, shoveling out the stalls, hauling in gray buckets of washwater. The muleteer hunched at his tack bench with a mallet and punch, fixing the traces, sullen, toothless as old shoe leather. He'd lived half a life in the gutters of cities Brynt couldn't even pronounce, in Argentina, in Bolivia, and there was a clarity to his meanness that made his presence bearable. The stalls reeked still of the previous night's smoke. The muleteer's overalls sagged loosely as he worked, cussing a blue streak, a music just under his breath. Not at anything in particular, not at anyone, just cussing almost for the sake of it, as if it were a thing needing its own attentiveness, like prayer, or poetry. *Goddamnmotherfuckingsonofawhore*, he blurted. And Brynt, tired, sad, nodded in time to his outbursts.

Marlowe never said a whisper, that last morning. Not one word. She'd walked beside him, not touching, all the way out to the cart where it sat in the half-light of the early field, the wet grass at their knees, her palm hovering at the back of the kid's neck protectively, her shawl wrapped at his shoulders, hoping he would say something, anything, even if it was just to say how damn mad he was about it all. But his little face just stared down at his shoes the whole way. He'd looked so small. It was almost the worst part of it, for Brynt, the way he said nothing, not even when she kneeled in the cold mud and held him and said goodbye, while the detective threw his little trunk up in the back of the cart and stood waiting, pulling her gloves off with her teeth, running her red hands over the mare in the chill. Then Marlowe climbed up, the detective clicked the reins, and the cart creaked bumpily out over the wet field onto the old road that led east, into the rising sun.

She tried to imagine Marlowe happy in that woman's company, Marlowe laughing at some foolishness she'd muttered, maybe folding himself sleepily into her coat at a fire in a roadside ditch, but she couldn't imagine it, and she crushed her eyes shut in despair. Eight years, his family had hunted him. The love in that gesture, surely that meant something?

If nothing else, she thought, at least he was safe.

Safe. She felt something then, a web of pain flaring in her abdomen, in her ribs, sudden and precipitous, so that she straightened and put a hand to her gut and stood gasping, staring around her. She didn't know what was wrong with her. It was like she couldn't breathe for a moment. And then the feeling was passing, or the worst of it at least, leaving her dazed with that same heaviness she'd been feeling ever since Marlowe had left, or been taken, rather: a heaviness that was three parts lonely and one part anger, and the anger in it was aimed squarely at herself. She shouldn't have let the boy go, not alone. Not without her.

Mr. Beecher lifted aside the flap of the tent with his silver cane, gingerly, as if he didn't want to dirty his fine clothes, never mind that he lived and traveled with a circus outfit in and out of the shittiest towns in the Midwest.

"Well, there you are," he called irritably. "Did you not get my summons?"

She wiped her mucky hands on her shirtfront, palms and knuckles, and glared down at him. She should've hated him, the pleasure he'd taken in giving Marlowe over to that detective; hell, she should maybe strip him out of his lovely little tweed and dunk his bare white ass in mule shit. But she didn't. What was the matter with her that she didn't?

"Never mind it, I shan't belabor the point," he was saying with distaste. "We're not a charity outfit. Your wagon is assigned for two performers. There's only just you in there now, yes?"

Brynt flinched, nodded.

"Nice and roomy now, is it?"

"No," she said.

He looked her up and down. "Ah. Nevertheless—"

"You're belaboring the point, Mr. Beecher," she said softly.

Beecher flushed. "The point is, I'm assigning Mrs. Chaswick to join you in your wagon. She'll be bringing her things over in the morning."

"Mrs. Chaswick."

"Is that a problem, Miss Brynt?"

"She's the one talks to the ghosts? What's wrong with where she sleeps now?"

"Not that it's your concern. But she sleeps at present in the mess wagon with old Mr. Jakes. Hardly appropriate. And they're spirits, not ghosts." He started to go, paused. He pinched the bridge of his nose. "One more thing. Don't come to me, complaining about how she smells. I know all about it; I don't care."

Brynt reached out a big hand to stop the paymaster from going. "Mr. Beecher," she said. "Wait."

He peered up at her, irritated. "It's not a negotiation, woman."

"That detective, the one Marlowe left with. Did she give an address for where she was going? Somewhere in Scotland, wasn't it?"

Mr. Beecher drifted distractedly over to the rails of a stall, scraped the sole of his boot against it. The horse within shifted, restless. The muleteer was muttering on the far side of the tent, swearing away. *Goddamnbitchfucker. Fuckfuckfuckfuck.* Beecher took no mind.

"Sir?" she said.

"Alice Quicke," he said. "That was her name. What, are you thinking of leaving us too? Are you thinking of going after the boy?"

He said it with a mean little smile on his face, his little mustache twitching, and Brynt for a long moment said nothing.

Then she said, "Maybe I am."

"You don't finish out your contract, you don't get paid," he said sharply.

"I'd just like to write him a letter, Mr. Beecher."

He sniffed. "Well, I can't help you. Perhaps Felix would know. Though God only knows how much of what she said was true. I can smell a lie like you just stepped in it, Miss Brynt. There wasn't half a dollar's worth of truth coming out of that woman's mouth."

Brynt lifted her face. She met his gaze directly. She could feel her face growing hot.

"And you let him go?" she whispered. "You didn't say a word?"

Beecher grinned.

"Aw, look at you," he said. He winked. "I'm kidding, woman. Lighten up."

After he was gone, Brynt stood a long while, brooding. Then she ducked out of the tent, clutching the shovel at her side, needing air. Her silver braid fell long and heavy over one shoulder. Her eyes drifted over the patched and sagging tents, the big top looming over everything, casting it all into a dull cool shadow against the evening sky. *Marlowe*, she thought.

And that was when she saw it. A figure.

Weaving between the guylines like a flicker of darkness.

Brynt started to shake. She dropped the shovel in the mud with a slap, her head swimming. It was him. The shadow man. The man from the Dream, with the long white fingers and the coat as black as tar, a muffler pulled up over his face, dusker's hat drawn low.

He did not look her way. He was striding through the puddles in the dusk and slipping between the tents and moving quickly, but there was some wrongness to him, a blurring, as if a dark smoke were seeping out of his clothes as he went. He was tall, maybe as tall as she was, though nowhere near as strong. She was filled with an awful, sickening feeling.

She knew what it was he wanted.

Marlowe.

She picked the shovel up out of the muck, turning its blade in front of her like a hatchet, wiping the mud on her sleeve. Then she started after him. She was huge, silver-haired, filling with a fury that she hadn't known before. No one seemed to be about; somehow the tents were quiet; she splashed through the slick, past cooling cookfires, following.

The stranger turned left, left again, reappeared on the far side of a wagon. Brynt hurried. Never once did he look back. She wouldn't have cared, wanted him even to look back, to see her, so great was her rage. She knew her strength; she had dropped a mountain lion once with a single punch in a wretched little town in Mexico. That was years and years ago; she was much older now; but she was strong enough to handle a man of his size. Fear was for small folk.

He stopped at Felix Fox's tent. Then he swept inside, was gone. Brynt glowered. She was swinging the shovel at her side and had her head low like a bull and her small eyes pinched tight and she didn't slow at all. She slid on a patch of mud, then regained her footing and at the tent she took a deep breath and lifted the flap with her shovel and went in.

Inside was dim. Quiet. She paused to let her eyes adjust. A desk, a filing cabinet. Three chairs, empty. The loose boards were grimy with crusted mud as she stepped forward. The back half of the tent was separated by a curtain and behind it Felix had his little bed and wardrobe and his washing pail and she went back there to look but the stranger wasn't there and Felix wasn't either, of course he wasn't, he would be rehearsing the acts in the big top at this hour. But she didn't understand; the stranger couldn't have left: there was only the one exit. She went back through and stood with her shoulders bowed to keep from banging the ceiling and the shovel loose at her sides and she listened but she couldn't hear anything.

"You're not crazy," she muttered, catching sight of her hulking figure in the pier glass.

All over the desktop lay a fine dusting of powder, and she stooped, uneasy, and ran two thick fingers through it, leaving a pale crooked trace on the wood. Her fingers came away black.

When Felix Fox left Mr. Beecher, with all his ledgers and his columns of little numbers and his railroad timetables, and walked tiredly across the muddy grounds to the big top, it was already night. His spectacles were folded in his trouser pocket. The lanterns blazed up ahead. He could hear the horses nickering off by the corral. They would need to be moving on soon, all of them, tickets were just not selling. That was the sum total of Mr. Beecher's complaint. But they had still not repaired all the wheel castings on the equipment wagons after that big storm caught them outside Bloomington, and the new blacksmith was drunk every morning by breakfast.

Well, let Beecher worry over that, he told himself. His partner handled the money, the organization, the schedules and bookings. Hell, he fairly ran the circus in its touring season. But if Beecher was its brains, Felix Fox was its heart. He was an artist. He'd studied Pierrot in Bologna, puppetry in Prague, he'd worked with acrobats in the sun-kissed villages of Provence. It was he, Felix, who dreamed up the styles and themes and choreographies of the acts, and he, Felix, who worked in the ring every afternoon training them up, and he, Felix, who painted the sets and built the cabinetry and double-checked the knots in the safety lines. Without Beecher, true, there'd be no circus; but without Felix, there'd be no show.

He lit a cheroot as he approached the big top. He could hear laughter from inside. Scooter was working the tickets at the door, cashbox at his neck, hands stuffed in his pockets.

"Slow night?" said Felix softly.

"Slowern a snail's asshole." Scootch shrugged, tipping back his hat. "I reckon it's near to dried up hereabouts, Mr. Fox, sir. If you don't mind me saying it."

Felix winked. "We'll be moving on soon enough, lad," he said. "Fresh pastures and all that."

He went in. The bench seats weren't even a quarter filled. Young Astrid in her greasepaint and ballooning pants was stalking the ring, blowing out a tune on her bugle as she went. A fine talent, that one. Not even fifteen yet, kid could juggle and ropewalk and clown as good as any. She had a bruise from a fall discoloring half her face but the audience would never know it, not when she was up there in makeup. It never ceased to amaze Felix, the beauty of it all, how a shabby tent spattered with mud could transform, in the firelights, into something so *beautiful*; how the performers with their weary shadowed eyes, their hungry ribs, could be made so *beautiful*; how the mules with a daub of paint here and there could transform into stallions as graceful as any that ever ran. Oh, there was a magic in it, beyond question.

He put on his spectacles and slowly walked the perimeter of the ring, counting heads despite himself. There were fire lanterns hanging from nails on posts above the bleachers and mirrored candles serving as footlights in the ring and the air was smoky and filled with shadows. Felix counted twenty-three heads, eight of whom he recognized as crew, meaning only fifteen tickets had sold, even at the new reduced price. Pitiful. He took off his spectacles, pinched his eyelids shut a moment. Perhaps the sideshow was better attended.

It did not help that the boy, Marlowe, the Amazing Shining Boy, was gone. Nor that Brynt seemed lifeless and depressed when she stood in front of the crowds. A bad business, he thought. Performers came and went, of course, though rarely did they break contract, and he'd never before lost a part of his show to a detective.

He made his way back through the dark to his tent, brooding, and dropped his cheroot into the mud and ground it out with his heel and then went in. He had already doffed his hat in the gloom when he felt something was wrong. There was a faint reek of soot in the darkness.

"Hello?" he said. "Is someone there?"

"Mr. Fox," said a voice. "I've been waiting for you."

"These are my private quarters, sir," replied Felix sharply. He wasn't sure where the voice was coming from. "You are here from the *Daily Almanac*, I presume?"

He sat at his desk and fumbled at the lantern until he'd lit its wick and then he closed the little glass door and peered up. The stranger was standing in the darkness beside the filing cabinet, his face wrapped by a black scarf. Felix swallowed, uneasy. He looked nothing like a small-town reporter. The man was tall, thin, wearing a long black coat or cloak, silk hat low at his eyes.

"Come, sir, state your business," Felix added, suddenly irritable. He was tired; it was no hour for a person to call unannounced. He fidgeted with his collar. "I have a circus to manage, if you don't mind. These are my hours of *work*."

"You need not concern yourself with this evening's performance, Mr. Fox. It has been taken care of." The stranger's voice was very soft, very low. He had an English accent. Before Felix could ask what the devil he was talking about, the stranger added, "You had a visitor recently, a man from England. Went by the name of Coulton, yes?"

Felix was starting to feel strangely short of breath. "Who?" he said. He looked for a glass of water but there was none.

"Coulton," repeated the stranger. "A detective."

"I never met anyone by the name of Coulton," croaked Felix. His breaths were coming quick now, shallow. "Tell me, sir, is it smoky in here? Shall we step outside?"

"Do not lie to me, Mr. Fox."

Felix got to his feet. He was feeling dizzy. "Forgive me, I just need some air—"

"*Sit down.*"

Shocked, Felix sat.

"You will answer my questions, sir."

Felix felt suddenly afraid. He stared at the stranger. He didn't know how, but all at once he understood it was the stranger's doing, this asphyxiating, this choking off of his air.

"The detective," the voice said again, patiently. "Frank Coulton. Tell me about him."

"It was a woman," Felix gasped. "Alice Quicke. Here. For Brynt's boy."

"Brynt's boy?"

"Marlowe. Was working. Sideshow. For us."

The stranger shifted in the darkness, nodding. "And what precisely did he do, this boy?"

Felix's eyes bulged, his heart was thundering in his chest. "Nothing. He glowed. Blue. Like a lantern. Please, I never asked—"

"Tell me about the woman, Alice . . . Quicke. She took the boy?"

"To England. Yes. Halliday. His name. Was Halliday."

"When did she leave?"

"Last week—"

"I'm afraid you've been lied to, Mr. Fox," said the stranger calmly. "There is no Halliday boy. This child, Marlowe, has been stolen from you. He will be taken to a manor house in Scotland. The Cairndale Institute. They will do things to him there, awful things. I'd hoped to spare him that."

Felix was scrabbling at his collar, pulling at his tie. The stranger had stepped forward now out of the darkness but somehow it still seemed to smolder up off him, as if ash were coming out of his clothes, out of his very skin.

"What I'd really like to hear, Mr. Fox," he continued, "is everything you know about this boy. His age, what he looks like, where he's from, who's been caring for him. Everything. Leave nothing out. Could you do that for me?"

Stars were flaring at the edges of Felix's vision. "Yes," he gasped.

"Excellent," said the stranger, coming closer. He sat in a chair facing the desk, folded one leg over the other, smoothed out his trousers. With each gesture a curl of black dust, like smoke, rose and dissipated into the darkness. "Let's not waste each other's time, then," he murmured.

He took off his hat, and unraveled the long black scarf, and that was when Felix saw his face.

Of *course* that bastard Beecher couldn't tell her anything, thought Brynt. What did he ever know that didn't fit in a ledger?

She lowered her powder and horsehair brush, stared into the looking glass Marlowe'd had her nail inside the door of their wagon all those months ago. Marlowe. The looking glass was for him, so she had to hunch on the floor to see. Her stage face stared out, white with powder, eyes blackened and fierce in the flickering light. She was otherwise naked. Her tattoos covered her flesh, each one a memory or a story of where she'd been, who she'd been. A dragon curled around a half-moon from the hand of a Chinese artist in San Francisco. That was the week she'd heard her brother died. A broken tree soared over her left ribs, a gift from a Gypsy artist in Spain. Roma, he called his people. They'd been lovers for two weeks, and then she'd woken one day in a field to find him gone, stolen away in the dark. He'd left her his gold chain. Foxes, phoenixes, pixies, sprites. Between her heavy breasts lay an ornate crucifix, Jesus in his crown of thorns, his sorrowing face turned away. That one she'd paid out her last dollars for in the days just before the reverend's death. Before Eliza Grey had vanished, and Marlowe became Brynt's to love. And there was a last space, uninked, just over her heart, which she would one day fill with the silhouette of a shining boy. Her boy. On the little table the candle stub guttered in its dish and she half stood, wrestled into her underthings, into her dress, swept her warmest shawl over her shoulders. She blew out the candle.

Never mind Beecher, she thought. If she wanted to follow Marlowe, she'd have to talk to Felix Fox himself.

At the door she hesitated, glanced back. The little wagon was dim, narrow. There was nothing in it she loved. She couldn't even stand upright. But everywhere she looked she saw Marlowe and heard him, his serious little voice. She'd packed a carpetbag of clothes and personal effects and she reached under the table and took out the book of engravings that Marlowe used to like to look at and she worked that into the carpetbag too. Then she looked around at the wagon. Let the woman who talked to ghosts have it. Brynt would be gone by morning.

Or maybe gone, she corrected herself, as she went down the juddering wood slats, stepped off squelching into the mud. Hopefully gone. It was night now, the circus was in full play. The air was cold. She could see the colored lanterns of the big top glowing behind the row of wagons. She'd hear what Felix Fox had to tell her first, yes. Then see. Though she'd traveled a fair piece of the world, and though she had little fear for her own safety, she'd still need somewhere to begin, some way of picking up Marlowe's trail.

She hadn't gone ten paces when there came a whoosh from somewhere behind her, almost like a sudden great sucking in of air, and then an orange glow backlit the sky. She felt a wall of heat roll out past the wagons, the tents, and turned her head. The big top was on fire.

For a long moment Brynt did nothing. Just stood in the eerie bloom of light and stared, trying to make sense of what she knew to be true. And then she started to run.

There were others running with her, past her. Men, women. Someone was hollering for buckets, for water. The big top was a curtain of flame, the fires blue and white and crawling across the tarpaulin and up the beams like a living thing. The heat was immense. Brynt could hear the screams of horses within, bloodcurdling, awful, and she stalked the perimeter, staring at the faces soot-stained and horrified and hollering at them to get water, to make a line, to start clearing everything out of the way. In the light everything gleamed garish and hallucinatory and weird, the shadows playing across the grass like a peculiar living tattoo. There were men and women from the town, from Remington, some only half-dressed, all of them running across the field to help. Brynt saw Mr. Beecher in his shirtsleeves hauling a bucket in each fist, chewing at an unlit cigar. She saw the muleteer leading a limping horse out of the shine, heard his cussing over the roar. She saw a towering clown in melted greasepaint throwing water on the fire, bucket after bucket after bucket.

But she didn't see Felix Fox. Not anywhere.

She paused. She stood in place and turned and looked all around but he wasn't there. "Who's still inside?" she shouted at a rig operator, a man she knew worked the big top flywheel.

He was black with smoke.

"Is Mr. Fox still inside?"

He gaped at her, he shook his head. "I don't know," he said. "I never saw."

She started to run then. She ran away from the fire feeling the awful heat at her back and she ran between the cool of the wagons, hunting for Felix Fox's tent. There was no light within. She burst in, calling his name.

"Mr. Fox? Mr. Fox, sir!" she shouted.

The tent was still, was dark. She fumbled her way to the desk, remembering it from earlier that day, and found the lantern and the candle and was surprised to feel it still warm. Somebody had been there not long ago. She looked for the flint and sparked it and lit the candle and closed the little glass door. And then she saw his body.

"My God," she breathed.

Mr. Fox lay sprawled in his chair behind the desk, his long legs cast wide, one shoe kicked off. His face was a dark red, his eyes flecked with blood, the eyelids and the skin under them bruised and ringed in black. His clawlike fingers were upturned in his lap as if seeking benediction, as if seeking grace.

He'd died suffering.

Over everything, like a fine dusting of black snow, lay that same strange silky black soot she had found earlier that day.

Brynt stumbled outside, dizzy. She was breathing hard. The fire was still raging across the circus grounds. She stood a long moment in the stillness of that part of the field watching the orange glow over the tents and then, without thinking, almost as if it were another person doing it, she walked slowly back over to her wagon and took the little carpetbag off the table, the one she'd packed earlier that night, the one with her clothes and the book of engravings for Marlowe, and she turned away from the horror and the roar and the slaughter and started for town.

But at the edge of the fire's light she stopped. There was something near the fence, a figure, standing perfectly still in the darkness, a figure holding a hat and almost indistinguishable from the darkness itself. Brynt, staring, her clothes streaked with smoke and sweat, knew him at once, knew who he was, what he'd done. Most of all, she knew who he was seeking. Her blood was loud in her ears. The monster stood unmoving with his hands loose at his sides and he just watched as the big top burned, crumpled, fell in on itself. After a while he put on his hat, and turned, and made his silent way out into the night.

And Brynt followed.

WAKING THE LITCH

Charlie Ovid had no memory of his father. Some nights when he was very small and his mother was still alive she would tell him about the man who had made him and loved him and he would listen in the moonlight of some crowded quarter house to her whisper. He was a good man, she said, but a troubled one. She did not ever know his family. He'd left everything and descended into London to make his way and it was there she had met him and fallen in love.

"His kind and our kind wasn't supposed to be together anyplace, Charlie," she would tell him. "But he didn't care about that. He thought there'd be a better world coming, one we could all be a part of. He thought we just needed to survive long enough to see it."

And Charlie would listen wide-eyed in the shadows as his mother ran calloused fingers through his hair. She was herself the daughter of Jamaican freedmen, her parents still young when they were brought to England from a plantation north of Kingston, their benefactor a white man of wealth and privilege but also, she insisted, with an outrage at the world as it was, not unlike Charlie's own father. Maybe that was a part of why she'd fallen in love with him, she'd whisper. And some-times when she thought it was safe she would take from her skirts the little silver wedding ring, given to her by his father, and press it into Charlie's wrist, so that he could stare at the strange markings in the cold moonlight, the twin crossed hammers and the fiery sun, until they faded up out of his skin and were gone.

Who was his father, what had happened to him, what had his life been before? It was all of it beyond Charlie's imagining. It was like this bone-deep ache inside him, what he remembered and what he couldn't remember. He thought sometimes about how his flesh could heal from anything but how the real hurts, the ones deep inside him, never got any better. When his mother died, he'd drifted seeking work, and there was in him some vague notion to find his father's grave off that wagon trail in the west, to stand bareheaded over the dry dirt and stones that held the man his mother had loved, and who had loved him, Charlie, and to pay his respects. But of course it wasn't to be; a half-black kid with no family and no name couldn't just wander through the counties of the South in his shirtsleeves without soon finding himself at the wrong end of a stick.

And then this Mr. Coulton entered his life, a man from England searching for him, Charlie, of all people. And he had the same crest— the twin hammers and the fiery sun—on an envelope in his keeping. Charlie was wary, he was careful, and he was filled with a fierce anxiety. Something at Cairndale would tell him about his father, who he was, what had happened to him, Charlie was sure of it.

He just had to find it.

The thing was, Mr. Coulton, in his bright yellow waistcoats, and his auburn whiskers, wasn't like any white man Charlie had known. It made him think of that benefactor from his mother's stories, all those years ago, that white man who'd helped his grandparents leave Jamaica. And when Mr. Coulton looked at Charlie all that long ocean crossing, in the lavish lower first-class cabin of the SS *Servia*, a steamship of dazzling brass fixtures and electric lights in the saloon and a hull that carved through the gray swells like a blade, the man really *looked*, not with disgust or anything, not in anger, not like he was looking for a rat to pulp. He just looked at Charlie like he'd look at anyone, at any person, that is, same as he looked at the ancient steward who delivered their hot towels each evening, or the red-faced boy who brought their ironed laundry, and Charlie, who all his life had learned to drop his eyes at the sight of a white man, and tremble, and wait for the lash, just plain didn't know what to do with it.

They disembarked in Liverpool on a drizzling morning and Mr. Coulton took his own travel case in hand and they walked side by side up the hill through the rain to the railway station, water running into their collars, seeping into their shoes, impossibly cold, nothing at all like rain in the Delta or the sweeping river rains he'd always known, and no one looked at them askance, not even the police constable swinging his stick in the drizzle. And Mr. Coulton, with his whiskers and big raw-looking hands and bruised bowler hat, purchased two tickets heading south, for St Pancras Station, London.

As the railway carriage rattled and shunted and gathered speed and the rain flecked the windows, Coulton drew the compartment slider shut with a click and sat opposite, and swept off his hat and ran a hand over his balding head. Smoothed out the few hairs he had. Sighed.

All his life, Charlie had lived in dirt hovels in Mississippi, in crowded communal rooms, in the field rows themselves in high summer. He got clean in cool rivers on Sundays, before trudging the long six miles through dust to church. He'd owned only a single pair of shoes in all his years, and those shoes had gone from being too big to too small to being nothing at all.

White folk, it wasn't just that they were rich, or talked however they wanted, or went wherever they wished to go. It wasn't just their geldings and coaches and liveried servants. It was more than that. They walked through the world as if it was a place that didn't have to be the way it was, as if it could change, the way a person could change. That was the difference, he'd always thought. He had to remind himself sometimes that his father must have been like that, too. And this man, this Mr. Coulton, who'd purchased Charlie a new set of clothes in New Orleans and paid for his meals and who talked to him calmly, quietly, asking nothing of him, this Mr. Coulton was no different in that respect. He just didn't understand how everything he had could be taken from him, quick as lightning. How his life wasn't worth a penny, once it was gone. He, too, was an innocent, when it came right down to it. Like any of them.

They'd been at sea for weeks; the train carrying them south toward London took a matter of hours. Yet the journey felt just as long. Everywhere Charlie looked he saw strangeness: deep green fields, stands of weird-looking trees, fence lines and sheep on distant hills like in a painting he'd seen once, stumbling into the courthouse in Natchez, right before his trial. Even stranger: everyone on the train platform, or shoving past in the narrow train corridor, was white, but they didn't flinch from him, like happened back home. They just nodded, tipped their hats, went on past.

For the first hour Coulton sat with his eyes shut, his shoulders and yellow waistcoat jiggering at the rattling of the train. He wasn't sleeping; Charlie could tell. They roared through tunnels—long clattering darknesses—then up out of the cuts, into gray daylight.

"Mr. Coulton, sir," said Charlie at last. "Did anyone ever leave Cairndale? I mean, went away and was never heard from again?"

"Cairndale ain't a prison, lad. You can leave it if you want."

Charlie wet his lips, wary. "No, I mean . . . do you know of anyone who ever *did*?"

Coulton cracked one heavy eyelid, squinting in the light. "I never knew of a talent what wanted to leave it, once they got there," he said. "But folk are free to go, if they choose. England isn't much like your own country. You'll see."

Charlie watched him.

"London's a right stew of folk. I seen every kind there. Oh, I don't mean just the Cathays and the Moors and the like. I mean card sharps and cutthroats and pickpockets what'll take a piece off you without your even feeling it. Aye. Heart of the bloody world, it is. And every bloody one of them is free to come and go as they please."

He didn't always understand what Mr. Coulton said. It wasn't just the accent. It was also the man's meaning. Sometimes it was like the Englishman was talking a different language.

"You don't much look like a lad what's killed two men," Coulton added.

No, he didn't always understand the man's meaning. But he understood that.

He looked away. He looked away, in part, because he didn't know what to say, but mostly because it wasn't true, he wasn't a lad who'd killed two men. That was the thing, that's what he wasn't telling. Stabbing that deputy in the throat haunted him, it did. He kept seeing it over and over in his mind's eye, what happened, how fast it was, how it felt. It made him sick. But you didn't grow up black and alone and unprotected in the Delta and get to keep your hands clean.

He'd fought his first man when he was nine years old and his mama wasn't even two weeks in the grave. That was to keep the little cloth sack of coins his mama'd pushed into his hands as she lay dying. The man had left him bloodied and walked out of the barn with the coins in his shirt and Charlie had nearly starved after that. He was ten when he left a man pinned under a cartwheel in the rain, taking the man's coat and a sack of his food and fleeing into the darkness. If that wasn't killing, it wasn't far short of it. He'd been hungry then, too, but felt so sick at what he'd done that he couldn't eat the man's food and when he went back two days later the man and the cart and all of it were gone.

But under the eyes of God there could be neither dissembling nor withholding and it was true, he had killed before. That was the awful fact of it. It was a boy like him, fourteen years old, a boy he was living with in a ruined warehouse, a boy who'd introduced him to drink. The boy's name was Isaiah. He had two teeth out in front and a funny eye, but he'd had a quick sense of humor and used to make Charlie laugh. They'd finished a bottle and in the way of kids and drinking they'd got to arguing and then to fighting and Charlie had knocked him backward against a wall where a spike stuck out, some sort of harrower for the old warehouse sacking, and the boy was dead before he even knew what was what. That one broke Charlie. He never touched a bottle again, never would.

Then there came the overseer, yes.

And now the deputy.

He knew the deputy was a bad man and a cruel one and if it wasn't Charlie he was tormenting it would be some other. He knew if he hadn't stepped in, the man might have hurt that white lady, the one who'd rescued him, Miss Quicke. Alice. He knew this and still he felt sick at what he'd done. Taking a life was just about as dire a thing as any thing there was.

But he couldn't talk about this to Mr. Coulton, to anyone. He kept what he felt close to his chest and he didn't dwell on it. That was the way to get by. And so, when they arrived at St Pancras Station, in a roar of steam and smoke, Charlie stepped down and looked all around in amazement. He was tall enough to see over the hats of the crowds. The air was black with soot; the ceiling of steel and glass soared high above. He followed Mr. Coulton close through the bodies, squinting, choking, past porters in slouch caps with trunks stacked high on trolleys, past men in black silk hats, flower girls with boxes on ropes round their necks, past workmen and sweeps and beggars and out into the murky brown darkness of a rain-thick afternoon, the rain falling darkly, at a slant, the cobblestones pooling in the wet and shining blackly up, for the gaslights were already on, and Charlie stared at all of it, at the roar and crush of humanity, as if all the world were coming and going from the cobblestoned square just outside St Pancras Station. As perhaps it was.

Mr. Coulton led him directly to a cabstand on the corner and ushered him up into a two-seat hansom and leaned out to get the driver's attention. The driver was across the square, at a food cart, clapping his hands for the cold, and he came at a run when he saw Coulton's wave.

"Twenty-three Nickel Street West, man," said Coulton, banging his walking stick at the roof. His cheeks were red and pitted in the chill. "Blackfriars. Make it quick, mind." He grunted, shifted his weight, and the hansom squeaked and shivered. He grinned at Charlie. "Welcome to London, lad. Welcome to the big smoke."

"The big smoke," Charlie murmured wonderingly, as they lurched into motion.

The dark city swept past. Rain ran off the hindquarters of the horse in front of them in silver ropes. The hansom jolted and creaked in the busy streets.

Slowly, so slowly, Mississippi, and all its horrors, the swampy heat and the vast sky and the meanness of it all, started to fade and come apart in his mind, like newsprint in the rain.

They pulled up at a tall, ornate row house at the corner of a well-kept street. The windows were dark. There were bollards blocking the pedestrian way, cobblestones shining in the brown gloom. Huddled figures hurried across the street. A small street-side entrance was visible, but Coulton led him through an iron gate, into a high dim carriage house, vacant, and across the cobblestones and up the steps to a set of grand oak doors. He did not ring, but simply turned the pull and entered, as if it were his own house, his own right to do so, and Charlie, nervous, followed. His eyes took in the elegant wainscotting of the entrance hall, the chandelier high above, the dense ferns around a clouded mirror, the empty hat stand like a skeletal watcher. Coulton's shoes left half-moons in the soft carpet as he set down his traveling case, wiped the rain from his face with an open hand, and went through into the house.

"Here we are, then," he said with a grunt.

A grand foyer, with stairs twisting up into the gloom. A tall clock made of what appeared to be bone was ticking loudly in the stillness. At the edge of the parlor Coulton paused, blocking the way, so that Charlie could not see past.

"What the devil," he muttered.

Coulton crossed to a table under a big window. The gloom was filled with the heavy draped shapes of furniture. He'd picked something up in both hands and was turning it in the low light and then Charlie saw what it was. A specimen jar, holding a human fetus, malformed, in a green liquid. It seemed almost to glow in the gloom.

"Do be careful with that," said a soft voice. "Aborted hydrocephalic specimens are not easily obtained. And where you go, Mr. Coulton, breakage tends to follow."

A stout woman in a black dress was standing absolutely still in front of the window, with her pale hands clasped before her. She came smoothly forward. Her shoulders were rounded and soft, her neck overflowing her tight collar. A birthmark covered half her face, like a burn, complicating her expression. Charlie had not heard her enter; she seemed simply to have glided, ghostlike, out of the air.

"Aye, Margaret," said Coulton, setting the jar heavily down. Inside, the fishy thing drifted and turned, drifted and turned. "I always did admire your taste."

"You'd be interested to hear how I acquired it. It was in the possession of a rather unusual . . . collector." She turned. "Who is this? This will be the boy from Mississippi? Where's the other one, the one from the circus?"

Coulton took off his bowler, shook the rain from his greatcoat, grunted. "How about, *Welcome back, Mr. Coulton. And how was your journey, Mr. Coulton? I trust everything was satisfactory, Mr. Coulton.*"

The woman exhaled very slowly from her nostrils, as if long-suffering and put-upon. "Welcome back, Mr. Coulton," she said. "And how was your journey, Mr. Coulton?"

"Plum as pudding," he said with a sudden grin, laying his hat on the sofa.

"There is a hat stand in the hall. As there has always been."

Coulton paused, one arm half out of its sleeve. Then, with a calm deliberation, he finished taking off his greatcoat and made a great show of folding it carefully, setting it too on the sofa. His yellow checkered suit seemed to glow in the dimness, like a moth at a lit window.

The woman sighed. "Charles Ovid," she said, turning her dark gaze on him. "My name is Mrs. Harrogate. I am your good Mr. Coulton's employer."

Charlie tried not to look at her too closely. "Mrs. Harrogate, ma'am," he said with a nod.

"Oh, I'll have none of that," she said sharply.

She crossed the parlor and took his chin in her fingers and turned his face so that he had to meet her eye. He was much the taller of them. He stared at the birthmark.

"There," she said. "This isn't America, Charles. Here, you will not be less than you are. Not in my presence, at least. Do I make myself understood?"

He nodded, alarmed, confused, afraid to look away. "Yes, missus," he whispered.

"Yes, Mrs. Harrogate," she corrected.

"Yes, Mrs. Harrogate."

"Now," she said, turning to Coulton, "*where* is the one from the *circus?*"

"Somewhere in the middle Atlantic by now." Coulton sat on a velvet sofa and put his boots up, leaving wet brown heel stains like horseshoes on the lacework. "I left that for Miss Quicke to handle. I reckon she's handling it."

Mrs. Harrogate sucked in her breath. "On her own?"

"Aye, she's capable. Is it a problem?"

"Those were not my instructions." She did not look pleased. "I've had no telegram, nothing. I will need to inform Cairndale."

"Listen, Alice Quicke can handle twice whatever I can. She's hard as nails, that one. And the Midwest is halfway to wilderness, Margaret. Give her time. I'd be more worried if you *had* heard from her."

"Did you quarrel? Is that why she went alone?"

Coulton smiled in calm annoyance. "I've known shoe leather more agreeable than her. But that weren't it." His voice lowered. "I heard talk, Margaret. In Liverpool. Before I left."

"Oh?"

"I think maybe our old friend's back. I think he's got an interest in our lad, here. In Charlie."

"Our old friend."

"Aye. *Marber.*"

"I know who you mean, Mr. Coulton. But he's been gone seven years. Why return now?"

Coulton shrugged angrily, his stout face reddening. "Well, I never read his bloody diary, did I? Maybe he got lonely."

All this Charlie, bareheaded, still standing, with trousers darkened from the rain, observed with careful attention. He was used to making himself still and unseen and he tried to do that now. But when Mrs. Harrogate let her gaze fall on him, it was as fierce and piercing as before, and he understood she hadn't forgotten his presence at all.

"Mr. Ovid," she called sharply. "There is a basin of heated water on a nightstand, and fresh towels laid out for you. I have taken the liberty of acquiring some more suitable clothes on your behalf. I thought you would be shorter of stature, but they will do. Yours is the first room off the landing on the second floor. You must be wearied from your journey. I will fetch something for your appetite shortly."

Charlie, uncertain, turned and went up the stairs. In the gloom the stained glass windows on the landing were lit weakly from the streetlights outside and cast his hands and clothes in a weird green light. His was a large wallpapered room, thickly furnished, its curtains drawn. A crack of light from the lane seeped under their folds. The bed was wide, tightly dressed. A mahogany nightstand held a covered porcelain bowl, a towel folded beside it. The towel, when he held it, felt impossibly soft. It smelled of lilacs. Last of all Charlie lifted the cloth from the bowl and watched the steam roll up over his hands and wrists like a dream.

He knew Mrs. Harrogate had sent him away to continue her conversation in private and he lingered in his room after washing his neck and face and hands, not caring. It felt so good to be clean. After a while he opened his door and stood peering along the corridor. There were other rooms, doors standing open. He had a feeling there was more to Cairndale and to Mrs. Harrogate but he couldn't imagine just what it was. It seemed to him he had stepped through into a strange world, a world of shadows and eerie deformations afloat in jars and secrets and soap and blessedly soft towels. The craziness of it staggered him.

He went out to the landing and leaned over the balustrade looking down and then up and then, for no reason he could explain, he continued upstairs to the next floor. Another hall, another door. Charlie pushed it open with tentative fingers.

What he saw made his blood run cold. In a slumped bed, identical to his own, lay a figure, gray, bald, his bedsheets twisted in sleep, his skin leeched of color. He made no sound as he slept. On the nightstand Charlie glimpsed a pipe, a candle, a dish with a small black gum smeared on it, like a thumbprint. The man's wrists and ankles, he saw, had been tied to the bedposts with rope.

"This ain't your room, lad," said a voice.

Charlie jumped. It was Mr. Coulton, standing in the opened door, his face hidden in shadow. He looked bigger, bulkier. In silhouette his squat head and long whiskers gave him a shaggy, gorilla-like shape. The floorboards groaned as he came in.

"I won't be tied up like that," said Charlie warningly.

Coulton grunted. "You? Jesus, lad. Course not."

"Who is he? What'd he do?"

"*Was*, you mean," Coulton corrected. "Who *was* he. A friend and confidant to a man what wants you dead, lad, if I know him right. This here is Walter bloody Laster."

Charlie hesitated. Anyone who'd would want him dead would be back in Natchez, angry about the overseer, and the deputy he'd slaughtered in that doorway, but he didn't think that was Coulton's meaning. He stared down at the skeletal figure tied there, bruised like a pugilist, his lips soft-looking and very red. The sharp fingers looked bony and strong.

"What's the matter with him? Is he sick?"

"Not sick, Charles," said Mrs. Harrogate. She swept into the room in her black skirts. "Dead."

Coulton looked over at her. "You never said you found him."

"Well. You only just arrived, Mr. Coulton."

Charlie was afraid they'd be angry he'd strayed from his room but neither appeared so. This surprised him. Mrs. Harrogate went to the window and parted the drapes with two fingers and watched the rain against the warped glass.

"He is a litch, Charles," she said. "He is both dead and not dead." She turned. "Oh, don't look at me like that. You yourself know something of what is and isn't possible, I think. We were led to believe Mr. Laster died of consumption, oh, what was it, seven years ago, Mr. Coulton? Yet it seems someone has found a way to preserve him."

Charlie stared at her, bewildered. "Preserve him—?"

But no one explained more.

"It's him, isn't it, Margaret?" said Coulton. "It's Jacob. It's got to be."

Mrs. Harrogate nodded.

And then Mr. Coulton stepped forward, reeking of pipe smoke and ash. He leaned over the sick man on the bed, the sick whatever-it-was, the litch. He laid a wary hand on the creature's forehead, took it away in wonder. "Did you know Jacob could do this?"

Mrs. Harrogate frowned.

"He's gotten strong," she murmured.

Margaret Harrogate left Coulton and the boy settled in the parlor and went up to the fifth floor, to the attic, drawing a shawl over her shoulders, pulling on her kidskin gloves. It was cold, this high in the house. She did not affix her veil. She unlocked a little iron grate at the top of the stairs and dragged it rattling open, and then went into the drafty stinking loft. The rain was still coming down, steadily, miserably, drumming on the roof. Beyond the little watch balcony, through the glass doors, she could see the cold brown haze of the city. One door stood always open. The tar paper was sticky and pooling under it.

As she neared the big wood-and-wire loft, she could see, behind the landing board, the dark shapes of the bonebirds, silent, unmoving, little fists of stillness on their staggered perches. A newly arrived one waited in the trap.

Carefully, she unlatched the door, stepped inside. She pulled the thick leather hawk glove onto her left hand and regarded the creatures. They were delicate, pale constructions of bone and feather, their hollowed eye sockets dark, their skulls tilting side to side. Gruesome, really. But they needed neither sleep nor sustenance, nor did they ever get lost. Dr. Berghast had built a strange clockwork breast piece to hold their ribs and breastbone in place, and the curious gears and armor enclosed their vertebrae and the soft backs of their skulls.

She took out the message from the bonebird's leg, tied with black thread, and unscrolled it. It read, simply:

Do not examine the M. child. Bring him north at once. Proceed with C. Ovid as usual. —B.

At the standing table she took out a small paper from the drawer and licked the stub of the pencil and wrote out a brief reply. She paused before adding that the second child, this *Marlowe*, was still en route. Then she rolled the paper tightly and tied it with a red string and slipped it into the little leather pouch on the nearest bonebird's leg.

Slowly, so as not to disturb the creature, she carried it out into the rain and threw it into the air. Soundlessly it rose, flapping, circled the roof twice, and was gone.

It was not like Henry Berghast to take an interest in the unfound talents, let alone to be agitated about any particular one. But this last boy, Marlowe, from the Illinois circus. The name was unfamiliar, but Margaret knew him all the same. She remembered the terror of that night, seven years ago, prowling the dark grounds of Cairndale with lanterns, dredging the loch, raking the underbrush with poles while Jacob Marber howled out there in the highland dark. The cradle stilled in the nursery, the nursemaid's bed empty. It was why Berghast wrote every few days, driven, furious, why he sent bonebirds south at speed, demanding updates: Had they yet arrived, and in what condition, and had she noticed anything peculiar? Oh, she understood.

Had her life been different, had her dear husband not been taken from her so soon, had they been blessed in that way—why, she too would've stopped at nothing to get her own child back.

When she'd seen the bonebird off, Margaret put on her veil and descended the rear servant stairs and went out into the city. On Thorne Street a cab went clattering past, very near, the horse's hooves splashing in the puddles, the smell of wet horsehair and iron in her nostrils. The streets were full despite the weather. She walked two blocks east and then turned north, away from the river, passing a tea shop and Wyndleman's Bank. She bought three beef-and-onion pies at a seller's wagon at the edge of the park and then trudged back through the puddles, the hot greasy papers folded up under her arm.

Jacob Marber, she was thinking. For God's sake. Hunting Berghast's son.

Well, much luck to him. The world was wide and the finding hard. Hadn't it taken Henry himself eight years to trace the child, and that with a glyphic to find the way? What made Jacob imagine he could do it quicker?

But there were pressing affairs here as well, she reminded herself. The examination, for one. Charles Ovid would need to be assessed for his talent, a plate of his likeness taken by the photographers down the street, a file made up. She'd prepared the room under the house already, even before she'd brought Walter back to the flat; all was ready. There was that, at least.

She stopped just inside the iron gate at 23 Nickel Street West and opened the pies with her thumbs and took out a small packet of powder and mixed it into the meat. Then, in the parlor, she gave the boy all three pies, and took up a candle in its dish and went upstairs. It would take some minutes for the powder to take effect, she knew. There was little rush. She found Coulton in Walter Laster's room.

A second candle burned at the bedside. Coulton stood over the litch, turning his hat in his hands, his whiskers wild and scraggly. In the candle fire his eyes were shining.

"So he's back, then," he said softly, not looking at her. "That's what this means. Jacob Marber has returned."

"Yes," said Margaret.

"Look what he's done. Walter, the stupid bugger." Coulton put his hat on the edge of the bed, ran his fingers through his thinning hair. "You can't keep him here, Margaret. It isn't safe. Not for the boy, not for any of us. Jesus, you don't even know if them ropes is strong enough."

"They're strong enough."

"Is there a lock on that door?"

"He'll stay put."

"Maybe when he's sleeping. But when he comes to? What do you aim to do with him?"

"Take him to Cairndale, of course."

Coulton laughed. "Sure. And maybe feed him a kid or two while he's waiting?"

She knew it sounded mad. She met Coulton's gaze and saw his expression darken.

"You're serious. To the institute? What the devil for? Can he even pass through the wards?"

She set the candle down in its dish and glanced out into the hall to be sure the boy was nowhere near and then she clasped her hands in front of her. "He's our only direct link to Jacob. We'd be foolish not to use him."

"Use him how? He's just a dog off its leash."

"He can be rather talkative for a dog, Mr. Coulton. He's already offered some interesting insights into Jacob Marber. For instance, it seems Jacob left him here in London with a task. He has been searching," and here Margaret lowered her voice, "for a keywrasse."

In the silence that followed, Coulton scratched at his whiskers. "Well . . . that doesn't sound . . . good," he said slowly.

She watched him. "You have no idea what that is, do you?"

"None at all."

"A weapon, Mr. Coulton. A very powerful weapon. It would be of great consequence to Jacob, should he acquire it. Needless to say, he will not succeed. Especially with his loyal Walter locked up at Cairndale. Besides," she added, "I rather expect Dr. Berghast will want to examine Walter in person."

Coulton massaged the meat of one hand, working its fingers in a fist. "Aye," he said reluctantly. "What's that you been feeding him? It isn't tar? Where'd you get a twist of the poppy?"

"I have my resources, Mr. Coulton. The same as you."

"We should just kill the bugger right now." He leaned over the unmoving form of what had once been Walter Laster. "If we even know how to do that. You got to dig around in there, cut out the heart. Isn't that how it goes?"

"You're the one who knows about litches. You encountered one before, didn't you?"

Coulton grimaced. "Aye. Years ago, in Japan."

"How did you destroy that one?"

"It weren't me what done it. It were the litch's maker."

"Mm. We could ask her."

Coulton sighed, and for a moment she saw in the candlelight the compassion that was in him, that was a part of him, that he hid with his gruffness. "It were a terrible thing, Margaret," he said, "what happened there. I wouldn't want to ask the poor girl. She don't need to go through it all again." He went to the window and lifted the gauzy curtain and stared out at the encroaching dark.

"So be it," he said at last, turning around. "And did our friend here offer any insight into where Jacob bloody Marber might be found, now? If he weren't in Natchez or anywhere on the way back, why was he asking after my destination? Where's he gone to, Margaret?"

She watched him closely. "Don't you know?" she said.

And then a flicker of understanding crossed Coulton's face. "The circus lad," he muttered. "Marlowe."

Margaret smoothed out her black skirts, interlaced her fingers before her.

"He wasn't coming for Charlie at all," he continued. "It was always Marlowe."

"And if he hasn't found him yet," said Margaret softly, "he will soon."

When it was time, Margaret led Coulton and the boy down to the cellar. Through a thick unmarked door, down a second passageway, damp and dark, through another locked door into an ancient room. One wall was stone and buckled and looked so old it might have been in use in the time of the Romans. The cellar was deep and had no windows. In this room Margaret examined the new children, had done so for years. Coulton didn't think it necessary this time.

"The lad's a haelan, Margaret," he'd told her earlier, "there's not much to examine. I saw it with my own eyes. Plucked a blade right out of his own forearm and cut a man's throat with it."

But haelans were rare, she knew, and there were varied degrees of skill, and it was best to determine such things for herself. She unlocked the door, lifting the lantern high. The examination room was soundproof, its ceilings and walls and even the porcelain tiles underfoot painted white; there was a drain in the floor, like in an abattoir. She'd been preparing for days now for Coulton's return and had set up a little table near the door with various sharp implements under a white towel, and a little red box, covered by a sheet, in the far corner. In the middle stood a sinister chair, positioned over the drain, with iron manacles screwed into its armrests and its legs. Its purpose was fear, not pain. Fear could be a useful trigger for latent talents.

Charles stopped in the doorway. "Mr. Coulton?"

He sounded frightened.

"Aye, lad, go on," said Coulton. "You ain't in any peril. I swear to it."

Margaret ushered them in, brisk, stern, rubbing her arms for the damp. That was the one thing about the place she'd been unable to change. A nice little stove glowing in the corner, that would just about do it. Might even be useful, too, for burning.

"Now, Charles," she said crisply. "What has Mr. Coulton told you? Have you been informed about Cairndale, its purpose?"

When the boy said nothing, only glanced nervously across at Coulton, she frowned in displeasure. It was Coulton's job to prepare the kids, wasn't it?

"Cairndale Institute is a refuge, a place of safety for people like you, a place where you'll learn to harness your talent. It is run by a man named Dr. Berghast. If this test goes as I expect it to, you'll be meeting him soon. But first, I must confirm what it is you can do. Is that clear?"

He blinked slowly. There was a careful intelligence in the boy; he would do well, indeed.

"I won't be put in irons," he said.

"You will," she replied. "The restraints, Charles, are for our safety, not yours. Why would we bring you all this way, only to make you suffer? You must see that would make no sense at all."

The boy looked at the chair, looked at her, hesitated. Then he sat. Coulton squatted next to him and fastened the irons with a little key, turning each little lock twice. He left the key standing in the second lock and gave the boy a nod. Then he stepped noiselessly back.

"Mr. Coulton tells me you are a haelan. That is the name for what you can do. It is a rare talent, but you are not alone. There *are* others. How old were you when you first knew what you could do?"

Charlie wet his lips. "My mama said I just always could do it. She said it wasn't a thing to show anyone. She said keep it safe, keep it secret."

"Your mother was a wise woman. How many people have seen you do it?"

"I don't know, Mrs. Harrogate."

"But many, you would agree?"

The boy nodded.

"I'd say a good dozen in Natchez alone," Coulton interjected. "All them what were present at the execution."

"Ah. But they won't believe what they saw," she murmured. "They'll find some explanation; they always do. It's no obstacle. Tell me, Charles. How many people have you killed?"

He looked quickly up. "Missus?"

"Killed, Charles. How many?"

His voice was small when he answered. "Two, Mrs. Harrogate, ma'am."

She clicked her tongue. He was lying to her, of course, she could see that writ clearly in his face. The powder she'd fed him hadn't yet taken full effect. No matter. She was pleased by the lie, pleased to see the shame he felt when he spoke of it. She'd seen too many kids in that chair, hurt over and over by the world, until their hurting and their being hurt no longer seemed shameful at all. Those were the ones that worried her.

She crossed the room, her black skirts swishing on the white-washed floor. She picked up a long surgical knife from the table near the door. "Does it hurt, Charles? When you heal yourself, I mean?"

"Yes." The boy paused. "It's like my insides are on fire."

"I must see it for myself, you understand," she said. "I must cut you now. But I would like your permission."

His eyes were clear. "Yes, ma'am. You can do it."

She crossed the room and cut the boy's arm. Bright red blood flowed slowly down over his wrist, his knuckles, it dripped on the white tiles. The boy was gritting his teeth in pain, gasping, and he turned his face and stared down at the wound. As they watched, the incision closed over.

Margaret Harrogate looked at Coulton. He shrugged, bored. She turned back. "There are five families of talent, Charles. You belong to the second. You are a haelan, what Dr. Berghast would describe as a regenerator. When your cells begin to die, any part of you, in fact, your body revivifies. It is a rare and extraordinary talent. You will age differently than the rest of us. You will understand risk differently, danger differently, love differently. Now, think carefully, Charles. Is there anything else you can do?"

"Anything else—?"

"Unusual. Special. Can you . . . manipulate your flesh? Say, reach objects that should be too far away? Did you ever slip into a space too small for you, that you shouldn't have been able to slip into?"

"I don't think so, Mrs. Harrogate. No."

"There is a box in the corner. Do you see it? I want you to try to reach it. Concentrate, now."

Ovid closed his eyes. Opened them. "I don't understand," he said.

"Close your eyes. I want you to imagine a white sky. Nothing is in it. Now, in that white sky is a dark cloud. It is shaped like a door. It is getting closer. Look at it. There is a keyhole in it, and you hold a key. What happens when you turn the lock?"

The boy looked confused, unhappy.

Margaret ran her tongue over her teeth, considering. Perhaps it was not a part of his gift, the mortaling. Perhaps he simply needed to learn control. No matter.

"Tell me about your mother," she said, changing her approach. "Tell me about your happiest memory of her."

"My mama?"

He peered suspiciously at Margaret, eyes hooded. She waited.

"My mama . . . ," he repeated, softer.

Now she could see the powder was taking effect.

"Mama's just about the only good thing there was for me," he said. "I don't even remember her voice now. She used to sing in the church, used to sing like sunlight was just shining on the angels. Like honey on your tongue. That's how it felt. This one day, she came back home smelling like flour and sugar because she was working in those days in this old kitchen, and they were making pies that week. And she rolled up her sleeves, and there was all this sugar on her elbows and arms, and we licked the sugar off them together."

Margaret smiled. "Could she . . . do things? Like what you do?"

"No."

"And your father, could he? He was white, obviously—"

"I don't remember my pa," said Charles abruptly, angrily, and he dropped his eyes and stared at the red starbursts of blood on the white tiles.

She could see he didn't want to say more, and she felt a quick pang of guilt, but it was necessary; she needed to know certain truths. The boy was struggling against himself but the powder was in him. "Pa died taking us to California," he said at last. "I always wanted to find where he was buried and tell him I'd grown up and tried to be a good person like Mama said he was. He was a good man, and he loved us, and he believed in a better world. That's what Mama always said. But he was afraid too, all the time, afraid for me. Maybe he knew what I could do, I don't know. I was just a baby." Charles looked up. His eyes were glassy. "Maybe it was just he knew there was no place on this earth for someone like me. Nowhere I'd ever belong."

"Ah."

"He was from here. I know it."

"From London?"

"No, ma'am. From *here*."

Margaret frowned, unsure of the boy's meaning. She glanced across at Coulton, who was listening intently. She was going to ask more but something stopped her, some instinct she had learned long ago to trust and to listen to, and instead she brushed her hands on her skirts and turned away. "That's fine, Charles, thank you. Now, I want you to concentrate. I know you're tired, but I have one last question for you. What is it you *want*, Charles?"

The boy's head drooped suddenly, then jerked back up. "I don't want to be hurt anymore," he said. His words were thickening.

"How much powder did you give him?" asked Coulton. "I reckon he's about finished here. Did you get what you needed?"

Margaret nodded.

"I want to know what he looked like ... what my father looked ...," mumbled the boy. "I want to hear Mama's voice again, I can't remember her voice...."

She unlocked the manacles on the chair, helped Coulton lift him, stumbling, to his feet. He was thin, gangly, his legs folding sideways under his weight.

"The poor thing," she said, stepping back. "All of them. They deserve better from us."

Charlie Ovid awoke in the parlor, on the velvet sofa, his arms folded up under his head. A fire burned in the grate. His head was aching. He lay still, trying to remember the examination, what had happened.

Wind was in the flue of the fireplace, like a low keening. A drunk was singing faintly streets away. Horses clopped by on the cobblestones outside. A slow steady dap of rain sounded against the window, easing for a time, coming back.

He shifted uncomfortably, then sat up in the gloom. He ran a hand over his face. Even at night, it seemed, Blackfriars seethed with life. Someone had opened the window a crack, and the rainy air left a chalky taste in his mouth. His nostrils when he picked at them were crusted with a black rime. He'd never known anything like this place, this London, the magnitude of such a city built by human hands, old, yes, impossibly so, like it had always been there, and going on for miles and miles like the great brown Mississippi he loved, and the filth, and the deep vanishing alleyways and crooked lanes and shadowy stairs into cellars where figures emerged like apparitions, all of it, only just glimpsed through the murky rain at speed as the hansom splashed its way through the crowded streets from St Pancras Station—

What was the matter with him? He rubbed at his wrists. Mrs. Harrogate had seemed pleased, in that creepy room in the cellar. He didn't trust her, of course, the way she glided in her black dresses soundlessly over the floor, her gaze dark, unblinking, the disturbing purple mark across her weathered face. No, he thought sharply, that wasn't fair of him, he knew what it was to look different too. But he couldn't shake the feeling that when she looked at him she was sizing him up, weighing him like a sack of dry goods for the value. Oh, he didn't trust Mr. Coulton much either; it was true. But at least he'd watched that man closely, and he'd come to believe he was a good man, whatever that meant. *A man ruled by compassion* is how the young pastor at his church might have said it. He supposed they'd both retired to their bedrooms upstairs, up where that creature too slept, that litch, tied and drugged, its gray-blue skin and bloodred lips like a thing out of a nightmare. Charlie lay back down, wondering about it, and the institute, what it all would be like. It filled him with dread.

And that was when he heard it.

A door, somewhere in the house above him, creaking open. Slowly. But no footsteps followed, no squeaking of the floorboards. He waited. No one came.

And then he heard a soft scrabbling sound, like little claws on wood, and he sat up and stared hard at the stairs leading up into the house.

Nothing. The grandfather clock made out of bone ticked out its soft seconds. No other sound beyond the rain at the glass. He got up and walked to the base of the stairs and put a hand on the banister and listened.

"Mr. Coulton, sir?" he called up. "Mrs. Harrogate?"

There was no answer.

In the stillness, he started up the stairs. The second-floor landing was dark, silent. So was the third floor. But on the fourth floor, the door to the litch's room stood open. Beyond lay an absolute darkness.

Charlie stopped, his heart beating fast.

"Mister?" he called softly. "You awake?"

Something pale and indistinct then moved at the top of that room's doorframe, as if it had been waiting, waiting for him, a blur against the darkness. It slid down into view and hung there, upside down, looking at him with huge black eyes. Charlie stared back, uncomprehending. And then slowly, very slowly, the thing bared its long teeth, and something shifted in Charlie, a terror, and he opened his mouth to cry out for Mr. Coulton, or Mrs. Harrogate, anyone, but no sound came.

He stumbled back. The litch dropped scrabbling to the floor and righted itself, the torn ropes swinging at its wrists and ankles.

Then it leaped.

Charlie took off. He threw himself down the stairs four at a time, sliding and stumbling, rolling when he reached the main floor of the house and righting himself and stumbling for the parlor and shutting the door behind him. He could hear nothing. Where was Mr. Coulton, Mrs. Harrogate? Were they okay? He'd fallen over himself, was crabwalking backward away. He fumbled for the sofa, tried to stand. For a long moment there was nothing; he told himself he was being foolish, his senses had deceived him.

Then the door thumped. Once, twice. In the sudden silence the hand-pull was drawn slowly downward, and the hinges creaked open, and then Charlie watched in horror as the gray litch crawled like a humanoid spider up the wall to the ceiling moldings and there peered down at him, cocking its head to one side, clicking its teeth.

Before anything else, before he could cry out for help, or fumble for a weapon of some kind, it had launched itself, lightning fast, and collided with him in a crashing of potted ferns and pier tables and splintering furniture. It was clawing at his throat, tearing at his hands where he fought it, the torn ropes in a blur of thrashing, the litch leaning its face down close and snapping its jaws. Charlie fought silently, wordlessly. He worked his knee up under it and kicked hard and it flew off him, eerily light, smashing against the far wall. Charlie was on his feet in a flash. He caught a glimpse, just a moment, of that strange fetus in its jar. It seemed to be staring at him, pressing its malformed hands against the glass in recognition. But when the litch came at him again Charlie lifted the jar over his head and shattered it in a great reeking crash over the litch's head.

The stillness that followed was terrible. The litch, stunned, lay in the foul matter turning its face this way and that, slipping over the glass, lifting the slimy thing in its claws. Charlie didn't stay to see more: he threw open the door and crossed the foyer and was outside, stumbling and catching himself and running onward for the iron gate, unlatching it, swinging it shut with a clang behind him. Then he backed up and stood on the dark rain-slick cobblestones of the street and stared at the darkness.

Already the rain had plastered his shirt to his skin. He didn't know if the thing could get through that gate but he didn't think so.

But then he heard a shatter of glass. It was the big bay window, in the parlor. Through the black rain he saw a pale figure clinging to the side of the row house.

Charlie ran. He ran sliding between the bollards and across the cobblestones and turned into a dark alley, stumbling over a pile of broken crates. There were figures in the doorways, turning, raising their faces in the gloom, but he didn't stop. He crossed a small court and turned down a lane past a little park with benches and a statue looming in the gaslights and then he stumbled halfway down a flight of crooked stairs and stopped. It had got ahead of him, somehow: the litch was hunched on the lowest stair, peering up at him, making that weird clicking noise with its teeth.

In the rain Charlie's forearms and chest were on fire where the litch had scratched at him, trying to get at his throat. He was gasping. The pain was strange to him, not like normal. He stood in the wet with his shoulders heaving, feeling his strength ebb, feeling his terror rising.

And then the thing scrabbled sideways and came at him, running up the stairs on all fours, very fast, the torn ropes at its wrists and ankles slapping against the cobblestones. Charlie turned, ran back up. There was an iron dustbin at the top and he seized its lid and turned and swung with all his might and he felt the lid smash into the litch, catching it under its jaw, and the thing screeched and spun off sidelong into the shadows. And then Charlie was running again, leaping the cobblestoned stairs, making his way out onto a road shining in the weak gaslights.

The river was just ahead of him, a molten darkness of orange lights and strange shapes, boats, skiffs maybe, and he saw a bridge off to his left and made for it. There was no one else about. His footsteps clattered off the cobblestones, into the gloom. He was halfway across the bridge when he stopped and looked back. He didn't see the litch. He wet his lips, breathing hard, and thought about it, and then he hurried to the stone railing and leaned out and saw it.

The litch was racing along the stone undercarriage of the bridge, upside down, a blur of gray in the darkness. Charlie started to run but he hadn't gone more than ten feet when it crawled up over the railing in front of him and crouched in a pool of hazy gaslight and it cocked its head and studied him.

"What do you want?" Charlie cried in the rain. "What?"

The litch crept forward. Its mouth was open.

"Get away from me!" he shouted. "Go on, get!"

The litch paused. For a long moment nothing happened. And then it leaped, its claws out, its teeth clicking, and Charlie, expecting it this time, fell sideways away, so that the creature only caught him a glancing blow in the side, and he struck at it with his fists as it went past, lifting it, so that it struck the stone railing at height, and went over. He could see it twisting there, dangling out over the gap, scrabbling at the bridge for purchase, finding none. Charlie was clutching his side, gasping, sobbing. He watched as the litch swung horribly out over the river and plunged down into the darkness of the Thames.

Then he slid down with his back to the freezing stone, in the very middle of the span, under a faint halo of gaslight in the rain, and he started to shake, he was shaking and shaking, and he didn't know if the water in his eyes was the rain or him crying or what.

Every Stranger is a New Beginning

Alice Quicke left Remington in the graying light with the shining boy half-asleep under a blanket in the wagon, reins looped around her thick wrists. Rain was misting in the gloom, a red glow fanning up over the tree line. The shadows were long when they rode through Merville and Oaks Hollow and they slept that night in an abandoned barn on the side of the road and in the morning they went on. They saw few riders. The next night Alice lay fully clothed in the bed of the wagon with the boy curled against her for warmth, and the night after they crossed into Indiana she slept in the dirt with her back upright against an iron wheel, her chin dipped, her boots kicking at the coals of the fire as she dreamed.

In Lafayette it took her two days to sell the horse and cart. She bought third-class tickets south to Carmel and from Carmel they shared a compartment with an old lady and her lapdog all the way through to Columbus, Ohio. And nine days later Alice and the boy were in Rochester, New York. She signed the leather-bound register under the name Mrs. Coulton while the rains came slantwise against the porch, the kid dripping beside her. Under a candle-wheel chandelier the whores leaned out, their balcony in shadow, silk fans folding and unfolding in their gloves like the wings of birds.

The next morning, Alice read about the fire.

The news was old. In the noisy breakfast room she counted back the days in her head and understood it had happened six days after their going. It had started in the big top and leaped from there to the menagerie and in all eleven people and twenty-six animals had died. There was a poor linocut reproduction of a big top in flames. She looked at the boy with his plate of steak and eggs and his small serious face as he chewed while the rain tracked shadows across the dormer windows behind and cast a gloom over the table in front and she decided, devastation in her heart, that he must never know.

They spent the day in the city shopping for clothes for the boy and ate in a tea shop overlooking a park where a small fair was lighting up the dusk. Later that night she stayed awake at the window staring through the curtains, her revolver on the little table at her elbow. She again read through the article about the fire and then folded it into quarters and put it away in her sleeve, like a handkerchief. She blew out the candles. In the long puddles in the middle of the road the orange lights of the railway station rippled and danced.

Marlowe wasn't one for talking. He'd hardly said two words all their first week of travel. She raked her fingers through her greasy hair. She thought about the fire, all those people. The newspaper had called it an accident. What would Coulton say of it? She thought of his grave pale eyes, his tired mouth. The darkness in his voice as he spoke of that man, Marber. Jacob Marber. The bounty hunter who was no bounty hunter. Behind her a black-haired boy breathed softly in the dark, alive.

Such things happened. The world was cruel. Still, something in it gave her pause. She thought of the asylum where her mother had lived out her days, the stillness of its scrubbed floors, the loneliness of its graveyard. Her mother. She tried to think of some kindness in the woman but could not. What kindness had she, Alice, shown in return? She ran a knuckle under her eyes. She didn't even have a daguerreotype of her, any recollection of what she'd looked like in life. She was just gone, just as if she'd never existed at all. What does anyone leave behind? She looked at the boy, burrowed in his pillow. She'd get him to old Mrs. Harrogate, in London. She'd do that much. The rain was blowing in sheets against the glass. Two figures crossed the street at a stagger, hats drawn low against the gusts. In her heart lay a shadow, like dread, a presentiment of some wrongness, and she raised her hand unthinking to the folded paper in her sleeve.

"What is it, Alice?" she muttered, troubled. "What aren't you seeing?"

While her face in the glass rippled ghostlike against the dark.

In the morning the boy slept late. Alice didn't wake him. She sat on his bedclothes and resisted running a hand through his tousled hair and just waited for him to stir.

"Good morning," she whispered, when he did.

"I dreamed about horses," he said sleepily. "Like you told me to."

He was so small. Though their journey had been uncomfortable he had not complained. For the first week he'd said nothing at all, and only in these last days had he started to talk a little. If he feared for his future he did not say it. She'd known few children in her adult life and was surprised by the good feeling in her whenever he touched her, or slipped his little hand in hers, or smiled up at her with his tiny crooked teeth showing. He slept with both hands raised up over his head as if he were in a holdup. He ate with a fork in one hand and a spoon in the other, scooping and scraping by turns. When he put on his new little black shoes, he was still getting them mixed up.

"Up up up," she said now. "Train leaves at noon."

He blinked his tired eyes, sat up. "You said we could stay here. See the lake."

"You'll get your fill of water when we sail out of New York. Let's go."

Under the blanket his little body lay very still. She thought he might say something more but he didn't. No complaint, nothing. He got up, started to get ready. She watched him at the washbasin, feeling a pang.

"You sleep okay?" she asked, guilt lacing her voice. She hadn't realized he wanted to see the lake so much. Why wouldn't he? Poor kid probably never saw much that wasn't next to a circus field.

He was scrubbing with great absorption at his little pink face, his pink ears, his pink neck. Rubbing the towel dry. He carefully did not look at her.

"It's just, there are schedules," she explained, drifting up behind him. "The liner departs in less than a week. I don't want us to miss it."

He frowned at her in the mirror.

"There are people depending on us, people who want to meet you," she added. "They've been waiting a long time. Good people."

Now he turned, looked up at her. "What are they like?" he asked.

She swallowed. "I don't know. Kind?"

"You don't sound very sure."

Alice wet her lips. She didn't know what to say. She said, "Marlowe, it's your family."

"Brynt's my family."

"No," she said firmly. "She isn't."

But she felt a catch in her throat as she said it. It was more than he'd said in their entire two weeks together. Fuck Coulton for putting her in this position. Fuck this job. The rain was blowing up against the glass. Marlowe was looking at her steadily now and there was in his face something sad, and wise, as if he knew the ways of the world too well and pitied her for what she was doing.

She reached for her boots in disgust.

One last job, she thought. Then she was out.

But the bad feeling that was in her didn't go away.

It just got worse, in fact, the closer they got to Grand Central Terminal. Three days later they were in New York City, stepping off the train into a cloud of white steam, the roar of the station overwhelming, a curving sky of smoke-blackened glass, steel girders. Alice was glancing warily all around at the pale faces passing, their dark hats, the flash of their silver-tipped walking sticks, heart in her throat. She had her right hand deep in the pocket of her oilskin greatcoat, working the hammer of a loaded Colt Peacemaker revolver.

As they descended, Marlowe reached up and took her free hand. She looked down in surprise. Maybe it was just that he was afraid of losing her in the crowd. But she liked it, was surprised by how much she liked it, and she gave him a quick tense smile as she shouldered their way through to the luggage porters.

At the edge of the platform lurked a blind woman, hair wild, face haggard. "Wrong way wrong way wrong way," she was hollering at the passersby. No one paid her any mind.

Alice could feel the kid's fascination. "Don't stare," she said. "She's mad, Marlowe. She's just talking to herself. Leave her be."

But as they hurried by, the madwoman turned her milky eyes upon them. She seemed to follow them somehow as they went, dialing her ruined face slowly in their direction, watching them go, so that Alice, who kept glancing uneasily back, shuddered. The crowds flowed past.

It had been weeks now of grubby rooms, of hotel grime and half-cleaned sheets. Alice was getting tired. But she took Marlowe down to the crooked streets near the harbor, where the huge passenger liners docked, and there she found a shabby little rooming house, meant for sailors maybe, or maybe for passengers paying steerage. An old wooden house, three stories, with gabled windows and a shingled roof mostly in one piece. Its hall was narrow, high-ceilinged. It might have stood in that spot more than a century, was once perhaps a respectable house in the years before the Revolution, before the city grew up all around it. Alice entered the dim office, the oil lamps above the wain-scotting casting everything in a weak orange glow, hearing the floor creak under her like a ship, and wondered at the thousands who had walked those very same floors.

The dread only increased when she tried to let the room. The man who ran the place was old, and hunched, and he walked with a stagger, carrying an oil lamp in his one hand, a ring of heavy keys in the other. His slimy hair overhung his collar. There were patches on his elbows.

"Where's your husband, then?" he said to her, suspicious.

Alice met his gaze. Her boots had stepped in a stream of green muck from the chandler-works next door and, carefully, she wiped them clean on his carpet. "He's dead," she said.

The man just grunted, studied Marlowe. "This your boy? I run a respectable house, I do. And there won't be no visitors, neither," he muttered.

Alice frowned at the implication. She could break his nose in six places before he could blink, but she couldn't do a thing to stop his foul thoughts.

"Will you take our money or not?" she said calmly. "We need three nights."

"You pay in full, up front." When she didn't argue, he gestured for them to follow.

And Alice, still with a feeling of dread in her, thought: *It will do*.

It was a single room at the top of the house, and when the man had opened the curtains, and turned back the moth-eaten blankets, and opened the door of the wardrobe cupboard so that the long clouded mirror reflected the daylight, he left them alone. The walls and floor were so thin, she could hear him go crookedly back down the hall, descend the stairs, cross the long corridor below and go back to the first floor.

She looked at Marlowe and he looked at her. "It'd be a palace for a mouse," she said.

He smiled.

There was much to be done. They spent the following days standing in lines at the docks, stamping their feet for the tiredness, or filling out paperwork for the customs offices, or finding a cabman to come up to the rooming house and collect their few pieces of luggage for the sailing. The docks were crowded, ropes and hoists and great flats of crates being loaded onto barges from warehouses, and police officers drifting grimly among the laborers, and families just in from Staten Island, huddled, miserable, wary. Alice led Marlowe through all of it, that bad feeling just getting stronger and stronger. It was almost like someone was following them, she thought. It was that kind of a feeling. But whenever she ducked into a doorway, or stopped at a dry-goods window to study the street reflections, there never was anyone.

On their last night in New York she didn't sleep. She lay beside Marlowe in the bed, listening to his breathing, staring up at the ceiling in the darkness. In a few hours they'd be climbing the gangway, finding their cabin, sailing out of the harbor. Away. It was after midnight; she'd heard the tolling of the sailor's chapel streets away, marking twelve bells. There was a water stain yellowing the plaster overhead from some leak long years before. It made her think of Mrs. Harrogate, the birthmark on her face. Soon, now.

And that was when she sensed it.

It wasn't a sound, not exactly. It felt more like a shadow going over the sun, a sudden drop in temperature, and she frowned and turned her face on the pillow and lay very still.

And then she did hear something. A soft creaking in the corridor below, as if someone were taking pains to be silent. She got out of bed, pulled on her trousers, her shirt, her boots. Then she stood listening. The shuffling was coming, slowly, up the stairs to the third floor, their floor.

Swiftly, quietly, she started shoving their few possessions into their traveling cases, scooping up Marlowe's clothes, the little traveling mirror she carried. She shut the lids, buckled them fast. She looked around her. She went to the window and opened it onto the cold night, feeling an anger rising in her. Last of all she took out her Colt Peacemaker and eased back the hammer and turned the oil-smooth chambers slowly and then she pocketed it.

"Marlowe," she whispered.

She shook him and he opened his eyes in alarm. She put a finger to her lips, looked at the door.

The rooming house was absolutely silent. Impossibly silent. There was no faint sound of snoring, of coughing, the low murmuring of other residents. It was this—the stillness of it—that had alerted her. Marlowe was already putting on his little shoes, wrongly, struggling into his coat. She went to the door, leaned her ear up against it.

Then they both heard it. Footsteps, clear, calm, unhurried, coming down the hall toward their room. Alice pressed a hand against the door, stepped back to arm's length, and aimed her revolver at chest-height directly at the door. The footsteps stopped.

Nothing moved. No sound.

Something, someone, a man, cleared his throat in the darkness beyond. A creeping horror came over her then, a feeling of anxiety, of dread. And she blinked her eyes rapidly to clear them and saw, weirdly, a black smoke seeping through the crack under the door, and dissipating, and then seeping through all four sides of the door, growing denser, darker. The door rattled softly as it was tried. Alice felt a sudden cold terror.

Just, she thought.

Fucking.

Go.

Go! She grabbed Marlowe's arm, dragged him across to the open window. "For God's sake," she hissed. "Hurry!"

She climbed up onto the sill and lifted their two small traveling cases onto the roof and then she picked up Marlowe under the arms and hoisted him out.

Whoever was outside their door must have heard. They started banging on it, kicking at it. The room was thick with a black smoke, it smelled of soot, of dust, and Alice held her handkerchief to her mouth and turned to go. Then she whirled back, ran across to the nightstand, took out from the drawer their tickets and documents for the passenger liner. She was making noise now, clattering across the room, not caring. The door thumped in its frame.

The roof was sloped and Marlowe was crouched on his heels clutching his knees to his chest and Alice grabbed him in one arm and their two cases in the other and she tottered and stumbled her way up to the crest of the house. She hurried along to the chimney, half slid down to the eaves on the far side, then threw their cases across the small gap to the building next door. Then she cradled Marlowe's head against her shoulder.

"Close your eyes," she whispered.

And she jumped.

She landed badly on her left knee and folded sideways and then got up quickly, looking back. She couldn't see any sign of pursuit. It was madness. This roof was flat and there was a wrought iron fire ladder and Alice hurried the boy down it, into the street. She could see from there the dormer window of their rented room and she stared hard up at the darkness. There was no one there. And yet a faint smoke was seeping into the night; and then, against the darkness of the room, a greater darkness stepped forward, a black silhouette in the shape of a man, and it watched them go.

For she was already seizing Marlowe by the hand and limping on her bad knee, limping at a half run into the darkness, into the night, away.

Her knee wasn't broken, there was that. But it was swollen, the skin mottled and purple and weirdly soft, like a monstrous eggplant, and it would take no weight.

She crept with Marlowe up to Washington Avenue and crossed limping between the sleek black carriages, theater traffic, but glancing back all the while, and in a small park behind a statue of some dead American Revolutionary she halted, slid down into the wet grass with her throbbing leg outstretched in front of her.

She was trying to catch her breath, looking off into the darkness, trying to think. She gave the boy a hard look. "Did you ever see anything like that before? Ever?"

He shook his head, his blue eyes wide.

She knew the kids they collected were different. *Talents*, Coulton called them. And she knew that person—that *thing*—back there was anything but normal.

"Don't you lie to me, Marlowe," she said tightly.

"I'm not," he said. His voice was little more than a whisper.

All at once her leg erupted in a fire of pain. She cried out, holding her knee. Her voice banged off the walls, the echo dying away into the darkness.

"Is he coming after us?" Marlowe asked.

She said nothing, just looked quickly around.

The park was small, really just a square of grass around the statue, a solitary streetlight burning on the corner. There were buildings on three sides, rear walls, windowless, judging by the dark looming forms. An occasional cab clattered by in the street behind them. If the man found them, there would be nowhere to run.

She must have passed out. When she opened her eyes Marlowe had changed positions, was sitting cross-legged close to her, and he had folded his coat and slipped it under her head for a pillow. In the darkness she could just make out his pale face.

She tried to sit up, fell back.

"Is it your leg?" he whispered.

"My knee. How long was I out?"

"You just kind of fell over."

She wanted to make some joke about the creature at the hotel but couldn't think of anything to say and after a moment she closed her eyes.

"Alice?" said the boy.

"Yes?"

"My name's not really Stephen Halliday, is it?"

She opened one eye, in pain. "Why—why would you ask me that?"

"I can tell. I know."

"No," she said reluctantly. "It isn't."

"Who am I, then?"

"Do we need to talk about this now?" She gritted her teeth, saw his face. "Listen, I don't know who you are. Who do you want to be?"

"Marlowe."

"All right, then." Her head sank back.

"Alice? Why did you say I was Stephen Halliday if I'm not?"

Her knee was aching again. The wet grass had seeped through her clothes and she was very cold. It'd be a hell of a thing, getting to the passenger liner in the morning. She grimaced. "I guess because the people I work for told me to. And I guess I thought it was the best way to get you to come with me. The way that would . . . hurt people the least."

"You mean Brynt?"

"Brynt, yes. And you."

Marlowe in the darkness was quiet. She could see him chewing at the cuff of his sleeve. "So where are you taking me, then?"

"London. Then to a place in Scotland. It's called the Cairndale Institute, you'll be safe there. There're other kids there, just like you. Kids who can . . . do things."

"Will you go with me?"

She winced. "Some of the way. Usually I just . . . find the kids."

He nodded. "You shouldn't have lied to me."

He got up then and he walked out into the darkness. She started to ask what he was doing but he came back, shoes squeaking in the wet grass, having walked carefully around the perimeter, and now he kneeled next to her and said, quietly: "I know why they want me. Why the people you work for want me."

It was such a strange thing for an eight-year-old kid to say. So eerie and composed. She felt the hairs on the back of her neck prickle. "What do you mean?" she asked.

But he didn't answer. He did something instead, something she wasn't expecting. He reached out his fingers; he touched her wrist. "What happened?"

"This?" She shook her head in surprise. "It's nothing. A sprain."

Remembering it as she did so. How she'd slapped the man's hand from her waist at the bar in White Rapids and how his friends had laughed. He was a cattle drover with pay, he'd told her with a grin, and he'd been alone with men for four months. Coulton was scowling from their table as if the attention were her own doing and that had made her angriest of all. When the drover reached for her hips again she had set her feet as Allan Pinkerton had taught her to do and had leaned her muscled shoulders in and punched the bastard hard in the face and felt something give under the force of it and then the drover's legs collapsed out from under him and he was down. The bar went quiet, men looked away, the bar started up again. Coulton had done nothing.

The boy sat with his knuckles interlaced, his hands crushed in his lap. Then he held both palms up in front of her, as if he wished to show her something.

"What're you doing?" she asked.

Very slowly he began to untie her boot, slip it off, roll up the leg of her trousers. She let him do this. When her injured knee was visible he looked at her with a question in his eyes and then he pressed both palms against it. He did so with gentleness. She felt a heat in his hands and it felt good. The warmth traveled the length of her thigh, aching. Then the heat got worse. Her knee got hotter and hotter and she looked at the boy. His eyes were closed. He was shining.

It was that same bright blue shining, his skin sigiling with veins of light. She stared. She could see through to the veins, the shadowy bones in his skull and hands. The wet grass and the outlines of the statue were blue in the glow. And then the heat in her knee grew very intense, and the pain sharpened, and she could not help herself, and she cried out and pulled away. The burning faded. The light in the boy went out.

"Marlowe," she gasped. "Marlowe—?"

But something was different. She felt it at once. The shine was still fading from the edges of her vision. She peered down at her leg and shifted her knee and turned it side to side. It had healed.

She stared in amazement. Her heart was beating very fast.

"Don't be mad," he whispered.

He looked pale. He was cradling his wrists gingerly now against his little chest and she saw how swollen they looked.

"It'll be okay," he said. His little face was clouded with pain. "I took your hurt away. I have it now. It goes away fast when I have it."

She was trying to understand what the boy had told her but she could not. She thought of Coulton, she thought of Charlie Ovid with the blade hidden in his smooth flesh. "It isn't possible," she said. Getting gingerly to her feet as she spoke, testing her leg, staring at him.

"She said you wouldn't believe me," the boy whispered.

"Who said?"

He didn't answer, he didn't need to. Of course Alice did believe. Her knee was proof enough. She thought of her mother, unbidden, the green fire in her eyes when her faith used to take over in her, that madness, and she thought of what her mother would believe, glimpsing the miracle of it all, and she closed her eyes in sudden grief. Her mom.

Within the hour he held out his arms and rotated his wrists and showed her. The swelling was gone. It was already beginning to get light. The city felt emptied, still.

"It doesn't take long," he said. "Little hurts like this."

She felt something then, a kind of disgust, which surprised her and shamed her. She didn't want to touch him. He'd trusted her with something important and helped her and her disgust felt like a kind of betrayal. She lowered her voice when she said, "Have you done this a lot, Marlowe?"

"Yes," he said simply.

"How did it start?"

He shrugged, uncomfortable. "I can't always control it. I didn't used to be able to."

"They'll help you with that. At Cairndale." She moved then and got stiffly to her feet and stamped the warmth back into her legs and then she said, "Your friend, Brynt. She knew?"

He was putting back on his coat and he didn't look up. "We didn't talk about it."

She nodded. She looked around at the empty square, the graying silhouettes of the buildings against the sky. Somewhere out there was a man, a creature, made out of smoke, a thing that was following them. It was madness and yet she knew the truth of it. She'd seen it herself.

"We should find you something to eat," she said. "We'll get down to the docks."

She picked up the little traveling cases and blew out her cheeks. Marlowe was peering up at her.

"Alice?"

"Mm?"

"Is it all right if I'm scared?"

"Everyone gets scared," she said. "I get scared."

"Like at the hotel?"

She nodded. "And other times too. Scared is just your head telling your heart to be careful. It's not a bad thing. It's what you do with it that matters."

He seemed to think about this. "The thing at the hotel scared me."

She gave him a long careful look. "We'll be on the ship in an hour. And we'll not see him again after that."

"Yes, we will," he said.

The boy had a way of doing that, of speaking with certainty about things that had not happened yet, and Alice found it unnerving. What she saw when she looked at him was a small, defenseless child, and her heart, which had never much cared for babies or love or human connection, was struck afresh and left singing with pain. But she felt at the same time a new kind of disgust, nervous at what he could do. She was not a religious person and did not ascribe spiritual causes to the gift of his healing, for she could not conceive of a god who would create a world so full of suffering. There were naturalists in Washington that believed all creatures were a part of a pattern of development, that people were once like the apes, gradually changing their characteristics. When she looked at Marlowe she saw the mystery of it all. Alice remembered how her mother had used to say there were wonders in the world and that most people were afraid to see them. *Look with your heart, not with your eyes*, she would murmur, running her cold fingers through Alice's hair. She said all that was needed was a little faith and the marvelous could be found. *Do you believe?* And Alice would say, very solemnly: *I believe, Mama, I believe it, I do.*

All her life such memories would flicker inside her, a second flame. It was the knowledge of a world beyond this one, of the impossible made possible, if only she would see it.

Just because you cannot see it, daughter—her mother would whisper angrily—*does not mean it is not there.*

Well, she'd seen it now. And she believed.

They went on board with the crowds in the early light, porters rolling trunks up the ramp, stewards in crisp white uniforms nodding to them gravely as they passed. Gulls wheeled in the gray, shrieking and filling the air with their cries. It was a gleaming new ocean liner and they'd taken a second-class stateroom and their little bits of luggage were already on board. The corridors were packed with men smoking cigars, women laughing into their gloves. Marlowe kept close. She felt the strange looks of the passengers at her men's clothes. She was still moving gingerly on her leg, feeling strange. In the stateroom she changed into a mauve dress and bustle, feeling awkward and hating the tight pinch of it, and Marlowe just sat quietly watching through the porthole as the ships in the harbor slid past.

When it was time to cast off they went up on deck with all the others and stood at the railing and watched the crowds gathered there. The sky was filled with clouds of gulls; the pier was packed. She could feel the engines thrumming through the floor. There was a bang and then streamers began to fall and at the same moment the ship's horn blared, deafening, and the crowds roared.

The boy was peering at something. It was a man, at the back of the crowds, almost invisible. He stood in the shadow of a warehouse, the darkness smoking up off him. Tall, his features obscured by a black scarf. He wore a silk hat and a long black coat and black gloves on his hands, and he was staring directly at the boy with an expression of pure hatred.

But the ship had already cast off, its great oceangoing turbines groaning in reverse, the city's oily waters churning up over the huge ropes where they were being cranked, dripping, on board. Alice twisted and leaned out over the railing to keep the stranger in view. She knew who he was. He'd started forward now and was shouldering powerfully through the onlookers and well-wishers toward the ship even as the gap widened and the streamers fell and fell and the band on the quarterdeck struck up a waltz, and in the roar she lost sight of him on the platform. And then there was only a sea of faces, hundreds of them, innocent, ordinary, their gloved hands flickering as they waved, and the skyline of New York beyond, and the dark stranger had vanished in the smoke from the ship's engines, drifting blackly out over the pier, thinning, gone.

Monsters in the Fog

Walter Walter Walter wake up Walter wake up—

Walter Laster squinched his sore eyes shut. Through his lids the brightness was blinding.

—*the boy Walter the boy what happened to the boy you didn't finish what you started Walter—*

So.

Cold.

He was so cold.

He shook his head, his cheek and left ear clumpy with muck, and rose up into the white light of the day like a creature arisen from the earth. He was squinting and peering about him. The river. The Thames. He was in filth at the edge of the Thames, in a deep thick gluey mud that was not like mud at all.

—*the boy the boy the boy the boy—*

The boy, yes.

He needed to find the boy.

He heard a low whistle and some laughter and turned. Mud larks, they were. Kids. Three of them, with their ragged trousers rolled up past their knees, their grubby faces raw and flushed in the chill, snot shining on their upper lips. He hopped and waded and fell over and clawed his way back upright. The kids, laughing, scattered. One threw a rock at him.

There'd been a bridge in the rain. He'd been drowning, yes. Drowning a long time. Days? He was barefoot and his feet ached from the chill and his clothing was stiff and caked with an evil-smelling yellow mud. Farther along the shore he saw a solitary figure in a long patched coat and hat, picking his way over the shallows, and Walter trudged steadily toward him. He was trying to remember something important. What was it?

You know what it is Walter you know what it is—

The figure glared in suspicion as Walter got close. It was an old man, bewhiskered, sunken-cheeked, rancid, mean-looking.

"Get off, youse," the old man hissed, waving a ragged arm. "Find your own bits."

Walter seized the old man by the collar. The old man was flailing there in the white daylight, under that white sky, with the great walls of the embankment rising up over them, and he just wanted the man to stop, it was too much, so he ground the old man's face into the muck, deeper, deeper. The limbs thrashed, went still. Then he rolled him over and studied the mud-encrusted face, the staring eyes. He scooped the muck out of the toothless mouth. Last of all he unlooped the sack from the shoulder, peeled the dead man out of his coat. He left the body there staring up at the sky. He trudged over and picked up the floppy hat and put the coat and hat on and then he made his way up to a sewer tunnel some twenty yards along.

The tunnel was tall enough to stand upright in. Foul matter was running in a slow-moving river along the middle and the walls were encrusted and slick. His eyes liked the darkness.

O come to us Walter come to Jacob he is coming Jacob is coming for the boy—

Jacob. His own friend. He wanted the boy for Jacob, that was it. Yes. The tunnel turned and divided into two and he heard a faint rustling from the easterly direction and climbed a short ladder and found himself on a platform, above a deep sewage-filled cavern. The far wall seemed to be moving and then he saw it was seething with rats.

Thirty feet on he came to a passageway. There was a flickering light within, a single candle guttering in a dish, casting everything into strange relief. It was an old cistern, with slots in the walls, most filled with the groaning half-stirring shapes of the sleeping poor. He stood a moment in the doorway, caked in muck. He saw the three children from the riverbank hunched in a corner, eyeing him warily, not laughing now. He stumbled to an empty slot, where a scumbled blanket lice-ridden and filthy lay in a tangled mess, and he lay himself down. He just wanted to sleep. That was all. Sleep.

He slept.

He awoke with a strange taste in his mouth, metallic, like iron. The candle had burned low, was guttering dangerously. Someone had put a knife in his ribs while he'd slept. It was sticking out. There was blood dried on his arms, his shirt. When he breathed, the knife handle wobbled back and forth. He peered down at it in surprise, then around at the shadowy cistern. It was empty. Where did everyone go? He gripped the handle with both hands and pulled and the knife came slowly out and then he staggered to his feet and saw the bodies. There were maybe ten, twelve of them. All piled bonelessly in their rags in a corner of the cistern. It looked like their eyes had been removed. The floor, striped with gore where they'd been dragged. Walter stared around in confusion.

He went out into the lightless sewer. Slowly, uncertainly. Retracing his steps. His head was thick and he wasn't thinking clearly. It was night outside, a thick fog had descended. He stood in the darkness, peering out across the river at the weird yellow lights haloing in the murk. Then he was climbing steep stone stairs up to the embankment. Then he was standing in front of a lighted window, staring at a shop-keeper's dummy behind the glass. He was so cold. Why couldn't he ever get warm?

Later he stood in the court where his rented room should have been. All was in ruined silhouette. The building had collapsed. There were charred timbers sticking out of the rubble and he ran a hand over his smooth scalp, hairless as a catamite, and stared helplessly out at the fog and the darkness and then, his bare feet sliding over the sharp rubble, he went back out into the night.

The boy. He could almost smell the boy, a sharp metallic scent in the thick of the city. He turned and turned, sniffing at the air.

For a long time after the litch plunged into the river, Charlie just sat hunched in pain, in the middle of Blackfriars Bridge, the night rain drumming against him, pattering on the stone railing and the dark setts and the puddles shining weirdly in the darkness. He couldn't stop shaking. His chest and arms were on fire. There was something wrong with his head, too, and he kept closing his eyes and waking up, not knowing where he was. The rain slowed, the rain stopped, a thin gray daylight filtered grittily over the wet. Then there were hansoms and coaches clattering across the bridge, and then clerks in dark suits and bowlers were trudging past, stepping over him, paying him no mind. Sometime later a constable tapped his knee with a truncheon.

"Walk it off, blackie," the constable said. "Less you want a night in the stone jug, like."

He got woozily to his feet.

The constable glanced, bored, out over the railing. "London Docks is that way," he said. He gestured off downriver with the truncheon.

Charlie stumbled away, feverish, retracing his steps, trying to. The sky was lightening. It would be morning soon. All around him stretched a maze of crooked lanes and dark alleys and streetsweepers in rags and horses shitting on the stones and a god-awful stink of sewage wafting up out of the gutters. The vastness of it all made him stagger.

He slept for a time in a rotting doorway and woke to find a monstrous rat crawling over his foot. He stole a meat pie from a wagon on a street corner, stumbling out into the traffic of horses and iron-wheeled cabs muscling past, narrowly avoiding collision. His arms and chest looked wrong, swollen, the skin soft and painful to the touch. He should have been healing by now. There was something in the litch's claws, some poison maybe, that went deep. He slept in a puddle in an alley somewhere near the river, soaked, and he awoke it was morning again. There was a girl in rags, crouched beside him, barefoot. A second, smaller girl stood behind.

"Ere, you," said the first softly. "You got to get up, like. Ere."

She dragged him up by his throbbing arm. He cried out, shivering, and got to his hands and knees, then stood unsteadily.

"There." She grinned up at him. She was half-black, like him. But so small. Maybe six, seven years old at most. Her hair was filthy, her face streaked with pale grime. The other girl was younger even, with long tousled brown hair, like a mouse, and she worked a knuckle into one nostril, rooting around, sizing him up, but said nothing.

"Me name's Gilly," said the older one, finally, and grinned. "This ere is Jooj. An you can quit yer gawpin, you look a bloody sight worsern us."

His head felt gluey, hot. He tried to say something but only swayed. They led him by the hands, one holding to each, drawing him forward like a reluctant goer at a fair. Into the gloom and damp shadows of Wapping. The river, reeking, was somewhere near. Gilly and Jooj would stop sometimes to let him rest, gasping up against a slimy wall, and they'd peer up at him in interest, those two small girls, or else sometimes they'd stop to pick a bit of metal or a button out of the open gutters, wiping it on their shirtfronts to clean it, pocketing it someplace in their rags.

At a peeling warehouse, its walls leaning unsteadily and creaking in the fog, he was ushered inside, and up a rickety staircase, and on the upper floor beneath a wall of broken windows he saw a small crowd of children turn to look him over.

"Bleedin hell, Gilly," a tall boy said. He got up, came over. He was younger than Charlie but nearly of a height. "What's he, now? Ye can't just drag any damn cockle in off the stones, like. What's Mr. Plumb to say?"

Gilly grinned up. "I got Plumb in me pocket."

"Sure ye do," said the boy.

"But, Millard," said Jooj, the littler one, in a tiny high-pitched voice. "You's always sayin we needs a lookout. He's right perfect."

The tall boy got close to Charlie, looking him over like a cut of meat. "Do he got a name?"

"Aye," said Gilly. "Rupert."

"He ain't no Rupert. Is you name Rupert?"

Charlie, clutching his pained chest, sank down to the floor. He grimaced.

"What's a matter with him? S'e cut up, like?"

"Aw, Rupert's just a bit faint, he is. Needs some pottage."

"Jesus almighty he ain't a Rupert, Gilly. Lookit him. Aw. E's bleedin."

Charlie clenched his teeth, glared in pain up at the squabbling kids. "Charlie," he whispered. "My name . . . is Charlie."

Millard grinned at the two girls. He was missing all his front teeth. "Told youse," he said.

"Hullo, Charlie," said Gilly, crouching down. "Don't pay Millard no mind, he's just a bitta worrier, he is. He'll come around."

A moment later Jooj appeared at his elbow, holding a battered tin bowl. Inside was a cold lump of porridge, a spoon sticking out of it.

"Go on, eat," said Gilly, taking it from the little one. "It ain't poisoned."

He ate, and slept again, and woke feeling somewhat better. The sharp pain in his chest and arms was subsiding. The warehouse was darker, the cracked panes glinting like frost. Millard was sitting beside him, holding his knees to his chest.

"I thought maybe you was dead." He grinned. "Ere. Eat this. It's like to help."

He gave Charlie a greasy waxed paper and inside it were three pale balls of dough, still warm. They tasted sweet; Charlie chewed them slowly, turning them from cheek to cheek, swallowing with difficulty. Gradually he felt more clearheaded, sharper, wakeful.

"There ye go," said the boy. "Ye thirsty?"

He had a tin cup he passed across and Charlie drank it and was surprised to see it was stout. Bitter, thick, filling. He ran a hand over his mouth.

"We got a job what needs doin," said Millard. "Ere's your opportunity to make a right use of yourself. Come on, then."

He led Charlie back down the ruined steps to the warehouse below. The child thieves were gathered there, four dim bull's-eye lanterns bobbing among them. Gilly came up, studying his face, nodding at whatever it was she saw there.

"Ready?" said Millard.

Gilly shrugged. "Aye," she said. She was looking with interest at

Charlie. "Feelin better? Right. Good. We need your peepers. Can ye whistle?"

"Whistle?" he said.

Jooj materialized beside her, clutching a lantern in both hands close to her chest, and she nodded up at him. She whistled a quiet little *coo-coo-coo*. "Like that," she said helpfully, in her tiny voice.

"I can whistle," he said.

"Aye. You just give er, you see them damn beaks comin up," said Millard. "Three wee quick whistles, just like Jooj ere. Got that?"

"Wait," he said. "Why me? Why do you need me?"

Gilly looked at him like he was simple. "Oh, Charlie. Because you's not a *littler*, like us."

"A littler?"

Jooj nodded up at him, eyes like saucers.

"Aye," said Millard. "Likes of us standin round, doin nothin? Them beaks knows somethin's up. But you, you's just a hand lookin for work."

"At night? In the dark?"

Gilly grinned. "You ain't been in London long, have ye, Charlie?"

The night was thick, cold. The urchins poured out into the blackness, scattering like rats. Charlie followed Gilly, and Gilly followed Jooj's narrow lantern shine as it cut its way through the dripping fog of Wapping. They saw no one. They slipped down narrow passages, along slippery wooden boards, over open trenches of sewage, clambered up a rickety staircase and crept along a stone wall between grim dirty yards. Then they were creeping through an abandoned building and turning left and hurrying down a set of wet steps and turning left again and scrambling over a wooden railing, which swayed under Charlie's weight. They came out underneath a jetty, in the mud, and Gilly put a finger to her lips, and Jooj slid the eye of her lantern shut and in the darkness led them slowly upside. Some of the others were waiting at the end, watching the river, the lights burning in the barges beyond.

Gilly pulled on Charlie's sleeve and he bent down to her.

"You go right along that way," she whispered, pointing. "Stand at the corner of them warehouses. Keep out of the light. Give out a whistle you see the beaks."

"What about you and Jooj?"

She shook her head, impatient. "Just go," she hissed.

He started away. But then he heard a ripple of water and turned and saw a dark skiff, with four small ragged figures poling it, approaching the pier. As it came alongside, Gilly and two others leaped across, soundless as shadows. The skiff rocked once, twice, then started its slow poling out over the river toward the tied-up barge.

Charlie lurked in the reeking dark, as he'd been told to do. The minutes passed. Once he saw a lantern swaying far out across the docks, weaving between the buildings, but it did not come his way. When he peered out across the water he could see the little figures shifting wooden crates, seven, eight urchins at a time on a single crate. They worked swiftly, efficiently, in plain sight. Clearly someone, somewhere, had been paid off. Once, he heard a shout, then a distant splash, and he crouched and stared and saw the skiff, mid-river, rocking from side to side. The urchins were swarming all over it, like ants. But soon they were on their way again, tying up alongside the jetty, hoisting the crates in netting suspended by a large pulley set up by the kids left onshore. And then they were all carrying the crates, six kids at a time, under the jetty into the rough muck, and piling them there. It took almost two hours with all of them straining to carry the nine crates back to the warehouse, taking several trips to manage it, and Charlie wondered at first what they'd stolen that could be so heavy, but soon the weariness and drudgery of it pushed all curiosity from his mind.

It was nearing dawn when they had all returned from the docks.

A short while later Charlie heard the squeak of ironshod wheels and the low nicker of a horse and then two grown men came in, big, grim, with long greasy hair sticking under their bowlers.

"Well, hullo, me littlers," the taller, thinner one called out.

No one moved.

"That's the bull man," said Millard quietly in Charlie's ear. He nodded at the taller, thinner one, who had stepped into the middle of the floor. The other hung back at the door. "Ye just keep yer gob shut," Millard added. "It don't do for him to notice ye."

The bull man ran a hand over his whiskers. "Bring round the cart, Mr. Thwaite," he called to his companion. "We got a delivery, looks like. My, my."

Then he walked around the crates, very slowly, making an exaggerated count of the boxes. "One, two, three, four, ah, very good. Five, six, seven, eight, nine. Magnificent," he said, beaming around at the frightened urchins. "Let me see, now. Nine . . . nine . . . nine . . ." He raised confused eyebrows, turned in place, lifting his bowler. "What's this? Ain't it ten? Does I count me numbers wrong?"

"We lost one, sir," said Gilly, soft.

He stopped. "Eh? I didn't catch that?"

"I said we lost one, sir," said Gilly, louder. "Fell in the drink."

All at once the bull man strode over to the little girl, his legs long and thin like shears, his oilskin coat creaking. He pressed his hands to his knees and leaned very low at the waist, so that he was staring right into Gilly's eyes. "You *lost* one," he said. "Fell in the *drink*, it did."

"Yes, Mr. Plumb, sir."

"The job was for *ten*, like. Weren't it *ten*, Mr. Thwaite?"

"It were ten, Mr. Plumb," said the thick man at the door.

"It's nearly all ten of em," whispered Gilly. "It's nearly all."

"*Nearly* all," said Mr. Plumb. He reached out and seized the little girl's wrist and held up her arm. He started pointing to her fingers, one by one. "Let me count, like. One, two, three, four, five. Yes? And on your other hand, six, seven, eight, nine." He took her littlest finger and bent it back, way back, so that she screamed and leaned sharply backward.

"It don't matter, this one though," he said. "You still got *nearly* all."

Gilly looked so tiny, dangling in front of the bull man. No one else moved, no one breathed a word.

"You ain't kept here on account of charity," he was saying. "You got yer jobs to do, an you got to do em."

But Charlie couldn't watch any more. He stepped forward, his heart in his throat. "Leave her alone," he called. "She's just a kid."

At once the thick man near the door, Mr. Thwaite, poured like a shadow forward and a club appeared out of the folds of his coat and it caught Charlie hard on the side of the head, sending him sprawling. Everything went sideways, then dark. He was gasping. Fumbling in the dirt, unbalanced, his ears ringing as he tried to get up.

"Who's this now? A fresh un?" Mr. Plumb had dropped Gilly in the dirt and turned to look.

"Don't never mind him, Mr. Plumb, sir," Gilly begged, clutching her hand. "He ain't but simple. Shut yer gob, you," she snapped at Charlie.

He fell back, confused, hurt. His cheek was stinging, the blood seeping down.

"He don't watch his yap, he's like to lose his tongue," said Mr. Plumb.

"I'll cut it out me own self," said Gilly.

Mr. Plumb laughed. "Aye you would, you damned sticker," he said. "That's the savage in ye."

When the men had gone, Gilly hurried over. The club had caught Charlie on the side of his face, tearing the skin below his eye, bloodying his nose. He shook his head, feeling the thick weight of it, like a sack of water.

"Your finger—"

"Never mind that. Here now, hold er higher," Gilly was muttering. She lifted his chin gently and he heard the quick intake of her breath and he understood suddenly. He pulled away, covering his cheek with one hand. But he was not fast enough. She was staring in horror.

"What you done?" she whispered. "Charlie?"

He looked at her, his eyes wet.

"Tain't human," she whispered. She took a step back. "Tain't right."

"Gilly—"

"Get away!" she cried suddenly. "Jooj! Lookit Charlie's bloody great saw!"

But before the mouselike waif got near, the tall lad, Millard, was pushing forward, grabbing Charlie's head, turning it side to side. The other kids were crowding round, dirt-streaked faces, big eyes staring.

"Bloody hell," Millard was saying. "He's a bloody freak, he is. He's a monster."

Charlie pushed him bodily off.

"Charlie's a monster?" one of the littlest ones said, maybe three years old. She started to cry.

"No—" Charlie whispered.

"He's Spring-Heeled Jack, he is!" a second kid burst out.

And they scattered from him then, squealing, all except Millard and Gilly, and Charlie himself stumbled backward, pain and anger and humiliation rising in him. He glowered in the dimness at the faces peering out at him from behind barrels, boxes, water-rotted timbers. Everything, the litch, being hunted in the darkness, getting beaten by that bull man just like in his old life in Mississippi, now this, being called a freak, a monster, all of it filled him with something he hadn't let himself feel, not in a long time.

Rage.

"The hell with you!" he shouted at the ragged faces staring. "The hell with all of you!"

His eyes were wet. He kicked his way out of the warehouse, into the dusk, into the settling fog, running through the chilled cobblestone streets, down shadowy lanes and crooked alleys and across the water-rotted timbers of footbridges. There were torches in brackets over the doors of drinking houses. Otherwise darkness, thickening fog. He felt suddenly uneasy, alone again in the city, thinking of that litch that might yet be out there, seeking him, crawling over the buildings like a pale spider.

He didn't know how long he wandered. But he came out, sometime in the night, to a wide cobblestoned road, lit by gaslights in the fog, the sound of laughter. Figures passed him. Men dressed in silk hats, ladies in fur stoles, drifting casually along the waterfront. He was back at the river. There were coaches gleaming in the fog. Faces looked disapprovingly at Charlie as he crept past, and he folded his arms over his shirt, knowing how ragged he must look.

Then he was at a bridge, again. He stopped at the railing in the middle of the span. It seemed familiar, but he had no idea if it was the bridge he'd fought the litch on, or if all bridges in London looked the same. The city was a world, he saw in despair; and he'd never find Coulton or Mrs. Harrogate in it, wander it as he would. The fog deepened around him like a living thing, as if it would take him, steal him away.

And then he heard a voice, a voice he knew. A burly bewhiskered figure in a bowler was standing over him, draping a chesterfield at Charlie's shoulders.

"Mr. Coulton?" Charlie blinked up in amazement. "Is it you? For real?"

Coulton grunted. "I been looking all over the damned city for you, lad."

"The litch, it—"

"Aye, lad. I know."

All of a sudden Charlie couldn't stop himself and he was crying, his back shuddering in great wracking sobs. Coulton held him tight. The dark fog curled around them, drifted past, across the span of Blackfriars Bridge and into the night.

And Charlie let himself be lifted. Charlie let himself be held.

At precisely the same hour, at Charing Cross station, a stranger stepped slowly down from an express train onto platform three. His boots left sooty prints on the ground. He carried no luggage; his silk hat was without shine, as if coated in grime; his long black coat and his black gloves seemed to suck up all the light surrounding so that porters and travelers alike shrank back, trying not to brush up against him.

He was not alone. Several carriages back, a silver-haired woman in a blue dress and shawl stood glaring. She was enormous, powerful, striking-looking. Her hands and wrists and throat were inked with tattoos. Over the echoing din, she could hear the hiss of steam, the clanking of steel pistons starting up. The man she followed was dangerous, true, but so was she; and as she had done since Liverpool, since embarking in the gritty morning darkness of New York Harbor weeks before, hell, since that blazing night in Remington nearly a month ago now when the big top had burned, she half wished he'd whirl about, and catch sight of her. Because what Brynt wanted was an excuse, a chance to do to him what he'd done to poor Felix Fox. What she wanted was to crush his windpipe with her bare hands.

But he didn't turn, didn't see her following, just strode away in the roar, his height accentuated by the tall silk hat, pushing past the crowds at the ticketing booths and along the carrier walk and through the great tunnel and out, into the murky gloom of London. He'd come for her boy, she knew: he was stalking her little Marlowe.

She bit her lip so hard it drew blood. At the Charing Cross entrance she paused, scanning the darkness. Skeletal shapes clattered past. At last she saw him, plunging into the fog.

And Brynt, cracking her knuckles one by one, went after him.

9

23 NICKEL STREET WEST

A lice Quicke and the boy reached London twenty-two days after leaving New York.

She'd been sick on the crossing, breathing the miasmic air, feeling more than seeing Marlowe where he kneeled at her bedside, holding a damp cloth to her face in the splintering light from the porthole. Now, thinner, hollow-eyed, she pushed open the creaking iron gate at Nickel Street West and knocked. She had the address from the papers Coulton had given her, all those long weeks ago on the riverboat out of Natchez.

Mrs. Harrogate answered, triumph in her eyes. Dressed all in black, with her dark veil over her face, the little silver crucifix shining at her throat. She looked past Alice to Marlowe where he stood.

There were workmen behind her, going in and out of the parlor, sawing, hammering, repairing all manner of destruction.

"Redecorating?" Alice said dryly.

The woman turned, clapped her hands, swooped down on the

workmen. "Out, out," she called. "That's enough for today, thank you, gentlemen, thank you."

The house was nothing like what Alice had expected. Cheerful, warm, with all the lights burning, its parlor heavily decorated with potted ferns and draped sofas and a clutter of pier tables and even a piano in one corner, ankles dressed. It looked like the workmen had been replacing a pane of glass in a street-side bay window. The caulking was still wet. There were holes in the walls, gouges in the floor. Alice read the struggle as it must have unfolded, writ large in the ruin around her.

The day was dim as it always was in London and she didn't see Charlie Ovid where he sat, his quiet face watching her, didn't see him there at all until Marlowe let go of her hand and went right over and sat next to him, swinging one leg and looking shyly up at him.

"Hello, Charlie," she said, taking off her hat. "It's good to see you here."

He managed a weak nod.

"Mr. Ovid is rather tired," said Mrs. Harrogate smoothly, stepping between them. "As must you be. I'd expected you here earlier, Miss Quicke."

She shrugged. "Slow crossing."

"Mm. It would appear so."

With the workmen gone, Mrs. Harrogate took off her veil. She crouched in front of Marlowe and took his chin in her hand and turned his face side to side.

"Marlowe," she murmured. "We've been looking for you for a long time, child. My name is Mrs. Harrogate. It is my job to see you safely back to where you belong."

Alice could see he was nervous. He was instructed to unloop his suspenders and lift his shirt so Mrs. Harrogate could examine the birthmark, and then she stood and interlocked her fingers over her belly and stared. Alice frowned, uncertain. Her task had been only to locate and escort the child but she found herself uneasy with Mrs. Harrogate's manner, as if the woman were checking out a horse she wanted to buy.

But then Mrs. Harrogate turned away, as if losing sudden interest, and asked in a cool dispassionate tone if they were hungry or tired, and led Alice across the parlor to a dressed table in front of a window. And her every gesture seemed ordinary, or nearly so, or at least neither sinister nor calculated, and Alice began to relax. She declined the cup of tea. Took off her hat, raked her fingers through her hair, rolled her neck and shoulders for the stiffness. Last of all she began to tell about the attack in the night in New York, and the burning of the circus, and the child's shining talent, and her own healed knee.

Mrs. Harrogate's eyelids flickered as she listened. But after that she tracked the boy's movements with a strange voracity, like a cat to a bird, and Alice felt all her old uneasiness again.

"His name is Jacob," said Mrs. Harrogate, turning a little spoon in her cup. Her eyes never left the boy. "Jacob Marber. He is not . . . like us."

"You don't say," Alice said acidly.

"Mr. Coulton and I feared as much, when he did not come after Mr. Ovid." Mrs. Harrogate breathed in sharply through her little nostrils, as if to contain her anger. "I wish you to know that Mr. Coulton's purpose is to prevent exactly what just happened. It is for this reason he is kept on retainer. I am most ashamed, Miss Quicke. You should not have had to confront Jacob Marber."

And Alice, who had been preparing her own outrage at being told so little, stoking it all across the Atlantic and overland to London, felt suddenly confused by the apology, mollified, and reached for a cup of tea she'd already declined.

As always, upon delivery of a child, Alice was paid in cash, twenty crisp paper notes slid into a billfold, left this time on the pier table.

Mrs. Harrogate made it clear that her services were still required. As she was putting back on her hat to go, Marlowe pulled her down so he could whisper in her ear.

"Don't leave me," he whispered. "Please."

She looked at his little face, his big trusting eyes.

"I'll be back soon," she lied.

And she went out into the fog, hating herself and the job and Mrs. Harrogate and Coulton, wherever he was, and she hailed a hansom across to her lodgings in Deptford. There she went through the rooms, looking for signs of entry, but all was as she'd left it, dim and shabby, though covered now in a fine layer of soot from the badly sealed windows. She went downstairs and paid the landlady several more months in advance and then went back up. She opened her wardrobe, changed into one of her two clean shirts, put on a new hat and then took it off and put back on her grimy traveling hat. In the cloudy mirror she studied her oilskin coat with a critical eye, fading and cracking at the seams. She pulled down a box of ammunition for her Colt Peacemaker and filled her pockets. She thought about staying the night, the rooms being so quiet, the bed simple and soft. Then she thought about Marlowe.

"Damn it," she whispered.

It was evening when she got back to Nickel Street West. All the windows were blazing with light.

"I knew you'd come," Marlowe said to her, when she walked into the warm parlor. But there was in his eyes something that said he hadn't known it, hadn't been sure of it at all. She felt a pang, seeing it. He'd eaten, washed his face, put on a flannel sleeping gown far too long for him. He'd been sitting with Charlie Ovid on the thick Persian carpet under the new window, talking maybe, or maybe just sitting, she couldn't tell, but whatever it was when she came in Charlie got up and went through into the bright foyer and upstairs without saying a word.

She gave Marlowe a tired smile. "I said I'd be back, didn't I?" she said. She gestured at where Charlie had disappeared. "Is he all right?"

Marlowe smiled shyly. "I like him. He's nice."

Nice. Not her word. She remembered how he'd cut the throat of the guard in Natchez, how he'd dug out of his own flesh the blade to kill him with, and felt something flicker across her face. It was clear something had happened to Charlie, not only because of the marks on his throat, only slowly going away. There was in his face a new sharpness, an unhappiness. She reminded herself to ask him about it directly. Or Coulton, if he ever showed up. Where the hell was Coulton, anyway?

"On an errand" was all Mrs. Harrogate would say.

And that only in passing, as she hurried out of the grand house, adjusting her hat and gloves, or made for the attic where she kept, she said, her pigeons, or else as she was coming back in from the shops, a package under her arm, disappearing into one of the rooms on the third floor. A day passed, then another. It seemed to Alice, in irritation, that the widow was avoiding her, as if she knew Alice had questions, as if she knew Alice would demand answers.

But if Mrs. Harrogate avoided Alice, she did not avoid Marlowe. Alice was with the boy one dark afternoon passing the entrance to the kitchen when the older woman, from within, called them through. A great pot was boiling on an ancient stove. Mrs. Harrogate stood at a long counter, chopping a row of carrots with a very sharp knife, *bang bang bang*, scraping them into the pot, chopping again.

"What kind of institute can't afford a cook?" Alice said.

"*Can't* and *won't* are not the same," replied Mrs. Harrogate. "Servants talk."

Alice smiled dryly. "They also cook."

"And you, Marlowe," the older woman said, ignoring this, "how are you settling in? I see you and Charles have become friends."

Marlowe, standing just inside the door, nodded.

She paused at her chopping. "Stand straight. That's better. We mustn't slouch like a layabout. Now, what did they teach you, child, at your circus? Did you learn your letters?"

Marlowe nodded. "Yes, Mrs. Harrogate."

"Your maths?"

"Yes."

"And your Bible? Were you raised a Christian?"

Marlowe bit at his lip, his face reddening.

"I see." She returned to her chopping but kept her eyes on Marlowe. "Show me your hands. They're filthy. Cleanliness is next to godliness, child. Did Miss Quicke not instruct you on how to wash, on the journey?"

"She took good care of me, Mrs. Harrogate."

"And yet you have been here several days in her charge and your hands still look like this. He is in England now, Miss Quicke. You must do a better job of helping him to blend in." She turned back to the child. "You will have questions about why you are here. You are a very special boy, Marlowe."

Alice watched as he met the older woman's eye boldly. She glimpsed in his expression something hard, stubborn, older than his years. "Because of what I can do," he told her. "Because there's other kids like me. I'm to go to meet them."

"Well, the other children are not like you exactly," said Mrs. Harrogate, selecting her words with care. She crossed the kitchen to a small pantry and came back with an armful of potatoes. "But they are talents, yes. That is what we call it, your ability, yours and the other children's."

"Talents," Marlowe murmured, turning the word on his tongue.

"We will be leaving for the north, soon. At the institute, you will meet Dr. Berghast. Do you know who that is?"

"No, Mrs. Harrogate."

"You were his ward. He is your guardian. Your family."

Alice looked up sharply. This was something new. Marlowe was regarding the older woman without fear. "You don't have to lie," he said. "I know there isn't any family looking for me."

"Who told you that, child?"

"It's okay, Mrs. Harrogate. Sometimes family is what you choose."

"Who told you that you had no family?"

Alice felt Marlowe's hand reach for hers. It was clear he didn't want to give her away, but he didn't know how else to answer.

"I did," said Alice.

Mrs. Harrogate frowned. A cold intensity seemed to rise off her, almost like a scent. "Miss Quicke is mistaken, child," she said softly, dangerously. She gestured and the knife danced fluidly in the air. "It is true that you were adopted. But that changes nothing. I assure you, your father is perfectly real, and quite anxious to see you. You were taken from him by your nursemaid when you were just a baby. Stolen away in the night, from the Cairndale Institute."

"My . . . father . . ." It sounded as if he were tasting the word on his tongue, trying it out, seeing how it felt.

"Yes. Until, as I say, you were taken."

"Why would anyone take me away?"

"Because a man named Jacob Marber was coming to kill you," replied Mrs. Harrogate matter-of-factly. "He had tried to do so once before. Oh, you were just a baby, child; it was none of your doing. You needn't look so. Jacob Marber was raised at Cairndale, but he would not learn how to be careful with his ability. His younger brother had died, years ago, at the hands of a cruel master, in a city far away, and his loss consumed him. Grief and hate are close cousins, child. When he came for you that terrible night, your nursemaid did not believe anyone at Cairndale could protect you. It was wicked of her to take you. But she was right to fear Jacob Marber."

Marlowe was listening, rapt.

"Something . . . happened. She died before she could return you. But you—you were found in a railway boxcar by a stranger, and spirited away, and might have been lost to us forever. We did not know what had become of you; but neither did Jacob Marber. When he could not find you, he vanished also. That is how it was, for your father. You were gone. His family was broken. Yet your father has borne it. Dr. Berghast has a great sense of purpose, a strength in him. As for Jacob, we have heard little of him for years. Now it seems he has returned. Your father, of course, fears for your safety; we must get you to Cairndale."

Marlowe said quietly: "Jacob Marber is who tried to hurt us at the hotel, isn't he? He's the monster made out of smoke."

Mrs. Harrogate's face glowed in the soft light of the kitchen. "Monster is rather an extreme way of putting it. You understand that he still wishes to hurt you?"

"Yes."

"Then you understand why it is important that you are here, with us. And why we must take you north as soon as possible, to the institute. You will be safe there; Jacob Marber cannot enter there."

"Why not?"

"It is . . . protected."

The little boy gave a visible shudder.

"Mrs. Harrogate?" he said. "What is my father like?"

The woman's eyes glittered. "He is as clever as the devil himself. You will meet him soon; then you will see for yourself. Now, I trust you will both eat a stew?"

After that, Alice didn't like to leave Marlowe alone. There was too much space for so few in that big house. The bedroom Charlie and Marlowe were using, on the third floor, was large and uncomfortable, furnished with lace doilies on the ankles of the chair legs and even on the handle of the door, and there was an ornate divan at the foot of the bed, and heavy silk wallpaper. They shared the bed, curling up together in the four-poster like brothers, just as if they'd always had each other, and Alice started sitting up in the night watching them. She'd been given her own room, a strange room with stacks of odd wheeled contraptions leaned up against one wall—her late husband's attempts at inventing a locution machine, Mrs. Harrogate explained— but the shapes were creepy in the dark and Alice was sleeping badly anyhow, waking often, feeling as if something was in the room with her, something watchful and hidden and filled with malice. So she sat up with the boys, wary. Harrogate herself slept at the end of the hall, her door permanently ajar, as if she was afraid of something passing in the night. On the fourth floor Alice had found, her first night at Nickel Street West, a stripped bed, and a wardrobe with a stained pallet stuffed inside, and knotted ropes, but no sign of whatever it had been used for.

Coulton, for his part, stayed gone.

The claw marks on Charlie Ovid's arms were on fire. Or at least that's how it felt, to him, as he lay in the half-light of the bedchamber, staring at the molded ceiling, trying not to think.

He should've healed by now.

He'd been back several days, but he still wasn't right. He'd started to tremble the moment Mr. Coulton brought him into 23 Nickel Street West, and Mrs. Harrogate, observing it, had put him to bed at once. That first night, she'd sat up with him, and he'd told her everything, surprised at her gentleness. No part of him wanted to trust anyone but it was hard, very hard, after the strangeness of all he'd seen, to go on not needing anyone. But after that night, he'd not spoken of the litch again.

It helped that he'd seen no sign of it since. Not in the house, not in the way Mrs. Harrogate talked. But Coulton had gone back out almost at once, his chesterfield buttoned fast against the fog, his gun in his pocket, and was hardly ever around, even after that other one—the woman, Miss Alice—had arrived, so that Charlie knew the man was out hunting for the litch in those terrible dripping alleys.

Where he lay now, in the bedclothes, he could feel the new boy breathing beside him. Marlowe, he was called. He hardly spoke when the adults were nearby but when they were alone he would talk about his life in the circus, his huge tattooed guardian, and he even spoke a little about something that had happened in a rooming house in New York, an attack. He talked about how alone he felt and how afraid he was of the city and on their third night he told Charlie about his adopted father, who was at Cairndale, and waiting to meet him. All this Charlie listened to with his eyes hooded and he said nothing about his own experiences, his mother, his father whom he'd never known and never would. And the kid watched Charlie closely, as if he had any kind of answer, as if he knew something about the world they were stumbling into, as if Charlie could keep him safe. He was still lit-tle, that kid, though he acted like he didn't know it. He wore his shoes on the wrong feet sometimes. One morning he forgot to button his fly.

Maybe it was the horror of what he'd suffered, the litch, its claws in the rain, maybe it was the feeling of being lost in a city as vast as a world. Whatever it was, when Charlie was brought back and was alone, he did something he didn't ever do. He took a letter opener from Mrs. Harrogate's desk and cut into his leg, ignoring the pain, and rooted around in the meat of his thigh until he found the silver wedding ring that had belonged to his mother. It was neither delicate nor effeminate, and he thought, now, it was maybe a strange ring for a bride. And while his wound closed over, he rubbed the ring clean and ran his fingertips over the markings and slid it onto his finger. It was tight, almost too small except for his second finger, and he'd taken it off again and looked at the strange crest, the twin crossed hammers and the fiery sun, thinking about his mother and the monster that had attacked him, and trying to imagine the cold fortress of Cairndale in the north, where he was bound. He knew his father'd had something to do with it, this ring was the proof. There was a truth buried there about who he'd been, what had happened to him. And Charlie swore to himself he'd find it out.

Since that night, he would lie awake, the ring turned inward on his finger and cutting into his palm like a talisman. It was on such a night that the new boy, Marlowe, whispered at him in the darkness, interrupting his thoughts.

"Charlie?" he whispered.

Charlie lay very still.

Marlowe wasn't fooled. "Charlie, I know you're awake."

"I'm not awake," he whispered. "Go to sleep."

"I can see you blinking."

Charlie shifted and turned his face. Marlowe was staring at him.

"I'm not awake," he muttered.

"Then how come you're talking right now?"

"I do that," he said, "when I'm sleeping."

"You're awake," said the boy.

Charlie sighed, closed his eyes. He could hear Miss Alice out on the landing, talking to Mrs. Harrogate in hushed tones. He knew she had started sitting up in the night, watching them. He was grateful for the sound of her presence, and hated it, both. But he didn't sleep when she wasn't there.

The boy made a small noise in his throat. "Charlie?" he whispered.

He opened his eyes again. "What."

"Are you going to Scotland too? Are you going to the institute?"

"You know I am."

"Mrs. Harrogate says my father's there. I'm going to meet him. Maybe yours is there too."

"My father's dead. I told you that already." Charlie grimaced, rolled up onto one elbow, holding his mother's ring tightly. "You never met your father before?"

"Uh-uh."

"How're you going to know it's really him?"

The boy was quiet, thinking about it. "I'll know. But he's not my real father, anyway. He's my . . . guardian. And family's something you choose. Brynt's my family. She's far away though."

Charlie looked at the kid. "Well, I got no family at all, Mar. And I'm fine."

"I think that's sad."

"That's cause you're little. It's not sad. It's not anything."

"I'm not little. How old are you?"

"I don't know. Sixteen."

"You don't know how old you are?"

"I said sixteen."

"I'm eight."

"Good for you," said Charlie, and then he said nothing more. For a long moment the boy too was silent and Charlie wondered if maybe he'd fallen asleep or if he'd spoken too roughly, but then the boy shifted closer in the darkness and reached his arm around Charlie's body. It was warm, and soft, and impossibly light. It had been a long time since anyone had touched Charlie in gentleness like that, and he didn't know what to do with it. His heart was beating very fast.

"You're like me," said Marlowe sleepily.

"I'm nothing like you," said Charlie.

"I mean different," murmured the boy. "You're different too."

And then the boy was asleep, curled up close to Charlie, his skin smelling of milk, and there was something in it all, something warm and sweet, that made Charlie, for the first time since he'd come back to the house, for the first time maybe in as long as he could remember, just close his eyes calmly, and a moment later he too was asleep.

Late, late into the night, Alice heard Coulton come stumbling in, the house dark and still, the boys unstirring in their bed. Marlowe's little arm was thrown wide, across Charlie, who lay curled up around a pillow.

She heard the front door open and close, heard Coulton's slow, heavy tread on the stairs. She knew it was him, knew the sound of his footfalls, and started to get up. But when he reached the landing she paused, listened. A thump, then a long soft scraping noise: Coulton was dragging something softly down the hall, into the back bedroom. After a moment she heard Mrs. Harrogate's voice, hushed.

She got up. The house was dark. She knew the sound of a body being dragged. She wasn't angry anymore, not exactly, her anger having cooled over the last two days into something else, something hard and sharp and grim, but she was tired of all the secrets. She went down to the second-floor landing and sat in a window seat there under the stained glass and waited for Coulton. But it was Mrs. Harrogate who came silently down in her black widow's gown, carrying a candle in a dish.

"His name," she said quietly, gliding onto the landing, "is Walter Laster."

Alice looked at her calmly. "Is he another orphan?"

"No. Walter is . . . something else."

Mrs. Harrogate's hard black eyes glittered in the candlelight. She was standing with the dish suspended before her, her disfigured face shadowy and strange.

"Where do you get the names of the kids?" Alice said suddenly.

"Ah. Mr. Coulton said you would have questions."

Alice ignored this. "I keep asking myself where. I can't figure it out. Charlie Ovid doesn't exist anywhere, not on a single damned registry. Don't tell me he does. And Marlowe was a foundling in a freight train. No one on earth can trace a kid like that."

"Well," said Mrs. Harrogate matter-of-factly. "Clearly someone can."

"You find this amusing?"

"Not at all."

"I think it's time," Alice said slowly, "you tell me everything."

"Your faith in me is most flattering. But I do not know *everything*."

Alice chose to ignore this too. "You can start with what the hell was *really* hunting us in New York. And don't tell me Jacob Marber's anything like Marlowe or Charlie. He isn't."

Mrs. Harrogate was silent a long moment, as if deciding something inside herself. "It is late," she said at last.

But she led Alice down to her study, opposite the parlor, and closed the door. Alice had not been in the study before and she was surprised by the smell of pipe smoke, by the dark leather furniture, by the enormous desk, all of it in a style preferred by men. She transferred the candle into an old lamp and the room softened in its glow. There was a cold fireplace behind the desk and Mrs. Harrogate went to the coal scuttle beyond and reached around into the wall and took out a bottle. Then she went to a cupboard, came back with two teacups, poured a knuckle of whiskey into each. She studied Alice in the lamplight. "Let us speak plainly, then."

In her fingers there appeared a shilling, flipping silently across her knuckles. She held it up, turned it in the glow.

"There are two sides to everything that is," she said quietly. "A facing side, and a hidden side, if you will. At any given time, it is so. But imagine that both sides are the facing sides. And that the hidden side is a third side, a side you never see. *Inside* the coin. The living and the dead are like the two sides of this coin. But there is a third side. And that is what these children are, these . . . talents."

"What happened to speaking plainly?"

Mrs. Harrogate smiled. "Jacob Marber, who hunted you in New York, was a talent once, not so different from Marlowe or Charles. A dustworker. But he fell under the sway of a creature of malice and evil. It has had many names, but we call it the drughr. It is, or was . . . oh, how can I explain it?" She pursed her lips. "The talents, Miss Quicke, are like a bridge between what is living and what is dead. They exist between states of being. Between worlds, if you will. The drughr is a corruption of all that. A darker talent. The part of it that was living . . . is gone."

"And what came after us in New York was a—"

"Jacob Marber came after you in New York. Not the drughr."

"But he was doing its bidding?"

"He is its servant. Yes."

"What does it want, this . . . drughr?"

"The children," said Mrs. Harrogate simply. "It eats them."

Alice, about to take a drink, froze with the teacup at her lips. She made an angry noise in her throat, halfway between a laugh and a growl.

"Understand, the drughr is not a creature of the flesh. But still it can decay. Its being must be . . . sustained. When it is strong enough, it will be able to walk in this world unmolested, it will be able to feed on the talents, both young and old."

"This is madness," Alice whispered.

The older woman frowned. "It's been thirty years since I felt what you're feeling. I forget how peculiar it all seemed, at first."

Alice looked away. She was remembering her first encounter with Harrogate, in the hotel room, when she'd been recruited. She was trying to understand how any of this fit with what she'd been told then. And then she remembered something.

"My mother," she said, picking her words carefully. "You said it was because of what happened to her, what she saw, that you . . . sought me out. You said—" Alice swallowed. "You said you *knew* about it."

"Yes."

"What my mother saw that day. When Adra Norn walked out of that fire, unharmed. Her . . . *miracle*. Was Adra one of your . . . was she like your orphans, a . . . a talent?"

Mrs. Harrogate smoothed out the skirts in her lap. "I've said too much already," she said reluctantly. "Dr. Berghast can tell you more."

"Dr. Berghast—"

"At the institute. He knows what happened at Adra Norn's community." Her hair fell across her face, obscuring it. When she spoke next her voice had changed, had stiffened, was colder and distant. "We leave for Cairndale in the morning. All of us. Mr. Coulton has suggested it is time you were told more of what we do. I agree. Come north with us. Ask Dr. Berghast yourself whatever it is you wish to know."

"I'm not going to Scotland," she said.

Mrs. Harrogate got to her feet. She was looking past Alice, and when Alice turned, she saw Coulton had come in, was watching in the gloom. She didn't know how long he'd been there.

"Get some rest, Miss Quicke," said Mrs. Harrogate, the teacups clinking in her hands, the bottle vanishing into her skirts. "I hope you will reconsider. The express departs early. It will not do to be late."

When she was gone, Coulton gave a long low groan and came forward. He sat where she'd been sitting. He looked awful, she thought, his face gray and lined with exhaustion. "Sleep for a bloody week, I could," he muttered. He managed a smile. "But it's good to see you."

Alice watched him. "You and Harrogate not talking now? Is that it?"

"We're good." Coulton pinched his eyes shut in the lamplight. "Or will be. There's just too much to say sometimes, it's hard to get started. Bit of a disagreement about old Mr. Laster. I see Marlowe's in one piece."

"He's better than Charlie."

"Aye. The poor lad."

"Marlowe's taken a shine to him."

"And it seems you've taken to Marlowe."

She was quiet at that. She'd known the child only a little over a month and already felt something intense, so that she was filled with worry and fear and anxiety half the time, and an overwhelming love the rest of the time. It wasn't like her to get attached. Ever.

"I pity him," she said at last.

"Hm," said Coulton, watching her. She wondered what he was thinking. But then he leaned forward and opened the little glass door of the lamp and lit a cheroot in the flame. "Margaret says you seen Jacob Marber. In New York City."

She nodded. "It seems so."

"I thought it were Charlie he'd come for."

"How could you have known?"

Coulton studied her in the orange glow, shadows playing across his face. "Well, it's my fault and I'm sorry. I knew him a little, years ago. We worked together, you could say. Tracking down our unfortunates. You wouldn't never have even known him then. He was gentle, like. Shy. Back then, I always said he'd of been better suited to the clergy. Had the most exquisite fingers, he did, like a pianist's. Ladies loved them. Used to embarrass him to no end."

"You said you hardly knew him."

Coulton looked at her with clear eyes, unembarrassed. "Some confidences just ain't a person's to tell," he said. "You know that as well as anybody."

"Was any of what you said about him true?"

"Aye, he *did* feel betrayed, Jacob did. Blamed everyone. Me most of all, maybe. Thing is, he were already turned by then. It weren't any tragedy what did it. It were just him. Jacob."

"Turned. You mean, by the drughr."

Coulton looked at her a long moment. "Margaret don't usually talk so much."

Alice gave a grim little smile. "Well. I was *courteous.*"

Coulton smiled grimly back. "Jacob were turned by the drughr, aye," he went on. "But he were a talent once, before that. A dustworker, his like's called. Them kids we been collecting, they ain't the only ones what can do things."

There was something in the way he said it that made Alice pause. He'd leaned back in the chair so that shadows swallowed his face. Only the coal of his cheroot, flaring and fading, could be seen.

"In Natchez," said Coulton, his face still obscured in the darkness, "you called Charlie a monster. All of them. But if they are, then I'm one too."

She swallowed. "You're like . . . them?"

"Aye."

He said it with a heavy sadness in his voice, and she wondered suddenly at what he must have seen, what he must have lived through. She knew nothing about him. What did he mean, what could he do? Rip knives out of his arm? She stared at her hands, struggling, wanting to ask, trying not to. It wasn't her business to know.

"I told myself this was the last one," she said at last. "I told myself I was out, after getting Marlowe here safe. I don't need this work. Not if I don't know what's going on."

"Maybe it's time you found out."

She looked away, suddenly tired. The house all around them was quiet. She thought of Marlowe, sleeping upstairs with Charlie.

"Harrogate took a bottle of Scotland's finest out from behind that scuttle there," she said. "You think she's got another one in there?"

Coulton leaned forward, his ruddy face coming into the light. He chewed at his cheroot, grinning. "I know that bottle. There's only the one." He met her eye, the smile fading from his eyes. "Listen. You want answers, you'll find them in Scotland. That's where you got to go. Did Margaret ask you along, yet?"

She nodded.

"So come. Come with us."

"To Cairndale," she said softly, as if to herself.

"Aye," he grunted. He inhaled deeply on his cheroot and held the smoke in his lungs, eyes glinting in the firelight. "Come to bloody Cairndale."

THE CALM
THAT COMES BEFORE

It was still dark when Brynt followed the monster to St Pancras Station and in the early rush of law clerks making their hurried way into the city she watched him purchase a ticket and then went to the same wicket and asked where the other was going. The ticketing clerk gave her a queer look, removing his spectacles to frown up at her. Brynt wore yellow kidskin gloves made special by a glove maker in Toledo, made to hide her tattoos in a country of peasant Catholics, and she still wore her only suitable dress, her size being hard to come by, though it was going shabby now under the arms and its petticoats were pocked with dried muck and because she'd lost weight it hung off her badly. But she met the clerk's eye and said she wanted a ticket on the same train and after a moment he shrugged and scrawled out a ticket to Horsechester.

"Where is this? Is it far?"

"It ain't but thirty mile north of London," said the clerk. "Quaint little village, it is."

The train was departing in the dark and she hurried down to the platform, not seeing the monster anywhere. Then she sighted him, climbing up the platform steps, vanishing into a clerestory car. Brynt shouldered her way through the crowds, hauled herself up. She tried to find a seat in third class that allowed her to peer out the window and that was near an exit. The carriage was nearly empty but for a man in tweed slowly peeling an onion with a little knife, and a governess with her ward seated with hands in their laps, neither speaking. The little boy made her think, with a twinge, of Marlowe.

At Horsechester the monster got down, smoldering with darkness, that black scarf obscuring his face still, and ignoring the alarmed stares of the other travelers he strode away, out of the little station in the predawn light, along the cobbled streets of the bucolic town. Brynt, grim, hungry now, hurried after.

He set out across the country, a dark solitary figure in city clothes. The sun was bleeding in the east. Brynt moved warily, anxious. She couldn't imagine his purpose. They were following the railway tracks across the countryside, and at a blind curve around a low grassy hill, she saw the man stop suddenly. He stood in the long grass, his arms dangling at his sides. Brynt, fifty yards away, sank down in the undergrowth.

There were insects buzzing in the grass. The breeze was cool. The morning sky turned blue, without cloud. Trains passed at intervals. The afternoon came, darkened into twilight. And still the monster stood.

Brynt would shift her position from time to time, first her legs cramping, then her back. The night turned cold. She slept badly. She was half-afraid when the night at last started to fade that she'd find the monster gone. But he wasn't; he still stood on the knoll, a shadowed figure overlooking the tracks, patient, unmoving.

It all made her very uneasy. Then in the early morning, under a blue sky, she saw the smoke of an approaching train beyond the curve, above the trees. Something felt different to her, though she couldn't say what. Soon she could hear it, the steady mechanical thrump of its rush, and then she heard the shriek of its whistle, alarmingly close, and she turned suddenly back and saw the monster had walked down the cut and up onto the tracks.

The train came into sight around the curve, a passenger express, tearing past at unbelievable speed, a great fury of fire and smoke and gleaming green and gold lettering. Brynt's heart was in her throat.

The figure, she saw, was standing in the middle of the ties, staring down the thundering train, his long black coat twisting around him. Calmly and deliberately he unwound the scarf from his face.

The train came on, its whistle shrieking.

He opened his arms wide.

Brynt got to her feet.

He didn't move, didn't leap away. And then—in a tremendous burst of black smoke and soot—the locomotive tore through him, tore through where he'd been standing, smoke pouring out around it like a great dark wing, then curling back into its airstream and enfolding the train and its coal car and its ornate wooden passenger carriages in darkness, before gradually dissipating out into dust, and Brynt saw the monster was gone, just gone, as if totally obliterated, and the whole screeching length of the train was roaring through the space where he'd been with sparks flaring in the wheels and the engine casing shuddering and the great brakes grinding down to a stop some fifty long yards farther on.

She started running.

At 23 Nickel Street West they'd all risen sleepy and irritable and stumbled through their ablutions and a meager breakfast downstairs and then out into the waiting carriages. Miss Quicke was the first awake. Margaret had been cautious and hired a second coach where Walter, smuggled darkly inside, would ride; but Charlie saw, and she saw that he saw, and his expression was all fear and betrayal.

The train departed on time. They were maybe an hour outside of London when it happened. The carriage jerked, groaned to a long shuddering halt. There was a crash of trunks and cases falling to the floor, a long squeal of brakes. Margaret grabbed at the windowsill for support, alarmed, and looked sharply at Walter. But he was still drugged and drowsing on the facing seat, gray and sickly-looking in his ropes, and he didn't so much as stir. She checked the knots, just in case. Then she went to the window and pulled aside the curtains. They occupied a sleeping compartment near the back of the train, just in front of the baggage carriage. She had also engaged a second compartment, clear at the far end of the train, at the very front, for the children and Coulton and Miss Quicke to ride in.

The train had come to a stop on a curve of track, and she could clearly see the gleaming locomotive at the front, the distant figure of the engineer in his coveralls as he jumped down, the cloud of black smoke drifting away from the fire stack. She hoped very much it was not a derailment. There were schedules to keep. A minute later she heard a rap at the compartment.

It was Coulton, of course. Glaring in past her, at Walter in his ropes.

"Everything all right?" he said.

"You're supposed to be with the children," she told him. "Your task is to keep them safe until we get to Cairndale."

"Aye." His gaze slid past her, again, to the litch. "I know the task. But we need to talk."

"Not here." She pushed the gruff man back out, into the side corridor, and slid the compartment shut behind her. She locked it, folded the little brass key into her palm, interlaced her fingers in front of her.

"Well?" she said. "If this is about Walter Laster, I do not wish to discuss it. The matter is closed, Mr. Coulton. Why have we stopped?"

Coulton blinked. "I don't know. Listen—"

"Did we hit something? Was there something on the tracks?"

"I don't know. Margaret—"

"If we are late for our connection, I shall be most displeased."

"Goddamnit, Margaret," he snapped. "Let a man speak."

She frowned in disapproval, glanced the length of the side corridor, then met his eye. "I believe I've let you have your say already, Mr. Coulton," she said in a deliberately quiet voice. "And such language is hardly appropriate."

"But you haven't," he said.

"I haven't what?"

"You haven't let me have my say. Walter said to me that Jacob's on his way. He said Jacob knows how to find him."

Margaret flared her nostrils in displeasure, lifted her chin. "I doubt that."

"You don't reckon it's possible? Or you don't want it to be?"

"Walter'd been smoking opium, he was quite drunk on it. You said it yourself."

"Don't mean it ain't true."

"We're on our way to the institute, Mr. Coulton. Jacob Marber couldn't get to him, even if he knew how to. He isn't on this train."

She watched Coulton glower.

"Aye," he said reluctantly.

She started to go, then paused. "Was there something else?"

Coulton flushed. "It ain't too late to change tack. If Jacob's looking for that bastard, he's like to have a way of finding him, if you take my meaning. He's like to follow him north. Why not let me escort him on a different train?"

"I think not."

"Or you, then. If it ain't too dangerous. It don't matter. But get him away from the children. You saw what happened with Charlie."

Margaret felt a flicker of regret at that. She had thought the opium stronger, the ropes more powerful. She'd been careful, this time, to increase the dosage and the restraints both. And she'd not leave the litch's side the entire way. It ought to be safe enough. More to the point, she didn't know how long they had until Jacob Marber came hunting, and she wanted Walter locked away behind Cairndale's walls before he did.

Through the windows she saw a conductor in his blue uniform and box cap walk slowly through the long grass, waving to someone up the line. Some of the passengers had got off, were standing on the slopes of the cut, smoking pipes, chatting in the sunlight. She shook her head.

"And what do you propose we do, Mr. Coulton?" she said softly. "Drag Walter off the train, here, and carry him to the nearest station? And who would do that—you? You would abandon the children? Or perhaps me, with my tremendous physical strength? No, I fear it is too late entirely to *change tack*, as you put it. Go back up to your carriage, sir."

Coulton rubbed at his whiskers. There was something in the way he was looking at her that she didn't like, a disappointment.

"Anything happens to those children," he said darkly, "you'll have to live with it."

At the front of the train, Charlie Ovid put a hand to the compartment window, watching the engineer and the conductors trudge back along the tracks, peering under the wheels, kicking through the long yellow weeds. A pale blue sky, clouds like wisps of cotton batting. After London's fog, he'd nearly forgotten what that looked like. Coulton's kidskin gloves were laid out, crosswise, on the soft polished mahogany seat, as if to remind them of his absence. A shelf of webbing overhead for hats and parasols. It was a modern compartment, with a sliding oak door that opened onto an interior corridor. Charlie let his eyes travel over the dark panels, imprinted and detailed, he studied the lace curtains obscuring the door glass. Marlowe had his face pressed to the glass, watching the men outside with interest.

"They hit something, that's all," said Alice, pinching her eyes shut. She tilted the brim of her hat over her face. "A sheep maybe. It's all right, Marlowe."

"They're looking under the carriages," said the kid.

Charlie furrowed his brow. Something was wrong; he could feel it. "Where did Mr. Coulton go, Miss Alice?" he asked quietly.

"You know where he went," she said, without stirring.

"He had to ask Mrs. Harrogate something, Charlie," said Marlowe. "He told us so. Before he went."

But Charlie wet his lips. It was because he knew who Mrs. Harrogate had brought along, why she was locked in a different part of the train. When she'd cuffed him to the chair in the testing room she'd said it was for her protection, not his. He knew that kind of fear.

"He's been gone a while now, hasn't he?"

"It's been twelve minutes, Charlie." She tilted the hat, opened one eye. "Try to get some sleep."

Just then they felt a sudden lurch, and the train groaned underfoot. The whistle at the front sounded three sharp blasts. Slowly, very slowly, the train started to creep forward, at a walking pace, not even that. And then the *clunk-shh, clunk-shh, clunk-shh*, faster and faster, as the train gathered speed. The green fields flowed past.

"See," said Alice. "Nothing to worry about."

But the bad feeling in Charlie just got worse. He studied Alice where she sat in her long oilskin coat, like a rancher. In the little traveling case overhead he knew she'd packed a revolver. He'd seen her clean it and wrap it in oilcloth, and he'd seen the way her hand lingered near it, and he knew the kind of person she was. It didn't make him feel any easier.

Suddenly Marlowe stiffened. Alice must have sensed it, for she took the hat from her face and uncrossed her legs and looked at him. The kid got down, went to the paneled door, pressed his hand against it.

"What is it?" said Alice. "What's the matter?"

The train was gathering speed, their shoulders jiggling where they sat.

Marlowe looked scared. "It's him," he whispered. "He's found us. He's *here*."

11

SHINING BOY

The train was moving again.

Lurching at first, shuddering, then starting to roll. In the narrow side corridor, Margaret Harrogate stumbled up against Coulton. The field outside the windows began to slide slowly past. She was tired, and irritated, not least because some part of her knew Coulton was right.

But the man had stopped arguing at least, there was that, as if maybe he'd given up on trying to convince her. He could be so insufferably sure of himself, at times. But then he held up a callused hand, and turned his head, and stood listening. The windows and fixtures were rattling softly now, the low clatter of the railway ties coming up through the floor. She put out a hand to steady herself, studying his stout red face as she did so, the soft flicker of his eyelashes.

"What is it?" she said.

He shook his head. "I don't know. I thought I heard something."

Her eyes shifted past him instantly, down the corridor, toward the compartment where she'd left the litch. The door was still locked, the blue curtains over its glass partition drawn. There was the quick dappling of sunlight and shadow as the train passed through a stand of oaks, emerged into open country.

And that was when they heard the scream.

It came from one of the compartments. Margaret whirled around at once in a swish of her long black dress and ran, and then she was turning the little key in the lock, sliding the doors wide. There were stains on the upholstery where the litch had lain. His ropes had been chewed through and left frayed, tangled. The curtains were flapping wildly, in shreds. Margaret went at once to the tall carriage window. It had been slid down and left open and the wind was whipping at her hair.

"Damn," she hissed.

Coulton spat. "How in hell'd he fit through that?"

Then a second scream came from the next compartment over and Coulton ducked back out, banged his fist on the lintel, but a young woman in spectacles and a schoolteacher's blouse with her hair loose in her eyes was already stumbling out, collapsing into his arms, shrieking.

"Dear God, oh dear God," she was crying.

"For the love of all that's holy, child," Margaret snapped, catching sight of her. "Speak plain."

But the young woman was blubbering too much to make real sense. "My window, out my window, it was a, a . . ."

Her face was ashen, Margaret saw. But she'd already told enough. The woman was shivering and leaning into Coulton's arms and he set her aside, just as if she were a sack of potatoes, and he drew his Colt Peacemaker from the pocket of his chesterfield and rolled his burly shoulders and went in. Margaret was right behind him. But this compartment, too, was as good as empty: a pincushion, stitching thrown in a panic underfoot, a half-eaten green apple rolling around under the window. Coulton tore off his bowler and leaned his head far out the window and squinted into the wind, then twisted to peer back the other way.

"Well?" demanded Margaret. She was furious with herself. She'd done everything she could think of to stop this from happening a second time.

"Bugger's gone," Coulton shouted, his face still in the wind. He leaned back in. "Right off the train, looks like. Could be he fell. Or jumped."

"He didn't jump," she said. "He's still on board."

Coulton checked the chambers of his revolver, snapped it shut. "All right" was all he said. He reached for his bowler. Then he paused.

"Say it," she said bitterly. "Go on. Tell me I should've listened to you."

He shook his head. "This ain't your fault, Margaret."

But she just scowled and held out a gloved hand and took the weapon from him. She turned it sidelong, expertly, and sighted down the barrel. "I brought him on board," she said. "So, yes. It is."

When she opened the door she saw all the disgruntled faces gathered now in the corridor, mostly gentlemen in silk hats, holding out handkerchiefs to the woman. A conductor was pushing his way through, demanding to know what was going on.

She turned back to Coulton, put a gloved hand on his wrist. "You make sure the children are safe. If he's after anyone, it's them."

Coulton nodded. "And you?"

She adjusted her little crucifix, met his eye. "I'll finish this," she said angrily.

Up at the front of the train, in the second-class carriage, Alice drew the window curtains, plunging them all into partial darkness. She was trying to understand Marlowe's meaning. *He's found us. He's here.*

Charlie was on his feet, swaying with the train, crowding the compartment unnecessarily. "Who's he talking about? Not Walter

Laster?" he demanded. "Mrs. Harrogate said he wasn't going to wake up."

Alice paused. "Walter . . . Laster?"

"Walter. The litch."

Alice went to the door and locked it. Then she pulled down her traveling case, unwrapped her revolver from out of its oilcloth, opened the little leather satchel she carried the cartridges in. She loaded it carefully, trying to steady her thoughts. Walter Laster: that'd be the one Mrs. Harrogate was riding with, in the rear coach. The man Coulton had dragged in, the night before.

"Mrs. Harrogate said he's dead. Dead and not dead." Charlie'd started to breathe sharp fast breaths, almost panting in his fear. "We've got to get out of here, we've got to go. We can't stay. I *seen* him, he's got these long teeth, and he can crawl on the walls like a spider, and his skin, it's all white—"

Charlie started to shake the door hard, so that the glass rattled in its bracket.

"It's locked, Charlie," she said, trying to calm him. "No one's getting through. Mr. Coulton will be back soon, it's all right."

"It's not all right," Charlie said, giving up on the door. "You don't know what he is. He's not a *person.*" His voice was rising now in pitch. "Nothing ever hurt me, Miss Alice. Ever. But *he* did. *He* hurt me." Charlie unbuttoned his cuffs, rolled up his sleeves. On each forearm were four deep, infected-looking claw marks. "Mrs. Harrogate said he was already dead. What kind of dead does that?"

"The kind that needs a little more encouragement, I guess. Like a bullet through the eye." Alice looked at Marlowe. "Is that who you were talking about? Walter Laster?"

Marlowe's eyes were big. "No," he whispered.

"Who, then?"

"The other one. The man from the hotel."

Alice went very still. "Jacob Marber's on the train?"

The little boy nodded. His voice was barely more than a whisper. "And he knows we're here too."

They waited. The minutes ticked by, Charlie and Marlowe looking increasingly scared. But Coulton didn't come. There was a thick, muffled kind of silence in the side corridor beyond, as if the railway carriage were emptied, as if all its passengers had fallen into a deep sleep.

From time to time Alice would lift the corner of the door curtain, glance out into the corridor. But there was no movement, nothing. No conductor came by. No Coulton.

Behind her, Charlie Ovid had pulled back the outside window curtains a bit and Alice could see they were passing through the outskirts of some gray industrial city, brick walls stained with soot, iron railings twisted into pained shapes. She caught a glimpse of dozens of smokestacks, churning a brown smudge into the sky. Dull sooty rooftops. Then they were rising again, up, out of the city's edges, northward.

Coulton should have been back by now, that was the truth of it. It was eerie, how quiet the entire carriage had gone. At last she heard the sound of the corridor door clattering open, the sudden rush of the tracks, and then the muffling as the door again snicked shut. Heavy slow footsteps. But they were coming from the front of the train, from the porter car and the locomotive beyond. She frowned, changed to the facing seat. Cautiously she lifted the curtain to see.

And dropped it, almost at once, in horror.

It was him.

A sooty darkness smoldered off his black coat, his hat, his black gloved hands. He was long and thin, with broad shoulders, and he wore a thick black beard, trimmed along the cut of his jaw like a barber. But his face was averted, and she could not see his eyes. He was dipping his head, peering into the compartments, and as he came forward the carriage itself seemed cast into gloom. Charlie and Marlowe had gone still, staring at her, at the look on her face, probably, and she met their eyes and she didn't try to hide it. Her heart was hammering in her chest.

"It's him," whispered Marlowe.

She didn't answer. She looked around, scanning their small compartment, the webbing overhead, the mahogany panels in the door. Her gun was gripped in her hand and she looked at it and then slid it into the pocket of her oilskin coat. She went to the window, fumbled the sash, wrestled the pane all the way down. The curtains sucked out and snapped along the outside of the train. She stuck her face out, into the roar of the wind, her hair flattening behind her. She squinted.

There was a conductor's handrail running the length of the car, and narrow protuberances that could be used for footholds. It'd have to do.

She ducked back inside the carriage, her head reeling. "Quickly, now," she said. "We need to get farther back in the train. Now."

Charlie looked at Marlowe, alarmed. "He's not climbing outside any train, Miss Alice. He's too little."

But she was already buttoning Marlowe's coat fast. She looked a long moment into the boy's face and then she nodded, satisfied by what she saw there. "You hold on to me and don't let go. All right? I need you to close your eyes and not to open them until we're in the next carriage. Just like we did in the hotel. Can you do that?"

Marlowe glanced fearfully at the locked door. A thin black smoke had started to seep in around its edges.

"Marlowe?" she hissed.

"Okay."

She folded her hat and stuffed it into her free pocket and closed up her coat and then she tied her hair out of her face. She put her hands on Charlie's shoulders. "You can do this, Charlie."

Charlie Ovid nodded. "It can't hurt me any, falling off a train," he whispered.

The compartment rattled around them. She heard a soft rap at the door. Even as they moved to the window, she knew there was no time. Where the hell was Coulton?

Alice picked up Marlowe against her chest, little arms interlocked around her neck, and she climbed out, out into the dizzying roar of the air, the full blast of it nearly knocking her sideways. She gripped the conductor's rail over the windows, inched back along the carriage. The wind was at their backs, shoving them onward. The gravel and railroad ties rocketed past, a blur under her. Charlie swung his long legs out after her, quick, lithe.

She could feel Marlowe trembling, his little face crushed into her chest. "It's okay, it's all right, it's all right," she kept murmuring into his ear.

As they clambered across the windows she peered into the compartments. They were all, somehow, impossibly, empty.

She was nearly at the back of the carriage when something hard and black banged and ricocheted past her, away. She glanced back. Jacob Marber clung to the outside wall of the carriage, at the front. His silk hat was gone. As she watched, astonished, he began to creep, slowly, gloved hand over gloved hand, sidelong toward them, his soft shoes slipping as he went. His hair was blown forward over his face obscuring it in the wind but she could feel it, somehow, his malevolent gaze, the way his eyes were fixed on Marlowe and Charlie.

"Charlie!" she shouted. He was maybe ten feet behind her still. "Charlie, hurry!"

Jacob Marber's long coat snapped forward around him in the roar, like a ribbon of darkness, reaching for them.

The baggage coach in the rear of the train was hushed, dim. Two raised air vents in the ceiling let in the only light, a faint trickling gray daylight. Margaret Harrogate crept slowly past the trunks and dark stacks of traveling cases, the shapeless bundles of goods in sacks, all tied off behind webbing, listening all the while to the faint clatter of the railway ties under the floor and for some sound, any sound, else. She held Coulton's gun cocked at her side.

In the middle of the coach she stood very still, glancing quickly behind her. Nothing.

"Walter?" she called out softly. "Walter, it's Mrs. Harrogate, dear."

He was close. She could feel it, *knew* that he was, though she couldn't have said how she knew. She walked calmly forward, her anger dissipating, her fear gone. It was as if she were empty. Shapes loomed up out of the dimness, cases and bags and baskets.

At the rear of the coach she drew the latch and slid the door open onto the rear platform, the roaring of the tracks loud in her ears, and she stepped nimbly over the railing and across, over the couplings, to the next platform. And in the rush of wind and amid the crackle of skirts she drew back the door of the last carriage. It was the Royal Mail coach. The lock had been ripped right out of its casing.

The wind from the open door threw up a million pieces of torn paper and they drifted in a slow descent of confetti inside the dimness. The bags had been shredded. She dragged the door shut with a clang, the bits of paper swirling.

Then through the weird snow she saw him. Walter. Hunched in the far corner, face turned away. His shirt had been ripped off so that the shoulder blades in his back stood sharply and the knuckles of his spine almost glowed in the dimness. He was barefoot, too. She could hear an eerie clicking sound, like knives clattering in a drawer. She moved the revolver behind her back.

"Walter," she said calmly. "It's cold back here. Aren't you cold?"

He went still at her voice. But he didn't turn his smooth and hairless head. His ears stuck out like dials. The papers were still spiraling around her. The litch was bent over something, she saw now, and as she neared she glimpsed a pair of shabby brown shoes, one unlaced, and a pair of hairy ankles sticking out of them. The mail clerk.

She tried to keep the anger from her voice. "Oh, Walter. Oh, this is most inappropriate," she said.

He shifted then, he crept across the body, deeper into the shadows. He raised his face, his mouth smeared with blood, blood all down his hairless pale chest, like a great red stain. His long teeth were clicking. His eyes, she saw, were completely black, as if he were still drugged on the opium.

"Jacob knows about the boy," said Walter softly.

Margaret paused.

His voice sounded like a rope drawn over stone. "He's coming, yes, he's coming closer now." He bared his teeth in what might have been a smile, or maybe just a reflex. "Oh I remember you, Mrs. Harrogate. Jacob used to talk about you. You and your precious Mr. Coulton."

She stopped, her heart in her throat. She started to shake her head. He seemed so collected, so much in his own mind. It was chilling. The revolver was still behind her back, low, and with her thumb now she very carefully cocked the hammer.

"Jacob Marber isn't coming," she said firmly. "That's the poppy talking. He left you, Walter. Left you in that awful city, alone. I found you, I was the one who found you. Not Jacob. Now, stop this nonsense and come with me. Let me help you."

He tilted his head then, as if thinking about it. But there was nothing human in the gesture. His hands when he lifted them from the floor left twin dark handprints of blood.

"My Jacob—" he said slowly.

"Has forgotten you."

The litch crept a little bit closer, the muscles in his legs coiling taut. "Oh, Mrs. Harrogate," he whispered, tapping the side of his head. "But I can hear him. He's already here."

For a long moment neither moved. Margaret watched his eyes. The train rattled and shook.

And then he leaped, right at her, his bloodied mouth wide, his long teeth glinting, and in the same instant Margaret Harrogate lifted the gun and fired.

Brynt was trying not to throw up.

She was huddled on the rear platform of the Royal Mail coach, her tattooed arms entwined in the railing, the wind roaring around her. There were steps on either side, closed off with a tasseled rope, and a strong door at her back. *Marlowe*, she thought. *You're here for Marlowe. Get moving.*

She kept telling herself that, over and over, as if it might help. But she didn't move. She was clinging to the very back of the train, watching the tracks scroll out behind her. She hated fast-moving things. Horses. Passenger liners. But being perched in the open platform at the back of a speeding train was maybe worst of all.

She'd picked up her voluminous skirts and ran for all she was worth down onto the tracks when she saw the conductors and engineer swinging back up into the stopped train, the sun at her back, her shadow long before her, and she'd just reached the step of the last car and heaved her great bulk up when the brakes groaned and the train started rolling again, gathering speed. She gripped the railing, gasping. She was sure someone must have seen her. But the train didn't slow, no porter came running back to shout up at her, and they were away.

Thing of it was, she'd seen that man, the shadow man, burst into smoke as the locomotive thundered through him. The engineer had seen it too, had braked hard and gone hunting under the wheels for the bits of him. She'd watched him walk the length of the train, swipe his cap from his head, squat, peer under each car. He'd found nothing, neither he nor the conductors, no part of the man. She'd watched this and thought about the smoke curling the length of the locomotive and its coal car and then vanishing. Whatever else, it wasn't suicide. That man—monster, whatever he was—somehow had got on board the train. Which meant Marlowe must be on it too.

Such had been her thinking, at least, as she lay in the long grass watching. But now, as she clung to the rear step of the postal coach, her thick braid battering away in the rush, her face screwed up in a grimace, it seemed near madness. Men didn't just explode into clouds of smoke. Circus ladies didn't go leaping up onto moving trains.

That was when she heard a muffled thump, as if something heavy had been thrown against the inside of the mail coach. She went very still. Then it came again, more violently. There was the clear unmistakable sound of a struggle inside. Brynt pressed her ear up against the locked door. Nothing.

And then something punched the wood siding of the car near her head, sounding like an angry wasp, leaving a small black hole. A bullet.

"Dear God in heaven," she whispered. Swaying from side to side, scrabbling away. And then a single clear thought formed in her head:

Go.

And Brynt checked her grip, glared up at the lip of the roof, and started to climb.

Alice shoved the rattling carriage door wide, pushed Marlowe through, out of the wind, then reached a hand back for Charlie Ovid. She couldn't see Jacob Marber yet.

They didn't stop. It was a carriage holding several more private compartments and they ran past all of them, stumbling from side to side as the train rattled on, the occupants turning one by one to stare in surprise as they passed. Alice kept glancing fearfully back. At the rear of the car she opened the door, stepped into the same familiar platform, the roar and clatter of wind and ties, and she lifted Marlowe across and then climbed over the railing and jumped across too. The next carriage was a third-class carriage, crowded, noisy, with wooden seats arranged in rows. The air was thick with pipe smoke and the creaking of newspapers and women in shawls shouting across the aisle at each other. Alice and the boys were all three disheveled now, wild-looking, with their heads bared. She took out her gun, not caring, and then she heard a quiet descend and she looked up. Row upon row of faces, pale, were staring at her. She hurried the two boys down the aisle, toward the back, ignoring the forward-facing passengers. Her forearms were sluggish and throbbing from the climb, and she was out of breath. She saw some of those she'd seen on the London platform, the two widows in black with their tight bitter faces, the man with the birdcage staring as they passed.

They were three rows from the rear when the door in front of them opened and Coulton came through. He'd lost his bowler hat and his ruddy face was flushed and his eyes were dark.

"You left us, you son of a bitch," she said. And shoved him hard in the chest.

He peered past her at the two kids. "You're all okay?"

"No," snapped Charlie.

Alice put a hand on the boy's sleeve to calm him. Passengers were staring. "Marber's behind us," she said. "We can't stop here. Hurry."

"Jacob is—?" Coulton gripped her shoulders, looked hard in her face. "Did you say—?"

But then he went silent, his glower sliding off her and along toward the front of the railway carriage. Alice turned to follow where he was looking.

Jacob Marber was standing at the very front of the aisle, a figure of darkness, breathing hard. Some of the passengers had got to their feet. Soot and smoke were coming off him, like a singed thing, like a thing drawn out of the fire only moments ago. His black gloves looked too long to be right and he'd lost his hat and his black hair was wild and standing out from his head. He made no move to come closer. His beard swept down before him like some Old Testament judge. Alice couldn't see his eyes.

"Get behind me," hissed Coulton.

He wrestled out of his jacket, rolled up his sleeves like a pugilist entering a street fight. His yellow waistcoat was tight at his shoulders and paunch. His neck, Alice saw, was very short and thick. And then he seemed somehow to ripple and condense, as if his skin were hardening, and she saw the middle of his waistcoat split, and his shoulders thicken. Something was happening.

"You should've stayed gone, Jacob," he called.

Seeing Coulton thicken there, seeing Jacob Marber wavering like some monstrous shadow, Alice had never felt such fear. It was sheer absolute terror. It seized her stomach, almost causing her to clutch at her belly in pain. She felt the boy clinging to her arm. But then Coulton took a step forward, and Jacob Marber opened his mouth as if to scream, and his teeth were black and a darkness filled his mouth like blood. And that was when Alice saw the thing appear on the wall behind him.

It could have been a sooty fingerprint, a dab of tar. But it began to grow inside the wood like a drop of ink in water and seeing it she started to tremble. It ate away at the wall, spreading fast, an absolute darkness, and then Jacob Marber raised his open hands like a preacher calling for some terrible sign and drew them slowly forward as if pushing against a great current and all at once that blackness poured toward them over wall and ceiling and floor, blacking the windows, snuffing out the lights, a shadow all consuming and alive and overtaking all those who sat in that carriage.

The car was shuddering. Passengers cried out, doubling over in horror. Alice had her Colt Peacemaker out but her hand was shaking and she had to grip it with her other to steady it and then she fired. She fired again and again into the darkness where Jacob Marber had been until all the chambers were empty and only a clicking came. It made no difference. The darkness came on.

Still she stood, going through the chambers uselessly, and only Coulton's hand on her arm, heavy and cold as a bag of sand, drew her back to herself.

"Go!" he shouted. "Go!"

His face was weirdly dense, as if his features had been overtaken by his flesh, and from deep in their sockets his eyes glittered out, small and hard as river stones.

And then he turned, and doubled up his swollen fists, and threw himself into the darkness.

Margaret Harrogate's first bullet went wide, punching through the wall of the mail coach. Walter was too fast, impossibly fast, scrabbling up the wall and across the ceiling. She watched the sudden penny of daylight open in the splintering wall, where the bullet had gone, like a flower of light, and she thought, strangely: *How beautiful it is.*

And then Walter was upon her, clawing, tearing, ripping.

She could feel the wet slash of her wounds. The revolver fell, was knocked scraping across the floor of the carriage and came to rest up against a mailbag. Walter was eerily light, so light Margaret could have lifted him with one arm, and she was not a strong woman by any stretch. And yet despite this his strength was immense, and she struggled and kicked and only just managed to get an elbow up under his chin, holding his long knifelike teeth away from her throat. With a sharp twist, she threw him off.

He landed on his back, flipped over, scrambled on all fours toward her. She was crawling for the revolver, trying to grab it, when he seized her ankle and she felt his long claws drive through the leather of her boot, into her leg.

They struggled in near silence, only the hard breathing and the slap and scuff of bone on wood. There was blood on the side of Margaret's head, in her hair, her arms were on fire. But she kicked out at his face, once, twice, feeling her heel connect with something that crunched, and then she was free and got to the revolver and whirled around and fired five quick shots in succession, directly into Walter Laster's chest.

The force of the impacts hurled him backward, hard up against a mailbag, in a tangle of webbing.

Margaret got shakily to her feet. Her left arm wasn't working right. There was blood getting in her eyes from somewhere and she wiped her face with her wrist, the sleeve torn and flapping. She stared at the litch, pale, thin, hunched, unmoving where it lay.

Then it gave a little shiver, like it was cold, like it had just felt a chill, and it lifted its face and looked directly at her. Its eyes were black, absolutely black. Obsidian and shining and inhuman.

She didn't hesitate. She pulled the trigger, again and again. But the chambers were empty. She turned it to use as a club and slowly, grimly, she backed up until she had her shoulder blades against the wall. She was looking for something, anything, to use as a weapon.

Walter got to his feet, his long teeth clicking softly.

He smiled.

Alice, frozen, watched as Coulton ran right into the darkness that was Jacob Marber.

And all at once it was as if whatever fear had held her fast just released its grip, and she seized little Marlowe under one arm, lifting him to her, his face turned away, and she threw open the rear door onto the roaring wind and climbed across the gap to the next platform. Charlie Ovid was right behind her, shutting the door, fumbling with it in the roar, looking for some kind of lock. There wouldn't be one, she knew. Already her head was clearing. The tracks hurtled past under her feet. *Son of a bitch*, she thought. If Coulton couldn't stop him, Jacob Marber would hunt them carriage by carriage down the entire length of the train.

She steadied her feet and spun the chamber and emptied the cartridges and reloaded as quick as she could. She couldn't hear anything from the third-class carriage. She started to go through to the next coach and then she stopped. She looked up. There were rungs bolted to the siding and all at once she lifted Marlowe back across and climbed with him up to the roof of the carriage.

All was sky and dazzling light. The wind knocked the breath from her lungs. Her long coat swept out behind her, tangling in her legs. She was on her hands and knees, Marlowe small and sheltered under her. Charlie was creeping up beside her, his mouth open in the wind.

"The engine!" she shouted. "We need to get forward to the engine! We need to stop the train!"

Charlie nodded.

The roof was wooden and nailed and sloped crazily. Alice hadn't gone more than a few feet when the little boy froze up.

They were crossing a river by then. The water glinted like silver far below on both sides and the way the light played off the surface made her head spin. There was the brown smudge of a city, off to the east. The boy had his eyes creased shut and he lay curled around Alice's arm so that she couldn't move.

"Marlowe!" she cried into his ear. "We need to keep going!"

She thought she heard the door bang open below. She glanced back in dread but saw nothing. Maybe it was Coulton, she thought.

Charlie was some ten feet ahead of them by then, clinging to the roof, his head down as if against a driving rain. Very slowly, with great effort, she nudged Marlowe forward an inch, two inches. Coulton would be hunting for them down in the carriages behind, by now. Coulton, or Jacob Marber. She nudged Marlowe forward, a little more. When she raised her face and squinted she saw they were maybe in the middle of the carriage. There were two other carriages ahead of them, and then the coal car and locomotive.

"Come on," she whispered.

And then she glanced back again. What made her turn? She glanced back and what she saw made her suddenly go still, wrap a protective arm around the boy.

It was Jacob Marber. He'd clambered up onto the wrong carriage and stood balanced on one knee in his slippery shoes, just across the gap, his black coat crackling all around him, his face and beard turned low against the wind. He was leaning forward into it, arms out for balance. Smoke ribboned away from him. Alice stared in horror. There was nothing in the man's eyes that she could see, nothing at all, not malevolence, not fury, nothing. Just twin pools of darkness, devouring the light, reflecting no shine.

He kneeled there, hatless, watching her, unhurried.

And she knew: Coulton was dead.

No one was coming to help them.

At the edge of the mail coach roof, Brynt slid sharply, started to go over. She just caught her fingers on the rail, pulled herself back up. Her bonnet was gone. There was a tear in her kidskin gloves. Her voluminous skirts were all wild in the wind. She paused before dropping down into the coupling platform between the carriages, and at that moment she saw the door of the mail coach slide back, and someone—some *thing*—leaped out.

What was it? Shirtless, pale, covered in blood. Its fingers looked too long for its body. She couldn't see its face clearly until it twisted its weight to throw open the door of the next carriage, and then she glimpsed the hatchet-like cheekbones, the dark eyes. There was blood all over its lips and chin and down the front of its trousers.

All this she saw in an instant, in the flicker of an eye, crouched on the edge of the roof, before the creature was gone, sliding into the baggage carriage, gone.

Marlowe! she thought in despair.

She was too late. He'd found him. She came down heavily, heart pounding, and burst into the mail coach, looking for the child. Everywhere was a mess of torn papers and crates strewn all over the floor and shelves knocked sideways and her eyes scanned it all quickly and then at the rear of the car she caught a glimpse of a small figure and she caught her breath.

It wasn't him.

It was a woman. And not the female detective from the circus either, the one who'd taken Marlowe, who'd promised to keep him safe. This woman was middle-aged, dressed in black widow's weeds, badly shredded now, her arms and face carved savagely up. She'd been cut in the belly and in the chest and her soft face was bloodied beyond recognition. Brynt kneeled beside her, hands hovering anxiously, afraid to touch her. The woman was still breathing, but faintly. Brynt glanced around the coach. There was a second body, several feet away, arms flung wide. The mail clerk's body. But no sign of Marlowe.

She turned her head grimly.

She glared in the direction the creature had gone.

Alice stared behind her, the roof's wind in her ears, tearing at her grip, threatening to throw her off-balance.

Jacob Marber still hadn't moved. He hadn't got to his feet, or struggled forward, or tried to leap the gap, anything, he just half kneeled there with his dead eyes fixed on her and his head down against the wind. It was exactly like, she thought suddenly, in dread, as if he were waiting for something. Or someone.

"Miss Alice!" Charlie shouted from up ahead. "Miss Alice, hurry!"

She didn't know how she did what she did next. But she scooped up Marlowe in her arms and got to her feet and ran into the wind, her boots banging over the wooden roof, one shoulder turned forward to cradle the little boy from the roaring.

She ran the length of the railway carriage and didn't stop at the gap but leaped at speed between the carriages and landed skittering on the roof of the next carriage. Charlie was already there, reaching for her, helping her up. She glanced back.

Jacob Marber was standing now, walking slowly forward. He was thin as a shadow, all dark. He seemed not to jump between the cars but simply to step off the edge of one and come down on the side of the other. And Alice saw something else, something worse.

A long white hand had appeared, over the lip of the roof, beside

Jacob Marber. Then a second. It was the litch. It dragged itself onto the roof, and then she saw the two of them together, nearly identical, one hairless and gray as a worm, both monstrous, both cruel.

They didn't glance at each other; they gave no sign or word. It was as if they just *knew*. Jacob Marber stood with his arms at his sides, that eerie dense smoke streaming out behind him. And crouched at his side, on all fours, spiderlike, malformed, Walter Laster glared. Shirtless, barefoot in the freezing wind. Walter was impossibly pale, his face and torso stained with blood. He opened his mouth, showing long swordlike teeth.

Alice looked for Charlie. He had his hands over his ears, staring in absolute terror.

"No no no no no," he was murmuring. She could see the shape of his lips but couldn't hear anything over the wind.

And that was when the litch—Walter—started forward.

He crawled slowly at first, lightly, as if the wind were nothing to him, as if scrabbling along the roof of a speeding train were nothing. Alice could see his long claws taking purchase, the quick sparks as he drove them into the iron runners fastening the eaves in place, scrabbling forward. She pushed Marlowe behind her, took out her Colt Peacemaker, kneeled for balance.

Walter came on, faster and faster, like a sinister white hound.

She cocked the hammer.

She'd unloaded on this creature's master and had no effect and she didn't think bullets would work on Walter either. But she'd be damned if she didn't try. She knew she had to wait until he was dead close. She'd get only the one chance. Her heart was steady. She took aim.

He was closing the distance rapidly, and she could hear now the scrape and click of his claws as he threw himself forward. Jacob Marber stood back, as if transfixed, just watching. Alice relaxed her breathing.

The creature leaped suddenly, fast over the gap between the carriages. But before it could come down on the other side, while it was still, somehow, in midair, something snagged its foot, and it twisted on its side, and then swung wildly, powerfully, backward, to smash onto the roof of the carriage it had just come from.

And then Alice saw an enormous shape rise up out of the gap. A woman, blood in her eyes, skirts flying. An enormous, powerful-looking woman.

Marlowe cried out. "Brynt! Brynt!" he cried. And the huge woman spun around, looking for the voice, her silver braid flying, and Alice recognized her, the woman from the circus, the tattooed lady, Marlowe's protector.

The litch was thrashing wildly in her grip, flipping about, its claws flailing. Alice saw it writhe and clamber around the woman's arm, quicksilver fast, fluid as a weasel, and get on her back and start tearing at her flesh. Alice could see gobbets of meat coming off in the creature's claws and the big woman was twisting, reaching up, trying to get a grip on the thing. Then she had it, and she dragged it over her head and smashed it onto the roof. But when she leaned back, it was clinging to her arm, and came up with her, its teeth snapping. It leaped again off her and forward, as if to get to Marlowe, and the huge woman, Brynt, threw herself forward and again caught it by one ankle.

Alice was trying to get a clear shot at the creature but couldn't. And then the woman raised her face and looked at Alice. They locked eyes for only an instant. There was nothing in her face, no expression at all. The litch was snapping and twisting, trying to get free. The big woman grabbed its leg with her other hand also, no longer holding on to anything, and she threw all her weight sideways.

"No!" Alice cried out.

For a long impossible moment the litch hung on. The woman, Brynt, was banging hugely against the side of the carriage. The litch snarled and looked at the boy with desperation, but Brynt's weight was too much, and then the creature that was Walter Laster was ripped bodily off the roof and the two of them, woman and litch, were blown out over the gap and were gone.

"Brynt!" Marlowe was screaming. "Brynt!"

Alice grabbed the boy, struggling in her arms.

Through his windblown hair she saw Jacob Marber, striding now over the carriage roof, purposeful, at speed, coming for them. A darkness fell over the sun.

Margaret Harrogate opened her eyes in agony.

Every part of her body hurt. There was torn paper sticking to the blood on her hands and her belly and something was wrong with her legs. She tried to stand, wobbled, fell back. Tried again. Groaned and peered woozily around.

Walter was gone.

The coach was quiet. In the dimness, she could feel through the floor the rear trucks rattling at speed over the tracks. She got to her knees, clutching her belly, then got to her feet. She stumbled for the door. She had to find Walter. Had to warn Coulton, warn the children.

Somehow she climbed over the couplings, into the baggage coach. It too was a mess. And somehow she staggered through that, making her slow agonizing way, and crossed the couplings again in the roaring wind, and entered the side corridor of the carriage where she'd drugged and tied Walter up, back in that fog-lit station in London.

That seemed like a lifetime ago. The carriage she found herself in, now, was in ruins. Doors were splintered open, ripped from their frames, windowpanes were shattered. Wind whistled through. There were bodies lying in the corridor, throats opened, blood greasy and black underfoot. Halfway down the carriage she slid in some congealed mess and just caught herself, gasping in pain.

Some of those lying there weren't quite dead and they moaned or cried softly to her as she passed. But she didn't stop, couldn't stop, not until she'd reached the crowded third-class carriage and glimpsed the rows of passengers still in their seats, asphyxiated, faces leeched and gray, their eyes bulging from their sockets, some of them still clutching their belongings to their chests.

She found Coulton lying facedown in the aisle, his skin white and chalky, shriveled, like a hand left too long in the bath, as if all the blood had been drained from him.

"Oh no, no, no, no," she whispered, cradling his head in her lap. The blood from her own wounds was getting on his skin, on his face. She closed his eyelids, leaving a bloody thumbprint on each. That was when she heard a scraping sound above her, and she looked up, uncomprehending, and something crashed mightily and the carriage shuddered and rocked side to side, and then she understood. They were on the roof.

She got painfully back up, made her way forward to the platform. The wind ripped at her. She fumbled across to the next car and gripped the railing hard, her teeth clenched, and looked up. She could see Walter, scrabbling and clawing at someone, a huge woman, her shredded skirts rippling out around her there in the wind. She heard Alice Quicke shouting from above the forward carriage, and she tried to think.

Then her eyes fell on the coupling between the cars, the chain rattling there.

It was, she knew, their only chance. She leaned out, tried to unscrew the turnbuckle. It didn't move, didn't even budge. The carriages were grinding and clattering together, the ties roaring past underneath in a blur. She heard Walter scrabble up above, heard the big stranger cry out, and then both plunged off the side of the roof, and Margaret gasped in pain and fell back.

It was no use.

She could feel the cuts in her stomach. There was blood all down her front. The wind was in her ears, in her eyes, stinging.

And then, as if from a long way off, Margaret Harrogate slowly grit her teeth, and got back to her feet, and leaned out and pulled at the coupling for all she was worth.

Alice pulled the trigger.

She watched the bullet go into Jacob Marber, strike him full in the chest, saw him shudder and spin sideways in the wind and then straighten and keep walking, steadily, quickly, toward them.

She fired again, and again, unloaded her weapon, and each time the bullets seemed to strike him and be absorbed by the dark core of him and just pass on and through, somehow, though it made no sense and broke every law of nature Alice had ever trusted in. Marber didn't react at all, just kept coming on, the air darkening in front of him.

Charlie had crawled to the far end of the roof, clinging to it, and was hollering at her. Alice tried to shove Marlowe after him but the boy wouldn't go, just peered up at her, his face smooth. It was like something had happened inside him, seeing that woman Brynt.

"Go, Marlowe," she cried. "Go with Charlie! Go!"

She glanced back at Jacob Marber. And that was when she saw it: a long curved scythe of darkness, like a tentacle of smoke, rising up out of the monster and then thrusting itself forward, toward her, and she couldn't get out of the way fast enough, and she felt something pierce her side, punch through her ribs with a searing pain, and then she was lifted impossibly up off her feet and held suspended there in the rushing wind, impaled by that darkness.

The pain was more than she'd ever known. She was clutching at the darkness, clawing at it, gasping. And that was when Marlowe reached up, and put both his hands on her ribs, his thumbs folded inward, shining suddenly. His skin was blue, transparent, brighter than she had ever seen it. And she felt the wicked point of the scythe withdraw, and all at once she fell onto the roof and crumpled. The darkness, whatever it was, was helixing around Marlowe now, getting sucked sideways by the wind but re-forming and spiraling all around and he just stood in the middle of it, hands upturned, his little face looking back at Jacob Marber.

Marber was nearly at the edge of the roof, nearly at the gap, not even fifteen feet from them. And Marlowe suddenly held out both his little hands, so small, defenseless, as if to warn the monster back, as if to tell it to stop.

Alice stared, stunned. And the darkness that was circling him all at once hurtled toward Jacob Marber, and surrounded him, and underneath it all the darkness was somehow glowing with that same blue shining until the man was lost utterly in the light and there was only a vague outline of a figure, struggling there, as if trapped in blue amber.

And then Marlowe collapsed.

There came a loud *whump*, and the blue light arced out and away, and Jacob Marber, on his knees, raised his slow face. His eyes seemed to be bleeding darkness. His expression was twisted in a rictus of pain and fury. He got to his feet. Alice crawled forward, her side ablaze with pain, and she cradled the boy in her arms.

And it was then, all at once, with a slow grinding screech, that the gap between the cars began to widen, the distance to open out, and she could see the tracks racing past below, and the back half of the train was sparking and slowing and pulling away from them.

Alice crouched on the roof, holding the little boy in her arms, her hair whipping out around her face. Far down the tracks, on the roof of the carriage, Jacob Marber stood facing them, motionless, while darkness swirled around him like a swarm of bees. He was watching, just watching, while they raced away, and all the while that he was still in sight it seemed to Alice he didn't move, until at last he was gone from view, and their train was racing on, northward, into Scotland.

The
VANISHING
of
JACOB MARBER

•

1873

12

KOMAKO AND TESHI

On the night before Komako Onoe—nine years old, twister of dust, witch child and sister to a dying girl—was to meet Jacob Marber in the flesh and witness something extraordinary, something that would change her life forever, she first lay with her little sister on their tatami and prayed.

She prayed to whatever god might be listening: *Save my sister, please.*

It was the month of hazuki. All of Tokyo was hot, muggy. Komako's wrist and the shadow of her wrist lifted and hung in front of the lantern, twinned and strange there in the glow of the brazier and the darkness of the sickroom floor.

"Show me, Ko," her little sister whispered, stirring, her eyes shining. "Show me again. Show me the girl in the dust."

The oak rafters of the theater creaked around them. Through the shutters, rickshaws rattled past over the wooden streets of the old quarter.

Komako did not think there was time. The third act was already half over and if the stagehands caught them underfoot they would be scolded or beaten or worse. She knew the kabuki and the tempers of its players the way other girls knew calligraphy and etiquette. But she slid back the screen with a soft click and crept in her slippers down to the trapdoor behind the ropes and pulleys, her little sister rising thin as smoke from her tatami to follow.

No one saw them go. The dark below the stage was sweltering and still. She waited until her sister was at the bottom of the crawl space and then went back up and pulled the braided cord of the trapdoor to shut it. Down through the slats drifted the singing of the ghost, the stamp and drag and stamp of the kabuki. Orange light from the stage fell in stripes over her mittened hands and face.

She could hear the rustle of her sister's obi dragging in the dust and she paused and turned. "Teshi," she whispered. "Teshi, do you need to rest?"

But her sister, five years old, stubborn, only set her pale face and crawled on past.

They found the paper box among stacks of props and old masks far at the back. It was filled with a silky gray dust, collected carefully by Komako. She unwrapped her hands. The skin was chapped and red-looking.

There was an old mirror, which she uncovered and laid flat for the smooth surface of it, and then she kneeled and dumped out the dust in a slow smoking pile and closed her eyes, waiting for the stillness to come. She could feel the sweat trickle down her rib cage. The dust was cool to the touch and then it got colder. A chill radiated through the heels of her palms and she bit her lip at the quickness of it. Then it came over her. The ache crept into the bones of her wrists, her elbows. She turned her hands slowly, and slowly the dust turned too, rippled across the dark mirror, and her reflection and her sister's reflection shuddered and dissolved in the swirling sand. Komako could not feel her arms. The cold was creeping into her chest. She opened her eyes and molded the air, gently, softly, and as she did so the dust came together into the shape of a little silhouette, doll-like, and it bowed its little head to Teshi, and she heard her sister laugh softly.

"Make her dance, Ko," her sister breathed.

And Komako, working her fingers like a puppeteer, danced the little dust creature across the glass of the mirror, its hands pressed demurely together, its legs sawing and folding in a perfect imitation of a kabuki princess.

In the gloom she heard a change in her sister's breathing and glanced across. Teshi's eyes were dark and big. Her lips looked very red.

"Teshi?" Komako whispered in concern, her damp hair plastered to her temples. She let the dust swirl and fold itself back down into an inert soft pile. Her hands throbbed. "We should go back up, now. You need to rest."

Her little sister was weaving, weakly, as if she might fall over.

"Oh, it's cold, Ko," she mumbled. Her white skin almost glowed in the darkness. "Why is it so cold?"

Gekijo mausu, the two sisters were called. *Theater mice*. The Ichimura-za had stood in the crowded Asakusa Saruwaka-cho district nearly twenty years, ablaze with fire lanterns, famous throughout Tokyo for its kabuki. The two girls lived there after hours and cared for the props and kept the doors locked and the braziers cold, the candles snuffed. The theater had burned to the ground in 1858 and the fear of fire was still real in a city of wood and paper. After the old master retired from the stage his son Kikunosuke kept the girls on. They went unpaid but ate what was left by the actors, balls of sweet rice, half bowls of broth, a fried dumpling on lucky nights. Winter mornings they would hunch over a charcoal brazier while curtains of rain swept the shop fronts outside, and the theater creaked emptily around them, and they'd imagine they were the only two in all the world. For their round eyes and pale skin set them apart. They were hafu and belonged nowhere and to no one. Many were the alleys they would not walk because of the urchins and rag boys who threw rocks and chased them. Yes, they knew what the world could be, its cruelty. Justice existed only on the stage. Their father had sailed off to his own country far in the west while Teshi was still in the womb and when work dried up their mother in despair had tied Teshi to her back and taken Komako by the hand and begged her way north to Tokyo. That was Komako's earliest memory, walking through the big city gates in the rain.

Their mother was the daughter of a poor calligrapher long in the grave and did herself die of a fever in the poorhouse just two years after Teshi's birth. Komako remembered little about her. The softness of her hair in the candlelight. A sadness crinkling the eyes. Stories she used to tell some nights of yōkai and the spirit world and of the girls' tall father, bearded, orange-haired like a dragon. All of that had faded with the years. Komako did not know anymore how much of what she remembered was real. But she would tell Teshi that their mother had cradled her in the night in a giant wooden shoe, and had sung to her, her little cricket, and she would watch her sister's face in the moonlight for the dream creeping over her features. Sometimes she would tell how she, Komako, only five years old, had carried Teshi through the rainy streets day after day and snuck into a theater for the heat and there crouched in the back listening to the kabuki and when it was all over how she'd hid under a bench and kept her sister quiet with a finger in her mouth. When they were caught she clung to Teshi and screamed and kicked out at the stagehand who'd been sweeping the house but was dragged backstage all the same. The old master just sat very still in his white makeup, staring. He asked nothing. With his wig already removed and the great folds of his robes pouring out around him he had looked like a living demon and Komako had been terrified. At last the master grunted, smoothed out his whiskers.

"That is your brother, little mouse?" he said, in his slow deep voice.

Komako clutched her sister closer.

"Sister, sir," she whispered.

"Hm," he murmured. He looked over at the stagehand kneeling at the screen. "There are already mice here in the walls. I do not think two more will matter."

"You must not ever talk about it," she used to tell her little sister. "Not what I can do. Not ever."

"But what if it helped people? What if there was a fire, and you could save someone?"

"How could I save anyone?"

"You could put out the fire. With the dust."

She shook her head firmly. "It doesn't work like that, Teshi. And they wouldn't understand, they'd be too afraid."

She said this in part because she herself was afraid. It was a kind of wrongness in her and it had never not been a part of her. Even as a very young girl she'd feared it, feared the door in her mind, the door into the dark. That's how she thought of it. If she held her palms over dust, that door would swing open inside her, and pull her through, and she would stand trembling in an absolute blackness turning her wrists blindly, blood loud in her ears while a chill set its hooks in her flesh. What she could do was not witchcraft; the dust was like a living thing. She'd believed for years it was a part of the spirit world she was glimpsing, but there was no beauty in it, and therefore it could not be so. Her gift worked only on dust, not on sand, not on dirt. But with dust she could twist and lift and turn and give life, creating silver ribbons in the darkness, blossoms of ash, and the older she grew the more precise her control. Always her little sister's eyes would be shining and she'd grip the edges of her threadbare kimono and stare and Komako would stare also, almost like it wasn't her doing it at all, almost like the dust had its own desires, and the two girls would just see whatever it was the dust wanted them to see.

"What's it like, Ko?" Teshi whispered one night. "Is it very awful for you?"

Komako ran her chapped fingers through her sister's hair. Those fingers were red and sore all the time and she wrapped them in strips of linen to hide their appearance. "Imagine a darkness," she murmured. "Imagine that darkness is inside you, but it's not a part of you. You feel it there. It's always waiting."

Teshi shivered. "Does it scare you?"

"Sometimes. Not always."

But Teshi didn't understand about fear, not truly. Komako knew this. The first time she ever saw Komako working the dust, she shrieked with laughter. That was before she started to get sick. She was three years old and holding an apple and the apple fell to the polished floor, but Teshi just stood, stunned, watchful, staring at Komako's hands, at the intricate forms they made in the air, at the dust in its dancing, and then she grinned a huge grin and clapped her hands together and shrieked.

"Komako, Ko! Look what you can do!" For her, Ko's gift was *play*. Everything was play. She'd poke her face through the wall where Komako squatted over the night pot, peeing, and giggle. Or stack boxes in the actors' room below and climb teetering to the top and reach up through the cracks in the ceiling with her fingers to wiggle them spookily beside her sister's tatami until Komako caught sight of them and screamed.

When the sickness came over her it did so gradually, and at first they thought she was just tired, and then that she had caught a chill in the autumn air, and that it must pass. Her little sister wasn't afraid at all. But Komako was; she was often afraid, mostly for her sister, who seemed so small and precious and frail. Her sister would lie awake coughing, blood flecking her lips, her skin going whiter and whiter. Komako took her to the Portuguese doctor at the free clinic, but he could not help her. She went to the witch in the old quarter, three times, the witch who calmed angry yōkai, who remembered the old ways, but that witch only gave Teshi a folded packet of dried moss and told her to drink it each night as the moon was rising, and nothing ever came of it.

"You must pay me better," she said, clutching Komako's wrist, "if you want the spirits to hear you. You must show me something rare."

As if she knew what Komako could do, as if she suspected.

After that Komako had kept Teshi away from the witch. But then there'd been that terrible summer night, a year ago exactly, when Teshi's skin had burned and her eyes rolled back in her head, and she lay in Komako's arms, gasping, unable to breathe, going still. Komako had driven her fists into her own eyes, tears on her cheeks, and *prayed*— prayed to the dead, to her mother's spirit, to any power that was—for her sister not to die.

This was in their tiny room at the top of the theater, late at night, alone, and Komako had felt the prickling cold come into her wrists and creep up her arms and begin to ache and throb. It had nothing to do with the dust, with anything. She'd just held her sister close to the brazier, felt her sister flutter in her arms like a trapped wing, and prayed.

And Teshi hadn't died. Somehow, she hadn't. But after that night some fire had gone out of her, and her skin had paled, until it seemed nearly translucent, and her lips had gone a blood-dark red. Three thin red lines had appeared at her throat, like necklaces of blood. Komako would wake to find her standing sometimes in the darkness, confused, peering down at her tatami as if trying to remember something important. A white silhouette looking strange, unearthly, in the moonlight. More spirit than flesh.

And she was cold, she said, all the time, so cold.

Cold as the dead, thought Komako.

That was the summer the cholera burned through the old quarter. It came in a fury, and faded with the autumn rains, but came back again the next summer, so that the dead were stacked like cut wood in the muggy streets and the shops stood empty and the hollow-eyed survivors burned incense to appease whatever angry spirit was killing their loved ones.

A year of fear. Teshi began walking in the night, sleepwalking, it seemed, if sleep she ever did, pacing the dark polished floors of the theater, barefoot. Komako caught her sister one night standing in the dark door to the street, staring unseeing out at the night, the warm air washing over her. Weeks later Teshi, alone, glided down into the alleys past the gambling dens and stood over the infected dead where they lay in pools of torchlight. Murmuring to herself about a door, a door she could not open. Komako had awoken to find the door standing wide and had hurried out and found her so, and folded a blanket over her shoulders, and steered her for home. There were workers and grieving figures in the firelight, watching. In the morning someone painted the characters for vermin on the theater door in red paint. Two nights later a folded note was delivered to Master Kikunosuke, after a late performance, warning of the demon child, and after that Komako saw what everyone saw, even the stagehands, even the actors who'd known Teshi since she was a baby.

"Cursed," they'd whisper. "The disease comes in the night on two legs, crying like a child."

And it was true, Komako knew it was true, that Teshi really was different. She hardly slept, ate nothing, was silent sometimes for days. It was not the cholera that was in her. But whatever it was, Komako at last gave in to her own fears and sent word to the witch, offering the one thing she could in exchange: the secret of the dust.

Three days she waited for a reply, and when it came, it was a folded paper delivered by a nervous boy in ragged pants. It was but a single word.

Come.

And she did, she took her sister out, into the dangerous streets, into the sickness, for the first time in months. A warm rain was falling. She led Teshi through the alley and across a cobbled road full of rickshaws abandoned and still and then down another alley, into the poor quarter. There were dead bundled in the back of carts, a reek of sickness and misery. The walking was slow, their wooden geta sinking in the muck. Her sister, bundled and cloaked to hide her appearance, coughed wetly.

The alleys of the poor were narrow and humid and crowded with workshops. Water dripped off sloping eaves. In the shadows figures paused at their labors to watch the girls pass.

The witch's house was a house long fallen into ruin. It stood surrounded by a tangle of dwarf bamboo at the back of a barren lot. The upper windows, long and low in the old style, had all been boarded over. The roof was missing tiles. There were bamboo blinds tied askew over the eaves of a deep verandah and when the girls walked across it the wood creaked and snapped with their weight.

They stopped at the doorless dark.

"Mistress?" called Komako.

Her sister coughed beside her.

"Mistress, hello? Are you here?"

There was a slow movement from the darkness within. A rustling, as of wings. Komako felt her sister press close.

"I did not think you would be back," called a voice. It was soft, almost beautiful. "What did you bring me, on'nanoko?"

Komako kneeled and untied a bundle from her back and laid it in front of the darkness. Slowly she unwrapped it. It was the paper box of silky dust, taken from the theater. It gleamed silver and black on the doorstep there and as Komako moved back the reflected light flared and wobbled and slid away.

"Closer," said the voice. "Bring it closer. My eyes are not what they were."

Komako rose then and brought the box into the hot darkness. Her eyes adjusted. She stepped up over the edge of the receiving room and kneeled and with her damp face bowed she inched forward on her knees and set the paper box down in front of the gray figure.

The witch did not touch it. "Yes," she said quietly. "Good. I do not know what can be done for your sister, but I will try. You understand?"

Komako nodded.

"Bring the dust." The witch rose smoothly and led them into the ruined house. Along a hot and airless corridor Teshi gripped Komako's hand. Her little fingers were cold, her fingernails sharp, Komako could feel it even through her linen wrappings. Most of the shoji screens had long ago rotted away and emptiness and darkness opened up on either side as they went. There was a smell of sour vegetables, of rodents. Ahead they saw daylight and then they stepped down into a courtyard garden. Despite the misty rain the day was bright after the dark of the house. The garden had been beautiful once but was weed-choked now

and sad. A stone memorial stood uncared for on a rock in the middle
of a green pond, reeds grown up all around it, and a little farther on,
a wood footbridge had collapsed. All this they passed in silence and
they went up onto a covered veranda and then back into the darkness.

The witch was not old. Her hair was very beautiful and worn
high and folded with twin bone hairpins glinting in it, the kanzashi
as sharp and white as her neck. She glided quickly and silently in a
stiff furisode decorated with patterned flowers and she did not turn
or slow for the girls. Komako had heard she was a widow by her own
hand, disfigured as a punishment for her evil, that she had stayed shut
up in that house since the days of the shogunate. She wondered if any
of it was true.

The witch lived in two rooms at the very back of the house. She
crossed to a brazier, lit despite the heat, and lifted a blanket from the
mesh and lit a lantern and set this at the foot of a tatami mat. There
was a teakettle half-corroded, sunk in shadow on the floor. A porcelain
bowl of darkness just visible.

She turned and was still. Her hands were lost in the long sleeves of
her furisode. "You have taken the child to a physician?"

"We are poor, mistress."

"The Portuguese clinic, then."

Komako nodded. "They cannot find anything the matter," she said.
"It is a chill. And a weakness. She is tired all the time. It is getting
worse."

The witch frowned. Her eyes, Komako saw, were strangely flat and
without expression, as if they had been painted on. "You. Child. Come
here, lie down."

Teshi came forward. She lay down on the tatami. The witch went
into the darkness and was gone a long time and when she came back
she was carrying a wooden tray in shaking hands. Its bowls and sticks
of incense and wax and the ancient knife with its bone handle all rattled

softly. She had drawn a line of ash across her forehead with one blackened thumb.

The witch took a white stone and pressed it into Teshi's palm and folded her fist around it.

"Hold this. Do not let it go. What is your name, child?"

"Teshi Onoe."

"And what is your age?"

"Five, mistress."

"From where do you come?"

"Asakusa Saruwaka-cho district. In Tokyo."

The witch made a clicking noise with her tongue. "From where do you *come?*" she asked again.

Teshi hesitated. She glanced at Komako. "I don't—"

"Dust, child. That is where you come from. And it is to dust you shall return." The witch lifted her face out of the darkness. "And what is it you seek?" she whispered.

Teshi said nothing.

The witch held out a cup of tea. "Drink this." Teshi drank. Then the witch unfolded herself from her knees and raised her arms and her voluminous sleeves fell back. She was holding two blocks. She banged them sharply over Teshi and a cloud of pale dust burst the darkness, faded. She walked all around the girl, banging the blocks. Then she began to sing.

It was a song unlike any Komako had heard, eerie and sad at once. Her little sister's eyes grew heavy and then closed. Her skin was like a furnace. The witch fell quiet and lit a taper of incense and the coal traced a red arc in the dark. Then in the stillness there came a soft click.

The white stone had fallen out of Teshi's fist.

"So it must be," the witch said quietly.

Komako felt a sudden fear. She didn't know what the witch could mean by that. Teshi's eyelids fluttered, her breathing came fast. Komako reached for her sister's sleeve.

The witch did not look away from Teshi when she said softly, "The dust is what animates your gift, on'nanoko. And that same dust is in your sister, making her sick. She must fight its nature."

Something moved in the darkness beyond the second room. Komako turned her face, the hairs at the back of her neck prickling. "Is someone here?"

The witch only gestured to the paper box. "The dust is drawn to her for a reason. Something attracts it, traps its essence. Something . . . remarkable. I have heard of this, but I have never seen it."

"The dust," she echoed, afraid.

The witch smoothed out her obi in the shadow, watchful.

"Please," Komako begged, "is it *me*? Am *I* making her sick?"

"But why would it be you, little one?" said the witch, in a tone of voice that suggested she knew far more than she let on. "Show me what you can do."

Komako unwrapped her hands slowly. Her palms were raw and itching. She could not keep from trembling as she opened the lid of the box. "It does not always work," she whispered.

The witch came closer. Komako could smell the sour milk smell of her skin. She hesitated, her hands hovering over the dust inside, its gathered darkness.

"You will help my sister?" she said bravely. "You must promise."

The witch made an impatient sound. "It is not easy, on'nanoko."

"But you can do *something*? Promise me."

A darkness passed across the witch's features. "Something can be done for her, yes," said the witch, choosing her words with care. "I will do what I can. I promise that."

Komako held her fingers, outstretched, high over the open box. She felt the familiar coldness seep into her wrists and winced.

And then the dust, in a long thin column, poured smoothly upward and formed, suspended in the air, a moving ball, quicksilver and beautiful in the gloom. The witch caught her breath sharply. Komako's wrists were already hurting. She was tired. She curled her hands around and around the dust, as if shaping it, holding it suspended like a tiny moon, and then she sighed and dropped her hands and the planet of dust collapsed all at once down into the box, lifeless again, inert.

The witch was staring at her. "It is true," she whispered. "You—are a talent."

"I'm not anything. I'm just . . . me." Komako, shaking, folded her red hands into her armpits for the warmth. She felt exhausted. Her face was wet. "You will help my sister, mistress?"

The witch had got to her feet and drifted to the edge of the warm darkness, and she stared out now, unseeing. "This is the girl," she said quietly. "You were right."

A voice replied from the shadows. "Ko-ma-ko . . . ," it said, slowly, as if tasting her name syllable by syllable. "Yes, Maki-chan. This is the girl."

Komako scrambled to her feet, stumbling backward.

Two figures stepped into the spill of light. They were men, Westerners. The taller had a thick black beard and wore a long black frock coat despite the mugginess and he turned a silk hat in his fingers. He had deep-set eyes, and a craggy worried brow, and ink-black hair raked back off his forehead. His clothes smelled faintly of soot.

"Do not be alarmed," he murmured. "We had to see what you could do; I had to see it. For myself. I had to be sure."

He seemed very tall. She stared at his companion—stouter, red-faced, mopping at his moist face—and then back at the man. "Who are you?" she said. "What do you want?"

He came closer. He stood looking down at Teshi lying on the tatami, small and deathly pale. "Your poor sister," he said. "She must be very cold?"

"What do you *want?*" Komako said again, fiercely now, stepping in front of Teshi. She clenched her small fists. She couldn't imagine what a foreigner would want of her. And then she thought of something. "Did my . . . did my father send you?"

"Oh, child," said the witch.

The stranger didn't answer. He was filled with an immense, slow concentration. He crouched down over the open box of dust and took off his black gloves. He had the most beautiful fingers, long and elegant and soft. The skin was like milk. He moved them in a series of strange gestures, as if he were writing in the air.

And then Komako gasped.

For the dust in the box was moving. She watched as it flowed up, up, into the man's pale hands, leaping playfully from finger to finger, twisting around his wrists, a silver ribbon of dust. He held it there a long moment, as if consoling it, as if it were a living thing. Then he let it pour back down, smoothly, into the open box, and he closed the lid with his long fingers, and he met her eye.

"I'm not here from your father," he whispered. He ran a hand through his beard. "What we can do, Komako . . . It is called dustwork, where I come from. It must frighten you sometimes? It must hurt you, to use your gift? And you cannot do it for long, without losing yourself in it?"

She nodded, fingers at her lips, afraid to speak.

"For me also," said the man, sadness in his voice.

13

JACOB REAPER, JACOB BLOOD

The bearded man was, of course, Jacob Marber. Young still, in those days, his world still full of the possible.

The summer light was going when he left the witch's garden. The mud streets beyond her house were quiet and there were crows on the wet roof tiles, watchful. He and Coulton hailed a rickshaw and made their bumpy way back, past darkening shop fronts, torchlights in the alleys, all the way back to the foreigners' inn above the harbor. The diseased city stank of decay. Jacob held his silk hat in his fingers and turned it, turned it, preoccupied, brooding about the girl Komako and what he'd seen her do. He felt strangely happy. He'd never met another who could work the dust.

The rickshaw hit a loose wood block in the street and lurched and Coulton put out a fast hand, swaying. "Well," he said, breaking his silence. "She isn't coming with us easy, that one."

Jacob glanced over in surprise. "I thought it went rather well."

"The devil it did."

"She'll come around. Give her a day."

Coulton gave him that look. Jacob didn't know the man well. Coulton was older by ten years and liked to remind Jacob of it and to use it to defend a cynicism Jacob suspected wasn't even entirely real. "Listen, lad," Coulton said now. "You get to my age, you seen a share of crazy in your life. I'm telling you, that one ain't picking up what we're putting down."

Jacob put on his hat, slowly, adjusting the brim. He watched the man in rags running their rickshaw, barefoot, his skin shining with sweat. The tall wheel whirred at his left elbow. He said, "There's always a way. She'll listen."

"There ain't *always* a way."

Jacob grinned.

He watched Coulton brush grimly at his sleeves. "You're like a bloody puppy, lad. I worry for you, I do."

The truth was, though, he wasn't half so sure as he let on. The rickshaw rattled on, into the coming darkness, the streets gleaming. It wasn't only their long sea journey, and it wasn't only this little girl and her sister. Lately, he kept seeing his boyhood self, struggling as a sweep in the grimy narrow chimneys of Vienna, half-starved, red-eyed, desperate, in those lonely years after his twin's death.

That was before Henry Berghast had come into his life, before he'd been plucked out of its horrors, taken back to Cairndale, clothed, fed, *guided*. But he'd already got sick from that first life; his breathing hadn't ever been right; and there was a different kind of sickness in his heart. He always thought: Why couldn't Berghast have come sooner, why couldn't he have come while his brother Bertolt still lived?

Hating himself and Berghast and fate and God even as he thought it.

Now, from the middle of the road, they heard chanting, saw a procession of monks in yellow robes banging wood blocks, singing in their strange intonations. The rickshaw puller waited at the side for the monks to pass. Jacob frowned, looked away. No, it wasn't just the old worry, the one he'd lived with all his life, as long as he could remember, that weighed on him. It was also the dreams.

At least that's what he told himself they were, dreams. He hadn't told Coulton yet. He didn't know why not. Maybe it was the peculiar vividness of them, maybe it was just he didn't think he could explain how real they felt, how undreamlike. They had to do with his dead brother, always, though his brother wasn't in them, didn't appear even as a memory. Instead there was always a figure, a lady, shrouded in darkness, dressed in an old-fashioned high-collared dress and a cloak and silk hat, talking to Jacob calmly, reasonably, in gentle tones, questioning him, speaking in riddles. Always it took place in whatever room he'd fallen asleep in, the ship's cabin on their voyage, the creaking old Japanese inn three streets up from the harbor here in Tokyo, wherever, and always it was just as if he were waking normally up, the woman seated across the room, a visitor, bringing news from a world unimagined.

"You're back," Jacob would say, frightened, in the dream. "What are you?"

Are we not all we can imagine, Jacob? would come the reply, low, soft, soothing.

He'd try to sit up in his bedclothes, try to see the woman's face. "What do you want? Why do you come to me?" His own voice sounding querulous and frightened to his ears.

And so would begin the strange call-and-response of the dream, like a catechism, the questions he seemed unable to ignore, the answers that came from him almost unwillingly, almost as if he couldn't help it:

What is it you want, Jacob?

"To know those that I love are well. To bring those I have loved back to me."

And are those that you loved not with you always?

"I fear, and I do not know."

It is your brother, your twin brother that I mean.

"I did not save him. I did not save him."

The woman's soft voice, filling then with love: *Death is not death, Jacob, and nothing is forever. I can reach him still, as can you. And if Berghast will not let you open the orsine, you must find your own way to me. . . .*

And the dream would turn then, melt away, into some more ordinary dreaming, and when at last he awoke, unsettled, he'd be half-unsure he'd even dreamed it at all.

When they got back to the inn, he and Coulton removed their shoes and took the offered slippers and went quietly upstairs, the dark polished wood floors gleaming, their bodies drenched with sweat. There was a smell of blossoms in the air, cut flowers in a bowl in the hallway. After a few minutes they heard a muffled greeting, and the innkeeper's wife appeared, a warm bottle of sake wrapped in a towel. She kneeled, opened the paper screen, entered, kneeled, and closed it behind her. Then she lit the lanterns, never once looking in their faces. There was such an unhurried grace in this country, Jacob marveled. So much beauty in the smallest of gestures.

When they were alone again, he said, just as if they hadn't stopped speaking of it, just as if he was continuing his thought: "She has my talent, Frank. The dust."

Coulton made a little movement of his head, said nothing. He was taking off his wet greatcoat.

"You saw what I saw."

"Aye," said Coulton reluctantly. "And I seen her sister too. *That* ain't your talent, lad."

"Maybe. Or maybe it's the dust that's done it."

"You never done nothing like that."

"I've never tried."

"Aye." Coulton grinned, pouring out a knuckle of sake. "Is that envy I see in you, lad?"

Jacob frowned, irritated. The man was teasing but, in truth, some part of him was fascinated by the possibility. He had never been able to find the limits of dustwork; who could say what it was capable of? But he said none of this out loud. Instead he said, "Easiest way to get her to come with us would be to promise to help the sister. That's her weak point. Tell her we could cure her at Cairndale."

"We can't cure what that girl is."

Jacob raised his face and saw Coulton watching him with hooded eyes and then he said it out loud, the thing they'd been avoiding naming: "Because she's a litch. That's what you mean, isn't it? The little sister's a litch."

"Aye. And the poor lass thinks her sister's just sick."

"She knows the truth," said Jacob softly. "Even if she won't let herself believe it."

Coulton crossed to the window. The wooden shutters were held up by a stick. "I just don't see how it were done. Making a litch, that takes a process, don't it? It don't just *happen*."

"According to Berghast," Jacob pointed out.

"Aye. According to Dr. Berghast."

"But what does he know? Has he ever even seen a litch, in life? Maybe it could work like this, too. Maybe there's something in dustwork that makes it possible—"

He faltered, didn't finish the thought. He was thinking of the woman in his dream but he hadn't realized he was until he'd spoken and now, blushing, he didn't finish. But Coulton was peering, troubled, out at the torches moving through the cobbled streets, and seemed not to have noticed. He lifted his shirt, wiped at his face. The locals were carting the choleric dead out of the city.

"Right. So this girl," he said, "this Komako. We're saying *she* made her sister a litch? And she don't even know she done it?"

"I guess we are."

Coulton turned. The anguish in his face made Jacob flinch. "And that would mean the wee girl, what's her name, Teshi—"

"—is already dead. Yes."

He heard Coulton sigh in the darkness.

"Fuck," he said quietly.

Jacob's earliest memory was of the dust.

He was four years old. It was a summer night, that grim children's home in Vienna. He was crouched sweating under a moth-eaten blanket, his brother beside him, both of them straining to hear the night nun's footsteps recede through the echoing halls. They were twins but not identical. His brother didn't have Jacob's gift, his talent, couldn't do what he could do. The light of a streetlamp from the open window was dimly visible through the blanket. He was working his little hands over the dust he'd scooped up from the corners of the room, making it swirl and shift and spiral, when one of the older boys tore the blanket from their cot. Jacob never knew what the boy saw, if he glimpsed his talent at work, if he even believed his eyes. His brother, Bertolt, was on his feet in an instant. Hurling himself at the bigger boy, tearing at his nightshirt and face in the dark dormitory, pummeling him with his fists, and though the other was older and bigger, Bertolt ripped at him with such a fury that it was the boy who cried for help and Bertolt who was hauled off by the throat, Bertolt who was beaten savagely, Bertolt who the nuns said had the devil in him.

The nuns never did forget that. But nor did the other boys, and after that, Jacob and his brother were left mostly alone.

Their days were spent picking oakum or sewing pieces of cloth and when they got a little older the nuns rented them out to factories on account of their size. They'd clamber between the machines, slide themselves into the gaps where the great whirring gears were punching away, in order to unsnare a loop of leather, or bang loose a jammed bolt. Bertolt never let Jacob go into the machines but went himself, even when he was getting too big for it. There were boys without fingers, boys without hands. A few years after, one Sunday afternoon, Bertolt took Jacob's hand and walked right out the open front doors of the factory, into the grime of the Unterstrass, to live as sweeps in the crews of kids working the chimneys of the great houses in Vienna's high streets. Bertolt was just like that, he'd walk into his own future and take Jacob with him, and Jacob loved him, admired him, wanted to be like him.

They became sweeps. Soot was different from ordinary dust, not as easy for Jacob to manipulate or draw into his hands, sticky and clumpy as it was, smearing over everything, and so the work was hard. He'd scrub and clamber and slide greasily along the shafts, gasping for breath, twisting as he went, a small boy in outsized clothes, the whites of his eyes showing. But he never cared much. Bertolt was the thing, the only thing that mattered, and they figured sweep work was safer than climbing inside the machines. They'd always had each other's backs. When he'd been sick with scarlet fever in the orphanage it was Bertolt, four years old, who mopped his brow and changed his sheets, not the nuns. It was Bertolt who brought him food scraps when he was punished with no dinner. It was Bertolt who gave him a reason not to give up. They had no recollection of their parents, had nothing to remember them by, and if there'd ever been a daguerreotype, or necklace, or memento, the nuns had not seen fit to preserve it. It was only the two of them, just the two of them, in all the world.

"Bertolt, what'll we do?" Jacob asked him one winter. They were freezing by then, starting to get too big for the sweep work, their knees and backs bruised and bleeding.

"We'll find something," said his brother. "There's always a way."

"What? What'll we find?"

"I don't know. But we'll find it."

Then two weeks later his brother suffocated in a chimney when he got stuck and the sweep boss left his little body unclaimed in a dirty alley and Jacob understood the only thing kids like them ever found was suffering and pain and death. And Jacob, in a rage he'd never felt before, had stalked the boss to a card table in a club in the dark hours of the morning and strangled him with the dust, strangled him until his eyes nearly burst from their sockets. He was ten years old.

He was alone after that, hiding, starving, afraid. That was the winter Henry Berghast found him, just as if he'd been searching for him all his life, the same winter he made the long journey, by railway and by coach, across Europe, across a slate-gray sea, to the chilly white halls of Cairndale.

Jacob was thinking about all that as he left Coulton, and went through the paper screen, to the adjoining room. The air was hot, unmoving. The sleeping mat had already been laid out on the floor, the strange hard round Japanese pillow at its end. He could hear Coulton clearing his nose, coughing roughly, moving about. He took off his shirt, unbuttoned his trousers, raked his hair back from his face. He didn't think he'd sleep.

The woman came to him that night, again, a brooding shadow in the corner of his dream.

"You're back," Jacob began, slowly, as he always began. "What . . . are you?"

And came the familiar reply: *Are we not all we can imagine, Jacob?*

But the words seemed hurried this time, as if she were impatient with the question. She lurked, shrouded in her usual darkness, but radiating a new and disturbing tension.

We are running out of time, she said suddenly, and folded her hands behind her.

Slowly, as if from a long way off, Jacob closed his eyes, opened them. He tried to shake his head. "This . . . is not a dream. I am not dreaming, am I?"

I wish there was more time. I must speak plainly.

"Yes—"

You are special, Jacob, you are not like the others. You have always known this. You will one day do great things, you will bring a great goodness into the world. You will help many people. And it will begin with Bertolt.

"Bertolt—?"

He is suffering, even now. His spirit is suffering.

Jacob rubbed at his face, disbelieving.

But there is a way to help him. Only you can do it, only you are strong enough. He can be brought back.

"What do you mean?" he whispered. "What do you mean, brought back—?"

Death is just a door. The orsine at Cairndale is the key, Jacob. Henry Berghast keeps it closed, his glyphic keeps it closed . . . but you must find a way to open it . . . The woman in the darkness seemed to pause. *I'm not what you think, Jacob. Remember that. There are those who will tell you I mean you harm. But you know—you can feel—that it is not so.*

"Wait. If the orsine is opened, the dead will come through—"

The best lies have truths inside them, Jacob. Henry Berghast is not to be trusted. He will tell you the orsine means destruction. It is not so. I want to help you, I want to help Bertolt. But you must let me.

He felt a dread go through him at that, even inside the dream, a cold and terrible foreboding, as if the words were a threat somehow, a promise of malice. And then he woke up.

The inn's timbers creaked around him. He lay on the tatami, drenched with sweat, listening to the darkness, to the absolute silence of the city outside. His heart was beating very fast. He wet his lips, feeling the dream fade. He opened his eyes.

There in the corner loomed the woman, radiating malice, impossibly tall and crooked like a shadow stretching across the ceiling, her face shrouded in darkness.

"*JACOB!*" she screamed at him, wild and fierce and horrifying.

He cried out, and scrambled instinctively for a weapon, anything, but there was nothing, and when he looked back, the woman was gone, the room was empty.

He was alone.

Frank Coulton knew how losing felt and he also knew what it was to be the last man at the table. He was thirty-four years old and a physical wreck, his lungs bad in the morning from a lifetime of smoking and his back bad in the night from everything else. He was losing his hair, would be bald in a few years. He had auburn sideburns that he'd grown out into a butcher's beard, and hands so thick and fat from punching that he looked sometimes like he was wearing gloves. He was stout of stature and thick-necked like a bull and he liked his waistcoats brightly colored. But he'd been alone more than not, and he didn't always know how to be with other people. He'd been a gambler, a riverboat operator, a soldier for the Union army; he'd been an apprentice bookbinder, and a carpenter in the great libraries of London and Boston. He'd had a whole lot of nothing good, and not a lot of something bad; and if you asked him either way, he'd take the something over nothing every time.

He'd never concede it but his heart, as the ballads would have it, was pure. He believed in the steadfast virtues. Goodness wasn't a matter of perspective and he'd seen too much suffering to want to see more of it in the world. But the wrong kind of hoping led to bitterness, and bitterness led only to the gutter. He'd seen it in the Union field hospitals, men giving up. His own talent was strength. He could contract his flesh down into a packed solid so dense that a single punch could crack a brick wall and not even split a knuckle. A bullet on a battlefield would lodge shallowly in his flesh, painful but harmless. Yet it felt to him, every time he used his talent, like the very walls and ceiling and even the open sky was closing in on him, a tremendous weight, so that he couldn't breathe. This being, Dr. Berghast had told him, a common condition on the continent, known to the new generation of mentalists as claustrophobia—a side effect, it seemed, of what he could do. He'd learn to live with it, Berghast had told him. Aye, he'd agreed, but how? *Simply by going on, Mr. Coulton,* Berghast had replied. *Just simply by going on.*

Well, he knew something about that, about going on.

He woke in the morning in the rickety old inn, high over the misty Tokyo harborfront, and he sat up at once, his nightshirt already damp. He glared around the empty room.

Something was watching him.

He *felt* it.

In fact, he'd been feeling it for weeks now, ever since they disembarked in Tokyo, before that even, while hugging the jungle coast on that creaking old bark up from Singapore, standing at the ship's rails, watching the sailors clamber through the rigging in the haze. As if some presence stalked them. He'd caught flashes of something from the corner of his eye, movement, a blurred figure, but when he turned to look, always it was gone. Lately it had got worse, more intense, the hairs at the back of his neck prickling so that he'd whirl around suddenly, at unexpected moments, trying to see whatever it was that followed, and Jacob would look at him like he was mad.

He got dressed now, uneasy, thinking about it, and he folded up the tatami and left it there on the dark gleaming floor. He could hear the innkeeper's wife running a brush over the stairs. Jacob's room was tidy, empty: had a habit of going his own way, that lad did.

Despite everything, he should've felt pleased. They'd been hunting the Onoe girl for weeks, on the thinnest of leads, trying to track her down in a humid city wracked with cholera. And now they'd done it; and they had only to convince her to go with them, and they could be gone, out of the damn country, back to the world they knew.

Coulton reached for his hat and suddenly paused, hand in the air. It'd been turned on end, upside down, left standing like that in a way he'd never do. He wondered if the innkeeper's wife had been in while he was sleeping, or if Jacob had done it, but neither seemed likely. Had he left it like that, in his tiredness? Maybe.

He ate a breakfast of rice and grilled fish out of the little wooden box left at his door, using his fingers, ignoring the peculiar little sticks for eating, and then he went out. The streets were eerily quiet.

In his billfold he'd kept an address for a brothel in the Yoshiwara district and he went there now, past the elaborate three-story gabled buildings, their wicker balconies, their horned tile roofs. There were a few Japanese in dark little suits, with silk hats, looking strange to Coulton's eye. But most of the men adrift in the street at that hour wore dark kimonos, or rough trousers, and went about in groups of two or three.

The brothel he sought, House of the Yellow Blossom, was dim, musty, deserted. A woman sweeping out the entrance stopped and looked at him a long sullen moment and then disappeared into the gloom, and then in her place appeared, fixing her hair, wearing a bright red robe with a white sash, a young girl, who said something in rapid Japanese.

Coulton took off his hat, shook his head.

"I'm looking for this man," he said. And gave her the paper he'd been given.

She bowed, took the paper, bowed again. And then she retreated into the house, and Coulton stood and paced and opened the door to peer back out at the muggy daylight in the wide street. At last the man he sought appeared, a middle-aged man with a beard already gray, a sour expression in his eyes. He was wearing a robe, blinking in the brightness.

"Captain Johannes?" said Coulton.

The captain grimaced, reached into his pockets, withdrew a pipe. "You'd be the Cairndale fellow," he said.

"Aye."

"The one wantin ship out to the Singapore colony."

"Calcutta, actually."

"I don't cross to Calcutta," said the captain. "Free ports only. I can get you to Singapore. But there's plenty of barks out from there. Steamships too, you want to book passage all the way through to England. Were you wantin to come in, talk it over?"

Coulton peered past him, into the interior. "Is there any need?"

The man grinned suddenly, showing two missing teeth. "Your employers already give me all I need. Unless there's a change of plan. There ain't a change of plan, now?"

Coulton thought about the girl, about what Jacob had said the night before. He looked at the captain, his gray eyes. "Give me one week more," he said. "Keep yourself reachable, like. I'll let you know if there's any change to be made."

"I'll be here, waitin. It don't hurt me none." He winked. "Unless I pay them to. Three passengers, was it?"

"Does it matter?"

The captain shrugged. "Not to me."

Before going out that morning, Coulton had rolled a ball of rice in a tissue paper and stuffed it into the pocket of his coat, and now, like an indigent, he drifted along the street in the shadow side, unwrapping the sticky rice and eating it with his fingers. He caught the unsettled stares of passersby and smiled angrily. It didn't matter what part of the world he was in. Folk just liked to look down on other folk.

In the afternoon he went back across the old quarter, through the cholera-stricken streets, past the sweltering shop fronts, empty now, dark figures huddled far at the back, the bodies wrapped in white cloth and left out in the yards, the rustling of crows lifting and circling and dropping again back down, the reek of sickness everywhere. At the ancient overgrown house where Maki-chan lived, he paused, then rapped sharply on the doorframe, and waited.

She fascinated him, true. Dr. Berghast had provided the introductions. She was a witch by local custom but Coulton knew an educated woman when he met one and there was in Maki-chan something formidable and attractive. She spoke a near flawless English. She knew things she shouldn't. She greeted him in the warm darkness and bowed and gestured that he follow her and then, shuffling in her tiny slippers, led him to the pavilion in the overgrown garden.

A tea had been set out, as if she'd been expecting him. The pot was still hot.

Coulton pulled from his waistcoat pocket a little leather drawstring purse. It clinked in his fingers, heavy with coin. He held the purse out but she did not take it and after a moment, uncertain, he set it on the floor between them.

"It's what we agreed on," he said. "It's all there, like. You maybe want to count it?"

She made no move to do so. She only inclined her head, then again met his eye with her steady dark gaze. Her eyes, he thought, were beautiful.

He cleared his throat. "It weren't what it looked like, yesterday," he said lamely.

Her expression didn't change.

"The girl," he tried again. "She's a queer one, aye. But not so queer as all that."

She wet her lips, and he fell silent. Then she said, in clear precise English: "You are, I think, an unusual man yourself, Coulton-san."

Coulton felt a heat rise to his cheeks. He wasn't an easily embarrassed man but there was something in this woman's gaze that unsettled him. He didn't answer. His knees were cramping from kneeling already and he shifted uncomfortably, trying to get the blood moving.

"It was not only Komako-chan, who surprised me yesterday," she said. "I did not expect Berghast-san to send talents to me."

Coulton looked at her in surprise. "You know about . . . talents?"

"The unseen world is all around us, Coulton-san. Though we do not often glimpse it." She kneeled very still with her delicate hands folded one atop the other in her lap. "My obaa-san used to say, we are each of us a house," she murmured. "Here." She tapped her breast. "And here." She tapped her forehead. "And every house will have its visitors. We must be gracious hosts."

Coulton felt himself starting to frown. "Talents," he said, "ain't like a person coming to call. It's just a part of a person, like a hand is. Or a thought is."

"Have you ever observed a water droplet roll into another?" she replied. "They are two, and then they are one. When a guest enters a house, it becomes the house."

Coulton studied her quietly. He didn't know quite what to say. Maybe it didn't matter. He wondered for a moment if she were a talent herself, if she had a gift also. Everything in this country seemed to go unsaid. After a long silence he asked, "How is it you come to know Dr. Berghast, like?"

Maki-chan smiled, and elaborately folded back her sleeves, and poured out the tea, taking her time with each gesture. "Oh, there are talents here too, Coulton-san," she said at last, again as if she could read his thinking. "It is not only your part of the world that knows of them. Though we do not gather above an orsine here, and we have no glyphic to help us find others. They must find us. But if this Onoe girl was revealed to Cairndale, then it is to Cairndale she must go. A glyphic's claim must be respected." The witch paused. "You did not imagine yours was the only such refuge in the world?"

He hadn't thought about it, in truth. He'd only always just gone where he was told, collected what kids he was told to collect. He knew there were talents in Paris because Berghast corresponded with them; but elsewhere in the world? He felt a sudden quick flare of anger, thinking that Berghast hadn't seen fit to inform him. Made him look foolish, it did. He frowned and he turned the little cup in his fingers and he blew on it to cool it. "So who is it you work for, then?" he asked.

Again, that smile. "Ah. I have been honored to work for *you*, Coulton-san," she replied.

It was no kind of answer. The little cloth purse with the strange Japanese coins in it still sat, untouched, on the floor between them. But Coulton felt something shift in that moment, a delicate balance, as if the payment had at last been accepted, and he marveled again at the precise customs of that land.

It was dark when Coulton got back to the inn. There was still no sign of Jacob and he cursed under his breath and then, standing with the inner screen open behind him, paused and turned slowly. He had the same creeping feeling, the feeling that someone was there.

"Hello?" he called softly.

The corridor was dark, the warm floor in shadow, the stairs and the polished railing visible in the gloom.

"I can *feel* you, like," he growled. "Don't think I can't."

Still there was nothing. After a moment, grimacing, he shut the screen with a snick and took off his hat and coat. Going mad his arse. He knew when there was a something, damn it.

The tatami again had been laid out and he stood looking down at it, irritable. It never did feel right, sleeping on a thin mat on the floor. But the inn was clear of vermin; and truth was, his back hurt him less in the mornings than it used to.

He was sweating lightly in his shirtsleeves, sitting cross-legged at the little desk, writing out their progress in the institute journal, when Jacob returned.

"Well," he said looking up. "Look at what the bloomin cat dragged in. Where you been at, all day, then?" But catching sight of Jacob's face, he stopped. "Lad? You all right?"

Jacob hovered for a long moment in the shadow, then came forward and crouched near the paper lantern. A faint orange glow cast his features into a strange relief.

"I was down at the harbor," he said quietly. "Thinking."

"Thinking?" Coulton grinned. "No wonder you look so damn tired."

But the younger man didn't smile. "I've been having . . . dreams," he said. "Most peculiar dreams. They're so real. It's like I'm not dreaming at all."

Coulton, quiet, watched Jacob's face, watched the conflict in it.

"There's a . . . a woman. I can never see her face. She keeps in the shadows. It's like she's there with me, in the room, while I'm sleeping."

Coulton felt a shiver go through him. He thought of his hat, upside down that morning. He said, "It's a queer place, this country. It'll be good for us both when we're back in England, in the right world."

But Jacob shook his head. "It's not the place, Frank. I've been having these dreams a while now. Even back at Cairndale."

"All right," said Coulton. "So what do she want, your dream woman?"

"She wants me to open the orsine. At Cairndale."

Coulton started to smile, stopped.

"But last night she said . . . she said I was running out of time. That my brother wasn't . . . gone. Not really. That I could still help him."

"Your brother. As in, Bertolt. As in what died all them years back?"

Jacob nodded.

Coulton leaned forward, suddenly concentrated. The room seemed to shift around them, to get smaller. "I ain't saying how crazy it sounds. I ain't saying that."

Jacob held his long beautiful fingers over the lantern.

"Did she tell you how it were to be done, then?" asked Coulton.

Jacob's voice was little more than a whisper. "No."

"Listen. I've had dreams myself, lad. Felt as real as a bullet in the back."

Jacob smiled faintly. "You think I'm going mad?"

"I think dead is dead. No matter how much we wish it weren't."

Jacob caught the tone of caution. He got up to go, paused at the screen. "She said last night: *I'm not what you think I am.* Does that mean anything to you?"

Coulton rubbed at his whiskers, raised his eyebrows. "Fuck all," he said.

"Yeah."

But after the younger man was gone, and the screen was slid shut, Coulton sat unmoving in the dim glow of the lantern and thought about it. He knew men who'd been afraid during the war who used to dream shadowy figures standing over their cots at night. He thought of the feeling he'd had for weeks now, of being followed, of little things being moved in the night. He remembered the flicker of something at the edges of his vision, on board the ship, in the streets of the old quarter, here in the inn itself. As he lay down to sleep he thought of something else, something one of the old talents had said once to him, in the parlor at Cairndale. She'd said every light makes a shadow and there can't be one without the other and there were stories told, old stories, about a dark talent, a talent that stayed in the shadow side, in the gray rooms beyond the orsine. The drughr, it was called. It appeared in dreams.

"Ach. Most likely it's just a story though," she'd added, unhooking the poker and raking at the coals in the dark. "Most likely it doesn't exist."

Get a grip on yourself, man, he told himself now. *The drughr's just a story. And a story can't hurt you none, can it?*

He shut his eyes in disgust.

14

Hope is a Clockwork Heart

Komako, seething, took her sister back.

Back, out of the witch's garden, to the old theater, bundled and shivering, Teshi's gray face hidden in the folds of her actor's cloak, and Komako steering her all the while through the dark parts of the streets. It had been a lie, all of it: the witch had no cure. Not for her. Not for Teshi.

Her face was pinched with fury. But she stayed quiet, for her sister's sake, only their wooden geta clattering as they stumbled through the muggy neighborhoods. She couldn't stop seeing what she'd seen, the dust curling over the man's beautiful fingers like smoke, dancing across his knuckles, and the other one, the silent one with the eerie auburn whiskers, who'd kept near the door, watching, listening, his eyes too old for his face.

Once, when Teshi was still very small, Komako had heard a sound from the old master's dressing room. A lady—a geisha—had come to visit him. The sisters had not seen her before. She was very beautiful. Her face was white and her kimono blue and gold and her delicate pale fingers fluttered like birds. She was tuning a samisen with a fierce concentration. On the kotatsu lay an unwrapped bundle of songbooks. The strings were melancholy and gray. But when she began to sing an emptiness opened inside Komako and the sound of the geisha's singing was an echo of some darker thing deep within. She felt Teshi's hand on her sleeve. They hardly dared to breathe. As she peered out from their hiding place, she thought it was like the geisha sat behind glass, so removed was she from the world, moved by it but not a part of it, and when Komako at last looked away she saw the master was crying.

That is how it seemed to her now when she looked at her little sister. As if she were behind glass.

Back at the theater, she put Teshi, shivering, into their small closet room and covered her with a blanket. She stirred the coals in the brazier. All that night she worked distractedly, brooding, unsure of herself. She snuffed lanterns while actors were still in the rooms, she spilled a bucket of washwater across a floor, she dropped a box of old masks during the first performance, making such a clatter that she'd hid under the stairs to keep from getting beaten. She slept badly, her dreams strange in the heat, and the following afternoon, still distracted, she tried to lose herself in her tasks. A junior stagehand found her and Teshi on their knees, kimonos folded up at their thighs, Komako grunting, Teshi moving slowly as if not of her own volition, both of them scrubbing the floor of the gloomy costuming room with a brush. The man handed Komako a small gray pouch.

"A gaijin left this for you," he said. "He gave no name." He fixed her with a long searching look, as if trying to understand what she might be involved in, then left.

Komako felt a surge of dread. The wrappings at her hands were wet and she wiped her wrists on her apron. The floor around her gleamed. She could hear the theater filling with voices. On the far side of the room Teshi, on her knees, was watching, a curtain of hair fallen across her face.

"Is it the man from before?" her sister whispered. "Ko? What does he want, Ko?"

Komako didn't answer, didn't say, *Me, it's me they want.* Instead she loosened the drawstring, pried open the mouth of the pouch.

It was filled with a silky silver dust.

Jacob waited two more nights, and then he went back.

He didn't know if the girl had got the little pouch of dust he'd left for her, didn't know if she'd be angry to see him, or suspicious of his motives, or what. He'd thought maybe, with the cholera raging, he'd find the theater half-empty, or nearly so, and that it'd be easy to slip unnoticed into the back halls, and find her. But it wasn't easy, not at all.

For one thing, he wasn't alone.

No one else outside the old theater seemed to notice the woman. She wore the same old-fashioned dress from the dream, with the ruffled linen collar, and the long dark cloak with the little silver clasp, and the same silk bonnet with the curved wire frame. And though he should have felt menaced, anxious at the very least, Jacob found himself instead feeling a strange dreamlike solace, as if she had come in kindness and in hope. And so he turned and joined the flow of people pouring in to watch the kabuki.

He wavered in the low entryway, amid the torch smoke, surprised that he was not stared at more, and then as the first gong crashed he slid back around the corner and saw the apparition watching him from a side corridor, and then she slipped away. He followed, a dreamlike slowness in his every movement. The dark woman led him through a labyrinth of dim airless passageways, sliding screens, crooked flights of steps, until at last he entered a small still room at the top of the theater, a brazier burning in the middle of the floor, and there she was, the girl, Komako.

She was kneeling at Teshi's side and she rose to her feet as he appeared. He glimpsed a rope, tied to an ankle, as if to restrain the little one.

"Who let you in here?" Komako demanded.

She didn't wait for his reply, but turned and opened the screen and led him away, into the creaking hall, then up a narrow stair that had been hidden in darkness, to a trapdoor in the ceiling. He found himself outside on the high roof. The city spread out below, a dizzying sea of little fires and colored lanterns. The muggy air smelled of rain. The girl was already ten feet above him, climbing nimbly across the clay roof tiles in her bare feet. She didn't pause, didn't look back to see that he followed.

When he reached her at last, she was on a sheltered balcony, gabled, with a low dark door behind her, looking locked and unused for years. The railing was a kind of wickerwork, very old and very beautiful, but Jacob didn't trust it with his weight.

The girl sat, dangling her feet through the railing, like a kid, exactly like a little kid, and Jacob was reminded again with a sudden pain just how young she really was. He took off his hat, sat next to her, his hair sticking to his temples.

"What is this place?" he said quietly.

"You shouldn't have come," she said. "I don't want to see you."

He didn't point out that *she'd* dragged *him* up to the roof, that she could've said that below, or just refused to talk, or even hollered for someone to remove him.

"Forgive me," he said. "I've angered you."

"I'm *not* angry."

He wanted to smile at that. But he just regarded her gravely, remembering how he was at her age, when Berghast had found him in the grime of Vienna, how old he'd felt, peering at the wealthy clothes and soft face of the older man, how he'd felt like that man couldn't know anything about the world, not really. And he'd felt such fear, too. He felt it still. He searched the girl's face and tried to think of some way to begin. "Your English is excellent."

She shrugged. "It was my father's tongue. My mother made me learn."

"I'm lucky that she did. What's wrong with your hands?"

She hesitated. Then she slowly unwrapped the linen bandages, held up her hands. Her small fingers were chapped and red. "They've always been like this. Yours aren't?"

"No."

"When did you . . . know?" she asked, choosing her words with care. "I mean, that you could do—?" She flicked her hands, as if shaping dust. Suddenly it was obvious to him how much she needed to talk, how many questions she must have. He determined at that very moment to be as honest and direct with her as he could.

"Always," he said.

"Can you do anything else?"

He paused, studied her in the darkness. "Like what?"

"Like anything."

He shook his head. "No. Just the dustwork."

"Does it hurt you?"

"It's cold, especially in my wrists. That hurts."

She seemed to think about that. "How did you learn to control it?"

He wrapped his arms around himself, leaned back to study the humid night sky. There were no stars. "On my own, at first," he said softly. "Like you. But when I got to Cairndale, they taught me things about it there too. Ways to use it safely."

"Cairndale. That's where you're from?"

"In Scotland. Yes."

"That is in Europe?"

"Yes."

"You traveled halfway across the world." Her voice was hushed. He nodded.

But she didn't seem pleased by this. She started winding the linen bandages back up, around her hands, in quick deft movements. "You traveled halfway across the world . . . for me? Because I can do what you can do. Why? What is it you want from me, Jacob Marber?"

It sounded strange, hearing his name from her like that. She didn't talk like a child, that was the thing. He looked at her. "I want to bring you back with us. To Cairndale."

She laughed a sharp, angry laugh.

"Why not?" he said. "What's here for you? Who can do what you can do? Who would understand it, even, if they saw it?"

She bit her lip, looked away. "I know nothing about you. You could be anyone."

But he knew she was thinking of her little sister, what would become of her. He turned the hat in his fingers. "You know one thing about me. Is that not enough?"

The girl's eyes flickered to his hands, away.

"You can't live here unprotected, Komako-chan, not forever. Our kind, we don't do well on our own. People fear us."

"Are there no people in Scotland?"

He smiled slowly. "Some. But the Scottish, they're very . . . practical." He looked at her and winked. He started to talk then, gently, about his childhood. He told her a little of how he'd survived as a boy in the alleys of Vienna, scared, hungry, until a man had come seeking him out, too. A doctor. The very man who'd written them in Kyoto about her. They'd been in Japan over a month now, he and his partner, and only sheer chance had brought her to them now. Chance, or fate. She could decide. He told her dustwork was not the only talent in the world and that his companion, Mr. Coulton, could make himself very strong. It was, he said, something to see. She listened in silence and never took her eyes from his face as he spoke and he didn't know how much she believed. He said to her that he'd had a brother, a twin, who died when they were maybe Komako's very age. That death had broken him and he'd never got over it and he never would. Lastly he told her about the glyphic, a man as old as the oldest tree, who lived in the ruins of an ancient monastery at Cairndale. They called him the Spider, because of what he did, because of his talent. He was, said Jacob, a finder.

"It is he who led us to you," he explained. "In his dreaming, he waits at the center of a kind of web, and every time a talent is used somewhere, he feels its vibrations and tries to locate it." The girl was watching his lips, as if fascinated by the words, and all at once he fell quiet, suddenly self-conscious. "I'm nothing like you, Komako-chan, it's true," he said. "I don't know your life, what you've been through. But somehow, you and I, we're the same. That must mean something."

He raked his hands through his beard. She was maybe the very age he'd been when Henry found him in Vienna. Her eyes were dark and sad. Her hands were wrapped in linen, as if burned.

"Your brother," she said. "He was sick?"

Jacob shook his head. "It was an accident."

"The doctor who found you. He did not save him?"

"It was before that. He was . . . too late."

"You would have done anything."

Jacob breathed quietly in the night air. "I still would," he said softly. And saying it out loud like that, hearing it said, suddenly he knew it was true, and he thought of the shadow woman and the orsine and what she'd said.

Komako took a long, slow breath.

"My sister is sick," she said. "No one knows what is wrong with her."

He nodded.

"I don't know what to do."

He tried not to look at her. He wasn't sure how to tell her. "Your sister," he began, and then he swallowed and tried again. "Your sister, Teshi. Did she have a . . . very bad sickness before? Was there a day, a night, when you were afraid for her life?" He studied her. "She must be very cold all the time. She's so pale. Does she ever sleep?"

"Never," she whispered. "She never does."

"Her teeth. Are they . . . sharp? Does she have three red lines around her throat, here?" His fingers worried at his hat. "Teshi isn't sick, Komako-chan. It isn't a sickness."

Slowly the girl turned her face, looked up at him, a terrible question in her eyes.

"Your talent. It isn't just dustwork. It's something else, too." He studied her face, the stillness of it, and he felt sick with what he was going to say. "It's you. You're keeping her here, your love for her has been keeping her here. It's not hurting her," he added quickly. "But . . . you need to let her go. You need to give her peace."

The girl was shaking her head, as if she didn't believe it, or understand it, or maybe both. But he knew some part of her did understand it, some part of her knew it was so.

"She's already gone," he said. "I'm sorry."

And he was, he felt it deep in his heart, a deep violent ache in his chest. He couldn't look at her. He thought she'd scream at him, strike his chest with her little fists, or maybe just sneer, or get up and walk angrily away, but she did none of those things. She only sat, observing the darkness, as if she hadn't even heard him. And that was when he felt it again, the presence, and he peered across the rooftop.

The woman of smoke was back, standing on the clay tiles, silhouetted darkly against the night's darkness. Jacob felt something cold and unhappy go through him. It started to rain, softly, a warm curtain of water dripping from the gables in front. The shadow's attention seemed taken by something in the street below, some flicker of movement, and she extended a long arm and pointed, and Jacob got to his feet to see.

A small shape, very white in the darkness, ghostlike and eerie, was running along the street, away from the theater, into the heat and darkness of the old quarter. He heard Komako breathe in sharply beside him.

It was her sister, Teshi.

She'd got loose.

15

THE GIRL WHO WAS SEEN

Komako flew through the trapdoor, taking the stairs two at
a time, fear and confusion rising like a hurt in her throat,
and then she was hurtling along the dark corridor, past the
empty chamber she shared with her sister, and she was cursing the
folds of her kimono as she leaped the next flight to the landing, leaped
again to the last. She could hear Jacob behind her, slower, heavier, his
boots banging over the hardwood, but she didn't wait, she couldn't, not
with Teshi going out into the poor districts in the dark while the cholera
raged, Teshi who was like a five-year-old silhouette of the disease
itself. Komako knew the superstitious poor, had lived among them all
her life; she knew what they were capable of. Stagehands stood at their
brooms, heads turning, as she sprinted past. She didn't care. It felt to
her already as if something she'd always had was ending. She threw
open the alley-side door, plunged into the warm rain.

She wasn't thinking about Jacob's words, what he'd been trying to
tell her. She understood, or thought she did, or understood enough
at least, to feel an indignant fury swelling in her at what he'd dared

suggest. *Let him be gone too,* she thought. *If he won't help Teshi, then he's no use either.*

The rain was lashing her face now, in her eyes. She wiped at it with an open hand. She could hear shutters banging closed all along the Asakusa district, as if worse weather were coming. There were still lanterns burning under some of the eaves, a few still lit and swaying on their ropes above the street crossings.

Then, ahead, she saw it: a wisp of white kimono trailing around a corner.

Jacob was calling to her to slow down. He was right behind her, a big dark shadow, bareheaded, his hat swinging in one fist. But she was close, so close to Teshi. She came around a corner and ducked down a narrow dripping alley, past the huddled poor, one woman under a ragged parasol, and then she saw her sister.

She was so little, so pale. She was standing very still, a tiny confused creature with her hair wet, shivering, cold in the swampy heat, staring at the wrapped bodies stacked like cordwood under the coffin maker's awning. Lanterns within were lit. There was a sound of steady hammering.

Komako grabbed Teshi by the shoulders, spun her around.

"You can't do this!" she cried. "You can't just come out here without me! It's not safe, Teshi. Do you hear me?"

Her sister peered dully up at her, her eyes very dark. "I'm so cold," she whispered.

Jacob had stopped some feet away and was standing in the rain, his hands on his knees, his face lifted to watch her. Gasping, his black beard dripping.

"I have to get her out of here," Komako called over her shoulder. "She isn't safe here."

But there came then a sudden spill of light, from the opening door of the coffin maker's. Voices. Someone in the mah-jongg den above slammed a window shutter back, peered out. She glimpsed movement from the shrine next door, the darkness there, and without thinking she stepped at once in front of her sister. They were widows, fathers, sons who'd lost their families to the cholera.

"Komako . . . ," Jacob hissed.

But his warning was already wasted. The grieving poor, the angry grieving poor, in rags and ragged straw hats, were already on their feet and leaving their vigils to step out into the rain, some of them now with torches, some with sticks, one man with the teeth of a rake held high.

At that precise moment, far across the old wooden city, Frank Coulton sat cross-legged in his shirtsleeves in the dead middle of his room at the inn, a paper lantern hanging from the crossbeams overhead, its shade casting a faint orange glow over his thinning hair and his big wrists and the battered leather traveling trunk standing open and empty against the far screen. He was gripping a loaded revolver in one hand, a pair of brass knuckles in the other, like he was of a mind to pray over them. All over the floor, over every surface, he'd sprinkled a fine silver dust.

Come on, you bastard, he was thinking. *Show your bloody self.*

He'd left the shoji screens on all three walls standing wide, in invitation. He closed his eyes, he breathed, he strained to listen in the gloom.

He'd let Jacob go to the kabuki alone, two hours earlier, had let him confront the girl alone, in part because it seemed an easy enough task, charm being a thing the lad carried in his pockets the way other men carried loose coin. But mostly, though, it was because Coulton had a task that needed doing, *this* task, and he wanted to be on his own to do it.

After all, it wasn't every day you set out to kill a drughr.

Because that's what it was, a drughr, and he'd come around to believing it, to believing in the unseen thing that stalked Jacob and himself. He didn't care how crazy it sounded. The drughr hadn't infected his own dreams, not yet at least, not like Jacob talked about, but he'd sensed its presence at his spine, a slow creeping dread. He knew little about the old stories, stories of the dead who'd never died, who'd crossed over into the gray rooms, still living; wielders of the dark talents, physically monstrous, impossibly strong; creatures that could pass through doors, and walls, and even human flesh; dream creatures and so, like dreams, invisible by the light of day.

Aye, should be easy enough, then, he thought dryly. *What could go wrong?*

And he gripped the revolver harder.

Two things had happened in the days after finding the girl that made Coulton believe what followed him was real. The first was at the base of the inn stairs when he turned back suddenly, having forgotten a list of supplies he'd wanted, and as he hurried back up the stairs he'd brushed *something* with his shoulder. He'd stopped and reached out a hand into the emptiness while the landlady, below, peered up at him, expressionless. The second was a murmuring in the corridor outside his room, in the dead of night, a low urgent muttering the words of which he couldn't make out, just as if he were overhearing one side of a conversation. He rose catlike and quick in his nightshirt and drew back the screen and stepped out into the moonlit hall. It was empty.

He didn't tell Jacob. If something invisible was stalking them, it could overhear anything at any time. But he began, from that moment on, to think about how to confront the monster.

His plan was simple. He had two desirable outcomes. The first would be the killing of the thing. But even if he only enraged it, provoked it, so that it revealed itself to him, that would be a success. He needed to know what it was.

And so he sat in the weak orange lantern light, waiting. He was afraid and it wasn't a feeling he was used to and he didn't know what to do with it.

An hour passed.

Nothing came.

And then, suddenly, somehow, it was in the room with him.

The hairs on the back of his neck prickled. "I know you're here," he said grimly, into the stillness. "I can hear you breathing, like."

Silence.

He grunted, closed his eyes. He was forcing his talent, making his flesh denser, thicker, incredibly powerful. His heart was going fast, the familiar suffocating feeling coming over him, as if the walls were leaning in. He didn't think his strength would be equal to the drughr's, not if the old stories were even half-true, but he had his revolver too and when had a drughr been shot in the face by a Colt at close range and walked away? He was breathing fast. He could feel the cords in his neck as he turned his face sidelong to listen.

"I been asking myself," he said quietly, "just what it were, haunting me all these weeks. Aye, I known you was here, even shipboard, when we was sailing out of Singapore."

His eyes swept the room slowly.

"And then we had our little moment on the stairs. Thing is, if I can touch you, then so can a fist. So can a bullet. You take my meaning?"

And that was when he saw it. A faint smudge of dust on the floor, entering from the dark corridor, coming nearer. Footprints. Passing the opened traveling trunk, passing the small writing desk with its bottles of ink. He felt a quick horror at the sight and he fought it down, wondering just how massive the thing could be, what it was he was confronting. What did it want? He was careful not to move.

"Thing about being invisible, now," he said, keeping his voice steady, "is it don't mean you ain't there. And if you're there, you ain't somewhere else."

He raised his eyes and looked directly at where the drughr stood.

The footprints froze. He saw the thing shift slightly, as if turning to peer behind it, and he understood in that moment that it knew he'd seen it, that it had walked into a trap, and he launched himself with all his force and speed directly at where he supposed it loomed. As he leaped, he knocked the paper lantern and it swung crazily back and forth, casting a wild moving shadow over everything. And then he struck, and felt his fist connect, a glancing blow only, and he was spun off sideways and crashed through a paper screen, tearing it down around him as he fell.

He was on his feet again at once, coughing, whirling about, trying to see where the drughr had gone. He'd lost his revolver. The dust was all kicked up into the air, floating downward. But he could see no outline or shape of the figure in the haze and he feared it had escaped.

Then his eyes came to rest on the steamer trunk, shoved sidelong against a beam. A slow noise came from inside it, almost like a groan. He hesitated only a moment. And then without thinking he jumped forward and slammed the lid shut, locking it fast, and then he stepped back and stared through the descending dust.

All was suddenly still. He could hear now the landlady hurrying through the inn below, starting to come up the stairs, pausing halfway up. But his glare was fixed on the trunk, silent, still. His blood was pounding.

It wasn't possible, he thought, it just wasn't possible. You couldn't trap a fucking drughr in a steamer trunk. Could you?

And just then, as if in answer, the lid thumped sharply, twice, and then a furious drumming started up from inside it, and Coulton doubled up his fists and took an involuntary step back.

Fuck me, he thought.

Before the first man in that mob had lifted his club, even before Komako could drag her sister by the wrist back, out of reach of his anger, the Englishman had stepped smoothly through the rain with his long black coat snapping at his knees and his silk hat dropped in the wet alley and raised his fists in challenge. Komako saw his eyes. They were black, the whites gone, the irises filled with darkness.

"Stay behind me," he said grimly.

She knew the superstitions of these people, knew they believed in demons and evil spirits, and knew they feared the cholera was a mark of witchcraft among them. She knew this, and she knew how they'd always looked askance at Teshi, and she was afraid.

She had one protective arm around Teshi's shoulders. Her sister seemed dazed, half-asleep, wholly unaware of the danger they were in, her face still dialed toward the bodies under the canopy. The mob was thickening. There were bakuto among them now, holding knives, their loaded dice in little pouches at their throats. Twenty, maybe thirty faces glared out at her, and when she turned her head she saw others had blocked the way they'd come. They were trapped.

And then the first man lifted his club and swung it in a long whistling arc through the rain and Jacob somehow twisted and caught it in his ribs with a terrible crunching noise. Komako winced, hearing him grunt in pain. But his hands were gripping the shaft of the weapon and he spun the smaller man sidelong off him, into the alley. He turned the club in his fists and rose to his full height and then, incredibly, he *roared*, there was no other word for it, he roared like a bear into the dark rain, a sound of absolute fury that made all there hesitate and shrink back.

"Go, Komako! Go!" he shouted.

But she couldn't, there was nowhere to go. An old woman came forward, an ancient woman in a shabby yukata, her robe hanging wetly from her, and she leveled a crooked finger at Teshi. A hush fell over the mob.

"Her," she whispered. "It's her, it's the demon child. . . ."

A ripple went through the mob. A voice from the back shouted something, then a second voice. A brick landed near Teshi, a rock struck Komako in the chest. The mob was gathering its courage, its anger rising again.

"Jacob!" she cried out. "We can't—"

But then he was beside her, sweeping Teshi up over one shoulder, striding through the rain toward a dark shop front and kicking the door down and dragging Komako forward with him, into the gloom. He stood in the doorway, a tall bearded figure of rage, and glared out at the gathering crowd.

Komako hurried through. The shop was just two small rooms, front and back, and there was no other way in or out. In the darkness she could smell something awful. The back room was filled with the cholera dead.

"We're trapped," she cried. "Jacob! We can't get out!"

Jacob just shook his head. "We only needed to be out of the rain, Ko. We only needed to be dry."

She saw him take off his gloves. The dust. He meant to use the dust.

"No," she whispered. "You can't."

He looked at her, his eyes completely black. He seemed to be waiting but she didn't know what more to say. She looked for Teshi and saw her little sister kneeling in the back room, a pale figure in the gloom, kneeling among the laid-out dead. In her head flashed, again, the words Jacob had said to her on the roof of the theater. Whatever was wrong with her sister, it wasn't illness.

Jacob turned back, raised his hands. And all at once the dust in that filthy shop poured toward his fingers, swirling around and around his outstretched arms.

A man had come forward from the edge of the crowd, swinging a torch, the flame guttering in the rain but not going out, and Komako saw that he meant to burn the shop, to let them burn inside it, and without thinking she ripped at her linen bandages and felt the icy pain in her wrists, and she gathered a skein of dust and sent it arcing out toward the torch. The fire went out in a quick strangled gasp of smoke.

The mob gave out a collective gasp. She looked over at Jacob and saw the dust spiraling around him, saw him step forward now under the dripping awning and raise his eyes and look at the angry mob. There was fear in their faces. They were witnessing the work of demons, of spirits, of an evil witchcraft. There could be no life for her and Teshi now, not here, not after this. They'd *seen* her.

Then came a glow from next door, and she glanced quickly over and saw someone had lighted the thatched roof. Despite the rain, the fire was already leaping toward them.

"Jacob—" she cried.

"Get your sister," he said, and his voice sounded strained.

But she didn't, not at once, and instead she watched as he fell to one knee and dragged his hands forward as if through a thick water, the cords of his neck straining, and the great whirling dust flew out in its billions of particles into the faces and eyes of that gathered crowd, descending on them like a swarm of locusts, and they cried out, clawing at their eyes, stumbling, suddenly blinded.

"Hurry!" he was shouting.

And then Komako was in the dark of the shop, grabbing her sister's wrist, dragging her out, and Jacob picked the little girl up and the three of them ran through the rain, away from the guttering shops and gambling dens, the frenzied mourners and all the silent dead, through the darkness of the district, toward the old kabuki theater and the only home she'd known.

Coulton stared at the trunk in the swaying light, the lid battering with a fury.

His heart in its cage was pounding. He could hear the landlady calling for Jacob from below, in a panicked Japanese. "Marubu-san? Marubu-san!" and he hesitated only a moment before picking grimly through the mess and pocketing his revolver and then kneeling down beside the trunk.

"I don't know if you can understand me," he growled softly. "But either you shut the fuck up this minute or I unload this Colt into this trunk. Do invisible stop a bullet?"

The lid stopped thumping. The trunk fell still.

"Right," muttered Coulton, glancing off.

He stepped out into the hallway, leaned out over the railing. He called down in a calm voice that everything was fine, he'd just fallen over and broken a screen, an accident, but he was fine, all was fine, not to worry. He would of course pay for the damage, yes, yes.

He could see her pale face peering up at him from the bottom of the stairs, in the half-light. She was holding a broom as if it were a weapon, in two shaking hands. Her eyes were expressionless. He didn't know how much she understood but she said something back in rapid Japanese and then she turned and went silently down.

Back in his ruined room, Coulton stared at the trunk, uncertain. He could hear the drughr shifting, moving its limbs within. But it no longer struggled.

He tried to make sense of it. He didn't see how a simple thing like a trunk could stop a drughr. Weren't they supposed to be able to pass through walls? Weren't they supposed to be huge, powerful, far too massive to stumble by chance into a trunk and not get out? Hell, his missed punch shouldn't even hardly of stunned it.

He glared at the trunk, unsure what to do. The inn felt very quiet. Slowly, always facing the thing, he began to pick up the mess, righting the furniture, stooping to sweep up the dust, the splintered pieces of the screen. When he was done he set his hands on his hips, peered about. The room still looked a mess.

When he could think of nothing else to do, he sat cross-legged in front of the trunk, and just watched it. He was of a mind to wait for Jacob. He got up and paced to the window and glanced out at the rain and then he went back and folded his arms and stared at the trunk some more. It was late. And that was when he heard his name.

"Mr. Coulton?" called a voice, muffled. "You still there? Coulton!"

He pulled the gun from his pocket, his blood pounding. Several minutes passed. It hadn't sounded much like a monster. He grimaced. *How stupid are you, man?* he thought.

"Please!" the voice called.

Mighty fucking stupid, Coulton thought. And then he stepped forward, and swiftly unbuckled the lock, and threw the lid wide.

Inside was a kid.

Folded awkwardly into the bottom of the trunk. A fucking kid. Scrawny and naked and dirty, with her freckled nose running and her cropped red hair all thatched and lice-ridden like it hadn't been washed in her entire bloody life. It was cut like a boy's and with her skinny neck and long narrow face she looked, Coulton thought, like a particularly bony, already-plucked chicken.

She was looking woozily up at him, surprised, her mouth open, a gap between her front teeth, as if she couldn't believe he'd hit her, the left side of her narrow face already darkening where he'd struck. And then all of a sudden she sat crookedly up, and scowled at him, and rubbed at her sore head.

"Jesus," she said. "What you gone and done that for?"

He kept his revolver aimed at her heart. "What are you?" he whispered. "Show me your real self. Show me."

She stared at him like he was crazy.

"Show me!" he shouted.

"Oy!" she shouted right back. "I ain't deaf! I *heared* you." She started feeling her jaw, gingerly, glowering up at him. "What you gone and hit me for, anyhow? Ow."

He frowned, suddenly unsure. He was watching her, turning it all over in his head. It didn't make sense. He reached carefully behind him, took out his nightshirt, threw it across. "Put this on, for God's sake."

She did so. It hung off her in a great pool of cotton at her feet. Her hands were lost in the sleeves. She stuck out a sleeve in greeting. "Me name's Ribs," she said, by way of introduction. Then she saw his face. "Aw, what. You ain't never seen a invisible girl before?"

He blinked. "Is that a joke?"

All of a sudden she gave him a quick sly grin. "You was so scared! Oh you was!"

"I weren't," he said.

"Near wet your pants, you did. Oh it hurts to laugh. But I can't help it. You should've seen your face."

"You should see yours now," he muttered. He rested the revolver in his lap but kept the hammer cocked. "What're you doin, followin us, then? I never heard of a talent what could make a kid invisible."

"Sweet holy baby Jesus," she said with mock seriousness. She opened her eyes very wide. "If *you* ain't heard of a thing, it can't be so, I reckon."

"You got a real nice way about you."

"Why thank you, Mr. Coulton, sir."

"Ribs ain't any kind of a name."

"Tell it to me mum."

"Where's she at, then?"

"Alas, I am but a poor unfortunate, Mr. Coulton sir. Me tale is most tragic." She curtsied in his long nightshirt, looking ridiculous. "I were born nowhere, I were raised everywhere. Poverty were me da. Loneliness were me mum."

"Hold up a minute," he said. "I got to have a cry."

She grinned again. "I won't tell no one."

He studied her freckled features, her sly green eyes. Then he nodded. "Right. There's no way the drughr could be this goddamn annoying. But I just might shoot you anyway."

Ribs seemed to find this funny. "Okay, right, listen," she said, regaining her composure. "I ain't never seen no one else can do what I can do. Or nothing like it. Then I seen Jacob one day with the dust. At the docks in Singapore. I wanted to see what you was. So I just climbed up on board an shipped out with you, I did. I never knowed you was comin to Japan."

"How'd a bloody lass like yourself end up at the docks in Singapore, anyway?"

She grinned. "O now that there is a woeful tale. It is sure to rend your heart, Mr. Coulton, sir."

"I damn near killed you, lass. I thought you was a drughr."

"A what?"

"A dru—" Coulton shook his head. "Never mind it."

"Oh! Here's a broadsheet for you: I ain't a unicorn neither."

Coulton blew out his cheeks. He was wondering if a gunshot would bring the Tokyo constabulary down on him and if it did would this kid's body be invisible or not and if it wasn't would it be worth it anyway.

Ribs, though, just looked more and more at ease. She rubbed her hands together, glanced briskly around her. Scratched at her red hair. "Okay. So where's Jacob at now, then? Is he talkin to that Komako girl?"

Coulton stopped. "You know about her?"

"Hard not to, the way you two carry on."

"How much you overheard, then? You know what it is we do?"

"Yup."

"You know where we come from?"

"Yup."

"Brilliant," he muttered. "Berghast is like to have me bloody hide." He looked at her, shaking his head. "What am I going to do with you, then? I can't just leave you wandering about."

Ribs blinked up at him, her short hair standing wild on her head. "Jesus, you. I ain't been hangin around here for me own edification. I mean to go with you, of course."

"What, back to Cairndale?"

She winked. "But not in that bloody trunk, of course."

The warm rain was coming down in sheets now, blurring the curved rooftops.

Outside the old theater, Komako left the Englishman in the deserted street. Around the corner, rickshaws were gathering in the torchlight, sheeted against the rain. She'd offered him nothing, no assurance, no thanks. Confused by what was in her heart. He'd saved her; he'd ruined her. She'd exposed her talent and there'd be no hiding now. She steered Teshi inside, up through the dark rooms, blessedly passing no one as she went, and in the little space they shared at the top of the theater she laid her sister down on a tatami. The brazier was still lit, pulsing with heat.

Last of all, she propped wide the wooden shutter, peered out. He was still there, Jacob, a dark figure in the rain, hatless, soaked, watching the door she'd gone through. In the night he seemed eerie again, unknowable, frightening. He would wait for her only so long, she knew.

She felt a presence beside her. It was Teshi, risen from her sickbed, hollow-eyed. She put a hand on Komako's shoulder to steady herself and the cold of it went through her.

"What does he want, Ko?" whispered Teshi. "Why does he stand there?"

"He wants me," she said simply.

She sat then, cross-legged, with her back to the wall, and Teshi crawled over and lay her little head down in her lap, like she used to do, when she was small, in those years before she got sick. Komako stroked her hair.

She was trembling, but not because of that. She was thinking of what Jacob had said, how it was her own will keeping her sister from finding peace, and how she must do it, she must let go, and she remembered the pale silhouette of her sister drawn to the dead in that alley and the unearthly sleepiness in her, even as the mob screamed, even as it attacked them. Her sister was so cold all the time. She never did sleep, and her teeth were, as Jacob had guessed, small and sharp, like a fish's. And she thought then of the doctor at the clinic and the way he'd stared at Teshi, as if in horror, and of the witch's cold distaste, and she saw all at once how she'd already known it, even before Jacob had told her, how she'd known for a long time now that what was wrong with Teshi wasn't an illness and that what had to be done would be, for her sister, a sort of kindness.

Teshi slipped her little cold fingers into Komako's. "It's okay, Ko," she whispered.

Just exactly as if she knew.

But she couldn't know, there was no way she could know. Komako searched her face, feeling as she did so as if she were being dragged forward, dragged toward a brightness that must hurt her and her sister, dragged toward the two strange men and whatever truth they'd brought with them, and though she swallowed and closed her eyes and tried not to think about it she could not stop herself, she couldn't, and then it was as if she were falling into a light that was like dying.

Oh, Teshi, she thought suddenly, fiercely, as she fell. *Oh, Teshi, I'm sorry, I'm so sorry—*

Something loosened inside her then, some hard knot of tension all at once was dissolving, and Komako felt an awful sickening in her stomach, and she gasped back a sob and opened her eyes, looking wildly about in the glow of the brazier. Teshi's head was in her lap, eyes closed, like she was sleeping, exactly like she was sleeping. But it wasn't sleeping.

16

THE DRUGHR

Years later, long after he'd ceased being what he was, after he'd stood in the gray rooms beyond the orsine with his skin steaming, and the apparitions with their mournful eyes had gathered to meet him; after he'd become, yes, what he'd always been fated to become, an extension of the drughr, the dust rising inside him like a smoldering darkness until he no longer remembered even his own name; after he'd killed those two children at the river crossing and been changed by it, changed utterly, the many betrayals and lies of the institute coming clear in that moment, and above all, after he'd gone hunting for the baby, the child at Cairndale, the shining boy— still, in a small locked room in his heart, Jacob would remember this day, this departure, and the voyage that was to come. For this was his second beginning.

They sailed out of Tokyo bay under the flat backlit white of a sunless sky, four passengers on board the Swede's smuggler's bark: himself and Coulton, Komako in her grief, and that strange stowaway, the invisible girl, Ribs.

As they cleared the bar, and the sails crackled and filled with wind, Jacob watched Komako at the railing. Her eyes were fixed on the receding rooftops of her city, her face was open and sad. She'd hardly spoken, had said nothing about her little sister, nothing at all, and he knew by her silence what she'd done and what must be in her. He thought of Bertolt as he'd been in the alley, all those years ago, his arms and legs loose and streaked with soot, and he wondered if he could have done the same and knew in that instant that he couldn't have done it, his love for his brother wasn't vast enough, or selfless enough, and he lowered his eyes, ashamed. He'd never known who he was in the world, without Bertolt there to anchor him.

After a time, he joined Komako at the stern. Gripping the railing hard in both fists as if to strangle it and staring out with her at the strange and beautiful city in its passing.

"You will not see it again, not for a long time," he said softly.

"I hate it," she replied.

And walked away.

Jacob watched her go, then lifted his gaze. The shadow woman, that creature of smoke and darkness, lurked silent and brooding in her black skirts beside the smooth trunk of the foremast. A sailor crouched next to her, picking oakum from a coil of rope, unaware. Jacob didn't even know her name. It was strange, not knowing what to call her. The drughr, of course. He'd figured that much out. But not evil, maybe. Was it possible? She was with him often now, not only in sleep but also on waking, like an eerie second shadow of what might yet be. She loomed behind Coulton at the captain's table in the evenings, while his gruff friend tore a bread roll with his thumbs. She stood unswaying on the sunlit deck while the bowsprit heaved and sank in the spray, weightless, the wind never in her skirts. In the dim cramped cabin he shared with Coulton, she often hung in the open doorway, as if not quite touching the floor, the smoke obscuring her eyes. Sometimes seeing her frightened him. Mostly, though, it just left him feeling unaccountably old, and sad.

He didn't speak much in those first days. He'd stare in the evening lantern light at Coulton's red face, his auburn sideburns, the way he sucked deeply on his cigar and held the smoke in his lungs with his eyes closed like a man profoundly satisfied with his lot. His friend was often in conversation with the girl Ribs, that skinny wastrel with her thatched red hair. She was always eating and she chewed with her mouth open and that gap in her teeth visible.

Coulton seemed easier, happier even. Certainly Jacob was happy for him. It wasn't only that they were sailing for home, he knew. It was the brash kid, too.

So Frank Coulton has a heart, he remembered thinking, seeing him like that in those days. *Who'd have guessed it.*

Ribs, for her part, flashed like a salamander in and out of any room Jacob wandered past. It was almost like she was avoiding him, almost like she knew something he didn't. She was everywhere, and nowhere, talking a mile a minute, her voice carrying to every corner of the creaking bark. Scrawny and quick, with eyes that weren't the eyes of a child. On that first morning she wore a yellow child's kimono, bought with care by Coulton from the silk district, but by the second morning she was wearing a rolled-up pair of sailor's pants and a shirt torn at the sleeves and still too long, and these she wore for the rest of the voyage. It hurt Jacob's heart to see her like that, wondering just what she'd had to put up with, what cruelties, how few kindnesses must never have been extended, but she didn't seem to dwell on it. The only times he saw her silent was when she'd sit with Komako on a lashed crate on the poop deck, both of them peering out at the sun-reflected water, its flaring blades of light, two girls maybe of an age, a friendship maybe blossoming between them.

They were already clear of Sagami Bay by then, tacking west of

Oshima Island, the wind strong and southerly. They were making for Taipei, and the East China Sea.

With little to do beyond keep tabs on the two girls, and drowse, and shield his eyes against the brightness, and observe the sailors swinging in the high rigging like macaques, Jacob's thoughts would drift ahead to Scotland and Cairndale and the lonely stone buildings there. He'd been away too long.

There was almost no alone on that ship. Always a sailor would appear, grunting, working away at some task, or Coulton would emerge out of a hatch, restless, or the girl Ribs would run past on her way someplace. Or he'd turn suddenly and see the drughr, ghostlike, watching him from across the ship. He was already sleeping less and less. What Komako had done to Teshi was inside him, somehow, too, and he couldn't let it go. He turned it over in his head, brooding, until it blurred with what the drughr had said about Bertolt's little spirit, suffering, alone, afraid, and about how he could bring his brother back.

And so it was Jacob summoned the drughr to him, on the third night at sea. He went up on deck under the stars to be alone and he sat with his back to the railing at the foredeck, the warm wind in his beard. He crushed his eyes shut and he willed her to him, and she came.

You told Mr. Coulton about us, she said. Her voice wasn't pleased.

Jacob, holding his knees to his chest, looked up. She was so close, he might have reached out and pinched her skirts between his fingers. Above the stiff ruffed collar, smoke curled and thickened where her face should have been. "There is no us," he muttered. "You said death is just a door. You said it can be opened and closed, by anyone who knows how."

Yes.

"Is he still . . . Bertolt? Is he still who he was?"

You must open the orsine. You must open it so that it does not close again.

"Will you give him a message for me?"

You will give it to him yourself. When you open the orsine.

"Why can't you do it? What do you need me for?" He rubbed angrily at his face and glared off at the darkness. "Anyway I don't even know how. You can't open something you don't understand."

It is easy, Jacob. You must kill the glyphic.

Jacob stared at her. "Mr. Thorpe?"

He has gone by many names. But it is one and the same. Yes.

"I know what you are," he said suddenly.

And what am I?

He swallowed. "Drughr."

She kneeled, demurely, with her gloved hands in her lap. *That is one name. There are others. I am old, older than your good Dr. Berghast, older even than your precious glyphic.*

"Coulton says you're evil," he whispered.

Her head tilted then, as if giving him a long flat look. Almost like she were human. *Evil,* she said softly, *is a matter of perspective.*

"It's not."

Oh? And is a tree evil? Is dust evil? We are a part of a greater darkness, Jacob, that is all. The second side to the coin. And what are you? What is dust, what does it mean to have a power over dust? Is that not evil?

"Talents aren't evil."

Yours is a very particular talent though. Is it not?

He saw the silhouette of a sailor rise from the forecastle and cross to the railing. The sea was calm, glowing now with the eerie blue glow of jellyfish under the starlight. After a moment the sailor drifted back to his watch.

Imagine if you had learned then, what Komako has learned now. You could have kept Bertolt alive, you could have kept him with you. It is a part of the dustworker's gift. Did Berghast not tell you? Of course not. He would not wish you to know. But I can give you that power.

"I wouldn't want it. I don't want it."

It is yours regardless. The drughr leaned forward, her face all smoke and blackness. *Dust is the power to bring darkness into the world,* she said. *You know so little of what you are, Jacob. You are still so young. I have seen sandstorms at midday in the Empty Quarter, how they block out the sun. You would think it the dead of night. Their roaring obliterates every sound. And the feel of the sand blown against your skin obliterates all other sensation. There is no smell, no taste, no sound, except the sand. The sandstorm strips away all of the human senses, until a person is no longer a person. They are cut off from their own self. That is the power of dust.*

"I don't want to hurt anyone—"

Of course not.

Jacob shook his head. He felt sleepy, almost drugged. The drughr had that effect on him, somehow. "You said . . . you said you knew a way—"

To find your brother, in the other world. To help him, yes. The orsine is the door, it is true, but there are other ways through too. Little windows. I can take you through, Jacob, I can do what Henry Berghast will not. But the orsine must be opened if your brother is to be brought back for good.

"You said he's suffering—"

It will not be easy. And there is a price. Will you pay it? That is the question.

"What price?"

Ah. The drughr paused, as if considering. *Why is it the smallest creatures, Jacob, the most defenseless, the mice and the voles, prefer darkness to day? Your Dr. Berghast wishes to preserve the world as it is, the powerful in their interests, the meek in their place. But I . . . I do not believe it has to be the way it is. Do you know why the dark talents are called dark, Jacob? Oh, it is nothing to do with good or evil, with rightness or its perversion. It is because they make it possible for the weak to conceal themselves, to live like the strong.*

"Bertolt wasn't weak," he whispered.

The drughr was silent, smoke swirling over her face.

"Why would you help me?" he said. "Why?"

The rigging creaked in the starlight. The drughr rose smoothly, a blacker shadow against the shadows of the ship's masts.

Because I need something too, Jacob, it said quietly. *I need your help, too.*

In the morning, Frank Coulton sat on a deck barrel, hearing the soft swish of the cards being dealt, a warm wind flaring in his shirtsleeves and crackling in the yards of canvas overhead. The shadows played across his face. He was distracted, thinking of Jacob, worried about the lad. His eyes looked ill, like he was no longer sleeping.

There were four Orang Laut sailors cross-legged and grinning, all leathery and tough, the second mate dealing out their hands. The sailors' poison was zanmai, a game using those strange little colored karuta cards so common in the Tokyo streets. The rules were basic: three cards, trying to add up to nineteen. The cheating, though, was exquisite.

Coulton, a connoisseur of skill no matter its nature, enjoyed the way the sailors peeled his coins up off the deck, one by one, with exhalations of surprise each time they drew nineteen.

Later, at dusk, Ribs said: "I can tell you how they done it. I been watchin."

He stopped what he was doing, looked at her. "You get caught working your talent, here on this little ship, an we'll all be swimming to Singapore. Just act like a normal kid. Can you do that, like?"

Ribs gave him a withering look.

"I *ain't,*" she sniffed, enunciating slowly, "a *kid.*"

But the sun-drenched days were long, the warm air soupy and thick. He couldn't really blame Ribs for her boredom. He too was fading. Increasingly sick of the sea's swells, eager for dry land and a cold bath, he tried and failed to smother his irritation.

They were two days past Taipei and Coulton was in his little cabin with the door closed and the hammock stowed, writing at the narrow desk nailed to the floor, when he paused and put down his pen and half turned on the stool.

"Right," he said softly. He stared up at the ceiling. "If you're wanting to go all the bloody way to Scotland with us, there's got to be rules, like. First rule is: no sneaking."

The cabin was empty. Jacob was up top. The ship lifted and fell, lifted and fell.

At last, out of the emptiness, came Ribs's voice. "How'd you know I was here?"

"I can *smell* you, lass."

"You can't never." She sniffed, uncertain. Paused. "You can't, can you?"

Coulton closed his journal, a knuckle marking the page, and rubbed at his face in exasperation. "You said you was done working your talent on board. You said you'd refrain, like."

She materialized suddenly, a scrawny naked thing right in front of him. "This better?" She grinned.

He recoiled sharply, the heat rising to his cheeks, and turned his face away. He fumbled for a moth-eaten blanket from the hammock. "For God's sake," he muttered. "What's anyone like to think, they see you wandering about like that? I told you to act like a normal person. This ain't normal."

She was grinning at him. "Frank, Frank, Frank," she said.

"You want to make the voyage in my bloody trunk? And it's Mr. Coulton to you."

She laughed, and in the blink of an eye vanished, the old blanket dropping to the floor.

But if Ribs was reduced to pranks and foolishness, Jacob in his moodiness only grew more disturbed. Coulton watched the dark rings under his eyes go from yellow to gray, he watched the way he'd pinch the bridge of his nose, and lean out of the sunlight, and he'd worry. The lad had unlooped his collar and taken off his cravat and his dark coat so that he walked about now half-dressed, in only his shirtsleeves, his hat half the time left in their cabin. It was the apathy of it all, the long sameness of the days, the way it ate away at your usual disciplines that made a person ship-mad.

Some nights he'd wake to find the lad's hammock empty, and go up on deck, and see him staring out at the starlit sea, his haunted eyes angry. There were nights at the captain's table when Jacob didn't show. He never wanted to talk about it.

And then, one night, he did. He came in and paced their narrow cabin, twisting his long beautiful fingers up in front of him. Coulton was at the little desk under the porthole, and he turned on the stool with the pencil in his fingers and he waited. His neck was sunburned, his big nose raw and peeling badly. But Jacob, somehow, looked almost pale.

When the lad spoke, his voice was vague, unhappy. "I couldn't help her, Frank," he said. "I couldn't do anything to help her."

It took him a moment to realize who he meant. Komako's little sister. "But you did help her," he said.

Jacob shook his head. "You don't understand, you weren't there. She *begged* me to save Teshi."

"You didn't do nothing wrong, lad."

"I told her to let her sister go. I did it. Me."

"Aye, and what choice was there? Were she going to bring a litch on board with us? All the way back to Cairndale? Or maybe not come at all, just go on living with a litch in that place? How long do you reckon she'd have lasted then?"

"Her sister didn't have to die."

"She were already dead, lad."

Jacob glared at his long fingers, twisting in his lap.

Coulton got to his feet. He made himself look at the lad, look directly at his hurt, when he said, "That ain't the kind of power you want. You think you do. You don't."

Jacob's eyes flashed. "Maybe it is. Maybe I *should* be more powerful. What's the point of these talents if we can't save anyone?"

"Save who? From what? From *dying?*"

"Yes!"

Coulton stared at Jacob, just stared at him, at the bitterness in him, and he didn't know what to say. It was because he understood. "But your Bertolt's already dead, lad," he said quietly. "He's dead, and there's not a thing what can bring him back."

Jacob turned away in anger.

"It weren't never for that purpose, our talents," he went on. "Death ain't the bad part. You know that."

But the lad, impulsive, unhappy, just kicked at the door of their cabin, and was gone.

Not really gone though. There was no going anywhere on that ship.

Jacob went up the ladder to the foredeck but couldn't be alone there and he paced instead at the stern like a cat, prowling the railing, watching the sun sink low in the west and fuming.

It wasn't Coulton's fault. He knew that. It wasn't anyone's.

He was glaring out at the fading day when Komako came up, and put a hand on his arm, and he looked down at her in her floral kimono. All at once he felt his fury drain away. She seemed so uncertain, so shy.

"You all right?" he said.

She shrugged. There were clouds in the north, darkening. The sky was streaked with gold.

"At the institute," Komako said, "will there be others like me? Like Ribs?"

He didn't understand, and then he did. "Oh. Children? Why, are you worried about it?" As soon as he asked it he felt foolish; of course she'd be worried. He recalled his own midnight dread, as he'd climbed into the railway carriage with Henry Berghast, all those years ago.

"Listen," he said, kneeling down. Sometimes he forgot she was just nine years old. "It's a place where you'll be safe, Komako. There's other children, yes. You'll make friends and you'll lose them and maybe you'll even find someone you like more than that, when you're older. There're teachers and classes and books for reading and you'll learn about dustwork and what it is and what it can and can't do. It's a big old house and there are fields and the dirt is red like blood and the grass is greener than the water in Tokyo harbor. You'll see. And there's a lake for swimming in the summer, and an island with ruins on it."

His voice faltered, remembering. The warm air smelled of salt, of sunbaked wood. Deckhands were running up the shrouds and bare-footed along the booms, furling sails, tying them back. They were shirtless and sun-blackened like figs. Their shadows leaned far out over the water.

"What about you?" said Komako, in a small voice.

He blinked. "Me?"

"Will you be there, too?" she asked. "You won't leave me?"

Jacob reached a slow arm out, and laid it around her shoulders, and she didn't flinch, or tense, or draw away. They stood like that in the light of the setting sun.

"I'm not going anywhere," he lied.

That night, in his slung hammock, in the narrow cabin he shared with Coulton, he dreamed of Bertolt. It didn't seem like a dream. He was in the long ward at Cairndale. All the beds were vacated, their mattresses and ticking upended and left leaning against the wall, all but one. Daylight came in a white glow through the muslin curtains. His brother lay in bed, his flushed face turned into the pillow, hands unmoving and pale on top of the bedsheet. He was the same age he'd been when he died. So small. A nurse whom Jacob did not know walked swiftly down the room, her heels clicking, and stopped at Bertolt's bed. She lifted a wrist and after a moment dropped it and then leaned across to open Bertolt's eyelids. The room got brighter, and then brighter still. And then Jacob awoke.

He'd sweated through his nightshirt. He turned blearily and saw Coulton's hammock hanging like an emptied sack and his friend nowhere. The lantern on its hook on the beam had been left burning low. Jacob swung his feet out, slid to the floor, rubbed at his face.

The drughr was standing in the corner.

"For God's sake," he hissed. His heart was hammering.

The invisible girl, she was watching you earlier, it said. *You did not see her. You must be more careful, she is too curious.*

"She's not the only one," he said pointedly. "Where's Coulton?"

Mr. Coulton will not be back for some time.

But Jacob scarcely heard her. Something about the way she was standing reminded him of something, a memory from long ago, from his childhood in Vienna. And then he remembered.

"I know you . . . ," he said suddenly. "I've seen you before. When I was little—"

Yes. In the Stephansplatz.

"Under the cathedral arches, that day Bertolt fell in the street. That day the horse kicked him."

Also the day you both first entered the orphanage. I saw you climb the steps; I saw the nuns take you inside. You looked back at me. Do you remember?

He shook his slow head. He was trying but couldn't.

Also in the railway carriage, when Henry Berghast took you out of Vienna. I was seated across the aisle, at the window, watching you. You kept looking at me.

"I remember that," he whispered.

I have always been with you, Jacob. I have always watched over you. You are precious, a great power is in you. Think of all the good you could do, the people you could help. If only you will let yourself become what you are meant to be.

"Bertolt always said tomorrow was a new start. What we were going to do hadn't been done yet."

But it has already been decided. What you will do, what you will become. Sometimes it is decided for us.

"I . . . I don't know."

You were meant for this. You were meant to help him. To find him.

He felt drained, like he hadn't slept in weeks. He didn't know what was the matter with him. The creature glided forward, her face a slow smokiness, all depth and dissipating clouds and drifts of shadow, fascinating, bottomless, like staring into a loch lit from far within by some eerie luminescent life, almost visible, so that he had to force himself to look away.

He is suffering, Jacob. He is still a child, as he was when he died. And he is alone and suffering. Unless . . .

"Unless what?"

The drughr'd removed her gloves.

Hold out your hands, she said. *Turn them.*

Her own hands were blackened, twisted like the hands of the dead. With her fingertips then, slowly, she brushed his palms. He flinched. She was *touching* him. It felt eerie, insubstantial, like an exhalation or a sigh, but it was a touch all the same. His shock turned to fear. All at once the drughr, that apparition, that *figment,* gripped his wrists and a searing pain ripped up his forearms. Her grip was strong. He staggered, shaking, a deep unmoored sickness washing over him, but she did not let go, she held him at arm's length as if an agreement were being sealed though he'd agreed to nothing, and his hands were on fire and an agony crackled in his knuckles and wrists and he could not stop himself and he cried out.

She let go.

He stumbled back, cradling his wrists, clawlike. His hands and forearms were stained a dark inky stain, as if he'd bathed them in quinine. It looked as if they were tattooed in swirls and patterns, but the tattoos were moving, shifting languidly inside his skin. His knuckles were deformed, his thumbs elongated and monstrous, his fingers yellow and cracked.

"What've you done?" he whispered in horror.

The coin is struck, Jacob Marber.

She gestured to the corner of the narrow cabin. The lantern at its beam swayed slowly. Jacob's heart felt heavy and hurting in his chest. His ruined fingers twitched, almost of their accord, and a small curl of dust on the floor lifted, suddenly, and came to him, and as he turned his hands he felt it, a forcefulness, a cold power in him that wasn't in him before. In wonder he worked the dust and to his astonishment it folded over itself and *grew*, it grew denser, darker, as if it were multiplying in front of his eyes, dust but not quite dust now, something else, dimming the lantern on its iron hook and blacking out the hammocks and filling the little cabin with a swirling, inky darkness.

The dust is a part of you now, Jacob, came the drughr's voice. He could no longer see her for the thickening air. *I sense a beautiful hunger. Feel it, feel what you are capable of.*

And he did; he could. He felt elated, as if he could do anything, as if through sheer will he could bring a darkness into the world.

He made a fist, the ink in his skin clouding and coming apart and drifting together again, like smoke, and then the dust was sucked down under his monstrous curled fingers in a swift whorl and was extinguished. The dust was *in* him, an electrical current.

Jacob studied his malformed hands. He felt different, older. "This can bring my brother ... back?"

That is only a taste, she said. *That is only a beginning.*

He wet his lips. Suddenly he remembered Coulton, and felt a pang of guilt, and glanced back at the door as if it might open any moment. His friend would never understand. He lowered his voice yet further. "Tell me," he said. "Tell me what I must do."

The lantern creaked above them. He could hear the water sloshing gently at the bulkheads. Something was happening to the air behind her, as if it were fraying, rending open.

The journey is long and the nights are short, murmured the drughr. *You must be willing to come with me. You must leave all this and follow. For you are not strong yet.*

"I will be," he said. "I'll get strong."

The strange opening in the air widened, large enough for him to step through. The drughr's reply, when it came, was a whisper.

Come, then; come, and make a difference in the world.

The
INSTITUTE

·

1882

17

THE GOOD WORKS OF CAIRNDALE MANOR

A lice Quicke awoke in a strange bed, her knuckles bruised. She didn't know whether it was morning or afternoon. Her clothes and hat lay folded and stacked on a night table beside her. Outside, she could hear the eaves dripping with rain, the sound of children's voices.

Her left side ached when she breathed in, where Jacob Marber had impaled her, but when she felt gingerly for it with her fingertips she could find no wound. She tried not to breathe. Just squinted up at the rafters, wincing, struggling through her haze to remember.

There'd been the windy roar of the train, yes, as it pulled away from that monster, smoke ribboning off Jacob Marber's upraised fists. And Marlowe, cradled in her arms. Later, a dreamlike wait at a railway platform somewhere, while conductors fussed about, frantic, and huge gleaming locomotives snorted on the tracks. And she remembered a second railway carriage, at night, and then an old Scottish barouche with collapsed springs, stinking of cigars, its wheels banging over bad roads. Then ... this. A dim room, high-ceilinged, sparsely furnished. Flagstone floors, the walls papered in a faded green Japanese pattern. She didn't know where she was.

"You're at Cairndale," said the nurse who came in to change her bedding. "And you look a fair sight better. How do you feel?"

"Cairndale," she echoed numbly. "Where's Marlowe, is he—?"

"The shining boy? He's about, I'm sure. He and his friend."

"How long have I been asleep?"

"Oh, not so long as that. Easy, now. Ups-a-daisy. There we go."

But it seemed to Alice that time had elongated, had stretched and shifted in strange ways since the attack in the railway carriage. It all felt so very far away. She watched the nurse roll up the bedsheets and stuff them into a basket on a metal cart, the door closing, the sound of the wheels and her footsteps receding. Then she got out of bed. Her ribs flared with pain. She stripped off the nightgown and slowly got dressed. Her Colt Peacemaker wasn't there, wasn't anywhere. She opened the curtains. Because of the rain the daylight was dim. And yet still the brightness of it hurt her eyes, made her skin tingle uncomfortably. Her side throbbed. She'd been beaten and kicked and battered dozens of times in the course of her life but what Marber had done to her, where his dust had hurt her, somehow felt different. *She* felt different.

It turned out not to be a window but a tall glass door, with an old brass pull and white paint gone yellow with age. It'd been opened a crack for the air, and despite her pain at the brightness Alice went out onto the covered balcony beyond. She was on the second floor of an ancient stone manor, its windows dark, a courtyard pooling with shadow in the rain below. A hoop and stick leaned against one wall, like a memory of childhood. Three kids in gray cloaks were playing some sort of game under the eaves, jacks or marbles, it looked like.

As she watched, one pulled a pipe from behind her back and puffed sneakily and then passed it around. A bull's-eye lantern had been left burning on a stone bench outside the porter's gatehouse. Beyond the gates she could make out a winding lane of red clay, dead brown grass, a cluster of distant outbuildings silhouetted in the gloom. They were high above a loch, and she could see an island there with a huge tree growing out of the ruins, the umbrella of golden leaves just visible. An ancient wall snaked distantly along the property. Altogether a chilly, lonesome sort of place.

Scotland, she thought grimly. *You're in fucking Scotland, Alice Quicke.*

She saw no sign of Coulton, or Charlie, or Marlowe. No sign of any other life at all, except, in a tall window on the upper floor of the east wing, she caught sight of an old woman, withered hands clasped before her, thin white hair wild on her scalp. After a minute the old woman pulled the drapes shut.

"I was beginning to fear," said a voice, "that you would sleep until midsummer."

Alice turned. Mrs. Harrogate was standing in the doorway. She wasn't wearing her veil. Her soft face looked badly bruised. Her left eye was purpled shut, a darker color than her birthmark. She wore a fine dress: black piping in scrolls down each breast, tight cuffs, an embroidered collar hiding her throat. But mostly it was the thick bandage wrapped around her head, concealing her left ear, and the fine web of dried scratches all over her face and hands that made Alice stare.

The older woman glided forward. There was in her eyes something drained and sad. "I *am* a sight, Miss Quicke, but you needn't gawp so. Come; you ought not to be out of bed."

"They took my gun."

"For your own protection, I am sure. How do you feel? It is a most unusual wound, but it will improve, I am told."

Alice put a slow hand to her ribs, absorbing this.

"Marlowe's safe," Mrs. Harrogate continued, guessing her thoughts. "I've sent someone to let him know you're awake. You'll find he's quite famous, here. The boy who escaped Jacob Marber . . . The other children, even the older residents, all are most curious. No one imagined he'd be back, I expect."

Alice grimaced. The nurse earlier had called him the shining boy. She remembered how it was in New York City, that night in the park, when Marlowe had healed her knee. How he'd taken the hurt into his own body. "Did he—?"

"Heal you? Mm. In the carriage, on the way here. I don't know that you'd be here at all without him." The older woman's face darkened. "Dr. Berghast was quite satisfied."

Alice wondered at that, but before she could ask, Mrs. Harrogate sat beside her on the bed and brushed her arm. "I must tell you, Miss Quicke. Now, while we are alone. Mr. Coulton is dead."

"Coulton?"

Mrs. Harrogate's little nostrils flared. "He was murdered by Jacob. On the train."

"Oh," said Alice, stunned.

"He was very strong. He thought nothing could hurt him. I . . . I thought the same."

Alice remembered Coulton shoving her and the children behind him, the screams as the carriage darkened. "The last I saw him, he was . . . changed. He was using his talent, I think. He ran at Marber in the carriage. Directly at him. It gave us the time to get out."

Mrs. Harrogate nodded. "Yes, that sounds like him." She turned her face so Alice couldn't see it. She adjusted the bandage at her ear, busied her hands. "Well, we must collect ourselves," she said in a thickened voice. "Mr. Coulton would hardly approve of a show of feeling, hm? Now. You are dressed for travel. Is it so?"

Alice glanced at her clothes. "I, I wasn't . . ."

"I'll be returning to London myself. I have business there, business that will not wait. There will be room in the carriage for another." She seemed to consider something. "You haven't yet seen Cairndale, of course. Would you like to?"

Alice, still shaken, nodded mutely.

The upper corridor was long and wide and they went slowly, like invalids. Had anyone seen them, Alice in her oilskin coat, both hands clutching at her ribs, and old Mrs. Harrogate in her widow's weeds with her swollen eye and her bandaged ear, they might've stared, or laughed; but there was no one, no one at all to see, and the two women shuffled instead through the badly lit hallway, every second sconce snuffed out, past the closed doors and along the dark wood wainscotting, until they came to a turning, and a wide staircase that descended down. She heard the distant voices of students, along the halls, the sound of running footsteps. But the interior of the manor seemed, she thought, larger than it should be. There were just too many doors.

"Because it is built beside an orsine," said Mrs. Harrogate, watching her from the corner of her good eye, gauging her reaction. "I am impressed; most don't notice it so quickly. It can be quite disorienting for some. There was a woman here whom it used to make physically ill." She raised an eyebrow. "The building is indeed larger inside than out. Cairndale Manor is a liminal space, a conduit between worlds. Here, the world of the living and the world of the dead touch."

Alice gave her a strange, uneasy look, but said nothing.

The stone staircase descended. A stained glass window drenched their faces with a bloodred light. Its panels showed the lives of the sainted dead.

"The orsine, Miss Quicke, is the last passage between those worlds. There were others, once; but Cairndale is the only orsine that remains active. It is our task, here, to contain it. It is Dr. Berghast's task. The orsine must be kept closed, you see."

"Why?"

"Or the dead will come through," said Mrs. Harrogate simply. "The dead, and worse."

Alice raised a skeptical eyebrow. It all sounded mad to her. "I guess it's a good thing you keep it closed, then," she muttered.

"Cairndale has always been here," Mrs. Harrogate continued. "The original structures are old, far older than you can imagine. It was a monastery once. You can see the ruins still, on the island in Loch Fae. You have seen it? From your balcony? The land was sold by its order centuries ago to the first of the talents, a man who claimed for himself the title of lord and constructed the manor as you see it around you now. He was the first of his kind; but when he learned there were others like him, he determined to establish a refuge for them. Ah. Here is his likeness." She stopped in front of a smoke-darkened portrait. Dark eyes stared out from a face now long-dead. "The property has been added on to, of course, first as a hospital for the poor, later as a sanatorium, now as a clinic. Or, at least, this is how we have wished it to appear. But in fact it has always just been a sanctuary, for its resident talents. Most of them are old now, too. You will see them, some of them, when they come out of their rooms. The ones who wish to be seen, that is. In recent years, it has also become a kind of . . . school."

"For the children."

"Yes. There are twenty-one of them now. As they come of age, some leave, of course. They must learn to control their talents, to focus them." She paused. "This must all seem rather strange."

Alice let her gaze drift upward, to the ancient candle wheels suspended from the coffered ceiling. "Stranger than what?"

The older woman smiled and went on. "There are fewer than twelve old residents here now," she said. "Excluding Dr. Berghast, and his small staff. The children are kept in small groups, taught by a few teachers only. They are . . . discouraged from intermingling. Dr. Berghast believes it best to keep their intimacies limited."

"Why?"

Mrs. Harrogate shrugged. "He does not explain his reasons. Not to me."

They came down into a grand entrance hall. Leather armchairs arranged around thick Persian carpets in each corner, immaculate, empty. A huge stone hearth, unlit, in the rear wall, and on either side, doors opening into shadows beyond.

"Meals are served through here, Miss Quicke. And here is the smoking room, for gentlemen only."

Alice snorted at that.

"Quite," said Mrs. Harrogate. "I expect a scandalous visit would give the older residents much to discuss. To your left is a passage leading to the little classroom where Charlie and Marlowe will study. It is run by Miss Davenshaw. She is strict but fair. Most of her instruction, however, is given in the outbuildings. It is of a more . . . practical nature. You are welcome to walk the grounds, but do not approach those buildings, Miss Quicke. For your own safety."

Alice gave her an irritated look.

But if Mrs. Harrogate noticed—and she did, Alice knew, she noticed everything—still, she gave no indication. She just interlaced her fingers, nodded grimly. "You will have more questions, of course. Dr. Berghast will send for you when you're stronger."

Just then there came the sound of running footsteps, and an ancient oak door across the hall was thrown open, and a girl with a long braid flying out behind her ran through, in a blur. Right on her heels came Charlie, long-legged like a camel. When he saw Alice he stopped, stared. For an instant he looked, she thought, almost happy, almost like the young man he could have been, in a different life, a different world.

And then, behind Charlie, straggling and trying to keep up, a smaller figure burst through, black hair tousled, shirt untucked, little arms plowing the air. Marlowe.

"Alice!" he cried. "You're awake!"

He ran to her, and she felt her legs give out.

"Oh thank God," she whispered. And pulled him fiercely into her arms, feeling the small good warmth of his little body.

It was late when Margaret Harrogate crossed the wet courtyard at Cairndale and entered a nondescript door in the east wing. She was thinking about Alice Quicke. Her head and her ear were hurting again, and she pressed a hand against the bandage as if to contain the ache. She walked quickly through the rooms, their furnishings shrouded in white sheets, drapes closed against the world. At a thick oak door, she knocked twice; a voice answered; she lifted the heavy iron ring, twisted it sideways, and went in.

A reek of dust and spices and moldering earth. Only Dr. Berghast liked it here. This was the institute's old storeroom. There were long metal shelves filled with jars, their labels yellowed and faded, and little wooden worktables pushed up against the walls, with old-fashioned weights and measures and scoops of various sizes.

She found him gazing out the window at the rain. When first she'd met him, his hair had been black as a raven's wing. Now, white hair fell long over his collar. His still-powerful hands were clasped behind him. The knuckles of his fingers looked swollen and protuberant, like knots in a tree. But he was still strong, broad-backed.

"I have been thinking about the creature you were bringing me," he said, not turning to look at her. "The litch, who was thrown from the train. Do you believe he is dead?"

"No," said Margaret, surprised. "It would take more than that to kill him."

"Can he be found?"

"It would not be easy."

"Nothing worth the doing ever is, Mrs. Harrogate." He turned and looked at her. His face was unlined, the face of a younger man. "And how is Miss Quicke?"

"It's too soon to tell," Margaret replied. "I informed her about what happened to Mr. Coulton. Perhaps I ought to have waited. When you see her, she will ask you about Adra Norn. What will you tell her?"

Dr. Berghast smoothed his beard with his palm. "I will tell her the truth," he said slowly, "or what I know of it." His eyes glittered like gray stones. "Alice Quicke's role in this is far from finished. Will she do for our purposes, do you think?"

Margaret, standing, thought about it.

"She isn't ready," she said. "But she will be. Have you seen the boys yet?"

"Not yet. Soon." Dr. Berghast studied her carefully. "You do know who he is, the little one?"

Margaret nodded.

Berghast tapped his thumbs over his interlaced fingers, brooding. "The boy has come back to me," he said, with a quiet satisfaction. "As you said he would."

There was something in his face, a dark hunger, and seeing it Margaret felt a shiver go through her.

18

THE YOUNG TALENTS

Safe. Charlie Ovid felt *safe*.

It was a peculiar feeling for him, safety, a kid who'd been stolen away to a fog-thick city by a mysterious Englishman with a gun and there, for God's sake, stalked by a *monster*. And yet he *did* feel safe; he slept that long first night at the institute in a narrow room with a slanted ceiling, Marlowe in the bed next to his, and the horror of their flight out of London faded like a dream. And all the menacing worlds he'd known—the sweltering prison in Natchez, the sun-drenched fields of cotton in the Delta, even the murky streets of Wapping at night, all of them—felt very far away.

Safe. That was the wonder of it. And so, on that first morning, when Charlie woke to hushed voices, to *girls'* voices, he wasn't afraid; he didn't leap to his feet, doubling his fists; he just lay groggy and still under the blankets, and tried to hear. They were two and they were talking about Marlowe.

"You reckon it's true, then?" whispered the first. "The shining boy? It's really him?"

"I expect so."

"Huh. Ain't much to look at, is he?"

"This coming from you?"

"Shh. He's like to hear you."

"Miss Davenshaw said they found him in America, however he got there. And this other one too. She said their train was attacked by Jacob Marber and they fought him off. He fought him off. Again."

"She told you all that?"

"Yes."

"She don't tell *me* that much. Why don't she?"

"You have to ask that? Really?"

A muffled snort, like a laugh. "Hell. They could've been found in the bloody arctic, wouldn't make no difference. No way old Jacob's done with them." A rustling, as the girl drew near. "Aw, Ko. Waked this one up now, you did."

Charlie cracked an eye. The room was filled with daylight. His tongue felt thick and he worked his jaw a moment, gulping air. He saw Marlowe asleep in the next bed, twisted in white sheets, his little trustful face smoothed in sleep, and then he raised his head and saw the girl.

She'd perched herself up on the narrow writing desk, so that her legs dangled free. She was maybe two years older than him, dressed in a plain gray pinafore. She wasn't white; he'd seen Chinese workers in the rail yards in Natchez and there was a likeness there, maybe. She had a slender face, wide shoulders. Her long hair was black and shining and had been plaited in a braid that fell all the way to her waist. She wore black kidskin gloves with the fingers cut out. Her eyes were as black as her hair. He'd never seen anyone like her. He realized he was staring and a heat came into his cheeks and he looked away.

"I knew you weren't sleeping," said the girl. "You're a terrible faker. Do you always pretend to sleep, so you can spy on a girl?"

"I, I never . . . ," he mumbled. "I mean, it's not . . ."

"So you're Charlie Ovid," she went on, unimpressed. She looked him up and down. "I thought you'd be older. I'm Komako."

Uneasy, Charlie glanced around. He couldn't see the second girl. "Who were you talking to?"

The girl Komako's face took on an innocent look. She tugged at her braid. "Hm?"

"Just now. I heard you. There was someone else in here."

"In here?"

He blinked, suddenly unsure.

But just then the air shifted beside his bed, as if the gloomy light itself, spilling in through the window, was rippling.

"Boo!" whispered the second girl, into his ear.

Charlie nearly fell out of his blankets. He scrabbled backward against the headboard, staring at the emptiness, his heart thundering in his chest. There was no one there.

"Aw, I'm over here, Charlie. No, here."

He turned his face from side to side, wild-eyed, like he was going crazy. Like he'd hit his head on the train and now he was hearing voices.

But the voice was real. "You ain't crazy," it said. "I'm what they call invisible, like."

Slowly he reached out a hand. It brushed only air. "Are you a . . . a ghost?"

Komako screwed up her face. "She's a *talent*, Charlie. Like all of us."

"The name's Ribs," the voice said cheerfully, several feet away now. "But you got to keep quieter. We ain't supposed to be in here. Ain't *proper*, like. Miss Davenshaw'd skin us alive, she known we was in here. So is that really the shining boy? The one what fought Jacob Marber off an lived, like?"

"Uh," said Charlie. "Yeah—?"

"Wait. You don't know who he is? Ko, he don't even know."

"Your little friend there is famous," said Komako. "Everyone thought he was dead."

"Famous?"

Komako shrugged. "Sure. He's the shining boy. Stopped Jacob Marber from killing everyone here at Cairndale five years back. He was just a baby. But he disappeared, got stolen away...."

Charlie glanced over at Marlowe, still sleeping. He was still sleepy and trying to make sense of what the two girls were going on about but it was hard, he was confused. They seemed to be waiting for him to say something more, so he said, "Who's Miss Davenshed?"

"Davenshaw. Our governess. She ain't *all* bad." The invisible girl, Ribs, made a clicking noise with her tongue. "You'll meet her soon enough. Go on, tell us: What were he like, on the train? Jacob, I mean."

"How'd you know about the train?"

"Aw, everybody round here knows. It's all anyone's talking about. Hell, Alfie in Mr. Smythe's class was takin wagers on it. You *was* on that train, yeah? You *did* fight off Jacob?"

Charlie wrapped the blanket around himself, sat up. "Marlowe did it mostly. Marlowe and Alice. I never did much."

"Well, you didn't die. That's something." Komako dropped to the floor, her long braid swaying, and she walked over to Marlowe's bed. "He's a little one."

"Yeah."

"How old is he?"

"Eight."

"Seems about right." Komako's face had a strange expression on it, part angry, part sad. "We don't have any little ones here. Not as young as that."

The mattress creaked beside him; Ribs had sat down. "Well, he's one of us again. And you is, too." She dropped her voice to a theatrical whisper. "So. What do you do, what's your talent, then? You ain't got a flesh giant under the bed now, do you?"

"Uh . . . what?"

"He doesn't know what that is," said Komako patiently. "You'll meet Lymenion soon enough, Charlie One-of-Us-Now. Though he's kind of . . . gross."

"Aw, he's cute, Ko."

"He's not cute. Even Oskar doesn't think he's cute."

"I, uh . . . I heal," said Charlie quietly. "I've always done. I don't ever get hurt, or killed, or anything."

Komako's dark eyes studied him. All at once he felt a sudden sharp pinch on his forearm, and he yelped. "Jesus! What'd you do that for?"

"You said you don't get hurt," Ribs complained.

"I get *hurt*. I just heal."

"Oh."

Komako was grinning. "Ribs can be kind of literal, sometimes," she said. "It's been a long time since we've seen a new haelan here."

"What kind of a name is Ribs, anyway?" said Charlie, glowering.

"A *fine* one, is what kind," Ribs's voice replied. "Charlie's a name for a bloody horse, so what's it to you?"

Komako seemed to be enjoying herself all of a sudden. "It's Eleanor Ribbon, actually. But she'll do worse than pinch you if you call her that."

Charlie was still rubbing at his arm when the bed creaked. It was Marlowe, sitting up in his nightshirt, rubbing at his eyes with his little fists. He looked around at them all and smiled a sleepy smile.

"Hi," he said shyly.

Later, while the boys were getting dressed, Komako Onoe lurked in the corridor outside their room, brooding. They weren't supposed to be in the boys' corridor, really; but Mr. Smythe and the other kids were down at breakfast, or already off to classes; and Miss Davenshaw need never know.

Fact was, Komako didn't know what to think. They *seemed* ordinary enough, if there even was such a thing at Cairndale. But seeing the shining boy in the flesh, Marlowe, brought a rush of memories back to her. That night, when Jacob had returned, changed, violent, dark as the dust that radiated at his fists . . . She and Ribs had seen him, at a distance, in the dark, but not been able to get close, not close enough to talk to him. The baby he'd come to murder, or steal, she'd hardly seen, only heard crying sometimes in the night when the window was left ajar. But she'd seen the smashed cradle, she'd seen the shattered window the morning after. She'd blamed herself, since. Maybe if she'd managed to talk to Jacob, maybe she could've stopped him.

All this was in her as she waited for the boys. She could feel Ribs watching her face, watching the quick play of her thoughts in it. "We should take them to Miss Davenshaw," she said quietly. "Now that they're awake. She'll be expecting them."

"Or . . . ," came Ribs's disembodied voice slyly. "We could just take a . . . *detour*. Give em a eyeful of the old haunt, so to speak. Find out all their *secrets*, like."

Komako blew out her cheeks, impatient. "We're not taking them to the Spider, Ribs. No."

"Loch's a lovely sight, this time of day. Could be *fun*—"

"No."

The Spider was their name for what slept in the monastery ruins. The glyphic. He never woke, it was said, not fully, and was so ancient, he'd grown into the roots of the wych elm that soared out of the old stones. It was said just to brush his skin was to see truth. The Spider located the lost children, in his dreaming; but far more important, he kept the orsine sealed fast, containing the dead, keeping all manner of evil on the other side. If something were to happen to him, the orsine would rip open; the dead would pour through into this world. No one could say what that would mean, but they'd learned enough to glean it wouldn't be pretty. The Spider's presence sheltered the very walls of Cairndale from creatures like Jacob, like the drughr. Disturbing him was strictly forbidden.

Which meant Ribs, of course, had already done it. Ribs with her sneaking, her poking about. No one else had dared. How often she'd gone, Komako couldn't guess, but Ribs swore she'd never touched his skin, never dared *that*.

There was a thrump as Ribs, still invisible, leaned into the wall. She cracked her knuckles, one by one by one. "That Charlie's handsome. I mean, in a scared rabbity kind of way."

"Don't be coarse," said Komako. She pulled her long braid forward.

"You think it too. I seen it."

"I don't trust him. You shouldn't either."

"You just don't trust nobody. I known bad sorts all me life, Ko. He ain't one." Ribs sniffed, then added mischievously, "Trust ain't half hard, you know. Just one touch by the Spider, an all sorts of gibberish'd come out . . ."

But just then the boys emerged from their room, hair mussed, eyes still sleepy, both dressed in the collared shirts and gray waistcoats given to all the boys at Cairndale, Marlowe's sleeves too long and flapping, Charlie tall and rail-thin with his bony wrists sticking out from his sleeves and one hand pinching up the waist of his trousers. Komako raised an eyebrow at that, and Charlie saw it, and all of a sudden he was looking with great interest at his shoes.

She glowered, to keep from smiling. So easily embarrassed, that one. The copper skin on his face and throat was so smooth and flawless, it almost glowed.

"I want to see Alice," said the little one, Marlowe. "Can we go find her, please?"

Ribs's voice answered. "Aw, she ain't even waked up yet. You want to see old Davenshaw first, anyhow."

Komako saw the boy glance, troubled, at Charlie. Both went quiet. She understood wariness, she understood fear. She'd been in Scotland nine years now and still felt it, though Tokyo, the old theater, her beloved Teshi, all of it had faded, faded into sepia, like an old daguerreotype. Oh, there were mornings yet when she'd wake with her throat sore, the dream of her sister's small hand in her own still real, still warm, and the ache she felt as it all was sucked down over the edge of sleep, as if being taken from her again, was almost unbearable. On such mornings she wanted to cry. Someone so small and so good shouldn't be ripped from the world, not like that. Mostly, though, Komako had grown used to Cairndale; she'd smoothed out her English easily; she'd grown close with Ribs and with Oskar. True, the weather was gray and chilly; true, the food was heavy and sour; true, the clothes were stiff and impractical. Her hands were still red and chapped. But Cairndale was not the only world; she'd grown up in another, a world of cruelty and hurt; and she was glad for the shelter of this place.

As, in time, would Charlie and Marlowe also be.

They passed the other boys' rooms, doors standing open, beds made tight and not an object out of place. She glanced at Charlie and Marlowe as they went along the corridor, down a narrow servant's staircase, on their way to Miss Davenshaw and the schoolroom. It was strange to think they'd confronted Jacob, that they'd seen him and even fought him. They still seemed so . . . innocent. She herself hadn't seen Jacob in years. She thought of him sometimes, mostly as he'd been in those first days in Tokyo, and on their sea voyage out of Japan—the quiet sadness in his eyes, the kindness, the calm silences as they stood at the railing together, watching the sun sink into the sea. He'd taught her how to control her talent, how to draw the dust in a way that cut her less, that eased the chill in her wrists. It had been a distraction, she knew, had known it even then, still reeling from the loss of her sister. She'd been grateful for it. But even on that first leg of their journey, along the coastline of China, before his vanishing, she'd seen how withdrawn he was becoming, how little sleep he could find. Mr. Coulton had seen it too, she knew. And then, at Cairndale, her new life had begun: lessons with Miss Davenshaw, arithmetic, literature, penmanship, geography. Her friendship with Ribs. The history of the orsine and the nature of talents. Practical classes of how to work the dust and how to control it.

Until, of course, that terrible night, when Jacob had returned, and what he'd done to those poor children at the river, and going after that baby like a man possessed, that baby who was here now, improbably alive, grown, the famous shining boy.

Through the glazed windows she could see rain. The daylight in the corridors was dim. They were nearing the schoolroom when Charlie caught up to her, asked about her talent. "You didn't ever say what *you* do," he said. "Your talent."

Komako studied him. Her covered hand was on the door pull. And then something in her, some stubborn thing, that same thing that pushed everyone away, and that Ribs was always telling her not to give in to, that same unhappy part of her looked Charlie square in the face and saw the openness in him and turned sharply from it.

"You know that thing that attacked you on the train?" she said. "Jacob Marber?"

Charlie nodded.

"I'm like him," she said flatly.

She didn't pause to see the effect of her words, didn't have to. She knew it would be disgust or revulsion or something like it. So she just opened the door angrily, and went through.

Except it wasn't disgust, or revulsion, or anything like that. Charlie heard the pain in her reply and knew it for what it was, shame, because he'd felt it too, all his life, and he just felt bad for even having asked the question at all.

The schoolroom might have been the old library once; it was well-lit, with a wall of glass panes at the far end, and bulleted leather sofas arranged under the eaves. As they stepped forward, Charlie felt Marlowe take his hand; then they were walking down between the rows of desks, a mezzanine above them to their left, and walls of books on either side.

At the end, silhouetted in front of the windows, stood a woman. Tall and severe as a slide rule. She wore a floor-length skirt and a white blouse that accentuated her bony frame and she stood to one side of her desk. It was Miss Davenshaw. She turned her face and Charlie saw that she wore a black cloth tied across her eyes: she was blind.

"Mr. Ovid. And young Master Marlowe. Cairndale is most pleased to have you with us. I trust Miss Onoe has shown you the manor?"

Charlie looked uneasily over at Komako. "Uh . . . a little?"

"I see." The old woman paused then and turned her sightless face to the wall, listening. "Miss Ribbon," she said sharply. "It is not polite to eavesdrop."

"I weren't, Miss Davenshaw," Ribs protested. "I swear it."

"Nor do we *lurk*, Miss Ribbon. And certainly not *in the altogether*." The blind woman walked smoothly to a cupboard under the window and felt around in a drawer there. She took out a folded pinafore. "You will please join us *suitably* attired, hm?"

"Yes, Miss Davenshaw," said Ribs meekly.

Charlie watched in wonder as the pinafore floated upward and away, around the standing chalkboard. A moment later and Ribs reappeared, visible now, her face flushed, her bright red hair clawed back off her face. She was smaller than Komako, and freckled, with soft lips. Charlie stared. Her eyes were very green. Beside him, Marlowe stared too.

"What?" said Ribs, narrowing her eyes. "I never growed a second head, did I?"

Charlie swallowed, looked away.

"It's just . . . you're pretty," breathed Marlowe.

Komako snorted.

Miss Davenshaw resumed her position at the front of the desk, standing. She crooked a finger. "Mr. Ovid," she said. "Come forward."

Charlie, uncertain, glanced over at Komako. Beside her, Ribs was grinning, nodding at him. He went to Miss Davenshaw and the blind woman reached out and gently, ever so gently, felt with her fingertips at the edges of his face. Her fingers brushed the bridge of his nose, the hollows of his eyes, they danced along his lips. Her touch was cool, soft, wonderful.

"Now I see you," she murmured, and there was a kind of benediction in it.

As she did the same to Marlowe, the little one spoke up. "Miss Davenshaw?" he said. "Is Alice all right? I want to see her."

Her fingertips traced his jawline, up to the shell of his ears. "Miss Quicke is resting, child," she replied. "You may look in on her later. I am told she is healing well and that it is because of you. Ah, yes. You are a fine young man also. I have wondered all these years what you would grow into. I am pleased to see you are not a monster. You may sit now."

"That's a joke," Ribs whispered to Charlie. "She's right funny, some-times."

But Charlie was still turning over in his head what the blind woman had said about Miss Alice and Marlowe. He didn't understand. "Because of you?" he whispered, as the boy sat back down. "What is she talking about?"

"I helped," said Marlowe. "In the carriage, on the way here. Alice was sick and I helped."

Now Miss Davenshaw was speaking again. "You will have ques-tions, I am sure. Let me set your minds at ease," she said. "Miss Rib-bon, what is the purpose of the Cairndale Institute? Would you care to enlighten our guests?"

"Um . . . it's our home?"

"A home is not a purpose, Miss Ribbon. Miss Onoe?"

"It is a bulwark against the dead."

"Indeed. Against the dead, and the drughr. We preserve the pas-sage between worlds and see that it stays closed. And what is Cairn-dale's purpose *in your lives?*"

"To equip us," said Komako. "To give us the skills we need, so we can be safe."

"The skills, and the knowledge. There are twenty-one students here. You will meet the others in time, no doubt. But most of your interactions will be with each other. To that end our days are divided into morning classes, wherein we receive an education, and an after-noon practicum, wherein we work on controlling and strengthening our particular talents. We have not had a haelan in many years, Mr. Ovid. We are pleased to have you among us."

"Yes, ma'am."

"And you, Marlowe. You would do well to remember that being *known of* is not the same as being *known.* Yes?"

The boy stared at her with big eyes. "Yes, Miss Davenshaw," he said, clearly confused.

Miss Davenshaw's face was impassive. "Now. Firstly, the rules. You will listen when you are spoken to; I will not need to tell you a thing twice, I trust. Lessons begin at half past eight each morning; you will not be late. In the classroom you are not to move objects or furniture around; I shall not look kindly on anyone who sets a chair in my path. Attendance in the dining room for each meal is mandatory. You will not leave the grounds of Cairndale under any circumstances, nor for any reason, except when accompanied by staff. It wouldn't do to have unusual children drifting about the countryside, alarming the locals. Our safety here depends upon our discretion. Now. The rooms of the older residents are off-limits, as is the upper east wing, where Dr. Berghast works. Do not let me hear of your snooping. The other children, with their tutors, need not concern you. *This* is your class here. Most important, the glyphic's island is strictly forbidden. You will not disturb it. Do I make myself clear?"

Marlowe put up his hand.

"She can't *see* you," whispered Charlie. "You got to just *say* it, Mar."

"Miss Davenshaw?" said Marlowe. "What's the glyphic? Is it the big yellow tree?"

She made a tsking noise. She tilted her blindfolded face as if she could see them all with a greater clarity. "I'd have thought Miss Onoe would have told you all about our resident glyphic, when she was waking you in your beds this morning. No? She did not mention the *Spider*?"

Charlie saw Komako tug at her long braid, her face reddening.

"The glyphic, child, is the one we all depend on here. He lives below the tree, in the ruins of the old monastery, on the island in the loch. It is he who keeps us safe, who harnesses the power in the orsine and keeps it sealed. Should anything happen to the glyphic, the orsine would tear itself open. It is a thin membrane; on its far side lies a different world, a world of the spirit."

"Aw, you got to at least tell em what he looks like, an all," Ribs burst out.

Miss Davenshaw frowned. "You have an unhealthy interest in our glyphic, Miss Ribbon. Indeed, in all manner of things that are forbidden."

"I don't."

The old woman arched a disapproving eyebrow.

"I mean, not *just* in them kinds of things," mumbled Ribs.

"I am sure Miss Ribbon will regale you with tales both fanciful and imagined about the nature and appearance of our glyphic," said Miss Davenshaw. "Listen to them at your peril. I expect none of it will interest you just now; but we shall speak of it later, when you are settled."

But Miss Davenshaw was mistaken, in saying that the darker machinery of Cairndale wouldn't interest Charlie, nor the strange creature the children called the Spider, nor the mysterious orsine itself. In the weeks to come he would, in fact, learn a considerable amount about such matters, and he would, in time, eventually learn more about the orsine, and the terrors loose beyond it, than almost any other talent in the world. But for now all of that would remain shrouded in mystery. For while they were meeting with Miss Davenshaw a pudgy boy came to the door, a boy maybe Charlie's own age, or a bit younger, with hair so blond it looked white, and white lips, and pale blue eyes. He looked like he'd rolled in flour.

"Yes, Oskar, what is it?" said Miss Davenshaw, turning her face in his direction.

The boy entered the schoolroom, out of breath. He had a string tied around his finger and he was wrapping and unwrapping it nervously.

It was then Charlie saw, squeezing in behind, a second figure, a hulking shapeless thing. It could have been the boy's shadow except it was massive and solid, or nearly so; it seemed in fact to be the consistency of jelly, shuddering slightly as it moved, but marbled and slick like raw meat: a faceless thing that turned its faceless head this way and that, as if trying to see whatever Oskar was seeing. Yet it had no eyes to see by, nor ears nor lips nor mouth nor nose. Flies buzzed around it; a reek of turned meat entered the room and lingered. Beside Charlie, Marlowe caught his breath. But Charlie had no time to wonder at the thing, at the—what had Ribs called it?—the *flesh giant*; for Oskar had been sent with a message.

Alice had woken up at last.

19

HOUSE OF GLASS

Marlowe and Charlie, Charlie and Marlowe.

They were what Alice had, now.

She was kneeling in the grand foyer of that manor house, as if to receive some sacrament, while the two boys came to her, and she took them into her arms, and she held them to her heart.

She could have held them like that forever. But there was much to discuss; and after Mrs. Harrogate had taken her leave, the boys walked Alice carefully, worriedly, back up to her room. They were wearing identical white shirts and gray waistcoats and gray trousers, unfussy, ill-fitting. She hated the anxious tenderness of it, but was grateful too. She would not meet the girl who had run in first until the following day; nor any of the other young talents, the girl who could disappear, the boy with the flesh giant. Instead she and Marlowe and Charlie remembered Coulton; they grieved him, Marlowe steadfastly refusing to talk about Brynt; and together the three of them, that first night, went out onto the lawn after moonrise and held hands and said a prayer in memory of their dead.

Not everything was sorrowful. Cairndale's crooked halls, its labyrinthine interior, the drift of voices and old persons disappearing around corners, all of it made their first days there eerie and lovely, somehow, as if they had stepped inside a children's story. They stood on the stony beach of the loch and peered across at the island, and the ruined monastery, the golden tree growing up out of the stone ribs. Alice herself slept, and continued to heal.

And on the third morning, as she was rising from her breakfast, she was informed that Dr. Berghast wished to see her.

She was taken by a servant through a rear corridor and outside to a glasshouse, domed and built of wrought iron, its thousands of little panes steamed over and opaque. Constructed against one side of the carriage house, with a bare sandstone patio facing south, it looked, she thought, more like a delicate landlocked ship than an orangery. Across the lawns she could see the stables, and far beyond that, the low stone wall marking the property.

The first thing Alice noticed was Mrs. Harrogate, waiting for her in the entrance, the bandages taken off her ear. Harrogate's face still looked battered, her eyelid marbled but no longer swollen.

The next thing she noticed was Mrs. Harrogate's outfit: a checkered cloak and a matching hat, a small traveling case clutched in both hands. She was leaving for London.

Last of all she noticed a powerful-looking man down one aisle, white-bearded, wearing a leather apron with pockets, whom she at first mistook for a gardener. A gray-and-white bird hunched on his shoulder. He was bent over a little iron cart, repotting a seedling of some kind. But under his apron he wore a black suit and a crisp high collar, too fine for such work.

"Oranges, Miss Quicke," he called. He nodded up at the trees beside her, his hands still working the soil in the pot. "And we have strawberries also, for consumption in January. The heating is the difficulty. I am told they construct boilers now that can run all the night through, far more efficient than steam." He glanced up at her. His eyes were a startling pale gray, as if lit from within.

Alice, uncertain, shot a questioning look at Mrs. Harrogate.

But Dr. Berghast, for that's who he was, only beckoned her closer. The joints in his wrist and shoulder popped softly as he did so. "A visitor once came to Heraclitus for advice and was embarrassed to find him warming himself in a kitchen. Kitchens, you see, were undignified spaces in ancient Greece. But Heraclitus only said, 'Come in, come in, do not be afraid. There are gods here too.'"

Just then the bird on his wide shoulder made a strange clicking noise and Alice saw, with some alarm, that it was made out of bones. An iron brace like a kind of armor held its delicate vertebrae in place. Its sleek feathers were stark against the armor.

"Ah," said Dr. Berghast, observing. "I call it a bonebird. A curious creation, hm?"

Alice, still staring, nodded.

"They were made for us by a bone witch, many years ago. We use them for messages. More efficient and reliable than the Royal Mail." He glanced sidelong at the creature on his shoulder. It clicked, tested its grip. "The lady who made them has, sadly, passed. But these wondrous things just keep on going. They are ninety-six years old, now. Older than the revolution in France."

Its eyeless sockets seemed to peer directly at Alice. She suppressed a shudder.

"Mrs. Harrogate informs me," said Dr. Berghast, "that you wish to know about Adra Norn. You should know, I have not heard from her in a long time. I do not know even if she is still alive. We are of an age, she and I; and that would make her very old indeed. But I will tell you what I can."

"How did you know her?"

"It is a small community of scholars, Miss Quicke, who share my . . . interests. Everyone knows everyone else. Adra and I wrote to each other for years, sharing theories and research. We did not discuss personal matters. It has been many, many years since last I saw her. That was in Marseilles, at a gathering of scholars interested in the intersections between science and religion. I, of course, approached the subject biased by science. Adra thought otherwise. But there was nevertheless much common ground between us. We both of us, for instance, believed in the invisible world."

"What is that?"

"It is not a *thing*, Miss Quicke. Merely an acknowledgment that what we see is not all that there is." Dr. Berghast scooped out a hollow in the black soil of the pot, pressed a seed in with his thumb, like a raisin into dough. "Adra believed holiness involved separating herself from the corruptions of the world. She believed if she could receive true grace, she could perform miracles."

"Like walking out of a fire."

He nodded. "Not, you understand, a very reasonable supposition, from a scientific point of view."

Alice gestured at the bonebird. "I've seen a few unscientific things myself, now."

"But not miracles, Miss Quicke, never miracles. Miracles are monstrous by their very nature, they are contrary to the laws of this world. The talents are entirely natural. Marlowe and Charlie are no more evidence of God's hand in the world than you are, or I am."

"For some, that's enough."

"For some."

Alice studied the man's unlined face. He could have been forty, despite his white hair. But she knew he was much older than that. "You're telling me Adra Norn never walked out of that fire?"

"I find it unlikely. Do you not?"

"I was there. I saw it."

"You were a child. You know what you *think* you saw." His eye-lashes were long, and dark, and beautiful. "Adra was not like our residents here. She was never a part of our world. You understand that Bent Knee Hollow was not the only such community she founded?" He watched her closely and Alice felt—despite the gentleness of his voice—the concentrated and dizzying power of his attention. "Adra gathered around herself those she thought most . . . susceptible. Such as your mother. Ah, you are surprised. Of course I have heard about you. Is it not the reason Mrs. Harrogate believed you would be suitable?"

But Alice wasn't surprised. She'd assumed Dr. Berghast knew all about her; would have been surprised, in fact, if he hadn't.

"You must understand, Adra was always looking for something *particular* in her followers," Dr. Berghast continued. "A *particular* kind of faith. She wished to know where the essence of a thing resided, in the cause or the effect. Is it a miracle because it happened, or because it is *believed* to have happened?"

"You mean, the Hollow was all just some sort of . . . experiment?"

"Miss Quicke, even the most saintly among us still burn when touched by fire."

"People *died.*"

He nodded, said nothing.

Alice bit back her anger. She saw now she'd been hoping Adra Norn had been a talent, that there'd been some truth in what she and her mother had seen that night, when Adra walked through fire, something *real* to account for what her mother had done. But there was nothing.

"My mother believed it," she said softly. "She believed it so much it made her crazy. She believed everything Adra told her. Adra used to say: 'A strong faith makes its own change.'"

"We cannot change what we are. Only what we do."

"How did she do it? How did she make it look like she could walk out of a fire?"

Dr. Berghast held out his palms, seamed with dirt. The bonebird clicked its wings at his shoulder. "That I do not know," he said. "Carnival tricks, I expect. I am sorry about what happened. I have always believed faith and madness closely linked. I warned Adra. But she was willful, and determined to dabble in dangerous currents."

"In her letters, did she ever . . . mention my mother?"

Dr. Berghast paused, studying her. His expression was calm, unreadable. He might have been searching his memory, he might have been considering how to answer.

"No," he said at last. "Never."

Alice, feeling a sudden fierce disappointment rise up in her, turned to go. "I appreciate your time, Dr. Berghast. And your candor."

"And I," said Dr. Berghast, holding out a hand to stop her, "appreciate all that you have done for young Marlowe and Charlie. Mrs. Harrogate tells me they would not have survived their journey north, not without you."

"That was Coulton," said Alice. "He's the one deserves your thanks. And Marlowe's guardian, who fought off the creature with all the teeth. Brynt."

"The tattooed woman, yes. I did hear about her."

"A terrible affair," said Mrs. Harrogate softly. "A terrible loss of life. But there will be more. An evil is loose in the world, Miss Quicke, an evil of extraordinary appetite."

Alice turned. She'd almost forgotten Mrs. Harrogate. "You mean Jacob Marber."

"I mean the drughr."

"Jacob is merely . . . its instrument," said Dr. Berghast. He reached up to his shoulder and lifted the bonebird by two fingers up onto a perch. It shifted its grip sideways, cocked its head, its fragile bones clicketing. "I blame myself. It was I who found him in Vienna, you see. I glimpsed his talent. He was already who he would become, not a child any longer. I just did not see it then. I taught him myself; and when he came of age, I sent him in search of unfound talents. There was one child in particular, nine years ago, a dustworker like himself, in the Japanese islands. On the return voyage, he vanished. Your Mr. Coulton was with him; he said it had been a disturbing journey, that the child's little sister had died." Dr. Berghast slowly brushed the potting soil from his hands, with great heaviness. "Of course, we didn't know then that Jacob had been seduced by the drughr. The following year, not far from here, a talent was murdered. A young mother. It was Jacob. He took her newborn child, right out of her dying arms, to feed it to the drughr. But I stopped him; I was too late to save the mother, but I saved the infant. I did that much, at least."

"Marlowe," whispered Alice.

"The boy you call Marlowe, yes. I stood as his guardian and father. But Jacob was not satisfied; he located two children bound for our institute here, and took the little ones instead down to the banks of the Lye, and cut their throats, and fed them to the drughr. And when the drughr was strong enough, it helped Jacob break into Cairndale. They were trying to steal Marlowe back."

"Why? Why him?"

"That, Miss Quicke, I cannot tell you."

Alice swallowed. "That is . . . it's awful."

"It was, yes. It still is. I blame myself. You must understand, at the time I knew so little about the drughr's appetites. I'd thought the worst stories were like fairy stories. Oh, some of the old ones here believed. But I did not. I knew only that *something* had got through our orsine, that *something* had escaped."

"What is this . . . orsine?"

"A passage to the land of the dead, Miss Quicke," said Dr. Berghast. "Or so it appears; no one is entirely certain. There are two, in fact. The Paris orsine has been inactive for centuries, but ours still has the unpleasant habit of . . . *opening*. But the worlds must be kept separate, you understand, they must be kept in balance. And so we are tasked with keeping it closed. The dead are mortal, just as we are. They wander the gray rooms slowly forgetting, until gradually, over centuries, they dissolve away into the very particles of the universe. Imagine if they wandered back over."

"How can you know all this?"

"How does a fisherman know what lives in the sea? I have lived alongside it all my life."

"You are talking about souls."

Dr. Berghast frowned. "I prefer to keep religion out of it. There are no hosts of angels, singing from on high. It is a world like this one, only different. And there is no returning from it."

Alice rubbed at her knuckles, trying to take it all in.

"No returning from it, that is," Dr. Berghast went on, his voice darkening, "except for the drughr. Somehow it *did* return. It is here now, among us, in this world. And it is growing stronger."

"What is it, exactly?"

"A soul that fears death, more than anything else. A soul that fears the obliteration death brings. According to the old stories, it was locked behind an iron gate, centuries ago, after a great war. It was hoped the drughr would eventually dissolve, as the dead do, and that its evil would cease. In the stories, it drifted on the other side, preying on lost souls. But on this side, it is subject to decay, as are all things. Here it must commit unspeakable acts, in order to sustain itself."

"The children," said Alice.

Dr. Berghast nodded. "Because it is still weak. When it is stronger, it will feed on all the talents. Where the drughr goes, slaughter follows.

Human life is of no consequence to it. It is a predator, and we are its prey. And Jacob Marber is its . . . host. It is not yet powerful enough to be in our world, without his assistance."

"Why are you telling me all this?"

"Because I need your help," said Dr. Berghast. "I would like you to find Jacob Marber."

Alice gave a surprised laugh. "Me?"

Mrs. Harrogate, standing quite still at the end of the row, spoke up. "As long as he is out there, Miss Quicke, your Marlowe is not safe. Charlie is not safe."

Dr. Berghast placed the seedling he'd been repotting back into place under the glass. "At present, it still must act *through* Jacob; he is its weakness. Without him, it will be as nothing again. Yet with each new feeding, with each new child it devours, its power increases. Soon enough it will come here. You've seen what Jacob is capable of; the drughr is worse."

"My methods are for people," Alice protested. "Jacob Marber could be anywhere. How does a thing like him even think? You'd have to think like him to find him." She shook her head. "Neither of you could find him before; what makes you imagine I can find him now?"

"We know he's in London," said Mrs. Harrogate.

"London's huge."

"And," added Dr. Berghast, wiping the black soil on his smock and looking up, "we now have something we didn't before."

"What's that?"

"You."

Alice scoffed.

"Your injury, rather," corrected Dr. Berghast. He bent over the little wood desk and poured out a jar of iron filings. He took a magnet from his pocket and held it between thumb and forefinger for Alice to see, and then he waved it over the filings. "See how the iron seeks the magnet. That is what Jacob's dust does, with him. It is a part of him. And he left some of it inside you, when he attacked you." Berghast's voice was calm but his eyes were bright, too bright. "You doubt me, of course. But close your eyes, Miss Quicke. Reach out. Let yourself *feel* him. Can you feel him?"

Warily, she did as he asked. Standing there in the glasshouse, her lips dry, eyelids fluttering. She could feel *something*, a prickling that wasn't there before. It felt like a fishhook in her ribs, tugging. She didn't like it.

Berghast was watching her. "The two of you are connected."

She was shaking her head, increasingly angry. She felt violated, disgusted. She let her gaze slide over to Mrs. Harrogate, waiting still in her traveling clothes, both hands clutching the little case in front of her. "If I do this, if I find him for you . . . what will you do with him?"

"I will kill him," said Mrs. Harrogate.

"How do you kill a thing like that?" Alice looked at the doctor. "I assume you have a plan."

"Not I," said Dr. Berghast.

Mrs. Harrogate smiled thinly. "There *is* a way. If you will trust me, Miss Quicke."

Alice looked at the clay pots, stacked in their rows. She looked at Dr. Berghast. His hard gray eyes, his mouth hidden by his beard, the power in his neck and shoulders. The sun came from behind a cloud and lit the glass around him so that suddenly she couldn't see his face.

Fuck it, she thought. She turned to Mrs. Harrogate.

"I'm going to want my gun back," she said.

20

THE DISAPPEARED ONES

Charlie had been at the institute almost two weeks, sleeping badly, when he first encountered the dark carriage.

It would prove his first glimpse of the other Cairndale, its invisible twin, identical down to the framed watercolors in the halls, the dust curling in its corners, but somehow sinister, as if filled with intention. And after that he started to wonder just what exactly was going on and how much he wasn't being told.

Alice had left for London a week before, in the early gloom, under a reef of red clouds in the east. She'd held Marlowe, held Charlie, while Mrs. Harrogate watched impatient from the footer, her veil at her face, her eyes hard as marbles. After that it was just him and Marlowe, just the two of them. Things between them turned more tender, tender the way a bruise is tender, tender like there was a deep ache inside it all and to touch it was to be reminded of the hurt. Komako and Ribs would show them around, and sometimes the pudgy Polish boy, Oskar, too, with his white-blond hair and his deep shyness, and his wet fleshly giant copying his every gesture. But Marlowe kept close to Charlie all the while, closer than usual, pulling his chair very near when they ate in the dining hall, climbing up into Charlie's bed after the lights were extinguished, that sort of thing, exactly like what a kid brother would be like, and Charlie was grateful for it. For the first time in his life, he didn't have to be alone.

But one night, after Alice had left, Charlie awoke and saw Marlowe silhouetted at the window seat, his knees folded up to his chest, his face turned to the gloom.

"What is it?" whispered Charlie. "You get a bad dream?"

The boy looked at him, his dark eyes soulful. "I heard horses."

Through the open window, Charlie heard it too: the faint whickering of horses. He got out of bed. Their room overlooked Loch Fae and the dock and the dark island out there with the twisted silhouette of the ancient wych elm. There was nothing to see though; Cairndale's courtyard was on the other side of the building, below the girls' quarters. In his nightshirt, Charlie shivered and folded his arms.

Marlowe chewed at his lip. "Where do you think Alice is right now?"

"In bed. If she's got any sense."

"Charlie?"

"What."

"Do you ever wonder how things could be different?"

"Sure." He sat down beside him, sighed. "But that kind of thinking is crazy-making. It doesn't help. You want me to get you a glass of water?"

But the boy folded one foot over the other, itching, and wouldn't be distracted. "I mean, what if Brynt hadn't taken me in? Or if she'd run from Alice back at Mr. Fox's? Or if Alice hadn't got me out of that hotel before Jacob Marber got in? If you just make anything just a little bit different . . ." His soft face was troubled. "Do you think we're *supposed* to be here? Is that why it is the way it is?"

"Not everything's got a reason for the way it is."

"My mama used to say, 'There's always a choice.' Brynt said it too. But it's not true, is it? We never chose to come here, not really."

"I did."

The boy thought about it. "Because of your father," he whispered.

Charlie nodded. "Not just that. But, yeah."

"Are you going to show Miss Davenshaw the ring? Maybe she can tell you what it is."

"That's a secret, Mar. Okay? I need you not to tell anyone about it. Not yet."

"Why?"

But Charlie just sighed heavily. "I don't know," he muttered.

The night was black in Marlowe's blue-black eyes and he blinked his long eyelashes and then he looked up at Charlie. He looked at him with a deep pure trust. "You know what, Charlie? I'm glad all those things happened the way they did," he whispered. "I'm glad because you're here with me now."

"I'm not going anywhere," said Charlie. He gave the boy's shoulder a squeeze. "Except to get you a glass of water. You go on back to bed, now. I'll be right back."

He went out into the corridor, silent as smoke. The wall sconces had been snuffed. There was a cut-glass jug of water on a pier table at the far end for all the boys to drink from and a tray of glasses over-turned on a dish towel, but the jug was empty. Charlie thought about it and then padded on down the cold hall and turned left, into the corridor where the girls slept. A second table stood there with a jug half-full and it was while he was pouring out a glass in his nightshirt and bare feet that Charlie looked out and saw the carriage.

The window faced the courtyard. A carriage had stopped near the entrance to the east wing. There must have been a light burning below, for a red glow reflected dully in the windows and Charlie could clearly make out the drawn curtains, the brass door latch, the footer unfolded beneath the door. Black wood siding glimmered in the shine. Otherwise, all was darkness and gloom. Its side lanterns were shuttered, its horses nickered softly in their traces.

He furrowed his brow, moved closer. His face was almost pressed to the glass. He was standing like that when he saw two men emerge from out of the east wing, carrying a long coffin-like box between them. They loaded it into the carriage on the far side and then stood talking near the horses. The driver was wrapped in black woolens with his face obscured by darkness and a rain cloak drawn over his head, his breath steaming in the cold. Something passed between the men, a small pouch. Then the driver climbed heavily up, unslung the whip. There came a jangle of harness, the squeak of ironshod wheels.

It was the passenger, though, that caught Charlie's eye. He'd turned to climb up also and for just a moment Charlie saw him clearly, his features lit up in the faint red light. A scarred face, beardless. Hard eyes. The man looked around, then raised his eyes. He glared directly up at Charlie.

Whether he'd seen him or not, or just the shape of him there, Charlie couldn't know. He felt a sudden deep fear. But it was then, sharply, with an unexpected force, he felt a hand on his sleeve and he stumbled and was pulled away from the window, into shadow.

He found himself staring into the face of Komako.

"What—?" he began, his blood loud in his ears.

He'd dropped the glass when he'd stumbled but Komako had somehow crouched and caught it, cleanly, just above the floor, so that only a little water had spilled and the glass hadn't shattered and no one had awoken or come running.

She looked at him grimly and, without speaking, handed back the glass. She wasn't wearing her gloves and he saw the skin of her hands looked blotchy and red.

The look on her face was fierce, alert, but also there was in it something else. Fear.

She raised a raw-looking finger to her lips.

"Shh," she whispered.

And then she turned in her white nightgown and slipped silently away, back up the corridor, like a ghost, her long black braid hanging to her waist as she went, past all the other girls' rooms, to the room she shared with Ribs. Charlie watched her go. Unbidden, Marlowe's words came to him again, how they didn't get to choose their lives, and all that happened was chance or fate, with no way of knowing the difference between.

It had been a strange encounter, almost like a dream. Whatever the rider and his passenger had been taking out to the dark carriage, Charlie couldn't guess at. But Komako never spoke of it, and he knew better than to ask. And anyway, in the meantime there was daily life at Cairndale, and the whole strange world of lessons and of learning.

There were maybe fifteen boys at Cairndale. The boys' bedrooms were all aligned along that same brief corridor with a master's room—Mr. Smythe's—at the far end, his door left ajar in the nights while the boys settled. Most of those boys were older, and white-skinned, though there were several Chinese and two silent brothers from the Gold Coast who kept to themselves. All of them snuck curious glances at Marlowe; even the older residents, and the teachers, would whisper and stare whenever Marlowe passed by. They'd all heard the stories; many of them had been there that night when Jacob Marber had broken into Cairndale. They seemed to think Marlowe half-miracle, half-monster, for having survived Marber's attack. The hell with it: Charlie and Marlowe stayed in the little room they'd been given that first night; and other than Oskar, they had little to do with other boys.

It was Komako and Ribs they spent their days with. Miss Davenshaw had set the five of them up in lessons together, liking, as she said, the different abilities of each. "You will teach each other," she said, "and learn that every one of us has our own gifts to share." If she had other, darker reasons, she did not say.

They woke each morning to Mr. Smythe in the hall, ringing a bell, calling them to dress. Then came breakfast in the dining room, bustling, noisy, the scraping of plates and the shouting and the laughter, and then the scattering of the kids to their various lessons. Marlowe and Charlie, Komako and Ribs and Oskar: the five of them began each morning in the book-lined schoolroom of stern Miss Davenshaw, under her unseeing gaze.

It was probably the most normal of all that they'd learn there, though Charlie couldn't know that at the time. Miss Davenshaw would stand rigidly at the front of the schoolroom and assign readings and tasks to each of them in turn, and they'd line up and take from her hands their assignments and sit back down and begin to learn. Charlie didn't mind it, liked it even, going through his letters and learning to read more quickly, more smoothly. Then came geography, the acquisitions of the British Empire, the countries of the east, and an endless litany of cities and nations and languages. After that, the history of the British Isles, a list of kings and queens and dates of battles. And last of all they'd go through their arithmetic on the chalkboard in the corner, while Miss Davenshaw, though blind, followed along their work and tsked at each error, and the pale morning light slowly filled the high windows and fell across the bookshelves and crept, gradually, down to the carpeted floor.

And after lunch they filed out through the dead English gardens, over the bloodred clay, to the outbuildings beyond, and there began the subtle study of talent work.

It was this Charlie had been most eager for, most dreading. The outbuildings were two long gray wooden buildings, like barns, or storage sheds, with roofs that leaked in the rain and floors of dirt. They were not heated and were only just barely—Ribs muttered with a grin—buildings at all.

There were others in the building, adults, some of them very old. Miss Davenshaw separated the kids and they each went off with a different instructor but Charlie she kept herself. "I have some experience with haelans," she explained. "I will teach you what I can. Ah . . . you are surprised."

Charlie, who'd been looking at her black blindfold, tied tightly across her eyes, and frowning at her, felt a heat go into his cheeks.

Miss Davenshaw smiled a sharp smile, just exactly as if she could see. "Oh, not myself, Mr. Ovid. I am obviously not like you. My great-great-grandfather was a haelan. He raised me. That was some time ago. He is . . . gone, now. But I do know a little of what he could and could not do."

Charlie, who had been using his talent all his brief life to stay alive, crossed his arms. "I know how it works," he said. "It just sort of does its own thing. It just sort of—"

"Reacts? Yes. But it can be controlled, too, Mr. Ovid, it is a greater talent than that. Though it will certainly take some effort, on your part. And much patience. If you are willing to learn, that is. Are you willing to learn?"

"Maybe," he said warily.

They were standing just inside the opened doors and the cold air was muscling over them and Charlie raised his eyes and looked at the loft at the far end. When he lowered them he saw Miss Davenshaw had started walking, through the doors, outside. For a sudden flickering moment he wondered if she knew where she was going.

"You are right to be cautious," she was saying, just as if he hadn't been almost left behind. "But you need not fear."

"I'm not afraid."

"Hm. Yes. Good." She led him across the brown grasses to the perimeter of the institute grounds. The sky threatened rain. It was Charlie's first close approach to the wall and he felt a low buzzing dread in his skull, like he was doing something wrong, like he ought not to be there. He tried to shrug it off but his anxiety only increased.

The stone wall looked ancient, waist-high, covered in black moss, crumbling in parts. It was loosely assembled with weird pancake-shaped stones that might have come from the bottom of the sea. It stretched off in both directions, over the furls and encircling the dark loch and its dark clay cliffs, as far as Charlie's eye could see.

Miss Davenshaw trailed a long pale hand over the stones as they walked. The red clay was slippery underfoot. Cairndale loomed off across the field, behind the outbuildings, forbidding, strange.

"Do you feel it, Mr. Ovid?" Miss Davenshaw asked quietly, her blind face turned away. "Do you feel the wards? Unpleasant, hm?"

He did; they were the source of his anxiety, his dread. They were like a prickle of electricity all around him, a hum in the air, at a frequency just below sound.

"That, Mr. Ovid, is the glyphic's doing," she said. "It keeps us all . . . safe. Talents such as yourself cannot cross through, from one side to the other, except that the glyphic wills it. It takes a tremendous effort from him to keep the wards strong, I am told. He is never at rest. That is one of the reasons a visit to the island is strictly forbidden. But it would not do to have Jacob Marber, or his litch, walk in here uninvited, would it?"

Charlie suppressed a shudder. That thing that had attacked him in London still gave him nightmares.

"But also," she continued, "the wards keep us safe from the prying eyes of ordinary folk. They would be most alarmed at what happens here, hm? If any person attempted to enter the grounds uninvited, they would find themselves overcome with a strong sense of unease, a . . . discomfort. Which would grow most overwhelming. They would turn back before they'd come ten feet, though they would not be able to explain why. Cairndale has a . . . reputation, because of this. Should you leave the premises, you would see. The locals would regard you with suspicion, with fear."

Charlie, who had lived all his life under the bitter eyes of white folk, nodded. "I reckon they'd do that anyhow," he said. "I don't look like—"

"I know what you look like, Mr. Ovid. You are not the only foreigner at Cairndale."

He paused, looking at her blindfolded eyes, angry at her rebuke. But he bit back his retort. He could see over the crumbling wall the world beyond, steady in its slow turning.

"What you do, Mr. Ovid, what all the talents do, is a kind of . . . necromancy. It is the manipulation of dead tissue. No one can manipulate living tissue. And no one can work their talent on another's flesh. Come. Walk with me, if you would." She drifted again forward, her face averted, as if listening to something.

"There are five kinds of talent," she continued, crisply. "Clinks, casters, turners, dustworkers, and glyphics. Do pay attention, Mr. Ovid, this is important. Firstly, the clinks. They can accentuate their own bodies. You, as a haelan, are of this order. As are strongs, like poor Mr.

Coulton was, who make their flesh so compact and dense it can even stop a bullet. Secondly, there are the casters, who can animate mortal remains. Bone witches, who whistle up skeletons, are casters. And Mr. Czekowisz—your friend Oskar, with his flesh giant Lymenion—is a caster. Thirdly, there are the turners, who can alter the *appearance* of their own flesh—Miss Ribbon, as you know, can make herself translucent. Others can even shapeshift. Fourthly, there are the dustworkers, like Miss Onoe, who can control and manipulate their own dead cells that go into dust, and bond other particulates to it. Lastly, there are the glyphics. But they are a strange and unknowable breed; they grow into their talent like a tree grows into a hillside. They are solitary and powerful and you must go to them, to find them. It is their gift—or curse—to be able to see the webbing that connects us all and follow the threads through. They are immensely powerful."

Charlie walked alongside her, trying to absorb everything. "Five talents," he murmured.

"You will hear some of your fellow students talk of a sixth talent. But it does not exist. I advise you to listen only to the facts and to resist rumors here, Mr. Ovid. There are many rumors, here at Cairndale."

He gave her a quick sharp look, furtively, but he couldn't make out her meaning. It didn't seem possible she could know about his suspicions, about his mother's wedding ring with the Cairndale crest, or the dark carriage and its rider.

"There is a substance in you," she continued, "which we here at Cairndale think of as 'dust,' though it is not dust, not in the ordinary sense of the word. It is this that animates your dead tissue, your dead cells. Why it is in you, and not another, I cannot say. There is much we do not know. But it is this 'dust' that makes your corporeal self . . . remarkable. It is *in* you and *through* you, and it leaves its traces wherever and whenever you use your talent. The body of a talent is a map of their dust, Mr. Ovid, and a glyphic can read it like a book.

"As a haelan," she went on, "your flesh heals itself. It stitches itself back together. It repairs the dead cells and in so doing it appears to restore the blood that is lost. You cannot stay drowned, you cannot stay burned, you cannot stay strangled." She paused, her long fingers reaching for his face, touching him quickly, gently. "Nothing comes from nothing. The talents are drawn from the lives of their users; the more they are used, the shorter those lives. You feel a terrible pain when your talent is at work? It is the same for all of us. That is the price being taken. Talents burn brightly, Mr. Ovid, but they burn out fast. All except you. When you come of age, around twenty or so, your body will slow down its aging process. You will outlive all of us."

"You're saying . . . I won't die?"

"Everything dies, Mr. Ovid. Except God and the angels and the idea of freedom in the hearts of the pure."

He furrowed his brow.

"A joke. No. You will live a long time. But nothing is forever; and your talent will weaken, eventually. And when it does, your body will begin to age. Slowly at first, then more swiftly. You will suddenly be old, and you will suddenly be dead. My great-great-grandfather was a strong man of thirty, two days before his death. When he died, he was paper-thin and frail."

Charlie swallowed. "How long does it take?"

"Dying?"

"The living."

"That depends on how powerful your talent is. They are not all equal. You will live at least one hundred and fifty years."

He wasn't sure he'd heard her right. He tried to do the numbers in his head. "That's not something I want."

"Then you are wiser than most. Nevertheless, it is something you *are*, Mr. Ovid; wanting has nothing to do with it. Now, there are limitations to your ability. Your limbs will grow back, should they be separated from your body, but severing your head will end your life rather swiftly. The greatest toll for you will be in your heart, and in your soul. It is a draining thing, outliving those you love. And watching the world change around you. But that is not something I can help you with."

Charlie nodded. Their footsteps squelched on.

"Control is what we will attempt, in our sessions together. Control is everything. Right now you have none. When you are hurt, your body repairs itself. That is all. But there is much more you can do, Mr. Ovid, many strange uses for a haelan's gift. I understand you already know how to conceal objects in your flesh. But there are haelans who have removed parts of themselves—bones, even—when their use was needed. And other haelans whose control was so great, they could bend the dead tissue in their bodies, rather than simply repairing it; they could *shape* their *bodies*."

"Shape their bodies?"

"It is called mortaling. You might even say it is the real talent, the purpose of the haelan's art. They could elongate their arms or legs, they could squeeze their flesh to pass through impossibly small spaces. They could pick locks by pushing their fingers into the keyhole. That sort of thing. The pain must have been extraordinary. Learning to bear it is a significant part of our training here." Her nostrils flared as she breathed in slowly. "As I said: an unusual talent."

All this Charlie listened to with an increasing sense of dread. Miss Davenshaw with her eerie watchfulness, her gaze that could see without seeing. He was remembering, as if through a haze, the examination by Mrs. Harrogate, in London, in that first week at Nickel Street West. She had wanted him to do something like this, hadn't she? He glanced back at the outbuildings, far behind them now, then he let his eyes drift around the empty field. Despite it all, he couldn't help himself, he was intrigued.

"How do I do that? This . . . mortaling?"

"You? You do not."

"But you just said—"

"You are not sufficiently trained, young man. I will show you. Come closer. Do not mind the feel of the wards, the glyphic will not harm you. He knows we are here, he knows our intentions. Now, here, where these two stones meet in the wall." She took his hand and moved his fingers softly along the crack in the stones. "Here is a gap you could slide through. It seems impossible, hm? Nevertheless. The mortaling will move a body without a body's moving. It will overflow your imagining."

Charlie felt the gap. He shut his eyes. His entire body was thrumming with the energy of the glyphic's wards. There was stillness; and all at once the silence was like a sound in his ears. Something was happening. He could feel his fingertips where they pressed up against the stones, seeking the space between, and he tried to envision that gap creeping open, a narrowness he might pour his fingers into. Nothing happened.

"I . . . can't," he said, breathing hard. "I just . . . can't." He felt, strangely, as if he'd disappointed her.

"Indeed, Mr. Ovid," she said. "One thing at a time. If you are ready?"

"Right," said Charlie, trying to keep the anger from his voice. "I'm ready."

Miss Davenshaw gestured to a ring of stones, laid out in the red clay.

"Then let us begin," she said.

The days passed.

Charlie was in the candlelit library one afternoon when Komako found him. He had taken to wearing his mother's ring on a cord around his neck, in part because it wasn't easy or painless cutting it out of his flesh. He was gripping it unhappily where he sat, brooding, on the wide sill of the window, when he heard the heavy brass pull of the door, twisting. Then he heard the click of Komako's shoes on the inlaid parquet and slid the ring back inside his shirt.

"Ribs is looking for you," she said, hesitant.

"What for?"

"Oh, not *for* anything." A sly grin, just at the edges of her mouth. "I just think she can't relax unless she knows where you are."

Charlie frowned. If she was teasing, he couldn't tell. She came forward a little and drew out a chair and sat, very close. He could smell the lye soap in her skin.

She was wearing the fingerless kidskin gloves again, protecting her sore hands. "How was your first lesson with Miss D? I hate to think what a haelan learns. Did she make you recite the five talents?" She lowered her voice to a whisper. "Did she tell you about the sixth?"

"There is no sixth."

Komako tugged at her thick braid. "Or is that just what they want us to think? Ask Ribs about it. Ribs has all sorts of theories about the sixth. The dark talent, she calls it. There's a story the old-timers like to tell, about the dark talent bringing about the end times, and destroying all the other talents. . . ." She paused, shifting to see his face more clearly against the window. "Hey, Charlie. I'm just teasing. Are you all right?"

"Yeah. I'm fine."

"When I first came here, I got sad all the time. It wasn't just the place. I mean, it was a little bit the place."

"I'm not sad."

"Well. I was." Her mouth was open just a bit, as if with anticipation, as if she knew how closely he was watching her lips. "I'd just lost my sister, Teshi. She was my little sister, she'd been sick for a long time.

And then she just wasn't sick anymore. It was Mr. Coulton and Jacob who found me, who purchased passage for me here. Ribs was there, too. She'd just sort of . . . attached herself."

Charlie raised his face. "Jacob—?"

"Marber. Yes. He was different then. I don't know what he is now. He disappeared while we were sailing south from Tokyo. He was just . . . gone, one night. The sailors all believed he'd jumped overboard. But for years after, he'd be seen near Cairndale, off in the valleys, just walking. Head down, like he was looking for something."

Charlie suppressed a shudder. He imagined that monster of smoke and darkness, stalking the walls of Cairndale, trying to find a way in.

Komako's face was suddenly serious. "I know what it looks like here. Dr. Berghast and Miss Davenshaw and the like all act like this is a refuge for us, for our kind. And they want it to be, they do. But nowhere's safe, not really. You be careful, Charlie One-of-Us-Now."

"You don't know where I've been," he said. "I can take care of myself."

"You're not the only one who's had it hard, Charlie."

There was something about the way she said it. He looked at her then, really *looked* at her. Wondering suddenly and for the first time just what she'd lived through. How her sister had died, or her parents, or how she'd had to leave her entire life behind to come here. He scraped at the sill with a fingernail, feeling ashamed.

"What you saw the other night, the carriage in the courtyard," she said. "You weren't supposed to see it. It makes deliveries sometimes. Crates. And sometimes it takes things away, too."

"I'm not afraid."

"Only because you don't know. You don't know what's happening here."

He lifted the candle from its dish where it was guttering and poured out the wax and set it back upright. "So tell me."

But he could see she was deciding some argument in herself. She got up and listened at the door. She was looking at him darkly as she did so and her eyes were shining in the candlelight. Then she came back and sat very close to him.

"Kids have been going missing," she whispered.

He blinked. "From Cairndale?"

She nodded gravely. "Maybe even being killed. We don't know. Last semester I saw Brendan O'Malley going out to that same carriage in the middle of the night. No one ever heard from him again. When I asked, I was told he'd come of age and gone back to his family. But he didn't have any family, none worth going back to, at least."

"Wait. What do you mean, what're you saying?"

"I don't know, not yet. But I'm going to find out. All of us are, me and Ribs and Oskar."

"How?"

Komako leaned in close. He could feel her breath on his cheek. "Well, that's what I wanted to talk to you about," she said softly. "We need your help, Charlie."

It'd been Ribs's idea, to approach Charlie, to ask for his help. Oskar and Lymenion hadn't liked it, true, but Komako could see the sense in it. He had a wary sidelong way of looking at you, the way of a kid who'd lived rough, that had made Komako think he just might agree. And he was, after all, a haelan.

It was that, his talent, which had finally convinced her. Because if they wanted to know more—if they wanted to get closer to whatever was going on—then they'd need a haelan.

The disappearances had started two years ago. Not many, not enough that anyone seemed alarmed; and always there was an explanation—gone down to London, or returned to their families, or sent on a journey to Romania, to Peking, to Australia. But no one ever said goodbye. And they left all they cared about behind. When Brendan was smuggled out to the carriage, in the dead of night, he'd been building a replica of Cairndale out of matchsticks in his dormitory; he left it unfinished. This other girl who disappeared six months before him, Wislawa, had just captured a rabbit and was raising it in a cage behind the toolshed; she left it unfed. Admittedly, Komako didn't know any of the disappeared well: Cairndale kept its kids apart, as much as it could; but she'd heard the talk and knew they weren't the sort to want to go.

Which meant there was something going on. And, worse, there must be someone at Cairndale who knew about the carriage, who was helping make it happen. The thing was, Cairndale itself was such a pit of secrets, the vanishings could be nothing, or they could be everything. Komako had lived at the institute for almost ten years now and it was her home as much as anything and yet there were parts of it she'd not even guessed at.

But she knew plenty else. She knew, for instance, that the old talents at Cairndale were dying. There were eleven of them left, gray old men and women, shriveled like insects under glass, and they moved with the slowness of death. Sometimes they would take a turn about the yard, their nurses pushing their wheeled cane chairs, or themselves shuffling slowly in slippers and bathrobes. And she knew some of them went across to the glyphic at night, in the old rowboats, and that a few never came back, or came back weaker, frailer. No, not everything at Cairndale was as it seemed; but, of the many secrets that haunted it, none were sadder than Dr. Henry Berghast himself.

Oh, he was a good man, she had no doubt of that. It was Dr. Berghast, after all, who kept them all safe. Where he came from, she didn't know. His age, his past, his family were all a mystery. He spoke with no accent at all, a curiously smoothed-out manner of speaking, as if he were from nowhere and everywhere at once. Strong-shouldered, fierce, he looked to be a man in his prime, but she knew he could not be. For there was a strain about his eyes; and his hair had all turned white. She'd heard the old talents talking: He'd been guarding the glyphic for eighty years at least, before even their memory. Seeing that the orsine stayed closed. But his obsession with the drughr was alarming. He slept little, leaving often in the night on business, no doubt in pursuit of the drughr and Jacob and what Jacob had become. Miss Davenshaw said he blamed himself for it. All Komako knew for sure was that this ancient, ageless man, this person with pale gray eyes and a deep sense of rightness inside him, this *doctor*, was slowly destroying himself, in his restless stalking of that monster. And it broke her heart to see it.

It was for this reason she hadn't gone directly to him, hadn't reported her suspicions about the disappeared, hadn't warned him about the dark carriage. They didn't *know* anything, not yet. But the three of them had taken to watching the skies for bonebirds, and creeping out to the wire loft where they roosted whenever they sighted a new arrival. Komako and Oskar would keep watch while Ribs snuck in, untied the message, read it swiftly, and then replaced it, all the while the bonebirds clicking and rustling and turning their eyeless sockets as if to see her better. So far they'd learned little, a few strange messages from Mrs. Harrogate in London, a message in garbled code from somewhere in France.

But then one morning Komako was sent as a runner to the old storeroom, Dr. Berghast's laboratory. Standing at the beakers and distillers and weird bottled potions, Berghast had rubbed his eyes tiredly, taken the letter, dismissed her. As she turned to go she saw, stacked on his work desk, several plain brown manila folders. She knew where those files were from; and they gave her an idea.

If they wanted to trace the disappeared kids, they'd need someone who could clamber up the outside of the manor, in darkness; who could climb through Berghast's study window; who could unlock the door from the inside. Then Ribs could get in, and bust open the big cabinet, and search through the files of all the talents who had ever been admitted to the institute until she found what she was looking for: the files of the missing kids.

In other words, they'd need Charlie Ovid.

Komako hurried through the halls of Cairndale, whistling softly to herself.

Because Charlie had just agreed to do it.

21

OTHER PEOPLE'S SECRETS

Alice Quicke found herself, as she traveled south to London, thinking of the dead.

There was Coulton, of course. She could still hear his voice, its dry reedy accent, she could see the wispy auburn sideburns he'd cultivated and the thinning hairs he'd comb across his pink scalp and the ruddy, pocked, jowly shape of his face. He'd made her crazy, true: secretive, insufferable, sarcastic half the time and smug the rest. But she'd trusted him, trusted him because he'd earned that trust and because he'd never treated her like a woman detective, just as a detective, and because above all he was a good man, and a good friend.

And yet, as she'd stalked the railway platform in Edinburgh, watching small groups of beggars fan out across the tracks, or sat unspeaking with Mrs. Harrogate in a candlelit dining car, their plates swimming with gravy and mutton and hash, it wasn't Coulton who came to occupy her thoughts, but her mother.

Why that should be, she couldn't have explained. Her mother's name was Rachel Coraline Quicke. Alice hadn't seen her in years; part of that was hurt, part of it disgust. She'd had no childhood at all. Her earliest memory was of Rachel in the mud of a Chicago street, screaming at the shutters of their landlord, flinging gobbets of muck because their tenement door was locked and she'd lost the key. There was such fury in her. Her hips were wide, her belly soft to the touch. She'd drink whole boots of lager at the Irish saloon off Declamey Street and stagger home cursing. She worked in a German bakery in the next ward, snorting like a horse in the early hours, shaping with clever fingers the little dough figures in the empty bakery, the night outside very black, the pretzels and pastries and jam-filled tarts warm and sweet-scented. It was the only time she seemed at peace. When she was very little Alice sometimes went with her, pretending to help stoke the stoves, wipe the flour from the tables, not minding the hour. Then when she was four, her father left. After that it was just the two of them. For a time she'd had a little Irish setter named Scratch but then one day he'd run off too, killed in a fight or kicked by a horse or maybe just he too decided he'd had enough and there were easier places to live.

Alice herself, in those early years, was already a gutter rat, haunting the tumbledown west side where they lived. She ran with a pack of older immigrant kids in the alleys, mostly Irish, all of them weaving between the wheels of the carriages and cabs, starting little fires in the produce market on Randolph Street, throwing rocks at freight yard windows and running from the watchmen. Her friends were seized, beaten; but she never was, being too quick even then. Chicago in that decade was a sprawl of mud and filth, of flooding and sewage. The river reeked in the summers, the streets thickened into a stew of muck in the spring and fall. Even the horses floundered in the deepest intersections. And everywhere were the railroads, the hotels, the supply stores, the vast yards of sheds and livestock pens and grain elevators, all lit up. It was a city of fire.

Alice was seven when her mother found God. What followed was a strange time of prayer and church gatherings and riverside picnics on Sundays in the summer. She had one dress, which her mother washed exhaustively. Her mother's temper didn't soften; but her faith, if that's what it was, filled her with a renewed intensity, so that she'd lash her pink back before sleep each night with a birch branch, the red welts angry and oozing. She'd take to the street corners on a wooden crate in the afternoons, when she got off work, haranguing passersby to look to the state of their souls. And maybe it all poisoned her work, too, who could say. Because later that year she lost her job at the bakery, the only job Alice had ever known her to hold, the one steadiness in their lives, and after that everything changed.

At the Church of New Canaan there arrived a woman from the West, from a small religious community in the wheat fields of Illinois. Her name was Adra Norn. She was tall, with long hair the color of lead, and a face like sun-dried fruit, and huge rugged hands, masculine hands, hands that could rip a Bible in two. When she spoke, even the men listened. She said their God was an angry god, a vengeful god, and that his anger was directed at the men of the world. Her community was a place for women only, a refuge from the world's corruptions. If Alice feared her mother, what she felt for Adra Norn was different, closer to awe. The woman would sweep past with the force of a hurricane, her gray skirts whirling, her huge raw hands scooping up whatever needed doing. Her speech sounded biblical and disturbing and her accent was but half-intelligible though her meaning was clear: *God does not love you, God does not need you. Risk his displeasure and be harrowed.*

"And yet for those touched by God," she would also say, "anything is possible."

Alice's mother took to saying that too, under her breath, over and over, when she thought she was alone. Then one Sunday Alice saw her mother deep in conversation with Adra Norn; and soon the tall woman was descending upon their apartment in the evenings. Two months later, when Norn prepared to depart, Rachel too packed up their few belongings and set out with Alice for the holy community of Bent Knee Hollow.

That journey, her first, Alice would remember all her life to come: the crows rising as one out of the stubble fields, quick and crackling like thought, exactly like what she imagined thinking was like; the low red sun sinking over the tree line; the dusty roads, deserted, filling with an ancient light; and always the leafy green oaks and willows lining the cool rivers. Five days they rode, Adra Norn's old Conestoga wagon creaking like a great landship over the rutted crossings, Rachel hunched next to Adra on the hard bench up front, lost in conversation. Alice was left to herself in the rear, sprawled among crates of seeds, grain, bolts of cloth, hatchets and spades and shovels and their like; and because it was summer she slept each night in the open, at the smoldering fire, Norn first blessing their food and their fate and the very fire itself before laying down her own steely head.

They arrived at Bent Knee Hollow at sunset; all around lay fields of gold, burnished red in the bloody light. Alice got down out of the back of the wagon and stood with her mother, uncertain, in the eye of a storm of women, all of whom had poured out of the buildings as they approached, some in aprons, some still clutching carving knives or hatchets or bundles of wool, their faces weathered but happy, their eyes clear. Adra went among them, embracing all. The women, suddenly shy, would stare at their feet as she passed.

There was a calmness, a gentleness in that place. It took Alice weeks to recognize the feeling that was in her, there: peace.

Seasons passed. Rachel began to change, imperceptibly at first, then noticeably. She cut her hair short, like Adra's; she dressed in the same gray burlap dress as Adra; she rarely left the older woman's side. Her anger, if it was still there, went underground; Alice no longer saw the same tense straining expression in her forehead, in her jaw. But Alice saw entirely less of her too—her own days were filled with the tasks of communal life, plucking and chopping and peeling for the great vats of soup, stacking firewood, mending clothes, beating blankets with sticks, stitching boots. At harvest they traded their labor to the local farmers in exchange for food and stores. The women worked in a monastic silence, and there were no other children at all. On Sundays the community gathered at dusk to light a great bonfire and to sing hymns and roast potatoes in their jackets. The fire was holy, Adra Norn taught, the fire would cleanse the world entire, when at last the end times came.

Only the pure, she warned them, would walk through the fires and be saved.

Margaret Harrogate knew about all of that, of course.

Or the greater part of it, at least. She'd heard tell of Bent Knee Hollow, and of Adra Norn's foolishness, and she'd read the reports written by Rachel Quicke's doctors, about what the madwoman had done to all those poor souls in that commune, and also a long letter by Coulton about Alice herself and the state of her mind. Oh, she knew. If secrets were currency at Cairndale, then Margaret's pocketbook was full.

But none of that concerned her.

What did concern her was Dr. Berghast—Henry—the Henry she had left at Cairndale.

He was not the man she had known all these years. That much was ominously clear. He'd changed, she could see it now, surely anyone could. He was becoming consumed by his obsession. Never mind grief or fear, sorrow or hope. The drughr was all. Did he sleep? She had her doubts. Did he dream? Only of the drughr. He blamed himself for its horrible deeds; he carried the guilt of it inside him, like a cancer. Oh, he sounded reasonable and calm in the day-to-day, yes. But shame and fury had slowly mangled his heart into a shape that no longer resembled anything good and which would justify anything, any act, if it led to the obliteration of the drughr. She was frightened for him.

As she sat in the small train compartment, heading south, the spattered windows rattling in their frames, Margaret watched her companion sleep. Miss Quicke had proved herself brave, beyond a doubt; and she had proved herself loyal, to the children at least. Mr. Coulton had always sworn she was capable, trustworthy. Margaret sighed. Well, she'd know soon enough.

They were passing now through the north of England. They'd changed trains twice, and each time Margaret had scanned the gloomy railway platforms, watching for any sign of Marber or his litches. She'd seen nothing, no one. The ticket booths, the reading stalls, the solitary men in their drab black suits and hats, clutching their cases close— none of it made her easy.

She cast her mind forward, to London. The first thing she'd need to do would be to let Miss Quicke rest, to let her gather her strength. Then she'd need to find Mr. Fang, her contact in the exile community. He'd be the way to finding what she wanted: the weapon that could kill Jacob Marber.

It was the same weapon Walter had been searching for, all those weeks ago. It would have been no use to him, or to Margaret. Neither could have wielded it. The keywrasse would respond only to a dustworker's touch. But if Margaret was correct—and she was nearly certain that she was—then Miss Quicke, because of the wound from Marber, because of the traces of dust that were now inside her, would be able to wield the weapon. She would be able to *control* it.

Margaret watched the younger woman's face, pale and drawn,

watched her shoulders shudder in time to the railway carriage. Shadows and daylight flickered over her. Miss Quicke slept on.

I only hope she is strong enough, thought Margaret.

But Alice wasn't sleeping.

She knew Mrs. Harrogate was watching her. Knew it, and didn't care.

Her ribs ached; her head ached; she was tired and sore and angry that she'd left the boys alone in that strange manor. Meeting with Dr. Berghast had not reassured her. She could tell there was something wrong with the man, something off—a kind of buried hunger, a fury he'd tried to conceal. She didn't know its source, nor what it meant. If he was really Marlowe's guardian, it disturbed her that he'd not mentioned the child in affection, not even once. She thought of the boy as he was in that circus, with Brynt, how hopeful and how afraid he'd been, and she thought of the life she'd dangled in front of him, the promise of a family, and she hated herself for it.

But all that could wait, she reminded herself. She kept her eyes closed, her head down, in part because she didn't want to have to talk to Mrs. Harrogate, not just now. It wasn't only that she was tired. She needed to think.

The first thing was to avenge Coulton. He was a good man, a kind man underneath it all, and an honorable one. He hadn't deserved his death. And what Harrogate had said was true: if she really feared for Marlowe's and Charlie's safety, she'd have to kill Jacob Marber, once and for all.

Well so be it, then. It's not like she hadn't killed before.

Alice was eleven when Adra Norn, at Bent Knee Hollow, had disrobed and walked naked into the fire. All the women, astonished, stopped their singing and cried out; some ran for buckets of water; others held hands and wept; but after only a few minutes Adra walked back out, unscathed, her hair steaming, her eyes bright, and she stood naked in the firelight with her triangle of hair and her heavy breasts and she held out her arms in triumph.

Alive. Whole. Holy.

Something changed in Alice's mother after that. Maybe in all of them, in all of those women. But Rachel Quicke became obsessed; young Alice would find her some nights staring into a candle flame, holding a hand over the fire, or else watching Adra across the sleeping lodge with an unreadable expression in her eyes, a mix of fear and wonder and rage.

"For those touched by God, for those touched by God," she would mutter, over and over.

Her old anger returned, stronger, fiercer; she'd chop firewood for hours at a stretch, drenched with sweat, her skirts heavy; she'd scrub dresses against the washboard so fiercely that she wore holes into them. The other women drew their bonnets close when she passed, they averted their eyes.

It was during a full moon some six months later that Alice was shaken awake by a rough hand. It was her mother, fully dressed, who held a finger to her lips in the moonlight and led her out of the sleeping lodge. Alice saw Adra asleep in the big bed at the front of the lodge. Her mother took her to the flower meadow and told her to wait and then disappeared again into the dark. The grass shone silver under the moon. Alice shivered, cold. Maybe fifteen minutes passed and then an orange light bloomed into being. It was her mother, carrying a torch.

"Mama?" she said.

Her mother didn't answer. She handed the torch to Alice and led her to the sleeping lodge. There were piles of straw from the barn under the windows, and her mother—with a look of cold ferocity—

gripped Alice's wrist hard and forced her to touch the flame to each pile of straw, walking the perimeter of the lodge, while the flames, with a soft whoosh, leaped up.

Alice, crying silently, shook her head as they worked, staring at her mother in confusion. She could see now that the lodge's door had been barred shut on the outside.

The heat was intense. They stumbled back, and back again, and her mother took the torch from her. The flames were spreading quickly, bending sideways over the roof like long grass in a wind, consuming the walls. The windows shattered in the heat, one after another after another. Alice staggered back, covering her face. She could hear voices crying out in agony from inside.

"Mama!" she cried, starting forward.

"You will *stand!*" shouted her mother. Alice froze. Rachel's eyes were shining weirdly in the flames. "You will *stand* and *see*, daughter! For they shall rise, they shall walk out on their own feet!"

Alice stood. She stood as she was told, in her nightdress, in the darkness, the heat like a wind at her face. She'd never told anyone of this, of what she'd done; and her mother never told anyone, not even the legal counsel, not anyone. Alice just stood and watched, crying, while the great machinery of her life turned, and her childhood neared its true end, her mother's trial, and incarceration, and Alice's hard hungry years on the Chicago streets. She stood, and she saw.

For the sleeping hut whooshed and crackled, and the roof fell in, and the conflagration roared on, and not a soul staggered out.

While the stars in their orbits wheeled and turned, and the sky in the east did lighten, and the fires ate and ate and did not die.

22

THE STUDY OF
THE IMPOSSIBLE

It was late when Charlie went down to the appointed alcove at the edge of the courtyard. There in the darkness he found Komako, pale as an apparition, already waiting for him. She had wrapped her long braid in a coil around her head.

The night air was cold on his face and cold on his hands and he folded them up under his armpits for warmth. Under his cloak he was in shirtsleeves to make the climbing easier. There were lanterns burning in some of the older talents' windows and the orange glow reflected in Komako's eyes like firelight. He saw no sign of Ribs nor of Oskar and Lymenion.

"Ribs is already waiting," said Komako softly. "She's been hiding outside Berghast's study since lights out. Don't let her get distracted. We need those files. When you unlock the door, you won't see her, but she'll be there." Komako paused. "Unless she got bored, that is. And fell asleep."

Charlie grinned. Then he saw her face and stopped.

"Wouldn't be the first time," said Komako, with a shrug.

"What if Dr. Berghast is still up there?" said Charlie. "Say I get up to his window and he—"

"He is not. I watched him leave."

"But if he comes back?"

"Why would he do that?"

"I don't know. Can't sleep? He forgets something?"

Komako peered up at him in the darkness. She was nearly a head shorter than he. "If you don't want to do this, Charlie—"

"I never said that."

"If you don't want to do this," she continued quietly, "you don't have to. No one will think the worse of you, if you're afraid."

"I'm not afraid," he muttered. He leaned out around the alcove, listening to the night, and then he gestured at the east wing. "It's that window there? Under that funny roof? Not much to hold on to."

"That's why we need you."

He knew her meaning. She meant it was dangerous and likely to lead to serious injury and what they needed was a body, any *body*, that could plummet thirty feet onto the cobblestones if a foot got put wrong and yet not make a bloody mess of it. Literally. What they needed, in other words, was someone who could break his bones, over and over again, and not get caught.

But he had something he wanted too. And he wasn't leaving Berghast's study until he got it.

You're still a damn fool, he thought to himself, as he crouched low and ran silently across the courtyard. *You just can't keep your hand out of the fire.*

At that very moment, Ribs was counting the flowers in the wallpaper in the east wing. She'd got as high as 612 and started to think they were moving around when she raised her face to listen and lost track and had to start all over. She was crushed up against the wall, knees to her chest, bored out of her mind. She was invisible, of course, feeling the pinprick of light on her skin almost like a current of electricity. It felt like rolling naked in a tub of nails.

The sconces had been doused at the going of Dr. Berghast and his manservant and the doors were shut fast and locked. The corridor was dim, creepy. When she was sure she was alone she got up and tried the door to Berghast's study just in case but it was locked, of course it was. She stood at the window. All was dark. She couldn't see Charlie or Komako and it occurred to her maybe they weren't coming, maybe it was all a setup, a joke, to get her stuck up here in the east wing all night and in a scramble to explain herself come morning.

She grinned to herself. That's the kind of thing *she'd* do, maybe. But never Ko.

In a nook in the wall stood an old glass cabinet filled with tintypes and etchings of Cairndale from decades past, bucolic and mild. She peered close, trying to find the windows of the girls' rooms, but the windows were all in the wrong places.

It'd surprised her that Charlie had agreed to help them. She'd told Ko and Oskar with perfect confidence that he'd do it, he was just the sort of person who would, but she hadn't believed it, not really. She wondered what Ko had said to talk him into it and felt a sharp ache of jealousy at the two of them alone.

The hell with it, she thought. He'd be coming soon. It was late, it was time. She tried to listen for sounds outside: scrabbling on the walls, the clink on the slate roof. Instead she heard something else: footsteps, unhurried, down the hall.

Someone was coming.

Charlie unlaced his shoes and rolled the cuffs of his trousers and left his cloak folded beside a drainpipe. Komako hadn't followed him

across the courtyard and when he turned to look for her he couldn't
see her.

He took a step back, peered up at the dark manor. Berghast's study
was at the top of a crenelated feature of bay windows, three stories up.
There was a balcony to the left and a covered entrance with slate tiles
on the ground floor, left of that. All along the facade loomed stone
sills, ancient brickwork, iron drainpipes.

It would be easy to fall.

Charlie blew out his cheeks, grimaced. Then he stepped lightly forward and reached up and swung himself onto the narrow slate roof
of the entrance. He could feel Komako watching him from across the
darkness and he tried to move slowly, confidently, like he knew what
he was doing.

Except he didn't, he wasn't much of a climber, never had been, and
he had the bad feeling that he was going to make himself ridiculous,
climbing the outside of a building in the dark.

At least it isn't raining, he thought.

He should have been more afraid of someone, anyone, walking past
a window in the west wing and peering out and seeing him creeping
spiderlike over the walls. Or someone crossing the courtyard for some
ungodly reason and hearing the chink and click of the slate tiles under
his feet.

He pressed himself flat against the wall and leaned out, far out,
reaching with the tips of his fingers for a handhold on the next sill. He
could just reach it. He firmed up his grip and dragged himself, heavily,
awkwardly, out over the gap, scraping the side of his body against the
bricks, gasping, heaving himself up.

There was a kind of corner beside him and he pushed his shoulder
into it and reached around and seized the iron spikes on the windowsill above and then he twisted his lean body and walked his feet up and

slithered—there was no other word for it—one knee, then the second, until he could kneel and rise unsteadily and stand.

He was maybe thirty feet off the ground now. It wasn't pretty, but it was effective. He'd need to climb to the third story and work his way out across the building to the bay windows. He eyeballed a leap to a balcony, four feet away, and the spiked railing there. Trying to be quiet, not knowing what was in the windows he would pass.

But as he made to jump, something went wrong. His toes slipped sideways, and though he lunged out with his fingers splayed, somehow, impossibly, he felt the edge of the balcony just miss his grasp, and then he was falling, the cold night air rushing past.

He thought: *Charlie, you're just a damn—*

And then the thought was cut short as the dark cobblestones rushed up to meet him.

A figure came around the corner in darkness, tall, hatless, in a frock coat, and Ribs saw at once who it was: Bailey, the manservant of Dr. Berghast.

Though invisible, still she shrank back against the wall. She thought: *Charlie, wherever you are, just don't come up yet, don't.*

Bailey frightened all of them. The man hardly spoke and glowered out from his skull-like head as if he'd gladly strangle anyone, kid or talent alike. He was part servant, part secretary, part ape. Ribs wasn't sure exactly what the man did for Dr. Berghast. Nothing pleasant, surely.

Bailey stopped outside Berghast's study door and slowly picked through a ring of keys. Then he paused and looked around, frowning. He stared at where Ribs was lurking, almost as if he could see her, and slowly he reached a big hand out, feeling the empty air.

Ribs pressed herself back against the wall, just out of reach. His fingers were millimeters from her face. But he seemed satisfied, and turned back, and found the key and unlocked the study door.

Ribs barely let herself exhale. Her heart was hammering in her chest. She was used to people sensing her presence, even peering around in suspicion, but rarely were they so precise in finding her.

Anyway, she thought. *You wasn't doing nothing wrong. You can stand in a hallway if you want to. It ain't against the law.*

While she was thinking this, letting her heart rate subside, Bailey had ducked his head and gone through into the little antechamber. Ribs slipped noiselessly to the entrance. Within stood the small desk where Bailey worked during the days, the two armchairs for visitors to wait in. And directly across stood the door beyond, the door to Berghast's study.

It was open.

Why bless your cold little heart, Mr. Bailey, sir, she thought, with a sly grin. She looked all around at the hallway and then back at the antechamber. Then she thought of Charlie. If he climbed up while Bailey was in the study—

She set her jaw. She'd have to warn him, somehow.

Invisible, on silent feet, Ribs slipped inside.

Charlie winced in embarrassment. Komako was kneeling over him, afraid to touch him, hissing his name. He could feel his shattered tibia already beginning to stitch itself back. Something was wrong with his hip. He had landed badly on his side and one shoulder had popped from its socket and he sat up in pain and wrestled it back into place and felt his body crunch and twist and shape itself anew.

Sweet Lord, it hurt.

There was blood on his face and hands and in his eyes and he wiped it away with his shirt. Komako fell back, watching him from the shadows. He saw fear in her face but also something else, fascination, and he was surprised that he kind of liked it.

"Charlie?" she was whispering. "You're okay, then?"

"Sure." He shrugged, tried to smile. "That balcony just doesn't like me much. Nobody heard?"

"No."

He got to his feet, grimacing. There was that, at least. His bare feet were damp and there was grit stuck to the soles and he wiped his feet on the inside of his trousers to clean them before starting climbing again. This time he went more quickly, with less dread, feeling as if he'd already done the worst and so there was less to fear. He scrambled from sill to balcony to sill, working his way steadily across in the darkness. There was in one window a candle left burning and when a shadow passed in front of it he stood with his back pressed to the wall, waiting. But when no further movement came he slid silently across, continued climbing.

Later still, his feet kicked an old lead drainpipe, as he made his way past where he'd fallen before. He listened to the rattle and clatter of it roll in the courtyard below, so loud that he was sure someone must hear. But no one came. No windows opened.

He climbed on.

Ribs watched Berghast's manservant at the desk, slowly going through the drawers. He'd lit a candle and the orange light cast its flicker over the desk and the surrounding carpet and the big man's features. He was taking out ledgers and papers in his enormous hands, stacking them, unhurried.

Ribs crept noiselessly to one side of the door. She made no other movement, breathing softly. Even the stir of air could make a target sense her presence. And Bailey, whatever else, seemed eerily aware of his surroundings.

She'd been in this study only twice before, both at Berghast's instruction: the first time shortly after arriving at Cairndale, by way of a kind of introduction; and later, amid the chaos and panic after Jacob Marber's attack, all those years ago. She remembered Berghast's pale gray eyes, as if lit from within, how he had studied her carefully as if looking inside her heart. She shivered, remembering.

His study was dim, oppressively furnished, very cold. A fireplace stood at one end, carved out of white stone, and near it the desk and several armchairs arranged in a half-moon. There were doors on three of the walls, too many doors, doors mismatched and strange and unlike any others she'd seen at Cairndale. She wondered where they led. On one wall hung a long strange framed painting, in ink, all slashed lines and overlapping circles. It resembled somehow the complicated inner workings of a vast tree. In one corner stood a tall birdcage with two bonebirds clicking and shifting inside. Last of all, her gaze fell on the bay window, its curtains open, the spiked iron bars on the ledge outside clearly visible despite the candle's reflection.

There was no sign of Charlie.

Finally Bailey found what he was looking for—a sheaf of papers of some kind—and began putting the rest back. He cleared his throat, passed a hand across his eyes, and in that moment he looked almost vulnerable, almost human, the shadows pooling under his hand and spilling out like a liquid darkness. Ribs watched in fascination. She liked such moments, liked glimpsing people in their unguarded states, liked the truth of it.

It was then, at that moment, that Bailey turned and stared behind him at the window and Ribs felt her heart lurch. For she had heard it too.

A scrabbling sound, exactly like a hand finding purchase on the wall outside.

Bailey got to his feet.

Charlie was leaning out over the darkness, breathing, just breathing. He had one hand gripping an iron railing and the other was cautiously feeling around the edge of a sloping stone sill. His toes were hooked around a window ledge, holding himself tight, too tight. He suddenly understood that if he let go, he'd swing out away from the wall, and fall.

And then his fingers found it, a deep groove, enough to lean his weight beneath. And with a grimace he let go and swung and swung back and then used the momentum to draw himself, grunting, upward.

His arms were sore. His stomach was sore. He was standing on a ledge, near the roof of the manor, and he could still feel the little fires in his flesh from when he'd fallen the last time. But he was close now, so close—he could see just around the edge of the wall where the bay window of Berghast's study loomed. The spikes looked vicious. He'd thought he would maybe have to scramble up onto the roof and work his way across, but he saw now a thin, nearly invisible ledge of brick between where he stood and the sill of the bay window.

There was nothing to hold on to, of course. But it wasn't far—he was thinking maybe, just maybe, if the momentum was right, he could propel himself across the gap using the penny-thin edge and hook himself onto the spikes, without falling past it.

Maybe.

He could see Komako now, standing with her hands loose at her sides, her face fixed upward on him. He wondered briefly how he must look.

Go on, he told himself. It's not going to get any closer if you wait.

He closed his eyes a moment and breathed and then he wet his lips again and crouched and leaped. He ran sidelong with two quick strides across the tiny ledge, not balancing so much as controlling his fall, and then he was reaching out for the window ledge and catching the iron spikes with his arms and puncturing his flesh on them and in this way catching himself, suspending himself bloodily in the air.

His legs kicked out over the gap.

He could feel the meat in his upper bicep and his hand and forearm all tearing. The pain was immense. There was blood soaking through his shirt and when he struggled he felt the spikes go through his wrist, through the small birdlike bones there. A wave of nausea passed over him.

And then he was up, somehow, through sheer force of will, up and clambering and ripping his arms free of the spikes and holding them close to his chest. He was kneeling and leaning against the window when he heard the hasp of the window turn, and the latch pull back, and the window was swinging outward, nearly knocking him off.

There was no one there.

But then he heard a voice, low and urgent: "Took your time, you did. Reckon you could make any bloody more racket out there?"

And something grabbed the front of his shirt and dragged him through and he fell in a bloody heap onto the carpet while Ribs muttered some unprintable blasphemy.

Fact was, Ribs had been thinking they were done for. Or Charlie was, at least. When Bailey rose like a walking tombstone and lumbered over to the window she was sure—absolutely *sure*—that it was Charlie the man was hearing.

But it wasn't, somehow it wasn't. A bird, a bat? Not Charlie. It was like he had twice the luck and half the dice to roll it with, she thought. He just always seemed to be slipping out of a bother.

It was one of the things she liked about him, truth be told.

Bailey had returned to the desk, collected the papers he'd been seeking, stuffed all the others back into their drawers and locked them fast. He snuffed the candle between his thumb and forefinger and in the sudden darkness Ribs held her breath, silent, invisible, listening. The door shut, and locked; his footsteps receded through the ante-chamber, and out into the hall, away.

She sighed.

Always it was something.

That was when she heard Charlie, the *real* Charlie, grunting and slapping and scraping his clumsy way up onto the window ledge. And she hurried over and unlatched the window and hauled him in.

A mess, he was. Ragged and bloodied and his arms all ripped clear up. But even as she watched she could see the cuts and punctures closing in around themselves, healing. He was holding them at strange angles, trying not to get the blood on the carpet or anywhere else. But there was a lot of it, even on Ribs's hands, and this was visible though the rest of her wasn't.

"How'd you get in?" Charlie was whispering, staring at the two bonebirds in their cage. Ribs was standing off to the side and she cleared her throat and he looked wildly in her direction. "Ribs? You're over *there?*"

"Keep your shirt on." She grinned. "You's lucky as a cricket, Charlie. Berghast's man were just in here, lookin for some papers. I reckon you'd of got to meet him directly if you was just a minute or two faster."

She watched as Charlie took this in. He nodded in that uncertain way he had. "I fell," he said. "Else I'd have been here faster."

Ribs laughed. "Then thank God you ain't agile like me. Else I'd of had to poke old Bailey with the fire sticker and run for the ladies' toilets."

The study felt eerie in the half darkness.

Charlie heard Ribs go to the big wooden cabinet against the wall, fiddle with the drawers. All at once a long heavy line of folders slid out into the air, staggered, tottered, dropped unsteadily to the floor. He couldn't see her, of course, only the lurch of the files. One of them slid up into the air, flickered open. It was empty. It floated back into place, and then a second one opened, also empty.

"We wasn't the only ones interested in them what disappeared, I guess," she whispered. "Weird. Who'd have taken all the papers but left the folders?" She left Charlie to lift the drawer back into position and slide it into its grooves. She was already pulling out the next drawer, riffling those files. Each file for the disappeared kids had been emptied. There were maybe ninety, maybe a hundred files in all. All the talents that had been collected by Cairndale, Charlie thought in wonder. Listed alphabetically. He leaned over the O's and found his own file and looked past it. But there were no other Ovids.

He flinched at Ribs's touch, looked up. A file was floating open in the air behind him, its pages turning. She'd had the same idea: it was her own file.

"I thought it'd be a bit thicker, you know?" she grumbled. "It ain't like I only just got here yesterday. Let's see. Intelligent, aye, resilient, aye. Why is this here skills part left empty? I got skills ... garrulous ... garrulous?" The file closed, was turned sideways, turned back, opened again. "Is this even the right file? 'Lacks discipline in her efforts ... Easily distracted ...' Huh." She laughed. "I guess it is. Look at this, Charlie, look. They reckon I might be from Cornwall! I ain't from bloody Cornwall."

She set the file down on the desk and fumbled for a fountain pen. "What're you doing?" he whispered.

"Just making it more accurate. How do you spell 'alluring'?"

"What?"

The pen scratched across the paper. "'Miss Davenshaw reports that Eleanor has exhibited a fine aptitude in all her studies, even surpassing Miss Onoe, whose scholarship has been rather a disappointment of late. . . .'" Her voice trailed off. "That's more like it." The pen paused. "You all right, Charlie? Your own file's right there."

His fingers hovered over it. But if he'd been hoping for a different Ovid, a second file, a hint as to who his father might have been, he was disappointed. He opened his file and read it carefully beginning with the first clipping but the details were sporadic and unhelpful. A list of the charges against him from Natchez. An interesting letter from Mr. Coulton describing Charlie and his talent. *A young man of integrity despite the cruelty he has been subjected to. A worthy candidate for Cairndale.* There was no mention of his parentage or place of birth.

But at the back of the folder was a second folder, misplaced, stuffed badly away. It recorded the details of one *Hywel Owydd.*

His father.

Charlie knew it at once, even before he began reading. He'd never known his father's name, not even that, and yet he had no doubts. His blood was loud in his ears. He turned away from where Ribs was standing and slowly, in the weak light from the window, he began to read.

His father, it seemed, was Welsh. He had come to Cairndale at the age of twelve, after manifesting as a clink, a strong. It was the most common of talents. He'd been laboring in a rock quarry for two years by then despite his age and it seemed some form of inducement—that is the word the file recorded, "inducement"—had been necessary in order to free him. He was described as *quiet, mathematically gifted, slight of stature.* He had been reprimanded twice for swimming naked in the loch. There were several pages of annotated notes recording results in his studies and a further page with dates and abbreviations that made no sense. At the back of the file was a paper dated February 1864, detailing his sudden absence from Cairndale.

Sighted in London by R. F., a cryptic note read. *Talent much reduced. Ex-73.*

Charlie stared, trying to understand the shorthand. He could not.

At the bottom of the page was a scrawled note, in blue ink: *H. O. disappeared. No further details. R. F. reports Thames is full. Subject presumed dead.*

The study was still, faint moonlight coming in through the window. All around them the manor was silent.

Hywel Owydd, Charlie thought bitterly. *Dad.*

And yet he still didn't know him, never would; his father, who'd walked these same gloomy halls when he was Charlie's age, who'd fled to London for some reason, who'd had no family in all the world who wanted him except the family he'd someday make and someday lose in the endless American West.

"What's that you got, then?" Ribs said at his shoulder. He tried to pull away but it was too late. "Owydd?" she muttered. "What, like ... *Ovid?*"

"It's my father," he said quietly.

He felt her lift the file out of his hands and she turned the papers steadily and then she grunted. "It don't make sense, Charlie, him bein a talent an all. That ain't how it works. Talents don't descend through bloodlines, they're random, like. Our parents is what usually throws us out, when they see what all we can do."

Charlie swallowed the lump in his throat.

"Huh. He were down in London?"

It was disconcerting, not being able to see Ribs as she talked. He looked at the file, floating in the gloom. "Does it mean something?" he whispered. "You ever hear of any talent ever leaving this place? You think he ran away?"

"All the way to London? Naw," she said. "But London's where they send the exiles."

"What are they?"

"Them what lose their talents, when they come of age. It don't happen to most, but to some. No one knows why." Her voice went very quiet. "It's just a awful sad thing. It ain't easy for them goin back out among ordinary folk, an not able to do what they used to do. It be like losing a part of yourself, I guess. Your poor pa."

Charlie rubbed at his nose with a knuckle. He tried to imagine it. "He was just a kid, like us."

Ribs closed the file, returned it to the drawer. Her voice was very close to his ear when she spoke next. "You ever want to talk about it, I'm a good listener," she said softly. "You ain't even got to know I'm there. We all got stories, Charlie. We all know how it is."

Charlie felt the heat rise to his face.

And then, mercifully, she was trying the desk drawers. All were locked. Charlie had turned away, confused, thinking about his father, when his eye glimpsed something on the carpet. It must have fallen out of the papers when Bailey was there.

Ribs picked it up. It was Berghast's notebook. They still didn't light the candle but went back to the window and in the weak glow from outside she turned the pages, struggling to decipher Berghast's scrawl. There were lists of dates, and numbers, and annotated letters that maybe meant something to him but not to Ribs or Charlie. Over the page: diagrams and what were perhaps maps, they couldn't say. Charlie's bleeding had stopped in his arms and he drifted around the study peering at the strange objects and trying the doors quietly. But when Ribs made a sudden surprised gasp he came back over, stood near.

"What'd you get?" he whispered. "What is it?"

The journal, floating in midair, closed.

"Ribs?"

"I think I just found who we got to talk to," her voice muttered. "An it ain't bloody Berghast."

"The *Spider?*" said Komako, later, in disbelief. She stared at Ribs. It was late; they were gathered in the classroom, keeping their voices down. She glanced at Charlie. "Is she serious?"

Charlie blinked in the candlelight. "I think so."

He seemed deflated. Maybe he was just tired. His shirt was torn, bloodied. He'd have to get rid of it, she knew. Seeing him fall had been awful, the plunging weight of his body in the darkness, the hollow crack as he struck the ground.

"I *am* serious," Ribs whispered. She was visible, wearing her gray smock, red hair standing up in thick tufts. "Cross me heart an hope to—"

"Okay, okay. I get it."

"I don't," Oskar said nervously. Beside him, Lymenion gave a low puzzled growl in his throat, as if in agreement. "What would the Spider want with, with, with the missing talents?"

Ribs winked. "Maybe he eats them."

Komako glared.

"Well the bloody journal never said, did it," Ribs protested. "There was just them names in the one column an the Spider's in the other. Course the next page had a list for a order of candles, an dates an times of delivery, so you tell me. I just reckon we got to just go on over an ask him."

Oskar gulped. He was winding and unwinding the string around his finger. "Ask . . . the Spider?"

Komako grimaced. Obviously Ribs was right, they'd need to see what they could learn from the glyphic. It might be as simple as him looking for the talents in that way he had, by *sensing* them. Maybe that was all Dr. Berghast meant, maybe he was searching for the disappeared kids too. She looked up. "Where's the journal?"

"Well, I put it back, didn't I? I weren't goin to just take it with me, like."

"You put it back."

"Yep."

"Okay. Yes, good. And there was no sign you were ever there?"

"Nope."

But something in the way Ribs said it made Komako suspicious. "Charlie? What isn't Ribs saying?"

"What?" said Charlie. "Oh, uh, there was blood. Some of it might have got into his carpet."

Komako wet her lips. "*Your* blood?"

He nodded, distracted.

"Old Berghast won't notice," said Ribs quickly. "An even if he do, he won't know who it's from. Charlie ain't got a scratch on him. An what would any of us be up to, in his study? It ain't a problem, Ko. We was like wind in the branches of a tree."

"How poetic."

Ribs's freckled face crinkled into a grin. "It's a gift."

Shyly, Oskar cleared his throat. He was staring hard at his finger and the string on it. "I don't like the—the—the Spider," he mumbled. "He scares me. But Miss Davenshaw says it's like a—a web. She says everything's connected. The Spider, he, he can feel when something on the web moves. The—the vibrations of it. That's how he finds the talents. When he's sleeping. Maybe he can find Brendan and Wislawa and all the other disappeareds?"

"Sure. In his stomach."

"Ribs—"

"I mean, that's what he—he does, isn't it?" Oskar went on. "He finds things? Kids, like us? He's the one who found Charlie and Marlowe. . . ."

"Mr. Coulton found me," said Charlie.

"Yeah, genius," said Ribs. "But how'd he know where to look?"

"Oskar's right," said Komako firmly, tugging at her braid. "Even if the Spider isn't involved, maybe he could help us. If we knew even just where to look, we could get some answers. None of us are safe here. That's what the journal means. It means all those we've noticed gone missing, they're all connected somehow. We're not wrong. And if they can disappear, so can we. We need to go talk to the Spider."

"Isn't that exactly what Miss Davenshaw told us *not* to do?" said Charlie, coming back to himself.

"Yep," said Ribs. She raised one hand. "So. Who wants to go?"

Komako raised her own. Then Oskar, Lymenion a moment later.

"Charlie?" said Komako.

"Char-lie," whispered Ribs. "Char-lie . . ."

Charlie blew out his cheeks, his face troubled. "You really think the Spider'll even talk to us?"

"We just got to ask nice, like." Ribs winked. "An he knows *loads* of stuff."

"When would we go?" he said.

"Tonight," said Ribs.

"Tomorrow," said Komako.

Near the fire, Oskar was staring at his lap. In the facing armchair, his flesh giant stared at its lap too, its oozing shoulders slumped in mimicry.

"Tomorrow?" whispered Oskar, miserable. "Isn't that a bit . . . soon?"

It was then a voice piped up from across the dim room. The coffered door was open; little Marlowe stood in his nightshirt, watching them, his face spookily pale, eyes deeply shadowed. "I want to go too," he said.

"Aw," muttered Ribs. "Where'd he come from, then?"

"Mar?" said Charlie. "How long you been standing there?" He got up and went to the boy and closed the door and kneeled in front of him. "What're you doing here anyhow? You get one of those dreams again?"

The boy nodded. He peered past Charlie, right to Komako, and he met her eye, and she looked away without being able to say why.

The thing was, Marlowe was so small, it nearly broke her heart. She looked at him and knew what she was seeing was her own little sister, Teshi. It didn't matter that Teshi would be twice as old by now, if she'd lived. She still felt Teshi's hand in hers, remembered how she'd hold out her arms to be picked up, and how Komako would hoist her up onto one hip, and how she'd sit some mornings behind Komako and run her little fingers through her hair, softly, like a warm wind. The way she'd smile before she even knew what Ko wanted. The way she'd yawn, with her whole face, her tiny little teeth exposed. All of it.

"I want to go with you, to see the Spider," Marlowe said again. He set his jaw, stubborn. "Don't leave me, Charlie. You said you wouldn't."

No one spoke.

The flesh giant raised its faceless head. There was something pitiful in it, something sweet. It breathed noisily, snuffling.

"Rrrh," it rumbled.

Charlie was tired the next morning. All of them were. But if Miss Davenshaw noticed, she said nothing. She did close her book however with an exasperated bang, when no one seemed able to answer her questions, and stand at her desk and inform them to follow her.

She took up a candle in a dish—not for her benefit, of course—and led them down into the shadowy cellars under Cairndale. The air was chilling; the candle guttered and righted itself; the stones smelled of decay. Broken webs drifted at their passing. Charlie kept brooding about the Spider, and his own file in Berghast's study, the eeriness of it all. Wondering what the creature would reveal.

They were in a wide flagstoned passageway, the walls slumping in places from the press of the soil over centuries. Their footsteps left tracks in the dust. Though she was blind, Miss Davenshaw walked swiftly, almost angrily, and Charlie wondered if her talent, whatever it was, granted her a kind of sight. She was dressed in a long green dress that swept the dirt and she wore her hair in a steely bun and her throat was long and pale and decorated with a single black ribbon.

The others had come down here before. Charlie heard Ribs's voice in his ear. "See, Oskar don't mind *this*," she murmured. "But you ask me, the jar babies is just about as disgusting as a slug in a pie."

"Do not dawdle," called Miss Davenshaw, impatient, as if she'd heard, and the darkness took her voice and whispered it off away.

She led them to a small storeroom lined with shelves and on those shelves jars and displays of human deformities, all of them fetuses. She set the candle down on a wall bracket and the light flickered and cast weird shadows over all. Marlowe moved closer, took Charlie's hand in his own.

"What, exactly, are we?" said Miss Davenshaw primly. "What is the nature of this creature, man? Are we made in God's image? Hm? Go on, look at the shelves, do. Consider what you see. Here, we leave squeamishness at the door."

When the others walked slowly along, peering into the greasy jars, Charlie and Marlowe did the same. There were babies with singular eyes, leaning as if asleep against the walls of their jars; there were babies with stacked knots of flesh where their skulls should be, babies with outsized heads, babies with two heads, even one with a single head and two bodies. In the candlelight they seemed almost to move.

"What is the correct term for these specimens, Miss Ribbon?"

"Teratologies, Miss Davenshaw," said Ribs meekly.

"Indeed. You will see here terminal craniofacial specimens, as well as conjoined twins, and cyclops syndromes. All of them monsters, in the eyes of medicine. But if we are to understand what we are, we would do well to consider how we come to be. What you see here follows its own rules of logic. These are not chaotic nor arbitrary malformations. Each of these aberrations swerve from the normal development in the womb in repeated, and predictable, ways. The womb bakes us, just as an oven bakes a cake; and if the recipe is flawed, or the ingredients poorly mixed, the result is not what we desire." Miss Davenshaw clasped her hands in front of her, she turned her blindfolded face toward them. "You are each of you different, in precisely this manner. But it was not a breakdown in the recipe but the addition of some other ingredient, which led to your talent. Look closely and feel pity. Difference, children, is not monstrous. It is nature at work."

Charlie looked. Pity welled up in him.

"And what of this?" she added. She gestured to a shriveled creature, half monkey, half fish. It looked mummified and fierce, its flesh drawn back off its fangs. "It is a mermaid, they say."

"It is a hoax," said Komako. "Someone just sewed a monkey and a fish tail together."

"A hybrid, my young ones, would be an aberration indeed. Dogs with wings. Great cats with the heads of eagles. And so on. But these do not exist. Miss Onoe, what are the causes of the monstrous, as related by the alchemist Paré?"

Komako wet her lips. "The first is the glory of God," she said. "The second is his wrath. The third, too great a quantity of seed. The fourth too little a quantity. The fifth . . ." She frowned, annoyed with herself.

"Mr. Czekowisz?"

"The fifth is the imagination," said Oskar shyly.

"And?"

"And the sixth is the size of the womb. The seventh is the posture of the mother while pregnant. The eighth is through injury, as when the mother falls, or is struck. The ninth is through illness. The tenth is through corrupt seed. The eleventh . . ."

"There is no eleventh," said Komako quickly, interjecting. "But Paré lists the influence of wicked beggars, and also of devils."

Miss Davenshaw nodded sternly. "Of course, Paré was writing in the sixteenth century," she said to Charlie and Marlowe, for whom all this was new. "He had not yet relinquished superstition, nor the influence of God. And yet already he had observed that the fetus develops in a material fashion. The flesh is physical, and grows over time."

"I don't understand," said Marlowe.

"The question, my dear," said Miss Davenshaw, gentling her voice, "is where do our talents come from? And the answer is, we are grown in the womb of our mothers, and all that we are, is given to us then. Anything different from the normal *appears* monstrous. But it is not. It is *not*."

Charlie couldn't be sure how much of all this made sense to Marlowe. He suspected almost none of it. The boy gripped his hand hard and did not let go. No wonder the kid was having nightmares.

"Tell me, Mr. Czekowisz, about this new concept of Mr. Darwin's, the production of species."

Oskar glanced across at Charlie, glanced away. He seemed embarrassed to be singled out. "Mr. Darwin has suggested that evolution is the result of—of constant changes over time to all animals."

"We are descended from the monkeys, then?"

"No, ma'am. Not exactly."

"Go on."

"There is a common ancestor. But our species split from the apes so long ago that we became humans. And they became . . . apes."

"Tell us, Miss Ribbon, how creatures change over time."

Ribs cleared her throat, stalling. "Um, wouldn't you rather ask Oskar that?"

"*Eleanor.*"

"Their environment," Oskar whispered.

"Because of their environment," said Ribs loudly.

"Thank you, Mr. Czekowisz. Miss Ribbon will be forever grateful. Miss Onoe, if you will?"

"Mr. Darwin believes that miniscule mutations are happening in species all the time, for no reason at all. But that whenever a mutation gives an animal an advantage in its environment—when it helps it catch food better, or find a mate—then that mutation is passed on to the next generation. And the old versions die out."

"And what, then, are monsters?"

A frown flickered across Komako's features. "Monsters are mutations that don't lead anywhere. They're too extreme to be replicated."

Miss Davenshaw moved now down the length of the shelves, running her fingers softly along the glass jars. "Yes," she said, "very good. And what are we, then, we talents? Are we monsters? Our differences are not passed on from mother to child. But they are variations that have existed as long as we have a history, variations that have continued in repeated and predictable ways. There have always been talents. And there will always be."

"Scientists don't know everything," said Komako quietly.

Miss Davenshaw lifted her blindfolded face, as if looking past them. "No one does," she said.

Charlie turned. There in the doorway stood a powerful man with a white beard, watching all of them in silence. It was Dr. Berghast. He bowed, and retreated back into the darkness.

23

THE EXILED AND THE DEAD

Margaret Harrogate arrived in London in the thick of a pea-souper, the fog dense and brown and choking. Miss Quicke was with her. Their hansom crawled through the streets, blind, its lantern illuminating only a corona of mist around itself. And the first thing she noticed, when she unlocked the iron gates and crossed the covered carriage yard and entered through the grand doors of 23 Nickel Street West, ushering her companion inside, was that someone had just been there.

She set down her traveling case softly, and stood listening. Then she crossed the foyer. In her study, the institute ledger was still hidden behind the coal scuttle. At her desk, her papers were undisturbed. In the kitchen the scarred counters stood empty and shrouded. True, the window on a third-floor bedroom had been left open, the drapes billowing slightly, but when she peered out at the fog she could see nothing, no movement. They were three stories up and the fall would be fatal. She knew Miss Quicke, in the doorway, was watching her with grave eyes. Margaret walked through the other rooms, touching nothing, the hairs on the back of her neck prickling, and then she found her small pistol in the drawer where she kept it and went up to the attic and checked on the bonebirds in their loft. All was just as she'd left it on that morning when they'd hurried for the train, on that last morning of Frank Coulton's life.

And yet: someone had been there, only moments before.

Miss Quicke immediately put a hand into the deep pocket of her oilskin coat, no doubt checking for her revolver. Then she went downstairs and out into the fog. She was gone a long while.

She came back shaking her head. "If there was anyone, they're gone now."

"There was," Margaret replied. "Did you not feel it?"

"Feel it?"

"In your—" She gestured to the younger woman's injured side.

"No," said Miss Quicke.

Margaret looked around, uneasy. The furniture, dark and still. The ghostly curtains. Outside the fog gathered, thickening.

They didn't stay.

Margaret thought of Walter and of her own nameless dread and she tried to be smart about it. Certainly Jacob knew the address. Miss Quicke stood at the window, waiting, while Margaret collected what she needed, and then the two of them left. They took a room just across the intersection, in a respectable lodging house for ladies, with a view of 23 Nickel Street West through the fog. The landlady's curfew might have been a problem: the lodging house locked up at nine o'clock; but the dormer window of their room let out onto a narrow ledge, and this ledge led to a low stone wall, and because of this Margaret knew they could come and go at any hour that suited.

The fact of it was, it had been fourteen months now since Alice

Quicke was hired, and yet Margaret Harrogate hadn't ever been close to her before, hadn't ever observed her firsthand, hadn't ever had the opportunity. The little she'd learned she'd gleaned from telegrams, reports, Coulton's wry and sometimes sarcastic stories. Quicke had rough-looking hands and a smile that didn't touch her eyes. Muscular shoulders. Greasy yellow hair, badly cut, smelling of whatever meal she ate last. But if her ribs ached, she didn't complain. If Coulton's death grieved her, she didn't weep. All the long rail journey out of Scotland and south through England she'd said very little, asked nothing, just glared out the coal-smeared window at the passing world, a fierce taciturn creature in a wide-brimmed hat and long stained coat more of a piece with the American West than the civilized violence of Britain.

But, too, she started to see what it was Coulton had come to trust, why he'd argued in her defense so many times, why he'd insisted on hiring her though she was an outsider and a stranger to their world. There was about her a great still strength, like a post driven into the ground. If she said she'd do something, she'd do it. Margaret liked that.

All that first day in London they stayed indoors, resting, collecting themselves, watching their house across the street. But Margaret watched the detective too, looking for signs of collapse, worried for her injury, worried for what it might mean. She was afraid whatever connected Miss Quicke to Jacob connected him, also, back to her; afraid that her presence would be felt on his end, too; afraid that even now, on their long murky first day back in Blackfriars, he would be prowling the streets, circling, *sensing* her presence.

While they rested, Margaret told Miss Quicke about the exiles. Sometimes, she explained, when a talent came of age, in late adolescence, their ability receded and died away. No one quite understood why. But when this happened to a child at Cairndale, he or she was sent away, usually to London, and it fell to Margaret to keep an eye on that community. They were often listless, sad on some deep level, as if they'd lost a part of themselves, turning to drink or to the poppy in solace. Among them too were those who had left the institute out of choice, who had walked away from Cairndale for one reason or another, to vanish into the maw of London's slums. And hidden among them, she went on, was the very woman who had once nursed her Marlowe as a baby, and who had stolen him away from Cairndale on that night so many years ago, when Jacob Marber came hunting the child. Her name was Susan Crowley; she could not be older than twenty-six; and in her possession was the weapon that could kill Jacob Marber.

The thing was, she was so well hidden, Margaret had no idea where to find her.

Miss Quicke raised her eyebrows at that. It was late, by then. The detective, tired, was slumped in her stained oilskin with her legs spread, running her knuckles through her hair.

"I did not want to betray her, you see," said Margaret. "I was the one who found her, all those years ago. She'd been discovered in a freight car and mistaken for dead and the rail workers had dragged her off to a little wooded place for someone else to stumble over. Didn't want the trouble of it, that lot." Her nostrils flared tightly with disgust. "Poor Miss Crowley. Burned all over her chest, her pockets turned out, her coat missing. It's no wonder they thought she was dead. If you'd seen her . . . Well. I knew Dr. Berghast back at Cairndale was in a fury, I knew he wanted her found on account of the child. But I was afraid for her, I didn't know what he would do to her. I could see the child—your Marlowe—was gone. So I said nothing. I told no one. Instead I took Miss Crowley south, into London, and saw that she was cared for, and I tried to forget I'd ever found her."

"Until you needed her, that is."

"Indeed."

"So. How do we begin?"

"*You* will sleep," replied Margaret, at the window. "That is your task. You must get yourself strong. I will go down among the exiles and make inquiries."

"Alone?"

Margaret smiled thinly. "I did not require your protection before we were acquainted, Miss Quicke. And I do not require it now. I will return in the morning with what we need."

"Right. The weapon you say can kill Marber."

Margaret inclined her head.

But to acquire it, she had first to find it. She knew Jacob Marber would not have forgotten about it, either. It was late when she left Miss Quicke sleeping in the lodging house. She slid out through the open window into the cold fog and dropped cautiously off the low wall and made her way east, to Bluegate Fields, her heart loud in her chest. The fog and the hour made the streets very dark. She had little patience for her own fear but it was there nonetheless, and real, and not always easily mastered. A fine result it would be, she thought, her out here and being stabbed on account of a few shillings in her purse. In Wapping, she drifted along the walls of sleeping indigents with a bull's-eye lantern outstretched in her fist until she found who she was seeking, a mean-looking boy in rags and grime. He could have been waiting for her, crouched as he was, barefoot, green eyes turned toward the light. He took her coin and led her down a maze of dripping alleys until they came to the rooms of Ratcliffe Fang.

She hadn't seen Fang in years: hunchbacked; a long, narrow skull fringed with long greasy hair; fishlike eyes bulging behind wire spectacles. Cotton gloves with two fingers cut out. His long wrists stuck out from his rags, hairy and bony, like an ape's. But he knew things others did not, and he walked the darkest lanes in London unaccosted and unafraid.

"Margaret Harrogate," he grunted, when he opened the door.

"Come in, and welcome. You'd best not stay long. There's them about what's been askin after you." His rooms were filthy, reeking of the rivers of muck just outside his doorstep, the floors sticky and creaking. He stumped back to his coal fire, drawing his blanket fast. "Shall I send round the corner for ale?"

Margaret declined. She sat with her handbag in both hands and told him what had happened on the train to Scotland, the slaughter Jacob Marber had caused, the child who had stopped him.

It was enough; she didn't need to say more.

Fang blinked and blinked in the firelight. "Do he understand about the child? Who he is?"

"Perhaps not yet. But he knows the boy is important. As for the boy, I am afraid *for* him, and *of* him. I shall kill Jacob Marber, Mr. Fang, but it is the boy I fear."

Ratcliffe Fang folded his fingers in front of his long face. "Ah," he said.

And Margaret listened then as he told her of the rumors raging through the flash world of Limehouse.

"They say there's creatures about, preying on those what ain't careful. At the docks, in the tunnels, under the arches. They say bodies is being found, mauled up, ripped to pieces. And there's unhappier rumors about, them what's sayin it's a man made out of smoke been at eating the bodies, drinking out the blood. An evil business, it is. I don't need to tell you what it means. The constables ain't looking into it just yet as it ain't anybody what matters, not to the City. Just knifemen and jillies and the like. But give it time. Already the locals go about in packs, terrified. Even the lighters and the fingersmiths is terrified, come dark."

Limehouse, thought Margaret with interest. That was close by. "What about the institute? What is said of it?"

"There's no gossip about Cairndale nor Berghast neither. Not in the flash world. Maybe there's some few heard of it, but they don't know nothing. The prevailing theory in the acre is it's Spring-Heeled Jack an his demons." Ratcliffe Fang ran his tongue over brown teeth. "It's them litches, course, what's making all the fuss."

"Litches? More than one?"

"They say there's a pack of the creatures. Hunt at night, like wolves."

"They're mistaken. Tell me, what do you think Jacob intends to do, Mr. Fang? Why has he returned now?"

"That I can't imagine. But there's purpose in it. Jacob Marber had a quick intelligence, but it wasn't never what guided him. His heart was just different. Every evil act he done, he done because of his heart. I don't expect he's ever got past the death of his little brother, to be honest. What do he intend to do? Nothing, I think, on this side of the orsine. But the gray rooms is closed to me, Margaret, an I try to concern myself with the things of this world. You know that. Lord knows they're foul enough. But you never come all this way to hear me opine on Jake Marber's character."

Margaret fixed the old man with a calm eye. She said, "I need to know the whereabouts of a young woman I left in your care. It was years ago, after that bad business with Berghast's infant. You will remember her, I think. Susan Crowley."

Ratcliffe Fang's expression didn't change, but she sensed his surprise. "You told me never to tell no one about her," he said. "Not even yourself. You made me swear to it."

She nodded. "And now I must ask you to break that promise."

"Ah."

"Is she still alive?"

Ratcliffe Fang peered into the fire. "She's alive," he said, reluctant. "Works as a seamstress, in Whitechapel. I can't tell you more."

"You must. There will be hundreds of such women."

Ratcliffe Fang narrowed his eyes. "It's not like you, Margaret, to come here like this."

"Then you know it must be important. Susan Crowley was in possession of something most rare, something I cannot proceed without. A tool, you might say, left in her care. I am certain Jacob Marber will be searching for her also."

Ratcliffe Fang's bulging eyes lit up in sudden understanding. "That's why Jake Marber's in Limehouse," he whispered. "She's got what can kill him, an he knows it."

"Indeed, Mr. Fang. And I must take it from her first."

Ten minutes later, she left Ratcliffe Fang's rooms, satisfied. An address was folded up in the wrist of her glove. Cold fog seeped in through her shawl. Her bull's-eye lantern was tightly shuttered so that its beam turned this way and that, shining off the slimy bricks of the tenements. She adjusted her veil. She'd been surprised at how Fang had aged; but then, she supposed, she too was no longer young. She walked deeper into the alley, holding her petticoats out of the muck with one hand, keeping close to the walls.

Whitechapel, she knew, was not far.

But she'd not gone twenty paces when something materialized in the dark fog ahead, at a dead man's corner. A silhouetted shape, lurking in the mist.

She opened her lantern and held it high but it was no good, the fog had thickened, and she could see only the drifts of fog turning and shifting in front of her.

"Who are you?" she called. "Give me passage. I'll not ask twice."

She heard the figure's boots scrape on the cobblestones, coming closer. Carefully, slowly, Margaret reached into her handbag for her small pistol.

It wasn't there.

She cursed and gripped the lantern and prepared to swing it hard at whatever cutthroat approached. The stones underfoot gleamed in the weak light.

"You're looking for this, I guess," came the voice.

Margaret stared.

And then the figure emerged out of the fog in an oilskin coat, hat drawn low over her killer's eyes, holding in her open palm the little silver-plated pistol. Margaret shook her head in anger. It was Alice Quicke.

"What?" said the detective. "You thought I wouldn't follow?"

"I'd have thought," said Margaret, taking back her weapon, "you'd have more sense."

Miss Quicke gave her a quick sly grin from under her hat.

"No, you didn't," she said.

Whitechapel was darker, more crowded. Hansoms creaked past like apparitions, drunken men weaved and hollered, swarms of pale children in rags crowded under the weak gaslights while their mothers, exhausted, stood in the doorways with their petticoats showing. Margaret went carefully, following Mr. Fang's direction. If it was the fog or Miss Quicke's dangerous look she didn't know, but they wandered unaccosted and unharmed. But the lanes were crooked and the muck soft underfoot, the puddles reeking, and they had often to duck past shreds of rags and linen strung up on lines in the miserable courts and alleys. Margaret felt better for Miss Quicke's company, grateful even, and when she realized this she was surprised, and made no further complaint.

At last they came to an unmarked door, dripping, slick with mold. It was the third doorway in, on the second alley up from the Black Fox drinking house. Margaret knocked, stepped back.

The door opened a crack. Eyes peered suspiciously out.

"Miss Crowley?" said Margaret matter-of-factly.

"What is it you want?"

Margaret removed her veil. "You will not remember me, but I am a friend of Mr. Fang's. I'd hoped we might speak. I have news about the child."

She seemed to know at once who was meant. "Where is he?"

"At Cairndale. But I fear he's in danger."

After a moment, the woman opened the door. She was tall, big-boned, but her cheeks had hollowed as if she'd fallen ill and never quite recovered. Thick black hair, astray under a bonnet. Her hands were wide and strong-looking. Visible across her collarbones was the stippled roughened skin of old scars, as if she'd been burned long ago. She was younger even than Miss Quicke but hard living had aged her badly and there was a stoop to her walk and a tremble to her chin.

"You," said the woman slowly. "You're the one who rescued me, from out that train car. You brought me to Mr. Fang. After the wee babe was attacked. After I . . . lost him." She put a hand to her scarred collarbone, as if remembering. She looked past, at the dark street. "You'd best come in."

When they were all three crowded into the meager sewing room, Margaret told about Marlowe, and how Henry Berghast had searched for him, and how Miss Quicke had taken him to Cairndale. And she told, too, of Jacob Marber's return.

"Then Cairndale isn't safe," said Susan Crowley, at once. The dim candlelight played across her features. "Jacob Marber will find a way inside. He always could find a way. He knew the child was special, right from the very first, that was why he did what he did. He will come for him again."

"That is my fear also."

Susan Crowley hesitated. "Why are you here?"

"I have questions," said Margaret. "And I must ask you for something. I mean to stop Jacob Marber before he can hurt the boy again."

"But he did not hurt the boy before, Mrs. Harrogate."

"Because of you. Only because of you."

"Yes, perhaps . . ." The woman looked away, her green eyes uncertain. "What do you know about Jacob Marber's history? You know that he disappeared, on a voyage back from the East?"

"Some said he'd drowned," said Margaret, trying to hide her impatience. "But Mr. Coulton said he'd fallen under the influence of the drughr and been spirited away by it."

"Yes. Into the other world."

Margaret blinked. "But that isn't possible, surely? His talent would twist. He'd die."

"And he should have done. But he did not."

"A living being in the land of the dead," said Margaret, thinking. "There has never been such a thing. I do not know what it would mean."

The woman picked at a piece of needlework, nervous. "But he is not the first talent to walk among the dead, Mrs. Harrogate. There have been others."

"What others?"

"Dr. Berghast's experiments." Susan Crowley paused. "I thought you knew."

Margaret felt a heat come into her cheeks.

"I do not know the particulars," Susan Crowley went on. She drew her ragged shawl tighter. "It began long before I arrived at Cairndale. Dr. Berghast was sending talents through the orsine. Into the other world. He did it for years. He was making a map, a map for his own purposes. That is how it began, using that poor glyphic to open the orsine just enough for his talents to go through. He had acquired something, an artifact, that allowed the talents to enter and return.

But then, one day, a talent did not come back out. He was lost. The artifact was lost too. Something had been disturbed, awakened in that other world, something had hunted him down and eaten him before he could—"

"The drughr," whispered Margaret.

The young nursemaid raised her frightened eyes in the candlelight. She nodded.

"But the experiments didn't stop," she went on. "They were just the more dangerous after that. Dr. Berghast needed to find the artifact that was lost inside the orsine. If it fell into the drughr's hands . . ." She shuddered. "But without the artifact, the talents he sent in came back sick, or aged, or . . . deformed. And the drughr just kept getting stronger. Eventually, after Jacob disappeared, Dr. Berghast stopped looking. He gave up."

Margaret had heard rumors of experiments, all those years ago. She'd refused to believe them. She felt a sudden deep shame. "Because of Jacob?"

"Because of the baby." Susan Crowley's lips thinned. "It is an awful part of the story. The last talents Dr. Berghast sent through were the baby's young parents. She was in the family way, though she didn't know it yet. While in the other world, she gave birth."

"I beg your pardon," said Margaret sharply. "How far along was she?"

"Ah. But you must remember, Mrs. Harrogate, time moves differently there. There are valleys and rivers where it slows down entirely, and hills where it speeds up." Susan Crowley's eyes darkened. "Jacob Marber found them, shortly after she'd given birth, and he killed the parents, and he took the baby. He brought it back out, through the orsine, into the ruined abbey at Cairndale. It is the only way out, you see, the only passage between worlds. The glyphic opened it for him. Jacob intended to steal the child, presumably. But Dr. Berghast stopped him."

Margaret did not look away from the nursemaid's face. She was still shocked. "Marlowe was born . . . *inside* the orsine?"

"In the land of the dead. Yes."

She shook her head in disbelief. But she knew the strangeness of Susan Crowley's account was its very truth, that Crowley was not lying. No wonder Berghast was so interested in the child. No wonder the child's talents were so bizarre, so different from any other's. No wonder Jacob and the drughr were hunting him.

He was something entirely new.

A stillness had descended. Susan Crowley lowered her voice. "I don't know as this is still true," she said, "but all the time I knew him, Henry Berghast nursed a grievance in his heart. When I think what he did—harnessing a glyphic, closing the orsine—I tell myself: if there was anyone who could find a way to destroy the drughr, it would be him."

Margaret tightened her grip on her handbag. "That grievance is there still."

"He is not changed, then?"

"Only for the worse. He is still obsessed with the drughr. Perhaps more than ever. I fear he will betray himself, betray Cairndale, betray everything he has built, in order to destroy it."

"That wouldn't matter to him. Not the Henry Berghast I knew."

She paused. "But it has been his life's work."

"No, Mrs. Harrogate. His life's work waits for him in the other world. Better for all of us if the glyphic were destroyed, if the orsine were sealed forever."

"Is that possible?"

The nursemaid's eyes hardened in the candlelight. "Not so long as Dr. Berghast lives. He would never allow it. Oh, he wants to be good. He *is* good, better than all of us. He's the one who's stood against the drughr, longer than any other could've done. But even back then, he'd already forgotten what goodness *meant*. It was always about the end result, for him. The method never mattered. I remember how he'd stand over the cradle, staring down, like the babe was a cut of meat. Like there was a *use* for him. But I'd . . . I'd vowed to keep that baby safe . . ."

Her voice drifted off.

"Which is why we've come to you now, Miss Crowley," said Mrs. Harrogate. "So you can keep that vow."

"What can I do?"

"You were entrusted with something once, by an old talent at Cairndale. You were wearing it around your neck when I found you, in that freight car."

Susan Crowley gripped her elbows in her big hands and sat with her head bowed as if thinking it over and then she rose and went into the back room. She returned with a leather cord looped around her knuckles.

"Is it this you mean?" she said.

She opened her fist, and Margaret saw the weir-bents. Instantly a cold wave of nausea swept over her. She began to tremble. They were shaped like two keys, blackened as if they'd burned once in a fire, both ancient-looking, both heavy. Miss Quicke too flinched at the sight of them, visibly recoiling, the wrongness pouring off them like a smell and affecting her powerfully, far more powerfully than Margaret. That was all for the good, she thought. But Susan Crowley just handled the weir-bents without concern, just as if they were ordinary keys, as if she couldn't sense any power in them at all.

Swiftly, using a handkerchief, Margaret lifted the leather cord from the table, careful not to touch the weir-bents. She folded the handkerchief in four, slid it all into her handbag.

"I can't imagine what they open," said Susan Crowley. "Such queer-looking things."

"Indeed," said Margaret, getting to her feet.

At the door, Susan Crowley drew the shawl self-consciously over her scarred collarbone and said, "Mrs. Harrogate, please. Tell me about the child. He must be eight by now?"

They stood in the open doorway with their backs to the fog-enshrouded lane. Mrs. Harrogate could feel the heavy weir-bents, weighing down her handbag. She nodded. "About eight, yes."

"I can't hardly imagine him. How tall is he? Is his hair still black? Yes, of course it is. Tell me, is he a good sort of boy?"

Margaret glanced at Miss Quicke. Behind and below drifted the night mists of Whitechapel, halos of yellow gaslight, ghostly figures.

"The best sort," she said firmly.

The young woman's eyes glowed then, remembering the baby he'd been, and for just a moment in the near darkness Margaret saw her hard features soften and fill with an old and undimmed love.

24

THE SPIDER

The thing about Oskar Czekowisz, the thing no one ever seemed to notice, or understand, was that he was terrified of being alone. Maybe it was because of Lymenion, his flesh giant, that no one thought it; for when was he ever alone?

And so, despite his own dread of the Spider, on that night when the others crept out into the cold hallway to go to the island—candles in the wall sconces snuffed, Miss Davenshaw already done her rounds and retired to her bedchamber—Oskar and his flesh giant were there, waiting, too.

At thirteen years old, he was short for his age, with soft shoulders and plump pale wrists. Everything about him seemed leeched of color. His hair was blond white, like an old man's, and very fine, and it fell straight over his ears and his forehead and into his eyes. Those eyes were large and trusting, but radiated fright.

Lymenion was his one companion, his true friend. He'd always been there, it seemed, as long as Oskar could remember, sturdy and quiet and watchful and loyal. Oskar could fashion him out of any dead thing he'd find in the ditches or farmyards or even out of the slabs of meat in a butcher's; he could make him and dissolve him at will, but always when he fashioned him anew and the meat and sinews took shape, it was Lymenion, his same friend, his only.

Lymenion liked the new kids, too. *But they have been through much,* warned his giant, the words forming directly in Oskar's mind.

"I just hope they like us back," whispered Oskar.

He hoped, yes; but he knew, too, how most people felt about Lymenion, the repugnant smell, the strange meekness of him, the way he copied Oskar's every gesture, like a meat shadow; and that was without seeing what could happen when he ran amok, when Oskar's own fury was aroused.

The fact of it was, until coming to Cairndale, Oskar Czekowisz and his giant Lymenion had been savagely, ferociously alone; not just alone but lonely: lonely in Gdansk, picking through garbage in the winding streets while the dogs lurked and kept their distance; lonely in the crumbling stalls of the old stables, behind that old couple's stone farmhouse, somewhere north of Lebork; lonely in the ruined tower above the windswept darkness of the Baltic Sea. He knew the locals feared him wherever he went; he knew the stories they told of a white-haired boy and his monster. So he kept away. Until one evening, when a stout man, red-faced, with auburn whiskers and a grim smile, came trudging up the long dirt road to the tower, oak staff in one hand, a windblown coat snapping sharply out behind him. He wore a bright yellow checkered suit and waistcoat, like a slash of color in that landscape. Oskar in those days spoke only Polish; he was ten years old; and the man, Coulton—for that is who it was—spoke only English. And so Coulton sat patiently outside the tower gate for three nights, waiting. And on the third night, when Oskar sent Lymenion to frighten him, Coulton just rolled his powerful shoulders like he was sore from sitting so long, and he stretched, and he smiled.

Now Oskar and Lymenion and the others crept quickly and silently through the manor, and out into the courtyard, and around the gatehouse and across the wet lawn. They were all wearing the same ghostly Cairndale robes, pale gray in color, thick enough to keep the chill out, and under these the white Cairndale nightshirts and nightgowns, woven of rough cotton.

A fog had descended. As they fanned out across the grass, they looked spectral and eerie in the gloom. They ran silent and swift and when the manor had receded back into the fog and its lights haloed and dimmed they slowed and, breathing hard, they walked.

Oskar was surprised to see Charlie fall in beside him. Lymenion struggled to keep up, his thick legs working, his stout arms swinging. He always had such trouble. Komako was out ahead across the grass, an apparition in her pale robe, Ribs's headless nightgown and robe flapping emptily through the grass beside her. If the girls spoke, it was only to each other.

"You've been to see the Spider before, Oskar?" Charlie asked.

Oskar cleared his throat, suddenly shy. "Yes," he mumbled. "I mean . . . no. Sort of? I mean, we all know what he is, we've all been to the island. But you don't get to see the Spider when you go. He's in a, uh, a different part."

"Why do you go to the island?" said Marlowe.

The boy was walking next to Lymenion, not bothered, looking with interest at his features, and seeing this Oskar felt strangely relieved.

"You'll go too," he said. "Both of you. Miss Davenshaw will take you. It's because of the orsine. She'll show you what it is, how it works."

"What's on the other side?" asked Marlowe. His skin looked pallid and ghostly in the dark. "Is it frightening?"

Oskar shrugged, embarrassed. "It's where the spirits are," he said lamely. Truth was, he didn't know much. "The world beyond the orsine is where the dead go, when they die. I heard Mr. Nolan talking about it once. He's one of the old talents. He said it's . . . it's like if this world was a sheet of paper, and you folded it, and then folded it again. And then you tried to draw a line over all the folded-up surface. It just feels . . . wrong. It just feels like a wrong place."

"Because you have to be dead first," said Marlowe.

In the fog, Oskar felt Lymenion turn his attention on the boy.

"But how would he know?" asked Charlie. "If he's never been there, how would he know?"

Oskar blushed, feeling suddenly foolish. "I wondered about that too."

"Maybe he did go there," said Marlowe.

But Oskar knew that was impossible. "No one can go inside the orsine."

They descended the dark slope, their feet hissing in the wet grass. The fog parted; Oskar saw the flat black table of the loch; the fog thickened again.

"You have to be dead first," Marlowe repeated softly to himself.

Charlie heard the soft wash of the loch on the stony shore but he didn't see it because of the fog, didn't see it at all, not until his shoes had splashed right down into it, and he felt Oskar's hand on his sleeve, pulling him back.

"Careful," said the boy, in his quiet way. "The dock is this way."

"Come on, you lot," called Ribs, from ahead. Charlie could see her disembodied robes stalking back and forth in the fog.

Near him, the flesh giant's breathing came thick and labored. There was something strange and dreamlike about it all, so alien was it from the world he'd known all his life, the cruelty of Natchez. He kept thinking about his father, not much older than he was now, losing his talent, going out alone into the world. Did his mother know anything about his father's other life, what he'd once been able to do? Did he hide it from her, that sadness, the sense of loss? Charlie saw a slender young man alone in a wet alley, his frock coat fraying, and he filled with a sadness all his own. He still didn't know what to make of it. He reached for Marlowe's hand.

The dock was a gray weathered contraption that had sunk on one side, maybe fifty years old, and it led crookedly out over the dark water. At its end was moored a solitary rowboat, big enough for the five of them, and Lymenion too, a cold lantern on a pole rising from its bow. Charlie heard a noise; then Komako came rattling along the dock, oars in her arms.

Marlowe was staring out at the loch. "It's big. I didn't know it was so big, Charlie."

"They say it has no bottom," whispered Oskar.

"Rrrh," mumbled the flesh giant.

"For God's sake," said Komako, brushing past them, climbing nimbly into the boat, her long braid swaying. "It has a bottom. It's just deep, is all." She steadied the boat's lantern on its chains, and opened the glass door. She peeled off her gloves, cupped her raw fingers around the little candle stub in its wax. Slowly she squeezed her hands into fists.

The candle bloomed into flame.

"Oh," breathed Charlie, amazed.

Komako blushed.

"Aw it's just friction," grumbled Ribs, from close by. "It ain't magic, Charlie."

He felt Ribs take his hand. Her fingers were warm. She half dragged him off the dock, into the back of the boat, the boat rocking and banging as they got in. Ribs held his hand a moment longer than needed and then she let it go.

Oskar's flesh giant took the oars. A shine of mucus dripped from the handles where it gripped them, and soon they were sculling away from the dock, turning, pulling powerfully across the loch.

The fog thinned as they passed away from the land. All was silence; the chill of the air on the water seeped through Charlie's robe; the soft splash of the oars and the sleek weightless sensation as they sped over the surface made him sleepy. They were halfway across when Komako reached back, shuttered the lantern. He snapped awake.

"Look," she said.

Above the island, in the air and in the leaves of the great wych elm, Charlie could see thousands of tiny glowing specks, like fireflies. Not drifting, really, so much as lifting upward into the black sky, a cyclone of fiery blossoms, winking and sparking as they went. Charlie had never seen anything so beautiful.

"It's the orsine," said Komako. "The Spider's generating the orsine."

"What does it mean?" asked Marlowe.

"Means he's awake," said Ribs. But there was a new tone in her voice, subdued, wary.

They tied up at an ancient dock even more sloped and crooked than the first, and followed a steep trail up the rocky face of the island. Komako had unhooked the lantern and its weak spill of light illuminated the root-strewn path. At the top of the cliff loomed the ruins. A vast dark canopy of branches soared up out of the broken stones. That was the great wych elm.

It had been a refuge of several buildings once, all of them now collapsed. The island had a creepy, haunted air to it, as if something watched them. Charlie followed Komako and Ribs into the only standing building, the largest, its roof long since rotted away. It had been the monastery chapel; now flagstones were missing from the floor, and shrubs and roots had burst up everywhere, desiccated leaves blown up against the shadows. Where the altar should have been, the huge dark silence of the wych elm now grew: a massive sprawl of roots, spilling out on all sides.

Komako didn't lead them that far. She stopped at a small apse in the southerly wall and set the lantern down and brushed away a layer of dirt from the ground. Underneath lay a wooden door. The flesh giant turned the ring, lightly, easily, as if it weighed nothing, and hauled the door groaning upward. A dank gasp of air came out. Inside was a stone stair, descending into a greater darkness.

"Uh," said Charlie, looking around at the others. "Wait. We've got to go down *there?*"

"You're not afraid of the dark, Charlie?" Komako grinned. "What can hurt you down there?"

"Charlie isn't scared of anything," said Marlowe.

Komako lifted the lantern. It cast her face into crooked shadow, it darkened the hollows of her eyes. "Is that right, Charlie?" she said softly. "You're not afraid of anything?"

Charlie swallowed.

"There's another way in, Charlie," came Ribs's voice, out of the gloom of the nave. "A proper door, like, just round the front. But it's locked."

"Dr. Berghast has the key," Oskar explained.

"Rrrh," mumbled his giant, sounding distinctly unimpressed, still holding the trapdoor.

"Let me guess," muttered Charlie. "This way leads to the crypt?"

"*Through* it," corrected Komako.

Ribs poked Charlie in the arm. "Hey, what'd the skeleton say to his sick neighbor? *Stop your bloody coffin.*"

Oskar giggled, a nervous high-pitched giggle that echoed off away into the crypt.

"Oh my God," muttered Komako. "I'm here with a bunch of children." She looked back at Marlowe, suddenly abashed. "No offense."

But Charlie was still staring down into the darkness. "Tell me again, whose idea was this?"

"Ribs's," said Komako.

"Ko's," said Ribs.

Marlowe reached up and took Charlie's hand. "Mine," he said, his voice almost a whisper.

They left the flesh giant in the apse of the ruined monastery, shreds of fog drifting past. Ribs suggested in her salty way that maybe the smell of it might put off the Spider from talking to them; when Oskar protested, Ribs suggested they put it to a vote. All hands went up.

And so they went down, into the catacombs, the five of them, ghostly and pale in their robes while the dim light of the lantern played off the stone walls and the dripping of the darkness reached their ears. Charlie kept Marlowe close, his hand on the back of the little boy's neck, steering him gently in the blackness. The stairs came out onto a narrow passageway, with little windows cut into the rock, and bones piled up crosswise with skulls laid out on top. Those were the monks of an age long passed, eye sockets hollow and dark.

As they went, Charlie peered around: the ceiling was lost in shadow, and there were more passages opening both to the left and the right. On the walls now he saw the mummified remains of monks, shriveled to the size of children, suspended somehow in their robes on the stone walls. But the floor was dry, and scraped softly as they went; the air was cold; the dark was quieter than any quiet Charlie had ever known, so quiet it seemed almost to make a sound, like a bell, in his ears.

They walked on for five minutes, ten. Soon Charlie noticed the passage had narrowed, the ceiling lowering so that he had to dip his head as he went. But the bones of the dead were no longer; there was only the long darkness of the tunnel. A thick tree root emerged out of one wall, near his elbow, snaking alongside them like a kind of marker, guiding the way. It was joined by a second, and then underfoot a third, until soon the floor and walls of the tunnel were strewn with roots, roots breaking through the stones and mortar and the soft collapsed coffins of the ancient monks. The deeper they went the more roots they had to clamber over, and dip their heads to avoid, until it seemed a tunnel of root and not stone at all, as if they were descending into the heart of a monstrous tree. Charlie felt Marlowe fumble for him, grip his hand hard.

"It's okay," he muttered.

But whether he spoke to the boy or to himself did not matter; it convinced neither.

A few feet ahead, Komako stopped short. Charlie could see stones and rocks and a great tangle of tree roots blocking the way. There'd been a cave-in.

Komako just stood with the lantern lifted high, as if perplexed. Charlie didn't understand her hesitation; it wasn't such a big job as that; he'd worked at harder hauling when he was half as big, back in Mississippi.

He strode past, reached for the biggest root blocking the way. It felt soft, almost furred, in his fingers. He yanked hard at it.

"Charlie, don't!" Ribs cried out.

But he nearly had it free. He leaned into it and pulled. Suddenly the walls and ceiling trembled. Dust sifted down around his face, got into the neck of his robe. A deep inhuman groan rippled through the tunnel, as if the blackness was a living thing.

Charlie stumbled back.

Komako grabbed him by the shoulders, spun him around. "Don't hurt the roots!" Her braid whipped angrily from side to side. "What's the matter with you? You'll bring the whole tunnel down on us. Just stand over there. No, *there*. Touch *nothing*." She said something then to herself, in a sharp angry Japanese; it sounded less than polite.

Charlie, staggering back to the others, could guess its meaning. He rubbed at his shoulder. "She doesn't like me much, does she?"

Ribs, her robe floating beside him, paused. "*I like you*," she said.

But he was only half listening, instead watching Komako hook the lantern on a tendril for light, and in her pale nightgown work to clear the rocks without hurting the tree; and he didn't take his eyes off her until the way was clear, and they could squeeze through, and go on.

At last they came to a chamber. It was very dark. When Komako lifted the lantern Charlie saw the floor and walls and low ceiling were completely covered in the rootlike tentacles of the wych elm, so that it felt like they had come to the hollow core of the tree itself. A musky scent of earth and wood filled his nostrils.

He stopped with the others just inside. Marlowe picked his careful way forward, at the edge of the pool of light, clambering over the lumpen roots. In the half-light of Komako's lantern, Charlie could just make out, suspended from the low ceiling, in a vast tangled knot of tree roots and clumps of dirt and dangling moss, a kind of *thing*—a *figure*—so ancient, it seemed to have grown into the very roots of the tree.

Komako lifted the lantern higher. Hanging in the center of that tangled gnarl was a face, a face that could have been carved from wood, elongated and strange and with a strange gaping mouth, except that its yellow eyes were open, and glittering, and intelligent.

Charlie caught his breath. Marlowe was standing directly under it, small enough that he could look up into its eyes without crouching.

It was the glyphic, of course. The Spider.

"*You . . . should not . . . be here*," it said, in a voice like a slow rumble, a voice as cold as the dark places of the earth.

Oskar let out a whimper; a moment later Charlie felt something too, a tightening at his ankle. One of the roots had snaked around his shoe and pinned him into place. The others too were ensnarled, all except Marlowe. A second, a third root wrapped up around Charlie's legs, over his waist, his chest, holding him fast. The more he struggled, the more the roots squeezed, impossibly powerful. They were coming out of the walls, out of the ceiling.

"Uh, Ribs?" called Komako, nervous.

But it was little Marlowe, standing directly in front of the glyphic, who spoke to the creature.

"We didn't want to come here uninvited," he said. "But we need your help, please. We have questions."

"*They . . . want to know . . . about the missing . . .*"

Charlie watched Marlowe step even closer, his black hair stark against his pallid face. But it wasn't the missing children he asked about, not first. "I'm afraid for someone. A person. Can you see, can you tell me, is she okay? Her name is—"

"*Alice Quicke . . . is not . . . a talent.*"

Marlowe half turned, peered back at Charlie through the darkness. Charlie could see a faint light in his eyes, like twin stars. "No," said Marlowe. "But she's our friend, mine and Charlie's, and she brought us here to you. But she's gone now down to London with Mrs. Harrogate, and they're going to find Jacob Marber."

The glyphic focused its eerie yellow eyes on Marlowe. Its face looked all of wood but the eyes were bright, wet, reptilian. "*We know . . . you. We have seen . . . you. In the Dreaming.*"

Several thick roots lifted and swayed near Marlowe. But they did not attack him.

"*Alice Quicke . . . ,*" rumbled the glyphic, craning its neck, "*is trying . . . to locate . . . Jacob Marber.*"

"Yes."

"*But he . . . will not . . . be found. It is he . . . who does . . . the finding.*"

"What does he mean?" whispered Charlie to Komako. The roots tightened.

"Marlowe," she called. Her voice was soft and urgent and there was something in it Charlie hadn't heard before. Fear. "Marlowe, ask him about the disappeared kids. How do we find them? Ask him about the carriage."

But Marlowe had drifted closer and maybe didn't hear. "I . . . I've been having these dreams," he said in a whisper. "I think Alice is in trouble. I think she needs me."

"Dreams . . . yes . . . we know . . . about dreams. You . . . are the one he . . . seeks."

Charlie could not see Marlowe's face, only the back of his head, the way he was standing in his dirt-smeared robe, the way he balanced on the balls of his feet.

"Closer, child . . . closer . . . put your hands . . . on our face . . . do not be . . . afraid."

"Uh, Mar—" called Charlie. "I don't know if that's such a good idea."

"It's okay, Charlie. He won't hurt me."

Komako had one gloved hand free and she reached for Charlie's wrist. Her fingertips felt cool, light. "It's how he communicates clearest, Charlie. It isn't dangerous." She closed her eyes, as if hearing a sound in her skull. "He knows why we're here. He knows what we came for."

And then Charlie watched the little boy stand on his toes, and reach up, and lay his hands gently on either side of the glyphic's skull.

Slowly, a faint blue glow grew and grew until it filled the chamber, casting everything into eerie relief, as if they were underwater. Charlie knew that shine; he'd seen it on the train.

Komako's eyes filled with amazement. Oskar had stopped whimpering and stared, his delicate pale lips half-open. Even the tree roots hesitated.

Everything went still.

But then the light got brighter, it kept on brightening until it hurt their eyes, and they had to look away, and Charlie squinted against the glare and understood. Something was wrong. Marlowe had stiffened;

and suddenly, without making a sound, his whole body wracked backward, as if in agony.

"Marlowe?" Charlie cried in the dazzle. "Marlowe!"

Or he tried to, at least; it was as if the words wouldn't come, or would come only sluggishly, drained of all sense, and everything was moving impossibly slow. He turned his slow blue face. He lifted a slow blue hand. Slowly the blue roots squeezed.

And then, just as suddenly, the shining flared out and was gone; all was absolute darkness and afterimage, burning into their eyelids. Marlowe had collapsed, released from whatever spell had held him. Charlie tried to get free, to go to him, but he couldn't move, and somehow was having trouble breathing. But his eyesight was adjusting, again; he saw the roots surrounding the glyphic coil and contract, coil and contract. The creature lifted its face, peered malevolently at them with yellow eyes. "*The child . . . may pass . . . ,*" it rumbled. "*But you . . . the rest of you . . . come with too . . . many . . . questions. . . .*"

Charlie felt the roots around his chest slither tighter. His lungs were on fire.

But then there was a movement, a sturdy powerful movement from the tunnel where they had come in. Charlie's eyes were watering and it was hard to see. But the roots were shifting, seeking purchase, something was lumbering around behind them, and all at once Charlie felt a slick strong grip pry back the roots crushing him.

It was Oskar's flesh giant.

He went calmly among them, ripping them loose, lifting them away in the shelter of his arms. Roots snaked out, snagged at his arms, so that he had to keep slowly and methodically pulling them away, as if picking threads from a sleeve. There were just too many roots.

As Charlie came free, he saw Marlowe get to his feet.

"Please let my friends go," said the child, hoarsely. "Please. You promised."

There came a pause; for an instant Charlie was afraid the glyphic would attack Marlowe too; but then, with a soft rustling noise, the roots retracted, one by one, slithering back into the walls and floor. The glyphic seemed to sink upward, into the writhing mass of roots, until it was lost to view; and then Charlie was tumbling, gasping, free.

On his hands and knees, he raised his face. The others were already staggering back into the tunnel, climbing over the roots, wheezing. Komako held her throat. Ribs was no longer invisible. The glow of the lantern was a corona of light on the walls as it receded. But Marlowe hadn't moved; he stood dazed, small hands loose at his sides.

Charlie stumbled over. "What happened, Mar? What did he promise?"

The boy peered up at him, eyes shining in the tunnel dark. "I . . . I saw Alice," he mumbled. "The Spider, he showed me—"

"What? Is she in danger?"

"Oh, Charlie," whispered the boy. "We all are."

And then Charlie was lifting him, carrying him as he fled back up the tunnel, back through the narrow opening in the collapsed stones, all the long way back toward the crypt, and the monks' skulls, and the natural darkness of the true night.

Henry Berghast closed the journal he'd been writing in and wiped the nib of his pen dry and sat back. Through his study windows the night deepened.

So.

They had gone to the island.

It was perhaps not entirely a bad thing, he reflected. They would have questions, questions he could answer. He rubbed at his eyes, nodded. The coal fire in the grate was burning low, and the gas sconces cast strange coronas of light up the walls. In its cage, a bonebird clicked, shifting its footing on a perch. Its wings rattled.

He unlocked a drawer in his desk and took out a roll of paper and smoothed it flat. Overlapping circles and lines, arrows, notations in his own spidery hand. It was a copy of the huge ink canvas on his wall. Here was his life's work: a map, a map he'd been composing for thirty years. A map of the world beyond the orsine.

Time was running out. He had given up on his experiments, had started to fear he would fail completely in his pursuit of the drughr. But then the glyphic had located the boy, after so many years lost, and he had seen that the child would be useful, more than useful; the child might even make it possible for himself—for pitiful Henry Berghast, weak Henry Berghast—to complete what he'd set out to do.

He rolled up the copy of the map, locked it away. "Bailey," he called in a sharp tone.

The manservant appeared, his long face impassive, his gray eyes glittering and intelligent. "Sir?"

"Our recent guests, the new boys. Do you know them by sight?"

"Indeed, sir."

Berghast turned in his chair, he peered at his own reflection in the window. His eyes were lost to darkness. "Bring them to me," said the reflection.

25

Night Creatures and Other Sorrows

The creature was pale and hairless with long knifelike teeth and it stood in the open door, absolutely still, like a thing shaped from clay. Only its eyes moved, watching the night fog of Wapping.

It was barefoot, but that in itself was unremarkable, in a corner of the city where bodies lay in any state of undress, and the living were often confused for the dead. In ragged rough-spun trousers and an un-collared shirt and a gray mud-spattered gentleman's coat, it could have been any kind of person fallen on hard times. But its mouth was lost to darkness, entirely lost; and there was about it a sense—an aura—of absolute calm that didn't fit with the fallen or the destitute. It needed nothing. The door behind it hung by a hinge, splintered and broken; and half-visible from behind a chair lay a cracked pair of wire specta-cles, and the outflung arm of Ratcliffe Fang, his blood congealing like black wax on the floor.

The litch was just leaving. But it paused to pick up a battered old bowler hat from where it had fallen from the body, and with an eerie delicacy it turned it, turned it, as if lost in reverie, and then dreamily put it on.

Only then did it step out, into the murky night, and turn north. Despite the fog it walked quickly and decisively over the mud and trenches of filth. But it'd pause from time to time, and crouch smoothly to sniff the air, before again standing and pouring forward. All the while it was trying to remember something, something important, but it could not do so.

Jacob, it thought. *Jacob Jacob Jacob Jacob—*

The air changed; the litch had reached the noisy darkness of Whitechapel High Street. Here the scents intermingled and bled together, the reek of unwashed bodies and rotting food and animals and excrement so that it had to raise its face, and turn slowly, sniffing; but then, rising like a solitary high note above an orchestra, the litch found it again, that scent, the smell of who it'd been sent to find, and it turned east and slipped between the hansoms and the passing horses and the figures like specters in the fog.

The lighting was poor and above the pub doors hung ancient greasy lanterns illuminating the fog and the litch slid like smoke through the darkness. On the far side of Commercial Street it turned north, and crept down a deep alley with arches and slick brick walls, picking its way over the huddled forms asleep in the doorways.

Then east again, and north, down passageways and lanes and up alleys and across courts, until at last it came to stand, absolutely still, in the drifting fog. It crossed to a shadowy doorway, where a man was sleeping; he raised his elbows in irritation, and the litch—without so much as a thought—crouched and clutched the man's forehead with one hand and smoothly drew a single sharp nail across his throat. The fellow's shirt bloomed red; he kicked out, shuddered, fell back, and was still.

Across the lane, scarcely visible through the mist, a door was opening.

Two women stepped out onto the stoop, talking to a third still inside. The shorter woman was dressed in black and wore a veil at her face; the taller, in an oilskin coat, scanned the fog with dangerous eyes.

The litch faded back into the shadows.

Fifteen minutes later, in the muffled fog, Alice Quicke could hear through the thick silence the sound of her own boots scraping across the cobblestones—a sad, grim sound, like chalk on a coffin marking the newly dead. She strained to make out any other sound. Something made her anxious, uneasy. Mrs. Harrogate walked beside her, head bowed, a silhouette lost in thought. In the older woman's handbag lay the two heavy keys, but it was not the keys that worried her. Every few feet Alice would glance over her shoulder, the hairs at the back of her neck prickling.

Something was following them.

She was sure of it, sure as anything. A cutthroat, maybe; maybe worse. She thought of what Susan Crowley had said about Henry Berghast and smoothly cocked the hammer of her revolver in her pocket and held it tight. But nothing emerged out of the fog, and she said nothing to Mrs. Harrogate, and they walked on until the older woman waved for a hansom and a cab stopped creaking in the soupy dark and both women climbed up. Then the cabman slashed his whip and the skeletal horse rattled and lurched on.

Back at their lodging house, with the window firmly shut and locked, Alice wrestled out of her long coat and slung her hat on the unmade bed and frowned.

"We weren't alone," she said. "Leaving Susan Crowley's rooms. There was someone following us."

Mrs. Harrogate, unpinning her veil, then removing her shawl, stood very still. She looked at Alice as if weighing a purchase, considering its worth. Alice didn't like it. "Did you feel anything, in your side?" Mrs. Harrogate asked curiously.

"No." She put a hand to her ribs. "I haven't sensed anything since we arrived here. What if it doesn't work? What if I can't find Marber?"

"You won't need to. The keywrasse will do the finding."

Alice sat on the edge of the bed in the yellow gaslight, she pulled off her mud-encrusted boots. She wasn't sure the woman's meaning but decided to leave it. She had more pressing questions. "Why is Marber so interested in Marlowe?" she said. "Why would he kill the parents at all?"

"Because the child is powerful. And because the drughr is interested." Mrs. Harrogate's eyes were lost to shadow where she paused, folding her shawl at the wardrobe, and Alice saw the older woman's reflection in the looking glass pause also. Her tone softened. "Forgive me. Miss Crowley's account was . . . disturbing. Much of it I did not know. And I do not like to be surprised."

"You believe her, then?"

"You do not?"

Alice thought about it. "She wasn't telling everything, but that doesn't mean what she said was a lie. She made it sound like Berghast scares her most. Not Marber or the drughr."

"Only one who does not know the nature of the drughr would believe that."

Alice took this in.

"Remember," Mrs. Harrogate went on, "it's not Henry Berghast who hunts children, who seduces away talents, who betrays and murders the likes of Frank Coulton. We are here for one purpose only. We shall see it through."

"Crowley said Berghast's real work lay in that other world. Why?"

Mrs. Harrogate sat primly in the velvet chair, adjusted her skirts. Her face was troubled.

"Son of a bitch. You don't trust him either," said Alice softly, beginning to understand. Then she thought of something else and her face darkened. "Why have we been collecting children, Mrs. Harrogate? What are they used for?"

"Calm yourself, Miss Quicke. You will have our good landlady listening at the keyhole."

"I left Marlowe and Charlie in Berghast's care."

"And they are quite safe behind the walls of Cairndale," Mrs. Harrogate said. "Henry may be misguided, but he is not mad. The same cannot be said of Jacob Marber. I am certain their sudden proximity to *him* would result in a rather different fate."

"You keep saying Cairndale's safe—"

"Because Jacob cannot enter. The perimeter is protected."

"But he got through before. Isn't that what Crowley was saying?"

"Its protections have been changed," said Mrs. Harrogate smoothly. "No one—absolutely no one—wishes for a repeat of what happened when your Marlowe was a baby. But the only way the children will be safe, truly safe, will be to kill Jacob Marber."

As Mrs. Harrogate spoke, she took out the folded handkerchief from her handbag. Alice felt once again the sudden dizziness but she forced herself to look at the two keys as the older woman unwrapped them. Mrs. Harrogate put them on the pier table. "They affect you strongly," she said.

Alice swallowed. "They feel . . . wrong."

"Excellent. Yes. It is because you are a sensitive, Miss Quicke. That is the injury from Marber affecting you. I had hoped for this. These are called weir-bents."

Alice, who had a long knowledge of keys, studied the weir-bents. "They're old. I don't recognize their like. They're not for a safety box or a vault. What do they open, a room somewhere? Where do we find the thing?"

"What thing?"

"The weapon. To kill Jacob Marber."

Mrs. Harrogate's eyes glittered. "Ah," she said, smiling a patronizing smile. "You are mistaken. This *is* the weapon." The older woman lifted the leather cord carefully, studied the weir-bents where they dangled in front of her. "There were three once," she said. "Now there are two. Someday there will be only one, and when the last key is lost, there will be no way left to fight the drughr."

"What are they?"

"Evil things, Miss Quicke. Unnatural things. These are not keys but vessels, Miss Quicke. They hold inside them, like a fly in amber, something that does not belong in our world. You understand the or-sine at Cairndale is a doorway, a passage to another world. What is trapped in these weir-bents is *from* that world." Mrs. Harrogate closed her fist around the keys and winced. Her voice lowered. "And they are conscious, Miss Quicke. They have their desires and fears, just as we do. You must resist them."

In the weak gaslight of that strange room, Alice watched the woman in her black clothes rise and pad noiselessly to the locked door, like a ghost. It all felt eerie, and mysterious, and unreal. But she had long since given up on real. That same awful dread was rising in her again.

"Show me," she said in a flat voice. "Show me what they can do."

But Mrs. Harrogate held out the leather cord, the strange weir-bents swaying like some hypnotist's charm.

"No, Miss Quicke," she murmured. "It is *you* who must show *me*."

So it was for this, then, that she was needed.

Alice turned the weir-bents in her fingers, feeling a coldness go right through her, like a knife. The room swam. And then she was staggering, reaching for the edge of the bed, while a black nausea washed over her and ebbed and came again, and the incision in her side where Marber had stabbed her bloomed in pain. In her fist, the weir-bents were so cold they burned.

"You must give into it," whispered Mrs. Harrogate, from someplace near. "You must not try to control the pain. Accept it. Let *it* become *you.*"

And gradually, though the awful feeling did not leave her, Alice did so, and was no longer overwhelmed. She opened her fist, shaking.

They were not identical. One, she saw, was made of black iron, or something like it, its surface porous and pocked and rough to the touch. The other was carved out of a black wood that looked like iron, but seemed somehow much harder. They were heavy, with shanks almost as long as her hand. In place of the bow on the iron weir-bent was a Celtic knot, seamless and intricate as a snowflake; on the wooden weir-bent had been carved a crosspiece, and inside it a disk that turned in place, the wood oiled and burnished so that its veins glowed. At the end of its shank each had a strange twin collar, finely shaped, unlike anything Alice had seen, and a single uncut bit with no wards at all, as if neither had ever been shaped to a lock. And now, looking closer, Alice saw interwoven in both a fine silver metalwork, shaped almost like letters in a script she didn't know, though the patterning was different.

Different, too, were the edges of the bits, sharpened to a knifelike sharpness, and edged by that same curious silver inlay. Otherwise the darkness of the weir-bents seemed to increase as she looked at them, almost as if the shadows in the room were being sucked in, so that it felt as if she were looking through them, into the darkness of a vast night sky.

"Miss Quicke," murmured Mrs. Harrogate, and Alice came back to herself with a start.

"Yes," she said quickly. "What. What do I do?"

Mrs. Harrogate indicated the iron weir-bent. "This is the weapon. It may be used in the keyhole of any closed door, in any lock. It will fit. And when you open that door, the keywrasse will come out. Its purpose is your purpose; but it does not simply obey your commands. The keywrasse will try to master you. You must not let it."

"I don't understand."

"You will. One last thing. The weir-bent does not work in daylight. It can only be used at night. I do not understand how, or why; I only tell you what has been told to me. You must return the keywrasse through a door, and seal it again in the weir-bent, before the sun rises."

"Or what?"

"The weir-bents are what hold the keywrasse in bondage. The longer the wrasse remains out of the weir-bent, the weaker that control becomes. When the control weakens too much, the wrasse will be free to act as it wishes, here, in this world. It will obey only its own desires. It will follow only its own appetites. You will no longer command it."

"What will it do, then?"

"Let us not find out, hm?"

"But why is it I can do this and no one else?"

Mrs. Harrogate gave her an angry look, almost bitter. "Because you are the one who carries Jacob Marber's dust. But you are not the only one."

She meant Marber, Alice knew. Jacob Marber could control it also. She shivered and went to the door and started to slide the iron weir-bent in and then stopped. "Wait," she said. "The other key, what does it do?"

"Weir-bent, Miss Quicke. It is called a weir-bent. The iron unlocks; the wood locks away. It is for closing. When it is time for the keywrasse to leave you."

"Before sunrise."

"Or you shall have to wait until nightfall, again. Yes."

Alice nodded and turned back to the door. She slid the iron weir-bent in, and turned it.

Nothing happened. A long silence followed.

"You must *open* the *door*," said Mrs. Harrogate, sounding faintly exasperated.

Alice, nervous, turned the door pull. The hall outside was narrow and dimly lit by a single gas sconce near the top of the stairs and Alice cautiously stepped out and peered in both directions. It was empty. Then she felt something slide against her ankle and she leaped back but it was only a cat, a black cat with one white sock, belonging no doubt to the landlady, and Alice glared at it and started to go back in, feeling a strange mixture of both relief and disappointment.

But Mrs. Harrogate, however, was standing transfixed in the middle of the room, staring at the cat.

And all at once Alice understood. She looked down, looked back, feeling ridiculous. "No," she said, "The *cat?*"

It had padded noiselessly into the room and leaped now up onto the bedclothes and there it curled up, its long tail sweeping in around it. Calmly it started to lick at its white forepaw. And that was when Alice saw that it had two extra eyes, four in all, shining with light in the smooth black fur.

"What does it do?" she whispered.

Mrs. Harrogate calmly clasped her hands in the small of her back. She did not move. "It understands you, Miss Quicke. You may ask it yourself."

"But it *is* here to help us, isn't it?"

"We must hope so. Be polite; speak to it directly."

"Hello, uh, kitty," she said, feeling vaguely foolish. The keywrasse, if that was what it was, just continued its grooming. "My name is Alice Quicke. I, uh, I opened the door. . . . The thing is, we need your help.

There's a man, a—a drughr, that's killing our friends. We need your help in stopping it. Please."

The keywrasse raised its whiskers and yawned widely, baring its long fangs, and for a quick moment Alice thought it might acknowledge her, she thought it might respond in some strange uncatlike way, but instead it just leaped noiselessly down and padded to the window and jumped up onto the sill. And there it sat, head raised, ears dialed forward, peering out at the darkness.

"This is ridiculous," Alice muttered. She had the creeping feeling that a joke was being played on her.

But Mrs. Harrogate did not seem to think it ridiculous. She'd moved closer to the window and stood now warily just behind the creature, trying to see what it sensed. "What is it? Is something out there?"

The keywrasse did not move.

"Yeah, there's something out there," said Alice. "A mouse."

Mrs. Harrogate did not smile. "My name is Margaret Harrogate," she said politely. "We have summoned you because we wished to introduce ourselves. We will ask your assistance tomorrow night; we will go out into the city, looking for the one we seek. A servant of the drughr."

The keywrasse's ink-black tail flicked, curled, flicked again. Otherwise it gave no indication of having heard Mrs. Harrogate at all.

"Miss Quicke," she continued. "If you would insert the wooden weir-bent in the lock, our guest would be able to leave us."

And Alice did so; and the keywrasse, or cat, or whatever it was, as if understanding Mrs. Harrogate perfectly, sniffed and lazily dropped back to the floor.

But then, as if to prove leaving was its own idea, it paused a long moment in the open door before sauntering out into the hall. Quickly Alice shut the door, and withdrew the wooden key, and tied the leather cord around her throat.

The room was still; Mrs. Harrogate had turned back to the window, peering out at the fog.

"What is out there?" she murmured.

But Alice, for good measure, opened the door a crack; the hallway was deserted; the many-eyed cat had vanished.

They did not go out again for several nights. Harrogate collected broadsheets by the dozen, scanning the headlines, then feeding the pages to the fireplace. She was waiting for another killing in Limehouse. At last a lighterman was fished in pieces out of the river, and it was time. After nightfall, Alice drew on her heavy oilskin coat and tied her hair back and pulled her hat low over her eyes. Across the room, Mrs. Harrogate set a small wooden case on the bed and took out a bull's-eye lantern and two long cloth-wrapped bundles. Alice came over.

They were two knives, identical, their blades evilly sharp, with little iron rings along the grips for knuckles to go through and a slender pipelike spike underneath. Killer's blades.

"Jesus," whispered Alice, lifting one. "Where did you find these?"

"The Crimea," said Mrs. Harrogate matter-of-factly. "They were taken from a Russian scout. They will be of some use, perhaps, if we encounter Walter."

Mrs. Harrogate slid the blades into her belt. They sat well. Alice checked her Colt Peacemaker and pocketed a fistful of extra bullets like loose change. She saw Mrs. Harrogate take out a little silver-plated pistol from her handbag and check its workings and then tuck it back in and button it fast.

Alice grinned. "Look at us. You'd think we were going to war."

"We are," said Mrs. Harrogate, attaching her veil.

Last of all, Alice went to the door and inserted the weir-bent and let the keywrasse, purring, slide through. It went at once to the window, as if it knew exactly their intentions, and there it paced back and forth in a tight impatient patrol.

"Now," said Mrs. Harrogate, lifting the window so that the reeking air of the streets drifted in, "let us go to the deadhouses, Miss Quicke, let us set this keywrasse on the scent."

The streets were wet and dark with a heavy fog as they made their way slowly over to Limehouse. The keywrasse kept close. There were crowds in the streets all shouting and selling and sneaking despite the hour and there were sailors curled in doorways drunk and waifs in rags sweeping the crossings and once more the city, as it always did, made Alice vaguely angry and sad.

But in the air was fear, more than anything, fear of the monster stalking the docks and lanes of Limehouse. There'd been seven killings now and maybe more to come and no constable seemed to care. It felt strange to Alice to be drifting under the protection of a little black cat. But she was past belief and doubt. She'd seen too much. There were shadows in the world that were alive.

They found the body at the fourth mortuary they tried and stood in the weak orange gaslight amid the reek of formaldehyde and gaseous fumes while the night embalmer wiped his hands on his apron and tried to understand their business.

"What, the one they drug out the Thames?" He scowled.

The room was small, shabby, with a door ajar in the beyond leading back, Alice supposed, to the unclaimed bodies. "We'll have no gawkers here, and no newspaper folk neither. This is a respectable establishment, it is."

Alice held out her papers. "I'm a private detective, licensed by Scotland Yard. I've been asked to take a look at the body. Unofficial channels and such. It won't take long."

He'd been at work on a man with a long black mustache much like his own and there were tubes running into the cadaver's arms. He kept going back and forth, checking the progress. There was a streak of something dark on the side of his face and Alice didn't care to wonder what it was.

"It ain't suitable for a lady's sensibilities, now," he warned, looking at Mrs. Harrogate.

"She'll be all right," said Alice dryly. "She's the least sensible lady I ever met."

Mrs. Harrogate stiffened with a silent dignity.

After a moment the night embalmer shrugged. "Suit yourself. But only for a moment now. My work don't finish itself."

He led them downstairs into a long cellar with rows of little doors along one wall and lit a lantern and proceeded past to a second, smaller room. Here on a steel table Alice saw what appeared to be a washbasin. Something was swimming in a stew inside it.

"Go on then, have your look," he said.

And he hung the lantern on an iron ring from a rafter.

It wasn't a body. Whatever it was, it wasn't that. The smell was of ammonia and alcohol and under these a sweet, sickly, wrenching scent, like rotting vegetation. The bits were half-congealed in a mess but Alice could make out an elbow and forearm and crooked hand, also what appeared to be a foot with the bone sticking out, also a face with the eyes cut out.

"Them's chew marks along the edges," said the embalmer. He drew a slow, steady finger to show. "Here and here. What done this weren't human."

Just then the keywrasse, as if from nowhere, leaped noiselessly up onto the table and put its paws on the edge of the basin.

"Mother of God, what's he doin in here? Get out, you!" And the man picked up a rag and snapped it at the keywrasse.

But the cat was already gone, in a flicker of darkness, out the door and through the long cellar and back up the stairs and gone. Alice looked at Mrs. Harrogate; the older woman nodded.

It was done.

Back outside, in the reek of Limehouse, the keywrasse was impatient. It led them swiftly through a warren of slick shadowy lanes, over courts and under arches, until it came to a sunken pier where several figures sat in the darkness, fishing lines slack. Alice held the bull's-eye lantern high, to see where they were. The keywrasse was padding back and forth, its tail high, ears alert.

"This will be where they fished the body out," murmured Mrs. Harrogate. "It's taking the scent now."

"Or maybe where the bastard went in," said Alice.

And then the keywrasse was off, again, away from the river, winding back through the gloom and fog and racing between the legs of the crowds, untroubled by the filth and the horses and the roar of the high street. Alice found it hard going, keeping up. The fog descended, a sharp bitter taste to it, as if the vast lime kilns were poisoning the air.

The yellow fog thickened; and then, like a rolling curtain, it parted for only a moment and Alice caught a glimpse of a figure cutting past a bollard and sliding like a shadow around a building, a figure half-hunched, wearing a long black coat and a bowler hat. But even at that distance and in the dark she could see the unnaturally white skin of its neck, the long sharp fingers hanging from the cuffs, and she knew it was this that they were seeking.

The keywrasse had already poured silently across and into the mouth of the alley. It was a thief's lane, so named for the hidden exits and sudden turnings, crooked and narrow and littered with the sprawled legs of the indigent poor. Alice shuttered the lantern and picked her way cautiously over the bodies. Half were children, half were barefoot. The keywrasse slid into the fog, reappeared, vanished.

She could see the greasy panes of upper windows dully reflecting the mist. All were barred. Her nerves were steady.

The lane forked and she went left after the keywrasse and she heard Margaret softly follow. There were puddles of slime underfoot. A sound of dripping water.

She nearly tripped over the keywrasse. She could smell the river, nearby. The lane had come to a dead end. Mrs. Harrogate appeared like a ghost, eyes veiled.

But now ahead Alice could see it, the pale figure from High Street, the litch. It was standing raggedly with its lean arms at its sides and its hat doffed and hairless head bowed, almost as if it were listening for something. For a moment she feared they'd been sighted. But then it turned, peering around as if to be certain it was unobserved, and the fog thinned just at that moment, and Alice saw its features, and she froze. The auburn whiskers were gone, the thinning hair was gone, but still she knew that face.

It was Frank Coulton.

Beside her Mrs. Harrogate caught her breath. "Oh God," she whispered.

And then the creature that had once been Frank Coulton put back on the bowler hat and clambered spiderlike up the wall and leaped lightly over and down the other side and was gone.

Alice's face was white with shock. "It was *him*," she said. "It was *Coulton*. I thought he died—" She turned angrily on Mrs. Harrogate. "You said he died!"

But the older woman, shaken, could say nothing.

Just then the keywrasse poured like smoke from between her ankles, and Alice watched it scamper up the high wall, impossibly fast, and pause at the top with its spine peaked and its tail high. It turned all of its eyes down toward them, as if to check that they would follow.

Alice turned in place, looking for a way up. There was a rickety ladder leaning against a wagon and she kicked it down and dragged it across and leaned it up.

A litch.

The ladder didn't quite reach.

Coulton's a litch.

She spat. She rubbed her knuckles and glared to keep from thinking about it; and then, with her oilskin coat crackling out behind her, the fog like a living thing all around, she set the grip of the lantern in her teeth and started to climb.

26

HOUSE OF DOORS

A figure in a black cloak was waiting for them on the dock when they rowed back from the island. The glow of his lantern was like coins of light on the dark water. No one spoke; only the soft splashing of the oar blades, the creak of the locks cut the stillness. It was Dr. Berghast's manservant, stone-faced and grim; and he lifted the lantern in his fist and shone it from face to face.

At Charlie he stopped; at Marlowe he stopped.

"You two," he said in a voice as deep as a bass drum. "Dr. Berghast will see you. Now."

He said no rebuke about their being out, about their clear trespass. And yet his displeasure was plain. Charlie felt Ribs's lips near his ear.

"Shit," she whispered.

Komako was looking ashamed. He knew she'd be blaming everyone for their going but it was her idea too, she was willing too. He remembered what she'd said to him, when they were alone: *I know what it looks like here. . . . But nowhere's safe, not really.* Suddenly he wondered if it wasn't shame in her face, but something else. Fear.

He reached out to steady Marlowe. But Ribs wasn't finished. "Don't you believe all what he tells you," she whispered. "Old Berghast, I mean. Slick as oil in peat, he is."

"Ribs, I don't even know what that means," Charlie muttered out of the side of his mouth.

"Come," the manservant barked.

He felt her cool fingers brush his wrist. "Just you be careful, Charlie Ovid."

He clambered out of the boat, leaving it rocking at the gunwales. Marlowe reached for his hand, and together they followed the manservant into darkness.

Komako watched them disappear off into the night. Then the three of them made their slow way back, trailed by Oskar's giant, Lymenion. No one spoke. In the quiet dark, Komako was troubled. She'd seen something—no, she'd been *shown* something—while in the grip of the glyphic.

She was finding it difficult to make sense of it. They trudged grimly back up into the dimly lit halls of Cairndale and slipped into their favorite hiding spot, at the end of a deserted corridor, under a big window that looked out across at the east wing. They could see a light on in Berghast's study.

"I saw something," she said at last. She looked up, looked at Oskar and Lymenion and at Ribs, who had materialized in the gloom. "On the island. The glyphic showed me something. I tried to ask about the disappeared kids and the carriage, but I don't think it made any impression. But he's dying. The glyphic's dying, and he showed me a kind of, I don't know—memory, maybe. Of Dr. Berghast, feeding him some kind of . . . medicine. I think it's what he's making in his laboratory. I think he's keeping the glyphic alive. And I saw the orsine collapsing in on itself. Cairndale was in flames." She frowned, shaking her head. "It was awful. I don't know if it was the future, or if it happened a long time ago, or if it was just what the glyphic was afraid might happen." She ran her hands over her braid, confused. "If the glyphic dies," she said slowly, "then the orsine will open. Anything will be able to get through."

Oskar was nodding at her, nodding as if he understood. "The—the dead will come through."

"You saw it too," she said.

"No," he whispered. "I mean, I saw some of that. I saw he was dying. . . ." Oskar's eyes grew wet. "I—I don't know how, I just sort of saw it, you know? And—and I saw how afraid he was. That's what I mostly saw, Ko. The Spider's fear. But there was something else, too. A shop front. It had ALBANY CHANDLERS written on it. And—and—I knew it, Ko. I knew where it was. It was the Grassmarket, in Edinburgh. Mr. Coulton and I stayed near there when he first brought me over, before we came on to Cairndale."

"Albany Chandlers. It's in Edinburgh?"

Oskar nodded. "Do you think . . . do you think the missing talents are there?"

"Maybe."

"Why else would the glyphic show that? I mean, if not—?"

Komako wet her lips. She did a mental checklist of what was in play, ticking each off on her fingers. "We've got the glyphic dying. Dr. Berghast is trying to keep him alive, but it can't be forever. We've got the dark carriage and the disappeared kids. It's coming from some chandler's in Edinburgh, looks like. And we've got the files on the disappeared being taken from Dr. Berghast's office. Someone here at Cairndale has to be working with the carriage."

"You reckon it's all connected?" murmured Ribs. "You reckon Berghast knows about them missing kids? He had their names in that book—"

"No," said Komako firmly.

Oskar's watery eyes brightened. "Maybe it's—it's—it's not as sinister as it looks," he said. "Maybe Dr. Berghast does know about it, but the kids aren't being hurt. Maybe it's for their own protection."

Ribs snorted. "Protection?"

"Maybe they're in some special kind of—of—of danger. From Jacob."

"More than Marlowe?"

Oskar blushed, fell quiet.

"Rruh," growled the flesh giant.

Komako tugged at her braid, troubled. "Ribs? What'd the Spider show you?"

But Ribs had a strange expression on her face, half-anger, half-disgust. "Hm?" she said, her freckled nose upturned.

"Your vision. What did you see?"

"Oh, lots. Lots an lots." Ribs nodded. "Plen-ty."

"And? Would you care to enlighten us?"

Ribs picked at a scab on her elbow, her brow furrowed. "Oh, well . . . there were that chandler's. Yep. In Edinburgh. An that bit about Berghast doctoring to the Spider, I seen that too. Whew. There were just, uh, lots of things, yep."

No one spoke.

Then Komako said quietly, "You didn't see anything, did you?"

Ribs scowled. Her voice fairly cracked in disbelief. "Why am I the one what never gets shown nothing? He bloody well picks *you* and—and *Oskar*, but he don't show *me* nothing? What's a matter with *me*?"

"Maybe he couldn't see you," Oskar said helpfully. "Because you were invisible?"

She gave him a poisonous look. "It were a *rhetorical* question!"

"Rrh," mumbled Lymenion.

Ribs glared at the flesh giant. "What. The Spider talk to you too?"

Komako smiled, despite herself. "It doesn't matter," she said. "We don't have much time. We need to find out what this chandler's is."

"What're you saying?"

"We need to go to Edinburgh."

Oskar blinked nervously. "Edinburgh! But we—we—we can't get through the wards. . . . Not without permission."

"Actually . . ." Ribs rubbed at her red hair, reluctant. "Me and Ko found a opening, a while back. I reckon it's still there. It's a gap in the wards, Oskar. Just near right big enough for all of us to crawl through. Even old Lymenion."

Oskar looked hurt. "You never told me."

Gently, Komako put her gloved hands on the boy's shoulders. "We need to find the place that carriage is coming from, Oskar. Albany Chandlers. Before whoever it is comes looking for *us*. You saw the place in your vision. You can take us there."

Oskar swallowed. "But we'll get in trouble. If Miss Davenshaw—"

"There's a reason you were shown that vision," Komako continued. "The Spider *wants* us to go. He *wants* us to see. There's got to be a link to what's happening to him, and the kids. . . . It's all connected, Oskar."

Oskar shivered.

"Okay," he said, trying to sound brave.

Only Ribs seemed not to be listening. She'd gone back to muttering, scowling to herself. "Not like I even care, *stupid* Spider an his *stupid* visions. . . ."

Scratching miserably at the windowsill with her nail as she whispered it.

After leaving the others, Charlie and Marlowe were led back across the grass to the manor, and along a corridor and through a door and up a stairwell, and then along a second corridor, this one punctuated by doors every twenty feet, until they reached Dr. Berghast's study.

"Touch nothing," said the manservant. "Dr. Berghast will be with you shortly."

Charlie, for his part, saw little worth the touching. It was the same room he'd been in just a few days earlier, but cozier somehow, less frightening. A great lump of coal was burning in the fireplace; the sconces along the walls were lit, casting the room in a golden hue; leather armchairs were arranged in front of the fire. The air was warm, sleepy, smelling faintly of cigar smoke. In one corner stood the wooden file cabinet, locked. In the other stood a birdcage, the silhouette of a bird unmoving on its perch. The strange ink painting of crosshatched lines and circles hung in the gloom. Marlowe stepped gingerly over the Persian carpet and stood in front of it, staring. In the very center of the room loomed Dr. Berghast's desk: sleek, dark, empty but for a tray with a decanter of wine on it, and a solitary glass still half-full. Charlie saw no sign of the journal.

It might have been a cozy room, that is, if not for its particular strangeness: the doors. Nine in all, all of them shut, all of them carved out of the same ancient heavy-looking oak, covered in strange scrolling marks, as if shipworms had eaten their way through. So many doors gave the study the feeling of a deserted railroad station, or of a post office after hours—a place that should have been full of bustle, interruptions, hasty exits. Charlie peered around, uneasy. He hadn't noticed them all, that night he'd snuck in. Then he saw the birdcage more clearly and stepped closer to see. The things inside were not birds—living concoctions of bones and brass fittings, they turned their skulled heads side to side, as if regarding him from their eyeless sockets. He shuddered.

Marlowe though, silent, sat on the big sofa and just swung his little legs and picked at his hands and waited. Charlie knew the kid would be anxious, that it was his adopted father they were to meet; what was in the boy's heart he couldn't imagine; and he wanted to say something, to ask if he was okay, offer some reassurance, but then all at once it was too late, for the door they'd entered by opened briskly and in walked Henry Berghast.

Charlie froze. Marlowe raised his face, a half-hopeful shine in his eye.

But the man walked right past him, right past both of them, giving them scarcely a glance. At his desk he pulled out a notebook, he unscrewed the lid of a fountain pen. For several minutes he sat, writing quietly. And yet all the while Charlie sensed how the man was aware of them, was observing them, weighing their silence coolly and finding them wanting. At last he looked up, frowning.

"Well," he said.

And that was all.

Charlie knew him, of course, had seen him lurking in the dark windows while they trudged to the outbuildings, had glimpsed him at the ends of corridors, moving quickly, had seen him deep in conversation with the old talents in the courtyard some mornings. But never close up; never so near that he could feel the man's electricity, the intensity coming off him, like a low hum. Berghast was tall, taller than Charlie even, and broad-shouldered, with big hands. He wore an expensive black frock coat, an immaculate white collar, as if he had just come from dinner. His beard was white, his eyes the gray of a river in winter, bright and reflective and piercing, his hair thick and long at his collar. There was an aristocratic air about him; he looked like a man who was used to remaking the world in his image. Charlie immediately felt afraid.

Dr. Berghast interlaced his hands on his desk. He was as still as an adder. "It is late, boys," he said quietly. "You will be hungry."

Both Charlie and Marlowe shook their heads. Across the room the bonebirds clicked and rattled.

Slowly, fiercely, Dr. Berghast's eyes slid to Charlie. "You are the new haelan," he said. It was not a question. "I am Dr. Berghast. Tell me, how do you like Cairndale?"

Charlie swallowed. "I like it, sir."

"And yet you seem incapable of obeying its rules. You trespass after curfew, you come to my rooms in a state of undress. Your nightshirt is filthy."

Charlie looked at himself, the heat rising to his face. It was true: there was mud and grime from the island in streaks all over.

"You have been to see Mr. Thorpe," Dr. Berghast continued. "It is not permitted."

Charlie blinked. "Thorpe—?"

"Our glyphic. He is . . . not well. I trust you knew it was forbidden and that is why you snuck across, after midnight. Did you find the answers you sought?"

"I . . . I don't know, sir," he mumbled. "We—"

"It was my idea," said Marlowe boldly. "I wanted to know if Alice was okay."

Dr. Berghast turned his intense gray eyes on the little boy. "And is she?"

Marlowe hesitated. All at once it was like all his boldness was gone, and he chewed at his lip, coloring. "I don't know."

"But that is not all you asked about, is it? That is not the only reason you disturbed the rest of a dying man. Do you know who I am, child?"

Marlowe nodded. He was staring at the floor.

"Look at me. Who am I?"

"You're my adopted father," whispered Marlowe.

"Yes." He smoothed his beard, weighing them both in his gaze.

"And what is it you do, when you are not sneaking around the institute? Does Miss Davenshaw instruct you in the use of your talents?"

"Yes, sir."

"Did she explain to you what it is the glyphic does?"

"Yes."

"Tell me."

Marlowe looked quickly up, a question in his eyes. "Miss Davenshaw says he keeps the orsine closed. But she's wrong, isn't she? He opens it sometimes too. You make him do that. But he's got to be careful or else any sort of a thing could come out."

"How do you know that?"

"The Spider. He . . . told me."

"I see. And what sort of a thing would come out?"

Marlowe furrowed his brow. "Is it Jacob Marber?"

Dr. Berghast folded his big arms and leaned back on the desk and regarded the boys. "There are worse things in that world than Jacob Marber," he said softly.

The boy lifted his eyes then, defiant. "But you sent them in there anyway, didn't you? You sent the old talents in, even though it was dangerous. All those years ago."

Charlie felt a sudden misgiving. He looked at Marlowe, wondering just how much the glyphic had told him about this place, what had happened here.

Berghast was obviously wondering the same thing. "Mr. Thorpe has been rather forthcoming, it seems. Despite his condition."

It had never occurred to Charlie that anyone could be sent *through* the orsine. But then Charlie thought of something. "That's what you want us for too," he said. "To go in there."

Dr. Berghast's eyes glittered in a way that made Charlie suddenly afraid. "Yes," he said.

"Because it is important," said Marlowe.

"Because it is important," echoed Berghast.

Charlie glowered. "Important for *who?*"

But if Berghast minded Charlie's tone, he gave no indication. His face was as cold and flat and emotionless as ever. "In the other world, in the land of the dead . . . nothing is as it is here. There, matter is dust and spirit is substance. It is a world as different from ours as the inside of your body is, from what lies outside it. Its dangers are various and changing. It is easy to become lost. There was a time when I sent talents through. The old ones, you call them." Dr. Berghast worked his hands in front of him, massaging the scarred knuckles as if they pained him. He looked up. "But then something terrible came out of the orsine and put a stop to it all. A creature. It is this that gives Jacob Marber his strength, and his purpose. It is this which we are trying to stop. The drughr."

Charlie shivered.

"Miss Davenshaw will have told you about the orsine. But not its essence. Where do we come from? What are we, really? We are connected to the orsine in ways you cannot imagine. The orsine was built at the behest of a man named Alastair Cairndale. He was the first of our kind, the First Talent. You will have seen his portrait in the great hall. After his talent manifested, others emerged, other talents who found their way to him. All of this was many centuries ago. But wherever there is order, chaos will press in. In time there was disagreement, a struggle between talents for how to be in the world. Whether we ought to reveal ourselves fully. Whether we ought to play a greater role in the fates of nations. The drughr emerged out of that chaos, seeking to destroy us."

Charlie watched Marlowe. The little boy was listening intently.

"Lord Cairndale and his . . . associates, constructed the orsine and banished the drughr through it. He was powerful, far more powerful than we are today. His talent could not merely *manipulate*, as ours do, but even *create*. In the struggle he was dragged into the orsine, along-side the monster. How he perished, under what circumstances, was never known. But somehow he managed to contain the drughr; it was trapped inside the orsine.

"Yet now it is back," he continued calmly. "And it falls to me to stand against it."

Charlie could sense the older man's seductive sadness, the intensity of it, and he didn't like it. "You mean it falls to *us*," he said, reproach in his voice.

"I am no Alastair Cairndale," Berghast replied, just as if Charlie hadn't said anything. "And yet I must become him. All of us must carry what we are, Charles. Whether we wish to or not."

Charlie glanced over at Marlowe, whose face was expressionless. "I'm getting tired of being told that in fifty different ways. It's always someone else saying what's got to be carried and who it's got to be carried for."

A subtle flare of the nostrils betrayed Berghast's impatience. "Mr. Thorpe is dying," he said. "Cairndale's glyphic is dying, Mr. Ovid. Your outrage will change nothing. The orsine will rip itself open; Cairndale will be defenseless. The dead will pour through the breach into this world, and there is no telling what will become of us then."

Charlie swallowed, abashed.

"When that happens, the orsine will have to be sealed," Berghast continued, in a soft angry whisper. He might have been alone. "Sealed forever. And then our only way of destroying the drughr will be lost. If I am to enter the orsine, if I am to confront the drughr, I must do it soon. Its powers are different there; I can stop it there."

"I don't understand, Dr. Berghast," murmured Marlowe.

The man smiled his cold smile. "I have been preparing for this for longer than you can imagine, child. I do not need your understanding. Only your trust."

"You mean our obedience," muttered Charlie.

Berghast unlocked the bottom drawer of his desk and took out a long metal box. He rested his hand on the lid. "There was a time when I would send the talents through, so they could map the world beyond the orsine. So we would be prepared, you see, if the drughr returned. I'd found an object, an artifact of immense power. I'd been searching for it for years, across oceans of sand, mountains of ice. At last I tracked it down in a community of talents east of the Black Sea." As he spoke, he opened the box and lifted out a strange glove, made of wood and iron and cloth. It looked heavy and clicked as he picked it up. "Once there were three artifacts; now there is only one. This is a replica."

He passed it across and Charlie took it and turned it in his fingers. Plates of iron and wood like an armored gauntlet. Sewn inside the wrist of the glove was a band of sharp studs, like little teeth. "The real artifact allows the talent who wears it to pass through the orsine, intact, and to survive in the beyond. It allows them to return alive. But not only talents. The artifact's power is such that it protects *anything* that wishes to cross between the worlds. From either side."

Charlie blinked. "You mean, the—"

"The drughr, yes. It would be protected *here*. In this world."

Charlie was running his finger over the soft wood plates. He saw there were delicate carvings, line work, like the trails left by beetles in bark. Each plate was different. Stamped into the iron palm was the same crest as his mother's ring, the same design as what hung over the gates of Cairndale. Twinned hammers against a rising sun. The wood was soft, warm. The iron was supple. Even this replica felt immensely old. Charlie offered it to Marlowe, who handed it back to Dr. Berghast.

The older man's face darkened as he studied the copy. "A beautiful thing, isn't it? But the real glove was lost, years ago. It was lost *inside* the orsine."

"You want us to find it for you," said Marlowe.

He nodded cautiously. "We must find it before the glyphic dies. While the orsine can still be controlled."

Charlie scowled. "Why us?"

"Because you are both . . . unusual. You, Charles, are a haelan. Your body, your very talent, sustains itself, regenerates itself. You can stay in that world much, much longer than any other talent. And you, child," he said, fixing his eerie gaze on Marlowe again, "you are another thing entirely."

Marlowe looked back at him, his eyes big.

"You are quite remarkable, child. You contain a spark from the orsine. You are a *piece* of it. You were born in that other world, your mother gave birth to you there, before she was murdered by Jacob Marber. You can survive there as long as you wish. The orsine cannot harm you."

All at once it was like all the air was sucked out of the room.

Dr. Berghast had said it so casually, with such easy disregard. It was shocking. Charlie gripped Marlowe's shoulder firmly.

The little boy was staring at Dr. Berghast. His mouth was open.

"My mother was—?"

"Murdered. Yes. You did not know?" Dr. Berghast grimaced coolly, and then he said, with a look of satisfaction playing at the corners of his eyes: "She was a kind woman, a remarkable woman. She would have loved you more than her own life, child. Marber took her from you, from all of us. And then he tried to take you. If you wish to avenge her, if you wish to make Marber suffer . . . then this is the way. Bring me that glove, and I will destroy his master."

After the boys had left, Henry Berghast carefully put the replica glove away and opened a second drawer in his desk and took out a ring of heavy iron keys. He went to one of the doors in his study and unlocked it and lit a lantern from a sconce on the wall and began to descend. His footsteps scraped on the stone stairs. The steps wound down into the earth and stopped at a thick oak door.

It was a bolt-hole, a secret room built centuries ago, to keep Catholic priests safe in a time when they were being persecuted by the king. Berghast had long since converted it to his own purposes. Only he and his manservant, Bailey, knew of it. It was damp, this deep under the ground, and cold, the walls carved out of the very rock itself.

He unlocked the door, shone the lantern into the dark. There came a soft clink of chains; a clicking noise, almost like the wings of an insect. A figure was suspended by its arms, on the far wall, its head drooping down onto its chest. The smell was terrible.

"Mr. Laster," said Berghast softly. "May I call you Walter again?"

The litch raised its face, blinked its liquid eyes. There was a black intelligence in them, something quick and cruel and no longer human. It watched him.

Berghast hung the lantern from a hook in the ceiling and looped his thumbs into his waistcoat and regarded the creature. Then he went to a small table in the corner and picked up a dish. It held a black gumlike substance: opium.

Walter gave a quiet whimper, watching.

But Berghast did not want him to suffer. No, such suffering—and Berghast's eyes, his every gesture radiated his sorrow—was the last thing he wanted for poor Walter. No, what Henry Berghast wanted most of all was for Walter to end his own suffering. Or, rather, to let Berghast end it for him. All Walter had to do was give himself over to Berghast's questions, all he had to do was tell him what he wanted to know, and his suffering would end. It would be so easy, surely—

All this Walter's quick loathsome gaze took in; Berghast saw it flicker and vanish, like a lizard under a rock.

"So Jacob *wanted* you to be taken by Mrs. Harrogate," he said, by way of beginning the night's session.

"No."

"But that is what you told me last time. Is it not?"

Walter licked his lips. He said, shakily, "Jacob knew she would . . . bring us. To you."

"It wasn't because of the child, then? He didn't send you to kill the boy?"

Walter was whispering something under his breath, something Berghast didn't catch.

"Walter?"

"Walter Walter little Walter . . . ," the creature echoed in a whisper.

Berghast studied it in impatience. "So he did not send you to kill Marlowe, Walter?"

Walter shook his pale hairless head. Berghast saw the thin red lines of blood where the iron cuffs had rubbed his wrists raw. "Jacob . . . knows. He knows where we are. . . . That's why we're here, yes. He wants this."

"Oh, Walter," Berghast murmured sadly. "You believe he wanted *this* for you?" His gaze took in the grim cell, the chains, the opium unsmoked in its little dish, with a profound disappointment. "I think not. No. You are here because Jacob has abandoned you. No other reason. Jacob has left you to perish because you are no longer of any use to him. But you are of use to me. It is I who had you rescued, I who had you brought here. It pains me to say it, of course, but your Jacob does not love you. Not anymore. You have failed him, and he despises you for it."

Walter coughed, the needlelike teeth flashing in the lantern light. His whole body shuddered with the effort. "But he is coming . . . he is coming here. . . ."

"He cannot. You know that he cannot."

"The voices . . . ," Walter whispered. "They talk to us, they tell us . . ."

Berghast took a step closer. He could see the clawlike fingers, the deep gashes in the litch's hairless torso, the terrible wet red lips. And the teeth. This was a creature that would rip him to pieces the first chance it got. "What do the voices tell you, Walter?"

"He knows they are coming for him. The women. Jacob knows."

"Who do you mean?"

"Mrs. Harrogate. And the other."

Berghast frowned. This was unexpected. Always, just as he was prepared to consider everything out of the litch's mouth madness and delusion, some strange quick detail of truth would emerge and leave him marveling.

He decided to change his approach. "It must be so distressing for you," he said in sympathy. "Jacob doesn't know how much he needs you. If only you could give him something, something he desires, something that would show him. Then he would come for you, then he would not abandon you. What would you give him, Walter, if you could? What is it Jacob most wants?"

Walter raised his head. His eyes were calm and intelligent and reflected the lantern's glow. "Cairndale," he whispered. "We'd give him Cairndale, yes. And then we'd give him you."

Charlie didn't say a word the entire walk back through the dark manor. There was too much. All the strange account of the orsine's history and the drughr and the terrible news of Marlowe's mother and what had happened to her, and the island before that, and the Spider, and that heavy toothed glove of Berghast's. He and the kid cut across the courtyard in the cool air and then back inside, up the big stairs under the stained glass windows, past Mr. Smythe's door. And still they never said a word. They could hear Mr. Smythe's snoring through the wall. Charlie cast quick worried glances over at Marlowe but the boy was lost in his thoughts, troubled, or sad, or just disappointed. Charlie didn't blame him. Berghast *was* a disappointment, as an adopted father, as a mentor. He remembered what Ribs had warned him, as he got off the rowboat, but he didn't say it to Marlowe. He didn't need to. They didn't speak as they undressed, they didn't speak as they washed down their necks and faces, they didn't speak as they climbed into bed and folded their arms up under their heads and stared, identical, up at the dark ceiling. The curtains were stirring, as if something were in them.

"Mar?" Charlie said at last, in a low whisper. "You okay?"

It was a stupid question, and he regretted asking it as soon as he said it. He turned in his sheets, he looked across. He still had the silver ring on the cord at his neck, the ring his mother had forced into his hand as she lay dying, and he rubbed at it now, brooding. "Your father, he—"

"He's not my father, Charlie."

Charlie nodded in the darkness.

"I know what you're going to say," Marlowe added. "I don't trust him either."

"Okay."

"It doesn't mean what he said isn't true."

"No, it doesn't."

"And it doesn't mean we shouldn't do what he wants us to do."

Charlie swallowed. "Yeah. But it doesn't mean we should, either."

He saw the little boy's pale face in the darkness. His eyes were open. He couldn't imagine what the boy must be feeling. All his eight unlucky years he'd been passed from adult to adult, like a bad debt, and it was that man, that unkind, clinical, cold man who'd started it all. Charlie felt a tight fury rising in him, at the unfairness of it all.

"Hey," he whispered. "If you want to go into that orsine of his, I'm with you, Mar. I'm not saying otherwise. All right? But we don't have to do this. There's always other options."

"Like what?"

"I don't know. We could leave. Just go. You and me."

The kid looked miserable. "I think Mr. Thorpe wants me to go through," he said quietly. "I think he ... *needs* me to. He's dying, Charlie. What Dr. Berghast said is true. I *saw* it."

Charlie blinked. "What'd the Spider say to you, anyhow?"

Marlowe turned his face, folded himself up onto one elbow. He seemed to be thinking about it. "It wasn't like words," he murmured. "It was more like ... pictures, moving. In a fog. I ... I think it was what's *going* to happen, Charlie. Or what *might* happen. I don't know."

"What'd you *see*?"

The little boy's voice was just a whisper. "Nothing about what we went for. The disappeared kids, I mean. I tried to ask about it, but ..." He paused. "I saw Alice, Charlie. She was dead. Jacob Marber'd killed her. I saw you, too, but you had that symbol, the one from your ring, and it was glowing in your hand. In your palm. Like the glove we saw but you weren't wearing the glove, and like it was on fire. And I saw Mr. Coulton, but he was like that other man, Walter, from Mrs. Harrogate's. The one who attacked you. All white and his hair all gone and his teeth sharp—"

Charlie swallowed. A flash in his mind of scrabbling claws, of that creature looming out of the darkness. He shook his head. "Mr. Coulton's dead, Mar," he said.

But the little boy was looking at him with haunted eyes in the gloom. "That's what I'm saying. I don't know that he is, Charlie."

Sometimes Charlie just didn't know what to make of the kid, he didn't. Like on the roof of the train. Or in the glyphic's lair. This was one of those times. He nodded as if he understood but his heart was full mostly of pity and what he was thinking was that the kid had been through a lot of crazy and there was no knowing what was true, not really, no matter what he'd seen.

He wet his lips. "So what do you want to do? What is it you want?"

The boy breathed quietly in the dark.

"Mar?"

"I want Brynt back," he said, his lip quivering. "I want Alice back. I want everything the way it used to be."

Charlie, who wouldn't have gone back to his old life for anything, didn't know what to say to that.

He closed his eyes.

But if he'd got up instead and gone to the window, he'd have seen in the moonlight three figures—silhouettes that were almost familiar—running silently across the grass in long coats and ill-fitting hats, a fourth figure lumpen and strange shambling just behind, all of them racing over the clay fields to the wall and its wards and the road south to Edinburgh.

27

HUNTING MARBER

Alice Quicke landed squelching in something soft. Mud. Just mud. They were in a dark warehousing yard beside the river. The keywrasse was crouched on a coil of rope, listening to the night.

Coulton was gone.

She lifted the lantern cautiously, shining a thin beam at the wall, the crates, the ropes and cranes in the fog. She could see the impress of Coulton's feet in the muck, the smeared grime where he'd clambered up onto the planking and padded into the warehouse.

In the distance they could hear the shouts of laborers on the docks. The fog hung thick and unmoving and Alice had little fear of being seen but still she crept warily up to the open door of the building, her oilskin coat shushing at her knees. She held the bull's-eye lantern in one hand, her heavy Colt Peacemaker in the other. The keywrasse purred against her ankle.

"Go on," hissed Mrs. Harrogate. "Hurry. We'll lose him."

Alice glared back at the older woman. But when she kicked the door open with her boot there was only darkness, the thick scent of oiled metal and lumber and wet ropes.

The air inside the building felt cold, and vast, as if it went on for miles. The light of the lantern shone barely ten paces. Coulton could be lurking anywhere.

"You go on," muttered Alice.

But she didn't really mean it; and when the keywrasse poured forward into the stillness Alice followed quickly, all of her senses alert, expecting a blur of white to leap at her at any moment, remembering in flashes the horror of that other litch. Whether Walter had died on the train or waited with Coulton up ahead, she didn't know.

The keywrasse padded swiftly along the rows of crates and barrels, the floor slick in places where brine had spilled, the boards creaking underfoot. Alice's side began to ache. She made no noise as she went.

If Coulton had sensed their presence, he'd be lying in wait somewhere. But if not, chances were good he'd lead them directly to Jacob Marber.

At last the keywrasse stood with its back arched in front of a closed door. It had the number twenty-one in white paint. Inside was a storage room, the lantern illuminating open wooden boxes of nails and screws and fasteners. The keywrasse went at once to a trapdoor in the corner.

"Fuck that," whispered Alice. "We go down there?"

The keywrasse flicked its tail.

Mrs. Harrogate slipped past in her black skirts and lifted the iron ring and pulled. A gust of foul air came out. "He does not know we are hunting him," she said softly. "They are the ones who should be afraid, Miss Quicke. Hand me that lantern."

There was a steel in her voice that hadn't been there before. It was the sight of Coulton, Alice knew, that had done it.

Harrogate withdrew both her long black knives and slipped her knuckles through their rings. She should have looked ridiculous, a middle-aged woman in petticoats with a killer's weapons. Instead, thought Alice, she looked fierce, deadly. She dangled her feet over the edge, then slid down into the blackness.

"Yeah," Alice muttered. "Perfect."

And with a quick glance around at the dark storeroom, she swung herself down, and in.

She landed in an old sewer tunnel, a branch line, the stones slick underfoot. Mrs. Harrogate hissed for silence and Alice stayed crouching, her blood loud in her ears, straining for something, anything.

The older woman opened the shutter of the bull's-eye lantern a crack. Her knives were held out low and flat at her sides.

"He is ahead," she whispered. "Coulton, I mean. The keywrasse is already following. Come."

And then the shutter snicked shut, and she heard the hiss of the older woman's skirts, and all again was darkness.

Or almost darkness; gradually Alice's eyes adjusted, and she could just make out the curve of the tunnel, the dark watery slime running down its middle. Other darker tunnels opened out on either side and the keywrasse would wait for them at each turning and then vanish again ahead. Alice thought of the stories she'd heard, of rats devouring people in the sewers, and shuddered. They crept on, wary, through the reeking labyrinth. Gradually a faint glow could be discerned, around a curve up ahead.

They came to an ancient chamber, part of a Roman bathhouse once, by the look of it, pillared and tiled and shrouded in shadow. A deep feeling of unease, of wrongness, was in that place. It might have been the haunt of some gang of waifs or urchins, once; the floor was cluttered with broken furniture, odd crates and boxes and junk dragged in from the back lanes of Limehouse. But good new candles burned now in brackets on the walls, their light dancing across the grotesque frescoes of bulls and half-naked boys and women in folded robes.

And at the center of the chamber, in the stone hollow where the baths had once pooled, was a man. He lay covered in blankets, on a faded green daybed, next to a small table and a collection of jars and flasks and suchlike. He was ill; slowly, with effort, he turned his head at their approach.

It was Jacob Marber.

At once Alice felt afraid. The wound in her side flared with pain.

"Margaret Harrogate," he said softly. His voice was like dark honey and when he spoke a whispering seemed to echo up from the cavernous darkness all around. He looked at Alice, baring his strong teeth, and there was a strangeness in it.

"Ah. Is that Alice?" he said, as if they knew each other.

She shivered, putting a hand involuntarily to her side. She was not used to being afraid, and it angered her; and because of her fear, she made herself observe him carefully.

The shadows liked his eyes. That was the first thing she saw. And he was confident, too much so, pleased by his own cleverness. That was the second thing. He wore a stained black suit, his cravat rumpled, his shirt collar loose, like a gentleman back from a night in the gutters. A silk hat stood upended on the cushion beside him, gloves folded beside it, the black scarf that usually concealed his face inside the crown. Alice knew its silhouette from the quayside at New York Harbor. His beard was black and groomed and thick like a pugilist's, and his eyes were long-lashed and beautiful. But his skin was gray, and old—far older than his years—and he was thin in the throat, and lean-cheeked, as if he had not eaten in a long time. Alice glanced around at the shadowed pillars and at the candles in their brackets but she did not see Coulton or Walter or any other. If the keywrasse was anywhere, it too had glided into the darkness and disappeared. Very deliberately, she took the revolver from her pocket and cocked it and leveled it at the sick man's face.

"Ah," he said again.

That was all. If he was frightened, he gave no sign.

"We saw Coulton," she said. "We saw what you did to him."

Marber's eyes glittered. "And what did I do? He was dying. I saved him."

"You *killed* him."

"And yet here he is, walking this earth still. Hardly killed, Alice." Marber's wrists and hands were covered in tattoos that seemed to move in the candlelight. "There is much you misunderstand, I fear. I am not your enemy. I do not wish for violence between us."

Mrs. Harrogate reached over and gently, firmly, lowered Alice's revolver. Her own knives had been tucked away. "And neither do we," she said.

"I do," said Alice.

But Mrs. Harrogate only folded her skirts and sat in one of the chairs and held her handbag upright on her lap and after a long sullen moment Alice sat too. She kept her Colt Peacemaker sidelong on her thigh, its barrel pointing darkly toward Jacob Marber's heart.

Jacob Marber had squinched his eyes shut, darkness leaking from their corners. "You are surprised to see me so unwell, Margaret. You imagine it is because of the child. What happened on the train. But you are wrong."

"Perhaps," said Mrs. Harrogate. "Perhaps."

"My body weakens because I grow stronger."

Mrs. Harrogate said nothing for a long moment. Then she replied,

"You are weak in body because of the drughr. And you are weak in spirit because of the drughr. In the end it will consume you, as it consumes everything. That is its nature. You just do not see it."

Something flickered across Jacob's face, was gone.

"I am not doing this for me," he said calmly.

"Of course not. You are doing it for the drughr," replied Mrs. Harrogate. "For the drughr, and only for the drughr. You just do not realize it. You have been useful for a time, but that usefulness will end. What will happen to you, I wonder, once your master gets its hands on the child?"

"She is not my master."

"Oh, Jacob." And there was such pity in Mrs. Harrogate's voice that Alice turned her face and looked at her.

And she saw then, slowly, materializing out of the shadows, pale as smoke, the white form of Frank Coulton. He stood at the tunnel opening, long clawlike fingers at his sides.

Jacob Marber's voice was soft. "Where are the weir-bents, Margaret?"

Alice, surprised, looked back.

"The weir-bents," said Mrs. Harrogate slowly.

She seemed to be considering what to say next and Alice thought she would plead ignorance but she did not.

"The weir-bents can be of no use to you, Jacob. Even if I had them. Which I do not. The child is protected by a glyphic."

"Ah. But that cannot last forever." Marber ran a slow hand over his face, tired. A fine black soot smoked up off him as he did so. "The glyphic is weak. Berghast has been using it for too long, draining it. You do know what it is he desires? Why he is doing all . . . this?" Marber gestured with a hand, as if their being in this chamber was Berghast's doing. He lowered his voice. "Our good Mr. Coulton has already called on Mr. Fang. Therefore I know the weir-bents were in the possession of that nursemaid. I know you escorted her here to

London and hid her away, even from Berghast. I know many things, Margaret, but most of all, I know *you*. What other object could you have acquired that would make you believe you could confront me?" He gave her a small unhappy smile. "And yet, even still . . . why would you risk it? That is what I do not understand."

Mrs. Harrogate folded her arms, the long black knives glinting incongruously from under her elbows. "You flatter yourself," she said. "We are not in London for you."

But Marber continued on in his soft flat voice, his mind turning over itself like water. "I do not understand why Berghast would permit you to rush headlong into this. Unless time were of the essence. . . ."

"I come in vengeance, Jacob," Mrs. Harrogate said, as if to settle the matter.

But he was unimpressed. "I think not. I think I am better disposed of now than later. Why?" He turned his intense black gaze on Mrs. Harrogate. Alice could feel the menace like a thrumming in her skin. Slowly, his eyes lit up. "Oh," he murmured. "Surely not? Surely not . . . that?"

"Surely not what?" said Mrs. Harrogate, almost despite herself.

Marber gave Alice a superior look, as if it were a game, and he had solved a riddle. Then he turned back to Mrs. Harrogate. "It is because the glyphic is finally dying, isn't it? Soon Cairndale will be defenseless. The orsine will rip itself open. There'll be no closing it again."

"You're mad," whispered Mrs. Harrogate.

Marber leaned forward. "Absolutely," he whispered back.

But Alice could see it too, writ plain in the older woman's face, the same thing Marber had seen: he was not wrong. Alice didn't know what it meant, the dying glyphic, not really, but the intensity of it was clear. It was as if Mrs. Harrogate were just realizing it also, just putting it together in her mind, what Berghast had kept from her. She looked devastated.

Alice scanned the chamber. There was only the one way in; they were deep underground; Coulton was blocking their exit. The pain in her ribs flared as if in response to her fear. Suddenly it all made sense.

"It's a trap," she muttered. She stood, the clatter of her chair echoing in the gloom. "He knew we were coming. He *lured* us here, he *wanted* to be found."

"Quite so," said Mrs. Harrogate calmly.

In that same moment, Alice raised her gun.

She'd meant to shoot him through the eye. She had shot many men in her life; she was quick, and accurate, and deadly. But as she stepped backward to take her balance, she saw Marber's expression change in a flicker, from malice, to puzzlement, to a sinister understanding.

And then something extraordinary happened. He flicked his wrist, just casually, just as if he were waving away a wasp, and Alice's own wrist flicked in response. She felt herself stagger in shock—the force of it, the *violation*. Her revolver leaped away, skittering off into the darkness.

Marber was looking at her gravely. His own hand was still suspended. He turned his wrist and Alice's wrist turned too. She felt it in horror, watched it happening, but it was like it was someone else's wrist, like it was happening in a performance, on a stage. A sudden fierce revulsion filled her.

Marber seemed transfixed, mesmerized.

"How is this possible?" he whispered. He rose slowly, painfully, to his full height. He looked so pale, so unwell.

Coulton stood yet among the pillars, white, hairless, unmoving.

"Of course. The train. My dust."

"Leave. Me. Alone!" With a great effort, clenching her jaw, Alice made her hand close into a fist, and she forced it down to her side. It felt as if she were pushing against a tremendous wall of air. She was trembling with the effort.

Slowly Marber's own fist lowered in response, as if against his will. His expression darkened; all at once he released her, and the connection between them was severed.

She stumbled back, gasping, her head spinning.

"Interesting," Marber whispered. He studied her. "What is that around your throat?"

Alice, suddenly afraid, put a hand to the leather cord, to the weir-bents there. Mrs. Harrogate began to speak but Marber just lifted a hand toward her and she fell silent. Her arms were stiff at her sides and she was arching her neck, turning her head in a halting circle, swallowing in discomfort, a black dust swirling around her.

"Alice," he murmured. "What have you brought me?"

She saw Mrs. Harrogate, struggling to breathe. A thick rope of dust began twisting around her throat, holding her body tight, half lifting her onto her toes. Her fingers were scrabbling at her knives, unable to work them free.

"Let her go," Alice cried. "Leave her be!"

But Marber just walked calmly over to her, to Alice, and with his long twisted fingers lifted the leather cord, pulled at it with a snap. He stood very close. Alice could smell the dust in his clothes. His eyes were wholly black, so that he seemed to be looking everywhere and nowhere at once. But then he turned away, studying the weir-bents in his palm.

Margaret made a gurgling noise, her face darkening with blood.

"Let her go, please," begged Alice.

And Marber, with a casual glance back at Alice, shrugged. "As you wish."

All at once the tendrils of dust lifted Mrs. Harrogate into the air and hurled her bodily across the chamber. She struck a pillar and fell crumpled against the stone floor. One of her knives clattered away across the floor. Her body looked strange, bent wrongly. The litch, Coulton, still had not moved. Alice heard his teeth clicking, clicking.

"These," said Marber, sliding them from the cord, "these are rather . . . unusual, yes? What do you know of them, Alice?"

She could feel the muscles tightening at her throat. She was breathing in quick shallow breaths. She couldn't seem to get enough air.

He was watching her with that same cruel indifference and now it was she clutching at her throat, trying to breathe, knowing that she would die. She wanted to shout, to scream at him, to hurt him in some way, but all she could do was fall, heavily, to her knees, gasping. The keywrasse, she was thinking, where was the keywrasse? She tried to summon it, silently. But she could do no more; for, at that very moment, Mrs. Harrogate lifted her head weakly from the ground and slid her small silver-plated pistol out of her handbag and leveled it at Jacob Marber's heart and pulled the trigger.

Everything erupted. The sharp roar of the gunshot ricocheted off the ancient walls. Marber recoiled and spun under the impact and fell back in a sudden explosion of black dust. The weir-bents flew from his grip. All at once the air rushed back into Alice's lungs, and she was wheezing and shaking her head and heaving with the effort, stars in the corners of her eyes.

"Miss Quicke!" Mrs. Harrogate cried. And she flung her other knife skittering across the floor.

Alice had turned her head in time to see the knife spin toward her, and to see Coulton scrabble, leaping forward, his long teeth clicking, his claws scraping at the stone floor. And she crouched and grabbed the knife and rose to meet him.

Coulton! she was thinking, her head spinning. *Frank!*

And in that mass of smoke: Jacob Marber himself. It would not be possible to fight both. She and Mrs. Harrogate would die.

But then, in a blur, the keywrasse came among them. Where it had been hiding, Alice couldn't imagine. It flew between the pillars on its swift catlike feet, its one white paw shining, and it seemed to grow in size as it raced in and out of shadow, now as big as a dog, now as big as a lion, and it had too many legs somehow, and then it was smashing into Coulton and knocking him weightlessly back against the far frescoes and propelling itself sideways onto his back snarling and driving its tremendous fangs into his shoulder, tearing at him under its weight, and still not slowing but leaping again, driving itself toward Marber, still growing, now six-legged, now eight-legged, a creature of darkness and nightmare and fury.

All this unfolded so quickly Alice barely had time to adjust her knuckles in the rings of the handle and raise the long knife in front of her.

And then the keywrasse had plunged into the swirling cloud of dust where Marber was, and Alice twisted back in time to see Coulton—the thing that had once been Coulton—rise up out of the gloom smeared with its own blood, and crouch on its coiled legs, and spring at her.

She fell back, heavily, cutting fast and hard with the blade. She needed to keep Coulton at arm's length. The candle fire caught the strange unreflective orbs of his eyes, glinted off his long yellow teeth. He was hissing and snarling and there was nothing of the man she had known, nothing of the man she had come to admire.

And then she leaned in too far, trying to cut his belly, and his claws caught her shoulder and raked across the side of her neck.

He was on her in an instant. Some part of her was aware of Mrs. Harrogate, across the chamber, dragging herself bloodily back up against a pillar. And the dark cloud where the keywrasse and Marber fought thickened in the air, and parted, and she saw the keywrasse hook a claw into Marber's mouth and pull, slicing his cheek in a great ragged tear so that his face blackened with blood and through the hole she could see the teeth in his mouth, as in a skull. He screamed in pain.

But mostly it was the weird, slowed-down sense of time that she noticed, as Coulton dipped his head, trying to bite her neck, her face, and she gripped his throat with one hand and plunged the long knife over and over into his side, his arm, his ribs, his throat, seeking for purchase in the slippery blood.

But she wasn't alone; she felt again an enormous powerful weight as something, some creature, smashed into Coulton, hurling him across the floor. It was the keywrasse, panting, its long fangs snapping, its many legs crouched to spring.

She saw Marber, splayed out on the floor. And she saw Mrs. Harrogate, crawling toward him on her forearms, a blade in one fist. Slowly, through a fog of pain, she started to understand that they might survive, that they might even destroy Marber and Coulton. The keywrasse might succeed.

But then something else happened, something . . . horrifying.

The candles in their brackets guttered, one after another, as if some invisible presence were rushing along the walls of that chamber. One by one they went out.

And then a sliver of gray light, like an incision in the air, slowly appeared. It widened, wound-like. Sliding out of that ragged hole came a thing, a monster, a creature of sheer and utter darkness. The only light left was the light of the bull's-eye lantern, upturned on the floor, and in its beam of light Alice saw the horror stand tall. It stood twelve feet high, its shoulders crushed up against the ceiling, and its arms were a blur of smoke so that Alice could not be sure if there were four, if there were six.

It was the drughr.

And then it screamed. The drughr screamed and the sound was the sound of death, of pain, of absolute terror. And the keywrasse roared in challenge and leaped forward and then Alice could see nothing, only the darkness, but she could hear the clash and ringing and shrieking of the two creatures in their fight, a sound of metal striking metal.

She fumbled weakly for her knife, then crawled over to the bull's-eye lantern. She opened the shutter wide. She turned it upon the chamber.

The air was thick with a choking black dust. She couldn't see Mrs. Harrogate. But she saw Marber on his feet, clutching his face, black blood pouring through his fingers. He had something in one fist, clutching it close. She saw him climb through the silver hole in the air. Then Coulton, bloodstained and staggering, followed him through.

The drughr had seized the keywrasse by the throat. It was twisting it this way and that, shaking it, screaming. Alice fumbled for her gun, trying to find it in the smoke. But the drughr raised itself up to an awful size and hurled the keywrasse against a far pillar so that the walls shuddered and dirt poured down around them and darkness descended.

And then the drughr, too, was fleeing through the tear it had made in the fabric of the world, and the silver hole closed like a mouth.

And after that, a long deep silence, into which Alice fell back, exhausted.

There came a darkness.

A greater darkness.

Then: movement.

Pain, blooming in her chest. Alice coughed, reached for the lantern. Somehow the candle within had not gone out and she turned it, swung its light across to Mrs. Harrogate. The older woman's dress was white with dust, her blood a vibrant red in her hair and hands and her ribs. Alice crawled over to her, cradled her head.

Mrs. Harrogate grimaced up at her. "You . . . look . . . awful."

Alice sobbed a bloody sob. "Yeah," she said, through the tears and the snot. "And you look fit for the fucking opera."

"My legs . . ." She gasped, wet her lips. She was fumbling for her knees. "I can't feel my legs."

Alice looked at them, twisted strangely in the dust. She blinked the blood from her own eyes. "You'll be all right," she said. "We just need to get you out of here. We'll find you a doctor."

But she knew it was not fixable. Mrs. Harrogate was shaking her head. "It wasn't supposed to be here, it shouldn't have been able to . . . I don't understand. . . ."

"That was your drughr, I guess?"

Alice heard a soft meow then and saw the keywrasse sitting nearby. It was again just a black cat. It turned its four glinting eyes toward her, narrowing them, then looked away, bored. And then, with the greatest drama imaginable, as if the whole world might be watching, calmly it lifted one paw and began to wash it with a little pink tongue.

The older woman looked up suddenly, her eyes bright. "The weir-bents, are they—?"

Alice looked away, remembering. She got painfully to her feet, the rubble clinking, and with the lantern she cast around in the shadows. She stumbled to where the silver door in the air had been and then she began to claw through the wreckage. She remembered Coulton's long teeth snapping at her throat, she remembered the thing in Marber's fist as he fled. She'd lost them. She'd failed.

But then she lifted away a piece of broken wall. And there lay one of them, the iron one, left in the dust like a broken piece of calipers. But the wooden one was gone.

"Then we have already lost, Miss Quicke." Mrs. Harrogate was nodding bloodily. "Without the other weir-bent, you cannot send the keywrasse away. You will lose control of it. Nothing else can stop Jacob.

He will be waiting for Mr. Thorpe to die now. He will be watching the glyphic. You need to get the weir-bent back."

Alice spat. "First we need to get out of here," she said. She didn't know where Marber and that drughr had gone, or if they'd be coming back. She wouldn't put it past him. "That's what we need to do. While we still have light to see by. We can figure out what to do about the keywrasse later."

But Mrs. Harrogate was shaking her head. "No, Miss Quicke," she whispered. "Alice—"

It was the first time the older woman had called Alice by her name and she was surprised to find herself blinking back tears. "What is it?" she said gruffly.

"I can't. My legs . . ."

Alice tried to think. She looked at the older woman's body, twisted like a bad nail, and she set her jaw. The lantern was flickering, going out.

A darkness came flooding in.

28

OVERMORROW

In the morning, Charlie and Marlowe went back to Dr. Berghast.

It was still early; through their window while they dressed they could see a pale mist hanging over the inky darkness of the loch; the island was lost to view. Inside, the corridors of Cairndale were dim, and cold, and deserted. They saw no one. The other kids were still asleep. As they went, Charlie gripped his mother's wedding ring in one fist for luck or consolation or maybe just out of habit until, reaching the upper corridor where Dr. Berghast would be waiting, he slipped the cord around his neck and tucked it all under his shirt, out of sight.

When they knocked, softly, at Dr. Berghast's study, the older man opened the door at once, just as if he'd been waiting, just as if he'd known they would be back, at that hour, with that resolve. He looked haggard and drawn; he stood breathing; but his eyes were bright.

"So," he said. "You will go."

It was not a question.

He let them in. The cage holding the bonebirds was covered by a sheet. On Berghast's desk was a tray holding plates of bacon and sausage and boiled eggs and butter cakes, still steaming. They ate ravenously; Dr. Berghast watched without speaking; and when they were done he rose and took up a lighted lantern. With a strange key he unlocked the leftmost door on the easterly wall.

"Mr. Thorpe weakens," he said gravely. "We must not delay."

The door opened onto a flight of stairs, winding down into darkness. They were in the walls of Cairndale, descending, and then they were below the manor, and emerging into a dark underground tunnel. The air tasted sour, hard to breathe. The floor of the tunnel was slick with muck and some sort of watery runoff. Dr. Berghast lifted the lantern and, wordlessly, started walking. The tunnel, as far as the light would reach, seemed to go on in a straight line forever.

"Where are we going?" said Charlie. His voice echoed off up ahead, over and over.

"This tunnel leads under the loch, Charles. We are going to the island."

Marlowe said, "But the loch is deep."

"Yes, it is, child." Berghast did not turn as he spoke, only led them swiftly onward. "Except where a singular ridge of rock connects the island to the shore. We are walking inside it now. Above you is solid water."

Charlie swallowed. He thought of the weight of that water, pressing down on the roof of the tunnel, he thought of the rock splitting and caving in, and the roar of it....

"Who made this tunnel?" asked Marlowe.

"The dead, child. As they made everything that comes down to us."

They were quiet then and walked on. The only sound was the splash and scrape of their shoes, the low hiss of the candle swaying in its own wax.

At last the tunnel seemed to slope upward, just faintly, and the air sweetened, and then they had reached a second flight of stairs. Dr. Berghast led them up to an old door, which he unlocked, and on the other side of it Charlie saw, again, the ruins of the monastery. The gray daylight was fierce, painful, after the darkness below. Charlie squinted, grimacing. They were standing in an apse, in a little shelter, the door cleverly hidden from sight.

"Come," said Dr. Berghast.

He led them through the tumbled stones and the long grass and outside, to the front of the time-ravaged building. And again, laboriously, he unlocked a heavy door, and swung the lantern high, and led them inside, out of the mist.

It might have been a kind of living quarters once, for the monks who had built the island: a long room, windowless, with shadowy little chambers on either end. Dr. Berghast led them swiftly to a broken wall in the back, ducked his head, slipped through. It was a narrow stairwell, carved out of the rock itself, curving downward to a kind of natural cavern.

The dim light within was blue. The first thing Charlie sensed was a kind of thrumming, like a low-grade electric current. There were roots punching up out of the rocky floor, climbing in tangles up the walls. There were stone arches holding the roof in place and in the center of the chamber was a deep stone cistern, tangled and overgrown. Steps on one side led down into it. Its surface looked dark, unreflective; then Charlie saw it was not water at all but a kind of coagulated sap, thickening there. From deep below the skin of the cistern glowed an eerie, startling blue light. The roots had grown into it, the way a tree's roots will grow into a pool of water. Charlie caught his breath.

"The orsine," said Dr. Berghast calmly, indicating the cistern. He held out a small old-fashioned knife. "You must cut through it, to the waters below."

Charlie took the knife warily. "Where's the glyphic?"

Berghast raised an arm. "Ah, Mr. Thorpe is here, all around you. All this is a part of him. That substance, sealing the orsine? It is a resin, from his roots. He is feeding off the orsine."

"We've got to cut through it?"

"Yes."

"Won't it hurt him?"

"I imagine so."

Marlowe took a step toward the orsine, then stopped. Something was happening with his little hands, where he held them out; they were shining, shining the same brilliant blue as the waters.

Dr. Berghast looked pleased. He set the lantern down at his feet and reached into his jacket and took out a roll of parchment. "This is a copy of the map," he said, kneeling in the dust to open it. "You will recognize it from the wall in my study, perhaps. Come closer, Charles. It will be difficult to read, at first. But it will make sense when you are through the orsine. Here are the gray rooms, where you will enter. And here are the dead stairs, and here you see the beginning of the city."

"The city—?"

"The city of the dead. Yes. In the third circle." Dr. Berghast pressed a knee to one corner to hold the map flat and in this way freed a hand, and then he drew his long finger across the map, to the white of its outer edges. "Here," he said, "is where I believe the Room to be. It was too far for the others to travel to. But not for you."

"Wait. How're we supposed to know it?"

"The spirits will not go near the place. You will see a white tree that bleeds. You must go into the Room. You must bring me what you find there. You must bring me the glove. And this," he said, withdrawing a small leather-bound notebook, and a nub of a pencil, "is for you to record what you encounter, where you go, everything. There is some-thing I have not told you yet. The talents who used to come back from the orsine . . . they had little recollection of it. What they'd seen was all confused, all mixed up. We began using these notebooks to keep track of what they saw."

He put the parchment and the notebook and the pencil in a small cloth satchel, passed it across to Charlie.

"Be careful, both of you," he continued. "That world will play tricks on you. You may think you see your loved ones, those you've lost, and wish to follow them. Many have been led astray, in the trying. They are shades only; they are not the ones you loved and lost, but only the memories of them. They will not know you."

"If they're just memories, they can't hurt us," said Charlie.

"The spirits are very dangerous," Berghast said sharply. "When they gather together they take the form of a fog. You must not let yourselves be caught in it. They are drawn to movement, to heat, to quickness, anything that reminds them, however briefly, of the sensation of life. It is a pure and absolute need: a need that devours. They will leech the life from you. Stay clear of them. And there are not only the spirits of the dead in that world. Remember that our world, and that other"—he raised his eyes to regard the orsine with a curious longing—"each is a house of doors. Everything is always only passing through."

He leaned back and blew out the lantern so that the chamber was bathed in the blue light. Shadows filled his eyes. "I do not know how long you can stay in there. Time moves differently in that world. For the others, with the artifact, it was a few hours of our time at the longest. But for you . . . a day? Two days?" He seemed to grow bigger in the darkness. "Know this: observe your fingers, your hands. If the fog has affected you, they will begin to shake, the color will go from them. When that happens, you must start back at once."

"If we don't?"

"You will be lost."

The skin-like surface of the cistern hummed and glowed its eerie electric blue, and Marlowe's little hands glowed the same. And then Marlowe, who still had said nothing, took the knife from Charlie and crossed the grotto floor and crouched at the edge of the steps. He punched the long blade through. A dark stain seeped up out of the cut and Marlowe sawed a long cross in the surface. His entire body was shining now, glowing and translucent.

"Yes," murmured Dr. Berghast, "good."

The little boy paid him no mind. When he was done he dropped the knife onto the floor and took hold of the roots like a kind of rope and waded down the steps, into the shining incision; his trousers darkened, then his shirt, and soon he was soaked to the shoulders. And then, with a quick look up at Charlie, the waters closed over his head and he was lost to view.

"Jesus—" Charlie hissed in surprise. The kid had gone under so quickly.

He hurried to the edge, scanning the dark surface, the weird light coming up from beneath, but he could see nothing. Marlowe was gone.

"You must hurry, Charles," called Dr. Berghast from the darkness. "Else you will lose him. Do not forget the knife. You'll need it to cut your way back out."

Something about the orsine made him hesitate. It wasn't fear, exactly. But as he stepped in, he gasped sharply. The water—if water it was—gripped his ankles with its cold. It felt almost like it was taking hold. The leathery flaps on the surface folded under his weight. He screwed up his face, he took a deep breath. He could not see Berghast because of the blue shining from below.

"Hold on, Mar," he muttered. "I'm coming."

And his clothes billowed up around him, and he went down into the water that was not water. And after a time he could no longer feel his feet nor his legs nor his hands nor his arms, and still the steps went down, and soon he could feel nothing at all.

He took a deep breath. His face went under.

He descended into the dark.

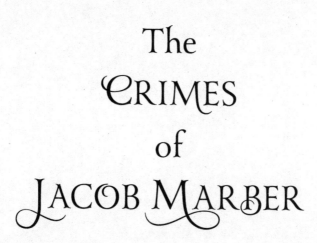

The
CRIMES
of
JACOB MARBER

·

1874

29

MAN, CHILD, MONSTER

Twilight, under a deepening sky.

Jacob Marber stood in his shirtsleeves and waistcoat in a slow river in the outer reaches of Scotland, watching the light fade from the silver-black water, knowing he did not belong, not among the living, not anymore. The strange smoke granted him by the drughr was coalescing in his skin, a part of him and yet not, like the breath of the dead.

He had wandered in the dead world for so long, month after month, that the world of humankind felt strange to him now. Small, too brief. He was no longer innocent but he had not yet done the worst he would do either. The water felt cold at his thighs, shocking after so long away, and the darkness in his skin tingled. He shuddered. This world of theirs, he thought. And turned away.

For he'd found his brother. In that other world, he'd found him. Just as the drughr had promised. And now there was no unfinding, no going back, he had to live with what he had seen. It had solved nothing. Redressed nothing. Like a ripple of air, like a sadness folding over itself,

Bertolt had come to him at the edge of the darkness three times, over three nights, summoned by Jacob's own grief. He looked still a boy, the very age he'd been when he died, his soft cheeks pallid, his dusky hair leeched of color, and Jacob had crumpled into tears seeing a face he'd loved and not hoped to see again. He'd begged, he'd pleaded, he'd told stories of their childhood in Vienna, of the nuns at the orphanage, of the factory, of their days on the streets. And on the third night he'd told in a quiet voice the story of Bertolt's own death, glimpsing for a moment a flicker of recognition. But then it was gone, as quickly as it appeared, and his brother just wavered, a curl of air, his eyes empty.

And the drughr had told him: *He has forgotten you; it is too late. There is no saving him now.*

Jacob breathed softly, remembering. From where he stood in the river he could see the road and the bridge in the dusk. He was watching for any sign of pursuit, but there was nothing, no one. No one had found the carriage in the trees, the dead horses, the dead driver. No one was coming.

He waded out of the river, his trousers clinging coldly. His frock coat was hanging on a bush. He raised his face as he heard a familiar voice in his head.

It is nearly time, Jacob. You are prepared?

On the mudbank crouched the drughr, animallike, savage, not in the form he had come to know her by, not a pale and beautiful woman, but hulking, and shaggy, fanged in shadow. She was staring at her own reflection in the water, fascinated.

Behind her, huddled in the low bracken, were the two children she had asked for. The two children he had brought her. He could sense her eagerness.

"Is there no other way?" he said quietly.

She did not reply.

The children were maybe thirteen, fourteen years of age—a boy and a girl, siblings maybe—intercepted on their way to Cairndale. They would be talents, of course. Located and sent north from Mrs. Harrogate in London, just as he'd used to do, as he'd done when he found the Japanese girl, the dustworker Komako, and that little invisible urchin. Remembering that, he felt a faint twinge of regret, of sadness. Then it was gone. He'd deliberately not asked the names of these kids, nor anything about them. He didn't want to know. He knew he should feel sick, seeing them, knowing what the drughr would do to them. But he didn't. They seemed curiously insubstantial, as if he could see time passing through them, like light, as if they might dissolve at any moment. Truly, he had been in that other world too long.

He was bonded now to the drughr. She was a part of him, as he was of her. That is how he thought of it. He could *feel* her desires, her fears, just as if they were his own, or almost so, just as if they were the shadow sides of his own longings. He felt, for instance, her raw hunger for the two children, for the power in their talents. She wasn't strong, in this world. Not yet. She would absorb the two children in her feeding. Drain them. And then she would do what she needed to do: weaken the glyphic's wards at Cairndale so that Jacob could smuggle the baby out.

You are certain you can get inside?

"I have it arranged," he replied.

The child is everything, Jacob. You must bring him to me. You must not fail me.

Jacob met her eye and nodded.

Him, meaning the baby. The boy without a name, the shining boy. The child whom Henry Berghast had stolen and was keeping now at Cairndale, locked away, to use, as Jacob feared, for his own sinister purposes. He didn't know all that child could do but he knew enough to fear its life would be an awful one and though he felt very little that was human and pitying he did feel for the baby, had felt for him, had held him in his arms and stroked his soft cheek and he'd felt it, a kinship, something close to love, and he'd thought: *You are like me. We are the same.* And he'd promised that baby right then that he would not suffer a childhood like Jacob himself had suffered.

The drughr knew none of that. And so Jacob was afraid, afraid the drughr would find out what he really intended, his betrayal, and afraid too that he'd fail, and what that would mean for the baby, and for himself.

For he didn't plan to bring the baby to her at all. He would steal the shining boy away, far away, to some place where no one could hurt him, not Berghast, not the drughr, not anyone at all.

The sky darkened. The hour drew near. In the dusk the drughr turned toward the children. They were huddled together, staring at her in terror. They had already shouted themselves hoarse.

Go now, she said to Jacob, dismissing him. *I will interrupt the wards as long as I can.*

He went.

There were no screams, no cries from the two children. But as he climbed away from the river, making for Cairndale and the baby there, Jacob heard the wet ripping sounds of the drughr, feeding.

In a large well-appointed room, overlooking the deep loch, in the upper east wing of Cairndale Manor, there came a knocking at the door. The nursemaid rose from the window seat and from the cradle she was rocking. She was still a girl herself, in most ways. She buttoned her blouse. Her breasts ached, heavy with milk, and she hesitated tiredly and tucked her black hair up under her bonnet. It had been the envy of the village girls until recently. She knew the baby would sleep now until she slept and then he'd awake and cry and only settle when she walked the length of the room again, crooning to him. Yet he was a dear and sweet thing all the same. She drew the curtains around the crib, around the baby sleeping warm within. Her name was Susan Crowley, and she'd worked in the kitchens at Cairndale until a year ago when she was herself with child. That was because of a dairyman's apprentice down in the valley, who was himself married; and though she'd done what she could to rid herself of the pregnancy in the French manner, nothing had worked, and she'd carried the baby to term. And then she'd given birth, and fallen at once in love with her tiny daughter and sure enough, that was when she was taken from her, taken by the good Lord like a kind of punishment. For that wee girl slept now in a churchyard in Aberdeen, dead of fever nine months ago, and Susan had cried herself sore every night after and still did sometimes, though she'd been engaged again here, and lucky enough for it, engaged for seven months now as a wet nurse to a foundling boy.

A boy unlike any other.

Oh, she'd seen him shine that strange beautiful blue shine, of course. She didn't know its meaning or its cause. There'd been no harm in it, no danger that she ever saw. Only beauty. But she'd seen how Dr. Berghast looked at the baby, the fear and the fascination flickering in his eyes, and she'd known: the child was special.

The knocking at the door repeated, soft.

It was Dr. Berghast. He stood in the hall, the sconces casting his craggy face in shadow. For a long moment he only looked at her. She didn't like the man, never had. It wasn't only his gray eyes, the firelight twinned within them or the eerie way they followed you around a room. It was something else too, some indistinguishable part of him, like a scent, a scent of dark suspicion.

She stood aside as he came in, taking his hat from his outstretched hand.

"He is sleeping, then," said Berghast, running a palm along his white beard, smoothing his whiskers.

"Yes, sir," said Susan, dipping.

He swept past. Henry Berghast was tall, powerfully built, immaculate in his dress. He wore his snow-white whiskers long and his hair long over his collar in an old-fashioned style Susan had sometimes seen as a girl on her grandfather and his associates. She knew he was old, far older than he looked, though she did not know his exact age. He was a man of science, it was true; a doctor, no less; but he was also a man of dark proclivities with a sensitivity to the impossible, like everyone at Cairndale. You couldn't live at the institute without seeing what shouldn't be seen and understanding the nature of what went on.

Where, exactly, the baby had come from, Berghast did not say. But she had heard rumors, bits of stories, and knew it had something to do with the dustworker no one spoke of, the one named Marber, who frightened the old talents. There were no other babies at Cairndale, never had been; the next youngest talent was nine years old and cut her own meat and changed her own bedding.

Dr. Berghast slowly drew aside the curtain and stood over the crib. He looked at the baby, sleeping there. He had given the boy his own name—Henry—but he never called him by it and neither did she, if only because she thought it didn't suit him, being the name of a man of ego and severity, and more like a stamp of ownership than a person's name.

"Would you like to hold him, sir?" she said now.

But there was wickedness in her, asking that, and she knew it, for she knew the answer already. Dr. Berghast had never once held the baby, nor even touched him, and there was a quick flash of alarm in his face as he registered her words. Then he turned away.

"The child looks healthy, Miss Crowley," he murmured. "You are doing well. I am grateful."

"Thank you, sir."

"It cannot be easy, being alone here."

"I don't think he minds it, sir."

"I meant yourself, Miss Crowley."

Had any other person said such a thing, she'd have thought it a kindness at best, rather too forward at worst; but with Dr. Berghast she knew it was neither, merely a statement of fact.

"Oh, it's no trial, sir. I like the baby's company."

"Mm." He stood looking down at the child a moment longer. She could not see his face. "My boy," he whispered.

Then he retreated back out, to the antechamber.

She followed.

"Miss Davenshaw tells me you are in need of extra coal and candles?" he said, when the curtain was again drawn and they were away from the sleeping baby. "I will see they are sent up. The child must be kept warm, yes. She tells me also that you are not eating."

Susan blushed. "I'm fine, sir. Only a wee bit tired. Tis to be expected."

He grimaced.

"I must tell you something, Miss Crowley. It has only just been decided, but I think it best you hear it at once."

Berghast's gray eyes bored into her own and she looked away.

"The child cannot stay here, at Cairndale. He will need to be sent away. I would like you to go with him, if you are willing."

She looked up. "Sent away? He is still very young, Dr. Berghast—"

"It cannot be helped. I have already written several letters of inquiry and am only waiting to hear back. I have two possible destinations. They are . . . remote."

"But . . . why, sir?"

She watched Dr. Berghast cross to the window and separate the muslin curtains with one hand and stare out at the gathering darkness. She had not lit any candles and she moved now to do so.

It was then he spoke.

He said, very softly, "Because the child is not safe here, Miss Crowley."

He is not safe anywhere. We must hide him, before they come for him."

She looked at him sharply. "Who is coming for him, sir?"

But that question, he did not answer.

At that same moment, in the lower foyer of Cairndale, Abigail Davenshaw was sitting upright and stiff in an armchair with her hands clasped in her lap, listening to the clock chime in one corner. She had been waiting almost an hour for the carriage from Edinburgh, the carriage that was carrying her two new wards.

Their names were Gully and Radha, twins, and they had come a great distance to reach the institute. She knew only what Mrs. Harrogate had told her upon arrival: they had come from Calcutta, purchased by Mr. Coulton from a spice trader, and they understood almost nothing of their talents.

Mrs. Harrogate had seen them in London, the morning of their arrival; their luggage had been delayed at the customs house at Gravesend, and Mr. Coulton had agreed to see them to the train when at last it was delivered.

As a general rule, Abigail Davenshaw did not like children to travel unaccompanied—one does not invite trouble into one's home, as her grandfather would have said—but it had been done like that since before her time at Cairndale, and there had never yet been any child lost or delayed, and so who was she to demand a chaperone be present?

She lifted her face. There came the sound of heels crossing quietly toward her.

"Mrs. Harrogate," she said.

"Miss Davenshaw," replied the older woman. "I have been looking for Dr. Berghast. He has not passed this way?" She paused. "What is it. The new ones? Have they still not arrived, then?"

Abigail Davenshaw inclined her head. "As you can see."

"Well. I am certain the carriage will arrive soon. It is Mr. Bogget, after all. He has been driving our new ones up from Edinburgh since, well, since my late husband's time. And he has not failed us yet. He has perhaps had some trouble on the road, or with the horses. He will be here. I am confident."

"Hm," she replied. For Mrs. Harrogate didn't sound confident, not at all, not to Abigail Davenshaw's practiced ear.

A long, uncomfortable silence passed. There came the faint rumble of children running along the corridor upstairs. The older woman made a sniffing noise, and then Abigail Davenshaw felt a hand on her sleeve.

"How late are they?"

"Fifty-six minutes."

"Ah." Mrs. Harrogate cleared her throat. "Where is Mr. Laster? Not at the gatehouse, I have just come from there. If there has been any word, he will have received it."

"There has been no word, Mrs. Harrogate. The carriage is simply . . . late."

Abigail heard steel in the older woman's voice when she replied. "You may choose to wait for word, Miss Davenshaw," she said. "But I do not care to sit idly by, doing nothing. I shall inquire of Mr. Laster. And inform you if there is news."

Abigail Davenshaw inclined her head. A long silence followed.

"Good evening to you," said Mrs. Harrogate, at last.

"Indeed."

Abigail turned her face as the older woman's footsteps crossed the foyer, heading outside toward the courtyard, toward Walter Laster's gatehouse beyond. She breathed calmly. Only when the front door had

boomed shut, and she was certain she was alone, did she allow herself
a quick, unhappy grimace.

The carriage was *never* late.

Impatiently, Walter Laster shut the gatehouse door behind him, locking it fast. Then he hurried across the courtyard to the delivery entrance, casting wary looks all around. It was growing dark.

No one saw him go. He was watching for that woman up from
London, the Harrogate woman, the one in black with her veiled face,
who seemed always to be observing him. As if she *knew*. At the delivery entrance he paused, quickly crushing a handkerchief to his mouth,
muffling his cough. He felt his body spasm with pain. When he took
the cloth away, even in the faint light from the manor house, he could
see the blood flecking it. His mouth and lips tasted of iron.

The carriage up from Edinburgh hadn't arrived. That had been the
sign. His heart was pounding, he shook his head weakly as he worked
through the ring of keys, finding the right one. He had to hurry. If all
would happen as he'd been told, then Jacob would be coming within
the hour.

At last he found the key he was looking for, and slipped inside the
delivery entrance, and stood listening. No one was near. He hurried
through the back halls and down the steps into the cold cellar, finding
the old lantern he had hidden behind a shelf. He struck a safety match,
lit the oil with his back to the cellar.

Jacob, Jacob. His dear and only friend.

Walter had always been small, crooked due to a childhood injury, a
loner who suffered for being alone. He had long greasy hair cut by his
own hand with a pair of shears borrowed once a month from the gardener's shed, and small hands, and two teeth out in back. He watched
the kids at Cairndale cautiously, keeping clear of them, disliking the

way they laughed around him, knowing the unnatural things they could do. But most of those at Cairndale paid him no mind—he was just queer Mr. Laster, who lived in the gatehouse and took care of any arrivals or departures that came through.

But Jacob hadn't been like that, no. Jacob, when he was at Cairndale, had immediately been drawn to Walter, or Walter to him—it was hard to know exactly—and it wasn't only that they were both different from the rest, or friendless in the same way. No, it was a deeper bond, not like friendship, more like what brothers could be. Or so it had always felt to Walter.

When Jacob had gone missing and not returned, Walter'd known something bad had happened. He'd watched that Mr. Coulton depart in a coach for Edinburgh, scarcely able to conceal his dislike. Maybe the man had abandoned Jacob, or killed him even, left his body in an alley somewhere. Certainly Coulton was the kind capable of it.

That was around the time the disease made itself felt. Consumption. He'd coughed sharply into his hand one winter and his hand had come away wet with blood and he'd seen it and known what it meant. Give him one year, give him five, it didn't matter. It would kill him sure enough.

But then came the dreams.

Jacob, whispering to him. Visiting him. Sitting with him, calmly, gently. His old friend, his only friend. And promising him that he could help, that he could make him better, make him healthy and no longer alone. That he was coming back to Cairndale. And he would take Walter with him, this time, when he went.

A door opened somewhere in the pantry overhead. Walter stood very silent with the lantern raised, listening, and then he continued to the cellar wall. It was cut into the rock, lined with shelves. He fumbled for a catch in the third shelf and found it and then the shelf slid smoothly forward, as if on rails, and then swung aside. A foul damp air poured past.

Walter was staring down into the utter darkness of a tunnel. It was perfectly round, as if it had been bored from the rock by a massive industrial drill. He wet his lips, nervous. Jacob was waiting for him, depending on him.

He lifted the lantern, and hurried in.

There were nights when Henry Berghast would walk the unlit halls of Cairndale, watching the darkness, feeling the movement of air across his skin and the way time moved around him and through him, like sand through a fist, and he would feel his body decay.

Aging. That is what it was, still strange to him, even after decades.

He would drift in his waistcoat and shirtsleeves with his collar stiff past the closed doors, the display cabinets, the framed watercolors and etchings on the walls, all of them strange in the night dark. And he would lose himself in his own remembering, remembering the way the sun had set over the mouth of the Nile in those early years when British warships were still unknown to the Egyptians, and how the air in the jungles of New Spain had smelled of rotting fruit. He would recall the many dead he had known, his colleagues, his friends, some of them famous now in the annals of science. Gradually, over the centuries, his friendships and attachments had fallen away. He had been alone a long time now, had watched those he loved grow old and die, abandoning him, leaving him with nothing, no one, only an ache where his love for them had been. There had been his parents, centuries dead; and a brother; and even a wife and child once, a little girl—what was her name?—who had liked white flowers and brought him joy, though all their faces were long since lost to him, and to remember them now was like reading of them in the pages of a book, a book written by someone else. He had been told many years ago that all talents, even the most powerful haelans, must age and die. He had waited for it. But he had not aged.

He had instead, he considered with a quiet detachment, slowly corrupted from the inside out, corrupted like an old piece of fruit, blackening and dying and the rot spreading, until what he was and what he appeared to be bore no relation. If you live long enough, you cease to be human, you cease to understand anything that fills the human heart. For the heart is made of time, and consumed by time, by the knowledge of its own eventual death, and Berghast could not die.

Except . . . *now* he *could.*

That was the cruel part of it, he thought, as he descended the stairs and drifted through the lower halls. *He* was the greater talent, *he* was the one whose existence ought to go on, it was *he* and no other who had seen and known true power. He had glimpsed a power like his own in another only once, in that ancient creature known as the drughr. She was beautiful, and terrifying, an intoxicating creature. Something of the absolute filled her, some deep inhuman purity, and Berghast had seen it and hated it and desired it. He knew the drughr was stalking the baby, just as Jacob was. And he knew, too, that there had been a prophecy long ago, from a glyphic in a cave in Bulgaria: a child would be born in the other world, in the land of the dead, a living child who would cut the fabric of the worlds and remake the talents in his own image. The Dark Talent.

Berghast had hunted that child for years, reducing his own talent in the process. And now, because of Jacob, the boy had been found.

Found, yes, and made safe; but Berghast was too weak to do anything with him, too weak to use him as he needed to, as he wanted to. It was a bitter knowledge. His talent had seeped away, so that he no longer healed, and now there was nothing but the long slow pain of his dying.

It filled him with a fury beyond imagining.

30

THE UNDER–TUNNEL

Jacob Marber found the cave entrance half-hidden by gnarled, wet undergrowth, on a low rise of rock, overlooking the valley. The entrance was narrow, the rock slick and cold. But just within, the roof lifted and the walls widened, and the tunnel opened right out.

He'd left a candle in a dish just inside the entrance. He took off his gloves, folded them twice, slid them into the pocket of his frock coat. Then he rubbed the dust between his fingers and a small blue flame erupted and he lit the candle and started forward, down the sloping cavern, scrambling and sliding to the back wall where a darker crevasse opened in the earth.

He was thinking about the two children at the river, the sounds of the drughr feeding. He gave a small shudder. *There is nothing you could have done*, he told himself.

And hurried deeper.

There were passages in the earth, all under Cairndale and around it. Few knew of them. No one had mapped them. Ancient tunnels, formed by the meltwater of the last glaciers, when the great pressure of the ice scraped out the lochs of Scotland and made the land what it was.

He walked on in silence, slipping on the wet rocks, his small firelight flickering over the stone. The air was cold, sour, unpleasant. He kept a careful eye as he went. He had some idea of where to go, a left here, a right turning farther on, but the going was uncertain, and he was afraid of getting lost.

Something in the narrow darkness of the tunnels made him think, for the first time in years, of those early happy days when he and his twin brother, Bertolt, had worked as sweeps in the chimneys of Vienna. They'd felt free. The orphanage was finished with. The crew of street kids they'd found was quick, and efficient, and well-fed.

It was autumn still, the weather not yet bitingly cold, and they'd slept tiredly together in a disused cellar among old casks, needing neither blanket nor fire. The other kids, the ones they'd joined, lay sprawled all around them each night, and each morning the sweep boss would meet with them in the alley and give out the brooms and pans and addresses for the day's work.

They were nine years old. It was the first time Jacob had noticed how beautiful the city was, the tramcars and the ladies in their finery and the smells of the vending carts in the parks. Bertolt showed him everything, as if somehow he knew the city, knew the world in ways Jacob didn't. He'd always been the bold one, of course, the clever one, Bertolt had, the one who made things happen. "Because you're special, Jake," Bertolt would say, "because you need someone to watch out for you. That's why. I can't do what you can do. I'm not special." He'd always talked like that, whispering it at night, his face on the orphanage pillow, while the nuns patrolled the hallways in grim darkness. He always made Jacob feel like living was worth it, like you didn't give up, no matter how hard it got. But Jacob knew it wasn't true too, what Bertolt said—his brother *was* special, he had a goodness and a cleverness that no one else had, especially not Jacob himself. All through his earliest years Jacob admired him and wished he was more like him and loved him more than life itself.

There came a sound from the tunnel behind him. Jacob paused, listening. A dap of water on stone. He wasn't the only creature down here, moving through the darkness, with purpose.

The sound didn't come again. The tunnel was impossibly black only a few feet in either direction. He stood in the dirty halo of candlelight, looking back and forth in both directions, feeling small and alone.

Maybe Henry Berghast knew he was coming. The thought came to him in a flash. But then he disregarded it; it could not be so. Anyway, there was no turning back now.

He crept on, his blood loud in his ears. The darkness parted to let him pass and when he had passed that same darkness closed in behind him, absolute.

After Dr. Berghast had left, Susan Crowley rose swiftly and threw on a shawl and lit a candle and went to the door. She listened. He was gone.

So. He wanted to send the baby away.

The wrongness of it startled her, angered her. She wasn't used to feeling angry, it wasn't an emotion that came easily to her, she'd lived all her life being told what to do and where to go and how to get there, and the right to be angry wasn't something she knew much about. But this filled her with a quick surprising heat. What did Dr. Berghast know of babies and their needs, their safety? He refused even to hold the child. She was blinking sharply, trying to think it through.

It's not like she hadn't imagined it, sometimes, fleeing with the baby into the night, away from Cairndale, away from Dr. Berghast. But always the baby was older, less delicate, hardier. And she knew, too, that her fantasies were only just that: fantasies.

She went quickly over to the cradle and checked that he was sleeping safely and then she went out into the hall. She was looking for Miss Davenshaw, not sure just what it was she'd say, but sure that the older woman would have something worth the saying. She knew Miss Davenshaw had her own misgivings about Dr. Berghast, and the way Cairndale was run. Oh, it was nothing the blind woman had said out loud—she was far too discreet for that—but rather the silences, the disapproving frowns.

But Miss Davenshaw was not in her rooms. Susan passed two girls, talents she did not know by name, hurrying down the hall, both in their nightdresses and looking guilty. She gave them a weak smile. They blushed, hurried on.

She knew that feeling, that fear of getting caught, whatever it was. Strange to think she was only a few years older than they.

On the landing she caught a glimpse of a woman in black, her face veiled. It was that grim woman up from London. Susan nodded politely, hurried past. That woman frightened her. She was a confidante of Dr. Berghast and did his bidding in the capital and was not to be trusted.

In the foyer, Susan found Miss Davenshaw seated on the long sofa, in front of the fire, her hands clasped in her lap. She might have been waiting for Susan, so quiet and patient did she appear.

"What is the matter, Miss Crowley?" the blind woman said, even before Susan could speak.

She cleared her throat. She didn't know how to begin.

"I find," said the older woman, "the easiest way to begin a sentence, is by opening one's mouth and speaking."

"Yes, Miss Davenshaw. I'm sorry. I just . . . I just had a visit from Dr. Berghast. He said he intends to send the baby away."

The blind woman turned her face. "Away?"

"Yes. He didn't say where."

"He wishes you to accompany the child?"

"Yes."

"Well, there is that, at least. When are you to depart?"

Susan shook her head. It wasn't what she wanted to say at all, it was coming out all wrong. "I don't want to go, Miss Davenshaw. That's what I mean. I don't think the baby should be sent anywhere. He's so small, still."

Miss Davenshaw lowered her chin. "And yet babies do travel, Miss Crowley." She smoothed out her dress. "Did he give you any explanation, any reason? No?" When Susan said nothing, the older woman lowered her voice so that Susan had to lean in to hear her.

"It is my own feeling, Miss Crowley," she said darkly, "that the child would be better off anywhere but at Cairndale. If you take my meaning."

The air under the earth grew thicker. Jacob spied the glow of the lantern, its splash across the tunnel walls and ceiling, long before he saw the man himself. He blew out his own candle.

"Hello, Walter," he said quietly.

The man gave a start and peered frightened around. He was short, slight of build, with a sickly pallor in his cheeks, as if he were already leeched of life. Jacob knew he was dying of consumption. His hair had thinned on top though he was not much more than thirty, and he wore it long around the crest of his scalp as if to compensate. More likely, he just didn't much care. Large nervous eyes. A tremble in his gullet. He believed Jacob his friend and Jacob knew this; it was pitiful; it was pathetic.

"Jacob? Is it you?" he whispered.

Jacob stepped out of the shadows, letting the dust dissipate, so the man could see him clearly. Walter peered up at him, half in awe, half in fear.

"I come to where you said to," said Walter. "I did. I been here I don't know how long. But I brung the lantern, like you said. You'll take me with you, this time? You promised, Jacob—"

"We haven't much time," said Jacob.

Walter nodded vigorously, but he didn't move. "Yes, yes, of course, you're right," he mumbled. "We must hurry. Yes." But then he cast a sly anxious glance sidelong at Jacob. "But you will, won't you? Take me with you, I mean? It's just—"

"Yes, Walter."

He swallowed. "Tonight? You'll take me tonight? Should I pack anything, a bag, maybe—"

Jacob looked down at the man, shivering with cold or fear or something else. He said nothing. He could feel his irritation rising.

"It's just, my lungs don't feel so great," Walter continued. "And you said, I mean I don't know if you remember it all that clear, but you said you'd um, help me with that? There was a way to—"

Jacob glared pointedly past the man, up the tunnel.

"It's just um, you're my friend and, I mean, you said you would—"

"Walter," Jacob said coldly. "I am your friend. Your one true friend. I have come for you, also. Now. You must go on ahead and make sure no one is near. I cannot be seen. Will you do that for me? When I have what I came for, we will go together."

The small man nodded and nodded. "Right, yes. The baby. Yes?"

"Yes."

Walter gulped. "Oh, yes, yes, you're right. I'm sorry. Yes. I'll go on ahead."

And he scurried off down the tunnel, in a queer ratlike fashion, the lantern swinging dangerously from his outslung hand. And Jacob followed.

The child was near. He could *feel* it.

The darkness in the tunnel grayed. Ahead was an opening. At last

Jacob slipped noiselessly through a broken wall, into the murky cellar of Cairndale. The familiar smell. The old creak of its floorboards. Walter was nowhere to be seen. Jacob brushed a gauzy web from his face, and a rush of memories came back to him, so that he stood at the threshold and swallowed and closed his eyes.

Home. He was home.

Abigail Davenshaw rose from the sofa in the foyer, where she'd been waiting well over an hour now, and she started grimly for the dining hall. Enough fretting, she told herself.

The children would arrive. They always did. If not tonight, then in the morning.

The dining hall was quiet, dark. It had been cleared hours ago. She had no appetite but perhaps a pot of tea would calm her nerves, allow her to sleep. She had asked to have something put aside for the children when they arrived but though she called out, no one answered. She made her way through to the back kitchens. They had all gone.

But as she was turning to leave she felt something, a faint chilled breeze, coming from the cellar. She thought at first a door or a window had been opened or broken. But the air smelled strange, damp and sour, like an emptied grave.

She made her way down the stairs, into the cellar. She did not know this storeroom well, and went with care, feeling her way along the shelves, following the breeze. And then she came to a shelf that had been clearly moved aside, and felt the cold edges of the tunnel entrance, and understood.

She'd been at Cairndale long enough to have heard the stories of tunnels under the manor. She knew Dr. Berghast had an underground passage leading from his study across to the island, to the orsine there. But she'd not heard of a tunnel here.

She withdrew slowly, thinking about it. And then she made her way back up to the kitchens. A serving girl, Mary, exclaimed in surprise at Abigail's emerging from the cellars, but Abigail had little patience for it.

"Send for Mr. Smythe," she said sharply. "And Mrs. Harrogate, if you can find her. Tell them to bring lanterns. There is something in the cellars that must be seen to. Hurry."

"Yes, ma'am," said the girl, catching the tone in her voice.

Abigail Davenshaw listened to the girl's shoes clatter away across the floor. What she was thinking was that some of the children, the young talents, must have descended into the tunnels on a lark. But it would be dangerous, she knew, and if they became lost . . .

It did not occur to her—not in that moment, at least—that the tunnel mouth had been opened for the very opposite reason: because something had come in.

Quickly, now.

Jacob hurried up the stairs, through the kitchens, along the back passages to the servants' stairs, up two more flights to the rooms at the top of the east wing. It felt strange, being back. He knew these halls, these rooms, the very shape of the manor as if he had always lived in it and never been away, even now, even with its differences, a strange shelf, a new wallpaper, a framed watercolor over a bureau that had not been there before.

He was surprised at how angry it made him. But surprised, too, by the longing that came over him as he crept through the dim halls. He saw no one. But he could feel through the walls the sleeping talents, the young ones dreaming of their unlived lives, and the old ones, nearly dead now, dry and thin as paper. They meant nothing to him. They had done nothing to help him, to bring him back from that other

world, to offer him refuge when he'd glimpsed the true nature of the
drughr and recoiled in fear. Somewhere ahead he could hear Walter,
moving with a surprising stealth, his lantern shuttered now, stifling a
cough now and then. Perhaps the man was not as useless as he seemed.
Jacob himself walked calmly, with long slow strides, as if these rooms
and this manor were his own.

But he was not calm, not really. He was listening with all his powers for a particular footfall. For somewhere among all of it, he knew,
stalked Henry Berghast, restless, fierce, suspicious.

He'd known men like him, even as a boy, even on the streets of
Vienna. Men who wanted what they wanted and let nothing get in the
way, neither pity nor scorn nor human frailty. His brother, Bertolt, had
fallen prey to such a man. Herr Gould, their sweep boss, had a huge
round belly like a drum, and a red face, and hands the size of shovel
blades. When he heard Bertolt had got stuck in a chimney across the
city, he'd come and tied ropes around the boy and dragged him clear,
despite his screams of pain. Jacob had tried to get up to stop it but he
couldn't, he was too little, there were men in the gathering crowd who
held him back, and it was raining that day and his talent just wasn't
strong enough to do anything. Bertolt came out dead, his head turned
backward. And Herr Gould had carted his twin brother away and
dumped him in an alley among the trash when no one was watching,
no one who mattered, that is, because Jacob and the other sweeps were
there to see it. Jacob had sat with his brother's body among the filth for
hours, while night fell around him, and when he rose at last he wasn't
the same boy.

That's how he thought of it, remembered it, now. If it was the truth
or not, who could say. But in his mind it was his brother's death that
changed him, that opened him, in time, to the drughr.

He'd laid his brother out flat with his little hands crossed on his
chest and cleaned the soot and grime from his face and neck and then

he'd got to his feet, only just nine years old, and gone in search of Herr Gould. Blind with fury. He was turned away from the drinking houses and brothels but he found the man at last in a gambling den off the Unterstrass. The man at the door took him for a messenger lad and let him through and Jacob stood in the roar and the darkness with his fists clenched and he watched Herr Gould laughing and drinking at his cards and whatever it was that was in him, whatever evil, or fury, boiled up out of him, and that talent he'd had for twisting the dust just exploded. He felt the dust come to him, swirl around his fists, and a pain and cold shot through his arms and made his head swim. He lifted his hands. His cheeks were wet.

And then the dust was shooting out from his outspread fingers, wrapping itself in ropes of darkness around the big man, his chest, his throat. And it started to squeeze.

The lanterns flickered all around the room. By then the patrons were falling over themselves, overturning tables, scrambling to get out of the way, the prostitutes screaming in fear. And Herr Gould's face reddened, then purpled, and his eyes half burst from their sockets, and the force of the dust had lifted him clean off his feet so that his big-knuckled hands were clawing at the air in horror.

When Jacob let him go, he fell in pieces to the floor. And Jacob turned, emptier even than before, and went out into the city, truly alone.

Somehow Berghast had heard of it. Somehow he'd come looking. Jacob had thought at first that the man had come to save him, but he hadn't, he knew that now. He'd come to use him, as he used everyone. Little Jacob Marber, dustworker, killer of men, was to have been his weapon.

Walter was waiting for him in a small alcove shadowed from the wall sconce nearby and he licked his lips and pointed to the nursemaid's door.

"It's in there, Jacob," the man whispered. "But the nurse is with it. She's always with it. Don't never leave it alone."

"*He* is a *baby*, Walter. Not an *it*. And why ever would she leave him alone?"

The man nodded obsequiously. "Yes, yes, of course, why ever *would* she, hm?"

But Jacob was unnerved all the same. Berghast had put the baby in Jacob's old room. He murmured instructions to Walter, telling how the man was to distract the nursemaid, and then he watched as Walter rapped softly on the door and stuck his hands in his pockets, then took them out, then smoothed his greasy hair.

Jacob slid forward, soundless.

The nursemaid who answered the door was young, a girl still, big-boned and black-haired. She watched Walter with a wary politeness as he spoke, asking after her, gesturing past her at something in the room, something needing repair, then stepping briskly through despite her protestations.

As she turned in irritation—"I beg your pardon, Mr. Laster, what do you think you are doing, I did *not* invite you in, sir, the wee babe is *sleeping*"—Jacob drew a fine cloud of dust around him, like a veil of darkness, and let himself silently in behind her. Then he crept along the perimeter of his old room. The nursemaid had lit only the two candles and it was easy for him to keep to the shadows.

Walter was making some nervous joke about a clock on the mantel, laughing weirdly.

Jacob slipped over to the curtain, moved it just slightly. Creeping like a nightmare toward the cradle. He held his breath. There, he saw, was the tangle of blankets.

And there, the helpless child.

31

THE BEGINNING

The fire crackled in the grate. Henry Berghast leaned back from his desk, uneasy, dissatisfied, unable to do any work at all. He screwed back on the lid of his ink bottle and drummed his fingers on his closed journal and then he put on his hat and took up a lantern and went down to the underground passage that led across to the orsine. If the drughr were to come, it would of necessity be through there.

He walked swiftly. He had not informed Bailey of his going. No matter.

What was troubling him was not, in fact, the drughr. No. He saw no reason to believe the drughr's reach could extend past the glyphic's wards. No; it was, he understood, the nursemaid Crowley. He did not like the way she had reacted when he told her the child must be sent away, for its own protection. Would she prove an impediment? He was not sure.

He was sure, however, of the danger. It would be only a matter of time before Jacob Marber came for the baby, before the drughr came.

He knew this with a certainty. The glyphic had hinted as much, some days ago. It was not the child's welfare of course but everything the child represented—the possibility of power, of redemption—that drew both the drughr and Henry himself to it, like lake pike to the scent of blood in the water. It was an old, endless game of strategy that he and the drughr played. The child might yet prove decisive.

The lantern was high in his fist. He ascended the stairs at the far end of the tunnel, his long legs taking them two at a time, and he paused in the night air. The scumbled stones and broken walls of the old monastery rose up around him in the darkness. He looked back across the loch at Cairndale, lit against the sky like a ship at anchor. Something was not right.

He frowned, brushed the worry from his mind. One could prepare, and then one could wait. But worry served no purpose.

He ducked his head and with the lantern held out before him made his way through the ruined monastery and down to the cistern below. Even before he had emerged from the curving stone stairs he could sense something was wrong. The chamber, usually lit a faint blue color, the reflected shine of the orsine, was furiously bright. The orsine was shining in full blast.

He held a hand to his eyes and squinted, uncertain. It had never been so bright before.

For a long impossible moment he stood, thinking. If the orsine was alight, it meant it had opened. If it had opened, it meant the glyphic's powers were—

And then, in a growing fear, he understood. He turned swiftly on his heel and ran. He ran for the tunnel and took the stairs three at a time and ran with his long scissorlike strides the length of it beneath the loch, the lantern swinging dangerously in his fist, and when he got back to his study he hurtled out through the antechamber and past an astonished Mr. Bailey and he did not stop, he did not slow, though his hat flew from his head and several old talents and a few of the young children stopped in the halls to watch him pass, unnerved, alarmed. He did not stop or slow until he reached Miss Crowley's rooms, until he reached the baby.

The east wing was quiet, calm. He tried to slow his breathing, he adjusted his waistcoat and combed his fingers with his hair and then he knocked firmly.

He heard Miss Crowley's irritated voice even before she opened the door. "Mr. Laster, sir, you really must—" Then she fell silent, staring up at Berghast in surprise. "Oh, forgive me, sir, I thought you were—"

"Laster. Yes." He pushed past her. Some part of his brain flickered at that, wondering why the gatekeeper would be bothering the nursemaid. But then it was gone. "Where is the child, Miss Crowley?" he said quietly. "There has been no . . . disturbance?"

"Disturbance, sir?"

"You have been here all this time?"

"Yes, sir."

He looked all around. The rooms seemed quiet, warm, just as he'd left them. He dialed his face slowly toward the curtain, toward the crib that would be just beyond it, willing his heart to calm down. Had he been mistaken?

"The wee thing's sleeping, sir. Not a peep out of him." Miss Crowley put a hand to her throat, her nose crinkling. "But what has happened, Dr. Berghast? Is something the matter?"

He did not answer her. A dread was rising in him. He went to the curtain, drew it slowly back, and stared down at the crib.

It was empty.

Jacob held the swaddled thing close to his chest as he ran through the halls. The soft warm weight of it. The smallness of it. He half feared he might smother it and he kept slowing and lifting its face away to peer down at it in its blanket and then looking up and around and running on.

He'd left Walter. He'd just scooped the baby into his arms and turned and slipped out of the nursemaid's rooms with the dust cloaking his presence as before, scarcely daring to look at the child, to marvel at its sweetness and wonder at his holding him again, but once in the outer hall he abandoned all deceits and he just ran.

The hour was late. He needed to get back to the cellars, to the tunnel. He feared being seen, of course; but more, he feared the drughr's power would fail, and the glyphic's wards would return to strength, and he would be trapped inside Cairndale's walls.

He slowed in the servants' corridor. There were voices ahead in the kitchens and he stopped at the door, lurking in the shadow, listening. He thought it must be the cooks or the serving staff but he was wrong, it was two men talking about missing kids, a tunnel in the cellars. He heard a third voice call up from below, then retreat away. They'd found the tunnel.

He melted back into darkness, alarmed.

The corridor was long, flagstoned, its walls peeling with ancient gray paint. There were candle sconces standing empty along the walls. Several doors, all shut, and then the stairs at the back. He was trying to think how he might get out. He slid his coat over the baby to muffle any cry it might make and then he turned at a sound. Footsteps. Someone was coming.

He swallowed, freed his hands for the dustwork. He had some confidence he could strangle whoever approached, unless they proved a talent of some strength.

But just then someone hissed his name. "Jacob, this way! Come!"

It was Walter, peering through a half-opened door just down the way. Jacob didn't hesitate. In a flash he was across and through and the door was closing. They were in a kind of narrow broom closet, the only light creeping in through a crack in the door. Jacob could smell the sour reek of sickness coming out of Walter's clothes. The small man looked up at him, held a finger to his lips.

Whoever hurried past did not slow.

Then Jacob felt a gentle tugging at his sleeve. It was Walter, leading him deeper back into the closet. At the far wall the little man pressed a hidden panel, and a door appeared.

Jacob followed him through. He was feeling wonder and a savage amazement. He'd seduced Walter because the man was weak, vulnerable, an easy mark. He'd not imagined the man also might be genuinely resourceful.

Walter's hidden passage led through to a small sitting room, its furniture draped in white sheets. Jacob caught a glimpse of the three of them—himself, Walter, the baby—in a tall clouded mirror standing near a window. Apparitions, each one. Then they were slipping soundlessly out into the grand foyer of Cairndale Manor.

It stood empty and dark. The great hearth had burned down to embers. Jacob moved quickly toward the front doors but he wasn't even halfway when Walter stopped in alarm.

There was a figure standing in front of the doors. A woman, thin, severe, with a cloth tied over her eyes. She was, Jacob realized, blind.

"Just where do you think you are going?" she said.

Walter was looking at Jacob in fear, confusion flickering across his face. He waved his hands in some furtive way as if to communicate something but Jacob felt a sharp impatience bloom inside him and he stepped forward.

"You have mistaken us for another," he said coldly.

And then the baby started to cry.

Jacob watched her face turn toward him in the darkness. She seemed to register his words. "I believe," she said slowly, "that is true."

That was all. And yet, it was as if she had said: *I know what you are here for, Jacob Marber. I know what you* are. Somehow—maybe from her expression, or the silence that hung after, broken only by the thin cry of the child—Jacob got the distinct feeling that she knew exactly what was happening. Blind or not, she *knew*.

And it was then he sensed a shift in the gloom all around them, and he looked down in surprise and saw the baby, the child, was flickering with a faint blue shine.

"Miss Davenshaw, ma'am—" Walter began.

"Mr. Laster?" she said, in surprise. "It was you—?"

Jacob acted fast. He drew the dust and smoke from within his flesh and crushed it tight in his fist and then he lashed it in a long slow arc out at the blind woman, like a whip, so that it struck her viciously on the back of her head, and hurled her forward across the floor. Her body knocked against the base of the stairs and slid sidelong toward Jacob and Walter and came to a stop.

And then Jacob Marber, dark with fury, smoldering, stepped over her crumpled figure, and kicked open the big doors and went out into the night, the baby shining brighter and brighter in his arms.

Henry Berghast glared down at the empty cradle, furious. And just then a sharp voice interrupted his thoughts.

"Dr. Berghast! I've been looking for you, sir."

He turned. Mrs. Harrogate was standing in the open door, peering in with an odd expression. She looked from Miss Crowley to Berghast and then back.

"There has been a discovery, in the cellars," she continued crisply. "A tunnel. Miss Davenshaw fears some of the children might have got out." Her voice faltered. "What. What is the matter here?"

Henry felt the blood move through his skull. He put a hand to the wall, as if to hold himself upright. Miss Crowley was wringing her foolish hands.

"No one has got out, Mrs. Harrogate," he whispered. "Rather, someone has got in."

"I beg your pardon?"

Henry went swiftly to the window and drew back the curtains and threw the casement wide. The night was cold, vast, deep. "It will be Jacob. Mr. Laster is assisting him. They have taken the baby, Mrs. Harrogate. They have stolen the child."

Miss Crowley gave a little whimper, sank onto the sofa.

"My God—" said Mrs. Harrogate. She sounded angry.

But Henry was already thinking. "He is still here. There is still time. You have discovered his path of escape, therefore he will need to leave by a different way. Across the fields, perhaps? No. No, he will go down by the loch and use the cliffs for cover. Somehow the glyphic's wards have been reduced." As he spoke he hurried from window to window and then he left the room entirely and hurried along the hall, stopping at each window to get a better glimpse. And then he saw it, he saw what he was looking for.

Out across the fields, on the low slope down toward the loch, just as he'd presumed, he saw a faint blue flickering in the darkness. The baby. The shining boy.

"There you are," he whispered.

Jacob knew they must have seen him, he knew there was no time. He gave no thought to the blind woman he had struck down, back at the institute. She was nothing to him. He ran, feeling his frock coat snap out behind him, the night air slapping cold on his face, his boots sliding crazily in the slick grass of the slope. Somewhere ahead lay the dark loch, beyond that the cliffs. If he could only reach them he could slip across the stone perimeter of Cairndale, out of the glyphic's grasp.

The baby was crying and would not stop. Walter was wheezing, falling behind, calling to him weakly to slow. But he didn't slow, he couldn't. His arms were fairly crackling with the blue shine from the baby now. The child was wrapped in a blanket and burrowed inside Jacob's coat and yet the shine still poured forth. There would be no hiding him.

He risked a glance back. Cairndale's windows were alight.

Then: something happened. He didn't understand it at first. It was a kind of prickling, a pain, all across his skin and his face and his scalp, so that he stumbled. The baby felt hot, impossibly so. He fumbled for the child in his coat and pulled him clear and held him and stared down into his shining face.

And the shine intensified.

He was no longer thinking, acting purely on instinct. Perhaps he would have acted differently, otherwise. But he kneeled down in the muck of the slope under a black night sky and he tried to summon the dust; he tried to enclose the baby in a sphere of darkness. He was thinking he might still conceal the shine. He might yet hold it in.

But the pain intensified. Soon his skin was stinging and then his eyes started to cloud over and an agony erupted in his flesh. Through the cloud of dust the baby's blue light grew.

Too late, he understood. There was no containing it.

And then came a blinding flash, followed by a wind that roared in Jacob's ears, and he was thrown spinning into the air, like a rag doll. And the ground came up to meet him in a rush.

Scorched earth, still smoldering.

That was all Margaret Harrogate could see in the eerie glow of the lanterns. Scorched and torn earth, and the raked-up marks of some manner of struggle. She, too, had seen the blue flash of light from the institute windows and come running.

"My God, what—?" she murmured, her breath standing out in the cold.

Dr. Berghast turned in place, staring around at the darkness. "The child," he whispered. "The baby did this. Where is he? Where is Jacob?"

"The baby did this?" Margaret doubted very much that it was the baby's doing. But who was she to say? She shook her head. "Your Jacob has eluded us, Dr. Berghast. The baby—"

"Is not with him."

She raised her lantern so that she could see his face clearly. There were nearly two dozen others coming down from the manor, lanterns and torches burning against the darkness. She watched them fan out and begin to search.

"Here," said Berghast, pushing at the mud with his boot. "You can see where Jacob fell. And how he left, this way, at a run. He's injured. Look at the way his boot prints stagger. But here"—and he walked some feet away, to a patch of scorched earth—"here you see a new set of prints. Smaller. A woman's. Or a girl's. This is who found the baby. She goes off in that direction."

Margaret listened to all this with incredulity. "A girl?" she murmured. "You cannot imagine one of the students here has taken the baby? One of the students has been in league with Jacob Marber? I do not believe it."

Dr. Berghast scowled. "Of course not, Mrs. Harrogate. Though Jacob did have his confederate here, among us."

"Mr. Laster will regret this."

"Mr. Laster is already dead," snapped Berghast. "He just does not realize it."

"His sickness—"

"Is most advanced. Yes."

Margaret paced between the two sets of prints, swinging her lantern side to side. "They do not go in the same direction. Marber's prints, and this other's."

"Because they are not together. I expect the young woman has stolen our ward and made off with him. She will be heading for Edinburgh, no doubt. And from there, south into England. Jacob will be . . . disappointed."

Margaret sensed there was much she did not understand. She could see the searchers moving across the grounds of the institute, combing through the undergrowth. "Who was it?" she asked. "Who took the child?"

But Berghast didn't answer. She watched him peer around at the lanterns alive in the darkness, their reflections in the black water of the loch. Slowly, his face filled with satisfaction.

"She'll not get far," he said softly.

Two miles away, in the darkness, Susan Crowley was stumbling and falling and getting back up, the baby snug inside her cloak for warmth, the only sound the gasp and frightened moaning that she herself made as she ran.

Cairndale was already far behind her. And somewhere back there was that man, that monster, Jacob Marber, who had stolen the child out from under her, and too Dr. Berghast, with his sinister unblinking eyes and his hungry manner. Oh, the poor babe. Dr. Berghast wished to send him away, to hide him from the world. He'd be safe only when she'd got him away, she knew, when she'd taken him out into the world away from that horrid manor with its talents and nefarious purposes. The poor creature ought to choose its own way in the world, choose who it wanted to be. And there'd be no choosing at Cairndale.

She stopped, listening. Her heart was pounding. She could hear no sound of pursuit but she knew they'd be coming. She'd left in a panic, throwing her cloak over her old clothes, ill-dressed for the weather and with no food at all. Well, she'd borne worse than hunger, hadn't she? So be it. There was no moon and that was maybe a good thing, even if it meant she had to keep to the middle of the mucky road as she went, her skirts heavy and clumped with mud. She was too afraid of losing her way to care. All around her in the gloom the strange wild blackness of the Scottish landscape pressed in.

Toward morning a farmer stopped for her, and she and the baby rode on into the Edinburgh markets huddled among sacks of vegetables. If he disapproved of her traveling unaccompanied he said nothing. She'd had the foresight to take the little money she'd kept at the back of her dresser and with this she purchased a third-class ticket south into England at the Princes Street Station, and she and the baby rode at the back of the railway carriage with their faces averted. There was a bubble of sadness around them that made them nearly unapproachable.

Long gray days, bleary with lack of sleep. The baby was hungry, the baby was tired. Susan fed him and washed him and changed him as best she could. Sometimes she would stroke his cheek and he would stare up into her eyes or reach out and grab her nose or poke her chin and she would smile gravely. She had lost one baby; she would not lose another. There was such innocence and such eagerness for the world in him. She didn't know what to do, where to go. She had a vague notion that Dr. Berghast would hunt her on the railways, that he would send his people after her, and so in Leicester she got on a passenger train heading east to Norwich and from Norwich she traveled south to Cambridge and sometime later when the money had nearly run out she snuck the baby aboard a freight train heading west again.

It was in that freight car, late one night, while the rain came down outside, that the baby started to shine with a fierce exquisite blue light, that same blue shining she had seen engulf Jacob Marber. She didn't know what to do, how to stop it. She was afraid her milk wasn't coming in right, that it hadn't been for days now. She was so tired. She opened her blouse to feed him, felt him begin to suck. She tried to close her eyes against the shine.

But then a terrible blazing pain erupted in her chest. Her skin started to boil. She cried out in agony and tried to pull the baby away, but it was too late, she was already falling backward, into the straw, the pain washing over her in waves, everything going black.

The train rattled and clattered on.

The baby, shining in the straw, started to cry.

Just then, outside across the passing fields, a brown-haired girl burst from the trees. She was clawing her way up the embankment in the rain, throwing herself forward for the door of the freight car, dragging herself gasping up. Dogs erupted out of the tree break, far behind.

And a man in a tall hat stood his horse in the dusk and raised a rifle to his shoulder and took aim.

INTO
SMOKE

·

1882

32

THE MAN ON
THE DEAD STAIRS

Charlie Ovid was descending, the knife in his fist.

A water that was not water was all around him and his shirt was suspended in it and he held his breath until his lungs nearly burst and he could not hold it any longer. Then he was gasping, breathing somehow; a ghostly blue light played upon his skin, the walls. He could make out stairs, a banister carved of wood, printed wallpaper. The stairs turned and turned as they descended.

Marlowe was nowhere.

But Charlie could hear a sound, like water in a pipe, all around. When he was thirteen and living along the Sutchee River in Mississippi he would go down on Saturday evenings after a week in the hot fields and lie in the quiet water and his head would sink so low that his ears were underwater. Going through the orsine was like that, exactly like that, like all at once his ears were filled with the sound of the pressure in his own skull, and it was his own blood he was hearing, frighteningly loud, but muffled somehow too. Except it wasn't just in his ears now, but all around him, in his whole body.

A quiet, thrumming inside him.

A quiet so terrible it left a high thin ringing in his ears.

There was water, and then there was not. As if the water had dissolved into air, into shadow. The stairs led down to a large foyer, dimly lit. A door with sidelight windows encased in polished wood, an oiled bench, a pier table with a cut flower wilting in its vase. The walls were covered in a strange green slime, a kind of mold maybe, and the carpet underfoot oozed water at every step. The light was strange, particled, grainy, and gray. He raised his face, slowly, slowly, as if underwater, and he saw Marlowe watching him from the doorway. The kid said something, but it was muffled, garbled, and Charlie could not understand.

"Mar-lowe," he tried to say, but it sounded like it was coming from far away.

There was something familiar about the foyer they were in. Marlowe turned, dreamlike, and opened the door and stepped outside. He crossed through a carriage house and slipped past a rusting iron gate, leaning crazily from one hinge, and out into the street. The cobblestones were overgrown with lush green weeds. There were dark puddles in the roadbed and water dripping from the eaves. Charlie walked out and turned in place, amazed.

It was a city but it seemed abandoned, given over to nature, so that bushes and trees could be seen growing out of the marshy street. All around lay a thick fog, the buildings vanishing into it. There were old hansom cabs leaning unused in the muck, some overgrown with moss. In a puddle near his shoe Charlie saw a scattering of coins, a rotting leather boot.

"Charlie," said Marlowe softly.

He turned, surprised. Marlowe was breathing heavily, as if he'd been running. His voice sounded normal, only just a little muffled. He put a hand on the child's shoulder, strangely moved. It seemed like a lifetime since he had heard anyone's voice.

"What is this place?" he murmured.

But even before Marlowe spoke he'd looked up at the gloomy facade of the building they'd come out of, and he'd known. He'd known it with a cold shock: it was Nickel Street West, in London. They were standing in front of Mrs. Harrogate's building, which he'd fled from that night when the litch hunted him.

"It's London, Charlie," Marlowe whispered. "We're in London."

And it was true, they were. But it was also, at the same time, not-London. Charlie knew it as sure as he knew anything at all. All around lay long green weeds, dripping water, black toxic puddles no deeper than his ankles. A wall of white fog was drifting all around them. He remembered what Berghast had said about the fog, the spirits of the dead, and he drew Marlowe back inside the gate. The stillness, the absence of people, and horses, and rats, all made it feel eerie and wrong. Charlie swallowed. He looked at the gritty brown bricks, the green of a velvet window sash overhead, the yellow and slick black of rotting wood beams. The city had no smell: that was the strangest thing of all. Just a faint charred tang, that sat in the nostrils like grime.

The fog drifted past, away. He took out the map from the satchel and turned it, trying to find a landmark.

"I think . . . I think we go this way, Mar," he said.

When he looked up, he became aware of shapes moving in the fog: narrow, shimmering columns of air. Not *in* the fog. They *were* the fog.

Marlowe took a soft step out into the street, staring. He could see them too. "They're spirits, Charlie," he whispered. "Look. They're pretty."

And they were: like twisting ribbons of breath, but shaped, and always moving, their blurred faces shifting and shuddering, one moment the face of a little girl, then that face blurring into an old woman's, then back. And Charlie, somehow, understood. Spirits, Dr. Berghast had

said, were memories, memories and forgettings; these were the faces
of a life lived, memories made real, but at the same time never staying,
never pausing, without any present to hold on to. There were hundreds of them, thousands maybe, all hovering very still in the street. A
city of the dead, Berghast had called it.

They were facing the building. They were facing the mouth of the
orsine, a great vast crowd of the dead. It was like they could sense the
world of the living beyond, like they were drawn to it. Charlie shivered.

"Can they see us?" Marlowe asked. "Do you think they know we're
here?"

"I don't know. We've got to be careful."

"There's so many, Charlie."

"Yeah." All at once the sadness of it overwhelmed him, and he had
to look away. "Hey. How're you feeling, Mar?"

The little boy furrowed his brow. "I feel . . . like I've been here
before. Like I know this place."

"Your hands aren't shaking?"

"I'm okay, Charlie."

"We've got to go fast, anyhow." Charlie glanced up the street, at the
specters swirling past. They were so beautiful. But something about
it didn't feel right; he didn't like how easy it was to get lost in them.
"Come on," he said, and started in the other direction, creeping carefully around the dead.

But all up and down the overgrown street, there were spirits adrift,
a wall of mist rising like heat shimmer over the setts, and finding a way
around them was not easy.

When they'd reached the end of the street, Charlie turned, looked
back. The fog of the dead was densely packed around the orsine. As
if waiting.

They hurried on. They skirted the dark puddles as best they could.
Always in the shallows lay strange objects, like memories, a fading old

tintype, a child's shoe. Charlie was afraid of getting lost but he didn't know what else to do. The city was like the London they had been in, but also not, crisscrossed with alleys and courts that he was sure didn't exist on the real Nickel Street. The buildings shimmered in places, sometimes looking new, sometimes crumbling, sometimes gone entire and in their place buildings of ancient wood. It was like the city was a dream of all its own pasts too.

Charlie led Marlowe down to the great river. The far bank was lost in fog. Where Blackfriars Bridge should have been, there was only embankment, and a slick, crooked, wooden stair leading down to a jetty. The water looked strange, black, thick like ink. Charlie turned in place, confused, and peered the length of the river. There were no bridges at all.

Instead he saw, crawling across the surface, small watercraft, moving sluggishly, poled by solitary cloaked figures in their sterns. If any passengers were aboard, they were spirits—invisible at such a distance—but the ferrymen themselves were solid, in black hoods, and cold-looking, and cruel, and Charlie drew Marlowe quickly by the shoulder away from the edge. He remembered Berghast's warning: *There are worse things in that world than Jacob Marber.*

He checked the map to take their bearings and peered past the cathedral, its dark mossy dome, and then led Marlowe unsteadily east along a street filled with watercress. Their footsteps splashed softly as they went. The gas lamps on the street corners were lit and shining in a corona of feeble light and Charlie felt again the strange almost-familiar feeling.

They turned down a covered alley and brushed past the hanging plants and waded across a watery court, the cold water reaching past their knees, and then a cobbled lane rose up out of the water and they stopped and wrung out their clothes and tried to get dry.

All the while the mists of the dead drifted past the mouth of the alley.

"How long have we been walking?" Marlowe asked, in a low whisper.

But Charlie didn't know. The light never changed. There seemed no day and no night in this world. He scraped a soft moss from a stoop with his shoe and then he sat and ran a hand over his face. He was tired. In the alley where they'd stopped there was a rusting ironshod wheel leaned up against a wall and a broken window with shards jagged as teeth. It was a cooper's shop; a sign hung over the door, blurred with weeds and grime. As he sat he took out the ring that had belonged to his mother and held it in his palm and stared at it.

And that was when the bad feeling came over him.

He didn't understand it. It was a feeling of pure fear, of panic. His heart was racing. He gripped the ring in his fist and looked over at Marlowe and saw the same terror etched into the boy's features and then he looked off at the mists and listened. He got to his feet and Marlowe did too and quietly, quickly, he tried the door of the cooper's shop. It opened easily, and in the darkness beyond he could see nothing. He and Marlowe splashed softly in, closed the door, held their breaths.

What was it? Charlie could feel his blood moving loudly in his skull. He had a hand gripping the door handle, holding it shut, and his gaze was fixed on the broken window to his right. Marlowe was in the standing water, clutching his elbows, shivering.

And that was when they heard it: a scraping out in the alley, like a metal bar was being dragged, coming closer. Something big and dark passed the window. There was a low snorting sound, as if a beast of some kind were rooting around where they'd been only moments before. Then a clanking, a splash; and the scraping noise gradually faded away until there was only silence, the slow dapping of water someplace in the darkness beyond.

Marlowe breathed and breathed. They stayed like that a long time, just waiting, in case something more was coming. But nothing did; and at last they went back out into the alley.

"What was it, Charlie?" Marlowe whispered.

"I don't know."

"You should write it into the notebook, like Dr. Berghast said to. Do you think it heard us?"

Probably, he thought. But he just looked at Marlowe and said, "It didn't hear us."

"I don't want to be here when it comes back."

He nodded at that. "Let me see your hands."

The little boy pulled back his sleeves and turned his wrists and Charlie looked. There was no sign of trembling or discoloration yet. He knew Berghast had said Marlowe was immune but he wasn't about to entrust the boy's welfare to the very man who'd sent them in here. He grimaced and took out the map and looked at it and peered around. The mists looked closer, the strange twisting figures ribboning away in them seemed almost to be looking for them. It was time to get going. At the mouth of the alley there was a sign nailed into the wall: FANNIN STREET. He reached into the satchel for the map. He couldn't see any Fannin Street anywhere.

"I reckon it's this way," he said, stuffing it back away. "It's got to be. Come on."

The dark buildings of the city loomed. They saw no sign of the creature from the alley. There was only the faceless dead in their turnings, and the water, and the cold.

The light never changed. They slept when they got tired, in the rotting second story of a tenement, somewhere north of the river. They were cold and damp and their feet were soaked clean through and they took off their shoes and dried their tender skin as best they could. It was a room with an old bedframe and no mattress, but the walls were nearly clear of fungus, the windowpane intact. They had no way of making a fire in the fireplace and no food to eat and they lay down shivering in the gloom. Time passed.

"You better put it away, Charlie," said Marlowe sleepily. "You're going to lose it."

Charlie opened his eyes. He was turning his mother's ring in his fingers again, tracing the twinned hammers on its face. He blinked. He hadn't realized.

He looked over, saw Marlowe's little face watching.

"I never told you," he said slowly. He looked away. He wanted to say nothing more but then he was talking and it was like he just couldn't stop. "I found him, Mar. My father. There was a file in Berghast's study. His name was Hywel. He was at Cairndale when he was young, just like us. A strong, like Mr. Coulton was. Ribs said there's this group living in London, exiles. Talents who've lost their powers. She said it's sad to see. That's what happened to my father. He ended up down there with them, alone."

"He wasn't alone," said Marlowe, with a quiet conviction.

Charlie, shivering, rolled over. "Yeah, he was. But it's okay. It was all a long time ago."

"He wasn't alone, Charlie. He had you."

Charlie swallowed a knot in his throat, unhappy. He was so tired. "I don't know where he got this stupid ring," he added. "He gave it to my mama when they got married. It was precious to her. It came from Cairndale, obviously. I don't know, maybe they give them out when you lose your talent."

"I don't think they do anything nice if you lose your talent," said Marlowe quietly.

"Maybe he won it in a card game. Or stole it."

Marlowe nodded, his eyelids heavy.

"I won't ever know though, will I? Not for real, I mean." The ring felt cold in his fist, unusually heavy. He did something strange then, he worked it free of the leather cord and slid it onto his finger. It glowed like a strip of silver light in the gloom. He didn't remember it fitting his finger so well before.

"Thing is," he murmured, "you waste all this time dreaming of where you came from, cause you know no one comes from nothing. And you tell yourself, if you only knew, then maybe you could see a reason for how you got to be the way you are. Why your life looks like it does. But there isn't any reason, not really." He worried the ring at his knuckle, feeling the bite of it.

"My father died a long time ago," he said, without pity. "I never got to know him. I don't even know what he looked like. He died, and then my mama died, and I was left all alone even though I was just a little kid. And that's just how it is. There's no changing it, and it doesn't mean anything."

"You got me though," said Marlowe sleepily.

It might have been the cold that woke him.

He was still wearing the ring. He sat up. Marlowe was standing two feet away, staring at the far wall. The fog had entered the room and was thickening there and Charlie scrambled to his feet.

"Mar!" he hissed, all his senses suddenly alert. He backed up, stumbling against the damp wall, glancing from side to side.

But the little boy hadn't moved. "Do you see her too, Charlie?" he whispered.

He wasn't sure what he saw. He was trying to make out the shapes in the half-light, frozen, staring, gathering his fear around himself like a blanket.

Marlowe didn't seem afraid at all, filled instead with sadness. "It's Brynt, Charlie," he murmured. There was wonder in his voice. "Look. It's her."

And he remembered then the enormous woman on the train, her arms and throat inked, her silver hair in a braid like a berserker out of legend, who had wrestled the litch down to its knees, who had held it fast and thrown herself off the speeding roof in order to save them all. And he remembered too Marlowe's words to him that first night at Mrs. Harrogate's flat, in London: *Brynt's my family.* And he looked at the little boy with pity in his heart.

"Has she said anything?" he whispered. "Did she say what she wants?"

For he was thinking again about Dr. Berghast's warnings, that the dead were not as they had been in life, as if the man had known what they would find.

Marlowe seemed afraid to breathe. "I think . . . I think she just wants to see me."

Now Charlie could see her too, the dark mist twisting and moving always, a huge figure, her arms tattooed with mysterious symbols, her face sorrowful, her eyes like twinned stars burning brightly in that mist. She was no longer human, that much was clear. Her features kept shifting, as if water were moving swiftly over her, and Charlie found looking at her dizzying. She seemed to be staring at Marlowe, staring with a fixed intensity. There was no love in it, no gentleness. An ache was rising in Charlie's throat; whatever she was now, this was not the Brynt the boy had loved.

He was colder now, much colder, and he saw his breath plume out before him in the ruined room. He reached out for Marlowe but the effort was strangely difficult. He looked around him. The fog had drifted thinly around them and now it was thickening and he saw faces flicker in the mists, lightless eyes, mouths that seemed open in some silent scream. He could hear a low hiss, like the whispering of hundreds of voices, indistinct but filled with want. He tried to cry out, but he couldn't. . . . The room was darkening. . . . He was cold, so cold. . . .

"Charlie!" Marlowe was shouting, from what seemed very far away. "Charlie! Charlie!"

And then a blue light was glowing through the mist, burning it off, the tendrils of fog dissipating and retreating before it, and he saw Marlowe with his palms outstretched, shining, and the boy was struggling to get him upright, and the two of them were stumbling over to the doorway and down the stairs and out into the street and away.

He didn't remember much of what happened next. There were flashes of images: a crumbling court, an alley under brick arches, a submerged street. He kept seeing the faces of the dead, their eyes, the longing in them.

He came back to himself sometime later, on the stoop of a tenement building on a crooked street. He could hear Marlowe kicking about in the damp room behind him, as if looking for something. The weird light in this other world hadn't shifted, hadn't changed at all. He sat up, feeling a clear cool hunger in his belly. His head was hurting. He looked at the fog of the dead drifting down the street and he wondered what would happen if he walked out into it, if he let himself get lost. Would his body lie in this world uncorrupted? Would he rise up out of it, a figure of translucence and already fading memory? He wondered then if this world meant God and all he had been told about heaven and the true order of the world was wrong or merely hidden by a greater veil and then he blew out his cheeks and rubbed his hands over his trousers as if to reassure himself that he was still alive. And that was when he saw his right hand.

It was trembling. He remembered Berghast's warning and folded his hand into his armpit and frowned with worry. He knew what it meant: Marlowe would have to go on alone.

After a time he heard Marlowe behind him. There were dried tears on his cheeks and his deep blue eyes looked red. "Charlie! You're okay."

"Yeah. You?"

The boy frowned bravely. "Brynt's gone."

"Yeah."

"But she knew me, Charlie. She knew who I was. I could see it."

Charlie looked at the kid, he shifted his hips. He didn't like seeing the hope in his face. He slid his trembling hand in his pocket, and stood.

"Yeah," he said. "Well, we got a room to find."

He started walking, tired, footsore. But Marlowe didn't follow. The boy was biting his lip with a haunted expression and there was about him something different, something changed, and Charlie looked once in the direction he'd been going and then turned and trudged back to the boy.

"Mar?"

Marlowe peered uncertainly behind him. "It's this way, Charlie. We got to go this way. I can . . . I can feel it."

Charlie raised his eyes in that direction and for just a moment he thought he glimpsed in the fog beyond the huge translucent spirit of Brynt, her eyes glinting, but then it was gone, whatever it was, and all that was left was that strange shifting curtain of mist.

"You're sure?" he said.

The boy shook his head. "No."

But he followed Marlowe anyway, along the crooked street and up a dripping alley, keeping as best they could to the shallow puddles, passing along under the dripping weeds and mosses hanging from the lintels and arches. He was no longer sure where they were.

It was a dead city, a London of stillness and loss, and the streets were labyrinthine and littered with the detritus of lives once-lived. Marlowe led him down a crooked set of steps, slick with a moss so black it shone almost blue in the weird light, and then he stopped under a kind of aqueduct and pointed. And there it was.

A white tree, bare of leaves, was growing up out of the muck in the middle of a fountain. Where its bark peeled away in thin paper-like strips, the new bark was a bright bloodred beneath. In its shadow stood an old-fashioned hand pump, made of wood, and on the far side of the square a sinister house, tall and narrow and crenelated with crooked balconies leaning out over the empty air. It had no door, only a broken opening in one wall.

"Of course," muttered Charlie. He ran his hand over his hair in disgust. "We got to go in there? Of course."

Marlowe was looking at him strangely. "Your hand, Charlie," he said. "It's shaking. Look."

But Charlie just stuffed it back into his pocket. "Don't you mind it, Mar. It's fine."

"Does it hurt?"

Charlie didn't answer. There were spirits gathering, thickening, off to the left of the square. He checked to be sure the way ahead was safe and then he hurried across, Marlowe half running beside him. At the stoop of the old house the boy pulled at his sleeve, catching him up.

"I know what you want to say," Charlie told him. "And you're not wrong. But we just got to get this glove Berghast wants. We're so close, Mar. You want to have to come back, do this all again?"

Charlie watched Marlowe think it through and then the boy gave him a quick reproachful glare. Then they went inside, taking care not to brush up against the slick stone lintel.

The house would have been dark but for the broken windows leaking that same eerie gray light. They stopped to let their eyes adjust and it was then Charlie saw they weren't alone. At the base of the stairs a vague column of air was coalescing. A spirit. He set a warning hand on Marlowe's shoulder. The spirit flickered, sharpened into the translucent figure of a woman, then twisted away again into air. Then it was a woman again, a woman in a bustled gown, her back to them. She made no sound but her agitation was clear. Slowly, she drifted across the room, as if underwater, and it seemed to Charlie that everything stilled and it was like he was standing in a cold street peering in through a window and then the spirit turned her face and Charlie saw her clear.

It was his mother.

Or, rather, his mother as she might have been, must have been, once, in those years before her loss and her hardship began. Her face flickered through its ages. Charlie fumbled for the wall, felt the cold ooze of the wallpaper under his hand. He was shaking. He knew every line of that face, he knew her every weather. The skin like dark eggplant and the tight hair drawn back into a bun. Her high cheekbones. Her sad brown eyes.

She seemed to be speaking to someone on the stairs, a second figure, though she made no sound, and then a second column of air was twisting, taking form, and a man emerged, pale, black-haired, slender as a shadow and with an old-fashioned frock coat. He descended and took her hands in his own and spoke to her in an urgent way, though Charlie could hear nothing. And he understood, at once, that here stood his father.

The face kept shivering and fading and taking on substance as it spoke. But Charlie stared at the thin lips, the little teeth, the creases at the corners of the man's eyes from long-smiling. He had a soft jowly face that was strange on such a thin frame, as if he ought to be heavy-set. His hair was long. The big pink shells of his ears stood out.

Charlie couldn't think; he couldn't breathe. He watched the two of them shudder and drift and go through a low doorway into the back of the house and he followed. The house was in a state of advanced decay and water ran in rivulets down the walls and the floorboards felt soft under Charlie's weight. There was a crib in the back room, a crib with a baby swaddled in it. He didn't understand. It was himself he was seeing, he knew it, and yet how could his spirit be here too, if he was alive and in the flesh and present and watching? Slowly his father twisted a ring from his mother's outstretched hand, his ring, Charlie's, the very one he wore on his own finger now, and then he watched as his father leaned over the crib and pressed the ring into the baby's tiny curling fist, and Charlie felt his vision blur.

And then his father raised his eyes, and stared at Charlie, *directly* at *Charlie*, with a look of dark confusion, and his mother turned and stared at him too, appalled, and then Charlie felt Marlowe's hand on his arm and the spirits both shivered and turned translucent and wisped away as if in a wind and there was nothing, no one, they were gone just as if they'd never been.

Charlie's heart was pounding. His cheeks were wet.

That was when he saw, behind where the ghostly crib had stood, a door.

"This is it, Charlie," Marlowe whispered. "This is the way."

Marlowe was standing at the open door, looking back at him with big solemn eyes. There were stairs beyond. Charlie turned and turned in place, peering around at the rotting house. Something was missing. He was having trouble shaping his thoughts.

"Charlie, come *on*."

It was a narrow back stairwell, a servants' passage through the house. They climbed the stairs to the second level and carefully edged around a hole in the floor and went down a hall and climbed more stairs to the third level. They kept to the seams of the stairs and they passed the third floor and kept climbing to the very top. And at the top they found the attic door. Charlie had a powerful sense of wrongness. They'd found the Room.

Marlowe, too, gave a little shiver. But he didn't hesitate; the little boy went through into the attic the way a person holds their breath and jumps into cold water.

The attic didn't look like much. A narrow room under a peaked roof. Beams had collapsed in one corner with a part of the outer wall gone so that gray fog and the silhouetted roofs of the city were visible through the hole. Charlie's footfalls clinked as he ducked his head, walked slowly in. A balcony door hung askew on one hinge. Rubble, collapsed masonry, the splintered bits of some long-smashed furniture all littered the room. Then Charlie froze. Slumped against the far wall was the body of a man.

It had been there for a long time. It was dressed in fashions from decades past, like some of the portraits in the upper halls of Cairndale. The dead man's skin had dried to paper and the eyes under their lids had sunk down into the skull and the mummified throat looked ropy and thin. And on one hand, shining darkly, as if it would absorb all the light it could find, was the wood-and-iron glove Berghast had sent them to find.

Charlie went over to the body, pulled the glove free. The little teeth inside snapped the hand at the wrist. Charlie shook the glove. The hand fell out in pieces among a sifting of dust. He stared, fascinated. The pieces of wood sewn into it gleamed, like black glass. The glove was heavy, and beautiful, far more beautiful than the replica Berghast had shown. Charlie's own hand, he saw, had stopped shaking.

"How long do you think he's been here?" said Marlowe. "What happened to him?"

Charlie frowned. "I don't know. I don't think I want to."

"Can I see it? Charlie?"

But Charlie was still holding it, staring into the deep unreflective black plates of wood and iron, and he could only tear his eyes away with a struggle.

"Yeah," he said, forcing himself to sound nonchalant. "Yeah, of course. Here."

And he gave it to the boy with a shrug and turned away. But in his heart he had a feeling like he shouldn't let it go, like he should keep it close, wear it for safety, because only he could understand how precious it was, only he could keep it safe.

But this feeling passed after a moment, and then it was like it had never been. He drifted over to the broken door, went outside onto the balcony. The air was cold. Both his hands were trembling now. In the square below, the spirits were denser and their veil of mist parted and closed again and the dark wet rooftops of the city seemed to go on forever. He wondered if there were other worlds besides this one, if there were worlds beyond worlds. Anything seemed possible.

They needed to get back. He turned to go inside when something stopped him, a feeling; and he peered down and glimpsed movement in the square below. A pale hairless figure, lurking under the strange white tree in the fountain.

And that was when he heard the scrape of shoes on wood, somewhere in the house. Someone was climbing the stairs. Inside, Marlowe had gone still. Charlie started to go to him but then froze and shrank back against the wall, his heart loud in his chest. For a shadow had filled the doorway.

It was a powerful man, all in black, vaguely familiar. He took off his hat, turned the crown in gloved fingers. Under his black beard, it was clear his mouth and cheek had been sliced open. There was blood all down his clothes. All at once Charlie knew him and shrank back.

"Hello, Marlowe," said Jacob Marber, his voice as soft as velvet.

33

THE GRASSMARKET

A dark rain had started in the night. The cart that stopped for them in the countryside was driven by an old peat cutter who sat like a figure carved from granite, pipe clenched in his teeth, rain runneling down off his hat and beard and slicker. He grunted them up and the three of them—Komako, Ribs, and Oskar—shook the water from their cloaks and scrambled up into the bed. Lymenion, reeking, soft as wax melt in the wet, stood down in the hedgerow in water ankle-deep, watching them go, his sad misshapen face unmoving. Komako looked at Oskar. The boy's face was turned away.

That peat cutter never spoke a word all the slow ride south into Edinburgh and they were themselves too tired to talk. It was almost morning when the cart banged to a stop on Princes Street. They were across from the Scott Monument. The three kids got down. Above them the castle loomed ghostlike in the downpour, like a city in the sky.

"Fair day to ye, then, travelers," the cutter called down in his thick Scots accent.

Komako, with her hood still obscuring her face, raised her hand in thanks. The man snapped the reins; his cart lurched off into the early dark.

There were coal wagons already at their deliveries and the shivering poor under arches and in doorways but mostly the city just felt gray, and lonely, and quiet. Komako scanned the buildings, looking for a public house open at that hour. The sooner they got directions, the better. They had a name: Albany Chandlers. And Oskar seemed certain it lay in the Grassmarket, wherever that was.

Of course, it was still too early for the chandler's to be open. But they could find it and wait, couldn't they?

Oskar was limping as they started down the street. Komako stopped, put a hand on his arm. "Lymenion will be all right. You know he will."

Oskar's bottom lip stuck out. He was blinking away the rain. "It's my shoe, Ko. It hurts."

Right there, in the middle of the street, Ribs kneeled and lifted the boy's shoe and looked at it. "You got a nail," she said. "Come, over here."

They crossed over to a park bench under a dripping elm and there Ribs took Oskar's shoe and reached in with her fingers and felt around. Still holding the shoe she got up and kicked through the twigs and bracken until she'd overturned a large rock and then she came back with the rock in one hand and the shoe in the other and started banging the nail down.

Komako watched all this and then stood and looked out along the street. "What do you think they told Berghast?" she said quietly.

Ribs grimaced, her red hair plastered to her face. "Charlie and Marlowe? Nothing. They ain't snitches."

But Komako wasn't so sure. "Berghast has a way of finding out what he wants to know," she said. "You remember how he was with the chocolate, that time you snuck into the pantry?"

Ribs paused in her hammering, wiped the water from her eyes. She seemed to be remembering. "Yeah but it were worth it." She grinned.

"What chocolate?" said Oskar. "I never got any chocolate."

Komako's fingertips were red in the cold and she folded them up under her armpits. "He looks so tired lately. Like he's overwhelmed. I don't want to make it harder for him, I don't want him to worry."

Ribs grimaced. "I reckon old Berghast can take care of himself, Ko. You ain't his ma."

"I know that," Komako said quietly.

"I don't trust him maybe, not like you do. But he ain't about to hurt Charlie or Mar none. An he wants the same things we want. We ain't working against *him*. Right?"

Komako chewed at her lips, thinking.

"Anyway," Ribs added, turning her face aside to spit on the cobblestones. "I reckon he already knows we was up in his office, pokin around. An he knows we was over at the Spider. Give him five minutes an he'll put it all together an tell us what we're up to and what we been thinking and what we had for lunch, an even whether we liked it and would eat it again."

They were quiet a moment, grinning in the steady rain.

"He wouldn't know what we ate for lunch," said Oskar.

When Oskar had put his shoe back on and stood in it gingerly and looked at Ribs in relief they crossed the now busier street, slipping among the creaking axles and the splashing hooves, and started their search for directions to the Grassmarket. There were young clerks under umbrellas and older shopkeepers with coats and hats greasy with rain but there were no women at that hour. They walked slowly, three small figures in identical cloaks. It was agreed, given Oskar's Polish accent and youth, and Komako's features, that Ribs would do the talking, and she looked pleased at the prospect and fiddled with her unruly red hair and licked a finger and smoothed out her eyebrows as if that would make a difference. She adopted a refined accent. Or what she supposed might pass as one.

"Pardon me, but would you be so grand as to share with me the general direction of a fine chandler's establishment in the Grassmarket?" she tried out, looking at Komako for approval.

"That's terrible," said Komako.

"Yes," said Oskar.

But Ribs just smiled and winked. "It would behoove you to speak more respectfully, my dearies."

"No one says dearies. That's not a thing."

"No one," echoed Oskar.

They were standing under the dripping eaves of a public house on a crowded corner by then. Ribs wouldn't be dissuaded. "Aw, you ain't like to know manners if they bit your bloomin nose off." She grinned. "I sound like a bloody queen."

And she pushed inside the smoky pub and the door swung to and she was gone. Komako rubbed at her chilled hands. Over Oskar's head she glimpsed a constable, in a gleaming dark slicker, drifting slowly past. His eyes under heavy brows flicked over her and Oskar, hovered a moment, then continued on. She was surprised at how fast her heart was beating.

Oskar had other worries. "Shouldn't we have left Miss Davenshaw a—a note, or the like? So she doesn't worry?" he asked.

"She can't see to read, Oskar," she said.

Oskar nodded glumly. "I know. I—I just mean a message of— of—of some kind. . . . I just don't like to think of her worrying, is all."

Komako didn't like it either. Miss Davenshaw was strict but fair, and there was a kindness in her like steel cable. She put a hand on the younger boy's shoulder. "Charlie and Marlowe'll figure it out," she said. "They'll tell her we've gone off somewhere. But all our things are there. It'll be clear enough we're coming back."

"But what if Charlie and Marlowe aren't at her class either?"

"Where else would they be?"

He shrugged unhappily in the rain.

A voice at her back snorted. "Thinks they're still with old Berghast, he does. Taking breakfast, like."

Komako turned. Ribs had come out while they were talking and was lifting the hood of her cloak up over her red hair.

"I don't think that," said Oskar.

Komako gestured at the pub. "So? What did they say?"

"Well, first," said Ribs expansively, "you'll be pleased to know they was impressed with my accent. Oh! Charming, it were! *Why hello, young lady,* they says. *An what's your like doin about on a day like this, unaccompanied as such?* An I tells them, *Oh, my governess is just outside, taking the air an the like,* and they says—"

"Ribs," said Komako. "What did they say about the *chandler's?*"

She shrugged. "They never heard of it."

"But the Grassmarket? They must know how to get to it?"

"We-e-ell," she began. "I never quite got the chance to—"

But just then Komako saw the police constable coming back their way. A hulking figure in his black rain slicker and with thick tawny side whiskers that made him look feline and ferocious in the gloom. He seemed to have an eye fixed on Ribs and Oskar and she quickly took the two by the elbows and steered them off.

"It's time we were going," she hissed.

And they shouldered their way through the thickening crowds of clerks, stepping down into the ankle-deep water below the bollards, trying to get around and get space. Vagrancy was just an excuse for a constable to do with you what he wanted and the last thing they needed, she knew, was trouble with the law. They weren't running but nearly so, going so fast as to draw reproving looks from passersby.

"You three! Oi!" the constable called.

He caught them not ten strides up from the corner of Hanover Street. Komako and Ribs and Oskar all shrank back against an iron railing, still in the wet. The man's eyes were hard to make out. He loomed over them, his face etched in a scowl, and Komako felt suddenly afraid. Here there were fewer pedestrians. But it was too wet for her to manipulate any dust and Ribs was fully dressed and so she couldn't make herself invisible and Lymenion, Oskar's flesh giant, was miles away. They were as powerless as any three ordinary kids, anywhere.

Stupid! she thought to herself.

The constable swung his stick—*slap, slap*—into the flat of his hand. A hansom rattled past. He looked off up the street, then back down at them.

"We wasn't doing nothing," said Ribs. "It ain't against the law to get rained on."

"'Tis true," said the constable.

"So . . . we'll just be going, then?" said Komako.

But he was blocking their way with his size and she could see the whistle around his neck and knew they weren't going anywhere without his saying so. His side whiskers were long and wet like a dog's fur and when he grimaced the water squeezed from them.

"I know ye," he said quietly. "You'd be from that Cairndale place, up the north now, wouldn't ye?"

Komako froze. She looked at Ribs, looked back at the constable.

"No," said Ribs.

But the constable ignored this. "My wife's sister used to deliver perishables up there to the estate, she did. Used to talk about the kids up there. Said it seemed a lonesome life, growin up on the edge of that loch. Just the few of you." He tipped the brim of his helmet with his stick and the water poured off to one side. "Ye needn't look quite so shocked, lassie. You're wearin them capes that come right out of the estate." He nodded to the insignia over their breasts. "Might be most here in the big city don't know it, but them what come out of the north know the Cairndale arms well enough."

"Yes, sir," said Komako politely. She was too surprised and confused to say anything more.

But Ribs wasn't. She stepped forward, as if taking the measure of the man, and said boldly, "We was lookin for a particular shop, sir. A chandler's, run by a Mr. Albany. It's in the Grassmarket. We wanted to buy a special something for our governess."

"From a chandler?" said the constable. "I might suggest a fine bolt of cloth be a better gift. Or maybe something from the teashop round the corner?"

"Mr. Albany is an especial friend of hers, sir," said Komako quickly. "It's a gift she'd appreciate, for reasons of sentiment."

"Ah. All right, then. Well . . ." He screwed up his face and turned in the rain and looked out at the gloomy street. "Let me see. I don't know a Mr. Albany, but if it's the Grassmarket you're after, it's off away behind the castle rock. Ye'll go over through them gardens to the Old Town and take a right on Victoria Street and follow it over toward West Port. Mind that. Most of the usual sort are there, dealers in pitch an tar an dyers an the like. And even if your man ain't, there'd be a one or a two to point ye in the right direction."

Komako memorized the names. Victoria Street. West Port.

"Ye'd be all right for coin, then? Ye've had a bite?"

Ribs's eyes lit up. "No—" she started to say.

But Komako spoke over her. "We are fine, thank you, sir. We ate before leaving this morning. And we brought all we need."

"Right, then," he said.

And he tipped his helmet and took his leave, strolling back off into the rain, cheerfully swinging his club.

But they *were* hungry, by then. They bought a newspaper full of penny cakes from a hot cart at the edge of the green and then they crossed through in the wet, none of them talking. The gravel walks shining, the stilled trees dark. The castle walls loomed above them, silhouetted and medieval, the battlement cannons just visible in the haze. The Old Town was grimmer and the streets narrower and when they came at last to the open air of the Grassmarket they were all of them tired and filling with doubts. In the old cattle pens, crows as big as ravens stood on the fence rails, watching. Komako could feel the water seeping around her toes with every step.

"Miss Davenshaw will be angry when we see her," Oskar said.

Komako put a calming hand on his arm. They were standing on the site of the old gibbet and she turned in the rain to peer across the span. A narrow alley, crooked shop fronts. A black horse hauling a wagon past in the gloom. And there it was, on a painted window glass on the corner, in large cursive:

ALBANY CHANDLERS,
Purveyor of Fine Candles Wicks Lanterns
Preserving Fats & Oils of All Kinds.
Edward Albany, Proprietor. Est. 1838.

A faded red awning with holes punched in it dripped over the stoop. A lidless barrel held God only knows what sort of effluent. There was a dead rat lying directly in the middle of the steps, left there by some enterprising cat. That, or poisoned. The shop looked dark, deserted, unwelcoming. But as they watched, the sign in the window flipped to OPEN. A pale face materialized in the glass, peering out at the street, then vanished.

Ribs grinned. She drew her hood up over her hair and affected her upper-class accent. "Well, my dearies. Do let's go pay good Mr. Edward a visit, shall we?"

Oskar made a face.

"She's not going to do it like that again, is she?" he whispered.

"Ribs—" said Komako. "Just . . . be careful. You don't know what's in there."

"I'm always careful." She grinned.

"If you see any sign of Brendan or any of the missing kids, you come right back. Okay?"

Ribs winked. Then she turned with a flourish, so that her cloak billowed out around her, and started across.

That same morning, at precisely five minutes past nine, Abigail Davenshaw rose smoothly from behind her desk and, running her hands over her skirts, crossed the quiet schoolroom to the hall. The manor was cool, filled with a scent of wet grass coming in through the opened windows. A coal fire burned behind her in the grate.

She'd seen no sign of the young talents all that morning, neither Komako nor Charlie Ovid nor anyone. Not at breakfast or in the corridors or in the yard. "Seen" being, perhaps, a strange word to use. For Abigail Davenshaw was, of course, blind; had been born thus, without sight; but because she had never known seeing, it was not a thing she missed, and she'd learned ways of navigating the darkness of her world with a swiftness and clarity that rivaled others' sight. She was fastidious with her appearance, wearing her hair off her neck and not a strand astray. She had learned the importance of this early in life. She was the illegitimate daughter of the housekeeper of an estate in the Midlands, and the reclusive lord who had retreated there had taken it upon himself to cultivate her intelligence. Why, she would never know. Kindness or charity, an experiment or something else entirely. When she was little, he'd read to her from the classics, Shakespeare and Dante and Homer, and later from the modern sciences, later still from the philosophers and modern poets. She'd learned the theories of light and of matter and the new laws of thermodynamics. She'd learned languages and music and dancing and even, strangely, the arts of fencing and boxing.

"It's not about seeing with the eyes, child," he would say to her, "but about listening with the ears and with your skin and using all the good Lord saw fit to give you."

She had a remarkable memory, and would quote back to him long passages word for word, and this, too, encouraged him in his education of her and in this way she grew, slowly, into a formidable young woman. How Dr. Berghast had found her, she'd never know. He'd written to her without introduction six weeks after her benefactor had died, and her mother, old by then, haltingly, had read out the letter in surprise. It seemed the Cairndale Institute had heard tell of her remarkable education and wished to employ her, in turn, in the education and guidance of their own rather unusual children.

She went now quickly along the corridor, tracing her fingers lightly over the wall, the familiar bumps and grooves that told her where the turnings came. She could feel the shifts in the air pressure, in the temperature, that warned her when a door was opened, when a person was approaching. In her rooms she kept a long switch of birch, very smooth, used by many with her impairment to scan their surroundings for obstacles. But she herself used it only rarely, only when she was going into unfamiliar territory.

She retrieved it, now.

The first place she went was to the girls' dormitory. There she stood in the doorway of the empty room, with her chin lifted, listening. The place was empty, she could sense it in the particular kind of silence and in the way the air moved around her. Drawing the switch back and forth through the air, tapping her way forward, she felt around Komako Onoe's bed, and then the rumpled poorly made bed of Eleanor Ribbon. Neither had slept there that night; she would swear to it. She sat very lightly on the edge of Komako's bed and felt around under the pillow. Nothing.

So. The girls had been gone since late the previous night.

She would wager Oskar and Charlie and Marlowe to be with them also. The latter two surprised her, somewhat; she hadn't thought Komako quite prepared to trust them. Oh, she'd observed Ribs's mooning about the new boy, Charlie Ovid, and knew Oskar wanted more than anything for a friend; but Komako was stubborn, and independent, and wary. Miss Davenshaw wasn't worried for their *safety*; whatever mischief they were getting into, they were more than capable of getting out.

Well.

She got to her feet and rubbed her left wrist with her right hand, thinking. There was, she considered, another possibility: Dr. Berghast. He hadn't yet interviewed the new boys, and it was just possible he had taken the lot of them aside for one of his chats, in his study.

She went swiftly down the stairs and into the courtyard, tapping her way across through the rain. She passed no one. She knew the way, though she did not often cross into the wing that held Berghast's rooms and the rooms of most of the older talents. The upper corridor that led to Berghast's study was punctuated with fire doors, every fifteen feet or so, and all stood closed, so that she had to go slowly and find the doorknobs, and push her way through.

She knocked at Dr. Berghast's study. No answer.

She tried the handle; it was unlocked. A scent of pipe smoke, coal, the spicy fug of brandy left out. And deeper, under this, a whiff of cracked leather, ink, mud, and stone. It was a room that made her shiver.

"Good day," she called boldly. "Are you here, Dr. Berghast?"

But only her own voice came back to her, and the hot unmoving darkness. She stepped forward, swallowing. She could smell something else, she was sure of it: the boys, Marlowe and Charlie. Their particular scents. They had been here.

"Boys?" she called. And then, to be sure: "Dr. Berghast? It is Miss Davenshaw, sir."

But the study was quite deserted. She entered and stood on the carpet feeling the warm air on her face and neck and listening to the sounds of the manor through the walls and floor, the distant movements of its inhabitants. That was when she felt something cool slide past her, a hiss of air, and she turned and went cautiously toward it and found herself at a door in the wall, a door that stood open a crack. She pulled it wide, called in, and her voice came back to her distorted. She could tell from the sound that she stood at the top of a circular staircase and that it descended a long ways. She furrowed her brow. The sensible thing, she knew, would be to turn around and leave. That is what she'd expect her wards to do. Instead, like a foolish student, she started down.

She went quietly, listening all the while. At the bottom of the stairs she found herself in a small antechamber, facing a locked door made of iron. She tapped at it softly, feeling a rising sense of unease. She had never heard of such a place. Cairndale was old, filled with secrets. And so, she thought sharply, was Henry Berghast.

She raised her voice. "Charles? Marlowe? Are you in there, boys?"

There came the quick rapid breathing of someone on the far side. The heavy clank of chains, shifting. Then more breathing.

"Who is in there?" she called, suddenly afraid. "Answer me. Are you in need of assistance?"

But whatever was within had gone very quiet, very still. The breathing, she thought, didn't sound quite right. It didn't sound quite . . . human.

Slowly, in the darkness that was her world, Miss Davenshaw pressed an ear to the cold metal of the door. She leaned in, listening.

34

World More Full of Weeping

The city of the dead was quiet. Mist swept the rooftops, rolling heavily over itself.

Charlie, crouched on the balcony, listened as Jacob Marber moved catlike and slow around the Room, circling Marlowe. Charlie wanted to leap out, throw himself at the monster. He had the knife Dr. Berghast had given them to cut through the orsine. And he was a haelan and not easily injured and though he didn't know the full extent of Jacob Marber's power he had a pretty good notion that his own body would recover, whatever happened.

But he didn't move, didn't breathe, just stood listening to the slow heavy footfalls on the planks. He didn't know if it was fear or something else that stayed him.

Just wait, he told himself. *Wait.*

He could just see Marlowe, staring down the monster. He was clutching the glove in front of him. His little shoulders were squared for a fight and despite everything Charlie knew about his powers, the kid looked defenseless in front of the monster.

"Imagine, finding you *here*," the man murmured. "Of all the places. Forgive me, we have not properly met. Jacob Marber, at your service." At that angle Charlie couldn't see his face, could only see the back of his black hair, the scruff of his thick beard. He kept raising one hand to his face, as if to hold his cheek closed. There was something wrong with its skin; the shadows across his knuckles were crawling.

"I wouldn't have found you either, if you had not used your . . . gift last night. It leaves a trace, in this world. Like blood in the water. Was it the spirits that attacked you?"

The boy hadn't taken his frightened eyes off Jacob Marber. Charlie's hands were trembling so badly he could barely make them into fists. He knew if he didn't leave soon, if he didn't get back through the orsine soon, something bad was going to happen to him.

"A strange place, this Room. Do you feel it?" Jacob Marber continued. "It is . . . protected. Hidden. You and I, we can find it and enter. But the drughr, she cannot come in. Nor can the spirits. Nor can your good Dr. Berghast, of course." He paused, set his hat back on his head. He was standing over the mummified body and he made a small noise, as if his wounds pained him. "This poor fellow must have crawled in here for refuge," he murmured. "What happened to his hand, I wonder?"

Marlowe pulled the artifact behind his back but it was too late. Jacob Marber curled his hand outward and a fine black tendril of dust curved around the boy's arms, wrenching his hands free. Jacob Marber took the iron-and-wood glove and examined it and then, to Charlie's surprise, he gave it back.

"Dr. Berghast sent you to retrieve this, I presume?"

When Marlowe didn't answer, the man resumed his pacing. Now Charlie saw his forehead was covered in scratches, his coat was torn at the shoulder. There was mud on his trousers.

"Do you know what that is?" he demanded. "What it will make possible, what Berghast will do with it? No, of course not. You would not take it from this room, if you did. And not only Berghast. *She* would wish me to bring it to her, also."

The floor creaked softly under his weight. Charlie was desperately trying to think of something to do. He had the element of surprise. He could leap at Jacob Marber, push him out of the broken wall. Maybe. But would a fall hurt such a monster?

Jacob Marber was speaking again. "You are angry with me. I daresay you might even hate me. Do you wish me dead?" Charlie knew he had circled the room and was facing his way now and he dared not peer around the door lest he was seen. "You believe you understand what you are fighting for, what you stand for. You believe you know your place in all this. But you are mistaken, child. Dr. Berghast is not your father. Not your real father."

"I know," Marlowe whispered. "He told me."

"Ah." Jacob Marber sounded like he would say something more but then decided against it and sighed and scraped his boots through the broken masonry. When he spoke next his voice had changed, softened. "I knew you once, long ago. Before you were called Marlowe. Did he tell you that?"

Charlie risked a glance. Marlowe was nodding angrily.

"What else did he tell you? Did he tell you I killed your mother? That I wished to kill you?"

"Yes."

"Do you believe him?"

"You killed Mr. Coulton. You kill lots of people."

"Ah. Sometimes it is necessary, if the one wishes to save the many." He was grim, quiet. He took something out of his pocket, turned it in his fingers. A key, carved of the same black wood as what plated the glove. "I did not kill your mother, child. And I did not try to kill you.

Henry Berghast has made me a monster, he has tried to destroy me. But I am not what he says."

"I don't believe anything you say," said the boy.

Jacob Marber's face twisted. "It doesn't matter. Truth is truth. Whether it's known or not."

Marlowe lifted his chin. "Are you going to kill me?"

"What nonsense is this? Kill you—?"

Marlowe glared.

"I've only ever wanted to keep you safe." Jacob Marber raised a regretful eyebrow. "Oh, child, what have they told you? What must you think of me?"

"What about New York? When you came after me and Alice?"

"Alice . . ." He was quiet a moment, brooding. When he spoke next his voice was softer. "I knew Henry had found you. Using his glyphic, I presumed. I knew you were being taken to him. I had no intention of harming Alice Quicke. But I couldn't let her take you."

The man seemed almost gentle. Almost.

Charlie knew what he had to do. He'd seen how carefully Marber had put that strange key into his frock coat. If he could do the mortaling, as Miss Davenshaw had tried to teach him, he might perhaps extend his arm far enough to pick the bastard's pocket.

He closed his eyes, steadied his breathing like he'd been told. But there was something, a fear, a loneliness, that kept rushing in, distracting him, and when he opened his eyes nothing had changed.

He couldn't do it.

Very near to him, Jacob Marber ran a hand over his beard, smoothing it, careful with the long gash in his cheek. Then he clasped his hands in the small of his back and turned and looked out the ruined wall at the city and the gray mists beyond. Charlie shrank back, his heart pounding.

"I was trapped in this world for years," Jacob Marber said quietly. "I learned to live here. I know it better than any living creature ever could, and yet I scarcely know it at all. You cannot imagine what it was like. I knew that there was a doorway—the orsine—but I could not use it. Henry Berghast kept it shut from me."

"You betrayed him. It was your doing."

"Mm." His shoes clicked through the rubble. "I was young still when the drughr first came to me. She offered to bring me through, into this world, to look for . . . someone. To help them. She needed my help too, you see."

Just then Charlie saw, at the edge of the balcony, an iron rod. Very slowly, very quietly, he leaned out and lifted it clear. It was long and thin but sharp on one end. He gripped it tight in one hand, the knife in the other.

"My brother died when we were children. We were twins. I was told by the drughr that I could see him again, that I could help him, here, in this world. If I grew powerful enough, I might even bring him back. But I was deceived. For years we wandered through this city, looking for my brother, trying to find any trace of him among the spirits. What do you see, London? For me, it is Vienna." He frowned. "It was lonely, and I grew strange, having no other living soul to talk to. Only the drughr, who was with me often, and with whom I grew . . . close. And she came to confide in me, and that is when I learned how much she hated the world of the living, how hungry she was to devour the talents. It consumed her."

"Did you find him? Did you find your brother?"

"Yes. But it wasn't Bertolt. Not anymore."

Marlowe was quiet.

Jacob continued. "My brother came to me three times, here in this world. I sat at the edge of the orsine, pleading that it be opened. All Berghast had to do was let us through. It would have changed everything.

But he did not; and my brother's memory of me faded. And then it was too late."

"Is that why you hate him?"

"A person grows peculiar, in this world," he said. "It's not the loneliness but the solitude. One day, the drughr, too, left. And I was truly alone. Devastated. Afraid. I set off in search of her. I had no one else, you see. And after a long time I found her, hidden in a tunnel at the edge of the river. She had a baby with her—a human child, it seemed. But it wasn't human. It was hers. Her own baby. And she looked magnificent. I could feel the power and fury in her. Somehow the baby was giving her strength, making her even more powerful. And I saw in that instant the horror she'd be capable of, and that the baby couldn't be allowed to live." He was breathing heavily now, and Charlie saw he had a hand pressed to his side. "It couldn't be allowed to. . . ."

Charlie could feel his blood moving in his head. He knew, even before the man spoke next, what he was going to say.

"I stole the baby. I'd meant to kill it. But I couldn't, I couldn't do it. I knew the horror of that child's life to come, how terrible its fate, and I couldn't stand that either. So I fled with the child to the only place the drughr couldn't follow—the orsine, which Berghast had closed to me—and I begged the glyphic to let us through. You were that baby, Marlowe. You were that child."

"No," the boy whispered.

"That is why you are different. And that is why the drughr is hunting you. She is your mother."

"You're a liar!" the boy shouted suddenly. "It's a lie!"

Jacob Marber went on in his low, pained voice. "But that doesn't mean you have to be *like* her. You can choose what you are, what you will be."

Charlie risked a horrified glance. Marlowe was trembling. Charlie could see how desperately he wanted to run away. But he didn't. And suddenly he understood why: *he* wouldn't leave *Charlie* either.

"When Berghast took you from me," said Jacob, "I was too weak, after years here in this world, to stop him. I came back for you, before I was strong enough. I wanted to take you away, to hide you away someplace where Berghast and the drughr could never find you. Someplace you could be happy and live a good life. But I failed you. I will not fail you now."

There was in his voice a genuine regret, as if he did not wish to happen what was about to happen. All at once his eyes turned entirely black, as if a black ink had spread cloudily through his irises and the whites of his eyes until there was only blackness, seeping and smearing around his lids. Slowly he rolled up his sleeves. There was a darkness writhing and twisting under his skin.

"Here we are like gods, Marlowe," he said, and his teeth showed through the bloodied hole in his cheek. "Here our talents are much, much more powerful. Can you feel it? This world doesn't like it, it senses that we do not belong. That is why our kind cannot stay here long enough to learn how to harness what we are, what we can do. But you, child, you can stay here. Because of what you are."

"I'm not, I'm *not*—"

Jacob Marber didn't bother to argue. He paused and lifted his face as if listening and then he said, "She is close. I must go."

"Who is close?" cried Marlowe.

But Jacob Marber was already spreading his fingers, almost gently, moving them in strange arcane gestures. A long thin rope of dust, tensile and somehow solid, snaked through the air and wrapped around Marlowe and held him fast.

Charlie clutched the knife and iron bar in his shaking hands. He felt light-headed, weak, like he couldn't catch his breath. But he just needed Jacob Marber to walk a few feet closer.

Then the monster spoke again and Charlie froze. "You will be safe here, child. She will not find you here."

"Wait! What're you doing? Stop it!" Marlowe was struggling, straining now against the ropes of dust. "Where are you going?"

"To lead her away from you. Then I will find Henry Berghast."

"Why? To kill him?"

Jacob Marber bowed his head in acknowledgment.

"You should kill the *drughr*," Marlowe cried angrily. "If you're really not bad, that's what you'd do."

Jacob Marber paused, his eyes shining. He looked overwhelmed by regret. "The drughr and I, we are bound to each other. I am sustained by her, as she is sustained by me. Killing her would not be so . . . easy." He lowered his voice. "But you must be careful, child. You are not alone in here. This is the world where the First Talent vanished. His power is still here. I can feel it. And Henry Berghast can feel it, too."

Marlowe ceased struggling, and stared at him. "So?"

"So why do you think Berghast wants that glove?"

"To stop the drughr."

Jacob Marber bowed his head, breathing. Then he looked up. "Be safe, little one. I will be back for you."

Then Charlie heard the banging of his steps descending through the strange house. A moment later, his dark shape appeared in the fog below, striding across the square. From the strange white tree a second figure detached itself, and scurried alongside, like a dog. Charlie knew that thing, the way it moved. He shuddered.

Marlowe was leaning up against one wall, across from the mummified talent, his arms pinned fast, his legs tied. The boy's little wrists were already red where the ropes stretched tight. Charlie at once kneeled and started worrying at the bonds.

Marlowe wouldn't look at him. "Charlie, did you hear what he said?"

"Worry about that later, Mar. Let's just get you out of this."

"He's going to kill Dr. Berghast."

"He's going to try. Hold still." But Charlie's hands were shaking so bad that he could hardly get his fingers around the cords of dust to try to pull at them. They felt soft, slippery almost, but also tensile and strong, and they flexed around the boy's arms and wrists and legs like living tentacles.

Outside, the fog slid past, ribboning with the dead.

Marlowe's voice was quiet when next he spoke and it was the quietness that made Charlie look at him. "I'm not a monster, Charlie," he said.

And then the boy was crying. Charlie dabbed at the boy's eyes with his sleeves. He said, "Don't you listen to him. Don't you let him get inside your head."

"I don't want to be . . . what he says I am."

"You're not."

The boy started crying again.

"Hey," said Charlie. "Hey, look at me. What about Brynt?"

Marlowe looked up. "Brynt?"

"She told you once you get to choose who your family is. So do it, Mar. Choose."

He lowered his face, miserable. "Brynt was wrong."

"You know she wasn't," he said fiercely. "She wasn't wrong at all. Now let me get these damn things off you. I don't understand how they're still here, aren't they supposed to just . . . disappear? If I can . . . just . . . get them . . ."

He was grunting, sweating with the effort. But there was no breaking them, no slackening them, nothing. They were not ropes. He couldn't untie a thing that had no end and no beginning and no knot anywhere and when he looked at Marlowe and saw the boy knew it too he saw a doubt creep into his face and he flinched and looked away. The kid was right to be afraid.

"It's no good, Charlie," he whispered. "Look at your hands."

They were shaking terribly. Charlie held them up in the eerie light. The skin was blotching, losing its pigment.

"You got to go, you can't stay here any longer. You need to get out. You *have* to."

"What if he comes back? And you're all alone here, tied up like this?"

But the boy was looking at him clearly, nodding his little black-haired head in that sad not-quite-a-child way that he had. And Charlie knew he was right, that he, Charlie, had to go back through the orsine, that he wouldn't be any use to Marlowe if he got sicker here. And the boy wouldn't be hurt, couldn't be hurt, not here, not like this. Charlie hung his head.

"I'll be coming right back," he whispered.

He picked up the strange glove from the soft floor, and it was almost like a sound was coming from it, a faint music he couldn't quite hear. The finger that wore his mother's ring started to ache. He stuffed the glove into his satchel.

"Do you remember the way back?" said Marlowe.

He did. He didn't even need the map. He'd find the river and then the dome of the cathedral and the building on Nickel Street and the dead stairs that led back up into the orsine. He'd be fast and he wouldn't stop for anything and he'd be back to get Marlowe before anything bad could happen. That's what he'd do. He stumbled to the door, swaying. He looked back at the little boy in his dark bindings, and he ran a hand across his eyes, and then he took the stairs two at a time with the satchel slapping at his side and he started to run.

35

STEAM AND IRON

B loodied, exhausted, Alice somehow managed to drag Mrs. Harrogate clear.

The drughr was long gone by then, Jacob Marber and Coulton gone with it. The weird shimmering gash in the air had closed over.

Alice wrestled Mrs. Harrogate through the dying glow of the lantern, their shadows crooked in the smoke. The black dust in the dark was choking. Mrs. Harrogate's feet left long dark streaks like a trail in the grime. Alice went back for the lantern and walked ahead and set the lantern carefully down and then went back and dragged Mrs. Harrogate farther. In this way, bit by bit, she made her slow return back up through the damp and the muck of the tunnel, toward the trapdoor and the warehouse and the world of the living.

They were maybe twenty feet from it when the lantern died for good and Alice, sweating, wheezing, her own wounds bleeding freely, just left it where it stood and hauled Mrs. Harrogate on. The keywrasse was padding alongside in the darkness, its one white paw seeming to glow as it went. There was a faint crack of daylight where the trapdoor didn't seal and she left the older woman moaning weakly and, because the ceiling was not high, she reached on her toes and pushed. The trapdoor opened lightly; no one had blocked it, thank God. Alice, grunting, hauled herself heavily up into the storeroom.

She could hear men moving about in the warehouse beyond, already at work. She was peering around for something, a rope maybe, something to help her get Harrogate out. Then she spied it: a ladder.

What she was thinking, as she grimaced and dragged the older woman out of that tunnel, back into the world, was how hopeless it all seemed now. Jacob Marber had escaped, with the help of the drughr; if Marber was a monster of terrible strength, the drughr was infinitely worse. Alice did not know fear but she'd known it when the drughr screamed. Coulton, poor Frank Coulton, had been made a litch; he seemed not to know her, let alone himself. Worse, Marber had vanished into thin air, through some kind of portal, and if he could move in such ways, how would she ever find him, corner him, destroy him? The only weapon she had was the keywrasse, and Marber had escaped with one of its weir-bents. Soon the creature would cease to obey Alice's commands; soon it would leave them, or turn on them, or both. Mrs. Harrogate feared it, and if Alice was learning anything, it was that what Margaret Harrogate feared, she too ought to fear. She thought of the monsters out there, stalking Marlowe and Charlie, and she bit back her fury. She could do nothing.

She sat a long time, just breathing, there in that storeroom. At some point Mrs. Harrogate lost consciousness. That was probably, thought Alice, for the best. At last she got up and somehow got the older woman over one shoulder and, with the keywrasse at her ankles, she staggered out into the roar and whoosh of the warehouse, a bloodstained and ragged figure carrying a body, her face streaked with muck.

Men stopped at their blocks of tackle to gape, men held a hand to barrels still suspended in the air to stare. The hell with it. Alice just set her jaw and stumbled past, out to the docks, and from there into the gray haze of morning carriages.

The first hansom refused on account of their appearance and the second refused to take the cat. The third was shabby and stained and charged her double but it took them directly to 23 Nickel Street West. Alice got out, ignoring the driver's disapproving look, the way he knuckled back his cap and sniffed, as if she and Mrs. Harrogate had been out drinking or worse. The driver didn't offer any help. Alice hauled Mrs. Harrogate through the iron gate and inside.

The house was dim, still. The keywrasse sniffed at a table leg, then vanished into the spill of shadow from the hall beyond. A door stood open. A stuffed boar's head on the wall hung undisturbed above a curtain. Alice waited a moment, listening. Then she carried Harrogate up and settled her in her bed, and at a basin she washed her own face and greasy hair, and then she went back downstairs and out into the street. She found a crossing sweep in front of Blackfriars Bridge and she gave the shivering lad two shillings and told him to fetch a doctor fast as he could. She held a third up between her fingers and told him it was his when the doctor arrived.

Then she went across to their rented room and collected up their things and settled with the landlady and dragged everything, roughly, through the intersection to No. 23.

Her head was aching, her knuckles were sore, the pain in her ribs was worse. She sat downstairs and waited for the doctor. He was an old man, Irish, out of breath even before climbing the stairs, and he sat with Mrs. Harrogate and pulled out a pocket watch and took her pulse and lifted her eyelids and frowned. He felt her knees; he turned her legs carefully at the hips. The crossing sweep lurked in the doorway, all eyes and grime, the third shilling in his fist.

"It was a fall from a horse," said Alice, standing. "She can't feel her legs."

"Some fall," the doctor grunted. He ran a hand over his whiskers. "And all these scratches?"

"Twigs. She was thrown in the park."

He picked something from his tongue. Tobacco. Then he unhooked his spectacles, tired. "She'll not walk again," he said bluntly. "I'm sorry." He took from his bag a small vial of medicine. "For the pain," he said.

Alice was past weeping. Weariness was all. She didn't know what to do; it was a feeling she wasn't used to, and she didn't like it. When Harrogate awoke, moaning, Alice administered the medicine, and the older woman fell back again, and slept again, and Alice washed the blood and dirt from Mrs. Harrogate's face and throat and left her. The last night she'd spent in this house, Coulton had still been alive, and she'd spent it sitting upright in the little room down the hall watching Marlowe's and Charlie's faces as they slept. That was in her too, and she didn't know what to do with it.

The keywrasse came to her all that day and rubbed against her ankles and leaped into her lap, purring. She would run a hand along its fur and scratch behind its ears and look down at it, a long wiry creature, its four golden eyes narrowing, and she would suppress a shudder, remembering what she had seen in that underground chamber, the size and many-legged frenzy of it.

"What are you?" she would murmur, stroking it. "You know Margaret is scared of you? Yes she is. Maybe I should be too, hm? What are we going to do, little one? How can we stop Marber now? I don't even have both your weir-bents anymore." She stared out the window at the poisonous yellow fog. "Margaret said you'll get strange if we can't lock you back away."

She was just talking, murmuring to herself. But something came to her then, almost like a sound, except it was in her mind. A flash of pain, an image all red in color, a sudden quick flare of understanding. *I am, I am, I am.* The voice was in her head, soft, accentless, insistent.

Then it was gone and there was something else, a kind of knowing: somehow Alice understood that the keywrasse was not only trapped by the weir-bents, made captive, as Margaret had explained, like a fish in a bowl—but also that it was wrong, deeply wrong, and that the poor creature oughtn't to be locked up. It ought to be *free*.

Her hand fell still. She was staring down at the keywrasse in shock. "What— Was that . . . Is that you?" she whispered. "Are you talking to me?"

The keywrasse flicked an ear, purred.

She stood abruptly and the creature leaped down, padded to the corner of the sofa, paused. Its tail stood high.

It can't be, thought Alice, watching it in fear. *Surely not.*

The next day she left the keywrasse locked in the front parlor and went out into the fog, alone. Though it was yet early, the mists had deepened, the streets were darker now but for the corona of lanterns, the blur of figures hurrying past. She came back with two small barrow wheels, of hooped iron and with stout oak spokes, and a small black case of woodworking tools. And she upended one of the contraptions stacked in the back bedroom and set about sawing and measuring and hammering. It was clean work and it gave her something to do. Her strong wrists were sore and scabbed where Coulton had attacked her but the pain didn't bother her. She was remembering something from her childhood at Bent Knee Hollow. There had been a woman there, very old, no longer able to walk, who had been put into an old wooden wheelbarrow, surrounded with cushions and blankets, and wheeled out to the bonfires every Sunday to be with the others. She was remembering that, and thinking of poor Mrs. Harrogate, a cripple now, and it felt good to be doing simple work again, work that had an end.

And when she'd built the axle and reinforced the under seat and attached the wheels at the right height she turned the cane chair upright and built an extended push bar for herself to use. Then she padded the seat and seat back with cushions and stood back and looked at her work.

A chair on wheels.

Mrs. Harrogate, for her part, had no interest in pity. She awoke angry in soiled blankets and Alice had to change her and wash her down and all the while the older woman was glowering and fighting back a disgust in her face. She wanted to know what had happened with the keywrasse (nothing), and what had happened with Jacob and the drughr (nothing), and whether Alice had made arrangements to notify Cairndale of what they'd been through (she had not). She had no interest in what the Irish doctor had diagnosed. She already knew.

"We must act at once, before Jacob and that creature can," she said, while Alice was rolling her to change her bedding. "I have remembered something, in my dreams. The glyphic. Jacob's deduction. I fear he is not wrong; and if the glyphic is indeed dying, then the orsine itself will tear apart. The drughr will come through."

Alice shuddered.

"Don't stand there gawping. Fetch me a pencil and a paper," Mrs. Harrogate said curtly. She grappled with the bedpost, dragged herself into a sitting position. "I will write out a message, and you must take it to the attic. There you will find a roost with my . . . messenger birds. Bonebirds, Miss Quicke. Like the one you saw at Cairndale. One will take my warning to Dr. Berghast."

When Alice still didn't move, the older woman paused and looked at her. Really *looked*. She put a hand to the marks on her face. "Ah," she murmured. "What is this? You have lost hope?"

Alice said nothing, ashamed. Whenever she closed her eyes she saw that thing, that drughr, huge and dark and screaming.

"Miss Quicke," said Mrs. Harrogate. "Let us be clear. Nothing worth the doing ever was easy. We shall prevail, but not if we give up now. You do not mean to give up, do you?"

"And what if I do?" said Alice suddenly, bitterly. She didn't mean it, not really, but all the anger and disappointment and guilt at having failed rose up to the surface, surprising even her with its vitriol. "Look at us, Margaret. What can we do to stop Marber now? He'll be nearly at Cairndale. You said it yourself, the glyphic is dying. Which means the drughr will . . ." She faltered, shuddering. "Meanwhile you can't even use a fucking bedpan."

Harrogate's eyes flashed. "And is Cairndale already overrun, then?"

"Maybe it is. Maybe Marber crawled through that fucking hole in the air and right into Berghast's water closet."

"He did not."

"Says you."

"He was injured, Miss Quicke. He will need time to recover, to gather his strength. As will the drughr. It will have taken much from it, opening that portal."

"You talk like you have a fucking clue. You don't."

"Ah," said Harrogate. "Here it is."

And it was true, Alice couldn't stop herself. "You have no idea what that thing even *is*," she exclaimed, "never mind what it can and can't *do*."

Mrs. Harrogate watched Alice a long moment. "I'd have thought you were made of stronger stuff," she said softly. "Mr. Coulton certainly thought so."

Alice blushed. The fury was seeping out of her, leaving her feeling embarrassed, petulant, tired. "Yeah, well, look where that got him," she muttered.

"Sit," said Mrs. Harrogate.

Alice, reluctant, sat.

"It is *not* finished, Miss Quicke. Despite what Jacob believes, Mr. Thorpe is not dead yet. And he is rather more resilient than most.

It seems Dr. Berghast has known of his condition; I expect he will have some sort of plan in place, should the worst come to pass." She fixed a steely eye on Alice. "Your Marlowe can still be saved, and young Charles Ovid. Unless we decide, now, *not* to act. Then it is indeed finished; then we will indeed have failed."

"But they're too powerful. What can we do?"

"We shall think of something," said Harrogate. "That is what we shall do." Her eyes alighted on the wheeled cane chair Alice had constructed, sitting in a corner under the window. "We shall begin by putting me in that *contraption*. You will pack a traveling case for the two of us. We shall go north, together, on the express."

Alice looked at the shadows on the wallpaper, looked back. It all seemed pointless. Even if they could get there in time . . . Just then the keywrasse slipped through the open door and padded over to the bed and leaped, lightly, onto the bedclothes. It curled up and began to wash itself.

"We will bring the creature," Mrs. Harrogate said.

Alice grimaced. "It . . . spoke to me. Last night. It showed me that it . . . it's trapped by the keys, hurt by them. It deserves to be freed, Margaret. It's in pain."

"It spoke to you?" Mrs. Harrogate pursed her lips. "The weir-bents are the only things that keep it in check, Miss Quicke, and keep us safe. Make no mistake. They are the bars on its cage, true. But would you have a wild beast walking free? The longer it remains among us, not locked away, the less our hold on it lasts."

The keywrasse lifted its face, flicked an ear. Yawned.

"It is listening, of course. Aren't you?" Then Mrs. Harrogate met Alice's eye with a dark and troubled look. "You saw what it is capable of. We must recover that key."

"Or?"

But Mrs. Harrogate left Alice's question hanging and did not answer it. She didn't need to; Alice knew only too well the older woman's meaning. *Or it must be destroyed.* It felt wrong to her though. When she looked at the keywrasse she saw not savagery but dignity. Did it not deserve to meet its own nature, to return to its own rightful place?

But the older woman was not finished. "We have another problem. If Jacob holds the other weir-bent, then the keywrasse will not be able to attack him. He is safe."

Alice absorbed this. It seemed it couldn't get much worse.

Last of all Mrs. Harrogate added, in a low voice, "Jacob is not going to wait for Mr. Thorpe to die. He intends to hasten his demise, Miss Quicke. He means to kill the glyphic."

"But he can't get into Cairndale, not while the glyphic is—"

"He will use Walter."

Alice blinked. "The litch? How?"

"He's already there. At Cairndale."

Alice rubbed at her face, trying to make sense of it all. "Walter's dead, Margaret. He died on the train—"

"He did not, unfortunately. Dr. Berghast has him at Cairndale. He was found unconscious off the railway line after the attack and taken north by Dr. Berghast's manservant. He was to be . . . interrogated." Mrs. Harrogate's eyes were black with disgust. "We thought we were being clever. But we were not clever. Walter is there by design. Jacob *wants* him there. And if Walter gets loose, and kills the glyphic—"

Alice wet her lips. "Then that monster can get in."

Margaret nodded. "Anything can."

The keywrasse, purring, lifted its four golden eyes.

At that very moment, deep under Cairndale, Walter Laster was scrabbling backward in the wet darkness, his chains rattling, until he was pressed up against the stone wall. He was cold. So cold. Somewhere in the dark on the far side stood the little table, the blue dish with its opium. He had always done right by his Jacob, hadn't he? He did love him, didn't he?

Oh, but Jacob had not abandoned him, not his own friend . . .

Time passed in the absolute. Lightless hours, lightless days. Sometimes the door would click, the bolts rasp back, and then a crack of light would groan and widen, and the tall silent man would come in, the servant, what was his name . . . Bailey . . . He'd peer down at Walter with a frightening look in his eye and Walter'd whimper, oh, Walter'd beg. Please, please, don't hit me again, please. Then the dark again, and the door. The click, the bolts drawing back, that same crack of lantern light widening, and the manservant, Bailey, would be back, bringing him water maybe, bringing him meat.

But the other one, the doctor, the one with the white beard and terrible eyes who pretended to be kind, *Henry Berghast*, yes . . . *he* did *not* come. And Walter waited, while all around him the air hummed with violence, the stones trembled faintly, and he felt the orsine like a living thing, eager.

Walter Walter—

"We are Walter," he would whisper. Feeling a sadness in his heart. Running his tongue along the needled points of his teeth.

Jacob is coming, Walter. It is almost time . . .

And he would whimper to himself, and rattle the chains at his wrists, as if the voices could see, could hear, and he would shake his head in frustration. "But we can't do it, how can we do it, look, look at us. . . ."

The thrumming in the air kept on. The voices did not cease.

Walter Walter little Walter, they would whisper. *Jacob is coming. Find the glyphic. Find the glyphic find the glyphic find the—*

36

THE ALCHEMIST'S TRUTH

Komako watched Ribs in her heavy cloak cross between the bollards on the far side of the street and go into the chandler's. The door closed behind her. The shop was dark and the windows reflected back the watery distortions of the street. At her elbow Oskar was sniffling, eyes creased with worry.

Five minutes passed.

Ten.

"All right," said Komako. "Let's go get her."

"Aren't we supposed to wait for her to come out?" said Oskar. "Isn't that what you said?"

She wiped the rain from her face. "Whose plan is this?"

"Yours?"

"Mine. And if you'd like to wait out here alone—"

"I don't," said Oskar quickly.

· · ·

The inside of Albany Chandlers was very quiet, very dim. The front windows were greasy with soot on the inside and a rainy daylight came through poor and thin. The door shut with a clatter of its bell behind her and Komako stood a long moment, letting her eyes adjust.

The air felt close, unhealthy. A reek of tallow fat and oils and something sharper and meaner, like lye, burned her nostrils. Tall stacks of industrial candles beside the door, wooden crates sealed and stamped. Komako stepped cautiously forward, peeling off her gloves as she did so.

It was a narrow corner shop, with the clerk's desk far at the back. Her eyes scanned the low ceiling, stained brown where the water had got in over the years. Gas sconces, turned weakly up, hung from the walls. When she could see better she started down a long aisle cluttered with tins and jars and stacks of ropes of all manner of thinness and she heard Oskar follow, his wet shoes squeaking softly. There was arguing from deeper in the shop. Two voices.

But neither belonged to Ribs. It was a man and a woman, old, married maybe. The woman sounded unhappy about something, affronted. Komako ducked her head as she neared but then, before she'd reached them, her eye caught on something under a shelf, and she froze. It was a wet cloak, neatly folded. Also a plain gray dress, a shift, a pair of very wet shoes.

Oskar crouched beside her, shaking his head. "She's got undressed, Ko," he whispered. "She's gone and made herself invisible."

"Brilliant." Oskar's real talent, she thought irritably, might be for stating the obvious. But if Ribs had stripped down it meant she might be anywhere. It also meant she must have seen something, heard something that required caution. She and Oskar should be wary.

"Oi! You!"

Komako looked up. An old woman in a leather apron and with a handkerchief tying off her hair was glaring down at her. She sounded

English, not Scottish. A wooden spoon was gripped in one wizened fist. Her other hand was missing.

"What're you lot sneakin round for, then?"

"We are not sneaking," said Komako calmly, enunciating each word. She pulled her hood back off her face. Oskar did the same.

"Why, it's a wee lascar girl, Edward," the woman exclaimed. She was looking past them and Komako turned now and saw at the other end of the aisle, blocking their retreat, an old heavyset man in shirt-sleeves. His beard was unkempt and stained by tobacco around the mouth. His hairy wrists were ringed black with dirt. "An if she don't speak the Queen's English!"

"Huh," the man grunted.

Komako lifted her chin at the man's name, ignoring the old woman's remark. "Mr. Edward Albany?" she said. "That is you, sir?"

"Huh," the man grunted again. His eyebrows came down in a suspicious glower.

"We've been looking for you, sir. We're from the Cairndale Institute. Do you know it?" She watched his face to see his reaction but there was nothing, not a flicker of recognition. She turned back to the old woman but she too seemed to be waiting for Komako to say something more.

"Go on," said the woman. "What of it?"

"Do you not make deliveries to the institute?" Komako said, suddenly uncertain.

Edward Albany frowned and peered helplessly over at the woman. Komako saw then that there was something childlike about him, despite his age. His other hand held several loops of wire and he hung them on a hook on one shelf, replacing them, and then he shrugged and shuffled off to another part of the shop. She could hear his heavy breathing even after he was gone.

Oskar was looking at her under lowered lashes, a question in his eyes. Ribs was nowhere.

"So what is it you'd be needin then, lass?" the woman asked, taking charge. "Deliveries, you say? We make aplenty of takeaways but only inside the city limits. It's just the two of us here, you see. An we ain't half what we used to be. Where did you say you was at?"

She'd drifted closer now and Komako could smell the lye and fat coming off her. Her one hand was scoured to the wrist and discolored and her other stump was raw-looking like meat. She had eyes yellowing with age or malnutrition or some darker illness and they wept slightly at the corners and Komako saw all at once that she'd been mistaken, that the woman's gruffness was not unkindness. She was just poor, and had lived a hard life.

"You're soaked to the bone, the two of you," muttered the woman. "You're drippin all over my floors."

Komako nodded. "Yes, ma'am."

"Come, come. I'm Mrs. Ficke. We must be at gettin you warm. Now, there's a wee stove in the back what gives off heat like a horse. An what's your name, lad?"

"Oskar, ma'am."

Komako could feel herself relaxing, too. "Mrs. Ficke," she said, "does the name Henry Berghast mean anything to you? We're here on account of him."

The old woman, close now, tapped the wooden spoon thoughtfully against her chin. "Berghast, Berghast . . . ," she muttered. Her eyes lit up. "Why, I believe it do."

Komako was drying her hands on her pinafore. "You know him, then?"

Something shifted in Mrs. Ficke's face, a flicker of shadow, just beneath the skin. She said, "White beard? Handsome as the devil?" She nodded. "A fair temper on him though. Oh, aye, I reckon I know him."

Komako hadn't worked out in her head what she'd say after that. She'd been imagining they'd have to sneak in, eavesdrop maybe—not meet the owner or director or whatever she was, and find her quite so . . . obliging.

"Mrs. Ficke," she began, "we're here on account of some deliveries Cairndale receives, every two weeks. And the, um, passengers the carriage takes on. We were directed here. We have some questions—"

"Directed *here*? To my shop? By who, love?"

"It's complicated."

"Most things are, I don't doubt it." A shrewd look came over her face. "Tell me true though. Do Henry know his wards is escaped, an is pokin around in his business?"

The old woman's yellow eyes flicked—for only a second—to the left of Komako. But it was warning enough. Komako spun quickly on her heel, drawing the dust to her fingertips.

But there was Edward Albany, already looming up over the top of the shelf, a heavy cudgel in his fist. Everything happened very fast then. Albany knocked over the jars as his heavy arm swung hard down and Komako heard Oskar cry out. She was summoning the dust but it was too late, his arm was coming down again, and then a searing pain filled her head and her eyes rolled back up in her skull and all at once everything went blessedly, painlessly, soundlessly, dark.

Ribs, invisible behind the counter, watched in silence as her friends were struck unconscious. She made no move to help them, nor, as the old chandler locked the front door fast and flipped the hanging sign to CLOSED, did Ribs stir and try to get closer. Manipulating her talent after a long night of no sleep was making her skin crawl, the seams in it feeling like they were on fire. She winced but kept the pain in check. What she needed now, most of all, was to be still.

Truth was, she was feeling irritated. Irritated at Komako's impatience, irritated by the old woman's sly questions. Sure, it'd been maybe a stupid notion, sneaking down to Edinburgh to find out what Berghast was up to. She could've told Ko that. Hell, she had. But did anyone ever listen to her?

Like to get them killed, it were.

She'd slipped into the shop quietly, reaching up to muffle the bell as the door closed behind her, and then started her slow way down one aisle. That was when she'd heard the old ones talking, and crouched suddenly, and listened. Almost the first word she'd heard was *Cairndale*. She stripped silently down and rubbed her hair dry with her shirt and then left her clothes hidden. She let the prickling come over her skin until there was only light and dust where her flesh ought to be. It was always a dizzying moment, looking down at her hands and feet and seeing nothing, and always there was that quick instant when she felt like she was falling. But it passed, as it always did; her head cleared; and she crept forward to hear better.

The old woman with the missing hand was talking about the deliveries. One was due that night, it seemed, and she was instructing the grizzled man as to the particular care of the crates. Whatever was in these ones, it seemed, it was breakable, and of greater value than usual. The man just nodded in time to her instructions, mute, grim. And that was when the old woman said it.

"Soon, now," she muttered. "That poor glyphic won't much longer live, an there's no solution here for it. Ye can't stopper a hole in a boat with beeswax, my old Mr. Ficke used to say. An them what's upstairs is beeswax, or worse. No, Henry'll not put it off much longer."

The old woman broke off, raised her yellow eyes. Ribs held her breath. The woman was glaring in her direction, almost as if she could see her.

But that was when the door clattered at the front of the shop; Ribs glanced back: it was Komako and Oskar, come dripping in.

And now they were struck down, the dolts. She ground her teeth. But watching the careful way the old woman and her companion handled them, the care they took not to knock their heads on the shelves as they carried them toward the cellar stairs, gave Ribs pause. Whatever else, the old woman didn't seem to mean them harm.

At least not just yet.

There was an old rickety staircase leading up from the back of the shop to the second floor, and Ribs hurried toward it. Upstairs, the old woman had said. Ko and Oskar would need rescuing, sure. But when she'd done that, there'd be no more chance to look around; best get an eyeful first.

Silently, keeping to the outer edge of the steps to avoid creaking, she went up.

Komako opened her eyes onto darkness. Her head was throbbing. She shifted and saw her blotchy hands were tied in front of her, her pockets turned out. Oskar lay beside her, similarly tied. They were on the floor of a badly lit cellar, the dirt under her cold and damp.

"Ah, she wakes. Excellent." The old woman was moving about in the darkness, shifting things, kicking through some rubbish, and her voice came creaking and muffled to Komako's ears.

She groaned despite herself, shaking her head to clear it.

"That'd be Edward's doing," said the woman. "I *am* sorry about your head. He don't know his own strength. But we can't be too careful. Just one moment as I finish with this . . ."

She must have found what she was seeking then, for she paused, and a moment later a light bloomed in the cellar and Komako saw where they were.

It was a laboratory workshop. There were glass pipes high up along the walls with some sort of liquid moving slowly through them and stoves in two corners with something bubbling there. A book-shelf slumped under the weight of thick tomes. Near Komako, in a long wooden trough, she saw hundreds of white beetles crawling over themselves. There were crates and barrels covered in dust, looming up out of the darkness, and jars of dead things along the far wall. And at a long table in the center of the cellar Mrs. Ficke was working, shifting jars and books out of the way, making some concoction. She had at-tached a strange apparatus, a kind of iron hook with moveable claws, worked by gears and levers, to the stump of her damaged arm. It was held in place using leather straps and buckles that crossed her chest and ran behind her shoulders. Deftly she used it to move jars and lift boxes and unclasp wires that held the lids to jars. Komako stared.

Oskar was stirring now, lifting his plump face, peering in sudden fear around him as their situation dawned on him. "Ko?"

"It's all right," she whispered. "We're all right."

"Hello, Oskar," said Mrs. Ficke softly. "I do apologize for the ropes."

"What will you do to us?" Komako demanded.

"Do?"

"Will you hurt us?"

The old woman grimaced. "Oh, child. Of course not."

"I don't believe you."

"As you wish." She was continuing to work at her long table, pour-ing out a fine powder onto a scale, measuring it with care.

"Prove it," said Komako. "Untie us now, then."

Mrs. Ficke paused only long enough to smile a condescending smile but she made no move to untie them. Above them the floorboards of the shop creaked as someone—Edward Albany, perhaps—walked heavily by. Dust sifted down in the lantern light.

"You would be the girl called Komako," said Mrs. Ficke. "The dust-worker. Yes?"

Komako blinked. "You . . . know who we are?"

"More than you can imagine. And you, Oskar. Where is your companion, your . . . flesh giant, is it? What is it you call him?"

Oskar glared. "He's coming for me. You don't want to be here when he does."

"I am sure you are right. A rather formidable creature. I expected Eleanor to be with you."

"She's going for help."

"Oh, I think not." The old woman looked around at the darkness. "No, I think she is here, with us, now. You *are* here, are you not, Eleanor? I trust you are not intending to do something foolish."

There was no sound from the darkness, no reply. It didn't *feel* to Komako like Ribs was near, though it was sometimes hard to tell. She was afraid for her friend. Then again, she supposed, wherever Ribs was, was probably better than here.

"No matter," said Mrs. Ficke. "Is it answers you are seeking? Henry never did like me much, but I don't expect he'd send his wards as a . . . warning. So I'll assume you are here of your own accord. What did you do, run off from the institute? Or have you come in search of something more . . . *specific?*"

Komako wet her lips. She felt the cold come over her wrists, the icy pain, and she breathed in sharply as the dust began to swirl around her fingers. If this woman knew as much as she claimed, then she'd have known ropes would be little use against Komako's talent.

But Mrs. Ficke made a soft clicking noise, as if in disapproval. "That is neither necessary, Komako, nor useful. Not if it is answers you are seeking."

And the old woman took out one of her alembics with her good hand and came around the table and poured a dark powder in a circle around where Komako and Oskar lay. All at once the pain went out of Komako's fingers, the dust settled, her talent was gone.

"What—"

"It is a muting powder, child. Of my own devising. I got the idea of it from study of a bone witch, oh, many years ago. It doesn't work for long. But it will allow us to be civil with one another, at least for now." Mrs. Ficke stumped back around her long worktable, shifted some bottles and jars, poked at the smoking liquid. The lantern was shining from a stack of ancient books beside her.

"You are afraid my intention is to harm you. But we are not at odds, you and I. Our kind should not be. It is not right. Besides, Henry will have his own punishments for you, when you return to Cairndale."

"Our kind?"

"I'm like you. Or used to be, at least. You look surprised."

If Komako's face betrayed her disbelief, she couldn't have helped it. She lowered her chin so that her hair fell across her eyes.

"I'm one of the exiles. Ah, you've heard of us? Not much though, I expect. They rarely spoke about it in my day either." The old woman frowned. "There's some as lose their talents, when they come of age. For no reason anyone can explain. They just . . . fade, one day. An if that day comes, it's the Cairndale way—it's Henry's way—to ask them, politely, to leave."

"She was sent away," Oskar whispered, understanding.

"Dr. Berghast would never do that," said Komako quickly, firmly.

But Mrs. Ficke just raised her face in the glow of the lantern. Her voice was soft. "You know Henry so well, then?"

"She's been alone ever since," Oskar whispered to Ko. "Imagine . . ."

"I'll have none of that, boy," she said, glaring at Oskar. "No pity from you. I've had a life more interesting than most. There's no shortage of experiments to be done, knowledge to be acquired." She gestured at the cellar around them. "It don't look like much, it's no fancy university. But it's mine. There's never been much room for a woman in the Royal Academy, anyhow. But their kind wouldn't much care for my interests. Think only what they're supposed to think, they do.

Whereas I have made a life's study of the opposite. I've studied what ought not to exist."

Komako glowered. "Yeah. Candles."

"Alchemy, dear. An older branch of knowledge than science, and a wiser one. Oh, the scientists are afraid of what we alchemists once knew. When Henry sent me away, I was nineteen years old. I was of little use to him then."

"You think he needs you now?"

The woman's eyes glittered. "Oh, I have made myself useful."

"Because of the glyphic."

"My tinctures, yes," murmured Mrs. Ficke. "I've kept him alive this long. You are a clever little bird, hm? But I've done more than just that, my pet."

The knots at Komako's wrists bit into her flesh. She glanced at Oskar in the lantern light; he was staring wide-eyed at the old woman, frightened.

"What're you saying?" Komako whispered slowly, dreading the answer. "What things have you done?"

Ribs stopped at the top of the stairs. Below her, the shop was quiet. She could hear the sound of the rain drumming against the roof, faintly, somewhere. She took a cautious step forward.

The upper floor of Albany Chandlers was unlit and dim. Ribs found herself in a long hallway running the length of the building, ending at a street-facing window. That window had been bricked over sometime in the past. There were several small high windows set in the right wall, casting what little light there was; on the left were many doors, as in a boardinghouse, all of them closed.

It was then she heard the sound. A kind of whimpering, coming from the nearest door. It might have been a kitten, crying. She tried the door pull but it didn't open and then she pressed an ear against the door. The mewling stopped; started again.

There were seven doors in total. Each of them was locked. She could hear no sound from the others, except for the penultimate door—a scrabbling sound, from within, as of a small animal digging.

She turned, unsure. Heavy footfalls were approaching up the stairs.

It was the large man, Edward Albany. He was carrying a wooden crate in his scoured fingers and something in the crate was clinking. Ribs watched him kneel, set it down on the floor with an unexpected gentleness, and then lift out a bowl of some kind of slop and a greasy drinking cup. Then he unlocked the first door and went in.

Swiftly, her heart in her throat, she padded back down the dim hall. A strong reek of unwashed flesh reached her. At the doorway she paused, trying to make sense of what she was looking at.

A small room. The interior was dark, the far window boarded over. Slats of daylight came in between the boards and fell across the floor in stripes. Ribs saw the small bed. The clothes chest. The ragged figure in one corner, hunched and turned away, shuddering, weeping softly. And she saw how Edward Albany placed the dish and the cup down just within the door and went in and loomed over the child.

Except it wasn't a child. She saw that now. It was soft and deformed and lifted a crooked arm up as Edward Albany crouched beside it. What looked like roots or branches had sprouted all along its back, and its gown had been cut away to accommodate them. Albany took it into his arms and held it and rocked it and crooned to it and slowly, slowly the thing stopped its weeping. The strange rootlike protrusions entwined all up Edward Albany's wrists and arms, but gently. It seemed the creature could not walk but only drag itself and after a time Albany lifted it effortlessly and carried it to the little bed and laid it down. There was a shelf with books on it, Ribs saw now, and he opened one and began to read. And it was then the creature lifted its face, and moved its tongue as if trying to speak, and Ribs saw in horror just who it was.

His features had shifted, melted almost. His nose stood crooked and the eyes were strangely sunken in their sockets, yes, but it was him, she knew his face, had seen it for the past six years in the halls, in the dining room, out in the fields.

It was the missing boy, the one they called Brendan. The one who'd been building the model of Cairndale out of matchsticks.

Edward Albany was reading gently to Brendan, one big scarred hand tousling the boy's hair. That hair was white and growing strangely from the side of his scalp. Ribs glanced down at the crate and saw six more bowls and six more cups and she peered back along the corridor at the six other doors and then she understood.

Below, in the cellar, Komako was rubbing her wrists, shifting closer to Oskar, watching through the gloom as Mrs. Ficke continued at her work on the long table. The old woman had gone mercurial, sly. She seemed like she wanted to say more but had stopped herself.

The air smelled scorched, strange.

"Go on," said Komako, frustrated. "Why help Cairndale, if you were sent away? Why work for Dr. Berghast at all, if you don't like him?"

"Like?" A flicker of a smile crossed the old woman's face. "What has liking a person to do with it?"

"You could just leave. Go to London, America, anywhere. You don't have to stay here, making . . . tinctures."

Mrs. Ficke sniffed. "Everything seems so simple, at your age. I remember it. But nothing is, not really, not when you bring time and betrayal and forgiveness into it. Truth is, I owe Henry a . . . debt. A debt I'll not repay in full, no matter how I try." She inclined her head a moment, then looked up. The gears of her iron hook whirred down. "My brother, Edward. Henry showed him a kindness that did save his life. It is the right thing to honor one's debts, even if they must be paid in blood."

"In—in—in blood—?" stammered Oskar.

Komako felt the heat rise to her cheeks. "I'm sorry," she said quietly. "What happened?"

Mrs. Ficke shrugged.

"You are right to be suspicious, pets." Mrs. Ficke's pale tongue poked out, as if testing the air. "I'd of been the same way, once. Now let's be frank with each other. You are here on account of the missing children. Do not lie to me."

Oskar opened his mouth, started to speak, closed it.

Komako shook her braid out of her face. "Where are they?"

"There's more at work here than you can imagine," Mrs. Ficke murmured. "You think you're hunting a lion. But it's the jungle what's hunting you both."

She paused then and stared at the shadows across the cellar, as if deciding something. Then she went over and untied their ropes. Oskar sat up, rubbing his wrists. Komako's own wrists were on fire and she stretched and worked the raw skin gingerly.

"Eleanor," called the old woman. "Do come out. You'll find I've brought your clothes down and left them behind that barrel, in the corner. If you'd care to dress and join us—?"

Komako smiled sharply to herself. She hoped Ribs was far from there, maybe looking for a way to help. But after a moment, to her surprise, she heard Ribs's voice.

"I seen them," the voice whispered, in a fury.

"Seen what?"

From behind a crate, Ribs appeared, her face streaked with dirt, her hair wild and stringy about her shoulders. She was already dressed. She walked slowly over and stood beside Komako and Oskar, her face radiating hatred. She hardly spared a glance for Komako; all her rage was directed at Mrs. Ficke.

"I seen Brendan. And them others."

Mrs. Ficke went very still. Her hooked claw was suspended over a fire and she withdrew it and blinked and frowned. "You wasn't supposed to go upstairs," she said.

"What you done to him, then, eh?" Ribs demanded. Her voice was rising. "What you done to all them? When Dr. Berghast finds out—"

"When he *finds out.*"

"When I tell him what you done—"

"When you *tell* him."

"You'll be bloody well sorry, then." Ribs had her fists clenched and she took a menacing step toward the old woman.

But Mrs. Ficke didn't even flinch. "Ah, pet, you really don't understand it at all," she said, with regret. "That'd be Henry's doing, what's up them stairs. Not mine."

"The hell it is!" Ribs shouted.

Komako pulled her friend back. "What's going on? Ribs?"

Ribs whirled around. Her eyes were wild. "They're *monsters*, Ko," she said in a rush. "They're all locked in little rooms an they, they been made all into . . ." She shuddered.

Oskar's mouth was open. "Who are? The missing kids?"

Komako stepped sharply away from the muting powder and drew in a thick fistful of dust. A quick fury was in her. She felt the lurch and sharp intake of pain rising in her wrists and up her forearms as the dust took hold. She glanced at the stairs but there was no sign of Edward Albany.

"Go on, then," said Mrs. Ficke, unimpressed by Komako's display.

"But there won't be none to feed or wash or change them, if you do. You think Henry cares to keep them alive? It ain't but me an Mr. Edward done that."

A strong black dust was swirling at Komako's fists.

"Show me," she said. "Show me what you've done."

Komako had never felt such anger, such power. It frightened her. They met Edward Albany on the upper stairs and despite his size she felt how easy it would be to snap his neck with a rope of dust. He was holding a crate of dirty bowls and cups at his belly and he stood blinking, staring down at the darkness spiraling around her fists, as if confused, until his sister shooed him impatiently aside and led them past.

Mrs. Ficke stopped at the fourth door along the barren hallway. "This here is Deirdre," she said, taking out a ring of keys. "She came to us, oh, some two years ago now. She don't know her own self, so stand back, you lot. No sense in frightening the poor thing more than she is already."

Komako's fists were smoldering. The cold pain was in her shoulders now, radiating through her bones. She knew she ought to let it go, release it, but there was in the pain something new, something she liked.

"Ko, your eyes," said Ribs.

"They've gone all black," whispered Oskar. He looked worried.

She didn't care. It felt good. But when she saw the shrunken girl in the room, and the way Mrs. Ficke kneeled next to her, and stroked her back, all at once the rage died. She let go of the dust, just let it go, and it collapsed instantly, settling like ash on her clothes and shoes and the floor.

For there was such tenderness all at once in the old woman.

The girl Deirdre was standing in the middle of the room. The window had been painted over with lime but still it filled the small room with a gentle light. The girl's hair had turned white and was long and pulled over her face, as if she were shy, as if she were ashamed. Her body was small, like the body of a little child, and there was something the matter with her lower half. Her ankles, her knees, her thighs, all had hardened and intertwined into a single gnarled tree, her feet like roots, her legs the trunk. Her fingers were long and husked and sprouted little green leaves. Komako felt a revulsion rising in her, despite her. Oskar gasped. Ribs's eyes were wet.

"What . . . is she?" whispered Komako.

"Glyph-twisted," said Mrs. Ficke. "That is what she is. An a horrible thing it is, too." There was a small sewn doll in the corner and the old woman retrieved it and slid it into the unmoving crook of Deirdre's arm. "This is all what's left of her, poor creature. Didn't seem right, letting Henry dispose of her. Any of them. So we done what we could, we brung them here to take care of them. They're just sad and confused, mostly. I don't know what's left of them on the inside. But on the outside there's no part of them is harmful at all."

"You . . . care for them?" said Ribs slowly.

Mrs. Ficke pulled the girl's hair gently behind one ear, revealing a pale heart-shaped face, its eyes closed. "No one else done it," she said.

"What is glyph-twisted?" said Komako.

Now the old woman's face hardened. "Oh, these are just exiles, like me. Except when they lost their talents, Henry gave these little ones a choice. He told them about Mr. Thorpe, an his sickness, an what all's like to happen to the institute when the glyphic dies, an the orsine rips open. An he said what if they could help. He said what if they could keep their friends safe. An in return, he'd give them their talent back. These here are the ones what agreed to try."

"To try what?" whispered Komako. But she already knew the answer.

"To be made a new glyphic. In his image, like. To take over for Mr. Thorpe when he dies, an control the orsine an the wards an such. Oh, it's never worked, of course. A glyphic don't get made like this. But Henry had his notion that the key to everything were us exiles. Except now"—the old woman ran her palm tenderly along the girl's cheek, her voice tired—"now he's out of time."

"What do you mean?" said Oskar.

"The glyphic's dying, child. The drughr's coming. An then the dead will pour through. The orsine needs to be closed for good, like, to be *sealed*, an there's only the one way of doing that."

"What way is that?"

"Carve out the glyphic's heart, an sink it into the orsine."

"Nope," said Ribs quickly. "I'm out."

Komako glared. "That's disgusting."

Mrs. Ficke allowed a grim smile. "The world's an ugly place, loves. Unfortunately, I weren't consulted when it were being made. But here's the truth: Henry Berghast can't allow the orsine to be closed. How else is he to bring the drughr to him, if not through the orsine?"

"*Through* the orsine?" whispered Ribs, turning. "Did she just say *through* the orsine?"

Komako wasn't sure she'd heard right, either. "He wants to bring the drughr *into* Cairndale? Why would he do that?"

Mrs. Ficke's voice was soft. "The drughr is the difference between horror and fear, my pet. It's the kind of fear what fills you with revulsion, what makes you prefer . . . obliteration. This," she murmured, stroking the girl's hair, "is preferable to the drughr's bite. And yet, even so—it's Henry Berghast what you ought to fear more."

Ribs, for her part, just scowled. "Maybe luring the drughr into Cairndale's the best bloody way to *destroy* it."

"You aren't listening," said the old woman, shaking her head. "Henry Berghast's been hunting the drughr since before you were born. The drughr's power has never been measured. If it could be harnessed, if it could be absorbed . . ."

Komako raised her face in shock. "Absorbed—?"

Mrs. Ficke gestured with her hooked claw. Daylight filled her eyes, sad and bright. "That's what I'm trying to tell you. Henry don't mean to *destroy* the drughr, pet," she whispered. "He means to *become* it."

37

THE STRANGE MACHINERY OF FATE

Something was coming, something awful.

In a second-class carriage north of Doncaster, Alice Quicke sat with her face turned to the window, brooding out at the early light. She could feel it approaching, a kind of dread, racing toward her over the spine of the world. In a basket at her feet lay the keywrasse, purring; in the pocket of her greatcoat lay the old revolver, its chambers loaded. She gripped it fast. They would not reach Princes Street Station in Edinburgh until evening.

Margaret Harrogate, in the seat across from her, did not permit herself to brood, not about her crushed spine, not about how she'd never walk again, not about the bad feeling that was in her. The wheeled chair Miss Quicke had built, wedged in a corner, bumped softly against the paneled door. Across the fields the white sky filled with light, darkened again.

At Cairndale, far to the north, Henry Berghast could feel it too.

He stood in the damp cell where Walter was chained, a lantern raised in his fist. For two days the litch had eaten nothing, drank nothing, refused even a dish of opium, and now it lay fetal and still on its side, in the weak lantern glow. Was it sick? Was it dying? He didn't know. He thought of the two boys who had passed through the orsine and not come back and he nudged the litch with his boot where it lay unmoving like a dead thing. He had the sudden feeling—the unfamiliar, unpleasant feeling—that events were spiraling out of his control.

When the cell door groaned shut at last, and the locks turned and double-turned in the darkness, Walter Laster lifted his head, listening. He was very weak. Jacob was close now, so close. The manacles spun loosely over his bony wrists but though Walter struggled he couldn't pull his hands through. In the absolute blackness he put a thumb between his teeth, and held it there a moment, like a baby. Then, ignoring the pain, he bit down hard, and wrenched and twisted and started to chew.

There was no one in the glyphic's lair to see how he trembled and thrashed up out of his dream. He could *feel* it, the white creature that did not belong in either world, devouring itself. But there'd been another presence, too, a living child, alone and in pain in the other world. Who was that? He tried to reach out with his thoughts but in his mind there was only the creature, its hunger like a mouth, the evil of it. They were not strong enough.

The spirits were gathering outside the Room. Marlowe lay cold and hungry, still tied fast in Jacob's ropes of dust. He could see the fog of the dead hovering at the top of the stairs, silent. Just waiting. Just watching. Brynt was with them, his Brynt. She never took her eyes from him and though her face was changeable as the light, and her form but a column of air, her stare was black and lifeless and did not change. The boy turned his face away.

Something was coming. Abigail Davenshaw, seated at her vanity, drawing a hairbrush through her long straight hair, was trying to make sense of it. It was after midday. The children were still missing. Dr. Berghast was nowhere to be found either. And there was a locked room hidden beneath his study. She'd felt a cold fear as she'd stood there, listening to whatever lay inside it breathe. She lowered the hairbrush. She unscrewed a jar of cream, thinking.

The white sky was blinding as Komako rode out of Edinburgh in Edward Albany's wagon, Ribs and a sleeping Oskar jolting alongside her on the bench. The midmorning roads were crowded. She was a poor driver of horses but the mare seemed to know its way and the mud was not deep. There was fear in her heart, and dread, and something else, too. Rage. Beside her, Oskar started to snore.

Meanwhile, miles away, across the rough Scottish hills, a creature of meat and sinew lurched unsteadily on, skin glistening wetly. Lymenion was strong enough to uproot a tree with his bare hands but his thoughts were filled with worry. *Oskar*, he thought. *Oskar—Oskar—Oskar—*

White clouds massed under a flat light. Shadows shrank and grew long.

Tick-tick-tick went all the gears in all the clocks in all the world.

With the last of his strength, Charlie Ovid forced a shoulder against the viscous skin of the orsine, feeling it stretch and shape itself around him, and desperately, with the knife gripped in his two shaking hands, he stabbed and stabbed his way through, sawing a ragged opening, bursting up out of it, gasping, soaked, shivering into the dim light of his world.

He'd got through. He'd made it.

That was what was in his head: relief. The *feeling* of it. His thoughts, such as they were, were sluggish, as if he'd been asleep a long time.

How long had he been gone? A lantern had been left burning on one wall; but the chamber was empty. He tried to stand, but couldn't. Instead he curled up on the floor, amid the roots, shaking, the cold smoking off him like steam. His hands were twisted into a rictus of claws and the skin across his knuckles was a dark gruesome shade and the ring, his mother's ring, burned where he wore it on his finger.

What had happened in that other world was a blur. Marlowe had been there, was still there. Yes. And there'd been a man, a man with a black beard and dark gloves. Charlie gasped, remembering something. He raised his bleary face. The *glove*.

He scrabbled at his satchel. The glove was there, safe, whole, its empty fingers curled inward, a strange artifact of gleaming iron and gleaming wood. All around him, the orsine glowed its mysterious blue, casting everything in an eerie light. Charlie got unsteadily to his feet.

He stumbled over to the stairs and made his way down into the tunnel, along the wet darkness, his footfalls echoing ahead of him, the satchel swinging heavily, and then he was climbing the curving stone stairs, opening the door to Dr. Berghast's study.

A fire was burning in the grate. Berghast was in his shirtsleeves, at his desk, writing in a journal. He glanced up and removed his spectacles in the same moment.

"Mr. Ovid," he said softly. "You are alive."

Charlie swayed in the doorway.

Berghast's eyes tracked down to the heavy satchel at Charlie's side. "You have found it, then. Remarkable." He rose smoothly and came around his desk, studying Charlie with a wary eye. "It has been two days, and yet here you are. How are you not dead?" Then he looked sharply up. "You did not use the glove?"

"The—the glove?" stammered Charlie. "No, I . . . I don't think so."

The man took the satchel from Charlie, removing the glove, holding it out in the light and turning it. His eyes glittered. "Mm. Where is the notebook?"

"Isn't . . . isn't it in the—?"

Berghast turned away. He upended the satchel on his desk and its contents spilled out. Notebook. Knife. Pencil. Parchment. He flipped through the notebook with a frown, set it aside.

"What is this? Did you write nothing down? I require directions, distances, details of the Room and its condition of—" But he must have seen something in Charlie's expression then, because he paused, and said slowly: "You are alone."

Charlie trembled.

"Is he dead, then? The boy?"

Charlie shook his head, struggling to remember. "I . . . I don't think so. He was in the Room. I . . . I had to go. I didn't want to leave him, but he couldn't come away. . . ."

Berghast's cold gray eyes were boring into him, a look of fascination and fury mingling there. His fingers crawled spiderlike over the glove. "You remember it?" he whispered.

Charlie felt sick, ashamed. He'd left Marlowe behind, he'd left his friend, and he couldn't even remember doing it. He tried to concentrate: shadows materialized in the fog, slipped away.

But Berghast was still staring at him, unfazed. "You shouldn't be able to remember anything, Mr. Ovid," he said quietly. "How is this possible? Tell me, what else do you . . . *remember?*"

The older man gave a peculiar emphasis to the word. It felt suddenly dangerous.

Charlie started to talk, but the words came out in a jumble, and Berghast held a hand up to calm him. He sat him down in front of the fire. Rang a bell. A few minutes later his manservant, Bailey— tall, forbidding, gloomy as ever—appeared with a tray of hot tea and afternoon biscuits.

"First you must drink. Eat. It will help." There was no kindness in Berghast's voice, only efficiency. When Charlie had eaten, the older man asked again. "Tell me. Everything."

And Charlie did, he told what he could. Haltingly at first, confused. But as he spoke he began to remember other things. His recollection before descending into the orsine was sharp and clear; but now he could piece together some of his journey to the Room, too. He described the city of the dead and the creature in the alley and the way Marlowe had fought off the spirits. He remembered the white tree that bled, and entering the crooked house. But after that . . . everything went hazy, no matter how hard he tried. There'd been a man in black, yes. And pain. Or was it fear? The feel of water on his face. Running. Then slashing and hacking his way back through the orsine. As he sipped the warm tea, Charlie felt the shaking begin to ease. But he felt light-headed still. He put his head in his hands.

"You should be dead," Berghast murmured. "Even a haelan shouldn't be able to survive so long. Not without assistance." He regarded Charlie where he sat with his head in his hands, and then hesitated. "What is that on your finger?"

Charlie turned his wrists. It was his mother's ring.

"Where did you get it?" Berghast demanded. He seized Charlie's wrist in a strong grip and turned his arm to the firelight but he seemed afraid to touch the ring. He took up a letter opener from his desk and for a terrified moment Charlie thought he meant to cut the ring away but instead he only scraped at the silver. It flaked away; underneath, the ring was made of alternating bands of black iron and metallic black wood.

Just like the glove.

"By God," said Berghast. "*This* is how you didn't perish in the orsine."

"Let go," Charlie protested, unable to pull free. "It's mine!"

"It is not," said Berghast. "It belongs to no one. The metal has been reworked, but I'd know its trace anywhere. This, Mr. Ovid, is one of the two missing artifacts. Immensely powerful and older even than Cairndale." He increased his grip. "Do not lie to me: *Where* did you *acquire it?*"

"It was my . . . mother's," Charlie gasped, reluctant. "My father gave it to her."

"Your father." Berghast released his grip.

Charlie withdrew his hand sharply, as if it had been burned. He folded it up under his armpit. "He was a . . . a talent, here. But his gift disappeared, and he got sent away."

"Impossible. Talents do not come from talents."

But Charlie just stared stubbornly back, refusing to look away. He knew where he came from. And not only because of the file he'd read. Somehow, he knew it with a new certainty, a new clarity. And it wasn't for Berghast or anyone else to tell him otherwise.

Dr. Berghast, however, seemed unimpressed. He rose to his feet still holding the glove and he went to the door and rested one hand on the pull. "I must think about this," he said. "This has been a most illuminating encounter, Mr. Ovid. You may keep the ring for now. Go. Get some rest."

Charlie got up numbly, not understanding. "But aren't we going to go back in?" he said. "For Marlowe, I mean? He's all alone in there."

Berghast frowned. "What would you have me do?"

"We have the glove. And, and now there's this ring. I thought—"

"You did *not* think," snapped Berghast. "There is nothing to be done. That boy was your friend, and yet you left him. *You* abandoned him, and now it is too late. Marlowe may be able to survive in the orsine. But the spirits will have come for him by now."

"The spirits?" Charlie was shaking. He'd had no choice; surely he could see that.

"Leave me now, Mr. Ovid," Dr. Berghast finished. "It is what you are best at, is it not?"

The disgust in the man's tone was final, was crushing. Berghast stood silhouetted against the firelight, his hands cradling the ancient glove like a thing from an unremembered past, a thing that had showed him once his truer self, and might yet show it again.

Charlie, devastated, went.

It had been a long cold day on the road as the cart led them back from Albany Chandlers, back along the green crooked ways, to the gate at Cairndale, and through.

It was late; the sun was low in the west. They'd slipped unhindered past the wards, and along the gravel drive toward the manor. Lymenion was waiting for them in the cold, his hulking shoulders slick in the moonlight, and Oskar had stood in front of him with a look of deep relief and then all of them had gone, troubled, in.

But they hadn't crept up to their rooms, hadn't bothered, but instead had gone into the schoolroom and shut the door carefully and drawn the curtains so as not to be seen. The dinner bell would be ringing soon, and anyway they were all too disturbed by what they'd witnessed in Edinburgh, by all that Mrs. Ficke had told them, to rest. Komako folded her hands together over a wick of candle and a flame bloomed and then the four of them sat on the floor behind Miss Davenshaw's desk.

Hopeless.

That's how it seemed to them all. Komako, when she let herself think about it, felt a quiet rage building in her. But she'd come to a decision, all the same.

"We need to seal the orsine," she told the others. "Mrs. Ficke knew it, too. That's why she told us how it's to be done. The Spider's afraid it won't be finished, that's what he was trying to show us. He's guarded it for centuries, and it won't have meant anything if it rips open now."

Ribs scowled. "Or . . . we could just grab any of them what would listen, an *go*."

"Go where?" said Oskar, rubbing at his reddened nose. "Running won't do any good, Ribs. If the dead get loose, where would be safe?"

"Rrh rruh," agreed Lymenion.

Ribs popped her knuckles, one by one, her green eyes staring gloomily into the candle flame. "How good are you with a blade, Ko? Cause I ain't cuttin his heart out of his body. Uh-uh."

Komako frowned. "We'll draw straws. That way it's fair."

"Come up with a different plan, then. I ain't doin it."

"I—I—I'll do it," said Oskar softly.

They fell silent, looking over at him. Ribs opened her mouth, closed it.

The boy blushed under their scrutiny. "Bodies don't bother me," he said. "It's what I do. It's how I make Lymenion. I just . . . I might need some help."

There came a sound from the darkness. They all turned as one, as the door pull clicked and opened silently in the gloom beyond. Charlie stood there, looking filthy and tired and like he'd maybe been walking the halls for hours, crying. His clothes were ragged and his hands were held out before him, the fingers clawlike and pained. He stopped when he saw them.

"Jesus, it's Charlie," Ribs breathed. "What—?"

Komako went to him. She felt a surge of something inside her, not relief, not worry, but something else, something like an angry kind of happiness, and it confused her. She touched his dirty sleeve and then she said, "Where've you been? What's happened, Charlie?"

"I left him," he whispered. "I left Mar. I did, Ko. Me."

She put her hands on either side of his face and tilted it down to look at her. "Hey," she murmured. "It's okay. Where is he? Where is Marlowe, Charlie?"

"I . . . I can't remember," he said, grinding his knuckles into his forehead. "We went through the orsine, Ko. Me and Mar. We went *inside* it."

Then in the candlelight he told them all that he remembered, broken as it was. How Berghast had drawn them into volunteering, and the murder of Marlowe's mother, and the cold fire of the orsine, and the city of the dead and the glove and what Berghast had revealed about his own mother's ring. They listened in silence. Komako's heart hurt when he talked about Marlowe, seeing the stricken look on his face. He couldn't remember abandoning him. That was almost the worst of it, it seemed. He couldn't remember it at all, only knew it was so, only knew his friend was in there still, alone, little, afraid.

When he was finished, Ribs told about Edinburgh. She left out nothing, not Mrs. Ficke and what she'd said about Berghast, not the glyph-twisted kids, not the girl Deirdre.

"It were Dr. Berghast what done it," she said. "It were awful sad to see, Charlie." Last of all she told about the orsine tearing open and the terrible method of sealing it forever. However a glyphic's heart was to be carved out of the thick armor of its bark, it had to be done. Oskar, she said, giving the boy a quiet appraising look, had already volunteered for it.

Charlie cleared his throat. "What about Marlowe?" he said softly. His eyes searched their faces. "If you seal the orsine, he . . . he can't get out."

Ribs was solemn. "We all want Marlowe back, Charlie. But what's he comin back to, if the orsine rips open? There won't be no one here."

"I can't believe I'm saying it," said Komako. "But Ribs is right."

"I'm not leaving him in there."

"Charlie?" said Oskar, nervous. "Marlowe can survive in the orsine, right? So we got time to think of something." He looked at his flesh giant, as if listening. "Lymenion says we could ask one of the old talents. They might have some ideas. He says maybe there's a way to get Marlowe out *and* seal the orsine."

Charlie lifted his face and his eyes were haunted. "It's worse than that," he said in a low voice. "I . . . I think Jacob Marber's on his way here."

Komako looked up sharply. "Jacob—? Here?"

"It's just a . . . a feeling. I can't explain it."

"Aw, hell," growled Ribs. "We ought to just go on over to the island and seal the orsine now. While we can, like. There won't be no drughr comin through then, an no dead neither."

"But the wards will fail too, when the glyphic is dead," said Komako. "Jacob Marber can just walk right in. There's no good side to this, there's no right way. Either we close the orsine and risk trapping Marlowe inside it, and Jacob being able to come into Cairndale as he pleases . . ."

"Or we don't," Ribs finished, in a tone of disgust, "an the dead come through, an the drughr, an the whole fucking world breaks."

Oskar breathed out slowly. "Dr. Berghast cares only about trapping his drughr," he whispered. "He won't help us."

Komako got to her feet, running her hands through her tangled hair. She was exhausted. She hadn't slept properly since before they went to see the Spider, hadn't eaten, hadn't washed. She rubbed at her neck. The others looked at her, expectant, like maybe she had an answer. Only Charlie didn't look at her. He seemed different from how he'd been before, older somehow. More determined.

The shadows in the room were thickening.

"Right," she said tiredly. "We need to find a way to get Marlowe safe. Obviously. But whatever happens, that orsine has to be sealed."

After the others had gone up to wash and change, maybe to try to rest, Charlie climbed onto the windowsill and stared out at the darkening lawn. He could just make out the mist moving across it. Like the spirit dead, he thought dimly, though it was nothing like the spirit dead, not really. The candle burned down. His heart was empty. He sat and he stared at his hands and he felt nothing at all.

It was Komako who came back, twenty minutes later, who found him like that. She didn't explain why. He was alone and then suddenly he was not and he lifted his face and saw her.

"I don't know what to do," he whispered, just as if she'd been there the whole time. "I don't know how to fix it. It's my fault, Ko. It's my fault Mar's still in there."

Komako rested her hand on his, watchful, quiet. And then, when he said nothing more, she leaned in and kissed him on the cheek. Her lips were as soft as flowers. He stared in surprise.

Her eyes were grave. "We'll find a way, Charlie," she said. "Somehow we will."

He swallowed. The heat had risen to his face and he was flustered and he swallowed again. "Yeah," he said.

"Just don't give up hope."

But he wasn't about to. Hope wasn't something he could afford to give up. "Marlowe's still alive, Ko," he said suddenly, fiercely. "I can feel it. He's, he's trying to—"

But then he broke off, staring out at the mist.

"What is it, Charlie?" she whispered.

"He's trying to get back," he said softly.

38

THE LAND OF THE DEAD IS ALL AROUND

The thought unfurled in the glyphic's mind like a flower.

Jacob Marber is coming.

Time was a mist all adrift around him, without future or past, and he dreamed as he had always done of the beginning and the end of things. He was dying. This he knew as he knew the soft give of the earth in his fingers, as he knew the feel of sunlight on the baked stones of the monastery above him. He had lived longer than there had been nations and he observed the workings of the living with a detachment. He had seen generations pass into dust and lived on and the greater pain in such a long life was the remembering. Now he stirred and he felt the slow tendrils of root stir and shiver all along the tunnel and through the stones and up to where the orsine lay.

Soon, now, Jacob Marber will be through.

There was that ancient haelan, Berghast, who had lost his talent, who feared the glyphic's dying and brought elixirs to keep him alive, and there was the terrible hunger deep inside him, like a fire that would not go out. And there were all those others, the talents in the big house across the loch, who used to come to him sometimes, to ask his permission to enter the orsine. And there were the dark ones in the other world, moving, always moving like water in a river, but with nowhere to go, and the evil that lurked just on the other side of that, desperate, furied, utterly inhuman and unknowable and black. It was she whom he held the orsine closed against, she alone who made him fear. And far beyond her, a darker power, banished so long ago it was like it had never been.

The glyphic turned his slow tendrils through the earth, feeling the cool soil shift. There, almost hidden, silent, was the man of smoke. Marber. A rip had opened in the fields beyond the wards and he was pressing through, even now. Cairndale's wards would not hold. The glyphic saw in an instant all he would lose, all he would gain, for what was to come and what had already been were as one.

Now he could feel fingernails, scraping at the skin of the orsine, fumbling, feeling for the soft scars where the other's knife had sawed. If it was a dream or real he couldn't say. But the pain in him was thick, real, spreading through his limbs like a heat, and he began to shudder, and in the shuddering he sent out dreams, like pollen in a wind, dreams that they might find their dreamers.

Soon.

"Oh," he whispered, into the darkness under the earth.

Let them know, let them see, let them come before it is too late.

Henry Berghast woke from the dream filled with an unfamiliar fear and he looked around, confused at first, coming back to himself gradually. A dream. It had been a dream.

He was in his study, his collar loosened, his shirtsleeves rolled. The hour was late, almost evening, to gauge by the deepening blue in the curtains. The fire in the grate was cold. The bonebirds clicked and rattled in their cage. He rubbed his face and he stood—his back stiff—and he rang for his manservant, Bailey.

He'd been waiting, yes. Ever since the Ovid boy had returned from the land of the dead, with the glove in his possession. All he lacked now was a lure to draw the drughr out.

But that, too, would come. He had dreamed it.

He went to the narrow water closet and poured out a basin of cold water and splashed his face and dried it on his shirttails and then he stared into the pier glass. His eyes were pouched and heavy-lidded and old. He held his palms over his white beard and stared as if at a stranger and he drew the hair back from his face and held it flat with his two hands. Then he opened the little cabinet and took out a pair of scissors and a razor. He shaved his beard slowly, pausing often to consider his reflection. It was a face he didn't know. It amazed him to think about the true faces of things, of what lay beneath the surfaces, how all he and everyone thought they knew was but appearance and illusion. His fingers worked away at his beard. Then he began to cut and shave away the hair over his eyes and across his forehead, at last drawing the razor in long sweeping motions across his scalp, splashing it in the cold basin, until he was standing with small cuts bleeding and his bony scalp weird-looking in the glass.

There came a knock at the door. His manservant, Bailey, betrayed no alarm at his changed appearance. The man—tall, bony, grim—merely nodded to him and held out a towel as if he had been summoned for that very purpose and Berghast took it and turned back.

You are going mad. He smiled to his reflection.

His reflection—hairless, blood-speckled where the razor had cut too deep—smiled back.

He caught Bailey's face in the mirror, watching. "We must be like water, Bailey," he murmured. "We must be clean, and empty."

He went back into his study, his manservant silent. It was then Berghast saw the door to the tunnels was open. Lurking in it was a small figure, ragged, with bloodied fingernails, his black hair wild. A blue shine seeping up out of his skin. He could have been standing there a long time. He could have been standing there but an instant. It was all just exactly as Henry Berghast had dreamed it would be.

The shining boy.

Marlowe.

Marlowe had come back.

Abigail Davenshaw, asleep in her rooms, woke suddenly. She went to the opened window with her heart in her throat and she felt the afternoon light fall across her face.

The child was back. Marlowe.

He had returned.

She knew it to be true. She was trembling. Outside, the grounds of Cairndale were quiet, the air tinged with a distant smoke like burning leaves. She could smell the loch below the manor. But there were no voices, no students calling to each other, no signs of life. She had dreamed little Marlowe so clearly and she knew somehow that it was not a dream, not really, and she had dreamed other things also. Rarely did she dream in images but this day she had. If it resembled sight, she could not say. But she had dreamed a man striding across a field in a hat and cloak and she'd known it to be Jacob Marber with that same clarity and she had dreamed flames and heard weeping and the weeping had been her own.

She knew she must go to Dr. Berghast, tell him what she had

dreamed. She couldn't imagine doing so, it seemed so foolish. *Forgive me, Doctor, I have been having bad dreams. . . .* And yet there was a fierce conviction in her that filled her with certainty. Go, she must. She put on her shawl and carefully ran her hands over her dress and her hair, smoothing out any strays, and then she tied the blindfold at her eyes and picked up the birch switch for speed and opened her door.

There were presences in the hallway, hurrying past. She could tell at once by the sound of their footsteps and the smells, like of dried cotton and the acrid stink of urine, that it was some of the old residents, the ones she thought of as ghosts.

"Miss Davenshaw," said a shaking voice. It was Mr. Bloomington, the ancient talent who lived down the corridor. "You would be best, my dear, to stay in your rooms. This is no time to be going out. We have told Mr. Smythe the same."

She bit back her pride and turned her face in his direction. "And why ever not?" she said. "You seem like you could use assistance, sir."

She could hear his labored breathing. It sounded like fear.

"He's back, Miss Davenshaw. He's come back. He's got through the east wards and is on his way here, Lord only knows how. The children . . . the children must be kept safe. We are all going out to meet him."

For a brief confused moment she thought he was talking about Marlowe. But Mr. Bloomington must have seen something in her face, for he added, in his croaking voice: "It is young Jacob, Miss Davenshaw. Jacob Marber is coming across the fields."

She felt the shock of it. "What will you do?" she whispered.

"What we should have done long ago," said the old man. "We will fight."

39

THE RISING DARK

It was the stillness on the long crooked road to Cairndale that made Margaret Harrogate afraid.

The quiet of it.

The road meandered past stands of trees and ribbons of plowed field and yet in the fading light she saw no crows, no creatures, nothing. Even the bushes and the twisted oaks seemed to shrink back away from the road, to seek out the coming darkness. Their hired carriage rattled on.

Miss Quicke's eyes were closed. She held the purring keywrasse on her lap, stroking its fur distractedly, as if it were an innocent, as if it were a pet. Margaret had seen cats with their eyes creased shut in pleasure and a quick glance might have made any think that was all this was, not a monstrous thing from a different world, four eyes where there ought to be two. Not a *weapon*. But that's what it was: a tool for killing. Margaret saw the gentleness in Miss Quicke's fingers and she scowled and looked out through the dusty window. Her own hands gripped her knees as if to hold her legs straight. She disliked immensely the feeling of powerlessness that was in her but she told herself it didn't matter. *Prideful,* she thought. *That is what you are, Margaret. What would good Mr. Harrogate say to see you now?*

But there was something different about the detective woman. Not only a new kind of kinship between them. Something else. It had to do with the keywrasse and the way Miss Quicke reached for it, the way it rubbed purring against her ankles, the long silent matched stare the both of them, woman and creature, held to. Margaret knew what she had seen, there in the underground back in Wapping, the keywrasse as large and swift as a lion and with eight legs and a coat that rippled like dark water, and then she saw again in her mind's eye the drughr roaring and looming over everything, physical somehow, *corporeal,* and she rubbed at her eyes with the heels of her hands.

It was no good. How could they stand against such a terror? And with one of the weir-bents taken by Jacob Marber, seized and stolen away, so that the creature Miss Quicke now treated like a companion would grow less and less timid, would become wilder and wilder, until eventually there'd be no controlling it at all. The carriage knocked suddenly and swerved to the left and then regained its balance and Margaret put out a hand to steady herself. Miss Quicke had opened her eyes, was watching her. Margaret said nothing. She thought of poor Frank Coulton, how horrified he'd have been if he'd known he'd end up a litch, a slave to his old partner Jacob Marber, and she thought of Jacob himself, who'd been so much calmer, so much sadder than she'd expected. She passed a hand over her eyes and last of all let her thoughts drift to Dr. Berghast. She didn't know if he'd have received her bonebird, warning about the litch and Mr. Thorpe. The nursemaid's account of his experiments had disturbed her, she saw now; but he was still, she told herself, the same man who'd fought to destroy the drughr all these years. He was still their truest hope.

And he had to be warned.

"We'll need to get the kids away," said Miss Quicke softly, opening her eyes. "They can't stay at Cairndale."

Margaret regarded her calmly. "Indeed," she said. "You will see to that. I will find the glyphic and keep it safe from Walter."

Miss Quicke, as if reading her thoughts, said, "And Berghast?"

"I'm angry about what he's done," said Margaret. "But it will wait. No doubt, he would tell us a right verdict justifies a wrong trial. And who is to say, were we in his position, that we would act any differently? He knows the nature of the drughr, what it will do to all of us, far better than we."

"You sound like you're making excuses for him."

"Never," she said sharply. "But first we must be certain the glyphic is safe and that the orsine is not in danger. Otherwise we will have worse to confront than Henry Berghast."

"Will the drughr come to Cairndale, then?" asked Miss Quicke.

"Jacob Marber will come. And he does nothing, except at the drughr's direction."

"Coulton will be with him."

Margaret felt a bite of guilt. "Yes."

"I won't fail him again. I'll kill him, Margaret. I'll put Frank out of his misery."

She looked across and saw the flat dead eyes of a killer of men and she sensed, not for the first time, what a dangerous person Miss Quicke could be.

They were nearing now the crumbling stone wall marking the Cairndale grounds and she unlatched the window and reached a hand out and banged on the roof for the driver to stop.

"There's one last thing," she said. "The wards on the perimeter walls will not allow your guest to enter with us. Not unless they . . . fall." She looked down at the keywrasse warily. "If you will forgive us, we must leave you here until such time as we can call for your help, or return."

The keywrasse, very slowly, extended its claws and arched its back and yawned. Its four eyes vanished into slits.

"What would happen," said the detective, "if we tried to take him through anyway?"

Margaret blew out her cheeks. "No one's ever tried it. Do you wish to find out?"

Miss Quicke didn't answer but instead opened the door and stepped out and the keywrasse darted off into the dusk. The driver said something then to her and the detective replied and got back up, the carriage swaying under her weight. But just before the door closed Margaret thought she glimpsed, far off along the snaking stone wall, a tall figure in a hat, striding away.

They continued on then, through the old gates and up the long gravel drive and past the gatehouse and into the courtyard of Cairndale. The manor felt different—chillier, isolated, abandoned. No one came out to greet them. There were no students playing in the courtyard. Margaret raised her eyes as they came to a halt.

A light was burning in Dr. Berghast's study.

Henry Berghast ran a hand over his smooth scalp, down the back of his neck, the skin prickling.

"Marlowe," he said softly. "You have returned."

The child stood in the doorway wavering, his face very white. Berghast could see abrasions on his wrists. He was staring hollow-eyed around him, as if he did not know the place, as if there was something he was trying to remember.

"Easy, child," murmured Berghast, coming toward him with his hands outstretched the way he would approach a skittish horse. "Come, sit. You will be tired."

The child came dutifully forward, sat in the big armchair by the fire. His voice when he spoke sounded cracked, thin, as if he hadn't used it in a very long time.

"I . . . want to see Charlie. Is Charlie . . . here?" he said.

Berghast was already moving around the desk, locating the glove, returning to gather fuel for the fire in the grate. His manservant, Bailey, had melted back into the shadows on the far wall and loomed there silent, watchful.

"Charlie is safe, child," said Berghast. "He will be pleased to see you."

The boy nodded to himself.

For just a moment Berghast felt a quick sharp twinge of guilt, seeing how little he was, how exhausted. He'd been afraid the boy would not make his way back out in time but his fear was not over the child's welfare but rather his usefulness and he knew, in that moment, that something inside himself had been lost, lost for good. But he'd been alive too long, had seen too many decades slide past, too many lives fade away, for him to dwell on it. Death was a part of life and did not distinguish between the very young and the very old. His death would come in due course too. He would not weep.

He saw the boy looking at the glove in his hands.

"Your Mr. Ovid brought it to me," he said smoothly. "We hoped it might help us get back to you, get you free. We were just preparing to come for you."

"It was Jacob Marber," whispered the boy. "He found us."

Berghast met Bailey's eye across the study and something unspoken passed between them. "You saw Jacob? You are certain?"

The boy nodded, his blue eyes watchful.

"What else do you remember?"

"I remember all of it."

Berghast felt a slow, deep satisfaction welling up inside him. "Of course you do. It is because you are a part of the orsine. I wish to know everything, child. I presume Jacob tried to steal the artifact?"

Again the boy nodded. "But he gave it back."

At this, Berghast frowned. He knew the nature of the drughr and how badly it wanted the glove and he didn't understand why Jacob Marber would give it back.

"He's coming here now," added the boy quietly. "He's coming to kill you."

Berghast crossed to the canvas on his wall, folded his hands at his back. In the dim light the lines seemed to track and drift and move. "So they have failed me, then," he said. "Your Miss Quicke and Mrs. Harrogate have failed me."

The boy's voice faltered. "Is Alice okay?"

"Well. She is resourceful."

The boy was rubbing at his face with the heels of his hands, obviously exhausted.

"This map," said Dr. Berghast, gesturing at the canvas, "is rather unusual. If you look closely, you will see it is not made of ink at all. That is dust, Marlowe. It is a map written in dust; and the canvas is human skin. Ah, you are disturbed? Do not be; it is the stretched skin of a dustworker, one of the oldest and greatest of their kind; and it was his wish to be used so. See how the dust moves, even now. It moves because that world you have just come from moves also, is in constant flux." Berghast leaned forward, filled for just a moment with a deep, liquid regret. He breathed softly. "This was a gift from someone I have not seen now in many years. Oh, we have all lost those we loved; it is a condition of this world. That person had an identical map hanging on her wall, and as this one changed, so did hers. They were connected, you see."

For a long moment neither spoke. The bonebirds clicked in their cage.

"Jacob didn't kill my mother, did he?" said the boy. He said it so quietly that Berghast almost didn't hear it, and when he realized, and looked up in surprise, he knew his face had betrayed the truth.

"No," he replied, reluctant. "He did not. Did he tell you that? Did he also tell you who your mother is?"

The boy stared at his lap. He nodded.

"Then you understand why I lied to you," continued Berghast. "Jacob Marber is a corrupted and conflicted soul. Your mother, sadly, is something far worse. But you do not have to be like her. I did not want you . . . confused by the truth."

"Charlie said it too. He said I didn't have to be like her, I can choose."

"Then he is wise." Berghast said it gravely, in a voice that was both his and not his. He went back to the fire, sat close to the child. He turned the strange glove in his fingers, stared at its lightless wooden plates. Every part of his being was electric with caution. He was close, so close, to completing what he'd labored so long to make possible. He must make no missteps now.

"Do you know what this is?" he said softly. "A glove, yes. But not only that. It is a repository of knowledge, a . . . book. A book, written before men had language. You can read, yes? Then you know. You know what it is to gain entry to another's mind. I have been asking a question for many, many years, and no one has been able to answer it. But this"—and he cradled the armored glove in his two hands as he spoke, the sleek black surface reflecting no light, utterly dark, utterly still—"this will tell me what I wish to know."

"How?" said the child, doubtful.

Berghast smiled. "I will show you."

He placed the glove carefully on the sofa and stoked the fire until it was burning very hot and then he dropped the glove into the fire. It did not burn, of course. But it heated until its armored surface was clear like glass and Berghast could see a gray smoke twisting and drifting inside the glass, and then he reached in with a pair of tongs and drew the glove out and went to where the child sat. "You must put it on," he said. "Do not be afraid. It is quite cool, I assure you."

The child, though afraid, did as he was asked; and when the glove had been slipped on, he looked up in amazement. His skin hadn't burned. The glove looked enormous on his little arm, still translucent, so that the boy's hand was like a stone in a river. Berghast kneeled in front of the boy, turning his wrist outward, staring into the glassy palm. "If you wish for the drughr to be destroyed, if you wish to keep your friends safe, you must hold your hand steady."

"How does it work?"

But it was as if the boy knew the answer already, as if he knew it and feared it.

"This was not made in our world," said Berghast, without looking away. "It requires a spark from the orsine, to function. It was not made by *us*, you see, to travel *there*. It was made by *them*, to come *here*."

"Them?" whispered the boy.

But Berghast didn't answer. He could see his own reflection now, a vague distorted visage curved and crazed in the glass palm. And beneath that, the beautiful folding patterns of smoke. "Show me," he whispered to the glove. "Show me what I seek."

Slowly then, all around him, it seemed his study walls were dissolving until there was only himself, staring with fierce intention deep into the glove, and all at once he was seeing all of it, how to lead the drughr to the orsine and contain it there and how to take its power into his own flesh. There were colors he could not describe and a dazzling light shining on his face and he couldn't feel his body, his muscles, anything, and instead there came an immense will, emanating from his mind, almost like a sound, a musical note. He did not understand all that he saw; it was as if it were being shown in a language he didn't fully understand, if pictures could be a language; and then all at once the plates of the glove darkened and he fell back, blinking, the feel of his own skin rolling over him like a hand over a mouth.

But he knew, now. He knew what to do.

The only way to destroy the drughr would be to infect it. He had known this for a long time, but he had not seen that it must be the blood of an exile, of a fallen talent, infecting the drughr. If the talents were its sustenance, the exiles were its toxin.

Trembling slightly, he rose to his feet. His stomach lurched. He took the glove from the child and then looked at the child in disgust. The glove had drawn out a part of the boy that had been hidden.

"I was a talent, once," he muttered. "Did you know? A haelan, like your friend Mr. Ovid. I thought my usefulness was ended, when I lost my power. But I see now it was only beginning. It was always in flux, my path, it was all a part of the same river."

The boy's hand looked red, raw where the glove had been.

"I will absorb the drughr's power, Marlowe, *because of* the emptiness that is in me. And that part of me that will go into her, will destroy her. For she cannot survive this world." He ran a slow hand over his shaved scalp and saw in the window his watery reflection do the same. "Those of us who have lost our talents, we are like emptied vessels. The shape is still there, but it is no longer filled. We are returned to a potential state. I will *become*, again; the drughr's power will fill me."

The boy looked at him, afraid.

"But Mr. Thorpe weakens by the hour. If he dies, the orsine will rip apart; and there will be no way to contain the drughr. Have you any idea how many of my friends she has devoured? It is because of her my talent faded. I will not fail. And you," he said, rising to his full height, "you must be the lure, Marlowe; you must draw her to me. She will come if *you* call to her."

"How will I know what to do?"

He made a fist. "It will be as easy as closing your hand. It is in your nature. Come, see." He picked up a candelabra from his desk and he led the child to a looking glass above the pier table by the door. "What do you see?"

And the child, weak, afraid, looked in at his reflection. A drughr looked back. Slowly, as they watched, the horns and thickened skull shrank back into the boy's own shape.

"You will know what to do," said Berghast, almost tenderly, his big hand resting on the child's shoulder, "because an abomination lives inside you. It is a part of you. And you cannot *choose* it away."

He was *here*. His Jacob had *come*.

Walter crouched in his cell, feeling the blood well up out of the meat in his palm where his thumbs had been. His face and chin tasted like sour iron, there was wetness everywhere, and pain, such pain, washing over him in waves.

But Jacob was near, Jacob had come. . . . Nothing else mattered.

Except that he hadn't yet done what Jacob had asked. He hadn't yet stalked the glyphic, he hadn't yet torn the glyphic's throat out for his own dear Jacob, no. He stood painfully feeling his knees creak and gingerly he paced the length of the lightless room. He'd slipped the loose shackles over his bloodied hands once he'd bit his thumbs off and nothing now would stop him.

He clicked his needlelike teeth. He closed his eyes, and he saw.

Jacob, his dear beautiful friend, Jacob. Walking slowly in the twilight along the perimeter of Cairndale, tracing a hand over the stones in the crumbling wall. The soot and dust smoldering up around him like a living smoke. The wards were weak, yes, even with the glyphic still alive, and Walter watched with his mind's eye as Jacob reached out and pushed his two hands against the invisible barrier, and it compressed softly, like rotten wood, it shivered under the pressure. It was no dream. He saw Jacob gather some strength into himself and then a slender crack appeared in the air before him and widened and split and then there was a tremendous roar and the stone wall burst inward and Jacob Marber, beautiful, shining, powerful, stepped grimly onto the grounds of Cairndale.

Oh, but there was another with Jacob, a second, a companion, skittering along crablike through the breach. Who was this? Walter felt a stab of envy and decided, yes, he would help his dear Jacob, that other litch was not good enough for Jacob, no, it would have to be removed. Eliminated. Gutted. Yes. For Jacob's sake, only to help his dear Jacob, yes.

But first: the glyphic. He must do as he'd been told. He could feel what was coming, the closeness of it, he knew there would be fire and bloodshed and horror and his lips tingled with the idea of it. At the cold door he pressed the shell of an ear to listen. The great deep underground of Cairndale was immense, and absolutely still. It was almost time. His blood was singing inside him.

Someone, yes, would be coming down the stairs soon.

And then Walter would be free.

Deep in the warm root tangle of the earth the glyphic felt his life loosening, unfurling bit by bit like the fingers of a hand, opening. He'd felt the shattering of the wards in his very skull, a sharp obliterating pain, and he'd known in that instant that Jacob Marber had come back. He had foreseen it and dreamed it and now here it was. But he was simply too weak now, too frail, to hold both the orsine closed and the wards along the walls at strength. And Jacob Marber had known it.

The warm darkness was all around. It was his own death he was seeing now. There had been a time far in the past when he had imagined he would feel sadness, and a later time when he'd thought he'd feel relief. He felt neither. A change was moving inside him like his own blood. He had lived so long on this earth that the lifetimes of men and women were to him as days and he regarded them as a child will an insect. He thought of the sunrise over the great ships of the Spanish Armada and the forest of masts that he had witnessed setting out across the channel and how the sunlight was like rigging and the trumpets at Valladolid were filled with longing. And he thought of the burning monasteries in Essex in the time of the invaders and the longboats that crept up the rivers, shields lining their walls, the dragon-headed prows cutting the air. The fear in the villages then. And he remembered the late dances in the formal gardens of Edinburgh in the time of King James, and the first hot-air balloon sailing over Glasgow and the Clyde and the last maypole on the village green in those days when he still walked above-ground. And the sunlight catching on the ice shards hanging from the gallows in Greenmarket and the cloud of steam that rose from the mouths of the newly dead when they were cut down at the dawn of the eighteenth century. And the blush in the cheeks of a newborn he'd held in Sicily once like the rosy color in a late-summer peach and the wonder in that while the exhausted mother slept in the straw behind him. And the way a child looked at him in the harbor at Alexandria as he climbed down the gangway and into the haze. All this, all this and more, would vanish from the world with his ceasing, all the ineradicable beauty that lived now only inside him would be lost, moments as fragile as coins of light on water, and this more than any other part of it made him feel alone and sorrowful and frail. For in all this feeling there was, he thought in his slow treelike way, the last remnants of what had made him human once, so that he was, still, one of them.

Something trembled in the earth. Far down the tunnel he felt it, a thing, brushing up against the walls and gnarls of root. Something was coming. His death was coming.

EVERYTHING AND NOTHING

The glasses rattled and danced softly across Henry Berghast's desk. He turned where he stood at the pier glass to watch them, and then he met Bailey's eye. Through the curtains, a quick bloom of light appeared. The boy Marlowe pulled out of his grasp and crossed the room and peered out. Something was lighting up the darkness; something was on fire.

"It's him," the boy whispered. "It's Jacob."

Berghast followed him across. He unlatched the window and swung it open. In the courtyard stood a strange coach, just arrived. He saw the woman detective, Miss Quicke, pause in the open door and peer out at the reflected firelight. *What is she doing here?*

But then came a distant shouting, the low muffled thrump of something detonating, and his thoughts went elsewhere. The outbuildings were burning. Those voices would be—must be—the older talents, gathering in the firelight. If it *was* Jacob Marber, if the wards had fallen . . . then they would not be strong enough.

He looked to Bailey, silent and forbidding in the shadows. "See to Mr. Laster," he commanded. "Then dispose of the papers here. I will take the boy. Come," he said to Marlowe. "We must hurry."

But the boy glared at him, suddenly willful, stubborn.

"*Come*," Henry snapped again.

"I won't go," the little boy said. "I want to see Charlie first. You said I could see Charlie."

Berghast forced himself to speak calmly. "There are things in this world more important than what we *want*, child. If we delay now, there will be no finding your friend at all. Jacob Marber and the drughr will see to that."

He could see the boy didn't believe it but he didn't have time to argue, not now. He turned and struck the little boy a powerful blow with an open hand and the boy's legs went out from under him. He collapsed, unconscious, to the floor.

Henry allowed himself his anger; he'd thought he had more time, he'd thought the glyphic's wards would hold longer. Perhaps Jacob was stronger even than he'd feared. He'd beaten Jacob back, years ago, before his own talent had faded. But he couldn't do it now.

Or not just yet, he thought in satisfaction.

He took the ancient orsine knife from the lowest drawer of his desk, the same blade he'd given the Ovid boy for his satchel. He slid it into his waistcoat. Then he put on the iron-and-wood glove. Its tiny teeth bit into his wrist. At the last moment he remembered the journal, his book of secrets, and just to be safe he unlocked it from his desk and went to the fire and threw it in.

Then he swung the unconscious boy up over one shoulder, unhooked a lantern from inside the door, and hurried down the stairs into darkness.

They were too late.

Marber was already inside the perimeter, Marber and his litch Coulton. Alice Quicke pushed Mrs. Harrogate at a half run over the flagstones, the wheeled chair squeaking and jouncing. The older woman made no complaint; she had her wicked-looking knives gripped in both hands on top of the blanket on her lap. Something was on fire behind the manor and they hurried around the side and through the portico and stopped at the edge of the field.

For a long confused moment, Alice didn't know what she was seeing.

Figures, silhouetted against the firelight, in a long line. They were in nightdresses and robes, and facing away, into the darkness. She counted eight. They were the old ones, the talents who had lived at Cairndale for decades, ancient and trembling and frail.

"What're they doing?" she whispered. "Margaret? What are they—"

"What they have always done," replied Mrs. Harrogate. "They are preparing to fight."

"They can't *fight*," she snapped. "Look at them. They can't even eat solid food."

And she fumbled angrily at the cord around her throat for the weir-bent there. She didn't see the keywrasse anywhere. But if the wards had fallen, then surely it could come through too? More and more catlike, less and less obedient, she thought. A small group of kids stood to one side, watching. There were other faces pressed to the windows behind.

"Remember why we are here," said Mrs. Harrogate. "We must warn Dr. Berghast. We must protect the glyphic."

Alice took her Colt from her pocket. "If that bastard's already here, I'd say we're too late," she growled. And then she heard a familiar voice.

"Alice?" it cried, urgent. "Alice!"

Charlie.

She turned and there on the stoop of the manor kitchens she saw him spilling out, all long awkward arms and legs like the adolescent boy he was, and there behind him the others, his friends, the Japanese girl with the sullen mouth and that little pudgy towheaded boy who hardly spoke and, what was it, something else, a figure of flesh and sinew lumbering out just behind them. She took a quick involuntary step back, lifting a cuff to her mouth at the smell. Last of all came the blind woman, the schoolteacher, turning her face this way and that in the faint glow of the burning outbuildings across the field as if she were seeing all.

Alice didn't see Marlowe.

But then Charlie was throwing his arms around her, and she was blinking in relief. He looked exhausted. The others were crowding Mrs. Harrogate, worried about her injury, clamoring to know what was happening out in the burning field. They'd come running down through the manor at the same time as Alice and Margaret had arrived.

It was Miss Davenshaw who spoke. "The old ones will not be able to stop Jacob Marber. He's grown too powerful. Even Dr. Berghast means to flee."

Mrs. Harrogate's head snapped around. "What do you mean?"

"He is gone," she said simply. "He has not been anywhere to be found all day."

Alice unbuttoned her oilskin coat, she adjusted the brim of her hat. Something was happening out in the field. The old talents had gone still. "We need to get out of here," she said slowly. "All of us. We need to go now."

But Charlie was looking past her, at the fire and the old talents standing in the grass. "We can't leave, Alice. There's something we've got to do first." His voice was quiet. "Before Jacob Marber gets to us, I mean."

Mrs. Harrogate wheeled her chair sharply into Alice. "We do not have time for this. We must find Henry. At once."

"I thought you wanted to protect the glyphic," said Alice.

"You can't," interrupted the Japanese girl. She was peeling off her gloves as she spoke. "No matter what you do. There's no way to stop what's happening to him. But you can still seal the orsine."

Mrs. Harrogate studied her with glittering eyes. "A litch has been sent to open it."

"A litch—?" Charlie stumbled back, fear twisting his mouth. "You mean, like what attacked me back in London?"

"The same."

"Charlie," Alice said, a dread rising in her. "Where is Marlowe?"

Charlie looked helplessly over at the Japanese girl. "I'm sorry, I'm so sorry. He's *inside* it, Alice. Inside the orsine. We both of us went in, only he never came back out. I tried to go to him, I did. Dr. Berghast wouldn't let me." He gestured out at the burning field. "And now if Jacob Marber's here, it means it's already started."

"What's started?"

"The glyphic. His dying."

Mrs. Harrogate was looking away, out across the field, scanning it. "Perhaps the child is safer in there, hm? At least for now. Tell me, girl, *how* does one seal an orsine?"

The girl smoothed out her long braid. "We have to get to the island. We'll need the glyphic's body."

"Henry will be on the island. With the drughr."

"Jesus." Alice shook her head. "Then it's too dangerous. We've seen the drughr, we know what it is. There's no fighting it." She reached up, took Charlie's shoulders in her hands and turned him square to her.

"Listen, if the orsine rips open, then Marlowe can get back through, right?"

"Yes—"

"Well. That's something, then."

"But back to *what?*" Charlie cried. "The dead will pour through. I've seen them, Alice, what they do to the living. They're . . . awful. Marlowe wouldn't want that."

"Miss Quicke," Mrs. Harrogate said from her wheeled chair. "We will get the child back. We will go *through* the *drughr*, if we must. It came through an opening in London, did it not? It . . . *made* an opening. We will find a way to do that, too. But the orsine *must* be *sealed*."

Charlie's eyes were wet. "Alice, we've got to *try*," he pleaded.

She didn't know what to say. She knew he was right, they all were. But just then there came a sound, a shriek, from off across the grass, and Alice spun in time to see the silhouetted figure of Jacob Marber—there was no mistaking him—walking slowly forward in his silk hat, his long coat crackling around him. She was already moving sideways, across the flagstoned walk, seeking a better angle to see him when he raised his hands, and a darkness seemed to grow from his upraised palms.

Something was happening to the old ones, too. They were changing, their talents manifesting. Three of them ran forward at a speed impossible given their age—no longer frail, swift now—and she stared in fascination as two of them seemed to thicken, grow larger even as they ran, their heads down like battering rams. The third, an old man in a nightdress, was increasing in height, his legs and arms lengthening, so that he had soon outpaced the other two and he was reaching a gigantic hand down as if to flatten Jacob Marber where he stood. An old woman, standing back, seemed to levitate up off the ground, almost to hover, and there was a strange white light like starlight shining from her. The others, too, were transforming, though Alice couldn't make out exactly how.

Something was wrong with Marber though, that much was clear. The great darkness around him, his dust, twisting up in a cyclone from his fists, seemed to hurl itself outward against the onrushing giant and the two muscled runners and then be sucked back in, surrounding him again, and she could see he was struggling. Then the giant too was pressing down with his big palms against the dust, leaning into it, forcing it slowly back down, and Alice started to think, to hope, that perhaps Harrogate was mistaken, perhaps they all were, perhaps the old talents were stronger than any had given them credit for.

It was then she noticed two things: one of the eight, frailer than the others, leaning into a cane and standing some distance away, with his head bowed; and a quick crawling thing, pale and almost unseeable in the eerie firelight, skittering crablike over the grasses toward him. She knew Coulton at once; and she lifted her revolver in a smooth reflexive motion and took aim, but it was almost like he'd felt her attention, her focus, for in that instant he skittered sideways, setting the old talent between them. And a moment later Coulton had leaped up, all claws and fangs, and driven the frail old figure ferociously into the earth.

She shot anyway, squeezing the trigger calmly, and the shot went wide; she'd been hoping to scare the litch off the old man, but it made no difference; and when Coulton next raised his face she saw a dark bib of blood and gore overrunning his chin and staining his throat and the front of his ragged shirt.

Whatever the old man had been doing was now undone. Jacob Marber, with a sudden explosive force, hurled the gigantic talent backward, and then a cloud of dust overwhelmed the others so that Alice could no longer see them.

It was the speed of all of this, the speed at which it all happened, that amazed her most. It seemed only a matter of minutes since he'd appeared. She glanced wildly over at the kids and saw they too hadn't had time to move, to do anything, and only stared in horror as that black storm of dust overwhelmed everything in its path.

"What is happening?" barked Miss Davenshaw.

"Where are they?" the Japanese girl cried out. "Do you see them?"

But no one did. There was only a great roaring storm of dust, cycloning over the field. For a long moment nothing happened. And then, striding forth out of the maelstrom, his eyes fixed directly on them, came Jacob Marber, the litch like a hound at his heels. The old talents were dead.

"We need to go," Alice said sharply. She spun around.

It was only then she realized Mrs. Harrogate was gone.

Charlie had watched Mrs. Harrogate wheel herself silently backward and away, off into the darkness, heading down toward the loch, the long knives like crescents of darkness in her lap. When Alice turned in surprise he didn't answer, he didn't speak up, tell her what he'd seen, where she'd gone. He didn't have to. They all knew.

But what Charlie was thinking, what he couldn't stop thinking about, was the spirit dead in that other world, listless, shimmering, gathered rank-upon-rank in a great thick fog on the far side of the orsine. Waiting. As if drawn to the heat of the living. His recollection of it was hazy but he had a sense of being swarmed, of a terrible cold seeping into his chest, of an unslaked hunger. He did not know what his world would be if they came through.

It wasn't a clear thought and it was gone as fast as it came because Alice was shoving him, shoving all of them, back toward the manor.

"Go, go!" she was shouting. "Hurry!" She was waving back the other students too. And then all were scrambling through the kitchen, past the big copper vats of stew and soup, cold now, maybe fifteen kids in total, spilling out into the dining room, crockery smashing in their wake as they hurtled past, into the foyer, up the stairs. Charlie glimpsed Mr. Smythe and his wards hurrying in the other direction but they were too far to call out to and anyway there wasn't time.

Upstairs, Cairndale Manor was quiet and still. They crept on. Through the windows the orange glow of the fires stained the walls and their faces and their hands with light. They heard a sudden shattering of glass behind them, and screams. Then the screaming stopped.

"He's coming," hissed Alice.

The other kids, the unnamed ones, had scattered into various rooms, shutting the doors, huddling in silence. But Charlie, glancing back, saw a shadow skitter across the walls, far behind, and knew there was no hiding. Not from the litch. It frightened him as much as anything in this world ever had and he started to shake. They were in a long straight hallway and the creature was coming fast.

"We need to face them," Komako whispered angrily. "We can't hide."

"Where's Miss Davenshaw?" said Oskar.

Charlie looked around. They'd lost her too somewhere, somehow.

"Son of a bitch," Alice snapped.

Everything was going wrong. Alice started to go back but just then the manor shuddered, the walls trembling, as if something were trying to bring it down around them. Charlie saw her hesitate. Then she pulled out a long key from her pocket and ran her hands over it desperately. He thought maybe she was losing it. But then a cat leaped lightly onto the sill of an open window almost as if summoned and Alice stared at it fiercely.

"Took your damned time," she snapped.

At the *cat*.

He stared. But he had no time to think about this. There came a sudden whooshing roar and Charlie glanced out the window and saw the other wing of the manor—the wing with Berghast's study—going up in flames. A darkness was whirling out there, blotting out the sky, and he realized it was dust. Jacob Marber's dust, surrounding them, enclosing them. They had to get to Berghast's study and into the tunnels before the fires made the going impassable. But then he felt Ribs's grip on his sleeve and he stumbled and turned. The litch was crawling toward them down the hall. As it went it swept the candles from their sconces. In one claw it held a lantern and Charlie watched as it swung the light high and then shattered it against a door. A splash of flames lit up the wood.

They would all be burned alive.

"We've got to go, now!" Alice shouted. They were sprinting then, heading for the turn in the hallway, a corner. Alice was glaring back in fury. "Why hasn't it attacked us yet?" she demanded. "It's faster than us, it should be here. It's almost like—like . . ."

Her voice trailed off in horror as they came around the corner.

"Like it's herding us somewhere," finished Komako, in a whisper.

Charlie followed her gaze. There ahead of them stood Jacob Marber, blocking their way out, the dark dust in ropes cycloning around his fists. Charlie couldn't make out his eyes because of the shadows but his chin was down so that his beard spilled out over his chest like an apron of darkness. A torn cheek flapped bloodily. He was walking slowly, unhurriedly, toward them.

"Charlie!" Komako hissed. She seized him by the wrist so that he turned to her and she said, in a calm cold voice: "You have to get to the glyphic, you have to seal the orsine. We can handle this. You need to go."

Charlie looked in a panic from Jacob Marber to Komako and back. "I don't . . . I don't think I can," he said. Far behind them, the litch's long claws scraped the walls.

Alice had overheard and pushed forward. "You heal, right?" she said sharply. "That's what you do?"

He nodded, confused. "Yes—"

And without waiting to hear more, she seized the scruff of his collar and turned him sharply toward the window and pushed him through. And then Charlie and the shattering glass and the splintered pieces of the wood frame all plummeted down into the fiery courtyard below.

Henry Berghast dropped the child onto the floor of the chamber.

He reminded himself not to rush. He'd hooked the lantern outside the door as he unlocked it and had forgotten it there but it did not matter, the chamber was lit by the blue glow of the orsine. Still, he must be more careful. He would not get a second chance.

It was then he realized they were not alone.

There were figures in the slumped in the gloom, dim silhouettes, as gray as dust, standing with their faces turned to the orsine and their shoulders rolled and their arms lifeless at their sides. Six in all. They took no notice of Berghast or the child.

The spirit dead.

Berghast crouched, glaring. As he watched, a seventh waded sleepily up out of the orsine. Its feet left wet prints on the stone floor. It stumbled a few feet away and then turned, and peered back at the shining blue surface, and went still.

Quietly, his heart pounding, he began to prepare what he needed. He was remembering the words he had glimpsed in the glove, the incantation, and he began to murmur them now, softly, under his breath. He was not one to believe in the spiritual or the unseen by nature and knew much of what the ancients had believed was nonsense and superstition, but he'd do as the glove had shown him. Better to be cautious.

He heard the child stir.

"You hit me," the boy whimpered.

Berghast allowed himself a quick brief frown. "You left me no choice," he murmured. "I did not like doing it. Do not make me hurt you again. Now hush; we are not alone."

The little boy must have seen them then, too, for he went silent.

Berghast hurried at his work. He approached the orsine warily but the spirit dead paid him no mind. He wore the glove on his left hand and he pressed it against the surface. The orsine's skin had thinned, split apart in places, already failing.

He ran his big roughened hand over his bare scalp, brooding. Then he began slowly to walk around the cistern, leaning down with the ancient knife and sawing away the roots where they dipped into the pool. The blade cut smoothly, easily, and the glyphic's roots hardly bled at all.

Still the dead did not stir.

Last of all he brought the boy to the edge of the pool and took off the little shoes and rolled back the trousers. The child was calm, turning his big eyes to the gray figures all around. Berghast plunged the boy's little white feet into the freezing orsine. They looked waxen in the blue shine.

"Now we wait," he murmured.

Marlowe looked up in fear. "I know you think you have to do things," he whispered. "But you don't. You aren't a bad person. You can choose."

"Ah, but I have chosen," he replied softly. "I have chosen *this*."

What the child thought, what he knew, was of no consequence. Jacob Marber was inside Cairndale, carving his way through the old talents. *Let him come*, he thought with a grim smile. *Let him see what will be.* The glove had started to ache on his hand. Its little teeth felt like they were chewing away at his wrist. Under his breath, he began to repeat the incantation, the words in their ancient tongue, thrumping like a drumbeat in the back of his throat.

Come, come, come, come.

How long did they wait then in the quiet? It seemed the world around them was receding in the stillness, so that there was no Cairndale, no Marber, no spirit dead nor fire nor ruin. There was only a man and a child, at the edge of a pool, staring in at their own watery selves.

And then, in the murky blue cistern: a shadow. Something was down there. A silhouette was rising up out of the depths, growing bigger, bigger, impossibly large.

"Ah," Berghast whispered, pleased. He curled his gloved fingers. "Your mother has come, child. She has sensed you, and she has come. Now we can begin."

The child turned his startled face downward. Berghast seized his little arm and slashed the blade across his wrist. The boy cried out; and the drughr, the beautiful drughr, swam up toward him.

And in that very instant the gathered spirit dead, all as one, opened their dark mouths wide and began to scream.

Komako watched Alice Quicke shove Charlie through the window, shattering the glass, all of it plunging onto the hard granite setts below. She knew he'd be all right, had seen enough of his talent to know that much, but her heart was sick with fear all the same.

She turned to face Jacob. "You deal with the other one," she said to Alice. "Jacob's mine."

Oskar's soft features hardened. Lymenion, hulking, glowering, stepped near. But Alice wasn't listening; she was kneeling in front of a strange dark cat, whispering to it, arguing. When she looked up, she looked right at Komako, and said, "He says he can't help us. Not against Marber, not while Marber has the weir-bent."

Komako didn't understand.

"A key, it's a key," Alice said hurriedly. "We have to get it off him, or the wrasse can't help us." She must have seen something in Komako's face, and frowned in quick irritation, and pulled out a cord around her neck and held up a long elaborate-looking key. "It's sort of like this. I can't explain it all now. Just look for a key, try to get it away from him."

"Right. A key—"

Her revolver was in her hand and she was thumbing back the hammer and turning so that her long oilskin cloak snapped behind her. "Hurry. Ribs and I will deal with the litch."

And she strode off back the way they'd come, murder in her eyes.

Komako could see Jacob Marber walking steadily now, calmly, up the long corridor. His face was savaged, his beard matted with his own blood. There was little about him she recognized from the young man who'd rescued her all those years ago, who'd saved her kid sister, Teshi, from that mob in Tokyo, who'd held her as she cried after Teshi was dead. She remembered how he'd talked about his own brother, his frantic search to help him, how he'd confessed that no matter the evil, if something could bring his Bertolt back to him, he'd do it. That something was the drughr. Maybe even while he was helping her, while he was holding her, that drughr had been courting him. She'd carried the guilt of it inside her for so long, the feeling that *she'd* failed *him*, that she might have sensed the ravenousness of his grief and helped him out of it except she was too overwhelmed by her own. All her brief life since she'd tried to remember that one truth: that her own suffering, her surrender to it, had increased the store of others' suffering in the world. But maybe, just maybe, Jacob could still be reasoned with. Maybe there was a part of him in there she could reach. And if not? She'd grown stronger than he could know; let him find it out.

Jacob came on. The candles in the hall smothered, one after another, into smoke. He strode toward them like a harbinger of some greater dark. Komako saw him and was suddenly nine years old again, in the crooked wooden streets of Tokyo, while the rain came down and her sister, Teshi, swayed and Jacob glared at her with an angry fear that was not so far off from love.

"Jacob—!" she cried. "You don't want this, I know you don't!"

He paused at her voice. His gaze slid past her to Oskar and Lymenion and then back.

"Komako?" he said, and there was a tiredness in him that nearly broke her heart. Slowly the smoke and dust faded. His eyes were glassy. "Please," he said, "go. Stand aside. I'm not here to hurt you, any of you. I came for Berghast."

"You killed the old ones. Out in the field. I *watched* you—"

"I tried not to. I warned them. They wouldn't listen. Alice Quicke has something I need." He studied her in the faint glow of distant fires. "You know nothing of all this, do you?"

Oskar whispered from across the corridor, "Don't listen to him, Ko. He's lying."

But she wasn't so sure. "Why are you here for Dr. Berghast?"

Jacob spread his hands. A darkness writhed under the skin. The brim of his hat was low over his eyes. "To kill him," he said softly. "And the keywrasse will help me do it. After Berghast—"

"Yes?"

"I'll kill the drughr. All of you will be safe."

"Why?"

"Because they're evil. Both of them."

She found the tiny pricks of light where his eyes were and stared at them hard. There was a lump in her throat. She made herself look at him and not look away as she said, "But so are you, Jacob. You've become that way, too. You've killed. Killing more won't change it."

All the while she was drawing closer, biding her time. Lymenion, near her, crept along the wall in darkness. She was maybe ten feet from Jacob when she saw it. On a chain in the watch pocket of his waistcoat, its knuckled head sticking out. The key.

He looked taller, fiercer, but there was also a slouched and twisted cast to the way he moved. He was favoring one side. He'd been savaged by someone, somehow, and the wounds were healing badly. All at once Komako let the chill seep into her wrists and her arms ached and she summoned the living dust to her and let it enter her, a great thick deep void that filled her and filled her, all of this in only an instant, and she felt the satisfaction of knowing Jacob couldn't have guessed at her power, at what she'd learned to do, at the speed and deftness in it. And she spun a thin strong tendril of dust out toward him, quick as a whip, and snarled the key, and snapped the chain and brought it back to her open hand.

He didn't even flinch.

He just sighed, as if it was this he'd been afraid of, and lifted the brim of his hat, and she saw what was in his eyes, all the tiredness and resigned fury and the years of cruel acts, and she knew she couldn't fight him.

She didn't have even a moment to try to run. Dust was seeping up *out* of him, long ribbons of darkness, it was *inside* him, a *part* of him. And suddenly it was snaking around her ankles, her knees, pinioning her elbows fast to her ribs. She glanced up and started to speak but couldn't, the dust was pressing on her windpipe, Jacob's dust.

Slowly he walked toward her.

It was then, bursting out of the darkness, that Lymenion struck. He struck with the force of a freight train and smashed Jacob backward, off his feet, and followed through with a tremendous fist, raining punches down on Jacob so that the floor shook and plaster fell from the ceiling and Jacob was crushed hip-deep into an indentation in the boards. All this happened so quick Komako could only glimpse it, a blur of fury. Jacob would have been smashed clear through into the floor below except at the last moment something checked Lymenion's fist, and it held stiff in the air, and then the mighty flesh giant staggered backward, turning its head this way and that, as if suddenly confused, as if some unseen force were harrying it from all sides.

"Lymenion!" Oskar was screaming. "Lymenion!"

Now the flesh giant was pummeling the air, batting at the dust swirling around him as if at a cloud of angry bees. The dust thickened until Komako couldn't see him. She could hear Oskar screaming, hollering something from down the corridor. And then Jacob raised his hands and squeezed them into fists and the darkness surrounding Lymenion squeezed itself down too and then Lymenion burst apart in a shower of reeking flesh, leaving only a stain on the floor and walls and ceiling.

Komako's ears were ringing. She couldn't move. The key was gripped in her fist but the ropes of dust and smoke were too strong for her. She looked at him desperately, her arms pinned to her sides. "What about Bertolt? Is this what he'd have wanted? Jacob!"

"Maybe," Jacob whispered.

She could see him deciding something, his expression hardening. "I loved you like a brother!" she cried. "Please!"

Jacob raised his hand, the tattooed darkness twisting in it. A black dust swirled, harrowing, beautiful.

"I know you did," he murmured sadly.

The dust when it struck her did so with the force of a terrible wind, snapping her head backward, spinning her sideways into the ruined wall. She couldn't see anything for the storm of soot in her eyes and when she opened her mouth to cry out it was filled with smoke and the living dust poured its darkness down her throat, into her lungs.

Margaret Harrogate knocked over her wheeled chair as she tried to get out of it, at the edge of the loch, where the sunken dock began.

She fell hard. She had to cast around in the gloom for the knives she'd balanced in her lap. But she'd been prepared for this and had worn thick wool sleeves to protect her elbows and she dragged herself grimly toward the rowboat and untied it and clambered in.

Behind her a wall of smoke roiled and flickered and the loch's reflection burned also. She allowed herself a quick pained moment to pray for Alice to get the littles away. All of them. *Just go,* she prayed, *go and don't look back.*

The hull rocked softly. She reached for the oars. Slowly the little rowboat pulled out into the lake of fire. There were flecks of blue light adrift over the wych elm, like glowing ash. Her shoulders ached, her arms ached. There would come from time to time the low muffled thrump of explosions up the hill at the estate. It stood enshrouded in a black cloud of dust and smoke, pulsing with an orange glow where it thinned. Something within was burning.

On the island she hauled herself out of the boat and tied it fast and crawled on her forearms along the rocky path, up the slope to the ruined monastery. Her elbows were torn and bleeding by then. In the firelight the monastery walls gleamed redly, as if drenched in blood. She paused and swung her dead legs around and sat up to think. The glyphic; the orsine; Dr. Berghast and his drughr . . .

When all at once a screaming started.

The scream was low and eerie and filled with the music of sadness and longing but there was hatred in it, too, and hunger, and Margaret shuddered to hear it. It was not the sound of anything human. She pressed her cheek to the cold rocks; it was coming from the earth itself.

Slowly Margaret clawed her way around the building. A heavy door stood open, a lantern burning on a hook beside it. The screaming grew louder. *Berghast,* she thought. She dragged herself in and through an antechamber and down a rough curving set of stone stairs and came out, gasping, into a large rocky chamber. A cistern. The light within was blue. The floor and walls were broken and crisscrossed with hundreds of roots, like tentacles, and the terrible screaming filled and reverberated off the walls. There were figures, gray, indistinct, standing all around in the gloom, their mouths open. The screaming came from them.

Her head swam. For there, at the edge of the cistern, his monstrous shadow cast huge from the strange light shining under him, loomed Henry Berghast. For a moment she didn't know him. His head had been shaved, his thick beard was gone. He wore a strange glittering glove, that ran halfway up his forearm. His broad back was to her, and pinned beneath his arm was the boy, Marlowe.

The child's wrist had been cut. Berghast held it stiffly out over the pool, the blood draining. The little boy's face looked ashen.

Margaret reached for her knives.

At that very moment, Abigail Davenshaw was walking softly across the carpet in Dr. Berghast's study, feeling her way with her birch switch, straining to hear any movement. There was the eerie soft clicking of bonebirds in a cage, as regular as machinery in the dark. There was the muffled thrum of the stillness. Footsteps far down a corridor, hurrying.

She made her careful way past the chairs, the desk. She could smell something, a scent of scorched leather and paper, very faint. A bite of cold air came from somewhere under the earth and she found the door she'd gone through before, the door to that strange locked room, standing wide.

"Hello?" she called down. Her voice clattered and faded into the depths. "Dr. Berghast? It is Miss Davenshaw. . . ."

Nothing.

She bit her lip, frowned.

So be it.

She started down. Feeling her way with her toes, slowly, cautiously at each step, willing herself not to fall here inside the walls, where no one would find her, while Cairndale burned itself to the ground.

But she didn't fall. And when she got to the bottom she knew by the way the air moved that something was different. The locked door had been ripped from its hinges.

"Hello?" she called uncertainly. She remembered the ragged breathing she'd heard before and she moved now with great caution, the fear she'd felt then filling her again. But whatever she'd heard was gone now, gone or dead; there was nothing alive but her.

When her birch switch touched the thing sprawled out inside the cell she wasn't sure what to make of it. A chain clinked softly. Her soles slipped in a puddle of some viscous fluid and she knew by the iron scent of it what it was.

She kneeled, fumbled for the face of the dead man. It was Dr. Berghast's manservant, Bailey. His throat had been torn out, there were deep wounds on his chest and arms. It was like he'd been attacked by a wild animal.

Abigail Davenshaw wet her lips and rose grimly and went back up the long stairs the way she'd come. In the study she made her careful way over to the fire and she fumbled for a poker and she carefully dragged a half-burned journal from the grate. It was this she'd smelled earlier. If Berghast had tried to destroy it, it must hold something of value, she reasoned. Then she went to the desk and tried the drawers and looked for anything more of value. The fires were getting nearer, she could feel the heat through the walls, and at last, with a hard expression on her face, clutching the scorched journal under one arm, Abigail Davenshaw crossed the silent study and fumbled for the door handle and hurried out into the burning building.

Charlie was scared, so scared.

He flew through the door of Berghast's study, his shattered collarbone still stitching itself together, the thousand cuts and nicks from the broken glass already healed. The glyphic. He had to locate the glyphic and carve out its heart. He knew he'd have to maybe face down the litch, Walter, the litch who had so terrified him in London and had tried to tear his throat out and whose claws had hurt him in a new way, so that he'd healed only slowly, only painfully. There was his memory of the litch, and there were the dreams he'd suffered in the months since, the dreams of its scrabbling across the ceiling, dropping down on him like some enormous white spider. He'd wake drenched, shivering.

And now he was seeking the very creature out. Everyone was depending on it.

But there wasn't time to think it through. He only paused long enough to stare around the study, making sure Berghast or his giant manservant were nowhere, his eyes alighting instead on the bonebirds at their perch, clicking their bones softly, on the coals in the grate still pulsing with heat, and then he ran for the door to the tunnels, the door that led below, and out under the loch to the island. If he'd been only just five minutes sooner, he'd have caught Miss Davenshaw plucking the burned journal out of the grate; he'd have seen her, and maybe been able to ask her advice, her help, but she was gone, drifting back out into the labyrinth of Cairndale, into the burning manor with that smoldering journal pressed tightly to her chest, half its secrets burned away, and he'd not see her again.

He descended the stairs three at a time. The tunnel was blacker than anything, the air foul. He'd forgotten a lantern or a candle. His footsteps splashed steadily in the standing water and though at every step he felt like he was about to collide with something he did not and he neither stumbled nor fell.

And then he felt the tunnel sloping gradually upward and the air cleared and a faint gray light was visible ahead. When he got out onto the island he clambered over the tumbled stones and saw a lantern left on a hook beside the open door. He could hear a low screaming from the orsine chamber. Something was in there. Whatever it was, it could spare a lantern, he decided, and he unhooked it and hurried around the back and entered the ruined cathedral.

Under the ribs of the roof and the night sky beyond it he made his way, tired, determined, the lantern in his fist. He found the crypt and there, left leaning against the wall, the old torch in its bracket. He opened the door of the lantern, lit the torch. The skulls grinned from their cavities. Bones in their ancient boxes lay at rest.

The roots thickened. He saw in the firelight signs of struggle, the roots torn or ripped to shreds, blood in a dappled trail leading deeper. That would be the litch. Walter.

He was half running by then, tripping on the roots and clawing his way upright, making too much noise. He didn't care. When he came out into the low tangled chamber of the glyphic he stumbled sharply and stared in horror.

The glyphic and Walter hung from the ceiling in a terrible embrace. There was blood everywhere. The roots of the glyphic had torn one of Walter's legs entirely off; a dozen other roots had pierced his body, punctured his arms and his chest and his spine; a thick knot of root was wrapped around his throat and his eyes were rolled back in his head. He was dead.

But so was the glyphic. Before he'd died, Walter had torn the glyphic's throat out with his teeth, and the ancient being's head now hung at a strange angle, blood all down his front.

Charlie was shaking, both devastated and relieved. At least he wouldn't have to be the one to slaughter the glyphic.

It was then he realized he hadn't brought anything to carve out the heart. He cast around in the torchlight. His eyes alighted on the litch's claws. The thumbs had been chewed off. He reached up and twisted the gore-drenched wrist and gingerly pressed one claw against the glyphic's bark-like chest.

It slid, sighing, in. A watery black slime oozed out. Charlie started to saw away at the chest, prying it wide, and when it was cut deep enough he reached in and groped for something soft, and rubbery, and he wrenched it furiously clear.

It came out with a sucking noise, the heart. It was still warm. The size of a fist, covered in a gelatinous black slime. He cradled it, breathing hard, feeling a terrible sadness welling up in him. Whatever else he was, the glyphic had been an ancient and good being, a being that had kept all of them safe. He'd lived chained to the orsine, as much a prisoner of it as any of the spirit dead. It didn't seem fair. Charlie stumbled back, wiping at the heart with one sleeve. Under the muck, the surface of the heart pulsed slowly, like an ember. It was shining.

That was when he felt it. He raised his face, and it came again: a low, deep rumble, like a train passing in the earth. The walls shuddered. Dirt sifted from the ceiling, all around. And then Charlie understood: the island was collapsing.

He swung the torch around and ran.

Alice sprinted back along the dark hall, feeling the manor tremble under her, knowing Ribs was close but not seeing the girl, of course, and she had her Colt out in her hands as she ran. Jacob Marber was somewhere behind her now, facing the girl Komako, and Oskar and his flesh giant. Here the corridor was quiet, cooler. She slowed, stopped. Tilted her head to listen.

She knew Coulton would be near. She could almost feel him there, waiting for her in the gloom, his terrifying long teeth clicking away. She thumbed back the hammer, turned in a slow circle. The lights had been snuffed in the hall.

"I know you're here, Coulton," she said calmly. Her eyes flicked to the darkened alcoves, the shadowy doorways. She had a sudden glimmer of doubt, wondering if maybe she was wrong, if he'd somehow got past her and was helping Marber up the hall.

"Coulton?" she said.

Then she felt it: a soft slick warm drop on her shoulder. With an impossible slowness, she raised her eyes and looked up.

Coulton was clinging to the ceiling, directly above her, his long teeth bared in a grin, some slickness gathering at his lips and dripping. And then he plunged down onto her, driving her with incredible force into the floor, striking the gun from her hand and tearing at her coat, her arms, her exposed skin, reaching once more for the weir-bent at her throat.

She fought silently, furiously, with a viciousness that surprised even her, biting at Coulton herself, tearing at his face, at his eyes with her thumbs. All at once he howled and spun away and leaped off her, clutching the base of his throat, whirling around and around like a madman. And then she saw the bloodied blade of glass, floating in the darkness.

Ribs.

Coulton saw it too. The litch hurtled itself against the wall and with a quick clawed toe pushed itself upward and landed right where Ribs must have been standing. But she was too fast; the glass weapon had dropped to the floor; Coulton screeched and swung about.

Alice crawled back against the wall, feeling with her hands in the dark for more broken shards. And then she found one and brought her fist around just as Coulton was throwing himself on her again, and she felt it go in deep into his stomach, and she slashed and stabbed and slashed again, cutting the flesh to ribbons, a great hot wetness drenching her wrists and arms.

He'd bit her shoulder badly and come away with a piece of her in his mouth but that was all. He slumped back, gripped his belly, kicked his legs out in agony.

She rose gasping to her feet. She looked for her gun, saw it floating in the air. Ribs had it aimed at the litch. She pulled the trigger. In a deafening roar, Coulton—what had once been Coulton—spun sideways and stopped moving.

It didn't seem possible. Alice swayed. She was holding her shoulder, and she looked over at where Ribs must have been standing and she nodded. And then they were both running again, slower now, but running nonetheless back up the hall toward the sounds of fighting and destruction.

They came around the corner. Alice nearly fell to her knees. Oskar was slumped unmoving against a ruined wall, his face bleeding. Lymenion was nowhere. There was a splatter of blood and pieces of flesh all over the ceiling down the hall and Alice felt herself stagger. An entire wall had given way and she saw in the ruined room beyond the huge dark whirlwind that was the keywrasse, eight-legged, double-toothed, battling Jacob Marber, Marber with the dust in ropes and tendrils snarling the keywrasse fast, dragging it by the throat backward, the keywrasse tearing at Marber's arms and legs with its long claws. Quickly Alice looked back. She saw Komako, kneeling, peering at her from under her tangled black hair. She held up one fist. She was holding the other weir-bent.

She didn't hesitate, didn't even think about it, but felt instead for the twinge in her side where she had been wounded by Marber, where the dust had penetrated her, and she leaned *into* it, embraced it, and raised both her hands open before her and spread her arms wide, feeling as she did as if she were pushing her way through heavy water. And she saw Jacob Marber, staggering back from the keywrasse, all at once lift his hands out from his body exactly as she was doing, a look of puzzlement crossing his face.

And then the keywrasse dragged itself up out of a pile of broken bricks and snarled and hurled itself at Marber's exposed chest.

Alice sank to her knees in the same instant. The force of holding Jacob Marber pinioned was too much; he turned his face, and spied her, even as the keywrasse leaped at his heart.

After that, everything happened at once. The keywrasse was struck sidelong by a wall of smoke. Alice felt a rope of dust enclose around her own throat with the tensile strength of iron, and then she was spinning, flying through the room and smashing through a door onto the little stone balcony. Everything was pain, fog, haze. She raised her face and saw the keywrasse, driving its jaws into Marber's throat. She blinked. Marber, smashing the keywrasse against the floor. She blinked. The keywrasse, swatting at his head. Suddenly the balcony was shuddering and Marber and the keywrasse were crashing past, and she saw Marber take a terrible swipe from the keywrasse, and his head snapped weirdly back, and then the balcony gave out under their weight and she grabbed for the edge of the door and somehow held on as Jacob Marber plummeted in a pile of stone and brick far down onto the courtyard below.

She felt something then, a great powerful set of jaws seize on the overcoat at the nape of her neck and lift her up, dragging her back into the room. She lay gasping and sobbing and not moving in the drifting dust and rubble. She'd survived.

When she raised her face, she saw the keywrasse was limping, favoring its left front paw. It was still big, the size of a very big dog, though it otherwise resembled a cat again, with only the four paws and the ordinary teeth. But there was blood on its snout and matted in its fur, though whether its own or another's Alice couldn't say. She reached up and wrapped her arms around its neck, burrowed her face in deep. The heat it gave off was tremendous. Its fur smelled of burned things.

"Thank you," she whispered, her eyes wet. "Thank you, thank you . . ."

Oskar and Komako emerged out of the smoke, bloodied, bruised. They didn't get too close to the big keywrasse. She saw Komako go to the edge and look down at the rubble, at the crushed hand of Jacob Marber just visible. The girl closed her eyes. Wordlessly, she gave Alice the second weir-bent, the wooden weir-bent that Jacob had taken from her back in London. The keywrasse narrowed its shining eyes, all four of them.

"Ko?" came Ribs's voice from nearby. Alice saw smoke curling around the girl's silhouette, faint, shading her in. "We can't stay here. If Jacob Marber come into Cairndale, that damn drughr's got to be close too."

"Ribs is right," said Oskar. He was bleeding at his forehead.

Cairndale groaned, shuddered all around them. They didn't have long. But Alice was peering out through the broken wall, past the dissipating dust, at the island, the vast canopy of its tree. It was all lit up with an eerie blue shine. "You think Charlie's sealed it?"

"No," said Komako, joining her. "Not yet. Can you walk?"

In a flash Alice saw the towering horror that had ripped a hole in the air, back in London. None of these kids had seen it. Only she. She looked at them and then at the exhausted keywrasse and knew they couldn't fight the drughr, not like this.

"We have to get down to the courtyard," she said, deciding something. She got shakily to her feet. "There's a carriage there; Margaret and I arrived in it. It can't have gone far. We have to get all of you out."

She turned to the keywrasse, and kneeled, so that it came limping to her and nuzzled her open hand. She was holding both weir-bents in her other hand and she set them carefully down in the broken mortar and stepped back.

"These are yours," she said quietly.

The keywrasse sniffed cautiously at the weir-bents, then raised its snout as if to regard her with wary consideration.

"Go on," Alice whispered. "Go."

And the keywrasse, as if understanding, suddenly angled its face sideways and gulped the weir-bents down its throat in two quick gulps, and then turned and padded noiselessly out into the fiery corridor with its shadow sawing over the walls and was gone.

The kids stood back, watching all this in silence.

Ribs, still invisible, groaned. "Bloody Americans! Always got to make the grand gesture, like."

"What's that mean?" said Alice.

"It means, maybe *next* time you could wait till *after* we get safe."

Alice started for the hall, checking her revolver as she went, her long coat flapping behind her. "No one's ever safe," she muttered, "and there's never a next time."

Just then, while Alice and the children ran through the burning manor, Margaret, on the island, was gripping the ringed knives in her hands and dragging herself slowly across the screaming chamber. The gray figures did not move. They filled her with terror. She knew only that she had to help the poor child, little Marlowe, she had to stop Henry Berghast from whatever it was he was doing. Somehow all this was her fault. She should have known him for what he was, she should have seen it.

She bared her teeth, crawled on. The boy lay slumped at the cistern, unhanded. Everything depended on surprise, on quickness.

But when she was still a few feet away, she saw in shock what he was doing. The drughr, like a stain of darkness, was pressed against the surface of the orsine, trapped there, filled with a fury. Henry Berghast had driven his hand into the muck of the drughr, feeding on it. Then, slowly, he seemed to drag the drughr up, up, so that it rose under the tar-like skin of the orsine, colossal, twelve feet tall. It was struggling and turning its unseeing face in the direction of Marlowe. And as it rose up the screaming gray figures suddenly ceased; they fell silent, with their mouths still black and lightless and wide.

The silence echoed in Margaret's ears, disorienting her. The blood from the boy's wrist was still leaking into the waters. She shook her head to clear it.

But then Berghast turned and rose fluidly as if he'd expected her. His beardless face was strained, the dark shadows under his eyes pronounced, the skin across his jaw and cheekbones skull-like and cruel.

His soft measured voice was both his and not his. "Ah, Margaret," he said. "You have come to warn me about Walter and Mr. Thorpe. You are too late. He is dead."

She tried to hide the knives but it was too late, he had seen them. He seemed unconcerned. At his back the drughr twisted slowly in its muck, a figure of agony and pity.

"I saw your carriage in the courtyard," he continued softly. "What has happened to you? You look . . . wretched."

He padded in a slow catlike circle around her and then crouched smoothly and seized her wrists. The gloved hand was rough, its wooden plates sharp-edged. It gave off a faint steam though it was cool to the touch. He twisted her knives easily away and she gave a gasp of pain and frustration. The drughr writhed above the orsine, folding over and over itself, like smoke in a jar.

Something shifted then, behind Berghast; he half turned away, and Margaret glimpsed Marlowe kneeling with both hands gripped hard on Berghast's bare arm. The boy was shining with a terrible brilliance, his skin translucent so that she could see the shape of his skull and his hollow sockets and the bones and veins in his arms. His teeth were clenched. The shine erupted.

And she saw Berghast's skin begin to boil where Marlowe gripped it. She didn't understand what she was seeing. It did not seem possible.

But Berghast stood suddenly and threw the child backward so that his head struck the rock floor and all at once the light in him died and he looked boneless and strange.

Berghast's own skin was shining.

"Why are you doing this?" Margaret cried, filled with a sudden helpless rage. "I came to *warn* you. I thought you'd try to *protect* them, all of them. Henry, I believed in you! All these years, I helped you! My Mr. Harrogate helped you! But you're just a—a monst—"

"I am not," he said. "There is a greater purpose to this."

He pulled her upright, twisting her wrists back so that she feared they might break. Then he let one go and brought his own knife up.

"Henry—" she said.

But he slid the blade painfully into her belly, paying her no mind. It went in slippery and without any give all the way to the hilt, and she gasped at the slow grinding hurt of it, her whole body filling with amazement.

"I am not a monster," he said again, looking into her eyes, forcing her to look into his own. "I take no pleasure in this."

And then he pulled the knife free and left her.

Charlie carried the dripping heart out of the crypt.

All around him a blue light shone. He held the glyphic's heart swaddled in his shirt like a newborn, feeling the warm slick of it, his cupped hands cradling it as he went.

Far across the loch, Cairndale was on fire. He watched the scaffolding of flames. His arms and legs were scratched and bloodied but the scratches were already closing and when he could breathe again he staggered around the ruined monastery and entered the dark monks' quarters and crept down the stone stairs. He had to sink the heart into the orsine.

The blue shine below was blinding. He stumbled at the edge of the underground chamber, wincing. The orsine was too bright. But as he turned his face aside he saw, lurking around the walls, strange gray figures. The light seemed not to register in their grayness, nor the darkness; and they turned their faces to Charlie where he stood, and he knew them. They were different, no longer beautiful, no longer ribboning with memory; but he knew them. The spirit dead.

Suddenly they swarmed him. They made no sound. But they moved at an incredible speed, and he felt the first one's touch with a tremble, as he tried to cradle the glyphic's heart. For it was as solid as anything in this world; and its touch glowed with that same blue fire; and he felt his own flesh begin to bubble and melt in agony.

And then a second, a third, was upon him, and as the spirit dead pressed in close, Charlie couldn't hold on to the glyphic's heart any longer, and it slid from his grasp, and suddenly the dead let him go and were swarming the small glowing blue heart. They were eating it.

"No—" Charlie fell to his knees, horrified. The dead paid him no heed, and soon the heart had been devoured entire. It was gone. Their mouths and fingers were stained with black slime.

It was then Charlie lifted his eyes and saw something was trapped in the orsine, a huge gluey giant straining against the orsine's surface. It looked thickened and elongated and covered in tar. And then he saw Dr. Berghast leaning out over the orsine, the artifact glove heavy at his side, his other hand plunged elbow-deep into the sticky thigh of the figure, as if gripping it, as if holding it in place. But something was happening to him, he was shivering, there was a low blue shine in his skin that looked almost like how Marlowe would look, sometimes, and Charlie understood. Berghast was draining the drughr's power.

The rip in the orsine was still widening. The dead were standing again, arms at their sides, watching the orsine. Charlie had failed,

failed everyone, he had lost the glyphic's heart and now the orsine would never be sealed.

And that was when he saw, huddled half in darkness, the unmoving bodies of Mrs. Harrogate, and his only friend, Marlowe. They were lying near a pillar and it looked like Mrs. Harrogate had somehow dragged Marlowe there. He could see a long smear of blood where she'd crawled and when he got to her he saw the blood in her belly and knew she was dying. Marlowe's left wrist had been cut and he was covered in his own blood and his face was very white. Charlie was too late.

But then Marlowe smiled weakly.

"Char-lie," he said, his voice soft and dry. "I knew . . . you'd come."

Charlie felt his chest swell with grief. He wiped at his eyes with the heels of his hands. "I'm sorry, Mar, I'm so sorry. I lost it, I lost the glyphic's heart, I was supposed to seal the orsine, but they took it from me, I tried to stop them—"

But the boy just sighed and closed his eyes again.

"Mar?"

He looked up and saw Mrs. Harrogate's eyes were open. She was watching him.

"My knives," she whispered. "If you can. Get to the edge of. The pool. You can still. Stop him."

He followed her gaze out, saw the long evil-looking things on the floor not far from Berghast.

"The glyphic, he's gone," Charlie said, choking back a sob. He couldn't see what good any of this would do. "The dead will get through now. There's no way to close the orsine. It doesn't matter."

Mrs. Harrogate's eyes flashed with pain. "It always matters," she hissed.

Charlie looked at Marlowe, looked back at Mrs. Harrogate. Dr. Berghast was still leaning out over the orsine, plunging his free hand into the muck of the drughr, draining it.

All at once Charlie ducked low, and at a crouch he started forward. He moved from pillar to pillar in the watery blue light. But he couldn't get to the knives. Almost without thinking, he closed his eyes; he breathed slowly and tried to empty his mind. There was stillness; silence; a feeling of great peace. And he reached out, calmly, and then it was like he was still reaching, still reaching, and he felt the muscles in his arm pull and cramp and pull harder, and it seemed his bones were being sucked from their sockets, and the pain was dizzying; then he felt his fingers close around the hilt of a knife, and he opened his eyes. The knife was heavy, heavier than it should have been, and the metal was warm to the touch. His arm looked weird, snakelike, and silently he drew it back into his flesh, the pain staggering. And yet his heart leaped.

He had done it; he had done the mortaling.

The enormousness of it, of what it meant, vanished in the moment. Berghast was still bleeding the drughr of its strength. He looked bigger, his back broader, he seemed filled with a frenetic energy. It was too late. It was always going to be too late.

Charlie ran forward. He plunged the knife all the way to the hilt directly into Dr. Berghast's back.

The effect was immediate. The shine flickered; the drughr slid bonelessly back down into the depths of the orsine. Berghast whirled around. His beard was gone, his hair was gone. His lips were drawn back over his teeth in a rictus grin, the eyes sunken and bright. An eerie blue energy was crackling over his skin, over his hand, just like Charlie'd seen with Marlowe. Berghast stumbled, and fell to his knees, as if the effort of whatever he had been doing was too much, and he had nothing left.

Charlie saw the second blade on the sill of the cistern and he lunged for it and came up holding it out in front of him. Berghast hadn't moved. He was kneeling with his shoulders slumped and his face down and just breathing.

But when Charlie stepped forward to stab him through his heart, Berghast's gloved hand rose to meet the knife and it clanged aside. He gripped Charlie's wrist and Charlie felt a savage agonizing fire. Something was happening to him, he could feel it in the old man's grip, a kind of hollowing out as if some part of his self were being scraped away.

"What—what're you doing?" he cried.

"You," gasped Berghast. "You don't . . . understand . . ."

For a long terrible moment the blue fire seemed to engulf both of them. Charlie shuddered in pain. The skin on his wrist was bubbling. But it was worse than that, it was like some part of his insides was being peeled slowly away. Berghast held on, not strong enough to do more. There was a flash of movement on the floor behind Berghast: Mrs. Harrogate had dragged herself across. Charlie watched as she reached up and pushed, ever so gently, on Berghast's shoulder; and as he wrenched his own wrist away, he saw the man who had done so much harm to all of them lean casually out, and pitch weakly over the edge, into the luminous pool.

It all happened so slowly, with such gentleness, that it didn't seem real.

But then Berghast started thrashing, trying to keep afloat. And Charlie saw, ascending from the depths of the orsine, a shadowy figure—the drughr—rising up through the cloudy blue water to wrap an arm around Berghast's throat, and drag him slowly down into the depths, away.

Alice and the others ran through the long corridors of Cairndale, stopping where the fire was too much, turning back, seeking a different way. There were bodies in the hall, small bodies. She tried not to look at them. Go! she was thinking. Just go!

The stained glass over the grand staircase had shattered and as they

descended the steps their boots crunched over the broken shards. The
fire was burning all around them. A part of the ceiling fell with a crash
and Alice stumbled but kept a hand on Oskar and dragged him clear.
Her hands and face were streaked with soot, her hair singed. Oskar's
eyes looked wild with fear.

And then they were outside, the night air whooshing around them,
and the light from the fire casting the landscape all around in an orange glow. The carriage was gone. She gestured at the gatehouse and
the gravel drive beyond it and shouted that the horses couldn't have
got far—they were still in their harnesses; they might have run the
carriage up the lane or even into the fields, but they'd find it, they
would. She didn't look to the right—she simply refused to—not at
the pile of bricks and masonry that had spilled out onto stones, the
clawed hand of Jacob Marber protruding from it. The keywrasse was
nowhere.

She was pushing the kids ahead of her, through the fiery courtyard,
her long coat heavy at her shoulders. There were too many for the carriage but they'd make do—they'd have to—and she'd drive the horses
into the ground to get them all clear.

It was then she saw a figure, collapsed in a doorway, gasping. She
slowed; she stopped. The others were some way ahead by then, slender
outlines, running across the cobblestones for the gatehouse. She went
to the doorway, kneeled cautiously down.

Komako had seen her stop. "Alice!" the girl was shouting. "We have
to go! Alice!"

But Alice didn't look around, didn't dare look away. It was Coulton. He was leaning with his back to a door, holding his stomach in
his clawed fingers. She looked at his blood-flecked face, the red lips
twisted in pain, the long needlelike teeth. His eyes were dark with
knowing.

"Al . . . ice . . . ," he gasped.

She leaned closer, breathing hard. She wasn't afraid. There was in his expression a recognition, some part of the old Coulton, the man she'd known and trusted. It was as if, with Jacob Marber's death, he'd come back to himself, and what he saw horrified him.

"Please . . . ," he whispered, almost crying. "Kill me. *Please.*"

She wet her lips. The manor was burning all around them, beginning to collapse. The wreckage was filled with the dead. She was blinking something from her eyes and she took out her revolver and cocked the hammer and held the barrel to his chest where his heart should have been. He wrapped his bloodied claws around it, and he held it with her. He nodded.

"Frank—" she whispered.

She'd been about to say something more when his thumbs found her trigger finger and squeezed. The Colt bucked once in her hand, recoiled in a slow cloud of smoke.

Charlie, weak, leaned over the stone rim. He was breathing raggedly, shaking his head. Berghast had done something to him. His wrist was an agony of fire. Deep within the orsine, down where Berghast had been dragged, he saw the blue shine flicker, grow fainter, and then suddenly it was like the brightness was rising up out of the depths, rushing up toward him. Charlie staggered back.

It was the dead, the spirit dead. Their gray figures were climbing slowly, methodically out of the orsine, one after another. There were twenty, thirty of them now. More kept coming. They gathered and turned and stood swaying, casting their gray heads from side to side, as if seeking something.

The waters began to rise too, overpouring the edges of the cistern, the strange glowing waters spilling out across the floor. Charlie splashed over to Mrs. Harrogate, pulled her by the armpits to the pillar where Marlowe lay. He kept an eye out for the gray figures. Some of them had turned their way.

But when he got Mrs. Harrogate back, he could see it was too late. She was dead.

"No, no, no, no, no," Charlie cried, holding her head. "Please, Mrs. Harrogate. No."

The waters pooled around them. Everything was going wrong. The ceiling shuddered. The island was shaking now, starting to come apart.

Marlowe sat up in the rising flood, his glassy eyes watching one of the gray figures. He looked so little.

"Hey," said Charlie, crouching down, getting right in his face. He forced himself to speak calmly. "I was coming back for you, I was."

"I know it, Charlie."

"I guess you just found your own way."

The boy smiled feebly. "I guess so."

The island shook again and there was a faint sound of explosions and Charlie blinked away his fear. Whatever Berghast had done to him, it left him feeling light-headed. The water was past his ankles. "Well, you got to tell me all about it," he said. "But we've got to go now, Mar. Can you walk?"

Marlowe shook his head. "I can't."

"Sure you can. I'll help."

But the boy gently pushed his arms away. Charlie didn't understand. He followed Marlowe's gaze back to where the orsine was flooding across the chamber floor and the earth shook suddenly and then he did, he understood, he knew what his friend was thinking.

"It's not possible, Mar," he whispered. "I lost the glyphic's heart. It's done."

"I can close it, Charlie."

Charlie tried to laugh incredulously but it came out sounding more like a sob. "What can you do? That's not something you know about."

But there was a calmness in Marlowe's face that unnerved Charlie and made him doubt his own words. "Brynt knows how," said the boy. "She'll show me."

And then Charlie looked again over his shoulder and saw the gray figure Marlowe had been watching. It was big, far bigger than the others, and stood facing Marlowe with her massive arms at her sides. It was her.

Charlie was crying and nodding and looking at his friend's face. "What'll happen to you?" he whispered. "There's got to be another way. *Please.*"

The boy bit at his lip. And even as he said it, Charlie knew there wasn't. Marlowe was struggling upright, gripping the pillar, leaving tiny bloodied handprints. Charlie stood with him. In the water at their feet Mrs. Harrogate lay in her ragged black dress, her bruised face turned away, her hair lifting slowly. Charlie set his jaw.

"Then I'll go with you," he said firmly. "I've got this ring. It's an artifact, like the glove—"

"You can't come with me," said Marlowe, in that same maddening calm way. He seemed different, not only because of the hurt and the exhaustion. He seemed more . . . centered. More himself. Like he'd glimpsed the person he would grow to be and was already becoming. He said, "You got to stay here, Charlie. I need you on this side."

"Why?"

Marlowe gave him a smile that looked strange on a face so etched with pain and blood and leeched of its color. "Because you have to find a way to bring me back," he said.

Charlie, devastated, couldn't think of what to say.

He watched as the boy waded over to the orsine, his small feet splashing in the glowing water, his wrists cradled against his chest and his little shoulders rolled forward. He looked so small. The huge gray figure of Brynt was with him. The shine was coming from Marlowe now, too, Charlie could see it, the brightness in him, and he saw in his mind's eye the boy as he'd been when they first met in London, how warm and soft the boy's hand had been in his own, and he saw too the prison cell in Natchez and he smelled the good smell of his mother's skin from before all that, when she'd held him, when he'd heard her heartbeat, and he had to turn away because he was crying.

The dead Brynt reached for the boy.

Charlie felt afraid. The blue shine intensified. It had a sound within it, mournful, in pain, and he could just see the silent gray figures gathered in that chamber swell with light as if from the inside, and disintegrate into light, just as if they'd never been, and then his friend, the only friend he'd ever known, as much a brother to him as anyone could have been, stepped down into the orsine and with a terrible strain drew the skin of the water over his head. His little hands were pulling, pulling, and then Charlie saw the furious blue shining from deep below shrink and narrow and sliver away until it winked out, and the chamber went dark, the surface of the orsine as cold and lightless as flowstone, and that strange blue shining of Marlowe's was gone, gone from the world, forever, gone.

Alice put a hand to her eyes and stared back at the burning manor. The great cloud of dust that Jacob Marber had made was thinning. Then she heard Ribs, hollering. The old carriage was down near the cliffs overlooking the loch. Alice came down the slope at a run, her boots sliding in the soft muck, her strong legs passing Oskar in the firelight. Komako was already at the wreckage, standing with her hands upraised on her head and not saying anything.

The horses must have spooked when the fires first broke out and galloped this far and then tried to turn hard when they saw the cliff in front of them. The carriage was overturned, two wheels splintered and askew. One of the horses was down tangled in its gear, not kicking, just lying quiet as if it had tired itself out. She didn't think it was injured. The other stood with its eyes rolling in fear as it caught Ribs's scent. There were three other horses, loosed from the burning stables, that must have followed these into the dark and that stood now with eyes rolling in terror, shying sideways whenever a kid got close.

"Stay back," she said to Ribs, wherever the girl was.

Far out across the loch she could see the island where the ruined monastery stood, the island where Charlie had gone. Something was happening there, something strange. There were lights rising from the trees like tiny moths, circling and spiraling upward. A strange blue glow was pulsing in the ruins, flickering out across the dark waters.

The first horse snorted, tossed its head. The second one suddenly kicked out, trying to get upright.

"Easy," Alice murmured. She had her hands up and stood so that the first horse could see her clearly. "It's all right," she soothed, "it's all right. You're okay. You're okay."

The horse was calming. She reached up and lay a hand on its damp neck murmuring all the while.

But then Oskar cried out in a panic. Alice stepped smoothly back and looked.

Ragged and smoldering, striding down toward them like a figure of wrath, was Jacob Marber. Even at that distance Alice could see the blood in his beard and the wounds where his ear had been torn away. His clothes were ripped. His big hands were raised.

"For fuck's sake," she snapped.

She took out her Colt and leveled it and fired five times directly into Marber's chest, staggering him. But he did not fall. Calmly, quickly, she opened the chamber and dumped out the shells and began to reload. She shouldn't have released the keywrasse so soon.

She saw Oskar lifted into the air and thrown like a child's toy down the slope, toward the cliff's edge. The boy lay where he landed, unmoving. Three other kids tried to run and were swept bodily out into the darkness, screaming. She saw Komako, hands raised, struggling, falling to one knee, then the other, her long braid sweeping out behind her. A cloud of dust encircled her. Still Marber came on, toward her, Alice. Then her revolver was loaded and Alice dropped to one knee and held her revolver over one wrist to steady it and she shot out Marber's legs.

That stopped him. His legs went out from under him sideways and he fell hard. Alice was already up and running for the others, for Oskar and for Komako, and she was shouting at Ribs to get the horses out of their harnesses. That was when the island exploded.

It blew in a vast blue fiery conflagration and the weird flames arced upward and spilled out over the loch. Alice staggered back, seeing it, thinking of Charlie out there, her heart suddenly breaking. But there wasn't time—Marber had got back to his feet, was screaming at her, coming at her now at a run just as if he hadn't been shot at all, or crushed, or torn up by the keywrasse, and she saw it and knew even as she lifted her Colt that there was no stopping him.

Not by her.

Something massive and dark bounded out of the night darkness and smashed into him. It was snarling and swiping at his head and then it and he tumbled and rolled down the slope toward the cliffs. It was the keywrasse: many-legged and fanged and clawed and filled with a fury Alice hadn't seen before.

But she didn't stop to watch. She was hauling Oskar up out of the dirt and running for Komako and lifting her to her feet and then they were all climbing onto the horses, unhitched now by Ribs, and they rode out bareback three on each; they rode fast and crowded and leaning low over the horses' necks and Alice, with her heart breaking, only looked back long enough to see the keywrasse seize Marber's skull in its powerful jaws and drag him kicking to the edge of the cliff, and then both of them plunged over into the brooding black waters below, the surface of the loch closing over them, rippling outward, going still. In the illuminated night, the island crumpled in upon itself, collapsing. Alice's cheeks were wet. Her bitten shoulder was on fire. Behind them the old manor burned and burned in the darkness. Their horses ran.

EPILOGUE

The sky in the east was red. Charlie found Miss Davenshaw in the ruins just as day was breaking. She was still alive, the only one. He helped her up the ridge and lay her down in the moss at the edge of the cliff, bloodied, streaked with ash and soot, her clothes torn. Carefully he covered her with a singed blanket salvaged from the smoking wreckage and gently he put a hand to her face and silently he begged her not to die. His wrist where Berghast had gripped him was still hurting. Below he could see in the gathering light the smoldering shell of Cairndale Manor, two walls standing yet, and he knew among its dead lay all the old talents and the beasts in their stables and others, servants, groundskeepers, young talents whose names he'd never learned. In the black waters of the loch the island had crumpled in upon itself so that nothing now remained but a deep scarred depression, filled still with the night's dark and slow to illumine.

Marlowe.

That was in his head. Marlowe. Over there on the island, lost. No matter how he tried not to think about it. Marlowe descending into the orsine, the spirit dead swept away before him, that fierce blue shine fading, all of it being drawn shut by Marlowe's fists and then the explosion. Charlie lowered his head to his chest, eyes moist. He'd gone back to the island and searched the ruins for his friend but of course not found him. There was for Charlie only this world now. Later at the manor he'd picked through the rubble calling for Miss Alice or Komako or Ribs or Oskar or anyone, anyone at all, but there was no one, nothing, no sign of life, until he glimpsed Miss Davenshaw under a collapsed beam in what once had been the doorway of the east wing. She was all white with the dust, like a litch, just exactly like a litch. But if the others had got away or fallen somewhere far or were buried right under his feet he couldn't tell and the not knowing was almost the hardest part.

It was all of it like that. He just didn't know what to do. Whatever had happened to Jacob Marber and his litch, they were nowhere to be found. He'd dragged Miss Davenshaw clear and tried to wake her and when that didn't work he'd looked around helplessly and then begun the long awkward climb with her held upright in his arms, up the ridge, away from the ruins, just trying to get away. There wasn't any clear thought in his head other than that. She was clutching white-knuckled to a leather-bound journal, half of it burned away, but when he tried to take it from her he couldn't pry her fingers from it and he gave up.

He went back down through the ruins and found in an unburned shed a planked wheelbarrow. The little panes of glass had been blown out in the explosion and he cut his hand on a shard and he stared at the blood welling up in his grimy palm and the way the blood dapped slowly on the handle of the wheelbarrow. That kind of pain didn't matter. Not to a haelan.

At the loch he got Mrs. Harrogate's body out of the rowboat where he'd left her and he wheeled her up to the ridge, her legs folded out over the front, her arms crossed at her chest, him not really knowing what else to do. It didn't seem right leaving her. Miss Davenshaw still hadn't stirred. He knew the columns of smoke would draw neighboring locals and that it wouldn't be long—midmorning at latest—before the constables and newspapermen arrived. He wanted to be gone before then. He knew Scotland wasn't Mississippi but still he didn't want to be the only one left alive, a young black man, surrounded by destruction and white bodies.

But then, as the sun cleared the loch, Miss Davenshaw woke up. She raised herself groaning up on one elbow and turned her face from side to side in the red morning.

"Who's that?" she croaked.

For a moment he couldn't speak. "It's me, it's Charlie," he said in a rush, suddenly overcome. All at once he was gulping air and sobbing, his shoulders heaving.

She was slow to reply. A quick complicated host of expressions crossed her face. "Charlie . . . Are we—? Did anyone else—?"

"It's just us, Miss D," Charlie said. "I haven't seen anyone else alive. It's only just us."

That was when he saw the smear of blood on the blind woman's sleeve where he'd reached for her, and he lifted his palm in wonder. The cut wasn't healing.

When he thought back on it later, he understood it must have been Berghast, at the edge of the orsine, who had done it. Somehow, with that burning grip, he'd ripped Charlie's talent right out of him, had gutted him, left him drained and husked and ordinary, as ordinary as anyone.

He wrapped his burned wrist in a strip of torn shirt, carefully, awkwardly, and then also wrapped his bleeding hand. Almost at once a spot of blood seeped through. The pain throbbed. He was too surprised, too exhausted, too filled with sadness and anger at all that had happened to make any real sense of this new loss.

"Maybe it'll come back?" he whispered to Miss Davenshaw, afraid.

She reached out a bloodied hand, as if to hold him. "Oh, Charlie," she murmured.

They left Mrs. Harrogate's body under a sheet in the courtyard at Cairndale, knowing the locals would bury the dead. That was Miss Davenshaw's notion. But they took what they could find out of the rubble, a traveling satchel, some foodstuffs from the pantry. The closest thing to a clean change of clothes. Miss Davenshaw instructed him to go to the standing shed and in an overturned pot he found a coin purse and a stack of banknotes and these he brought to her. The bodies out in the field he stayed clear of and later when he found the little hand of a boy sticking up out of the wreckage he looked at it and then walked down off the slope and sat and he didn't go back up.

By the time the long shadows had retreated halfway back across the loch they were already walking. Charlie could see riders on horseback approaching even as he and Miss Davenshaw left the grounds for good, clambering over the low stone wall of the perimeter, the columns of smoke still rising slowly from two of the outbuildings behind them.

Later in the morning they were picked up by a market wagon and rode the rest of the way into Edinburgh and when they got to Princes Street they went at once to the railway station and bought a ticket direct to King's Cross, in London. "We can disappear there," Miss Davenshaw explained. He didn't ask why, or from whom, or for how long. He just kept touching his bandages, feeling the prickle of a pain that would not leave him. She told him they'd go south to an address that had belonged to the institute and stay there for a time while they decided what to do next.

She meant, of course, the building at Nickel Street West.

. . .

Gradually he got used to the idea of what he was now, an exile, a lost talent. He was what his father had been before him. If he did not heal, he was no different than Alice, or his mama, and he had loved and admired them both. Nevertheless it amazed him that he wasn't more devastated by the change. Each morning he awoke, and felt the dark London air on his skin, and laced his boots, and felt the heat of his blood in his fingers, and thought of Marlowe alone in the land of the dead. His own misfortunes diminished at such times. Instead he'd remember a destitute boy, sentenced to death in Natchez, confused by his talent and frightened of it and thinking himself alone in all the world. That boy felt almost like a different person, someone he wished he could find, and talk to, tell him: *It's not okay, but it'll get better.*

Because it had. He saw that now. Even after everything. After meeting Mar and Ko and Ribs and Oskar, after learning about his father, after entering the orsine and walking through a dead world. His first life seemed like a dream. What he'd seen since was the more real. He'd witnessed the spirit dead rise up out of the orsine, had felt the icy swarm of them scrabbling for the glyphic's heart. He'd seen a drughr drained of its power, and he'd watched his best friend descend down into that other world, sealing it up behind him. There was a new quiet sadness inside him now. Not just his own loss. Charlie's only refuge in all the world had burned down around him. His friends were lost, likely dead. Whatever he was now, whoever he was becoming, it was nothing like the boy he once had been.

For several weeks they stayed at Mrs. Harrogate's old lodgings, eerie though it was for Charlie, haunted by the crooked shadow of what had happened there, the litch scrabbling across the walls, its claws at his throat. He remembered too the strange not-London of the other world, the foyer of that watery building, and had to suppress a shudder every time he went out. But they went out only for food and necessaries. They'd had to break the lock to get in, and though Charlie did his best to repair the gate, it still would not close properly, and they were both of them wary. Miss Davenshaw was quiet, brooding, obsessed with the burned journal she had carried out of Cairndale. Charlie would read passages to her for long hours at a time, the gas lamps turned high, a candle sometimes lit in the sconce beside the sofa.

As for him, he couldn't shake the feeling that Marlowe was not gone, was not dead, that he was somewhere inside the orsine, on the far side, still alive. He had no reason to think it and every reason to think its opposite, except for his friend's parting words, and the feeling he had. One night he told Miss Davenshaw what he felt, about how maybe Mar wasn't dead. Miss Davenshaw only pulled him close, and held him.

The journal he read from each night had belonged to Dr. Berghast. It was charred and there were pages missing and the entire back cover had been ripped off and the papers smelled of smoke and oil and dead things, and when he rubbed his fingers together they smelled of it too. Sometimes he would have to put the journal aside. It felt like a relic from that terrible night. Little in its pages made sense to him. There were columns of numbers, or dates, and half-legible scrawls observing colors and times of day, all of them records of some kind of experiment. All this he dutifully read aloud. There was an entry recording three names, with described locations, which Miss Davenshaw asked him to reread several times while she sat with her face turned aside and her brow furrowed.

"They are from the glyphic," she breathed at last. "Mr. Thorpe's last findings. Children. Talents. They're still out there, somewhere."

Charlie remembered his own rescue by Miss Quick and Mr. Coulton, from that jail cell in Natchez. It felt like a lifetime ago. "How's anyone going to find them now?"

But Miss Davenshaw only urged him to mark the spot and go on reading. Many of the later pages were missing but he could sometimes still read parts of entries and it was one such that he read that made Miss Davenshaw scowl and sit up straighter, as if she'd been waiting for that very passage. It seemed like a kind of diary entry. It made mention of a woman named Addie, of a community built of bones. *Addie believes it possible to guard the passage and keep its monsters at bay,* Berghast had written. *It is not possible. If there is a door, it will be opened. Sooner or later. For that is its purpose and all things of this earth both animate and not must fulfill their purpose in time. One cannot shut one's eyes and trust the horror will flee. The only way to slay a monster is to confront it in its lair.*

Slowly Charlie understood. He lifted his eyes. Berghast was writing about an orsine.

A second one.

Then one day a hand was forcing the big front door, and there came the sound of footsteps in the foyer downstairs, and then Alice Quicke was standing in front of Charlie, staring amazed and speechless, her clothes filthy and her eyes lined and her wide shoulders tired. She looked ten years older. Before he could say anything, pouring around her on all sides, came Komako and Oskar and Ribs, though Ribs's left arm was in a sling and her angular face looked paler than usual. They were all of them laughing, talking over each other, and even Miss Davenshaw was smiling gravely.

"And where's Lymenion?" she said, when they'd quieted down.

Oskar drew his pale eyebrows low in a frown. "He helped us stop Jacob, Miss Davenshaw. But I can make him again. I just need the right . . . material."

"He means he needs some dead uns," said Ribs helpfully. "Aw, Lymenion ain't gone for good. You can't kill a flesh giant now, can you?"

"No," replied Oskar sturdily.

"Thank you, Eleanor, that will do," said Miss Davenshaw. There was a faint smile at her lips. It seemed some part of herself was coming back to her, and she had drawn herself up in dignified pleasure. "First things first. I expect none of you have eaten. And when was the last time you washed? What are you wearing?"

As Miss Davenshaw's fingers began to investigate her wards' condition, Charlie saw Komako looking at him intently, searching his face, a deep sympathy in her, and he felt a heat rise to his cheeks. What did she see? Her eyes lingered on the swollen new scar on his palm. He folded his hand away, uncomfortable, shy. He liked the look of her, even rumpled and unwashed and tired. She had her long braid wrapped around her head.

"What happened to your hand?" she said quietly, so that only he could hear. "Charlie—?"

He started to answer her, to tell her about his talent, and then he couldn't. He shook his head, looked away.

"We thought you were dead," she said. "I thought you were dead. We all saw the island blow up."

"Yeah. I . . . I got away."

"Obviously." She arched a thin eyebrow and for just a moment Charlie saw the old Komako, the sarcastic girl, the one who'd given him such a hard time. But just as quickly it was gone again, and that new worry descended over her face like a veil. It made him sad to see it though he didn't understand why. It was only later that he realized she hadn't asked about Marlowe, none of them had. It was as if they knew. There was a distance in her now, some unspoken thing, and he knew then that they were all of them changed, changed utterly, and there was no going back to how it had been.

That night they gathered in front of the grate in the parlor and there Alice told about what had happened. She told about the killing of

Jacob Marber and how Lymenion fell and of the attack by the litch Coulton. The keywrasse had saved them all. Ribs was bleeding badly by the time the island collapsed and they'd taken the horses and fled the burning ruins of Cairndale for Edinburgh. There were fifteen of them who'd got away. They'd stayed with the alchemist, old Mrs. Ficke, while Ribs healed. The newspapers had been wild with speculation about the institute's destruction. The local police were seeking witnesses. Alice had been afraid that Berghast or the drughr or something worse might still be hunting them and she didn't want to stay in Scotland. So she'd come to London and left the other kids, all eleven of them, in the care of Susan Crowley. If anyone could keep them safe, it would be Miss Crowley. Of course Ribs and Oskar and Komako had refused. So they'd continued here, to Nickel Street West, because Alice hadn't known where else to go.

When Alice had finished talking, Charlie told briefly about Marlowe and Mrs. Harrogate and Dr. Berghast and the orsine. He told about losing his talent and held up his hand to show them the scar. He didn't have it in him to talk much about it. His friends' faces were drawn and tight and Oskar looked like he might cry when they heard how Marlowe had got out, had been there the whole time, and sacrificed himself.

After that Miss Davenshaw told about the aftermath, about Mrs. Harrogate's body and their journey south and the journal she'd taken from Dr. Berghast's desk. Last of all she told about Berghast's writings regarding a second orsine. It was real, she said; it had existed once; perhaps it still did. The rest of that entry was missing. But there were surely clues still to be discovered in the journal. "Somewhere there is another portal," she explained, sitting very erect and still. "There is another way into that other world."

Komako was shaking her head. "Why does that matter, Miss Davenshaw?"

Charlie looked at her, he looked at all his friends. "Marlowe sealed the orsine. After Berghast . . . fell. It might be he's still alive in there. I've got to find out, Ko. I've got to know for sure."

"You think he . . . survived?" whispered Oskar.

Charlie nodded.

"And Berghast?" said Komako. "Do you think he survived also?"

Charlie paused. "I don't know."

Ribs's green eyes narrowed. "What can you hope to do, Charlie? That bastard took your talent."

"Indeed, Miss Ribbon," said Miss Davenshaw, turning her stern face in the girl's direction. "But there are other ways of being in the world. Not all change is loss."

Charlie's own expression was fierce. He knew they would try to talk him out of what he was about to tell them. "I'm going to look for the second orsine," he said. "I'm going to find it. And then I'm going to get Marlowe out."

No one spoke. Alice took off her hat and clawed her hands through her greasy yellow hair. Then she put her hat back on. Her eyes were hard as granite.

"All right," she said. She met Charlie's eye. "So let's go find him."

ACKNOWLEDGMENTS

Firstly, Ellen Levine, agent and friend, without whom this book would not exist. No writer could ask for a fiercer, kinder, better advocate. Also: Audrey Crooks, for her tireless assistance, Alexa Stark, Martha Wydysh, Nora Rawn, Stephanie Manova, and everyone at Trident Media who helped make this book possible.

Megan Lynch at Flatiron Books has been a godsend, as brilliant and sensitive and delicate an editor as any author could hope to find. It's been my greatest good fortune to work with her. Also: Kukuwa Ashun, organizational guru, who has kept everything on track throughout. Keith Hayes, designer of an absolutely gorgeous cover. Malati Chavali, Marlena Bittner, Katherine Turro, Nancy Trypuc, Cat Kenney, and Claire McLaughlin, for their exhaustingly brilliant ideas. Erica Ferguson, copy editor extraordinaire. Ryan Jenkins and Hazel Shahgholi, invaluable proofreaders. Flatiron is amazing.

Jared Bland at McClelland & Stewart, stalwart supporter of this book from the beginning. I feel incredibly lucky to have fallen into his orbit, and to have his eye on my writing. Also: Tonia Addison, Erin Kelly, Sarah Howland, Ruta Liormonas, and everyone at M&S.

Alexis Kirschbaum at Bloomsbury, whose warmth and enthusiasm for this project helped get me through. Also: the rest of the team at Bloomsbury, especially Philippa Cotton, Emilie Chambeyron, Stephanie Rathbone, and Amy Donegan.

Rich Green at Gotham Group, wonder worker, for all his faith and support.

Above all others, always: Jeff, Kevin, Brian, my parents. Cleo & Maddox, who dream up worlds in words every day. And Esi, my love, my talent, with whom everything begins and ends.

ABOUT THE AUTHOR

J. M. Miro lives and writes in the Pacific Northwest.